Home Sweet Home

BY LANI MOKU

Home
Sweet
Home

Lani Moku

Copyright

Dedication

To all who have dreams that never end.

Preface

The concept of the book is based on a recurring dream I had many years ago. It all started way back in 1998 when I lived up in the mountains in Colorado. In February, we got hit by a massive snowstorm, and it was below freezing for the whole week. With over three feet of snow, I was stuck in the house with nowhere to go.

Since my contract job was coming to an end, I had enough of the snow, ice, and freezing weather. I started looking for my next job in a warmer climate. Ever since I was young, I always had this big dream of living on a tropical island. I must have been influenced by the Disney movie 'Swiss Family Robinson' and 'Gilligan's Island.'

I stumbled upon a few jobs in Marshall and Kwajalein Islands while browsing the Internet. Once I saw all those beautiful photos of the island life, I knew it was for me. That's all I had thought about for days. That's when the dreams started.

Day after day, I had the same recurring dream. I never made it to Kwajalein in the dream and ended up stranded on some remote tropical island. I had visions of walking along a sandy beach, feeling the warm water rushing over my feet. It was an absolute paradise. Influenced by the Gilligan's Island TV show, lucky for me, it was Mary Ann on the island with me in my dreams.

Once the winter storm passed, some friends stopped by to pick me up to go skiing in Breckenridge. They all laughed when I told them about my weird recurring dream. They said I was spending too much time watching Gilligan's Island or getting cabin fever after being stuck in the house all week. I think they were right about that on both parts.

One friend, who was a little superstitious, told me it was an omen or premonition, and I should stay in Colorado. After I told her the details of my dreams, she suggested that I should write them down. As the weeks passed, I jotted down a few notes about my dreams. A year later, I finished transcribing that recurring dream, and it became 'Home Sweet Home.'

Many of the story's events are loosely based on actual events or misadventures that happened to me or someone I knew, altering the time and location.

The inspiration for the island life came from my early days on Padre Island, surf fishing, and camping on the beach. While living in Colorado, hiking on the many trails and camping in the wilderness inspired many of the events in the story.

LM

Home Sweet Home

SECTION 1

The Adventure

Chapter 1

Job at Marshall Islands

For Ben Hughes, it's another dismal and frustrating day at work. Sitting in front of his computer, he stares at the monitor, wondering why the network is down again. Everything is at a complete standstill. He doesn't care anymore because it's just another day on the job. The life of a system analyst is not glamorous at all. For him, this is a downright boring job. If it were not for the money, he would leave in a minute.

To pass the time, he closes his eyes, thinking about his last camping trip in the mountains. None of this computer stuff interests him anymore. Being out in the wilderness, hiking the many trails, fishing, and camping is the lifestyle he loves. He longs for the weekends to be outside among all the trees and the clean air.

This is not the lifestyle he had planned. Back in his college days, computer science was really exciting, working with the latest technology. Back then, everyone was always enthusiastic and extremely knowledgeable about computers and software. Now, he is one of the very few who even have a computer science degree. Most of his coworkers are rejects with degrees in English, history, psychiatry, and the worst of the bunch, political science. There is good money in computer programming jobs, but it attracts too many people who have no talent for it at all. He knows he is spending way too much time cleaning up the mess that one of these rejects had made.

* * *

After another long day at work, Ben leaves the office feeling depressed. He is dreading the long drive home. Even after leaving work late, the highway is still bumper to bumper, going only five miles per hour. When winter arrives, he knows it's going to be worse with all the snow and ice. Living in Denver is getting worse, not only with the pollution but also with all the traffic. There are way too many cars and too much development. He is ready for a change, hoping it will be soon.

Arriving at his apartment, he stops by the mailbox at the main gate. Being the first of the month, he has to pay the bills again. His mailbox is overflowing with junk mail. Surprisingly, no one else wants any of this meaningless junk either, seeing it all tossed in the garbage cans next to the mailbox. He feels sorry for the poor old postman who has to deliver all this, and it ends up being tossed directly into the garbage.

Flinging one envelope after another into the garbage, he sees one that is definitely not junk mail. His heart is pounding fast with anticipation. It's the one letter that he is so glad to see. Out of all the jobs he had applied for, this was the one he wanted the most. He doesn't dare open it, quickly putting it in his back pocket. If this is bad news, he'll be screaming out loud, mad at the world.

Walking into his sparsely furnished apartment, Ben is glad the day is over. Sitting in front of a computer all day long makes him so sleepy. Rummaging through the refrigerator, he discovers there is no food except for a couple of frozen TV dinners. Too tired to go back out to get groceries or stop at a fast-food joint, the frozen dinner is looking a little better. He tosses one into the microwave, making a mental note of all the food he needs to buy.

He remembers the envelope still in his back pocket. Quickly pulling it out, he sees the return address 'Keen Tech Agency.' He knows this is it. Months had gone by, waiting to hear about the job of a lifetime. After never-ending phone interviews and forms to fill out, this is the moment of truth. He keeps staring at the envelope, hesitant to open it. It's going to be good news or very bad news. All the waiting is over. The content of the envelope has the answer.

After spending months searching for that special job on the Internet, Ben finally found the one he wanted. He stumbled upon a job posting advertising the adventure of a lifetime. A job in the middle of the Pacific Ocean over 2,400 miles southwest of Hawaii, a place called Kwajalein, in the Marshall Islands. A small group of islands where the U.S. military tests missiles, among other things they don't want to advertise.

Staring at the envelope, he wonders if this is his ticket out of here. Maybe the beginning of a new adventure. The alternative is to go back to work again, totally bored to death of a mundane day-to-day job. He knows that most companies usually call to inform you when you get the job, but a letter is typically bad news. Most times, it's just a thank-you letter for applying, but that's usually a single page. This envelope is thick and heavy. He lets out a long sigh, wondering if there are more forms to fill out.

Opening the envelope, he prepares for the worst. Reading the cover page, looking for that old line, 'Sorry, but you were not selected, and good luck in your efforts.' This time is different. To his astonishment, he got the job. He gasps out loud, flipping through all the pages, reading flight schedules, security clearances, and a list of things you can and cannot bring. What is so surprising is finding out that he has to be in Hawaii in less than two weeks. They also included airline tickets. No more forms to fill out, no more interviews, no more waiting around. He can finally relax. Now, he has the job of a lifetime.

Ben is on the phone, calling everyone he knows and telling them the good news. The last call is to his parents. He knows that's going to be the bad one. They're going to be disappointed since they were hoping he would get a job in Texas to be closer to the family. This job is even farther away, which means fewer opportunities to visit his parents.

* * *

Within two weeks, Ben tosses out almost everything he owns. What he couldn't sell, he had Goodwill haul off. Most of it was junk collected over the years. He knows it's time to get rid of it all, anyway. He would rather live with just a few possessions so there won't be anything holding him down.

An avid outdoor adventurist, Ben loved living in Colorado with all the camping, biking, rock climbing, canoeing, and hiking. Getting to go out skiing every weekend in the winter is even better. The small Pacific island has plenty of new adventures. He can't wait for all the sailing and scuba diving, but mostly all those pristine beaches.

All he can take with him must fit within two standard military duffel bags. Trying to decide what to bring that will fit in the bags is a tough job. On top of the list are his camera, fishing, and camping gear. Choosing what clothes to bring is simple. It's nothing but lightweight summer clothes. He sent all his winter clothes and ski gear to his parent's house for storage. If he decides to return to Colorado, at least he won't have to buy it all again.

After reviewing the guidelines of what to bring, he selects his seven days of clothes. He packs a couple of good slacks and one white dress shirt since there might be a few formal parties to attend. Luckily, he can squeeze all his clothes into one duffel bag, leaving the other one for all the fun stuff. He hopes they will have a dry cleaner on the island, or he'll be wearing wrinkled clothes every day to work.

Selecting all the fun stuff to take with him is the hardest part. The one thing he will carry on the flight is his camera bag. He doesn't want to risk losing his camera or getting it damaged in the cargo hold. This trip is a photographer's paradise. He is going to get some fantastic photos like never before.

Camping and fishing are his favorite hobbies, and it's the one thing he doesn't want to leave out. His survival gear is also part of the package. He has been caught in big snowstorms several times while camping up in the mountains. Too often, he ended up getting snowed in, spending days in a blizzard waiting for it to pass. Although moving to an island, his attitude is still the same: always be prepared for the worst.

His friends always teased him about his fancy, high-tech camping gear, but he was always there with the right tool or gadget to save the day whenever they were in a bad predicament. He had everything from fire starters, rechargeable batteries with a solar charger, flashlights, a small radio, compact cooking ware, and even a cutting wire to cut small wood for the campfire.

Luckily, all the camping gear fits easily into the other duffel bag. There is plenty of room left over for his fishing gear, sleeping bag, and mattress pad. Ben hopes the people at the airport won't be dragging it all out. Having to repack it all will take a long time. If the security at Kwajalein inspects the contents of his bags, they might think he is crazy seeing all the camping gear he has brought with him.

* * *

On his last day, Ben's best friend Kyle arrives at the apartment. They have been good friends for years. He is here to say goodbye and see what else he can take off Ben's hands. He doesn't want Ben to throw out any good fishing gear that he might use himself.

"Man, it looks like you just got robbed!" Kyle blurted out, walking into the apartment. "I can't believe you got rid of it all so quickly!"

"Yeah, I have been dumping it all. Goodwill got most of the stuff no one else wanted. I sold my car and got a rental for the last few days. That was a load off my mind, finally getting rid of it!"

"You got lucky there!" Kyle said. "I thought you were going to leave it here."

"No, one guy at work wanted it for his son," Ben explained. "I broke even on it, so I don't feel too bad."

"Well, at least you won't be needing any of that where you're going!" Kyle said, pointing to all the camping gear on the floor. "If you don't mind, I'll take it off your hands."

"Oh, I bet you would! I'll be using that more than anything. Camping on the beach is one thing I know that I'll be doing out there. The fishing will be great too! I got one of those small, compact fishing rods. It's not the best, but at least it won't take up too much space."

"What about all the fly-fishing gear?" Kyle asked, going through it all. "You can't use any of this on an island."

"Yeah, you're right... OK, you can take that. I guess all I'll need is the spoons and spinners. It's a shame I can't bring my good rod and reel. It'll probably get busted up anyway, trying to get it there," realizing his friend has his eye on all the fly-fishing gear.

"I kind of figured that. I'll take real good care of it. You can have it all back when you return," gathering up all the fishing gear.

Kyle, an avid fisherman, will take good care of it all and put it to good use. They spent many weekends camping together out by the lakes and rivers throughout Colorado. Fishing is always a big part of a camping trip. Camping and fishing go hand in hand, and there is no other place better than up in the mountains in Colorado.

Ben hands out the last of the beer. Looking at his empty apartment, he is getting second thoughts. He is not sure he is doing the right thing. If things don't work out, not only will he be out of a job, but he will have nowhere to live. Almost all of his possessions are gone. Down to a couple of duffel bags, he feels like he is starting life all over again.

"You know," Ben said, getting a little nervous. "After being out there a year, and I don't sign up again, I'll be unemployed. With no job, what will I do?"

"Just come back here for a while. You'll have plenty of money, and you'll need a vacation, anyway. You can stay with me until you get a job. With all your experience, it shouldn't take you long."

"You think they'll hire me back?" dreading the thoughts of working back at his old job again.

Kyle laughed. "I wouldn't go back to that place if I were you. You need to get a job as a fishing guide for all those tourists looking for that special fishing spot. We need to start up a business together! Just the two of us. Do nothing but fishing and camping. I have wanted to do that for a long time."

"You've been talking about that for years. I bet you anything you would never take them to your favorite fishing spots!"

"You got that right!" Kyle boasted. "Those are golden spots out there, and not for the amateur fisherman," taking another swig of beer.

"I remember that time you saw some tourists fishing in your favorite place," Ben recalled. "I can't believe you told them about all the wild bears attacking people in the area just to get rid of them!"

"It did the job, didn't it? I have been telling everyone for years about all the wild bears and mountain lions out there. If that doesn't scare them, then I'll tell them about all those people who had been mauled or even killed. I even showed them my scar when I got attacked," holding out his arm.

Ben laughed. "Oh, that big scar on your arm. Yeah, I remember that day! Didn't you get that when you fell off your bike on the way to the store to get more beer?"

"Like hell!" Kyle boasted, laughing out loud. "That was the biggest bear I'd ever seen in my life!"

Ben knows that most of the big wildlife scares were schemes to keep people away from the best fishing spots. He always laughed when he heard reports on the news, knowing that some local nut was trying to keep the tourists out. Kyle is the worst of them all. When they saw a small brown bear while out fishing, years later the story ended up being an epic tale of them fighting off a huge grizzly, chasing them for miles. Those tall tales keep getting better and better as the years pass.

Ben unloads the last of his possessions onto his old friend. Kyle makes out like a bandit with all the fishing gear, the odd books, and furniture. After the last goodbye, Ben returns to his empty apartment. The last of his possessions are stuffed into two duffel bags. Everything is now behind him. No more worries about rent, electricity, and car payments anymore. All the possessions that tied him down are now gone. He feels good about getting rid of it all, and he is looking forward to his new life.

* * *

Chapter 2

Hawaii, Job Briefing

A fter twelve long hours, Ben finally arrives in Honolulu. Having spent the last five years in Denver at 6,000-foot altitude, he feels so exhilarated being back at sea level again. Although it will take time to get used to the heat and humidity here. At least there is no more snow and blizzards. With the temperature in the mid 80s all year long, it will be a pleasant change.

Following the instructions in his travel guide, Ben takes a taxi directly to the Marine Corps Base, Hawaii (MCBH) at Kaneohe Bay. He wishes he had made his own travel plans and arrived here a few days early. What he needs more than anything is a couple of days out on the beach, especially after spending the last two weeks packing.

The trip to MCBH is a short thirty minutes. The scenery is spectacular with all the mountains and the ocean view. For a small island in the middle of the Pacific, he is so surprised to see all the people here. What is even worse is all the traffic. Even Denver had its bad times, but this is far worse.

At the base, the taxi stops in front of building twelve. The driver quickly gets out, takes the duffel bags from the trunk, placing them on the curb. Ben immediately feels the heat and humidity. The sun is fierce. Even with the breeze, it doesn't help at all. Such a dramatic change compared to Denver.

Walking into the building, Ben is so glad to feel the cold blast from the air conditioning. His clothes are completely wet with sweat, and that is just from a 30-foot walk dragging in the two duffel bags. He feels as if he has just gotten out of a sauna. Now, he wishes he had worn shorts and a T-shirt on the plane, and not his warm winter clothes. What he wants more than anything is a quick shower and to change into some clean clothes.

"Hi, is this the place to check in?" Ben asked the man behind the information desk. "I'm supposed to meet with Captain Scott for orientation."

"Yes, you're at the right place," the sergeant replied, laughing at Ben. "Looks like you just came right out of the mountains."

"How did you know that?" Ben asked, unable to think straight, wondering what was so funny.

"The thick plaid shirt, for one thing. I haven't seen one of those in years. I can't believe you're wearing all those heavy winter clothes. No wonder you're sweating like mad. It looks like you walked all the way from the airport," then laughs again.

"Well, for one thing, it was 15 degrees when I got up this morning," Ben explained. "I should have brought a change of clothes for the flight. I didn't think it would be this humid. Anyway, I'm Ben Hughes… Here are all the papers I got," placing the paperwork on the desk with his driver's license and Social Security card.

"Well, don't feel bad. You're not the only one who made that mistake. I hope you brought some summer clothes to wear. That's all you're going to need, especially where you're going."

The sergeant flips through all the papers and examines the driver's license photo, making sure it's the same person. Then he stamps every page 'Arrived' and then checks off the name on his clipboard.

"These are your forms, Mr. Hughes," the sergeant said, handing over a large sealed envelope. "Please wait over there with the rest of the crew. Captain Scott will arrive at fifteen hundred hours for the orientation meeting," pointing over to a weary-looking crowd.

Ben finds a vacant chair and drops his duffel bags, using them as a footstool. Looking around, he can easily spot the ex-military ones. He saw plenty of them in his last job. They all have the same look. It's all short hair and tight T-shirts. At least there are a few ladies in the crowd. The last thing he wants is to be on a small island for an entire year with no women working there.

A man in a uniform briskly walks up to the group. "Welcome, everyone! I'm Captain Scott. I see you all made it here with no problems. Just leave your bags here and follow me. We'll have a quick briefing, and then you'll be filling out some standard forms. Once you're done, you can check into your rooms to rest up and get a bite to eat," trying to usher them all down the hallway.

Ben feels so groggy. He drags himself up with the rest of the group. They all shuffle down the hall, grumbling about having to fill out more forms. No one wants to go to a meeting after arriving from the airport. Everyone is tired, hungry, and not in a good mood. With the beach less than a mile away, the last thing they all want is to be stuck in a room attending a boring meeting.

* * *

The military is very good at keeping things on schedule. Exactly two hours later, it's over. After filling out various insurance and security forms, watching endless videos, everyone is exhausted, ready to fall asleep. No one is in the mood for socializing. They all return to the lobby, not saying a word.

"The shuttle bus has arrived!" Captain Scott announced, walking into the lobby. "It'll take you to the barracks, where you can rest up for tomorrow's sessions. They will serve food at nineteen hundred hours. It'll give you time to freshen up."

A big sigh of relief comes from the weary group. Everyone drags themselves up. Grabbing their heavy duffel bags, they haul them outside to the bus.

Ben sits next to a man who must be over six feet tall. "Hi, I'm Ben!" trying to be sociable.

"Tom's the name," the tall man fired back, shaking Ben's hand with a firm grip. "I'm from Vegas. What brings you out here? Everyone seems to be escaping someone or something for this stint!"

"Just looking for something new and different," Ben explained. "I have been in Colorado for a while. I thought I might try the tropical beach scene for a change."

"I can't believe anyone would leave Colorado! I have been skiing up there a lot over the years and loved every minute of it. Man, you're going to have some bad problems with the climate after all that cold, dry weather where you're from!"

"Yeah, I know! I can feel it now. I'm going from one extreme to the other! Growing up in Florida, I thought I would be used to it. After being here just a few hours, I'm now starting to wonder. I didn't think it would be this bad."

"I heard they having Kona winds today," Tom explained.

"Kona winds? What the hell is that?"

"That means all the winds are coming from the south. That's why it's so humid. Normally, they got these nice cool trade winds from the north. We just happened to get here on a bad day!"

"Just my luck!" Ben said, already tired of the humidity.

Tom laughed. "Shoot, this ain't nothing. Kwajalein is down near the equator! That's going to be a burner out in the midday sun. It's going to take me a while to get used to this humidity, too. Out in Vegas, we just got the heat and not much humidity. Shit, it's like being in a damn sauna out here!" pulling on his sweaty shirt.

"You got that right!" Ben said, looking down at his shirt. "Going from winter to summer in less than a day is not a good idea. I'm already missing that nice, cool, dry weather back home."

* * *

The bus stops at an old three-story barracks. Not much has changed over the years. Everything still looks as if it's been here since World War 2. At least they have air conditioning units in every window. Ben is glad to see that so he can get out of this stifling humidity.

"Welcome, everyone!" the corporal barked out, sitting behind the desk. "This will be your home for the next couple of days. Since you're on a military base, you'll need to get used to all the security here. The barracks will have a twenty-four-hour guard keeping track of everyone who enters and leaves. You all must sign in and sign out. There are no exceptions. Posted on the wall are your room assignments. You have two hours to settle in. Dinner will be at nineteen hundred hours sharp."

Everyone rushes to see their assigned rooms. Immediately, there are a few disgruntled groans. They quickly discover that all the women are on the second floor, and the men are on the first. All the women complain after finding out there are no elevators, as they drag their heavy duffel bags up the stairs.

Ben sees his name next to his new bunkmate, Tony Wilson, assigned to room A-9. So tired, he slowly makes his way down the hallway, dragging his duffel bags. The room is small, with two single beds on opposing walls, looking like a typical dorm room. His roommate is already there, lying on a bed.

Dropping his duffel bags by the door, Ben flops on the bed. He is too tired to go through his bag to find something to wear. He feels so filthy, needing a shower. Not knowing where the bathroom is, he is too tired to care.

"You must be Ben!" Tony blurted out. "Welcome to paradise!" waving his hands about in the air.

Ben chuckled. "I hope this isn't what it's going to be like here every day. I'm so hungry and so tired. Don't know if I'm going to keep awake for dinner."

"I'm the same way. Don't worry about it. I heard the corporal at the end of the hallway will make sure none of us will miss it."

Ben lets out a long sigh. "Thank God! At least I can get a few minutes of sleep. So, I guess he's the dorm mother as well and will have his hands full, making sure we don't get in trouble! I bet he's pissed off joining up for that big adventure to see the world, and he's out there babysitting us!"

"Yep, he didn't look like he was in a good mood," Tony explained. "They're all like that around here. It's the typical military mentality, especially with this being a Marine base. We'll be monitored twenty-four hours a day until we leave. Nothing goes on out here without them knowing about it. These guys don't trust us one bit. It's funny how we're supposed to be stationed on a high-security military base, but out here, they treat us like a bunch of foreign spies."

"I noticed that. I had a feeling they can't wait to get rid of us."

Tony laughed. "That's for sure, especially for you civilians! Kaneohe Bay is somewhat of a pseudo boot camp for three days being part of our indoctrination. You can tell they don't want us here at all. I think it was imposed on them, and they don't like it one bit. It's politics as usual. Army, Navy, Air Force, and Marines, and they don't want to play on the same team. We're stuck in the middle, and no one wants us. I have seen this before way too many times."

* * *

By seven o'clock, both are sound asleep. Tony was right about the alarm clock. The corporal walks down the hall, beating on a metal trash can with his mallet. The clanking sound reverberates down the hallway, making sure no one will miss the mess call.

"Mess call nineteen hundred hours!" the corporal barks out loud, stomping his feet down the hallway, making as much noise as possible. "Let's go! Everyone up and out!"

Everyone slowly follows the corporal to the far end of the hallway. He opens the door, revealing a large dining room. Someone has already set up a huge buffet on long tables.

"Help yourselves!" the corporal shouted out. "We have chicken, steak, salmon, and all the fixings!"

Everyone quickly grabs a plate, rushing to get in line. Being so hungry, most start sampling the food while waiting. For Ben, it's a sight for sore eyes. He loads up his plate with almost everything they have after only having had a snack at the airport before the long flight.

Looking around for a familiar face, he sees Tony and Tom on the far side of the room, walking over to join them. Both are too busy stuffing their faces to talk. They also have huge piles of food on their plates.

Mrs. Burns slowly walks around the room, talking to everyone. She is the administrator who attended all the interviews and set up all the travel arrangements. If anyone has questions or problems, she is the one in charge.

"Hello, I am Mrs. Burns, and I am glad you all are here! I hope you enjoy the meal. I know it's been a long day, but it's almost over. We have a couple of days of medical exams and, unfortunately, more forms to fill out, but then you will be on your way. But first, I want everyone to stand up and introduce yourself. Tell everyone where you are from and why you are here."

Ben can't believe it. They won't even let everyone eat without going into another session. He wanted to talk to Tom and Tony. No one complains. One by one, everyone gets up, introducing themselves. They tell why they are here and what they expect this adventure will mean to them.

Ben is listening to everyone's story trying to fix their name to the face. All are from different places, but most are ex-military. Only five of them out of the twenty are civilians, and that worries him. He knows these ex-military types. They always act as if they are still in the military, and they expect anyone who works with them to be the same.

After all the introductions, Mrs. Burns asked all five of the civilians to stand. Jenny, Tom, Samantha, Liz, and Ben reluctantly stand up. The rest of the group are already cracking jokes about them.

"As you five can see, you're surrounded by a bunch of jarheads," Mrs. Burns explained. "You will need to attend an extra class on military formalities and etiquette. It sounds unnecessary, but it will take time to get used to working with these military types."

Laughter fills the room. The rest of the group knows who they'll be picking on for the next couple of days. The five civilians are all promptly assigned their new nickname, 'Newbies.'

Ben is feeling a little better after meeting everyone. He doesn't like being one of the few nonmilitary ones here. All the military people are giggling and taunting them. To make matters worse, Mrs. Burns gets all the newbies to sit at a table together for more paperwork to sign and more material to read.

Ben is used to being around these ex-military types. In most of his jobs, he always had to deal with the military in one form or another. He knows what all this extra paperwork is going to be. When civilians mix with officers, there are always problems. They expected everyone, especially the civilians, to treat them accordingly. All it takes is for one of the civilians to call a general a gomer to set off a war with the contractors.

He finally notices Jenny, a beautiful blonde, sitting across from him. He can see she is all business and no fun. Everyone at the table is laughing and having conversations, but Jenny mostly keeps to herself. She is too busy reading all the new material and ignoring everyone else.

Ben constantly glances over at Jenny. Occasionally, she smiles at him but goes straight back to reading the material. That usually intrigues him. At parties, for some unknown reason, he is always attracted to the women who seem most unapproachable. They are typically shy and not very outgoing. She doesn't look like the shy type at all but more of a business manager. That usually means all work and a no-play attitude.

As time goes by, everyone gets tired after the long day. One by one, they go back to their assigned rooms. The five newbies all leave together. The three women said goodnight, walking up the stairs together. Ben and Tom walked down the hall, grinning at each other. They don't have to say a word. Both know what is on each other's minds, women.

* * *

The next day, it's nothing but complete physicals, dental exams, and psych tests. After a big breakfast, the men go one way, and the women go elsewhere. For those who were in the military, this is nothing new, where the women were often separated from the rest. It all makes sense when they are all standing in line, wearing only their underwear, waiting for their medical exams.

Everyone is poked and prodded all day long with the inevitable endless vaccinations in both arms. No one questions why, all taking whatever is given to them.

Ben doesn't have to worry about the dental exam. He knew he had a few problems and went to his dentist and had everything done before leaving Denver.

Ben had no problem passing all his medical tests. Climbing the mountains in Colorado put him in great shape. A few of the others are worried. High blood pressure, high cholesterol, and being overweight are some of the conditions for being rejected for the job. No one wants to get this far only to be told, 'Go home. You are too fat and out of shape for this job'.

After lunch, it's time for the dreaded psych tests. All are sitting in front of the psychologist's office, holding their medical records. No one talks at all. Everyone had heard the horror stories about this test. They quietly wait to see the person's reaction coming out of the office after completing their test. The reaction is always the same. It's just a blank stare, and they quietly walk away. No one smiles or gives any indication that they passed or failed.

Ben is finally called in. He quietly sits in the chair in front of a large desk. Lying out on the desk, more paperwork to be filled out and a box full of number two pencils. The idiot test is first. Having seen this one before, he knows it's no big deal. Then, there is the inkblot test. Trying to describe an image from nothing more than a splash of ink on a folded piece of paper is ridiculous. After a while, he says anything for this to end.

The final test is with the psychologist. She is the one to determine if any of the candidates might have problems being on an island. She sits behind the desk, asking what seem to be endless, unrelated questions. The main thing she is looking for is the inability to be away from friends and family for a long duration. Also, everyone has to make new friends and work under constant stress for this job.

With a yearlong assignment and working in shifts for ten hours a day for fourteen days straight, it's not for the weak-minded. Some people do not last the first month. That is why everyone has two weeks off every three months, and they must leave the island.

After almost an hour, the psych test is finally over. Ben has no clue about the purpose of these frivolous questions. The psychologist doesn't let on to anything. All she did was write endless notes on her steno pad.

"So, did I pass?" he asked. "Am I normal?" getting a little frustrated with the psychologist.

"I'm sorry," she simply replied. "We'll let you know after we review the results. That will be all. Please do not discuss any of this with the others. You can leave now."

He is a little shocked by her personality. He thinks she is some kind of nutcase. She is supposed to be a psychologist, but it looks as if she can really use one. He can never work with anyone with a personality like that. He gets up and heads out the door, so glad it's over.

As Ben steps out into the hallway, everyone looks at him, hoping for a clue. With his strange sense of humor, he looks down at the floor and pretends to cry. Before walking out the door, Ben glances back to see all the stunned looks on their faces. He can't help but laugh, feeling so sorry for all those having to wait hours in agony, not knowing what is in store for them. He knows it was all for nothing and a complete waste of time.

* * *

Chapter 3

Last Day in Hawaii

The tests are finally over, and everyone has passed with no problems. The graduation party is at the Beach Hut. A trendy local hangout next to the beach lit up with Christmas lights. It's a very primitive establishment, but it sets the right mood for a Polynesian party out on the beach.

Ben and Tony arrive late at the Beach Hut. The music is blaring out loud, and it's already packed with people. Ben sits with his new friends. They're already on their second order of barbecue ribs and hot wings. A few are up dancing, but most are sitting around in small groups celebrating their last day in Hawaii. Tony and Bob paired up with Mary and Samantha, all drinking heavily. Tony has his arm around Mary, and it looks as if they are getting really serious.

Jenny Mason sits in the corner all alone. As usual, she has her notebook out, constantly writing something down. Most of the time, she keeps to herself, not socializing with the rest of the team. She is pretty and blonde, and smart as hell. She also aced every test and finished the entire program before anyone else.

Ben watches as Jenny shoots down all the men who approach her. The rumors run wild about her. Since she didn't care for any male companionship, lesbian was the first label she got. Most referred to her as being stuck up and not too friendly. Even the women noticed she had been distant, even with them.

Seeing her all alone, Ben wonders how she made it through the psych test. The whole idea of the test is to make sure everyone will work well with one another. It looks as if she is already having problems associating with other people. She might be one of those who will not make it through the first month.

* * *

Late into the night, Ben decides to make his move. "Guys, it's my turn! I'll show you how it's done!" boasting to everyone, seeing Jenny as a real mystery and a challenge.

They all laugh because everyone else has struck out. After a few beers, Ben loses all of his inhibitions. He buys two beers and then walks over to Jenny. Sitting down at her table, Ben places the other beer right in front of her. He stares at her without saying a word and has a big smile on his face. She ignores him, not even looking up, acknowledging he is even there.

"So, what's your line?" Jenny asked, getting irritated with him.

Ben thinks about it for a few seconds. "I'm not sure," he said, with a sheepish smile on his face. "Give me a little time to think of one. Actually, it looks as if you could use a drink and maybe talk with someone here."

Jenny smiles back. "No, thanks... You know, I have noticed you sitting up at the bar with all the guys making fun of me all night."

Ben laughed. "Not me... I have been watching you break the hearts of all those guys."

"So, now it's your turn. You've been staring at me for most of the night. Well, I have been watching you too. I wondered how long before you decided to make your move. So, what's your plan to sweep me off my feet?"

"None to speak of, now that I think about it. You know it's going to be a long haul, stuck on that small island. You may want to get to know some of the guys."

"It's just a job like any other," she blurted out.

"Well, from what I hear, Kwajalein is nothing but one big party when we're not working."

"It's just not my style," she said, shaking her head. "I'm not the party type."

He stares at her, wondering what to say next. Almost lost for words, he picks up his beer, holding it in front of her face. At least he knows this conversation can't get any worse.

She has a feeling he is not going to leave her alone, then picks up the beer, tapping it on his bottle. "Cheers," she said, taking a sip.

"See! That wasn't so hard, was it?" he replied, with a big smile on his face.

"I know all about your plan. You guys are all looking to get some action before getting shipped out. I heard it all before, and I'll tell you now, it ain't going to happen!"

Ben can't help laughing. Jenny stands out from the rest of the women here, and he likes that. She is honest and tells it like it is. He knows this is a good sign. He never lets up and finally gets her to start talking. Surprisingly, they had a lot in common and talked for hours.

Jenny is starting to admire Ben. After all this time, he never once tried to hit on her as all the others did. He is still a mystery to her, not fitting the mold that he was placed in his psychology review. She is glad to have someone to talk to and knows all about him after reading his dossier. He is a rugged mountain man of Colorado. Spending most of his time alone in the mountains is one of the key points they look for in people living and working on a remote island.

"I noticed you're always out on the beach real early," Jenny mentioned. "Are you one of those early-morning joggers?"

"Oh no, not me!" Ben explained. "I do a lot of photography and have been trying to get a good sunrise photo since we've been here. I was hoping to get a few sunsets, but we're on the wrong side of the island. So, the sunrise is all I have to work with here. Also, that's the best time, anyway. With no people about, I got the whole beach to myself."

"That explains a few things."

"So what's all this writing you've been doing? Every time I see you, you're always jotting down something in your little black book."

"It's part of my graduate work," she explained. "I'm a psychologist. I'll be working on Kwajalein to see how people work in isolated conditions."

His eyes open wide in disbelief. "No wonder you've been keeping a distance from the rest of us," he jokingly said. "You're one of those shrinks watching our every move. It's just like that nutcase in the psych test. We're all nothing but a bunch of guinea pigs to you guys!"

She laughed. "No, it's nothing like that! Although I am the first to admit it, she is a little strange. We just monitor how people react to one another, especially in the work environment. It's not an easy assignment. That's why even after all the tests, there are always one or two that crack and get sent back home."

"So, what's your evaluation of me?" he asked. "Am I one of those wacko types?" getting a little apprehensive.

"No!" she said with a big smile. "You're the mountain man who seeks out isolation in the wilderness. You're also easy to get along with, so you'll do fine."

"Yeah, but what about after we've been there a whole year!" he quickly replied.

She laughed again. "That's why they have all those parties and entertainment. It gets your mind off of work, but it does make it a fun place to live! If it weren't for that and all the good pay, no one would want to work out there."

"I know. It's all they ever talk about, but I'm looking forward to it. It'll be fun!"

* * *

Late into the night, the party dies down. Ben looks at his watch, surprised to see it's well past two in the morning. He has never been up this late since arriving in Hawaii. With the sunrise just a few hours away and being their last night here, they might as well stay up all night. With the long flight to Kwajalein, he can sleep on the plane.

"So, what do you think about going to the beach to see the sunrise?" Ben asked, finally getting the courage to ask her. "It's only a couple of hours from now."

"I haven't done anything like that in years," she replied, her eyes opened wide, loving the idea.

"That's great! Let's go! I need to make a quick trip back to the room. We need some warmer clothes, plus I need to pick up my camera," a little surprised that she didn't hesitate at all and wanted to go.

"I'm ready! It'll be fun!" she said, finishing the last of her beer.

As they get up to leave, everyone is chanting. All the women are already gone, leaving just the men. They are all up at the bar getting drunk. All the men who struck out with Jenny are still there. Ben is the one who is leaving with her. They all waited in vain for him to strike out so they could get a second or third chance.

Ben has been oblivious to everything going on around him since he first sat down with Jenny. Neither one of them has noticed that they are the center of attention in the bar. Bets are being placed all night on whether Ben will strike out or not.

"Way to go, Ben!" everyone yelled out, holding up their beers and cheering him on.

Ben smiles, waving back, a little embarrassed. Jenny starts blushing with all the attention and can't wait to leave. They rush out to the beach, still listening to all the chants coming from the bar.

"Does this normally happen when you leave a party with a guy?" he asked amusingly.

"Well, they just had a little too much to drink," she quickly explained. "For the record, this is just a walk on the beach so we can see the sunrise. So don't think you're getting any more than that!"

He noticed she was smiling the entire time while telling him he was not getting anywhere with her. Deep down, he is still wondering about her. She is letting her guard down. She is not as stuck up as the others made her out to be.

They rush back to the barracks, surprised that no one else is around. The only person around is the guard, who is too busy reading his book. Since this is the last night on base, there are no more restrictions and no more reason to check people in and out.

Grabbing his camera bag and a fleece jacket, he runs out to the main entrance. He is not sure how this is going to end. He is just happy to have some female companionship. With this being the last sunrise in Hawaii, he wants it to be special and to have someone to share it with him.

Looking at herself in the mirror, Jenny cringes seeing what the humidity has done to her hair and makeup. After a quick wash and reapplying fresh makeup, she rushes out front. Seeing Ben with a camera bag assures her a little that he is not just coming on to her.

* * *

Walking hand in hand on the beach into the darkness, they take their shoes off, occasionally venturing into the warm water. The night is beautiful, with just a slight breeze off the ocean. The sound of the crashing waves fills the night.

Ben is terrified that she is analyzing everything he says and does. He wishes he didn't know about her profession and now feels so awkward. Every word is carefully thought out. Somehow, he knows she can read him like a book.

Jenny, however, is pleased just to be out with a man who is not constantly hitting on her. It's a pleasant change since she had a few bad experiences and stopped dating for a while. She spent so much of her time with her education and job, not wanting to get back into a relationship too soon. This new job is a significant change in her life, and she wants to take her time and not rush into things.

They walk up to the small bench where Ben usually waits for the sunrise. Both sit down and discover they have a lot in common. Jenny is slowly dropping her facade, revealing a very shy woman.

Ben takes her hand, then leans over to kiss her cheek. He is a little shocked and unprepared as she kisses him back with one long, passionate kiss. She rests her head on his shoulder, putting her arms around him, holding him tight. It's a dramatic turn of events. He was not expecting this at all.

"Look how beautiful the sky is," she said, noticing the clouds over the horizon. "It's really turning red."

"Now, that's going to be a great sunrise from the looks of things. I better get things ready," realizing that so much time has passed.

"The sun is coming up already? That can't be!" looking down at her watch.

"Yep, it's time. It should be coming up over there in a few minutes," pointing over to the red glow on the horizon.

The sky quickly brightens up. Ben rummages through his camera bag. He sets up his tripod, locking the camera on top of it. Jenny watches him, intrigued by his fancy camera equipment. She thought all he was going to do was take a few snapshots and didn't expect all this.

"Now, this is going to be a great shot. The clouds are in the right position," Ben explained, placing the camera and tripod in front of a group of palm trees.

"Why are the clouds so important?" not understanding what he is doing. "I would have thought you would want a clear sky for this?"

"Just wait and see! Once the sun is in the right position, the clouds will light up, turning into a fiery red color! It makes the photos even better!"

"Aren't the trees going to be in the way?" she asked, looking over at where the sun was supposed to rise.

"Composition is very important in photography. Take a look for yourself," motioning Jenny to look through the viewfinder.

"Wow! That looks pretty good! I would have just snapped the picture of the sun coming up," looking through the camera, seeing how the palm trees would be on the right and the red clouds just above the sun.

"I know. That's what most people do. It's all in the planning. I have been out here several times, scoping things out. For these things, you have only about five minutes, so you need to be in the right place at the right time. Once the sun starts coming up, it's too late to move the camera. This is by far the best spot. It looks like this one might be a winner."

"Yep, you're one of those perfectionists," she said with a little smile. "I think that's what they look for in these jobs."

He laughed. "Ha, I got you fooled! I'm only that way in my hobbies, never for work!"

As the sun slowly rises above the horizon, Ben takes countless photos as Jenny looks on. The last sunrise in Hawaii is by far the best one yet and was worth the wait.

"Let's get some people shots in while we're at it," he said, motioning her to step in front of the camera.

"I don't know," she replied, feeling a little awkward. "I'm not very good at these things."

"How about standing over there right next to the tree? It'll make a great silhouette shot."

Jenny obliged, running over to the group of palm trees. He takes several more photos, calls out instructions, and poses for her to do. She has never done anything like this before. It's like a modeling session, and she loves it.

"This is fun! How about letting me take one of you?"

Ben agrees, showing her how to operate the camera. He runs out to the beach, standing with his arms out with a big smile. She takes a few shots then the camera makes a high-pitched whining sound.

"Oops! I think something is going on with this. All I did was push the button!"

"Oh, it's not a problem," hearing the noise from the camera. "It just means we're done. We just used up a roll of film."

"What? You got to be kidding. You just took an entire roll!"

"Yep, all in less than five minutes. On a good day, I can go through three or four rolls. Hopefully, if I get one perfect shot, I'll be happy."

"Do you think we can get it developed right away?" she asked. "I like to see how they came out!"

"Hey, wait a minute! Don't we have to leave this morning?"

"Oh God! That's right! I can't believe I forgot! We're late too! We need to get back!" looking at her watch.

"Let's run for it! We can't miss that flight!" quickly dismantling his camera gear and puts everything into the bag, running back to the barracks.

* * *

Arriving at the barracks, they stand facing each other. Ben is feeling a little awkward, not knowing what to say or do next. Seeing him hesitating, she quickly leans over, giving him one long, hard kiss. Again, he had not been expecting this at all.

"Thank you for a great night!" she said with a big smile. "It was a lot of fun! I had better go pack. Luckily, we're still a little early. Do you want to meet me for breakfast in ten or fifteen minutes?"

"You bet! Let me put this stuff away, and I'll meet you here," kissing her again before rushing back to his room.

He frantically gathers all his clothes, stuffing them all back into the duffel bag. Feeling so tired after being up all night, he is now paying for it. Lying on the bed is a big mistake. After a few minutes, he is sound asleep.

Jenny walks down the stairs, looking for Ben. Not seeing him at the entrance, she walks down the hallway to see if he is still in his room.

"So much for breakfast!" she shouts out, seeing him on the bed with his hands folded across his chest, sound asleep.

"Maybe breakfast was not a good idea," she mumbled, also feeling exhausted after being up all night.

With the long day ahead, she wants to take a nap more than anything. Gently shutting the door, she crawls up on the bed, snuggling up to him. Within a few minutes, she also falls sound asleep.

* * *

As the morning draws on, most of the team members wake up with massive hangovers. One by one, they pack up and head out to the airport. Most had spent the night in someone else's room. Several had slept in the bar, while others were on the beach. Since so many in the group never came back to the barracks, no one noticed that Ben and Jenny were missing.

With everyone at the airport, Mrs. Burns walks the corridors, checking all the rooms to make sure no one left anything. Someone always leaves a bag behind, and it has to be rushed to the airport. Walking up to room A-9, she opens the door, shocked to see both Jenny and Ben sound asleep on the bed.

"What are you doing here? You're supposed to be at the airport!" Mrs. Burns shouted.

All the yelling startles Jenny. "What time is it?" she asked, barely able to sit up.

"It's seven o'clock! Your flight leaves in less than an hour! You should already be there! You're going to miss your flight!" frantically, waving her arms up in the air.

Jenny and Ben slowly crawl off the bed, finding it so difficult to stand up. Both have massive hangovers. Jenny runs back to her room to get her gear. Luckily, she had packed everything the night before. Ben is not as organized, stuffing everything he can find into the open duffel bag. Mrs. Burns helps him pack, constantly scolding him for being late.

"I'll have to drive you two to the airport!" Mrs. Burns shouted. "There is no time for a cab or bus!"

Ben thanks her as he drags his duffel bags down the hallway. They meet up with Jenny, who is already in front of the building.

"Wait here while I get my car," Mrs. Burns said, running out to the parking lot.

Standing on the sidewalk, still in a daze, neither can believe they fell asleep, almost missing the flight. It's not the way to start a new job being late on the first day.

"Is this one of your typical days on the job?" Jenny asked, laughing at him.

"You should know," he said, joking with her. "It's all in my dossier!"

"We better not miss this flight. We'll be in big trouble," she added.

"No shit... After what we've been through in the last couple of days, we better not lose this job! It'll be a long trip back home."

Hearing the screeching tires, it startles them. Mrs. Burns has arrived and pops the trunk, waving them to hurry. Ben tosses the bags in. As soon as they are in the car, she stomps on the gas, burning rubber.

The drive to the airport is an absolute nightmare. Mrs. Burns doesn't stop at any traffic lights or stop signs. She constantly weaves in and out of traffic down the highway. She keeps hitting the horn, yelling, and screaming at anyone who gets in her way.

The car races up to the private terminal at the airport. Then, it screeches to a halt right in front of the entrance. The security guards automatically stand at attention, recognizing the car, but mostly the driver. Seeing two people getting out of the car frantically throwing white duffel bags on the ground, they laugh out loud. They have seen this all morning, more of the D-4 replacement group being dragged to the airport.

Ben thanks Mrs. Burns for the ride. Jenny gives her a big hug and apologizes for being late. They run through the terminal entrance to the Island Airways check-in desk.

With only a few minutes to spare, they both slapped their tickets and photo IDs on the counter. The woman behind the counter is not too happy. She takes the tickets and then enters the information on the keyboard.

"You'll be boarding in a few minutes," the woman said, handing out the boarding passes. "I'll take your bags."

"Good, that means we haven't missed our flight," Ben said, so relieved.

"No, but it was a little too close. You two are really lucky."

"So, where is the plane? I thought it would be here by now?" Ben asked, looking out the huge window, seeing only small planes out on the tarmac.

"Oh, the regular 737 shuttle already left," the attendant explained. "Some hotshot general and his staff had an emergency meeting at Kwajalein, so you all got bumped. Your group is taking the backup flight."

"You mean to tell me they just showed up and took our plane?" Ben asked.

"Sorry, but when the general wants a flight, it's his for the taking. They don't care much for contractors. Luckily, the backup flight is available. Otherwise, you could have been stuck here for a few days."

"I wouldn't mind a few more days in Hawaii," he said, joking with her. "So, what flight do we have then? I hope none of those out there is the one we'll be on!" looking at all the small airplanes sitting out on the tarmac.

"Oh yes, it's the white twin-engine one with the blue stripe," the attendant points it out for him.

"You got to be kidding!" he blurted out. "We're going to be on that small plane to Kwajalein?"

"It's not that bad," she said. "Some of the big executives use it to get around the islands. Even movie stars from Hollywood have used this shuttle. So, in a way, it's like you're getting your own private flight."

Ben is getting nervous traveling over 2,400 miles over open water in such a small plane. He has been on some of these shuttle flights in Colorado, and it's not too comfortable, and he hopes it has a bathroom in it. After a few hours, it's somewhat tolerable, but they're going to be stuck on this flight for almost eight hours.

After checking in their bags, he makes sure to keep his camera bag to carry on the plane. There is no way that he will let his camera gear get crushed under all that luggage. He is also hoping to get some good island photos from the air.

Ben turns to Jenny. "Well, I guess we got a few minutes. I need to get this film sent home before we leave and get some more for the trip. Do you want to get some food? I don't know about you, but I'm starving!"

"Yeah, I'm going to need something to eat, or I'm not going to make it. I feel light-headed already. I'm so tired, having a hard time keeping my eyes open."

"You'll have plenty of time to sleep. This flight is about eight hours long. At least we can get something to read and snack on before we get on the plane," he added, seeing a newspaper stand not too far away.

They rush over to the small newspaper stand. While Jenny is grabbing the snacks, Ben goes straight to the counter, seeing they have some padded mailers and stamps for sale. He grabs one mailer, dumping all six rolls of undeveloped film into it.

He writes his parent's address and adds a small note: 'Mom/Dad, about to catch my flight to Kwaj. These are the photos I took in Hawaii. Apologize for not being able to get them developed. We're running late. I'll call you when I get there. Love Ben.'

"I need to send this to the mainland," he said, handing the mailer to the clerk.

"This should be enough!" Jenny said, walking up with a huge stack of candy bars, drinks, newspapers, and magazines, dumping them all on the counter.

"You weren't joking about being hungry and wanting something to read," he blurted out, seeing all the junk food and newspapers she had dumped on the counter.

"It's a long trip, but I might share if you're nice!" she said, winking at him.

"Sounds like a deal to me. I'll get it," paying cash for it all.

"Thanks... I hope you didn't send the roll you took of me this morning! We can get those developed at Kwajalein."

"Sorry, too late... I just dropped it into the mailbox. I didn't mark the rolls, anyway. So, there is no way of knowing which one it was."

"Oh well, it doesn't matter. You're the one who will have to do all the explaining when your mom and dad see the photos of me. Good thing I decided not to do any topless poses for you, or did I?" winking at him, then smiled.

Ben's mouth drops wide open, hearing her remark. "We didn't take any of those, did we?" he asked, his mind almost blank with lack of sleep and one hell of a hangover.

He is trying to remember all the photos that he took that morning. His mind is still a blur from being so tired, and he's having a hard time remembering anything. He hopes there are no risqué photos he just sent to his parents. That will be extremely embarrassing.

They run to the gate, hearing the final call for their flight. Jenny keeps glancing back at Ben with a little grin on her face. Ben is now wondering if he missed out on an opportunity while on the beach with her. At least life on Kwajalein is going to be a little better, knowing that he might already have a girlfriend before he even gets there.

* * *

Chapter 4

Flight to Kwajalein

J enny and Ben frantically run out onto the tarmac. As usual, they are late and the last ones in line. Ben is getting nervous seeing the airplane close-up. The small turbojet is mostly used by the rich or for shuttling politicians around. It might be great to go from one city to the next, but not on an oceanic flight.

Stepping inside the airplane, Ben cringes seeing how small and cramped it is. There is only a single row of seats along each side of the aisle. At least everyone will get a window seat.

"Hey, Tony!" Ben yelled out. "Wow, it looks like you got one hell of a hangover. So, what happened to you guys?"

"Hey, Ben! Went out with Liz and had our own little party. Woke up on the beach this morning. It was great! I see you two hooked up?"

"Oh, we went out to the beach too," Ben explained, glancing back at Jenny. "We had a great time as well."

Jenny blushes, then looks away, not saying a word. Ben knows it's best not to boast, especially in front of her. Although not saying anything can imply a lot more happened. Tony winks at Ben, glad to see he hitched up with her.

Being the last ones on board, everyone else has the seats up in the front. The last two available seats are at the very back. At least they will get to sit across the aisle from each other during the long flight.

Ben puts his camera bag under the seat. "Oh, looks like we got the best seats!"

"How is that?" she asked.

"We're right next to the galley. We'll get our food first. Our meals will still be hot when they hand them out. We might even get to sneak back for seconds before the others even get their food," glancing back at the small galley and storage area right behind them.

"I think you're in for a big disappointment. All we have on this trip are sandwiches, coffee, and soft drinks. I think we even get to serve ourselves," she explained, trying not to laugh.

He let out a long sigh. "Oh, great! I was hoping for a good hot meal. I'm starving!"

"Remember, my mountain man... You should always be prepared!" she boasted, holding up the small bag of snacks.

* * *

The pilot starts the left engine. The noise and vibration are going right through the airplane. Ben holds his hands firmly against his ears, trying to block out the painful noise. Everyone else is doing the same. He knows this will be one long, miserable flight if it's going to be like this all the way to Kwajalein.

After what seems like an eternity of waiting in line for final clearance, the airplane races down the runway and then rapidly gains altitude. Ben looks out the window and sees the beautiful Hawaiian Islands. With all the mountains and pristine beaches, he is a little frustrated that he didn't get to spend more time there.

The pilot gets on the intercom. "Welcome, everyone! Our flying time is approximately seven hours at an altitude of 25,000 feet. We have one refueling stop at Johnston Island about three hours from now. Because of the security situation there, no one will get off the plane during refueling. So just sit back, relax, and enjoy the flight."

Once the flight reaches cruising altitude, the copilot slowly walks to the galley. After a few minutes, the smell of freshly brewed coffee emanates through the small airplane.

Ben gets up to stretch his legs, then looks into the galley. "Is any of that coffee ready?" he asked, surprised to see the copilot was also the steward.

"Sure! It's ready to go. Just help yourself. The name is Rodger," the copilot said, holding out his hand. "I'm glad to see you all made it. We heard some wild stories about you guys. Is any of it true?"

"I don't have a clue... We left the party early and spent the night out on the beach."

"I heard they're clamping down on the partying because of you guys. The people at Kwajalein will be watching you for a while," handing Ben a cup of coffee.

"Who is supposed to handle the food and drinks?" Ben asked, sipping the coffee, hoping it would help his throbbing headache.

Rodger smiles. "Well, you got the back seat, and you also know where the coffee is. That means you just got volunteered for KP duty!" then laughs.

"You got to be kidding!"

"Nope... Whoever is in the back seat gets to serve the goodies. That's why it's not too wise to be last in line around here. I need to get back. Finish up your coffee, then get to work. All you have to do is walk up and down the aisle looking real pretty, handing out the coffee or soft drinks."

"I was planning on taking a nap since I've had no sleep," Ben explained.

The copilot laughed. "Sorry... Those are the rules!"

Jenny can't help overhearing the conversation. "Oh, Ben! I'll have mine with one sugar and plenty of cream, please!" seeing his well laid out plans are falling apart.

Rodger returns to the cockpit, leaving Ben to handle the refreshments. He takes his new assignment in stride, giving him something to do while on the flight. He plays the part walking down the aisle with a stack of Styrofoam cups in one hand and a big pot of coffee in the other. Everyone is laughing at Ben, seeing him wandering about with his new duties. Countless remarks are being thrown his way. Handing out all the food and drinks is a full-time job, and he will not get much rest on this flight.

* * *

At the halfway mark, the airplane starts its descent to Johnston Island. Not getting off the flight to stretch their legs is not sitting too well with the passengers. Since they are on an unscheduled flight with their original plane being absconded by the military brass, there is no choice in the matter. Johnston Island is the only place where they can get fuel to make it to Kwajalein. No one has security clearance for this island, so no one is getting off the plane.

Ben is in the cockpit at the time Johnston Island comes into view. He is so relieved to see land again, but this place is not much from the looks of things. The island is only 1,000 feet long and 200 feet wide. It's almost like landing on an aircraft carrier. The runway is about half the size of the island. If this is what Kwajalein is like, he knows it's going to be a long year.

* * *

When the airplane turns off the runway, several military vehicles quickly pull alongside. To everyone's surprise, they have an armed escort to the refueling station.

"Welcome to Johnston Island," the pilot announced over the intercom. "We'll be here just long enough to top off the tanks, so sit back and relax. As you can see, we're not welcome here. Don't attempt to deplane or even open the hatch. You'll be arrested before your foot even touches the tarmac. They are very serious here. If you knew what they do on this island, you sure as hell wouldn't want to get off the aircraft."

That gets everyone's curiosity going. Now, everyone is staring out the windows.

As the fuel tanker approaches, several military police are very irritated walking up to the plane. They are mad about something, trying to signal to the pilot, pointing up at the aircraft.

Rodger rushes down the aisle. "Sorry, we have to close all the shades. We might see something that we're not supposed to!"

After several moans and groans, everyone obliges, closing all the window shades. After the pilot shuts off the engines, no one complains anymore. Now that it's so quiet, everyone decides that this is a good time to get back to sleep.

"Ben! Don't even think about getting that camera out!" Rodger shouts out. "You'll lose it big time out here."

"You got to be kidding? I wanted to take a photo of the armed escorts."

Rodger shakes his head. "If they see you with a camera, they'll come in and confiscate it. You would get reprimanded when you arrive at Kwajalein."

"What's all the fuss about?" Ben asked, placing the camera back in the bag. "It's not like we're spies. We all work for the same people, don't we?"

"That's the problem... We're not supposed to be here. This is an unscheduled flight. People around here don't like surprises. Your original flight would have been nonstop to Kwajalein. It looks like the people here at Johnston just found out about us not too long ago. They're asking way too many questions."

Ben laughed. "I bet it's all turf wars with the big generals. They forget we're all supposed to be on the same side. We saw a lot of that back at the base we were staying."

"You got that right. Those guys will be mad as hell when they find out this flight and the fuel are coming out of their pockets! Anyway, just sit back and relax. We'll be out of here soon."

* * *

After the brief pit stop, they are back in the air again. With all the excitement over, everyone wants this long flight to end. The people at Johnston Island are glad to see them go before there are any security breaches.

As time goes by, the weather changes for the worse. Large thunderhead clouds are developing all around. The turbulence is jostling everyone about in their seats. Most airlines can fly above the storms, but the best they can do with the twin-turboprop is go around the bad weather.

"Sorry, folks," the pilot announced on the intercom. "We got some serious turbulence up ahead. We'll be diverting our heading a little to get around these storms. Please return to your seats and fasten your seatbelts."

"Oh, Ben!" the pilot added. "Can you get a garbage sack and collect up all the trash so it doesn't roll around the aisle? Please!"

Everyone laughs as Ben is quickly volunteered for garbage detail. "Come on, Ben, no slacking around!" someone yelled out. "Back to work!" with more laughter coming from the rest of the passengers.

Ben gets up, finding it more difficult to keep on his feet with the plane constantly buffeting around. He grabs the trash sack, slowly making his way to the front. They all dump their cups and half-eaten food into the bag. He enters the cockpit and finally gets to talk with the pilot, Pete Smith. An extremely young-looking pilot, Ben thought.

Rodger turns around to unload the empty cups and wastepaper. "Thanks, Ben! You did a great job. Remember to add it to your resume."

"So, when do I get to help fly the plane?" Ben jokingly asked.

Rodger laughed. "After only one flight as a steward! It took me an entire month of handing out coffee before I got promoted to copilot!"

Ben likes these pilots, and they have a good sense of humor. He gets a quick tour of all the complicated instruments. He loves being up in the cockpit, especially getting to look out the front windshield at the fantastic view.

The clouds are enormous and very ominous looking, billowing up higher and higher. The sun drops behind a huge cumulonimbus cloud right in front of their flight path.

Ben looks down at the instrument panel and sees one massive line of storms on the radar screen. "That doesn't look good. How are we going to get around that mess?"

"Hard to say," Rodger replied. "The weather people got it wrong again. It's supposed to be more to the east, but it must have stalled. We may have to find a small opening and punch through it."

"What about going back and trying another day?" Ben asked, getting a little worried.

"Yeah, right!" Pete blurted out. "You're just looking for an excuse for another party! From the sound of things, that was one hell of a party. I just sat around watching TV last night."

Ben laughed. "It was a good one. I wouldn't mind going back so I can spend another day in Hawaii."

"Sorry, we can't do that," Rodger explained. "We are past the point of no return. That means we're more than halfway there. We can't even get back to Johnston. If we have any problems getting through, then we might have to divert to Ailuk, Likiep, or Rongelap Atoll to wait it out."

"Oh, great," Ben mumbled, seeing this flight was dragging on forever.

Pete is talking with the regional control on the radio. Ben listens in on the conversation. He is hoping they are not diverting their flight to another island. He can't understand most of the chatter. They seem to speak a different language with nothing but three-letter acronyms.

Pete finally gets off the radio. "Ben, you need to get back and buckle in. It's going to get real bumpy."

"So, we're going for it?" Rodger asked.

Pete nods. "Yep! We got the OK to try to punch through all this mess."

"Ben, can you store everything away in the galley while you're back there?" Rodger asked.

Ben just nods, then quickly makes his way back to the galley, storing all the trash through a slot marked 'Waste.' He puts everything else away, closing up all the storage bins and locking them down. Looking out the windows facing west, he sees the massive dark thunderhead with lots of cloud-to-cloud lightning. This storm is enormous, and it looks like it's getting worse.

The pilot turns to the west, looking for an opening in the massive storm. The radar displays a large, bright red line smeared across the screen, showing one continuous storm front. Rodger closely watches the radar, adjusting the magnification level until he sees the small opening. That is their doorway through the storm.

"What do you think? Does this look like a good one?" Rodger asked, pointing it out to the pilot.

Pete looks down at the display. "Yeah! That looks good. That's the one the controllers want us to fly through. How far away?"

Rodger does some quick calculations. "About fifteen minutes... Turn to heading two, three zero."

"We better get there quick. I hope those guys in regional control know what they are doing. I don't like the way this storm is building up."

As the small plane heads straight for the storm front, the pilot notices two large cumulus anvils high above, showing that the storm is still building up. They hit their mark, and the pilot turns to the south, right between the two massive thunderheads. He sees two large, bright red blotches on the radar screen. To the right and left, massive clouds loomed well above. The turbulence dramatically increases as they try to get through the storm front.

Jenny wakes up after hitting her head on the window. "What's with the rough flight? How much more time before we land?" she asked Ben.

"It's hard to say... We got a big storm between Kwajalein and us. They're trying to get through it now."

"I can't wait for this flight to be over!" not feeling good with everything being jostled around.

"I know... At least you had some sleep. I have been up the whole time."

"Why don't you try to get some sleep? Just close your eyes and stop looking out the window."

"There is no way anyone can get any sleep now with all this," he said, getting a little irritated with this flight.

"You think it'd be OK for a bathroom break?" Jenny asked, looking back at the rear of the plane.

"Only if it's an emergency!" Ben said, so shocked at hearing that she needs to go.

"I think I'll wait until we get there," she said, seeing everything bouncing around the cabin.

"Good idea... The bathroom is not the best place to be right now."

Ben feels a little nauseous as the plane bounces up and down. To make matters worse, he can smell the aroma of vomit as it flows through the small cabin. Things are bad enough getting tossed about, but the smell is not helping the situation. He is so glad that he didn't eat much on this flight, knowing he would have lost his lunch.

* * *

Rodger glances down at the radar and sees the small corridor closing up. A new bright red blotch develops directly ahead. A thundercloud has built up right in front of their flight path. The pilots realize the storm has engulfed them, and there is nowhere else to go.

"Damn!" Pete yelled out. "We should have gone to Rongelap!" regretting his decision to continue and not fly to the alternate landing strip.

"There was no way of knowing this was going to happen!" the copilot explained. "We had a big opening for a while. It just built up too quickly."

"Contact control and inform them of our situation," Pete orders. "See if they can get a fix on our position. Tell them we need to get out of this mess, and fast! Find out which is quicker, Kwajalein or Rongelap. If we can't make either one, tell them to find us the closest airport!"

As Rodger tries to contact the regional controller, the plane gets hit by a massive uplifting force. The nose lurches up, and the airplane stalls. To gain speed, Pete forces the controls down to stabilize the aircraft and slams the throttles forward to put the plane in a nosedive. The pilot struggles to keep control, descending into the depths of the storm.

Rodger is on the radio with the controller. A flash of brilliant light fills the cockpit, blinding them, accompanied by a massive explosion.

"Damn! We just got hit!" Pete yells, quickly realizing they just had a direct lightning strike on the nose of the aircraft.

"I can't see a damn thing!" Rodger replied. "How about you? You OK?" stunned by the brilliant burst of light plus the blast of the instant thunder.

"I can't see anything... Hell, I can barely make out the controls! Just give it a minute!" Pete replied, trying to focus on the instruments.

The pilot slowly regains his sight, looking over the instruments, evaluating the situation. Alarms are blaring so loudly, and red lights are flashing all over the instrument panels. He checks what systems are still operational. Most of the control panel is still dark. He knows right away that it's not good.

"Navigation is out, and so is radar! Rodger, see if you can reset the breakers!" Pete orders, still having problems with his vision.

"We have a major power supply problem! I can smell something burning!" reaching down, resetting the fuses one by one.

"I smell it too! Try the radio! Tell them we have an emergency! We need a vector to the nearest airfield."

Rodger works the dials on the transmitter. "Communication is out! Damn, I think we have a small pressure leak!" feeling the pressure on his ears.

Pete reaches over to put on his oxygen mask. "Get your mask on! Check the back and see if they dropped. The indicator is not working on the panel."

Rodger quickly places the oxygen mask on his face and then leans over to look down the cabin. "Damn, the masks didn't drop! We need to descend to 10,000! At least it's a slow-pressure leak. I don't think they noticed it!" seeing how scared everyone is.

The pilot is getting so frustrated. "Can it get any worse? We're flying blind in a storm. Instruments are out and losing cabin pressure. At least the basics are still working. The altimeter, climb rate, and pitch are still good. Recheck the breakers and get that radio working. I sure hope they're tracking us on the radar."

Rodger nods. "They should! We've deviated from our heading, and we're dropping altitude like mad. They know we're in the middle of this storm, anyway. They're probably trying to contact us now."

"I'm dropping to 10,000 feet. At least they'll know we have cabin pressure problems when they see our altitude. Luckily, it's a small leak and not a massive decompression. That is the one and the only thing we have on our side."

* * *

Chapter 5

Mistake

Zeak Davis, a regional controller at Oakland ARTCC, is on the last hour of his shift. He had been watching the storm for most of the day. He has been redirecting air traffic over, under, and around the worst of the weather. One flight, Ace 191 from Honolulu to Kwajalein, is in the middle of the storm. He redirects the flight west to run ahead of the leading edge of the storm. He hopes the storm will move farther east, as the meteorologist projected.

After only an hour, the storm dramatically builds west of the Flight 191 location, leaving them with nowhere else to go. Now, it's one long squall line blocking their path. Zeak closely watches the small blip of the flight on the screen in the middle of the storm. When the call comes in, it's no surprise. Flight Ace 191 needs assistance to get around the storm.

Flight Ace 191 is having problems trying to get through the storm, searching for a hole to punch through. The controller notices an opening just west of the aircraft's position in a long red line of thunderstorms. He radios the coordinates to vector them between the two huge storm clouds.

Moments later, while Zeak is redirecting other traffic, an indicator is flashing on the screen. The flashing marker for Flight Ace 191 immediately catches his attention. Their altitude is dropping dramatically. He notices the problem right away. Another storm has emerged right in front of their flight path. He unknowingly directed them into another thunderhead. With two on each side, it all quickly closed up, engulfing the small aircraft.

Zeak hit the microphone button. "Oakland ARTCC, Ace One Niner One!" he said, watching the altitude drop dramatically.

After a long pause, Flight Ace 191 responded. "Mayday, Mayday, Mayday, Oakland ARTCC, Ace One Niner One. We need assistance —" then gets cut off in mid-sentence.

"Ace One Niner One. Say again your last transmission," Zeak calls back, after a few seconds.

He stares at the screen, seeing the altitude still dropping for Flight Ace 191.

"Ace One Niner One, Oakland ARTCC, are you receiving? Ace One Niner One, if you read Oakland ARTCC, squawk Seven Six Zero Zero!" Zeak said a few seconds later, still getting no response.

With no reply, Zeak repeats the call several times. The blip of Flight Ace 191 disappears from the screen. The controller's screen immediately starts flashing alert messages, still pointing to the flight's last position. He quickly presses the distress button to alert his supervisor for assistance. He regretted his decision to move the flight through the storm. It's going to be a bad day for a lot of people on that flight. Maybe the end of his career as well.

* * *

Chapter 6

Disaster

T he pilot struggles with the controls, trying to maintain altitude. The constant cloud-to-cloud lightning is blinding. Large hail cracks the windshields as they descend through the storm. A massive vibration emanates throughout the aircraft. Right away, the pilot knows that this is not a stall indicator at the rate they're descending. This new problem is far worse.

"OK, we are below 10,000 feet," Pete said, taking off his oxygen mask. "Check the passengers and see if they are OK!"

Rodger removes his oxygen mask, looking into the back cabin. "The pressure leak must not be that bad. The masks didn't even drop. I don't think they even noticed it anyway with the damn vibration we got!"

Rodger notices a red glow coming from the engine over his right shoulder. "We have a problem with number two! Oil pressure looks good! RPMs are... What the hell. The gauge shows 1,400! That can't be right!" wondering if it was correct.

"No red light!" Pete replied. "Check the indicator manually. Could be just a burnt-out light. I wouldn't trust anything at the moment. Some are working, and some are not."

"No light on either engine," Rodger said. "Damn, this panel is dead!" after pressing the fire indicator manual test switch.

"With this much gone, it has to be a major electrical malfunction. Hit the fire extinguisher switch anyway, and pray it works. We can't take much more of this vibration!" pulling back on the throttle, shutting down the engine.

Rodger looks out the window, seeing a white mist enveloping the engine. The propeller stops, but smoke still blasts out from the cowling. The vibration stops, but now, with only one engine and in the depths of the massive storm, it doesn't look good.

Descending at the structural limits of the aircraft, Pete pulls back on the controls and throttles back on the remaining engine. Looking at the altimeter, he notices they are extremely low. Breaking through the cloud base, they are now in heavy rain. Lightning is still striking all around, not helping their situation.

At a 900-foot altitude, the pilots do not know their location or even direction. Flying under the clouds, they still can't see much of anything. The heavy rain limits their visibility to a few miles. They frantically look around for any bright areas indicating the edge of the storm. Flying in a circle, it all looks the same, just dark gray with nothing but rain and constant lightning.

Rodger works the instruments, checking to see what systems he can bring back to life. He frantically resets one breaker after another. A flash erupts from under the instrument panel near the copilot's feet. Smoke quickly billows out. He reaches behind his seat and grabs the fire extinguisher, trying to put out the fire. Smoke quickly spreads throughout the cabin.

Pete turns to his copilot. "Well, that's not good... She is falling apart on us. There is no way we can get above this storm or get out from under it. I don't know how long we can keep her in the air, and we're flying blind out here with no navigation. We might have to ditch if I can't find a place to put her down. Get someone from the back to help with the procedures."

Rodger turns around, looking down the aisle to the rear of the plane. "Hey, Ben! Get your ass up here! We need your help!"

Ben can't believe the copilot is waving for him to come to the front. It is not a good time to be serving drinks. He slowly makes his way to the front, holding onto each seat to keep his balance. Seeing all the terrified faces, he wonders how bad things are. Sitting at the back of the plane, he is unaware of all the problems they are having.

Ben grabs the back of the copilot's seat. "What's up? You can't want another drink?" seeing the pilots struggling with the controls.

"I wish I had a stiff drink right now!" the pilot replied. "I can sure use one!"

"Damn! What the hell happened?" Ben asked. "I smell smoke! Looks like you got some serious problems," seeing the cracked windshields and the state of the instrument panels.

"No, we got some major problems here!" Rodger explained. "We took a direct hit! We may have to set her down on the water. What I need you to do is make sure everyone puts on their lifejackets. Get the two life rafts out of the rear storage and place them on the floor in the galley. All the instructions are on the label on the back hatch. Also, once we're down, we'll need you to open the back hatch as fast as you can and toss the rafts out. Make sure you pull the cord before tossing them out!"

"You're going to do this now?" Ben asked, so stunned at hearing this.

"Not yet," Pete added, "but once the sun goes down or we run out of fuel, we'll have no choice. So we need to be prepared for the worst. We're going to try to break out of this storm, but once it gets dark, that's it for us. I'll have to put her down on the water!"

"What do the people on the radio say?" Ben asked, getting scared. "Aren't we close to an airport?"

"We have no idea," Rodger added. "The radio isn't working. With no instruments and one engine, there is no way we can fly like this. We're going to keep her in the air as long as possible, but when the time comes, you need to get everyone ready. Make sure you read all the emergency procedures."

"Is there going to be a rescue plane or ship coming out here for us?" Ben asked.

Both pilots look at each other. "Let's hope so!" Pete said. "They'll be tracking us on radar, so they should know where we are. Better get back and get everyone ready."

Ben turns around, crawling to the first row of seats. Grabbing the handrail, he lifts himself up, standing in front of everyone, holding on tight to keep his balance. Seeing all the terrified faces looking back at him, he knows it's no secret. They all know something is very wrong.

"OK, guys!" Ben shouted out. "Everyone, put on your lifejackets! It should be under your seats. They might have to land on the water if they can't get out of the storm. Read the emergency instructions for evacuating the plane. Everyone must know what to do!"

Ben makes his way back to Jenny. "This is yours!" she shouted, holding up the lifejacket.

"I'll put it on later. I need to get a few things out of the galley."

"No! You need to put it on now! Please!"

"OK, if you insist," seeing how serious she is.

"What's going on?" Jenny asked, getting scared. "I can smell smoke. Is everything OK?"

He slowly shakes his head. "No, it's a real mess up there. That lightning must have knocked out most of the instruments. We're down to one engine as well," he explained.

Her eyes are wide open, hearing the bad news. "So, what's going to happen?"

"I think they're going to get as far from the storm as they can. The last option, they're going to try to land on the water."

She is so stunned. "They can't do that! We're miles from anything out here!"

"I don't think they have a choice. I think they prefer a controlled landing to the alternative. If things don't get any better, they want to put it down while it's still light out. Once we get out of this storm, I don't think it'll be a problem. Let's hope this storm clears up fast," then rushes to the galley.

He read the instructions on the rear hatch several times. Opening an airplane door is something he has never done before, and he wants to make sure he gets it right. Somehow, he has a feeling he might have to do this in the dark.

Behind the galley, he finds a cabinet marked with a large red arrow labeled 'Emergency Locker.' Pulling out two large red plastic containers, he reads the instructions repeatedly on how to inflate the rafts before placing them next to the rear hatch. He goes back to the emergency locker, grabs the medical and survival kits, placing them on top of the rafts, praying they won't need them.

Ben sits down, buckling his seatbelt, pulling it tight, turning to Jenny. "Don't worry... We're probably not that far from the airport," seeing how scared she is.

"I got a bad feeling about this," she said, reaching over to take his hand.

He holds her hand tight. "It'll be all right... Don't worry," feeling her hand trembling.

* * *

Hours later, the two pilots are still struggling with the controls. Unable to break out of the storm, they're flying blind in the direction they hope is to the southwest.

"Something is wrong!" Pete yelled out. "I can't hold altitude anymore. We're slowly descending. One engine should be enough, but in this weather, I don't think we're going to make it!"

Rodger looks down at the remaining instruments. "I'm not surprised. We're hitting some major downdrafts. Although the number one engine is still looking good, we need two good engines to get out of this storm."

"Yeah, we're just bouncing up and down out here. There is no way we can get above all this. We don't have much fuel left either. With no navigation instruments, we're just flying blind! Hell, as far as I know, we could be flying in circles."

Rodger rechecks the charts. "I think you're right... I don't have a clue where we are. We got to be close to something. We should have flown over one of the islands by now. I don't see anything but water out there. We can be just a few miles away from Kwajalein and not even see it!" looking out the windshield at the dark gray weather.

"We'll just keep going until we have no choice," Pete explained. "Let's get as far away from this mess as we can, and then we'll set her down," realizing the situation they are in is getting worse.

"We'll need plenty of light for when we ditch," Rodger said. "Look at those swells down there. It's going to be a little rough. We'll need as much light as possible if we are going to do this. Once we're down, we don't want anyone drifting off in the dark."

"Yeah, you're right!" Pete agreed. "The longer we wait, the less daylight we'll have, or the storm might get worse. Right now, she's holding up, but if something else goes out, we might not have a controlled descent."

"We're having a bad enough time keeping her level now," the copilot replied.

After feeling another massive jolt, Pete struggles with the controls. "I guess I spoke too soon... I don't think she'll last much longer!"

"What happened?" feeling the slight shutter.

"Something else just broke," the pilot added. "OK, let's get it over with, and I'll set her down as gently as I can. She'll float for a while, but we need to get everyone out fast."

Rodger nods. "I'll go back and brief the passengers."

"Better do it quick! I need you up here!"

Rodger makes his way back to the cabin. He has a hard time keeping on his feet with the plane buffeting around. Seeing the faces of all the passengers, he wonders how they are all going to make it.

"OK! I'll give it to you straight! We had a major instrument failure because of a lightning hit. We're also down to one engine and are having a hard time maintaining altitude. It'll be dark soon, so it will be best to land while we still have some light out there."

"You mean we're going to land on another island?" Mary asked, sitting in the very front seat.

Rodger turns to her. "No, I'm sorry... We're not going to make it to Kwajalein or anywhere else. We're going to make an emergency water landing. I want you all to take out the emergency procedure cards in the pocket in front of you and read it! Your seat cushions float so they can be used as life preservers. Once we're down, get out fast, but don't panic. Ben will open the rear hatch and deploy the life rafts. It'll be a little rough out there. We all must keep together once we're out in the water."

"When we're ready to ditch," Rodger added. "I'll turn the lights on and then off to indicate that you should take the crash position!" quickly regretting using the term crash.

He turns the switch on, illuminating the cabin, then flips the switch back off. "Next time you see that, take your positions. I'll leave the lights on, but they may go out once we're in the water. Those of you in the back, use the rear exit. The rest of you use this forward exit. Just remember to keep together. We have two life rafts ready to go. Oh yeah, Ben, you remember what you have to do?"

Ben looks up at Rodger, giving him the thumbs-up sign. He looks over at Jenny. She has been crying. She wipes away the tears, trying to read the emergency information on the card.

"Don't worry. You'll be OK. I'll be by your side," reaching over to hold Jenny's hand.

"Ben, I really had a good time last night. I just wanted you to know."

"I had a great time too! I was hoping to spend more time with you," looking down at her small, gentle hand.

Jenny cries uncontrollably, which makes Ben so uneasy. He falls apart whenever a woman cries and is fighting back his own tears. He has seen things like this on the news, but experiencing it firsthand is absolutely horrible. In just a few days, he made good friends with many of the people on the plane. What makes it worse is that he is now very close to Jenny.

* * *

Their luck has run out. The airplane shutters violently. The pilots know that the remaining engine is going out. Pete makes the final approach. He lowers the plane down to about 200 feet above the massive swells. The good thing about having whitecaps on the ocean is that it gives him a perspective view of the direction of the wind.

"Give me verbal altitude readings," Pete said. "Don't want to take my eyes off the water. Shit, talk about making a visual landing. I haven't done this since my old training days. I'm going to try to time it with the ridges of those waves, and set her down right on top of a wave, then slide into the trough."

"Sounds like a good plan! OK, we're at 175, 160, 150 feet," Rodger said, reading off the altitude.

Pete reaches over, setting the flaps to 30 degrees, then pulls back on the throttle. With one bad engine, it's a constant fight to keep the wings level. With a full left rudder, it's still being pulled to the right. He turns on the landing lights, relieved to see they are still working.

"OK, Rodger, this is it! Warn the passengers!"

Rodger reaches over, flipping the cabin lights switch off, then back on. All the passengers bend over, putting their arms around their legs. No one said a word. The only sound comes from the droning of the single-engine.

As Ben leans over, he looks over at Jenny. They stare into each other's eyes, not saying a word. He feels so numb, looking at her while waiting for the inevitable.

"We're at fifty feet!" Rodger shouts.

"This is it! I'm going to set her down on the top of the next wave!"

Pete moves the flaps to the full position, pulling back on the controls, throttling back the engine. The plane slows to the point of stalling, with the nose pointing up higher and higher. He can feel the controls vibrating, indicating a stall. The stall alarms sounded. He watches the white crest of the enormous wave in front of them get closer and closer. Just before they reach the crest of the wave, a blast of wind lifts the aircraft.

"Shit! We missed it! I'll go for the next one," the pilot pushes the throttle forward, trying to gain altitude.

"We're still dropping! Thirty feet!" Rodger yelled.

"We're still too low! We need altitude fast! I got to drop her right on top of the next one!"

"We're at fifty feet! Hold it there!"

"Are we too high?" the pilot asked. "I can't make out anything!" trying to see the top of the next wave, seeing nothing but darkness.

"We're at forty-five feet! I can't see the white water either! What the hell is happening?" unable to distinguish anything outside the windshield.

The landing lights reveal that a massive wave is coming straight at them. They know they have dropped too low. The wave is approaching fast, towering high above.

"Oh, my God!" Rodger cried out, seeing the upcoming wave towering over them. "Pull up! Pull up!"

Pete slams the throttle full forward, pulling back on the controls hoping to gain altitude. The airplane goes into a vertical climb. With only one engine, there is not enough power, then it quickly stalls. The top of the wave slams into the tail section, tearing it off from the rest of the fuselage.

Ben feels a massive jolt. The impact feels like being dropped from the top of a building and slammed into his seat. Right away, he knows this is not the controlled landing they had planned on. A loud popping and ripping sound comes from the plane. All the lights go out. He can feel himself spinning around end over end in the total darkness, holding on with all his might, knowing the end is near.

With only one engine at full throttle, the airplane quickly lurches over to the right and then dives straight in, nose-first. Plunging deep into the ocean, the force of the impact rips off both wings. With the tail section gone, water quickly rushes in, trapping everyone inside. With all its crew and passengers, the airplane slowly sinks into the dark depths of the Pacific Ocean.

* * *

Chapter 7

The Ocean

Ben finally regains consciousness. Nothing makes sense to him at all. Still buckled in his seat, totally disoriented, he stares straight up at the dark clouds. His eyes are burning, and he can't focus on anything. He then realizes that the seat right in front of him is missing. He turns to look to his right, so confused. Not only are the windows gone, but the whole side of the airplane.

Sitting out in the open and being pelted by the rain, he has no clue what is happening. After a few minutes, his mind starts to clear. All at once, he realizes the entire front of the airplane is gone. Leaning over to look down the side, he is so shocked. The ocean is only six feet below, so the aircraft must have broken apart while trying to land, and he is still in the tail section. The wind and the waves are rocking it back and forth. He is panicking, knowing it won't take much to flip it over, and it'll quickly fill with water, sinking to the bottom of the ocean.

Ben quickly looks over to his left, so relieved. Jenny remains buckled in her seat, but appears lifeless. He unbuckles his seatbelt, crawling over to her.

"Jenny! Jenny!" he keeps yelling out, gently slapping her face.

She slowly opens her eyes in a daze. She finds it difficult to focus on anything, but mumbles a few words.

"Are you OK?" he frantically asked. "Jenny! Are you OK?" shaking her arm.

"I think so," she mumbled. "What's happening? Is it over?"

"Not yet! We're still on the plane! You need to get ready to jump out. Stay here while I get the life rafts out."

He looks down, seeing that the galley is full of water. At least two life rafts are still there, so he carefully slides down to the back of the airplane. Luckily, the water is only knee-deep. He quickly grabs the raft, pushing them up on his seat.

"Where is everyone else?" she cries out, realizing the rest of the airplane is gone.

"I don't know! Look around. They got to be out there somewhere. We need to get the life rafts out to them."

She frantically looks around. "I don't see anything! Where are they?"

"Just keep looking while I get everything from down here! They may have jumped out. Look for the lifejackets!"

"I can't believe this!" she screams. "There's no one out there!"

"Don't panic! We'll be OK. Can you help get these up?" pushing up the second life raft.

"You want me to push these over the side?" she asked, reaching down to help.

"No, not yet! Just put it on top of the other one. Let's get everything together first," handing up the medical and survival kits.

Once he makes it back to his seat, he desperately holds on to the life rafts and survival gear, trying to keep it all together. He knows it's just a matter of time before the whole thing just tips over. Since it will get dark soon, they have little time left. They need to get the rafts out on the water before it's too late.

Looking over at Jenny to see how she is doing, he sees this strange darkness looming behind her. Blinking several times to clear the rain and salt water from his eyes, he quickly realizes what is coming their way. His mouth drops wide open, seeing a huge wave towering over them.

"Hold on!" he shouted, tightening his grip on the seatbelts.

Jenny does not know what is happening. With her back to the wave, she doesn't see it coming. The huge wave slams into them so hard that it flips the tail section over. Ben finds himself in the ocean, turning end over end. Luckily, still wearing his lifejacket, he pops up to the surface, gasping for air.

He quickly turns around, looking for Jenny. All he can see is the bright red life raft floating right next to him. He grabs the life raft, using it as a flotation device.

"Jenny, Jenny!" frantically looking around for her, knowing that she should be nearby.

With all the massive waves and the rain, he can barely see anything. With the wreckage from the airplane still floating about, it's difficult to distinguish one thing from another.

Being lifted high on the crest of a massive wave, he sees the plane's tail section about thirty feet away. He is so shocked to see it floating upside down with the tail and elevator barely sticking out of the water.

He quickly ties the cord from the life raft around his waist so he won't lose it. He ignores all the pain, frantically swimming to the remnants of the airplane. The entire time, he looks around, hoping to see Jenny nearby.

Resting for a few seconds, he calls out to her. Waiting for a reply, but there is nothing. He realizes he is no closer than when he started. The wind and waves are pushing it away faster than he can swim.

Ben keeps on swimming, but to no avail. Utterly exhausted, he just can't reach it. The tail and elevator are sticking out of the water, acting like a big sail pushing it farther away. No matter how hard he tries, he can't catch up with it.

Another massive wave crashes over him, pushing him deep down below the water. Tumbling end over end, he feels the cord around his waist come loose. Luckily, the life raft is just a few feet away, and he quickly swims over to recover it. The life raft is his last hope. Without it, he knows he doesn't have much of a chance.

He loses sight of the tail section again and has no clue where or even how far away it is. Swimming is not an option anymore. His only hope now is to inflate the raft and get out of the water before he is too exhausted.

Quickly reading the instructions, he wonders why it says to tie the cord around his wrist before inflating. He is too tired to think about it, attaching the end of the rope to his wrist. With one pull on the release handle, a burst of air quickly discharges, popping open the life raft. The brightly colored red and black raft inflates within seconds.

Once fully inflated, the wind picks it up like a parachute. The life raft tumbles end over end, dragging Ben through the water. He is so glad that he read the instructions first. Otherwise, the life raft would have blown away with the wind.

Finally, the life raft stops rolling on top of the water. Ben uses the cord to pull himself to the raft, only to find it upside down. He is so tempted to get on top of it to rest, but he knows it won't be long before the next wave tosses him off.

At the crest of the next massive wave, he pushes up the edge of the raft as high as he can. A gust of wind gets underneath it, and that's more than enough to flip it over. The wind is so strong it pulls him straight out of the water as the raft flips over and slams him hard onto his back against the water. Coughing like mad to clear his lungs, he is hoping like hell it will not flip over again, dragging him with it.

At least one thing has gone right. The life raft is the right way up. The dome quickly pops up. Examining all the handles and ropes attached to the raft, he sees the entrance. Placing one foot on the rope, Ben grabs a handle, pulling himself inside.

He glances around, surprised at how big it is. The eight-foot diameter life raft has a built-in dome four-foot-high at the center. There are so many handles, ropes, and compartments, all neatly attached to the sides.

There is no time to rest. Seeing how dark it's getting, Ben needs to find Jenny. Looking around inside the raft, he finds a small red box attached to the side. Opening it up, he rummages through the contents, so glad to discover it's filled with all the essential survival gear.

"All right! Glow sticks. Just what I need!" pulling out the small plastic package.

Slapping the glow stick hard against the box, it quickly lights up. Seeing a small cord hanging from the center of the dome, Ben knows what it is. All tents have the same design. He is so glad this life raft is like the tents he got at home, quickly tying the glowing stick to the cord.

Rummaging through the box again, he pulls out two flares. He had seen these before but had never used them. After reading the instructions on the side, he pulls one end off, using it to ignite the flare. That is his first big mistake. A blinding white light emanates from the flare, and smoke quickly fills the raft.

He crawls to the doorway, gasping for air. The smoke is so bad that he has to hold the door flap wide open to let the wind clear it out. Lighting a flare in a closed area was not a good idea.

"Jenny! Jenny! Anyone out there!" he shouts, holding the flare up high, so he can now see through all the rain.

Floating wreckage from the airplane is all that he sees. Bits and pieces from the airplane surround the raft. Most of it is nothing more than Styrofoam cups, paper, and other unrecognizable debris.

Feeling sick to his stomach, all he thinks about is Jenny being out there all alone. He knows she has to be close by but doesn't understand how they got separated. Constantly yelling out for her, but the only sound he hears is the wind and the rain hitting the dome.

When the life raft rides on the crest of the waves, it allows him to see farther out. He notices something extremely bright in the distance. Right away, he knows it's the fluorescent-painted medical and survival kits from the airplane.

He knows the life raft should have a paddle. Then he remembers the rectangular gadget in the netting next to the red box. While still holding the flare out the door, he reaches back, grabbing the flat object. He quickly discovers that not only is it a paddle, but it also has a telescoping handle with a hook on the other end.

Ben fills the raft with whatever he can find floating out on the water. Using the paddle with one hand and the flare in the other is getting to be a hassle. He knows there has to be somewhere on this raft to put it. After a quick look around, he notices a round plastic holder above the doorway. He is so glad these people thought of everything, placing the end of the flare inside the holder.

Out of all the debris from the airplane, he finally sees something that looks familiar. Several seat cushions are floating nearby. He grabs as many as he can, knowing they make good flotation devices. If he sees someone in the water, he can quickly toss it out to them.

The rain finally stops, and now he can see farther out into the darkness. He lights another flare, holding it up high. He feels so sick knowing Jenny is out there somewhere. Thoughts went through his mind of what could have happened. Maybe the rest of the people are on the other raft. Jenny can be in the same situation, sitting in the other raft, looking for him.

"Hey! Anyone out there!" waving the flare high into the air.

To his astonishment, he hears what sounds like a distant cry. He carefully listens again. The sound of the wind, the hissing of the flare are the only things he can hear.

"Hello! Hello!" waving the flare slowly back and forth.

"Jenny! Is anyone out there? Jenny!" then he swears he hears the sound again.

His heart beats hard after hearing a faint cry for help. As another enormous wave lifts the raft, he sees a bright yellow reflection in the distance. He waves the flare from side to side, yelling out over and over. He can't focus on anything with all the smoke and salt in his eyes, but he knows someone is out there swimming towards the life raft.

Ben reaches back, putting the flare inside the holder above the doorway. He paddles hard, trying to get closer. Lifted on top of another wave, he hears someone calling his name.

He knows it's Jenny and starts frantically paddling with all his might. Once he gets close enough, he can see that she is exhausted. He reaches out to her with the long paddle. Luckily, she grasps the handle but barely holds on. Carefully, he pulls her in close enough, then lunges out, grabbing her lifejacket. She goes limp, having no energy left.

Ben doesn't have much strength left either, but it will be up to him to get her in the life raft. After all the times he had been white water rafting at home, he knows there is only one way to get someone in a raft. Reaching down, he takes hold of the handles on the top of her lifejacket, then falls back, dragging her safely inside.

"Thank God!" she cried out. "I thought something had happened to you!" putting her arms around him, and started kissing him.

Ben gives Jenny a long kiss. "I thought you were gone. I'm so relieved," he cried out, then passed out from exhaustion.

So relieved that she has finally found him, she holds him tight, not wanting to let go, and starts crying uncontrollably. She had been swimming for what seemed an eternity. After being in the water for so long, her arms and legs are numb. Her muscles are stiff, showing symptoms of hypothermia, and then she loses consciousness.

* * *

Jenny slowly wakes up. Sitting up, she looks around, seeing an odd collection of boxes and seat cushions. No one else is in the raft. It's just the two of them. She expected to see other people here.

"Ben! Wake up! Have you seen anyone else?" wondering what happened to their friends.

He slowly sits up. "No, only you... There are two rafts. Maybe they're in the other one."

She crawls over to the doorway. "Maybe they're out there, not far away. They could be out there drifting in the ocean."

"I don't know... I haven't heard or seen anybody. What happened to you? I looked all over and kept yelling out. I can't believe you disappeared like that. The tail of the plane flipped over, and dreaded to think you got caught under it!" he explained, feeling sick to his stomach.

"I was!" she replied. "When that wave hit, it knocked me off the seat down to the galley. Then it rolled over with me still inside it."

His mouth drops wide open. "What! You were really inside it!"

She nods. "Luckily, there was an air pocket near the top. I was scared to death! I thought I was going down with it. There was one window just above the water, so I knew it was still floating. But I was still trapped inside."

"How did you get out?"

"Well, I knew it wouldn't stay afloat for long," she explained. "I was getting tossed around so bad. The only way out was to dive down, but it's hard to do wearing a lifejacket. So, I started grabbing things to help pull myself down to get out. It was horrible! Once I got out, I started looking for you."

He is so shocked at hearing this. "If I'd known that you were in there--"

"We're both lucky!" she interrupted him. "I thought you were gone too and was yelling and screaming, looking around for you. I was out there for a long time. When I saw the flare, somehow I knew it was you! I kept swimming and swimming. I can't believe how far away you were."

"Jenny, I thought I lost you... I don't think I could have gone on without you. I hope the rest are OK. At least they might have the other raft. Without that, it'll really be bad."

"The other raft was on the plane with me," Jenny quietly whispered in his ear.

He pulls back, looking deeply into her eyes. "Oh God! Don't say that! Then we need to keep looking for them!" realizing they might be the only ones who made it.

"You're right! We made it out of the plane, so they should have gotten out as well. We need to keep the flares lit so they can see us. That's how I found you!" noticing the flare had burnt out.

Ben reaches over, pulling out another flare from the box. Crawling over to the opening, he makes sure to light it outside the raft this time. Jenny rummages through the red box. She finds various survival gear, a small medical kit, an inflatable plastic water jug, glow sticks, and a survival booklet inside. Also, it has another smaller container. She opens it, finding a flare gun with three shells.

She crawls over, kneeling next to him. "Would this help?" Jenny asked, showing him the contents of the box.

He is so glad to see the flare gun. "It's a good thing we have one of those! Maybe we should use that instead of the hand flares. They go up really high. If someone is still in the water, at least they'll know they're not alone. It'll also let them know where we are. You know how to use this?"

"Oh, no, you do it!" handing it to Ben.

"Let's see how it works," he said, reading the instructions on the box.

Ben points it in the direction of the wind and pulls the trigger. A brilliant glowing ball shoots up high into the air, lighting up everything. They are so shocked, seeing so much debris scattered everywhere. After 10 seconds, the flare hits the water, and everything goes dark.

The rain starts again, reducing their vision to only a few yards. The conditions are getting worse. Huge waves lift the small life raft. The wind picks up as well, driving the rain hard against their faces.

The last flare burns out. Without the flares, it's so dark they can't see anything. The only light they have is from the glow sticks. Looking out on the ocean, it's now nothing but darkness.

Jenny, so exhausted, reluctantly goes inside the raft. She is overwhelmed with emotions. All she can think about is their friends somewhere out there in this massive storm. Unable to keep her eyes open, she collapses from total exhaustion.

Ben stays out a little longer, trying to look for their friends, but deep down, he knows there is nothing more they can do. The raft is slowly filling with water from all the rain and the massive waves. After several hours of searching for their friends, reluctantly he closes up the small oval door of the dome, sealing them inside.

* * *

Chapter 8

The Search

The operators at the regional control center are diverting all aircraft away or around the storm's path. They are directing any flights unable to fly over the storm back to Hawaii. Controllers dispatched rescue planes after losing contact with Ace Flight 191 and the numerous distress calls from dozens of ships.

In the flight control center at Kwajalein Island, the supervisor learns about Ace Flight 191. Lieutenant Fred White gets the order to set up a rescue mission from Kwajalein. He immediately sets up a meeting in the briefing room at the command center. They currently have two aircraft on hand, a Convair HC-131A and a Learjet 25, to help with the rescue.

Lieutenant White plots the path of flight 191 from Honolulu to Johnston Island, then to Kwajalein, marking the position of the last contact. The entire area has hundreds of small islands, hoping they landed safely on one of them. He is so infuriated at learning about the alternative aircraft instead of the original flight using the 737. He knows they won't have much of a chance in a storm of that size.

In the briefing room, Lieutenant White explains the situation to the flight crews. Flight 191 was west of their flight plan and over 350 miles from Kwajalein. The aircraft may have attempted to land at Rongelap, so the search will begin at that location and will expand from there.

Paul Rutherford, the personnel manager, was getting ready to greet the new D-4 replacements. Now, he is waiting with everyone else to hear from the rescue flights. Gathering all the names of the crew's next of kin and passengers on the flight, he needs to be ready to contact the families with either good or bad news.

Paul knows it will be best to contact the families right after they find the aircraft. If there is any delay, the press will jump on it, broadcasting it live all over the country. The last thing he wants is for them to find out from watching television or hear on the radio that someone in their family has died.

Time is still on their side. The flight could have landed on one of the many small runways on the neighboring islands. In all the flights arriving and departing Kwajalein in the last thirty years, they never lost one. The flights with problems always managed to return safely to Hawaii or one of the other airports. All they can do now is wait for any information about the flight.

* * *

Chapter 9

The Dream

In Texas, Ben's parents are waiting for the phone call from their son, letting them know he has made it to Kwajalein. Ben's mother, Mary, goes to bed early. She is so worried about her son traveling so far from home. She cannot understand why he never settled down close to the family. Suddenly, for some reason, she is crying uncontrollably.

"Mary, what's wrong? Why are you crying?" Walter asked, rushing into the bedroom, wondering what was going on.

"Oh, I don't know," she replied, brushing away the tears. "I got this strange feeling that something is just not right."

"You do this every time he travels somewhere," he said, knowing how she gets all worked up when one of the kids is traveling.

"I don't like the idea of him so far out over the ocean. I wish Ben would just get a job closer to home."

"Oh, you know how he is... He just wants to travel the world. Don't keep worrying. He should be calling soon, and he's probably there by now. Try to get some sleep."

"Are you going to stay up and get the phone when he calls?"

"Sure, I'll wake you when I hear from him. Don't worry. He's probably having the time of his life!" giving her an aspirin, making her get back in bed.

Walter had seen this too many times before. There will be no peace until they get a phone call from their son. His wife is a worrier, but this time, even he is a little concerned. With his son flying out in the middle of the Pacific Ocean, he is anxious for the phone call so he can finally get some sleep. For some reason, he is getting worried as well.

* * *

Chapter 10

The Raft, Day 1

Ben wakes up totally confused. His arms are so numb after being wedged into the straps all night long. Everything is extremely bright. The green glow of the light stick is gone, replaced by the brilliant red color of the dome.

Crawling over to the doorway, he opens the vinyl door, revealing a calm ocean with a slight cold breeze. The sky is overcast, with dark gray clouds from horizon to horizon. The cool breeze feels so good, filling the raft with clean air. After being sealed up all night, the life raft smells a little musty.

Rummaging around, he takes an inventory of everything that is in the raft. There is one small towel to dry off with, which is no bigger than a tea towel. There is also a desalination pump and some fishing gear. The big survival kit he got from the plane has a few things for them to eat. Unfortunately, it only includes vitamin-enriched wafers, but at least it's better than nothing.

Ben pulls out the desalination pump and reads the instructions on how to operate it. It looks more like a bicycle pump with two vinyl hoses attached, but it's easy to use. Just drop one tube into the water and start pumping, and filtered water comes out the other end.

He sets it up, placing one end into the ocean and the other end into a plastic water container. After pumping the handle a few times, water flows into the container. He wonders if it's drinkable, trying a little. He's surprised it works, although it tastes odd, but not bad, considering it came from the ocean.

"What time is it? What are you doing over there?" Jenny asked, slowly sitting up.

"It's morning time, and this is a pump that makes drinking water. It works pretty good, too."

"I feel so horrible. It's all clammy and sticky in here. My hair is all knotted up too!" slowly running her hands through her hair.

"Yeah, I opened the door to get some fresh air in here."

With the humidity being so bad, he feels the same, needing a good wash. He feels all grungy as well after wearing wet clothes all night long. Jenny looks as if she has been through hell and back, but he knows it's best not to say anything and continues filling the water container.

After filling the water bottle, he hands it over to Jenny. "Here, drink some... I guess we can have some of those rice cakes for breakfast I found in one of those boxes."

"I wonder where we are?" she asked, crawling over, taking the water bottle, looking out at the vast ocean.

He shakes his head. "I have no idea," handing her one of the rice cakes.

"You think anyone else made it?" she asked, looking out at the ocean.

"I don't know... After what we went through last night in this raft, it's one thing, but being out there in the water with just a lifejacket. That would be a nightmare," thinking about all their friends.

"How long do you think we'll be out here?" she asked, trying to change the subject.

Ben thinks about it for a while. "It's hard to say. They'll be sending out rescue planes or ships to look for us. With this bright red life raft, it should be easy to see. If it clears up, they should be able to see us from miles away. They're probably already looking for us."

He doesn't want to tell her what he really thought. This ocean is vast, and being so far off course is not helping. Without a radio beacon, they are going to be hard to find. He knows it's just going to be a matter of time and plenty of prayers.

Jenny reads the survival booklet she found in the red box to see whether she can learn anything that will help. The raft is well-designed. There are various handles and straps connected to the sides and the floor. The cargo netting attached to the front helps keep everything together. She wished they had known that last night when everything was tossed about during the storm.

With nothing else to do, Ben stares out at the ocean. There are no rescue planes, ships, or even other islands. There is nothing to see but the vast ocean surrounding them. He is getting scared, wondering how long they are going to be out here.

* * *

After several hours, Ben stands up just within the doorway to stretch his legs. He is curious to see what is on the outside of the raft and how it's constructed. There is netting connected at various places on top of the dome. He wonders why it's on the outside.

"Ben, don't stand up! You'll tip over the raft or fall out! Would you just sit down!" she yelled, panicking.

"Are you OK?" he asked, looking at her a little concerned, wondering what brought on the outburst.

She doesn't reply, continuing to read the booklet after giving him a mean look. She sits on the far side of the raft, agitated.

Ben finally sits down in the doorway. "So, what's up?" seeing she is a little on the quiet side.

"Have you read this book yet?" she asked, holding it up.

"Nope, why?"

She glares at him. "I got to go! From what I found in this book, we're basically on our own!"

"What do you mean you got to go? What are you talking about?"

"Well, from what it says in the book. You have to get in the water and go," she blurted out, being vague about all the details.

"Oh, I haven't thought about that!" he said, realizing she had to use the bathroom. "Don't worry about it. It's just like pooping in the woods on a camping trip. Just drop your pants and do your business!" trying not to laugh.

"It might be easy for you, but I'm not the camping type! I'm used to the civilized world! I don't know how you can be so calm about all this?" getting even more irritated.

"Back home, I used to do a lot of camping. One time, I went rafting for an entire week. That was great! It wasn't much different from this, except this raft is way bigger and has a top on it."

"You did this for fun?" she asked. "You spent a week living like this on purpose?"

"Oh yeah! We spent seven whole days out on the water. The best part was the Class Five rapids. We usually drifted down the river for about eight hours a day. Before the sun goes down, we would find a good sandy beach to set up camp."

"What did you do for food?"

"We had freeze-dried packs," he explained. "They are easy. Just put in hot water, and you got a nice hot meal. But on most days, we caught fish for dinner. The food packs were usually the last resort when we had nothing else to eat."

"What about the bathroom?" she asked.

"The bathroom was usually a tree nearby, or you dug a hole in the sand. If you had to go while out on the water, then you were in big trouble. We had this one guy who had a few stomach problems while we were going through some rapids. He couldn't wait any longer, dropping his pants and sticking his butt over the edge. I always felt sorry for the people on the raft behind us. Not only did they have to watch it, but they had to paddle through the crap in the water!"

She shakes her head. "I can't believe you do this for fun! This is absolutely horrible. I don't know how you lasted a whole week. When I get out of here, I'm never leaving my apartment ever again!"

Ben feels sorry for her. She is a typical city girl, but she needs to learn how to survive in the wilderness. He is used to being out in the middle of nowhere without all the modern amenities. He never thought much of it when he was out camping. Going to the bathroom outdoors is just another weekend event for him.

"OK, give me the book. Let's see how we're going to do this," he said, knowing that Jenny has to go really bad.

Jenny hands him the how-to booklet for the raft. It explains everything they need to know. The raft's bathroom is nothing more than leaning over the edge while hanging on to the handles. There are even special handles attached to the side just for this purpose. At least they thought about privacy. All you have to do is scoot over on the edge of the raft away from the doorway. The only problem is the raft has everything but toilet paper.

He hands back the book. "It's not too bad. Let me check things out."

Ben stands up in the doorway, getting a good look around. The raft is nothing more than a large round inner tube with a floor and a dome attached. The dome connects to the inside part of the tubing. That creates a small ridge that will collect the rainwater. It also can be a place to sit and lean back on the dome in the warmth of the sun.

He crawls out, sits on the edge of the raft, then scoots himself over far away from the doorway. Safety ropes are on the sides of the raft. He discovers one long cord with a loop around the end. That must be the safety harness in case someone falls over, preventing them from drifting away. That will be helpful during bathroom breaks while in a storm.

Ben returns, explaining it all to Jenny. He ties the safety rope to her, helping her outside. Once she figures it out, she promptly orders him back into the raft. He waits inside, hoping not to hear a big splash with her falling in. She will have a balancing act out there to stay on the edge of the raft, but it's better than nothing.

After a long wait, she finally climbs back into the raft. "That wasn't as bad as I thought!" looking very proud of herself.

Ben laughed. "I'm glad to hear that. I was hoping you didn't fall in!"

"I was worried about that! I'm glad I had that rope tied around me. You know, it's really nice to get out in the breeze. This place is getting a little stuffy."

"I noticed that when I was out there. We need to keep the door open to air this place out."

She sits down, extremely proud of herself. She continues reading the survival booklet, eager to learn more about the raft and its safety features.

Ben can't resist teasing her. "Oh, by the way... You did check for sharks first before you stuck your butt out over the water?"

"You're not serious, are you?" looking up at him, so scared.

He just shakes his head and turns his back to her, looking out the doorway. He can't help laughing, not wanting to let on that he is pulling her leg. She is doing really good for a city girl. Being on the raft for a whole day is not easy. He is so proud of her. She doesn't complain much at all, spending most of her time reading the survival booklet.

For the rest of the day, they sit together in the doorway. They are scanning the horizon, searching for a rescue ship or an airplane. Not seeing anyone else is bothering them. They are wondering what could have happened. At least they don't see any empty lifejackets, or worse, one of their friends face down in the water. Maybe a rescue boat picked up the others, and they survived this horrible nightmare.

* * *

By nightfall, it's very discouraging. Jenny and Ben didn't see or hear anything. The one thing they were expecting to see was a rescue airplane in the distance, but there was nothing out there. With it getting dark, they prepare for another night in the raft. The cushions are a godsend, placed together to use as a makeshift bed. At least they don't have to sleep on the cold, damp vinyl floor.

"It's so uncomfortable with all these wet clothes on!" Ben said, pulling off his pants and shirt, throwing them on top of the cargo netting.

"You better keep your undies on!" feeling a little uncomfortable with him lying there in just his underwear.

He let out a long sigh. "Now, that's a lot better... What about you? Are you going to keep your wet clothes on?"

"I think I'll keep mine on. It doesn't bother me much," she blurted out, then giggled.

"Suit yourself, but at least my clothes might be dry in the morning."

The darkness sets in fast. Ben can hear Jenny moving around. She does the same, taking off most of her clothes and storing them in the cargo netting. She lies next to Ben, realizing how much better it is. So tired from their ordeal, it's not long before they both are sound asleep.

* * *

Chapter 11

Notifications

T he last search and rescue flight landed at Kwajalein. The C-131 had been out all day searching with no contact or debris sighted. Paul Rutherford contacts Captain Scott in Honolulu to inform him of the news.

"I'm sorry," Paul said. "The initial search came up with nothing. It's been twenty-four hours. It doesn't look good."

"We heard," Captain Scott replied. "Someone must have leaked it to the press. We're getting calls wanting confirmation before they go live with it."

"Did they say when they're going to broadcast the information?" Paul asked, so frustrated, hearing that the news media was already on top of it.

"Maybe on tonight's late news, but with the cable news, it's probably out now!"

"How much do they know?" Paul asked.

"Not much more than an aircraft went down," Scott replied after a long pause. "Well, it won't take much to figure out what flight it was. There are not too many flights from Hawaii to Kwajalein. Most of the families will start calling anyway to ask why they haven't heard from anyone. It's already after midnight on most of the mainland. It'll give us about six hours before the morning news on the East Coast. You better get a response ready for the families and the press."

There is another long pause on the phone. "I'll make the official announcement," Paul reluctantly said. "I had better start making the calls to the families before it gets any worse."

"If you need anything from us. Just let us know."

"We're going to need a lot of prayers," Paul promptly said.

Paul contacts each of the twenty-two families of the crew and passengers, informing them that the aircraft is missing and there is no news of any survivors. For each call, he has their personnel file open on his desk. He looks at all twenty-two photos from the records as he talks with the families. The sounds of their voices and the crying will haunt him for a long time.

Of the twenty-two people on the flight, some were married with families, while others were single. The youngest was 25, and the oldest was 56. The allure of good pay and benefits on a tropical island attracts many people, and some on this flight were simply looking to work for a year to catch up on bills. They were a diverse group, all seeking adventure, but their journey ultimately ended in tragedy.

At dawn, they will resume the search again with additional aircraft from Hawaii. Along with the loss of Flight Ace 191, dozens of small ships reported damage, calling for assistance. It turns the rescue into a massive operation because the area involved is over half a million square miles. With limited resources, the search and rescue flights are currently looking for Flight 191, but the priorities can change over time.

* * *

2

Chapter 12

The Raft, Day 2

On the second morning, Jenny is up early. Feeling so filthy, she longs for a hot bath. The humidity is unbearable. Her clothes are still wet with salt water and extremely uncomfortable to wear. She finds it's best just to wear her blouse while on the raft. Luckily, her blouse is long enough, so it won't be a problem around Ben.

With nothing else to do, she thinks this will be an excellent opportunity to wash while Ben is asleep. She gets the soap from the survival box. It does not resemble any mild soap, but from its design, it will do the job and probably last for years. She is a little wary of jumping into the open ocean for a bath, but there is no other choice with their limited supply of drinking water.

Before taking off her blouse, she makes sure Ben is still asleep. Tying the safety harness around her waist, she slowly slips into the water. She lathers up with the soap for a quick wash. Something as simple as a bath is a big hassle. She finds it extremely difficult to stay up above the water to wash and keep close to the raft and not lose the soap.

Seeing plenty of small fish under the raft is unnerving. The comment Ben made about the sharks really haunted her. With all the little fish swimming about, larger ones might not be far away.

After a quick wash, Jenny drags herself back into the raft. Luckily, Ben is still asleep. It gives her more time, and much needed privacy. She sits at the doorway, drying herself off with the small towel but keeps a constant eye on him. Dreading having to put on her wet, dirty clothes, she washes everything with soap while she has the chance.

After wringing out all the water, her clothes are still wet, tossing it all back on the cargo netting. Reluctantly, she puts her silk blouse back on. At least it's the one thing that's almost dry and somewhat comfortable to wear.

22222

* * *

Ben wakes up in a daze. When his eyes adjust to the light, he notices Jenny is already up, sitting next to the door. The sun is shining right through her blouse, outlining the silhouette of her body. He is a little shocked and can't help but stare. After what he has been through, this is definitely a sight for sore eyes.

"It must be washday," he mumbles, seeing her folding up her clothes. "I could really go for a long hot shower right now," feeling all clammy.

"Well, I have been meaning to mention it... I think it's time you had a wash too," a little embarrassed having to tell him.

"Yeah, I feel horrible and sticky all over. This humidity and salt water is making it worse. When was the last time I had a shower?"

"It's been way too long! Why don't you do what I did? Just jump in and have a good wash, or you can sit on the edge. It's not that bad now that the big waves are gone."

"When did you do all that?"

"Oh, while you were sound asleep," she boastfully said, sheepishly looking him over.

He notices the strange look on her face. Then he realizes he is lying out in front of her, wearing nothing but his underwear.

"I hope you're going to put some clothes on!" she added, seeing him getting embarrassed again.

He quickly tries to cover himself up. Seeing all his clothes tucked away under the netting and nothing close by, he realizes it's too late, anyway. Since Jenny has been up for a while, she has seen it all by now.

Ben slowly crawls over to the doorway next to her. The cool breeze feels so good and refreshing. After breathing in all the fresh air, he notices the raft is getting a little funky. With the raft closed up all night, the smell is getting worse.

"OK, I'll take a bath!" noticing how she is politely keeping her distance from him.

She let out a loud sigh. "Thank you!" handing Ben the soap.

He can't help laughing. Looking down into the water, he is a little hesitant. Knowing it might be a mile or two deep makes him a little nervous.

"Don't be shy!" she promptly said. "If I can do it, so can you! You'll feel much better after a good wash."

"OK, no peeking," he then stands up, slips off his underwear, jumping into the water. "Ah, this is great! It's surprisingly warm," splashing around in the water.

"You didn't tie the rope around your waist! Stay close to the raft and hold on to the ropes!" concerned about him getting too far away.

"You worry way too much… You know, there are a lot of fish under here! Nice big ones, too! That fishing gear might come in handy," he mentions, quickly swimming back to the raft.

"I noticed that when I was out there. Oh, by the way, Ben, don't forget about the sharks."

"Oh, I forgot about that!" he said, glancing around, feeling uncomfortable and ready to get out of the water.

She laughs, seeing how scared he is. "Just climb up over there. You can sit on the edge and have a good wash," pointing to the right side of the doorway.

He drags himself up onto the edge of the raft, dangling his feet out in the water. Leaning back, resting against the side of the dome, he basks in the warmth of the sun.

"Ben, don't you fall asleep out there, and don't lose the soap! You didn't use the safety rope either!"

"Stop worrying!" closing his eyes, enjoying the sun and the fresh air.

Jenny, still a little concerned, leans out to check on him. Seeing him sitting on the edge of the raft doesn't help. She keeps an eye on him, so worried he might fall in. She thinks it's so odd how he can sit out there naked, just staring out at the ocean without a care in the world. Being in a raft, drifting in the middle of nowhere, she doesn't understand how he is not worried at all.

"Hey, talk about a peeping Tom!" noticing how she was gawking at him while he washed.

"Don't forget to wash behind your ears!" she yells, seeing how embarrassed he is, then goes back into the raft to give him some privacy.

Ben jumps back in the water to rinse off, keeping a close eye on the fish underneath the raft. He slowly makes his way to the entrance, tossing the soap in before pulling himself inside. Quickly trying to dry off, he realizes Jenny is sitting at the far end of the raft, watching him with a big grin on her face.

He quickly covers himself with the towel. "Oh well, I guess we better get this out of the way. Have a good look!" getting up on his knees, holding out his arms, exposing himself to her.

"OK, Ben! That's enough!" covering her eyes with her hands, then laughs.

"You know, it feels great not having all those wet clothes on," lying down on the cushions using the towel to cover himself.

"You're not going to be lying around here like that!" she said, getting all flustered. "Put something on!" turning her eyes away.

"What's the problem? I got the towel covering me up."

"No, you need to put your clothes on," she promptly said, blushing.

"OK, I'll put my pants back on," seeing she is getting a little uncomfortable.

"Thank you!" Jenny replied but still sneaks a peek when he got up.

He takes all his clothes from the netting only to find they are still damp. He knows there is nothing more uncomfortable than having to wear wet clothes. While putting on his pants, he quickly notices Jenny has her hands over her eyes but is peeking through her fingers. She is giggling, seeing him fumbling about, trying to put on his wet clothes. He doesn't care. After being cooped up in this raft for days, privacy is the one thing they don't have.

* * *

Another day has come and gone. With the sun just above the horizon, they get ready for another night in the raft. After two whole days adrift and not seeing any rescue airplanes or ships, Ben knows things are only going to get worse. Their food will be gone in a few days. The fishing gear will be helpful, but eating raw fish is going to be a last resort.

Ben thinks about tomorrow and what it's going to bring. Hopefully, someone will find them. The alternative, he doesn't even want to think about it.

* * *

Chapter 13

The Raft, Day 3

On the third day, drifting in the middle of nowhere, another storm is on the horizon. The wind is slowly picking up, and the waves are getting bigger. Getting out of the raft for a swim or a wash is too dangerous. Even sitting on the edge of the raft is impossible.

Ben stares at the dark clouds, getting so depressed. Cloud-to-cloud lightning is not a good sign. He knows they are in for another big storm, and this one is approaching fast. Ben stowed everything away in the cargo netting. A lesson learned on their first night in the raft.

They don't have to wait long. The storm comes in fast and strikes hard. The wind is howling, and the lightning is relentless, accompanied by deafening thunder. Huge swells lift the small raft, dropping it down repeatedly. At least this time, they are more prepared now. Knowing how all the handles and straps work keeps them from being tossed around.

The sky turns black as if it were night. Luckily, Ben put one of the glow sticks in the holder on the dome. He never thought they would need to use it in the middle of the day. At least having a little light helps, so they are not being tossed about in total darkness.

* * *

After several hours, the conditions are slowly changing. For some strange reason, the waves feel different. These are not the big rolling waves they had for the last few hours, but now they are very steep, where the raft is almost vertical. The winds are getting so strong, it's lifting the raft up and rolling on its side. They hold on for dear life, praying the raft doesn't flip upside down or get torn apart.

The situation is getting worse as the waves start crashing down right on top of the dome. The weight of the water quickly flattens the dome. Within seconds, the dome pops back up as the water spills off. The waves are so huge it feels as if the entire raft is being pushed underwater.

The green glow stick falls out of the holder, disappearing behind one of the storage boxes. Their luck is running out. Now, they have to ride out the storm in the dark since it's impossible to get another one. In the complete darkness, all they can do is hold on and hope for the best.

Another huge wave hits, squashing the raft like an accordion. Jenny loses her grip on the handle but is still holding on to Ben. The next wave is far worse than they have ever experienced. The raft lifts entirely out of the water, flipping upside down.

Ben slams hard against the dome. He is in so much pain, especially with Jenny landing on top of him. With the raft upside down, the thin plastic material of the dome doesn't support their weight. To make matters worse, now the vinyl floor is pressing down on their heads with about a foot of clearance. Luckily, he still has a tight grip on the handle, pulling himself up.

"Ben! I'm sinking!" she yelled out in a panic, grabbing his leg as the vinyl dome enveloped her up to her chest.

"Just hold on!" grabbing her arm with his free hand, trying to pull her out.

"I can't take much more of this," she mumbled, wrapping her arms tightly around Ben's waist.

"This storm won't last much longer! It'll be OK... We'll make it through this. It might flip back over on the next wave," trying to keep a positive attitude.

Without the glow stick, it's pitch black. Ben can't believe he didn't put an extra one in his pocket. They need some light to see what is happening to the raft. With the way things are going, it will not be long before the raft disintegrates, and they'll be out in the ocean on their own.

"Ben! I felt something hit my foot!" she cried out after another wave slammed into the raft.

"Try to keep your legs flat above the water! Don't push your feet through the dome! We don't want to puncture it! Keep calm!" he yells, knowing that the sharks might be waiting for them if the raft falls apart.

She tries pulling her legs free, but the vinyl dome is clinging to her. She feels as if she is in quicksand, slowly being dragged down. All she can do is keep her arms around Ben until this nightmare is over.

"Ben, what are we going to do?" she asked, panicking.

"Just hold on! It can't go on forever!" he explained, trying to get a better grip on her arm.

When the next wave hits but it's noticeably different. The raft is not being lifted as before, but it feels more like being pushed along. The wave pattern has changed, but at least it's for the better.

Holding each other in the total darkness, they hope the storm will be over soon. Another wave hits the small raft, but this time, their luck runs out. Something is definitely wrong. Everything comes to a complete stop, but a horrible ripping sound comes from the raft as the wave rushes over them.

Air rushes out of the raft, and they know it's over. The raft is being torn apart, and the water rushes in and slowly starts sinking as the air escapes. The floor of the raft is just above their heads and getting lower. Knowing that the raft is their only hope for survival, they both know the end is near.

As another wave rushes over them, Ben feels something odd under his foot. Right away, he knows it's not a shark or anything like it. It feels more like something smooth. At least it's a good sign.

"Ben, I can put my foot down on something!" trying to stand up.

"Yeah! I feel it, too!"

"I think we're on land or something!" she said, so relieved.

"You're right! That's sand underneath us! That's probably why the raft got ripped open. We hit some rocks or coral--"

Another wave slams into the raft, and they are violently tossed about. Right away, it becomes apparent that they are on land, but in the dark, they are not sure of anything. The biggest problem is that the raft is upside down, and they are still stuck inside it. The vinyl dome is in shreds, wrapped around their feet, making it impossible to move around.

Another wave hits hard, causing the raft to roll end over end. Ben loses his footing, frantically trying to get untangled from the torn remnants of the dome. Once the wave rushes by, he feels something odd under his hands. For the first time, his hands are digging into the sand. Right then, he knows they finally made it to a beach, but the worst is not over yet.

Jenny struggles to get free. Submerged under the water, she gets tangled up in the vinyl dome. She holds her breath as long as possible. In complete darkness, she feels someone grabbing her, pulling her out of the water. Then the loose vinyl is being ripped away from her body.

She gasps for air. "Ben! Thank God you're here. I thought I was going to drown," constantly coughing to clear her lungs after breathing in the water.

There is no response. Then Jenny feels the hand on her back slowly pulling away. Frantically looking around, she is so frustrated not being able to see anything in the complete darkness. In a panic, she reaches out, trying to find him, but he is not there. A flash of lightning illuminates the raft. She expects to see Ben but discovers she is all alone and still inside the raft.

Ben, feeling a little dizzy, holds his breath while rolling end over end under the water. Once the wave rushes by, he realizes the water is only a few feet deep. To his surprise, he finds himself outside the raft.

He quickly turns around, searching for Jenny. Everything is pitch black, unable to see anything at all, but at least he can hear the torn remnants of the raft flapping in the strong winds.

"Jenny! Jenny!" he yells, walking toward the rustling noise.

"Ben! Where are you?" she asked, struggling to stand up.

"I'm outside the raft! I can't see a thing. Where are you?"

"Still in this damn thing! Help me get out of here!"

"Keep talking so I can figure out where you are!" he replied, getting so frustrated, not seeing anything.

Following the sound of her voice leads him to the remnants of the raft. He crouches over, moving his hands back and forth, trying to find her. A small part of the raft remains inflated, but it's still upside down. Standing upwind, he reaches down and grabs the handle, lifting it up high. The strong wind promptly gets underneath it, flipping the raft over.

"Jenny! Where are you?" still unable to see her.

He can hear her coughing, but with all the howling wind and the crashing waves, it's difficult to judge the direction of the sound. Luckily, lightning strikes in the distance. The blinding white light illuminates the entire area. Right away, he sees her white blouse several yards away.

He runs over to her. "Are you OK?" he asked.

She gags after breathing in some water. "Yeah, I'm OK," she mumbled, wrapping her arms around him.

"Thank God! It's over!" he cried out, helping her up.

"It's a good thing you pulled me out when you did. I couldn't hold my breath any longer. I got so scared when you disappeared like that. How did you get out so quick?"

"What do you mean?" he asked.

"When I was all tangled up in the plastic dome, under the water, you grabbed me, pulling me up. Then you were gone!"

"I don't remember doing that... I got knocked out of the raft when that last wave hit us, about twenty feet back over there. You were still in the raft?" he asked, so confused.

"No, you were with me the entire time. I could feel your hands on me, helping me get untangled from all that plastic. I thought I was going to drown!" she explained.

So exhausted, Ben can't think straight. "I guess... We're on land, so the worst is over," not understanding what she was telling him.

Jenny and Ben drag themselves onto the sandy beach in the total darkness, cold and exhausted. Lying on the beach, they hold each other for warmth and protection from the ferocious wind and pelting rain. Neither one complained, now safe on solid ground after suffering three horrible days in a raft in the middle of the ocean.

* * *

Chapter 14

Envelope

A large envelope arrives at Walter and Mary's house just days after hearing Ben's flight is missing. Mary's eyes widen in disbelief as she sees the return address. It's from Ben, and it's from Hawaii.

She runs back to the house, yelling and screaming. "It's from Ben! He's alive! Look, he's sent us something!" waving the envelope in the air.

"Oh, thank God!" Walter said, eagerly examining the envelope. "It's from Hawaii! Maybe this will explain what happened."

"I wonder why he didn't call?" she asked. "Hurry, open it! I want to see what he sent us!"

Walter notices the postmark. "Oh, no... This was sent out days ago when he flew out of Hawaii. The day his plane went down."

So disappointed, he slowly opens the envelope. He pulls out several rolls of undeveloped film and a small note.

"He must have written this while waiting to board the plane. These are the pictures he took while he was in Hawaii," reading the note from his son, then handed it to his wife.

Mary reads the note. "Why did Ben have to get on that plane? He didn't need to go to that island. He should have come here to be with us," then cries.

"I know... Ben should have stayed home. I want to see what's on these rolls of film. Let's get these developed right away."

Walter and Mary rush down to the one-hour photo to get the film processed. Mary persuades the clerk to process the film right away. She doesn't care about the cost. They eagerly wait at the photo counter, not wanting to leave.

Finally, the woman behind the counter brings out six packages of prints. Mary quickly opens them, flipping through all the photographs of various places in Hawaii. She finally sees the photo of Ben standing out on the beach. She cries, wondering if this is the last photo taken of her son.

"I think he met someone while he was there!" Walter said. "I wonder if she was on the plane with him?" seeing several photos of a young woman on the beach.

"There's nothing in the note. We'll have to ask that man at Kwajalein who called us," staring at the young woman on the beautiful beach.

He looks at the rest of the photos. "They look as if they were having a great time. Why did this have to happen? Why?" he asked, knowing that his son had been taken too soon in life.

Mary wonders if this young woman could have been someone special in her son's life. She might have been her future daughter-in-law. The tears flow from her eyes again. The nightmare is not over, and not knowing makes it worse.

After going through the photos, Mary selects one of Ben standing on the beach. She has the clerk at the counter make four 8x10 prints. Again, they sit and wait. They don't know what else to do, so emotionally drained by the notion they might have lost their son.

* * *

SECTION 2

Island Life

Chapter 15

The Island

B en wakes up shivering, feeling so cold and numb all over. His clothes are soaking wet and covered with sand. His eyes slowly focus on a blinding light in the distance. He realizes the bright light is the sun slowly rising above the horizon. The sky is clear, with not a cloud in sight.

Looking around, he is so surprised to be on a desolate beach lined with tall palm trees. The ocean is so calm with small gentle waves. After what they have endured for the last few days, now everything is so quiet. Such a dramatic contrast, but he is not complaining. They made it to land. The nightmare is finally over.

Jenny is still sound asleep, lying on top of him. He gently rolls her over, placing her on her back. Sitting up, he can't help but admire her beautiful body. Her white silk blouse clings to her skin, revealing every little detail.

Jenny slowly opens her eyes. "You never give up, do you!" she said, seeing him gawking at her body. "You kept staring at me like that while in the raft!"

"Well, I was just," he mumbled, feeling a little awkward, getting caught staring at her.

She slowly sits up. Every muscle in her body ached. When she looks down, she panics. Her blouse is up to her waist, and she is not wearing any panties.

"Oh, great! No wonder you got that look on your face! How long have you been staring at me?" she asked, frantically pulling down her blouse.

He promptly turns away. "I just woke up... I wasn't really staring," feeling so embarrassed.

"My God!" she shouted, realizing they were on a beach. "Ben, we finally made it! Where are we?" looking around.

"We're on an island, is all I know. A real nice one too!" as he looks around, glad she has forgotten about him staring at her body.

"Oh, Ben, it's so beautiful! I wonder what island this is. It kind of looks like Fiji."

"It does, but that's way farther south from Kwajalein. There are so many islands in this area. It's hard to say which one we're on. It looks pretty high, maybe 1,500 to 2,500 feet. That will be a good thing for us!" looking at the cone-shaped peak that dominates the island.

"Oh, why is that?" she asked.

"The higher the island, means it'll collect lots of rainwater. That means there are probably a few streams around here. If there's water, then there will be people here too!"

She is so relieved to hear that. "There should be a few resorts around here from the looks of this beach. It's so beautiful with all the palm trees! There has to be a small town or something nearby. We need to find who is here and contact someone at Kwajalein, letting them know we're OK."

Both struggle to get up, feeling a little uneasy, slowly walking down to the edge of the water to inspect the remains of the raft. Now, it's nothing more than a pile of red and black vinyl. The dome is in shreds and spread out all over the beach. The main part of the raft is still intact, but for the tube surrounding it that is supposed to be full of air, there is not much left. They know that there is no way they can repair it. They are lucky it got torn up on the rocks near the beach. Otherwise, it would have meant the end for them.

"We'd better see what we still have left. We need to pull it out of the water before it goes out with the tide," Ben said, seeing how the waves are already trying to drag it away.

"I don't think we'll be using this again," she added, seeing how torn up it is.

"Nope, it's had it... I hope we still have some water and food left until we find someone here. I wonder how much of the supplies we lost. I don't see anything else out on the beach."

"Maybe it all sank or got washed away last night," looking down the beach, not seeing anything.

"I hope not!" he said. "We'll be needing that, especially out here."

Together, they drag the raft onto the beach. The cargo netting is still intact, and the contents are still in the raft. Luckily, they didn't lose anything, and all the containers are watertight, so nothing got ruined with the saltwater.

"Ben, just look at this place! It's breathtaking! I wonder where everyone is? You'd think people would be out here by now," looking up and down the beach.

"It's still a little early. The sun just came up. Maybe there's something farther down the beach. I don't see any telephone poles or electric lines. Maybe the hotels are on the other side?"

"Yeah, it doesn't look like there's much on this beach. We'll have to check things out once we get situated. I need to get cleaned up first before I go anywhere. I'm not walking into a luxury hotel looking like this."

He can't help laughing. "I wouldn't worry too much about how we look. We've been through hell and back. We're really lucky to be alive!"

"You're right, but I have never felt so filthy in my entire life!" she said reluctantly.

"OK, come on... Let's go in the water!" seeing how badly Jenny wants to get cleaned up.

"I can't believe how clear it is," she said, walking into the water. "The turquoise color and the gentle waves. Oh, I'm really going to enjoy this!"

"So, how are we going to do this?" Ben asked. "We have nothing to hide behind," remembering how she always hid from him while they were in the raft.

She quickly looks around. "Well, there's no one else here. What do you say? Maybe we should celebrate our arrival here. You fancy a little skinny dipping?" giving him a little smile.

"You got to be kidding? You really mean it?" he asked, so shocked.

"Why not! We're adults, all alone out here on this beautiful beach. Besides, you can almost see through this damn blouse anyway," she slowly unbuttons it, then tosses it on the sand.

"Wow! Oh my God!" seeing her standing naked in front of him, not expecting this at all.

She holds out her arms, slowly turning around, showing off her body. "This is a first for me! I have never even been outside naked before!"

He can't help laughing. "I see you're really getting into this!"

"Oh, the sun feels so warm. I'll tell you one thing. It feels great not having to wear those damn wet clothes!" jumping up and down.

"That's why I sat outside on the raft in the sun. Feels a lot better without all those wet clothes on, doesn't it?" unable to take his eyes off her body.

She slowly walks up to him. "You're right about that, especially with all this sand. Anyway, it's your turn!" pulling off his shirt, unfastening his belt, pushing his pants down to his feet.

"Ben, I can't believe you!" seeing him getting aroused. "I thought you were supposed to be the big naturist!" then starts giggling again.

"Hey! It's not my fault. With you jumping about like that, it would get anyone going!"

She can't help smiling, seeing his feeble attempt to cover himself up. "OK, let's put all our clothes out in the sun. We'll just do without them for a while until they dry out," picking up all their clothes, running up the beach, draping them over a tree branch.

Ben stares at her fantastic body. Just in the way she is walking about, he knows she is trying to incite him and is doing it very well. With her walking around like that, it's more than he can handle, and he loses control.

"What are you doing?" he asked, seeing Jenny rummaging through the raft, looking for something. "Let's hit the water!" wanting so much to get off the beach so that he can hide his problem.

She finds what she is looking for, then turns, holding up the soap. Seeing Ben standing out in the open, trying to cover up his full erection, she can't help laughing out loud.

"What's wrong? You exposed yourself to me while we were on the raft. Looks like you can dish it out, but you can't take it!" she boasted, slowly strutting towards him, swinging her breasts about, really tormenting him.

He is so embarrassed. "I didn't do it like that!" gawking at Jenny's big breasts as she swung them around.

"Come on! It's bath time, so no need to be shy. Remember, I've seen it all before!" she said, giving him a sultry look, taking his hand, leading him into the water.

They walk into the surf up to their waists, then wash each other. Ben is in his glory. Lathering up the soap, he runs his hands all over her body. She is also enjoying every minute of it. It is their way of celebrating their survival. From their plane going down and drifting on the open ocean for days, they can now enjoy life on this pristine beach in the South Pacific Ocean.

They stand facing each other, not saying a word. Jenny is sheepishly looking down, seeing he's extremely aroused. Ben is a little hesitant but pulls her close, then gives her a long kiss. She passionately kisses him back, tightly wrapping her arms around him.

"Come on, let's go!" Ben said after a long kiss, quickly picking her up.

She laughed, kicking her feet up in the air. "Where are you taking me?" she asked, putting her arms around Ben's neck and looking deeply into his eyes.

"To the beach!" carrying her out of the water.

"And what will we do there?" Jenny asked, with her little innocent voice.

"It's a surprise! A really big surprise!" he said, with a big smile on his face.

Reaching the edge of the water, Ben gently places her down. She lies on her back in the sand, looking up at him with lust in her heart, slowly opening her legs before him. They make love for the first time on the beach with the small waves washing over their bodies. Oblivious to everything around them, they have no concerns at all about having sex on the beach. Caught up in the moment, they just don't care.

* * *

Jenny stares at the small puffy clouds without a care in the world. She realizes how wonderful it is to lie out on the beach totally naked. Getting goosebumps all over her body as the occasional wave rushes over her. She never understood the point of nudism until now. Being out on a tropical beach with no one else around makes the experience even more exhilarating.

Jenny rolls over on her side, propping her head up with her hand, looking at Ben's body. She slowly runs her hand up and down his torso.

"You never give up, do you?" Ben jokingly asked, noticing how she was staring at his body.

She laughed at him. "You've been gawking at me for a long time. Now, it's my turn!" leaning over, kissing him again.

"Wow!" he yelled out, looking into her eyes. "You've really changed. What happened to that shy little girl I used to know?"

"She's gone! This is my second chance in life. There were times I thought we weren't going to make it. I kept thinking about all the things I have always wanted to do in my life. Well, now I'm doing it all!" lying on her back, looking up at the clouds, stretching her arms above her head.

"Having sex on the beach and laying out naked in the sun was on top of my list!" he boasted.

She laughed. "Live for today is going to be my motto from now on," she said, taking Ben's hand.

Ben can't take his eyes off her as she stretches her body out on the sand. This is all so surreal. After what they have been through in the past few days, they are now lying naked on this beautiful beach. He is wondering if this is all a big dream and will wake up back on the raft again. If it is a dream, he doesn't want it to end.

* * *

"It's only eight in the morning, and it's already getting hot out here!" Ben remarked. "I wonder how bad it's going to get by the afternoon," walking back to the raft.

"Yeah, I can already feel it," she replied, putting on her blouse. "This white sandy beach is going to make it worse."

"Oh hell, my clothes are still damp!" Ben said, putting on his boxer shorts and shirt. "I'm so tired of everything being wet. It feels awful!"

"Luckily, my blouse is silk, so it dries fast, but it's still covered with sand. We can't seem to get away from all this sand. It's getting into everything. Anyway, let's keep everything out in the sun. It shouldn't take long for things to dry out in this heat."

"My luck, all my clothes are made of cotton. Once it dries, it'll be worse. Everything will be hard as a rock after being in that salt water. Well, we better move everything up next to the trees while we have a chance. From the looks of the waterline, the tide comes in up to here. We don't want all of our supplies getting washed away."

"Can we take a break and rest for a while?" she asked, too tired to do anything else.

"Well, if the tide comes in, we're going to have to move it all, anyway. We can do it later, but it will be a lot hotter than it is now. You can take a break if you want?"

"No, let's do it now while I still have the energy!" she said, standing with her hands on her hips, looking it all over. "We also need to get something to eat and start looking around for help."

After emptying everything from the raft, they moved it all up to the tree line. They drape their clothes over various trees and shrubs in the sun to dry. They then drag the remnants of the raft up onto the beach, tying the rope to a palm tree so it doesn't get blown away by the wind.

Once everything is out of the way, there is nothing else to do. They sit among the trees, resting in the shade, eating one of the dry rice cakes, hoping to get a big hotel breakfast later. Until they find something on this island, it's all they have to eat.

* * *

Hearing his watch chime, Ben turns to Jenny. "Well, it's nine o'clock. What do you want to do?"

"I'm ready to start looking around to see what's here. I'm getting hungry. What do you think?"

"Yeah, we might as well start now. The quicker we find something, the better. My stomach is already growling. I could go for a big steak right now!" looking down the beach.

Jenny agreed. "It would be great to find a nice resort and have a hot bath. I have had enough of this sleeping outside and in that damn raft. I would also give anything right now for some dry, clean clothes!"

Ben uses the desalination pump to fill the water container. Already feeling dehydrated, he makes sure they both drink as much as possible. With all their supplies safely stored away, they walk down the beach, looking for any signs of civilization.

"I could really go for a good hot meal right now," Jenny said. "Although if a resort is near us. They could have seen us out on the beach while we were running around naked. They might have taken pictures of us too!" looking about in the trees, worrying.

"I think I found your trepidation!"

"You noticed! Well, I have never done anything like that before."

"Well, you're doing pretty good for your first time! It looks like you were really enjoying it too!"

"It was nice... Being on this tropical island makes it a little easier. Just think, I would never go out without a bra on, and look at me now!" she boasted, turning around in circles.

"I am!" he replied. "I can't believe that's all you're wearing. That blouse of yours doesn't leave much to the imagination. From here, I can tell you're not wearing anything underneath it!"

"Is it really that revealing?" she asked, getting a little concerned.

"Oh, no... No one would ever know!" gawking at her large breasts bouncing about underneath her sheer white blouse.

"You're not supposed to stare at them like that!" she shouts, reaching over, slapping the back of Ben's head, feeling a little frisky.

"You just can't wait to show them off," he jokingly said, hoping she would take her blouse off again.

Jenny said nothing. She puts her arm around him, resting her head on his shoulder as they walk. Ben puts his arm around her waist. The walk along the beach is the one thing that they need the most after being cooped up in the raft for days. Their nightmare is finally over. Now, it's just a matter of time before finding help on this island.

* * *

By noon, Jenny and Ben had found nothing. They are also having a difficult time trying to determine how big the island is. The beaches are small, so they can't see very far. Every time they reach a bend, there is always another tiny stretch of beach, making them even more depressed. After a while, it all looks the same.

Ben is keeping track of the time and distance. On top of every hour, he puts markings in the sand. He also keeps an eye on the peak of the island and the shadow it casts. That is their best reference point, and it gives them a clue about the size of the island.

Ben notices that the sand on the beach looks a little odd. He has never seen such a smooth sandy beach with no footprints at all. On Hawaiian beaches, you can always see footprints after several days. Here, it looks as if no one has ever walked on this beach. Even the palm trees are not like the ones in Hawaii. No one has ever trimmed these trees. He is getting a bad feeling about this island. Things just don't look right.

Jenny suddenly stops. "You know... Now and then, I keep thinking I see something in there," she mentioned, looking into the trees. "Have you noticed anything?"

Her comment startled him. "No, I haven't... You think someone is watching us?" quickly scanning the tree line, looking for anything out of place.

"I don't know... It's like I see something in the corner of my eye. When I turn to look, there is nothing there. I noticed it several times."

"Maybe it's someone checking us out," he explained, walking up to the edge of the trees to look around. "Seeing how thick this jungle is, it'll be easy for anyone to hide in there."

"Hello!" she yelled out. "Anyone there?" waiting for a response.

"We were washed up on the beach!" Ben shouted after several seconds of silence. "We need help! Do you have a phone so we can call someone?"

They both listen, but there is no response. After waiting quietly for several minutes, no one emerges from the trees. The only sound is of the wind blowing through the tall trees.

Ben doesn't like this at all. His survival instincts kick in. Too many times while camping in the wilderness, bears or mountain lions have tracked him. Luckily, on these small islands, there are no such animals. The only thing it can be is another person watching them, which is the one thing he fears the most.

"Jenny, what did it look like?" he asked.

"Well, that's the weird part. It was small, like a young child, maybe around five or six years old. It's kinda dark in there, so I couldn't see much. Like I said, it was something moving in there that got my attention. Every time I look, I'm not seeing anything. It's so weird."

"The only thing I can see that's moving is the shadows cast by the trees," he explained, seeing the wind blowing the trees around. "You think that could be what you saw?"

"Maybe," she said, looking at the shadows.

"We'll keep an eye on it," taking her hand, rushing down the beach to get some distance from whoever it is. "If someone is checking us out, it'd be hard for them to keep up with us if we walk fast. We should be able to hear them trying to walk through all that mess in there."

"Maybe it's some kids playing?"

"Well, if it is some kids. I hope they didn't see what we were doing back down the beach. Maybe that's why they're hiding. The little perverts want to see another sex show!" he jokingly said.

She gasped out loud. "Oh no! I didn't think about that. That's all we need."

"Don't worry about it... Let's keep on walking. We'll keep an eye on the trees. Maybe they'll get tired and come out. Could be some local kids wary of strangers."

"Well, I hope we find somebody soon. I'm so tired and hungry. I just want to go home," regretting making this trip.

"We'll find someone or something. Just give it time. It's a big island, and someone has got to be here. By the end of the day, we'll be out of here and on the way home," putting his arm around her waist, trying to cheer her up.

* * *

As the day draws on, Ben's watch beeps again, indicating another hour has passed. "Damn! We've been walking for four hours now. From the looks of things, I think we're on the other side of this island. Check out those shadows way up there on top of the hill."

"Already?" she asked. "That can't be right! That was too quick," looking somewhat puzzled.

"Yeah, but unfortunately, I think we are. You can see those boulders up there. They are now on the right side," pointing up at the peak.

"I noticed it when we started," he continued. "They were on the left side of that peak, and now it's on the other side. That means we're on the opposite side of the island from where we started. We've been walking a little over four hours, and at three miles per hour, that's about twelve miles."

"Maybe we should turn back?" Jenny asked, looking back down the beach where they had just walked.

"No, I don't think that's a good idea," he said, shaking his head. "We know there's nothing back there, so we need to keep going. We're probably closer to our starting point if we keep walking this way," pointing down the beach ahead of them.

"So, what are you really saying?" she asked, getting irritated.

"This island is a lot smaller than I thought. It might take less than a day to walk all the way around it. If it's this small, there's probably no resort or even a hotel here. Even if there is a small village, we should have seen something by now."

"Ben, don't you say that!" she shouts, getting so frustrated, turning away, not wanting him to see her crying.

She fights back the tears. Her hopes of ever getting out of this mess are slowly diminishing. She doesn't want to think about it anymore. She just wants this to be over and to go home.

Ben knows he shouldn't have told her. "We still have a long way to go. There might be something just down the beach," trying to comfort her.

She pushes him away and takes a few steps, then turns towards him. "I'm so fed up with all this! When is it going to end? I want to go home! I should have never come out here! It was all nothing but one big mistake!" then she struts down the beach at a fast pace.

Ben feels her pain, and it's another big letdown for them. He has been trying to keep his hopes up, but deep down, he knows the smaller the island, the fewer chances they have of finding anyone here.

Jenny briskly walks far ahead of Ben. She is in no mood to talk and doesn't want any more bad news. With the airplane going down and drifting on that raft for days, she can not hide her emotions anymore. The stress from all this is getting too much. The reality is setting in that they might indeed be all alone here on this island.

Ben tries to keep up with her but can't keep up the pace. He feels a little light-headed. He stops for a while, trying to catch his breath. The heat is getting to him, and there is not much of a breeze. Then he gets tunnel vision and knows he is in big trouble.

"Jenny!" he called out, feeling so weak, barely able to stand up.

As soon as she hears his voice, she knows something is wrong. She turns to see him far behind, lying face down in the sand. "Ben! What's wrong?" running back to him.

She rolls him onto his back. She panics, seeing he is unconscious and looks so pale and fears the worst.

"Oh God, no! Please be all right! Ben! Ben!" splashing water on his face, gently slapping his cheek, trying to revive him.

Ben slowly opens his eyes. "What's up? What happened?" seeing Jenny kneeling over him and crying.

"I don't know... You were lying face down in the sand! Are you OK?"

"I guess… I just felt a little dizzy, kind of weak."

"You were unconscious for a few minutes! I was so scared. I didn't know what to do!"

Jenny looks at the water container, seeing it's still half-full. "I think you're dehydrated. You need some water," making him drink as much as he can take.

"Yeah, it's been a long day," he said. "I thought I could pace myself better. I guess I'm not used to this heat."

"Well, we haven't had a good meal in days, and this is a long walk. Maybe we should have walked a little slower and taken more breaks."

"I'm OK... We need to keep going down the beach. I'm just a little tired," Ben mumbled, slowly closing his eyes.

"No, you need to rest... We'll stay here and rest up for a while. Let's go sit in the shade by those trees over there."

Jenny helps him up, helping him over to the shade. Ben quickly falls asleep, so exhausted from this ordeal. Jenny sits next to him, keeping an eye on him. She knows they tried too much too fast. After hours of walking in this heat, it was just too much. With limited food and water, they need to be more careful and pace themselves a little better.

* * *

Chapter 16

Rest

Ben wakes up, a little disoriented. Looking at his watch, he realizes how late it is. Seeing the shadows cast by the island out on the ocean, he knows he must have been sleeping for a long time.

"How are you feeling?" Jenny asked, running her hand over his chest.

"A lot better now," he replied, sitting up. "Felt like the heat got to me."

"Yeah, that and going days without food and water. You need to make sure you drink enough water."

He agreed. "I thought I could conserve the water, but out here, we need a lot more. How are you doing?"

"I feel tired but OK... I must have fallen asleep, too. I guess we both needed a rest. We also need something better to eat than those old rice cakes. I must have lost several pounds," looking down at her waist as she stands up.

"Me too... No wonder I feel weak. I guess we better keep moving," trying to get up.

"Do you think you can walk?" she asked, putting her arms around his waist, trying to steady him.

He quickly puts his hand on her shoulder. "I'm fine... Let's not go so fast this time," walking down the beach at a much slower pace.

* * *

The hours go by, and it's more of the same, nothing but a desolate beach with no hotels or houses. There are no signs of any civilization. Ben expected to see some old remnants of airplanes or buildings from the Second World War. Now, he is wondering if anyone has ever been on this island.

Almost giving up hope, they finally stumble upon a beach that looks promising. Tall palm trees line this long stretch of beach. The clouds are building up on this side of the island. The top half of the island is now covered with clouds, looking like it's raining up there. A clean water source will be helpful. Their luck is changing for the better.

Jenny sees a bluish object in the sand about a hundred feet down the beach. "Look at that!" pointing it out to Ben.

"What the hell is that?" trying to focus his eyes on it.

"Civilization is what that is!" she cried out.

They frantically run down the beach. After hours of nothing but sand and coconuts, it's the first sign of civilization. Once they reach the object, they recognize it right away. Lying on the sand is a blue seat cushion.

"There must be a hotel close to here! This probably got blown away in the wind!" she said, looking further down the beach for anything else.

He picks up the cushion, examining it. "Oh, hell... I'm sorry, but this looks like it might be from our plane," a little hesitant about giving Jenny more bad news.

"I thought we put the ones we had up by the raft?" she asked, carefully examining it.

"Maybe it was blown down here by the wind," he replied, looking down the beach for the raft.

"Ben, I know for sure I put them near the trees in the sun to dry. Look, this one has a big rip in it. None of ours did."

"You're right! It's not one of ours. I bet there is a lot more stuff from the plane getting washed up here!"

"Let's keep going down the beach! Maybe the others made it here too!"

"That's just what I was thinking!" he said, hoping to see all their friends alive and well.

Walking down the beach, they discover more debris from the airplane. Most of it is small pieces of plastic, paper, and Styrofoam cups scattered all over the beach and in the water.

"Looks like most of this stuff is garbage," Jenny said, feeling so disappointed.

Ben picks up some of the Styrofoam cups and empty plastic bottles. "Well, it's not all garbage… We can use some of these for our drinking water," he explained, showing her one of the plastic bottles he found.

As they continue down the beach, Jenny notices a strange ridge far ahead in the sand. "Does that look a little odd to you?" she asked, pointing it out.

"Yeah, it does… I wonder what it is?"

They rush down the beach, and to their surprise, they discover a small dry creek. The creek runs from the trees down to the ocean.

"Now, this is interesting! I guess when it rains, the water has to go somewhere," he said, looking over the small creek.

She looks up at the clouds covering the island. "If it rains up there, the water must come down here and go out to the ocean. Let's see where it leads. Maybe there's a house back there in those trees."

"You might be right about that. If someone lives here, they'll need to be near drinking water!"

They follow the dry creek up into the dense trees. Once they're off the beach, it's like a jungle with all the plants and ferns covering the ground. The palm trees act as a canopy, blocking out the fierce sun, but it also blocks the breeze from the ocean. The humidity rises dramatically, making it extremely uncomfortable.

The dry riverbed leads to an opening in the trees, revealing a small pond at the base of a massive rock cliff. They stand in awe, looking at this fantastic scene. The cliff is nothing but moss and flowers and must be thirty feet high. The pond is only a foot deep and about twenty feet in diameter. Water trickles down from the rock cliff, splashing into the small pond.

"Ben, can you believe this? Look at that waterfall and all those flowers. It's so beautiful! There's not much water flowing down, but during a rainy day, I bet it would make a great place to have a shower."

Ben kneels near the edge. "It's fresh water too!" splashing the cold water on his face.

Jenny runs into the middle of the pond. "Oh, this feels so good!" she shouted, washing herself with the clean water.

"Jenny, this could be our only source of fresh drinking water," seeing the silt being stirred up.

"I know... Isn't it nice!" lying in the water.

"Well, this can be our drinking water or bathwater. Which one would you like?"

"Sorry, I didn't think about that. Can we use that desalination pump to filter out the water?"

"It should work better here because it's not saltwater. It'll filter out the viruses and stuff, but it'll still be bathwater."

"Maybe you're right... I'll just rinse off my blouse. It'll make it more bearable, not having to wear something that feels like sandpaper!"

"Just remember, we may be drinking this water later on."

Jenny removes her blouse, swishing it around in the water. Ben can't argue with her. She makes a good point since all their clothes had been in salt water for days and covered with sand. His skin is getting chafed, wearing damp clothes for the last few days. He quickly takes off all his clothes, rinsing them in the pond as well.

He can't help staring at Jenny while she is cleaning her blouse. She is standing naked in the pond, with an abundance of flowers on the cliff behind her. That is one fantastic sight to see. She is secretly glancing over at him as well. For both of them, it's a big adjustment to be around each other naked in this tropical paradise.

Ben drapes all his wet clothes over a tree branch. He then realizes he has nothing else to wear. He can see Jenny is in a worse predicament by only having a blouse. After rinsing off their clothes, they are secretly admiring each other's bodies. Standing naked in front of each other in this tropical forest is incredibly alluring, but neither wants to admit it.

"So, what do we do now?" Jenny asked, feeling a little uncomfortable not wearing any clothes.

"I guess we can fill the water bottles," glancing over at the small waterfall.

"Is it clean water?" she asked.

"It's as clean as it's going to get out here. We can still put it through the water filter first before we drink it. It'll probably taste a lot better than the ocean water we've been filtering out."

Ben takes the empty water bottles that they collected from the beach over to the waterfall. He rinses them out really good, then tries to fill them with the water trickling down the cliff face. The water is streaming down in too many places. It will not take long if he can get it flowing in one spot, but it's just not enough to fill anything fast.

After several minutes, he gives up. "This will take all day," promptly dunking the bottles into the pond to fill them up.

"I guess we can use that water to wash with later on," not liking the idea of drinking murky water.

"My thoughts exactly!" he said, filling the remaining bottles.

Stepping out of the pond, Ben takes one of the larger bottles, holding it up over his head, letting the cold water run down his body. He repeats it several times, having a good wash trying to keep the water in the pond as clean as possible. From his camping days, Ben knows you should never contaminate your drinking water by bathing in it. It might be the only water available on the island, and he doesn't want to ruin it.

"You were on about me gawking at you!" he mentioned, realizing she was staring at him with a big smile on her face.

"Sorry... I guess it takes a while to get used to this," she explained, averting her eyes away.

"Now, you see how I feel!" he added, making it obvious that he was staring at her body.

"Stop it! I wasn't looking at you like that!" she said, getting all flustered, trying to cover her body with her hands.

He laughed. "I think you were... That little grin on your face said it all!"

"I'm new at this, so don't tease me."

"I'm about the same... I've been out skinny dipping a few times, but nothing like this!" he shouts, standing with his hands on his hips, posing like Superman.

"Yeah, right! You're one hell of an exhibitionist. It feels a lot better not having to wear anything. I think I'll keep my blouse off until it dries out if it's OK with you?" feeling a little apprehensive, standing naked in front of him.

"I won't complain! I guess I'll do the same. To be honest, I don't think I can put on my wet clothes, anyway. They're rubbing me raw!" he explained, so surprised that she had opted not to wear her blouse.

"Maybe we better get back to the beach," he added, picking up the various bottles, wanting to get away from this humidity.

"Yeah, I'm ready to get back to that nice cool breeze out there. We need to remember where this place is. It would be great to be near this pond. I could spend hours lying in here to cool off."

"Looks like a good place over there," he said. "At least there's no sand," pointing to a flat grassy area nearby.

"That will be perfect if we don't find anything else. I know I'm not going to be sleeping on the beach again," looking over at the grass area shaded by the tall palm trees.

He now knows that she is coming to the conclusion that they might be all alone on this island. So far, they have found nothing to indicate anyone else is here. He doesn't say anything, wanting to keep a positive attitude.

They stand for a moment, looking at each other's naked bodies. "OK, let's get this out of our minds!" Jenny shouted out, getting a little flustered. "This is not sexual. We're hot, and our clothes are all wet. We're just doing this to stay cool!"

He let out a long sigh. "Right! You can say what you want. But this is going to take a while for me to get used to!" staring at her breasts.

"Well, at least I am trying! Come on, get serious. We need to keep moving. Remember, we're supposed to be looking for a hotel or other people here!" giving him a stern look.

He sighed again. "OK, let's go... You lead the way!" making damn sure she would walk in front for the magnificent view he would have.

Walking out to the beach, Ben admires her hourglass figure. He is in awe, watching her nicely rounded butt jiggle slightly as she walks, and is still having a difficult time controlling himself. He has seen this in movies and heard all the stories, but experiencing it firsthand is a dream come true.

Their luck has changed with the discovery of the pond and the abundance of fresh drinking water. Ben makes a note of the time and the location. He looks up at the top of the island to get a reference to where they are. They might have to walk back here if they don't find anything else.

They walk together, holding hands, occasionally strolling into the warm ocean water. They both feel so refreshed after cooling off in the pond. Not wearing any clothes makes it more comfortable. Now, they are a little more energetic with a better outlook on their situation.

"I can't believe I'm doing this!" she said, feeling like a different person.

"What?" he jokingly asked. "Walking on the beach? You need to get out more often," teasing her a little.

"No, you know what I mean! Look at us! We're out walking around, not wearing any clothes! I have never been outside topless before, and look at me now! You know, I never knew why people would go to those nudist camps just to walk around naked. Now, I know! This is absolutely fantastic!" flinging her arms up in the air, doing circles in the sand.

He looks at her in disbelief. "I'm glad you like it. It does feel a lot better with the cool breeze. It sure beats having to wear those horrible wet clothes!"

"Yeah, it just doesn't make sense to wear clothes out here. If my friends back home could see me now. No one will believe I'm doing this!" dancing about in front of him.

"I'm having a hard time believing it now!" he jokingly said, trying so hard not to get aroused with her romping about naked on the beach.

* * *

A short time later, they discover more debris scattered all over the beach. Seeing all the stuff from the airplane reminds them of why they are here. Ben picks up a small briefcase, half-buried in the sand. Only the front half of the briefcase is there, and the contents are long gone.

He reads the inscription on the tag still attached to the handle. "It's the pilot's briefcase," he said, slowly shaking his head.

Jenny gasped out loud, covering her mouth with her hand. She turns away, not wanting to look at the first object that belonged to someone they knew. She can't help thinking about all their friends. For a short time, they had forgotten, but the reality of their situation is coming back to haunt them.

Pieces of insulation, cabinet doors, and papers are all over the beach. Then, they notice a large white object rolling in the waves about thirty feet from the shore. Their worst fears had come true. They are hoping not to find any bodies. Having to deal with it is just too much.

"Oh God, Ben, I hope it's not what I think it is!" dreading that it might be someone from the airplane.

"Stay here!" placing everything into the briefcase shell, slowly walking out into the surf.

He cautiously approaches the large, white object. The only thing it can be is a body, bloated after days drifting in the ocean. He doesn't want to deal with it, but he knows he can't leave it out in the water. Whoever it is will need a proper burial.

As he gets closer, he recognizes what it is. "Thank God! It's one of the duffel bags from our plane!"

"Oh, what a relief!" she said, so glad it was not one of their friends. "Bring it in, so we can see what's in it!" hoping for a change of clothes.

"It's extremely heavy! It's in one piece and still sealed up too!" he then grabs the handle, dragging it back to the beach.

Jenny runs out to help. "Do you see any more?" looking out at the ocean.

"I don't see any... Maybe they're slowly washing up. If there's one, then there's got to be a few more around. Let's get this one on the beach before the tide takes it back out. Can you help me drag it in?"

Struggling to get the duffel bag out of the water, they don't get far before the handle rips off, causing them both to fall flat on their backs.

"It's waterlogged and heavier than hell," he said. "For some reason, it didn't sink."

"Ben, this weighs too much! We can't even roll it out. It's so heavy. We're not going to be able to drag it out of the water."

He staggers back, examining the duffel bag. "You're right... The only thing we can do is open it up and drag it all out one piece at a time," untying the drawstring.

"Does it say who it belonged to?" she asked, seeing the identification tag they all had to fill out.

"No, it's blank. The ink must have washed off," looking down at the tag.

"I guess it doesn't matter," she said. "I don't think I'd want to know, anyway."

"Oh, my God!" he shouted out. "You're not going to believe this!" staring at the contents.

"What's wrong?" she asked, taking a step back, startled by his reaction.

He looks up at Jenny as if he has seen a ghost. "You're not going to believe this! It's my bag! Look, it's all my snorkeling gear and camping things! Talk about lucky!"

"You got to be kidding," she said, so surprised. "What else do you have in it? I hope you are my size! At least now we can have something else to wear," leaning over to get a closer look.

"Oh, it's better than clothes! Out of the two bags I had, this is the one that's got all my good stuff in it! It's all my fishing gear, snorkeling stuff, binoculars, and all my other goodies, too," laughing out loud.

"I can't believe you brought all that junk. I hope you got some clean clothes in there. We can use those now since we have been wearing the same clothes for over three days. Just look at us! We're standing out here naked because our clothes are all wet and covered with sand," looking at him, a little shocked.

"This is way better than clothes. It's all my camping gear!"

"Why the hell would you pack camping gear?" she asked, so confused. "You were supposed to pack clothes to last you a whole year like I did!"

He laughed out loud. "Well, I was hoping to do a little fishing and maybe spend a few days camping on the beach. On our time off, I was planning to do some camping in New Zealand and Australia. So what did you pack? Just clothes?"

"Yes, I did! My two duffel bags were packed with nothing but clothes. Normally, that would only be enough for a couple of weeks for me. What were you planning to do? Wear the same clothes every day for a year!"

"I had all my clothes in the other bag. That would be enough to last me for a week or two. You know, they do have washers and dryers there. I bet half of one of those bags of yours was nothing but shoes!"

"Just hurry up and empty it!" she shouted, giving him a mean look, not wanting to admit he was right about the shoes.

Ben is so thrilled with their find. He drags out the contents, placing everything on the beach. The sleeping bag expanded, saturated with water, wedged so tight in the duffel bag. They both struggle to drag it out of the water, careful not to damage it.

"Damn, it's soaking wet! We can use a sleeping bag. How long will it take to dry it out?" dragging it on the beach, trying to wring out all the water.

"Out here in the direct sunlight, it won't take long," he said, feeling the heat of the sun. "At least it'll give us something nice and soft to sleep on."

"I'm still hoping for a real bed. Remember, we're supposed to be looking for a hotel. We still have a long way to go. We're not going to stop here, are we?"

"You're right!" he said, forgetting about that. "We need to keep on moving. Let's unload all this first. There are a few things that we can use."

"Didn't you pack any clothes in this one? It seems as though you got everything but what you're supposed to have in it," getting a little annoyed.

"Now, you mention it. I may have my swimming trunks in this one," dumping out the rest of the contents.

"Only swimming trunks! I was hoping for a change of clothes. Don't you have a T-shirt or anything?" seeing nothing but the odd camping gear and little bags filled with strange objects.

"Sorry, it's all packed in the other bag. I got my sleeping pad in this one. At least now I know why it didn't sink. It still got some air in it," tossing out the thin brown air cushion on the beach.

"So what exactly is this?" she asked, not understanding any of this high-tech camping gear.

"It's like a thin air mattress, but this one is filled with foam. It's like a big sponge compressed and sealed up in a bag. Once you release the valve, it sucks in air. Then you seal up the valve, and you have one nice little air cushion plus all the foam in it. You can even blow it up to make it nice and firm."

"So, why would I want one of these?" she asked, looking at him a little odd.

"Oh, this is great for camping. You put it under your sleeping bag so you don't have all the rocks digging into your back. It's also good insulation from the cold ground. I can tell you've never been camping. I thought twice about packing this. Luckily, I did. Otherwise, all this would have probably sunk to the bottom of the ocean. It's a lot better than a bag full of old clothes!"

"So, in other words, all we got is a bag full of your toys!" she said, a little amused by all this.

"Toys? Hell no!" he blurted out. "This is the top-of-the-line camping gear! I have a folding saw and a wire saw, and they'll come in handy around here. Now, we can cut up some wood for a fire. It's going to help us out. Especially my fishing gear!" knowing that she still doesn't fully comprehend how lucky they are to find the duffel bag loaded with his camping gear.

"So, what are we going to do with all this? Are you going to leave it all here?" she asked.

"Yeah, it's too much to take with us. Let's move it all up by the trees and dry everything out like we did with the raft. We don't want to lose any of this. We can come back for it later."

After storing everything from the duffel bag up by the trees, they also leave their clothes behind. There is no point in carrying wet clothes, putting them out in the sun to dry, including all the things they have collected.

They continue down the beach, not being burdened with carrying anything with them. Not wearing any clothes is a bold move, walking hand in hand down the beach.

* * *

The sun is near the horizon, with a few hours of daylight left. With just a gentle breeze, it cools down dramatically, and it ends up being a beautiful day. The late afternoon is better than the midday sun that they have endured.

Walking down the beach feeling a little better, now their luck is changing. Ben's duffel bag will be an asset in addition to the freshwater pond. If no one else is on the island, at least they know they can wait it out for a few days until a rescue plane shows up.

Ben can't help staring at Jenny as they walk along the beach. She has one fantastic body. Seeing her big breasts bouncing about is getting to him. When she bends over to pick up a shell, it's just too much. He has been fighting like hell to keep things under control, but it's a losing battle. His worst fear comes true. He gets an erection, and he knows there is nothing he can do to hide it from her.

Walking along the beach, Jenny pretends not to notice and tries so hard not to laugh out loud. She can't believe he gets so horny just walking along the beach with a naked woman. It's the type of thing she expected from a horny teenager but not from the big outdoor mountain man. Secretly glancing down, she is so amazed by his stamina. He has been erect for a long time, and it doesn't look like it's letting up at all.

"So, you got a big date tonight?" she asked, then started laughing.

"It's not my fault!" he explained, getting so embarrassed. "A man can only take so much of this."

"I'm sorry for laughing, but it's hilarious with you walking around like that!"

"Unfortunately, there is no way to hide it out here," he said. "Having you walking around me like that isn't helping my situation!"

She laughed again. "Next time, I'll be more careful and not bend over in front of you. I can't believe that's all it takes to get you going!" glancing down at Ben's erection with a big smile on her face.

"Come on, horny boy!" she added, taking Ben's hand. "We still have a long way to go. Try thinking about something else. Maybe that will help you out down there."

"I don't think I can," he mumbled, glancing at her breasts, which were constantly bouncing up and down.

"I'm new at this naturist thing, and you don't see me having issues!"

"Oh, really!" he said and turned to look toward the trees. "Look, everyone! She's naked! She's out on the beach running around naked! Everyone, come on over and check it out!" pointing at Jenny.

"Would you stop that!" she shouted, hiding up behind him. "That's not funny!" looking around, making sure no one else was there.

He just laughed. "Come on, nature girl... We still have a long way to go," taking her hand, continuing down the beach, and letting her know that he can take a joke, but he can dish it out, too.

* * *

They don't get far before discovering another ridge on the beach. This one is not a dry creek but more like a small river, about a foot deep and twenty feet wide. The waves crashing on the beach roll up the shallow creek, following its path into the trees.

"Now, this looks promising!" he mentioned, walking halfway across. "Hey, check it out! It looks like another pond back there in the trees. It's a big one, too!" pointing it out to her.

"You think there might be a house in there?" she asked, a little concerned.

"Hard to say. From the looks of how big that pond is, there is a good chance we'll find something!" walking into the trees to check it out.

She quickly chases after him, grabbing his arm. "Ben, wait... What were we thinking? We can't go in there like this," hiding up behind him.

"Oh hell, our clothes are all the way down the beach!" he said, noticing how she is trying to cover herself up. "That wasn't a smart thing to do, was it? Just think, if there is a big hotel in there, we'll have to walk in naked asking for help," then laughs out loud.

"Well, you got a bigger problem to worry about!" she shouted. "I ain't going in there with you looking like that!"

He looks at her, a little startled. "Awe, come on... It's not like the beaches back home. It'll probably be like one of those European resorts where you'll see a few naked people running around. Most of the women there go around topless, wearing nothing but thongs. Even the men wear those tight little Speedos."

"I don't think that's the issue here. Can you imagine what people would say when you walk up to them not only naked but with a big erection too!" pointing at his crotch.

"Oh hell, I forgot about that... Well, you ain't helping much, jiggling those in front of me all the time. If there are people in there, I bet all the ladies will be thrilled!" swinging his erection around, teasing her.

"Yeah, right!" she fired back. "You never know... It might be a gay resort, and the guys will be thrilled to see you!" and starts laughing.

He turns, giving her a mean look. "Hey! That's not funny!" feeling so uncomfortable.

Getting concerned about their predicament, they decide to get close enough to see if anyone else is around. If there are people here, they'll rush back to get their clothes and come back later.

Slowly, they make their way along the edge of the small river, hiding behind the trees. They listen and look around for any signs of people, but there is nothing. Making their way through the dense trees, there is nothing unusual. Once they are close enough, they stand silently in awe. It is nothing close to what they were expecting.

In front of them is a large lagoon, surrounded by palm trees, with a huge waterfall cascading down the cliff. This pond is enormous compared to the last one. Not finding any houses or people is a big letdown, but the scene is absolutely breathtaking.

Since no one else is around, Ben jumps into the small river, walking toward the lagoon. Cautiously, he moves on, getting deeper with every step. Not even close to the center, the water is already up to his waist. He stops, wondering how deep it is by the waterfall.

Jenny walks on the edge of the pond in awe of the scenery. "I can't believe this place. It's an absolute paradise! I have never seen anything like this before. I wonder if this water is drinkable?"

He cups his hands, tasting the water. "Oh yeah! If you like saltwater. You can see it in the shimmer on the surface. There is a mixture of fresh and saltwater here. When the tide goes out, and with a good rain, this will probably be all fresh water."

"Oh, Ben! Look at that!" she cried out, pointing to all the flowers running up the cliff.

"This is the best place we have found so far. It's going to be hard to top this one!" looking at all the flowers on the moss-covered cliff face.

The lagoon is about forty feet across, at the base of a massive rock cliff. The cliff face has numerous ridges filled with various plants and flowers. A small waterfall runs down the cliff, apparently from a major stream coming down from the island.

Ben feels a little uneasy being waist-deep in the water. "I'm getting out of this before something bites my toe. There is no telling what else may be in here," quickly making his way out of the pond.

Jenny laughed. "Your toe? You better watch out for your tallywhacker. I hope there are no hungry fish in there thinking it's a nice little snack!" walking to the cliff face.

"Your sense of humor is getting annoying!" he shouted, quickly jumping out with his hands covering his manhood upon hearing that.

"Don't dish it out if you can't take it!" she replied with a big smile on her face.

He realizes he has met his match with Jenny. She has a strange sense of humor. After seeing a small school of fish swim by, he is glad he got out. He quickly joins Jenny, who is trying to climb the cliff.

"I think they're orchids! It's so beautiful! Look at all the colors!" picking one of them.

"Jenny, you better be careful!" seeing how high she climbed.

"So what do you think?" she asked, placing the orchid behind her right ear.

"Wow! What a sight! If I only had my camera!" he shouted, seeing her standing up there naked with a pink flower behind her ear surrounded by tropical flowers.

"That's a shame... I'm out here posing for you, and you forgot your camera!" swinging her breasts about, taunting him again.

He just stares at her in awe and can't believe his eyes. The once shy girl he knew is now a bona fide naturist but an exhibitionist as well. To make matters worse, she continuously torments him with her body. She is driving him nuts, as well as keeping him extremely horny.

* * *

After a quick swim in the big pond, they continue down the long stretch of beach. There are no houses, hotels, or any signs that anyone has ever been on the island. The freshwater ponds are the best place for a home or hotel, but nothing is there.

"I wish I had my camera. That sunset is one hell of a shot," he said, trying to be upbeat about their situation.

"It's so beautiful! It ended up being a nice day, considering," she said, putting her arm around him.

"I know," he said, holding her tight. "That sunset is the kind of thing you only see in travel books. Now, that's something I can get used to watching at the end of a long day. I think it's a good time to go for a little swim," feeling how warm the water is as it rushes over his feet.

Jenny quickly noticed a bright red object on the beach. "Oh my God! Look over there! I think that's a raft!" pointing it out to him.

"It sure looks like it! Maybe the others got washed up here too!" seeing the black and red object in the distance.

"Thank God! That means they made it!" getting all excited.

"Maybe we should go back and get our clothes?" he asked, wondering what they should do.

"Hell, no!" she blurted out. "I'm just too tired to care anymore. I'm not going all the way back there just to get my clothes. You can do whatever you want. I'm going to check it out," then runs down the beach.

Ben chases after her. He is so surprised to see her running down the beach naked. The last thing he wants to do is meet up with the rest of the people from the plane while not wearing any clothes. That would be very embarrassing.

As they get closer, Ben has to blink his eyes a few times, trying to get a clear view. Not believing what he is seeing, he comes to a complete stop.

"Oh, hell!" he shouted. "I think it's our raft. Those are the clothes we put out to dry."

"Oh, no! We're back where we started! Don't tell me we walked around the island! All that for nothing!" feeling so distraught.

"I know," he said, looking at his watch. "I can't believe we did it so quickly. It's almost six-thirty. That's almost nine hours to get around the island. If we didn't stop, we could have done it in maybe six or seven hours."

"Just our luck!" she cried out. "We walked the wrong way around. If we had gone in the other direction, we would have found the freshwater ponds in no time!"

He nods his head. "I know... At least we don't have to go far for water now," feeling so depressed.

Slowly walking up to the raft, they find everything is still as they left it. Not saying a word, they just stare at the raft as the truth sinks in. After a whole day of walking around the island, they found nothing here. There are no signs that anyone has ever lived on this island.

Jenny turns. "We are stuck here, aren't we?" she asked, the tears running down her face.

"There might be something up on the hill," he explained, not wanting to admit it. "We have only seen the beach so far. Maybe there's something up there," glancing up at the island.

"So, what are we going to do now? It's getting dark, and I'm so tired and hungry. I don't want to sleep outside on the beach again," then cries, feeling everything is going against them.

"Remember, we got all my camping gear down the beach. We might as well go back and get it."

"How far is it?" she asked.

He turns to look back down the beach. "Well, considering all the breaks we had, and we weren't walking that fast, maybe thirty minutes or less."

She shakes her head. "I don't think I got the strength to go all the way down there and back again. It'll be dark by the time we get back here. Wouldn't it be better just to drag all this stuff down there where we left your camping gear?"

"That's a good idea. It'll be a lot better than staying here. At least we'll be near the drinking water, and we don't have much daylight left. Once it gets dark, we better make sure we're set up for the night."

"Let's take a break first," she said. "I'm so tired. I can barely keep up on my feet."

"Me too... Oh, by the way. We didn't bring any extra water either. It's going to be hard work hauling all this back without having anything to drink," feeling dehydrated.

Seeing how tired he is, she reaches into the raft, pulling out the desalination pump. "Here's our water. It's the one thing we did right!" giving him a big smile.

He is so relieved. "Thank God we've got that… I totally forgot about it. It's been a long day," ready to fall asleep.

He notices she is staring at the trees with a concerned look on her face. "What is it?" he asked, quickly looking at the trees.

She keeps staring at the trees. "It's nothing... You know... Ever since we've been here, I have had this strange feeling we're not alone. It's like someone is watching us," pointing to the trees.

"Is our little friend back? Did you see something?" looking into the dark jungle.

"No, it's just a feeling," she replied, shaking her head.

"We haven't seen any signs that anyone is here. I haven't heard anything. No footprints on the beach, but there could be someone up on the island. You've seen something?" he asked, seeing the odd look on her face.

"No, it's just that funny feeling I get once in a while. I keep thinking someone is hiding in there, watching us from a distance. There are so many trees, and it's so dark in there. Anyone could be hiding, and we'd never know it."

He laughs. "Maybe there are little kids in there peeking at us, or mostly you!"

"Why would they be spying on us?" she asked.

"You forgot, haven't you?" staring at her breasts.

"Oh, God! I forgot!" trying to cover her body with her hands. "Oh, I got the rest of my clothes here!" running over to get her bra and panties on.

Ben does the same, grabbing his pants. "Talk about uncomfortable! These are going to rub me raw!"

"Yeah, my clothes feel horrible. I think we need to soak them in that pond for a while to get all the saltwater out so they don't get ruined."

"Well, if there is someone here," he said, feeling a little uneasy. "I'll feel better if we see them first. I don't like the idea of someone secretly watching us," hoping there are no violent people on the island.

"I wouldn't like that either! Maybe there's a house up there. It could be some big rock star or a celebrity who had bought this island, and this is their little hideaway. They could be checking us out before they call the cops and have us arrested for trespassing!"

He laughed. "Let's hope so! I hear that a lot of them are buying islands in the Caribbean. That might be what we have here. It's too small for a resort but big enough for a private island. At least we know there's plenty of fresh water here. That's a good thing. That means there's got to be people here as well. I guess we'll have to check it out tomorrow. Until then, let's eat!"

"Good idea... Just forget I mentioned it. I'm just tired and need a break," seeing he is getting a little concerned about being watched.

Grabbing the last of the food, they walk down to the shore to sit by the water. Jenny sits in front of Ben, leaning back against his chest. He holds her while they look out over the ocean. The clouds just above the horizon are turning a deep red. Such a calm, beautiful day, so unlike the last three days they had on the raft.

Sitting on the edge of the beach, they try to be positive. No matter how beautiful this island is, deep down, they keep thinking about the fate of their friends. Now, their future is unknown. Since no people are living near the beach, they only hope to find something up on the island. All they can do now is hope that someone is here or wait it out to be rescued.

* * *

With everything packed away in the raft, they grab hold of the ropes, dragging it down the beach. Dragging everything across the loose sand is exhausting. They move down by the shoreline, where the sand is easier to walk on, and pulling the raft in the shallow water is less work. The raft is in shreds, but it floats a little, even with all of their supplies on it.

With only minutes of daylight remaining, they reached the spot where they had left all the camping supplies. There is not much time left to set everything up. It is not what they wanted, but it's better than nothing.

The one thing Jenny doesn't want to do is sleep on the sand again. She tosses everything out of the raft so they'll have room to lie on it. Ben places the cushions together on the raft for Jenny and sets up his trusty sleeping pad next to her.

In the complete darkness, there is nothing more to do but sleep. The moon is rising, emitting a soft light on the beach. Lying naked together on the makeshift beds, they look up at the stars.

Ben's mind is full of doubt. He can't understand why no one is on the island. With the abundance of water, there should be a small village or at least a few people here. This island is an absolute paradise, perfect for a hotel, but there is nothing here. He just can't figure it out.

Jenny snuggles up to him. They hold each other to keep warm. She gently kisses him, then realizes he is already asleep. So exhausted after the day trip around the island, it's not long before she is sound asleep as well, dreaming about their day together.

* * *

Chapter 17

Making Camp

The next morning, Jenny awakens, hearing music, wondering if she is still dreaming. Still feeling exhausted, her body aches all over. She slowly sits up, so startled. She laughs out loud seeing Ben brushing his teeth, and is totally naked, wearing only an Indiana Jones hat.

"Am I going to be waking up every morning seeing you like that?" she asked.

"Sorry, didn't think you be up this early... So how did you sleep?"

"Oh, not too bad, but I would give anything for a nice soft bed right now. Oh, my God! We got a radio?" hearing the music.

"Yeah, it's my little portable camping one."

"Can we talk to someone and tell them we're here?"

"Sorry, not that kind of radio. It's a regular one with FM and shortwave, but no transmitter."

"Where did you get all these things?" she asked, seeing all the new supplies next to the raft.

"It's all my camping gear," Ben explained, holding up his toothbrush. "I went through it all this morning."

"You had all this in your bag! My God, why would anyone want to pack all this for a contract job?"

"Like I told you... I was thinking of doing a little camping. It's all small and lightweight, so I could pack most of it in my bag. I figured I might as well bring it all instead of buying new stuff. Good thing I did! It's sure going to come in handy out here."

"Have you looked around with these yet?" she asked, picking up the binoculars. "Any boats or planes?" scanning the ocean with them.

He shakes his head. "Didn't see anything. It's so weird! There is absolutely nothing out there. No boats, planes, or any other islands. Although we might see something on the other side."

"So why would you bring binoculars?" she asked, still not understanding the things he packed for this job at Kwajalein.

"They always come in handy. I mostly use those for looking at the stars at night. Nowadays, it's hard to find a place with clear, dark skies. You'll see more stars here at night than anywhere back home. I bought those, especially for this trip. Luckily, they're waterproof, so they weren't ruined by the salt water. We can use those here to explore the island and look for rescue boats and planes!"

"Toys! Nothing but toys," she mumbled.

"Well, it could be worse," Ben added. "If your bag got washed up, we would be sitting here wondering what to do with twelve pairs of shoes and a bunch of fancy bras and panties!"

She glared at him. "You're not funny!"

He laughed. "You know I am right... You're definitely a city girl. You'll see. These toys helped me survive out in the wilderness in Colorado. They'll do the same here."

"I hope you have another toothbrush?" she asked, standing up, brushing off the sand. "We might have to share," realizing how long it's been since she brushed her teeth.

"Of course... I always pack extras," sifting through a small bag, pulling out another toothbrush still in its original package, tossing it over to her.

"Thank you! You're full of surprises. I can't wait to see what else you brought!" shaking her head in disbelief.

"I have lots of goodies stashed away. I'm still going through most of it. With everything in these little storage bags, I'm finding things I forgot. I probably bought some of this stuff a long time ago and never used it."

She stretches out her arms and legs, feeling the pain from the previous day's walk. Seeing the look on Ben's face, she keeps forgetting she is not wearing any clothes. She promptly grabs the cushion using it to cover herself up.

"Ben, would you stop staring at me like that? After yesterday, you should be used to this! When are you going to start wearing some clothes?" feeling a little awkward.

"I tried when I got up... It was too painful to put anything on with this bad sunburn. Maybe later on, when the sun gets too hot. So it doesn't make it worse. I'll probably just wear my swimming trunks, but for now, this suits me just fine. It feels great after having a wash at the small pond."

"What!" she blurted out. "You've already had a bath. How long have you been up?"

"I was awake as soon as the sun came up. It's hard to sleep when you have the sun in your eyes! But it's the best time of the day. So nice and cool out here, and it sure beats the midday sun."

"So what do we do now?" she asked. "Do we start looking around the island again?"

"No, not yet... We're not on any schedule, especially after yesterday's walk. I guess we can take it easy today."

"I don't feel like doing anything. My whole body aches like mad."

"Well, we do have that small pond," Ben suggested. "It's so nice, and it's a good way to start the day. I feel all nice and clean. I guess you're next," tossing her the soap.

She drops the cushion to catch it. "Oh, that's right! So, is it OK if I use the small pond for bathing?"

He nods his head. "Sure! The big pond is a lot better for drinking water. We'll use the little pond as our bathtub."

"That's great! I can't wait to wash my hair, and I feel all clammy after sleeping on the beach. I'll be back shortly!" making a fast pace down the beach towards the small pond.

"Check it out!" he shouted, pointing at Jenny strutting down the beach naked.

She quickly stops, looking around, wondering why he is shouting. She laughs, seeing it's just Ben gawking at her again with a big smile on his face. Tormenting him even more, she sticks out her butt, jiggling it back and forth as she walks.

"Oh my God, what a way to start the day," he mumbles, seeing the way she is strutting naked down the beach.

Jenny is playing it up for him, swinging her hips from side to side, making long strides like a model walking on the catwalk. He is in awe, watching her, so surprised at how much she has changed since they first met. He never thought they would be out prancing on the beach naked together like this.

Jenny is enjoying her morning walk on the palm-lined beach. With the sun just over the horizon and the gentle breeze, she can see that this island is an absolute paradise. It's a perfect day with a blue sky and small puffy clouds on the horizon. With the water so calm and clear, it's almost like glass. She can even see the coral in the water. The beach looks exactly like all those vacation posters of Hawaii, Fiji, and Tahiti.

She can't believe she is romping around naked out on the beach. Never in her life would she ever have thought about doing something like this, especially frolicking around in front of Ben, constantly teasing him. She can't get him out of her mind. After all the hell they have been through, none of this bothers him one bit. He is not scared at all, taking everything in stride. She wonders if it's part of being a mountain man and his love for the outdoor life.

Jenny finally reaches the small pond, a sight for sore eyes. She quickly jumps into the water, lying on her back. Beautiful flowers cover the cliff face. The birds are singing and fluttering about in the tall palm trees far above. It's more like being in the Garden of Eden. Bathing outside, surrounded by the lush tropical setting, she had never felt so exhilarated. It's almost like a beautiful dream.

* * *

Ben leans against one of the palm trees, sipping a cup of coffee and enjoying the beach. Jenny is finally on her way back from the pond. Seeing her strutting down the beach with her breasts bouncing about is one hell of a sight. He can't help but stare at her, surprised that she is walking about with no clothes on and doesn't have any problems with it. He has been reluctant to put on any clothes since it's far more comfortable without them, especially now with a sunburn.

"Oh Lord, she's going to drive me crazy walking around like that," he mumbles to himself, watching her with delight.

"Oh my God! You made a campfire! How did you do that?" she asked.

"It's easy... Just rub a couple of sticks together, and it lights right up. Just like in the movies," he said, joking with her.

She kneels next to the small campfire. "You got to be kidding! Is this a mountain man thing? You can really do all this with a couple of sticks?"

He laughed. "Yeah, right, I used my Flint starters. I'm a modern techie mountain man with all the latest toys, gadgets, and cooking pans. I already got some water boiling for the coffee."

"I can't believe you got coffee!"

"Sure, it's breakfast time! I don't do anything before I have a cup of coffee in the morning. Try this out. It might make your day," handing her an apple fruit bar and a cup of coffee.

"Ben, where did you get all this from!" so shocked by all these little surprises.

"It's from my camping things. It's not much, but it's a change from what we've been eating the last few days."

"How come you didn't get these out last night? I was starving."

"I wish I knew I had these. I got so much stuff packed away in all these little Ditty bags. Back in Colorado, I used to buy things and put them in my backpack and forget about them. At least now we have something different to eat. It's not much, but it should last us for a few days."

She sits down in front of him on the cushion. "Oh, this is great! You really made my day!" taking a sip of the coffee, devouring the fruit bar.

"I also found some bananas. There's a tree not far from here. They're a little small, but they'll do. There are lots of coconut trees around here as well."

"Oh, I can use a few of those too! The bananas will give us plenty of vitamins A, C, and potassium. The coconuts have the same, but also have vitamins B1 and B2."

"Wow, you sure know a lot about the vitamin thing," surprised by her knowledge of food.

"My family had a seafood restaurant. I spent most of my life in a kitchen. My parents taught my sister and me how to cook at a very early age. By the time we were in high school, we were running the place."

"So, why are you out here?"

"For eighteen years, that's all I did. I went to college for something different. I just couldn't see myself being in a hot kitchen for the rest of my life."

"That doesn't sound too bad. I used to work at a pizza place back in my college days. It was fun, and we got a lot of free meals!"

She laughed. "When it's your family's business, it's different. You start at ten in the morning, prepping the food. We would do lunch, then dinner, and that was seven days a week! I would be in school all day long and then help at the restaurant. I learned how to cook and do homework at the same time. So, what do you know about cooking other than pizza?"

"I usually just order the biggie meal from the drive-through window or maybe splurge on one of those frozen meals."

"Oh, you are one of those," she mumbled, shaking her head. "I can't believe you eat all that junk food. When we get out of here, I'll show you what proper food is. Once you taste real cooking, you'll never eat those horrible frozen meals ever again!"

"After eating nothing but those horrible rice cakes, I could really go for one of those frozen meals right now. Hell, anything would be better than those damn things!"

"So, what do we do now?" she asked, looking out at the ocean. "We just wait here for a rescue plane or something? Have you heard anything on the radio?"

"All I heard is that they're still searching for us. We are not the only ones. Several boats were lost as well, and they were rescuing people all over the place. From the sound of things, it was one hell of a storm. At least it means they're out looking. They should be around in this area. We need to keep an eye out for rescue planes."

"That means they will eventually find us here then!" so elated to get back home.

"Well, if they knew what's waiting for them here, they'll all be here real soon!" he jokingly said, gawking at her breasts.

"Would you stop that!" she shouted, covering herself with her arms. "I'm still new to this naturist thing," feeling uncomfortable not wearing any clothes in front of him.

* * *

With the sun getting higher above the horizon, the heat is getting unbearable. "It's time to start covering up!" Jenny said, putting on her blouse. "We need to make sure we don't make the same mistake like we did yesterday. We don't need to get sunburned again."

"Yeah, I don't want to get burnt more than I am now. I'm glad I have my swimming trunks. It'll be better than my old clothes," he said, slowly getting dressed, feeling the pain.

"You're going to need a shirt too!" she said, tossing it over.

He doesn't argue, hurting so bad after putting on his swimming trunks. "Yep, our days running around naked on the beach are over!" he mentions, putting on his shirt, hat, and clip-on sunglasses.

"You got sunglasses too?"

"I'm never without them! I always keep extras, just in case. These are my clip-on ones, but I might have some regular sunglasses. My contact lenses were in my camera bag, so they are long gone. I got an extra pair here you can use."

"It's just amazing. You got everything!"

He searches around and grabs one of his many small Ditty bags. "Here you go… Always be prepared!" pulling out not only a pair of sunglasses but a baseball hat too.

"Thanks! It's going to make a world of difference!" putting on the hat and sunglasses.

"Luckily, I have everything one would need for a big camping trip."

"This is great!" she said, looking at all the gear scattered on the ground. "You have everything but a tent. Was that in your other bag?"

"Here you go... This is it!" picking up a small brown vinyl bag only four by ten inches long.

"You got to be kidding! This cannot be a tent!"

"It sure is! A good one, too. When camping up in the mountains, everything you bring is small, compact, and lightweight. I used to carry all of this in my backpack. It's smaller than the duffel bag. That's why I didn't have any problems bringing everything."

"So what kind of tent is this?" she asked, examining the small brown bag. "It looks too small and doesn't look like it's going to help us much. Is it a kid's pup tent?"

"A pup tent!" he replied, somewhat insulted. "This is the latest in camping technology. A two-person tent designed to withstand the wind, rain, snow, and even this heat. It's about four-foot-wide and seven-foot-long. It'll be a little cramped for two, but it's better than nothing."

"I'm not going to complain! I dread the idea of sleeping out in the open again. Hopefully, we won't be needing it tonight."

"How is that?" he quickly asked.

"After all this time, there's probably a plane or boat coming soon. There has got to be someone out there checking out all these islands around here. We can't be that far from Kwajalein. At least now, we can wait it out."

He let out a long sigh. "You're right about that... I guess we need to keep an eye out for them, but we can still look around the island as well. There's got to be something here. With all the water we found, I'm surprised no one is living here. If someone is up on the island, maybe they'll be on the beach today. So, what do you think we should do next?"

"First of all, we need to get organized. I don't want to get caught in the dark like we did last night. Maybe we can move all this into the shade. We can set the tent up just in case we have to spend another night."

"That's a good idea," he said, looking up and down the beach. "You know, this is not a bad place to be. We're right between the two freshwater ponds."

"What about that nice grassy spot near the small pond?" she asked. "It'll be great being right next to the water."

"It's nice but way too humid. There is no wind at all back there. We need something close to the beach, so we'll have a little breeze but plenty of shade. Also, we need to be near the beach. If any boats or planes go by, we'll see it, and hopefully, they'll see us."

"So, what do we do? I don't want to sit out here in the blistering sun all day waiting to be rescued," she added.

"Let's do a little exploring around here. We need to find a better place to set up camp. Something in the shade," feeling the heat of the sun.

"I'm ready when you are," she said, picking up one of the water bottles. "As long as we keep it short. My legs are so sore from yesterday!"

"I'm sore as well," picking up the other water bottle. "We'll just look around here. There should be something close by. All we need is a little shaded area. Let's go check things out," walking towards the dense palm trees.

* * *

Exploring the dense trees is not an easy task. With all the underbrush and fallen palm leaves, walking is almost impossible. Just twenty feet from the beach, it's almost like a tropical rainforest. They quickly realize there is no way to clear an area big enough to set up a small tent.

After a while, they discover a perfect shady spot for a campsite. There are fewer trees and less underbrush but plenty of hard sand to put the tent. The location is perfect, being right between the freshwater pond and the big lagoon. It will give them some shade but still have a gentle breeze and be close enough to the tree line to see the ocean.

Ben knows this is the perfect spot to set up camp. "This is great! It's big enough for a campsite. It's even got a big shade tree out by the beach."

"I think that's a Milo tree," she explained. "I saw those on the beach in Hawaii. That will give us plenty of shade during the day. I don't know why we didn't see it yesterday. It'll be a nice place to take a nap, right on the beach with the cool breeze."

"Just what I was thinking... It's really low to the ground with about a four-foot clearance. The sand underneath it will be cool even in the midday sun. That's where I'm going to be taking my naps!"

"No more naps... We need to set things up first," running back into the trees, getting excited about their new campsite.

"This will be a good starting point to explore the interior of the island," Ben said after walking to the back of their new campsite. "Looks like we can start walking up from here. It's not too steep either," looking up at the gradual slope leading up to the island.

"Maybe we can do that on another day," she said, looking up the hill. "I don't know if I have the strength to walk up there. I'm still worn out from yesterday. We need to stay out on the beach so when someone comes by, we can signal them."

"I think you're right," he said, walking back to the beach. "Maybe we should take it easy for a while. Yesterday was a little too much for me. I'm still tired. You know, I lost a lot of weight," pulling on his swimming trunks.

"Me too! I have never lost so much weight like this. So, what are we going to do about food?"

"We have some granola and fruit bars," he explained. "We also have some coconuts and bananas. There are plenty of those around here to last us for a long time."

"So, we have enough for a couple of days then?"

"We should be OK for a while until someone finally decides to show up here, or we find someone on the island."

"Ben, I think the next thing we need to do is move all our things to the shade. I've had enough of this sun. I don't need this sunburn to get any worse, and you don't either."

"Yeah, we overdid it yesterday," he said, feeling the pain from his sunburn. "Let's drag it all in here and sort out what we have."

They drag everything off the beach into their new campsite. It doesn't take them long to realize the benefits of being in the shade, especially with the cool breeze flowing right through the trees. The beach is already getting too hot. The last thing they want is to be standing in the direct sunlight for the rest of the day.

Rummaging through the camping gear, Jenny picks up the compact fishing rod. "Do you think you can catch something with this? You know, I can cook almost any fish in the ocean! A good hot meal is something we can use right now. So, what kind of fish are you going to catch?"

"To be honest, I have no idea... I should have done a little research on that before I left."

"It doesn't matter... Whatever you catch should be good enough. Just make sure you clean it."

Ben hesitates for a moment. "Well, I usually throw them back after catching them. I'm not too good at cleaning and cooking them either," not wanting to tell her the truth.

She giggles. "You got to be kidding me. You're one of those! I thought you were a real fisherman."

"I am! We just toss them back in. You never heard of catch and release?" hoping to convince her.

"Well, if you catch one, I'll clean and cook it."

"It's a deal!" he blurted out, not having the stomach to clean a fish. "So, you don't care what type of fish?"

"It won't matter... Considering how long it's been since we've had a decent meal, I'll guarantee it'll be the best fish you've ever had!"

* * *

Clearing an area big enough for their campsite is exhausting. Dead branches, coconut husks, and the occasional fallen tree cover the ground. None of it is going to waste. They pile everything up for the campfire.

Ben gathers as many rocks as he can find, placing them in a small circle. The campfire is always at the center of the campsite. He places everything else around it. From his old camping days, he knows the campfire is the most important thing. The campfire is for cooking, heat, and at night will produce plenty of light.

The small tent is the latest in mountaineering technology, a small wedge-shaped tent with mosquito netting on top and both sides. It has a separate plastic canopy that is attached to the top and covers the entire tent to keep out the rain. Ben wishes he had brought his bigger tent. With two people, this one might be a tight fit. The tent is perfect for a weekend camping trip, but not for living in for days or weeks.

"That's it?" Jenny asked, seeing the tent set up for the first time. "It's rather small," somewhat disappointed.

"I know, but it's designed for two people. It's just for sleeping, anyway. I use this all the time back home. There are doors on both sides. The netting keeps out the flies and bugs but lets the wind flow through."

She examines the strange-looking tent, wondering if it's going to work. "The entire top looks like it's made of mosquito netting. What if it rains? It's all open. You can even see right through it!"

He pulls on the strings attached to the top of the tent. "There you go... The cover is attached to the center ridge, so it rolls down, covering up the tent, keeping out the rain."

"I had to ask," she said, seeing he had thought of everything.

"It's small but functional... I have been out in the snow, torrential rain, and even the hot summer with this one. It should work great out here. Even if it rains at night, you just reach up, pull on the string, and the cover rolls down. All you have to do is attach the ends to the stake. You can even do it when you're inside. It's easy!" showing her how the tent works.

"Oh, this is great!" she said, giving him a big hug. "I have never seen anything like this. One day, when we get out of here, you're going to have to take me up to the mountains for a weekend camping trip."

"It's a date! You'll love it there," hugging her again.

* * *

At about four in the afternoon, their campsite is ready. "I think this is a good time for a break," Ben said, taking off his shirt and placing it up on a tree branch to dry.

"I can use a break too. I'm not used to this humidity! It's like living in a sauna," removing her blouse.

"Wow! I see I'm not the only one who got a little too much sun!" seeing how red her breasts are.

"We need to make sure we don't overdo it from now on. We're going to be in a lot of pain for a couple of days!" looking down at her chest, seeing how bad it is.

"Oh, no... Check this out!" pulling down his swimming trunks, seeing how burnt he is.

"That's got to hurt!" she said, seeing his sunburned penis and trying not to laugh.

"I'm a little sore, but mostly from wearing all those damp clothes. Although it's going to feel a little weird when it starts to peel."

"You better keep it out of the sun for a while. That means you need to keep your pants on! So, you want to go for a swim? I'm getting a little hot after hauling all this stuff around."

"You read my mind," he said, taking her hand, "but I think this is called skinny dipping!" glancing up and down at her body.

"Ben, don't keep looking at me like that!" she shouted, smacking his butt hard, running to the beach, laughing hysterically.

"Hey! That really hurt!" tossing away his swimming trunks, chasing after her.

The water is so clear and calm. Running into the surf is a big mistake. With the bad sunburns, they are in constant pain.

"Just jump in and get it over with!" she said while floating on her back. "It's not so bad once you're in."

"I can't believe you dove in like that. I bet that hurt!" slowly crouching down, lowering himself into the water.

"It hurt like hell! You're just prolonging it. Come on, jump in!"

"Oh God, it hurts so bad!" slowly sitting down in the water.

"You'll get over it... You know, this place is an absolute paradise! Just look at the beach and all those palm trees. At least now, I can relax a little better knowing we have all that camping equipment."

"We'll be OK for a while… All we have to do is wait it out until someone shows up. We have enough food for about a week. After that, we need to start worrying."

"So, what about the fish out here?" she asked. "You think you can catch something?"

"I should be able to get a fish or two. I did a lot of surf fishing on the Texas coast. It should be no different here."

"Well, if you can catch a fish, then that will solve our biggest problem. That's the one thing we can use right now. A good hot meal!"

"You got that right! Especially after days of eating nothing but that horrible food rations! Even the fruit bars are getting a little old. We need something different to eat. I could go for some freshly cooked fish right now!"

"I can too! When is a good time to do some fishing?" she asked.

"Not sure... The end of the day might be better. That's usually the best time, or early in the morning. Either way, we should get something. Can't be much different from the Texas Coast," glancing down at the clear water and seeing a few small fish swimming nearby.

They both feel a little better after seeing what they accomplished with their new campsite. All the work is done. For the rest of the day, all they can do is sit in the shade of the Milo tree, looking for rescue airplanes or ships.

While Jenny takes a nap, Ben uses his binoculars, scanning the ocean, but nothing is out there. He is getting curious about what island they are on. They must be near Kwajalein, which is dotted with small islands. There are no other islands out there, even way out on the horizon. Deep down, he knows something is just not right about this island.

* * *

By the end of the day, it's a perfect setting for a tropical island with just a few clouds on the horizon. The ocean is so calm and extremely clear, with a turquoise blue color. They can't resist another swim. Ben dives into the water, gliding inches above the ripples in the sand.

"Man, there are so many fish out there!" he said. "You'd be surprised how close you can get to them! It's a shame I don't have a spear gun. It would be so easy out here."

"Ben, why don't you see if you can catch one? My stomach is starting to growl. I'm getting hungry!"

"I'll catch them, then you cook them, right?" he asked, hoping she would.

"You can do both if you want," she jokingly said. "I don't mind."

"Well, I'll let you do that part since you're the chef," not liking the idea of having to clean a fish.

She giggles. "Don't tell me the mountain man is so squeamish about preparing a little old fish?"

A little embarrassed, he just smiles, quickly diving back into the water. He would rather eat berries and fruit than cut up a fish, even if he is starving. Following a small school of fish, he finds himself in the middle of the most beautiful coral scattered about in the shallow water. With sand at the bottom and the coral at least three feet high, it creates a natural maze, allowing him to swim through the corridors. Not only does this provide shelter for an abundance of fish, but it's also going to be the best place to catch fish on the island.

He swims over to investigate the lava rocks situated right in front of the campsite. The smooth black lava rocks are just inches beneath the water, remnants of an old lava flow that extends hundreds of feet out into the ocean. At low tide, they'll be able to walk far out into the ocean on this and use it as a pier for fishing.

Curious about the huge boulders on the shoreline, he walks over to check them out. With no other rocks on the beach, these stand out. About six feet high and fifteen feet long, he wonders if these had rolled down off the island or had been part of the original lava flow. On the side facing the island, there is a small natural pond five feet across with sand at the bottom. What is even more surprising is seeing all the little fish and crabs swimming around inside it.

"Hey, check this out!" he called out to Jenny.

She runs over, looks into the little pond, and sees all the fish swimming in there. "Oh, my God! How did they get in there?"

"They must have gotten washed up in it during the storm. You know… I never realized it before. These boulders are right in front of our camp."

"It sure is, isn't it? That was some good planning on our part. At least now, we'll always know where the camp is and won't get lost."

He puts his hand into the water. "You should feel how warm it is. This will make a nice little bath for us. It's about the right size, too."

She laughed. "Not with all those fish and crabs in it. Oh, wait a minute! How do you feel about eating a crab dinner tonight?" eyeing the huge crabs.

"You're the chef! I had never eaten those before. Taste like chicken?" he asked.

"Much better! It's going to be great. We're in for a big treat tonight!"

"The best part is we don't even have to go out and catch anything. All we have to do is pluck them out of the water."

She laughed again. "You're just glad you won't have to clean a fish! I wonder how many more of these little pools are around?"

He looks at the lava flow going way out into the ocean. "You know... During low tide, I bet there's a lot more of these out there."

"You think so?" she asked.

"There are lots of little pathways between all the coral and lava rocks. It's more like one big maze. It'll be great for snorkeling. When the tide goes out, I bet there are lots of fish getting trapped in all those shallow pools. All I need to do is stand on the lava rocks and dangle the lures in front of the fish. It's going to be easy."

"That sounds like a good idea. Although, I think we'll keep with the crab for now. We don't have to do anything other than yank them out of this little pond."

He laughed. "I know... Let's go for the easy meal!"

"Tomorrow, you can go fishing, but tonight it's going to be a fresh-cooked crab meal!" giving him a big hug.

They return to the campsite, getting things ready for their first hot meal. Ben uses his flint starter to light the campfire. With all the dry wood, it doesn't take long to get it started. They put all their clothes on the makeshift rack next to the campfire. The sleeping bag is the only thing that is taking the longest to dry. Even with it out in the sun all day long, it's still damp.

Camping out in the wilderness is something Ben loves to do. After years of camping in Colorado, he learned from his mistakes. Everything needed is always in his backpack. He has all the cooking utensils and cutlery that will be sufficient for most meals. He is not sure what is involved in cooking the crab meal. Good thing Jenny knows everything about seafood since he has no clue how to prepare a freshly cooked meal, especially one that is still crawling around.

* * *

The sun is setting with another beautiful red sky. They are getting depressed after another day with no signs of any rescue airplanes or ships. Knowing they are going to get their first hot meal in days makes them feel a little better. Now, with the campsite ready, at least they won't be sleeping on the beach anymore.

Jenny is so impressed with all the compact cookware. With the best in camping gear, it's all self-contained, with one pot fitting inside the other. With the variety of cooking pots, pans, and utensils, it's all a chef would need to prepare any meal. She is so glad to see it also included the essential spices.

Ben grabs the small radio, wanting to hear the latest news. Jenny is puttering around, preparing their first meal. He is amazed by her skill in cooking a meal with such simple camping gear. While out camping, the only food was from dehydrated packets, where all you had to do was add hot water. He is so glad just to sit back and relax, not worrying about food anymore. There are no more rations and no more Styrofoam wafers. Now, it's freshly cooked seafood.

"OK, soups on! Come and get it!" she shouted out.

"You made soup! Oh, it smells so good. Finally, we got a nice hot meal!" looking into the bubbling pot.

"It's called peppered crab soup," she explained, handing him a bowl. "It's really hot, so watch yourself. There's plenty here, so eat up. We're going to have to eat it all since we have no way to store leftovers."

"This is fantastic!" he said after several mouthfuls. "You cook like this all the time?"

"Sure, it's a quick, easy meal. There's not much to it. You can do wonders with a few spices, but it's mostly pepper and a lot of crab meat. You have a good selection of spices in that bag. I noticed most are unopened except the salt and pepper," giving him a little smile.

"That's about the only ones I know… It's good you know how to use them. I'm ready for seconds!" getting another helping.

"Glad you like it! Seafood is my specialty."

"This makes up for those wafer things we've been eating. Tomorrow, I'll use my fishing gear and see what kind of fish we got around here."

She gives him a big smile. "You catch them, and I'll cook them!" so thrilled to see he is enjoying the meal she prepared.

After the big feast, Jenny cooks up the last of the bananas for dessert. "They still haven't said much about us on the radio."

"I noticed that," Ben said, staring at the flames of the campfire, deep in thought. "You would have thought we'd see something by now. We haven't even heard a plane in the distance. There should have been something out there. I just can't figure it out!"

"Don't be negative," she replied. "We must keep a positive attitude. There are many people worse off than we are right now!"

"I'm sorry... I need to keep remembering that," he said, knowing Jenny is right, thinking about all those who were on the plane with them.

"We've been really lucky! We can't complain. It's just a matter of time. We still have to see what's on this island. So far, we've only looked on the beach. We don't know what else is here."

"It'd be funny if we found out there's a house not far from here, and we've been sleeping out on the beach," he jokingly said.

She laughed. "Yeah, and they have hot and cold running water and a nice big soft bed. I can really go for that right now," dreading the notion of having to sleep outside again.

Jenny puts a couple of cushions together, lying on her side facing the campfire. She is so tired after the long walk from the day before and weak from the lack of food. She can't get used to going to bed once the sun goes down, but there is nothing else to do.

"If only you had your camera," she mumbles, noticing how he is staring at her body again.

Her comment catches him off guard. "Stop reading my mind!" he said, getting caught again staring at her naked body.

She laughed. "You better get used to it! I'm not covering up tonight! With this campfire, we don't need to worry about it getting cold. It's so nice and warm."

"Oh yeah, this is great... A campfire to keep us warm at night. A big, hot meal. It doesn't get any better than this, especially having a woman sprawled out naked next to the campfire."

She laughed again. "Don't tell me you didn't do this type of thing while camping in Colorado!"

"Having a naked woman lying next to the campfire? No... It gets freezing up there, and you would get frostbite. Back home, you would have at least three layers of clothes on. Although I think we did pretty good today. You're sure one hell of a cook, and you make a good camping companion for a city girl. I would love to take you out in the mountains when we get out of here."

"If this is what it's like, I'd love to go! I have never done anything like this before. Maybe tomorrow, you can teach me how to catch a fish."

"That sounds like a good idea! We make a good team. It's funny, but in less than a week, it seems as if I have known you forever."

"I thought the same about you, too," she said, getting a little flustered. "I have done more with you these last couple of days than I have in my whole life! Not in a million years would I have dreamt of doing all this."

"They did say this would be an adventure of a lifetime!" remembering the brochure for the job.

She laughs. "I'll never forget this adventure!"

"I don't think I will either," he said, seeing a tear running down her cheek. "Considering our situation, it's been great! Being with you has made it a lot easier. Ever since our first night together in Hawaii, waiting for the sunrise, I knew you were special."

"I guess that was our first date!" she said, giving him a big smile.

"Now that I think about it, I guess it was… You know, I don't think I could have made it without you."

Jenny, getting very emotional, starts crying. Ben crawls over, lying next to her, snuggling up to her. They both lie quietly together, watching the fire and listening to music. Thoughts of their family and friends run through their minds until they fall sound asleep.

* * *

Chapter 18

Worried

Mary wakes up in the middle of the night with a disturbing dream. She cries uncontrollably. She had another bad dream of Ben calling out to her from a distance.

"What is it?" Walter asked, waking up after hearing the commotion. "What's the matter?" still feeling a little groggy.

"I had that dream again," she explained. "It was Ben! It was so real. He's trying to tell me something! I can't make it out, but I know he's out there waiting."

"They're still looking for him. Don't get yourself all upset again. They'll probably find him in a day or two. It's a big ocean. It'll just take a little time."

"I know he's alive! I just know it! He's out there somewhere! I can feel it. I can really feel it," she yells, lying back down sobbing then slowly falls back to sleep.

Walter tries to be strong. His wife's nightly dreams worried the entire family. The notion of not knowing their son's whereabouts is a heavy burden for them all. There's nothing they can do but wait. He lays back down after seeing his wife is asleep again.

"Please come home, son," he whispered, looking up into the darkness. "Please, God, bring my son back home," the tears running down his cheek.

* * *

Chapter 19

Exploring

Just as the sun appears above the horizon, Jenny slowly wakes up. Lying on her back, she stares up at the palm trees towering high above against the deep blue sky. She finds it's so odd waking up in the morning with no irritating alarm clock. The only sounds are of the gentle waves in the background. Now, she is seeing why Ben loves the outdoor life so much.

Seeing a fine layer of ash covering her body, she discovers the downside of sleeping next to a campfire. Everything smells like smoke. Getting up, she brushes herself off, glancing over at the tent, still empty and unused.

"Can't believe we slept outside again with a tent just a few feet away," she mumbles to herself.

Looking down at Ben, she can't help laughing. He is lying on his back, sprawled out naked with another erection.

"If I had a camera," she quietly whispered. "What a shot that would make. Now, that's what I call a true mountain man," then giggles.

Jenny lets him sleep in late. Grabbing the soap, she makes her way to the small pond for her morning wash. Walking along the beach, she enjoys the solitude. The outdoor lifestyle, where you are up at sunrise and in bed by sunset, is not a bad life. She now knows what she has been missing after all those years living in the city.

Arriving at the small pond, she quickly emerges herself in the clean water. The pond is the perfect natural bathtub with soft sand at the bottom. She can lie back and soak while admiring all the beautiful flowers on the cliff face. At least now, she can relax, not having to worry about being stranded on this island. After having a good hot meal and with all the new camping supplies, being here for a few days is not so bad. A rescue plane should show up in a day or two.

After her wash, she walks back to the campsite. She doesn't think twice about walking around naked. Having to wear clothes is now more of a burden. Their clothes are so uncomfortable to wear, always covered with sand.

Walking into the camp, she can't stop laughing. Ben is still sound asleep, sprawled out naked, right next to the campfire. She wonders if he is having a wonderful dream because his erection isn't going away anytime soon.

Ben stirs from his deep sleep. "Morning," he grumbled, reaching over, caressing her thigh. "You're up early. You want something to eat?"

"Good morning, sleepyhead! Are you still hungry after all that food we had yesterday? Sorry, there is nothing left but those fruit bar things," reaching back, pulling out one for him.

"Thanks, I can't wait to get some more of that cooking of yours! That was a great meal!"

"Ben, I'm getting concerned. You've lost quite a bit of weight," running her hand over his stomach.

"I know... We both have! I have never been this skinny since I was a kid," glancing down at his flat stomach. "I see I got another problem down there too," he replied, noticing his erection.

"Yeah, am I going to be waking up to that every morning?" she asked, then started snickering.

"Don't know... Are you going to be walking around like that all the time?" smiling at her, somewhat embarrassed.

She grabs her baseball hat, putting it over his erection. "Anyway, I think it's important to eat a big meal like we did yesterday," she said, trying to change the subject. "We need the calories. The seafood will help out, but we need fruit for vitamin C to keep us going. We need to eat some of those coconuts, too. They're loaded with vitamins and minerals."

"Sorry, I didn't pack anything to open up those damn coconuts! I think it takes something like a hammer or a machete. Yesterday, I kept hitting one with a rock for hours and couldn't get it open. There's got to be a trick to it."

She laughed. "You mean to tell me there is something we need that you didn't pack in that bag of yours? Maybe we can look around on top of the island to see what else is here."

"You mean I don't get to rest after all that work we did yesterday?"

"Nope, get up and take a bath!" she said, slapping his stomach with her hand. "We have a big day ahead of us, and get some clothes on! You don't want your willy getting more sunburned than it already is. You never know, you might want to use it again if you know what I mean," giving him a sheepish smile.

"It's starting to hurt now. Why didn't I pack any suntan lotion?" getting worried, seeing his sunburned penis.

"My boobs are starting to hurt too!" feeling her breasts. "It's time to cover up... Walking around on the beach is not an issue. But to go through that jungle up there, we are going to need to wear all our clothes."

He nods his head. "If it's anything like down here in these trees, it'll be a rough hike."

* * *

After a quick breakfast, they decide it's time to explore the rest of the island. They start at the most convenient place, right behind the camp. With no cliffs or rocks to climb, the hike is a little easier. The gradual slope looks as if it leads up to the top of the island, and it might be something they can easily handle.

They make their way through the palm trees to the back of the camp, then walk straight up the hill. After walking through the thick underbrush, they are so glad they elected to wear all their clothes and their shoes.

The sweat pours from Ben's face. He is not used to this humidity, constantly having to stop to catch his breath. Trying to find a decent path up this hill is a chore. He is not used to this type of hiking either. In Colorado, there was always a trail or dirt road to walk on. But out here, there is nothing but wilderness.

The climb is more difficult for Jenny. She takes a few steps at a time before having to stop to rest. She is far behind, struggling to keep up, and it doesn't take long for her to realize this is a big mistake.

"I'm sorry," she said once she finally caught up with him. "I don't think I can go on," then collapses, gasping for air.

"I'm worn out too," handing her his water container. "Drink some more water. I think we've gone far enough, anyway. Maybe we should try walking along the hill instead of going up higher."

"Rest first," she uttered, still breathing hard. "I need a break," lying on her back, pouring water over her face.

"Yeah, it's a good time for a break. We're in the shade, and there's a good breeze up here. Just lie back and take it easy," not wanting to push Jenny more than she can handle.

He notices it's not long before she is sound asleep. She is sweating profusely, and he is worried about her. Her face is so pale. Opening up her blouse, exposing her bare skin, he pours water over her chest to help cool her down. Checking her pulse occasionally, he lets her sleep for a while so she can have a good rest. He wants to make sure she doesn't overexert herself as he did on their first day.

* * *

An hour later, Jenny finally wakes up. Sitting up, she finds it amusing seeing her blouse open and her breasts exposed.

"We need to talk about your obsession with my boobs!"

He laughed at her comment. "Hey, it's the only true cure for exhaustion. You can't keep wearing all those tight-fitting clothes in this heat. You got to be bare-chested to help cool down, but it only works for women with big boobs!" reaching over patting her right breast.

"It's going to take me a while to get used to your sense of humor," she said, snuggling up to him.

"Are you feeling any better?" he asked, handing her more water to drink.

"I'm still so tired... It was a good nap, but I would like to sit here a little longer. It's so nice and cool up here. That breeze feels so good. Is it OK with you if we stay here for a while?"

"We're in no hurry... Just keep drinking water and enjoy the view," putting his arm around her, holding her close.

"What time is it? How long was I asleep?" she asked.

"A little over an hour," looking at his watch.

"My God!" she shouted. "I thought it was about ten minutes. You should have woken me up!"

"It's a tough climb. I needed a break too. We're going to have to slow down with this humidity. We'll just do a little at a time. Let's relax in the shade and enjoy that spectacular view of the ocean."

* * *

After an hour, they decide it's time to move on. Too tired to walk up the hill, they turned left, walking to the west side of the island. They know there won't be any houses higher on the island, especially with this steep hill. From this height, they can easily see any houses below.

They finally see something intriguing. There is a large open area about a hundred feet away. On the far side of the open space, there are trees filled with huge yellow flowers. Ben knows this is something they need to check out. At least now, they have a goal. No more blindly walking through the jungle as they have been doing for most of the day.

Finally, reaching the edge of the dense jungle is a clearing covered with long grass in front of them. Running to the trees in disbelief, they discover these are not flowers but large oranges.

"What a find! Ben, look at all these oranges!" she quickly picks one and then devours it.

"The ones over there look different," he said, looking at one of the other trees. "They're a little bigger and more of a yellow color," pulling one off the branch, cutting it open with his pocketknife.

"Ben, that's a grapefruit! Look at the size of that thing!"

"What's all this doing here?" he asked, taking a bite of the sour grapefruit.

She shrugs her shoulders. "Don't know and don't care. Let's remember where this place is. We need to bring some of these back with us!" finishing up another orange.

"Jenny, look at that!" he shouted, noticing the view. "Now that is one hell of a sight!" seeing the unobstructed view out over the ocean.

He rushes through the tall grass to the edge of a cliff. "What a view, and we can see everything from up here! We must be hundreds of feet above the beach. I didn't think we walked this high up on the island. It must be at least a thirty-foot drop just to the top of those trees down there. Jenny, you got to come over and see this!" looking down at the trees far below.

She walks over to see what all the fuss is. Still eating an orange, she is not watching where she is going. She stumbles on some rocks hidden in the long grass, falling flat on her face.

"Be careful!" running over to help her up.

"Oh, didn't see the rocks. Too busy eating these oranges," brushing herself off.

"Now, this is interesting!" Ben said, seeing a couple of black burnt rocks that she had tripped over.

"What is it?" she asked.

"Oh my God! It's an old campfire!" he shouted, pushing the long grass away, revealing a small circle of rocks.

"There's more, too! Ben, look at this! An old metal barbecue rack! We can really use this."

"That means someone is here or has been here recently," giving her a big hug.

He finds a tin can with two-triangle indentions on the top. "This is an old beer can. In the good old days, you had to use a can opener. They stopped making these in the '70s," showing it to Jenny.

"Well, it's still a good sign," not understanding the disappointed look on his face.

Ben tosses the old beer can over the cliff. "Whoever it was probably stayed up here to be close to the fruit trees. It's also nice and cool up here, plus you have this clearing. If I had to choose, I'd live up here. Let's see what else is around."

Packing down the long grass with their feet, looking for more clues, they work their way over to the mountainside. They quickly discover there is not much else other than tall grass. At the end of the clearing, they stumble upon a steep trail that leads up to the rest of the island.

"Now, this looks promising!" he said, discovering a small dirt trail leading into the trees just up the hill.

"What's so great about it?" she asked, looking at the dirt trail.

"Jenny, look at it! It's a trail! People have been walking on this for a long, long time."

"Oh my God! You're right! I wonder where it goes?"

"Well, just think about it! Orange trees over there, a campfire out on the grass. This trail leads somewhere up into the trees over there!" Ben said, pointing it out to her.

"There might be someone living up there!"

"You got it!" he said, nodding his head.

"Look, Ben! There is another trail going all the way over to where we just came from!" pushing back the tall grass.

"Oh, hell... Just our luck! It looks like we missed that trail by twenty feet or more when we were walking up the hill. We need to check it out. It's going to the east," he said, quickly walking down the trail.

"No, let's explore up here first," she said, grabbing his arm. "This looks more promising... If nothing is up there, then we can follow this trail going down the hill," looking at the dirt trail leading up the hill.

"Yeah, let's keep going uphill. I think we're almost at the top, anyway. We don't have far to go now," knowing she is right about it.

The dirt trail is very steep, but it's easier to walk on, not having to climb over fallen trees and through thick brush. The path leads to a large open area at the top of the ridge. It's as far up on the island as they can go. The trail then splits three ways. One leads down the hill to the north side of the island. The other one turns left into the trees. The one on the right leads to the peak of the island.

With all the trees and tall grass, it's hard to tell exactly where these trails are and where they go on the island. They know they are just west of the peak, but again, no signs of anyone on the island. The path leading to the peak doesn't look too promising. There is not much of a chance of anyone building a house there.

"From the looks of things," Ben mentioned, taking a break at the top of the trail. "We must be more than halfway up the island. I didn't figure we would get this far. Since we're here, if we try the trail leading up to the peak, we'll be able to see the entire island from up there. It might be easier than wandering about aimlessly."

She shakes her head. "There's no way you're getting me up there. It kind of looks like the Devil's Tower out in Wyoming. It's nothing but a big rock that's flat on top."

"It does look like it, doesn't it? I guess that's the remains of the volcano. I have seen a few of those at Monument Valley in Utah."

"I'm not going to climb that!" she sternly said, looking up at the peak that towers over them. "If we're going to stay for a while, I want to check things out around here. Are you going to take a break?" knowing Ben is about to fall asleep.

"Sure... It's a good place for a break. Plenty of shade, and the breeze is so cool up here. It feels like air conditioning! I really can get used to this after what we've been through."

Jenny continues exploring while Ben takes a nap. She cautiously follows the dirt trail leading to the west. The path leads to a large clearing with a massive rock outcropping.

"Ben! Quick! Come and check this out!"

Ben rushes over, seeing her standing in front of a small cave. "Be careful, Jenny! We don't know what's in it!"

"It's not that big," she explained, peering into the dark cave. "I think I can see the back of it from here."

Standing next to the entrance, he can make out the remnants of a campfire just inside the cave. "This looks interesting," he said, slowly walking in.

"Don't go in too far! There might be snakes in there!" she yells, panicking.

"Don't yell like that!" he said, startled by her screaming. "I'm just looking around," hoping not to see or disturb any bats or other rodents.

"You see anything?" she asked.

"Not much... Some old empty tin cans and a small stack of firewood."

"Then someone did live here!" she said. "You think they're still here on the island?"

He shakes his head. "No, I don't think so. It looks like this stuff has been here for a long time," trying to make out a dark object in the far corner of the cave.

He waits for his eyes to get used to the darkness, and it's not long before he recognizes what the object is. "Awe, this is great! You're not going to believe what's in here!"

"Would you just get out of there!" she shouted, fearing the worst. "You've been in there too long!" standing back from the entrance, hearing clanking sounds.

"Why are you getting all panicky?" he asked, walking out of the cave. "There ain't nothing in there but these," carrying two large metal containers.

"Ben, there could have been some snakes or spiders in there. You need to be more careful!" running up, so thrilled to see him walking out of the cave.

"I hope there were no snakes in there, but I did find these. What do you think?" holding up the metal pots.

"It's a large wok, and the other one is a cast iron cooking pot! Is there more in there?"

"No, just these," he said, shaking his head, "but mostly old tin cans," handing the rusty wok to her.

"Oh yeah! This is great. They just need a little cleaning up. They'll be great for cooking!"

"With this big pot, we can fill it with water and put it on top of the fire," he explained. "We'll have all the hot water we need. That's what we used to do on our camping trips. Maybe what they used it for as well."

"Oh, it'll be great to wash with hot water. We can really use these! So, what do we do now?"

"There is nothing more up here," he said, looking around. "We can go down to the north side of the island, but I think I'd like to walk back down the way we came. I want to see where that other trail leads to. That's going back to the east, but it's on our side of the island."

"If we continue to the north side, we can see if someone lives down there. It's downhill, so it wouldn't be that bad," she suggested, wanting to continue exploring the island.

He thinks about it for a while. "From here, both the trails go downhill. The only problem is that if we go to the north side, we will have to walk around the island to get back. The other option is walking up the hill again to get back up here, then back down to our camp. That's going to make it a long day."

"Yeah, that might be too much," she said, shaking her head. "I don't want to walk around the island again, and I know I don't want to walk all the way back up here either. I vote to go back to the orange trees and see where that other trail will take us."

"OK, you're the boss… You just want some more of those oranges, don't you?"

"Oh, yeah!" she said, nodding her head. "Those were great! They've given me a boost of energy. Let's go get some more oranges!"

Carrying their new cooking utensils, they make their way down the trail to the orange trees. After walking through the jungle for hours, now they know where they are going.

"Let's take some back with us," she said, eating a few more oranges. "We can carry a few back in the big pot."

"We only need a few," he said, seeing her filling up the pot.

"Stop whining… The more we bring back means not having to come up here again when we run out."

"That's way too many. My arms are already tired after carrying it with nothing in it," not liking the idea of Jenny making it heavier.

"It'll be nice to have orange juice in the morning. Even better, grapefruit for breakfast!" she added, still filling up the iron pot.

With a full load of fruit, they walk down the trail. "Are you sure you want to take all this with us?" Ben asked. "We don't know where this trail goes. We might have to drag all this back up the hill again," worried about hauling the heavy cooking pot around all day long.

"I want to see what's on the other side of this trail. Don't complain... I'm carrying the wok, and it's also heavy. At least we are going downhill. You never know. This trail might lead us back to the beach. Where else is it going to go?"

He thinks about it for a while, seeing she is right again. "OK, you lead the way," following behind her, struggling with the big cast-iron pot.

Jenny leads the way through the jungle on the winding trail. The trail gets narrower, and the trees tower over them. Plants and flowers are covering the ground. The path, well-worn and etched into the hillside, looks a little overgrown. The trail leads to the fruit trees and the cave, so that the other end might be just as interesting.

Ben is glad that Jenny is handling this so well, especially for a city girl. He knows that living out in the wilderness is rough for anyone. After what they have been through, she is stronger and has not complained much. He can see that she has changed a lot in the last few days. He is so proud of her being thrown into this mess with no experience. She will even show up some of his camping buddies back home.

* * *

They venture further down the trail. The path is on the edge of a steep hill, which allows them to check out the island. There are no signs of any buildings or structures. All they can see is just more trees far below and the beach.

"Ben, just look at that view!"

"Feel that breeze too! Let's take a break here. I'm so tired," dropping the heavy fruit-laden pot.

"I'm tired as well, but it's not so bad going downhill. It sure beats trekking through the jungle. There's a good spot over there. We can sit and look at the view for a while."

Ben sits down next to her. "I think my arms are a few inches longer carrying all this stuff. You need to eat a few more of these oranges to help me out. I think we got way too many," handing her a handful.

She laughed. "Sorry, I guess I got carried away."

"I hate to see what you're like at the mall during a sale," resting against the hillside.

She gives him a big kiss on his cheek. "This is nothing... You should see me at the supermarket! When I go shopping for food, I don't play around. Remember, I used to shop for the restaurant. Try filling four shopping carts, and that's just for the weekend. Besides, when you see what I'm going to cook you for dinner, you won't be complaining!"

He just nods, closing his eyes for a quick nap. Jenny keeps on talking, and he tries to listen, but it's not long before he falls asleep.

"Come on!" Jenny shouted, waking him up. "Eat an orange. It'll give you more energy. We need to move on," massaging his arms to help him out.

"I hope this path isn't a dead end. I don't think I can walk back up there again," feeling the pain from every muscle in his arms.

"I'm not going back up there either. If it doesn't go anywhere, then we'll have to walk straight down the hill until we reach the beach."

"Let's hope it's not like this the rest of the way," he said, leaning over to look down the steep hill. "That's a long drop down there and way too steep to walk."

"Maybe it'll level off a little farther down. Here, this will help you out a little," taking out a few grapefruits, placing them in the wok, and giggling at him.

"Thanks, that'll really help," regretting, dragging the metal pots out of the cave.

At a fast pace down the foothills following the trail, they are back in the dense jungle again. Feeling the humidity, they know they are getting close to the beach. Since there are no signs of any houses, they now accept that they are alone on this island.

The dirt trail abruptly changes to what looks like a rock ledge. A small creek cuts across it, splashing down the cliff far below. There is not much water, but enough to refill the water bottles. They continue down the trail until it finally levels out to a large opening. To their surprise, they are standing in a shaded grassy area.

"I think we've been here before! This is where we thought it would make a good campsite. Look, that's the small pond over there!" running over to her favorite bathing spot and stripping off her clothes.

"The trail leads directly from the cave to the freshwater pond!" he shouted, dropping the heavy pot, feeling so exhausted. "No wonder that trail is old and well-worn. It was a good find!"

"I wonder how long they've been living out here?"

"The big question is, where are they now?" he asked, looking around the area.

"No telling, but what a find! We found all those fruit trees and the cave, too," lying on her back in the cold water.

"Maybe they're on the other side of the island. I wonder what else is around here," looking around for more trails.

"Ben, take a break. Get those clothes off and get in! This feels great!"

Seeing Jenny floating naked on her back, Ben can't say no to that. He strips off his sweaty clothes, tossing them aside, then slides into the cold water.

"At least we're close to the camp. I was dreading that we would end up on the other side of the island. I don't know if I could have walked much more, and I'm so worn out!" she said.

"I couldn't have either. My arms are aching so badly after carrying that pot. We're lucky the trail wasn't a dead end higher up on the island."

She sits up behind him, rubbing his shoulders. "Don't be a pessimist! We found signs that people had been here. The fruit trees were a great find, too. Even the cave is something we can use!"

"Yeah, I guess you're right," still wondering what happened to the people who were here.

"It makes sense now that I think about it... The cave is for shelter, and the pond is for drinking water. Then there are all those fruit trees. The trail links them together. I'm really curious where the other trail leads to, that goes down to the north side."

He thinks about it for a moment. "There could be something on the other side of the island. That will be a hell of a walk."

"Maybe another day," she reluctantly replied, feeling tired.

"Now I think about it... This trail has been well used, and I don't mean just for a few years."

"How long do you think?"

"I bet it goes back to the old Captain Cook days. Those guys had been roaming around this part of the world for years. This island has plenty of drinking water and fruit trees. Hell, we might even find some old cabins or shacks scattered around. We just got to find where they are."

"At least we saw signs someone could be here. We need to keep looking. I bet they're on the other side."

"There might be something just within the trees," he explained, nodding his head. "We might not have seen it from the beach and walked right by it the other day. It's just like this place. If the dry creek bed didn't go out into the ocean, we wouldn't have known this pond was here."

"So how are we going to find out?" she asked. "You can't see more than thirty feet in this jungle."

"Smoke!" he blurted out, thinking about his camping days. "It's just like our campfire. Not only can you see the smoke, but you can smell it, too. We need to walk up and down the beach tonight, looking for any light or smoke from a campfire. It'd be easier that way."

"And if they're on the other side of the island?"

"I think that's another day," lying back against her chest, closing his eyes, ready for a nap.

* * *

After a brief break at the pond, it's time to move on. Jenny and Ben slowly walk down the beach, gathering all the wet clothes, fruit, and cooking pots.

Ben drops the heavy pot when he walks into their campsite. His arms ache so much. He thought he was in good shape from his mountain hiking days in Colorado. This is far more strenuous than anything he has ever done before.

"We made good time getting back," Jenny said. "It only took a couple of hours," feeling good about her day out.

"Yeah, but it took us more than five hours to get up to the cave!" he explained, looking at her a little shocked.

She laughed. "Well, next time, we'll start at the small pond and use that trail. I'm not walking up that hill through that jungle again!"

"That was a tough climb. We'll definitely use the trail next time. It'll cut down the time to the cave to maybe an hour or more."

"Well, that's another day," she said, standing in front of him, stretching out her arms, feeling the chilly breeze over her body.

"I think you're going to have some big problems when you get home!" he mentions, admiring her naked body.

"How do you mean?" she asked, standing with her hands on her hips, looking at him puzzled.

"Just look at you! It's getting to the point now where I hardly ever see you wearing any clothes. I think you're so used to it, and you don't even notice it anymore."

She slowly struts up to him and then rubs her body against his. "This is the only way to go! I love it! Come on, let's go for a swim!" noticing he is already getting aroused, then turns running to the beach.

"Hey, wait! You can't do that, then run off, leaving me like this!" realizing what Jenny really wanted, then chases after her.

Ben doesn't know where she is getting all this energy. She runs down the beach like a bat out of hell, wanting him to chase after her. After the trip to the top of the island, he is so exhausted but chases after her as fast as he can.

Once she is in the surf, he finally catches up with her. They play around in the warm water for more than an hour before lying together in the shallow water. They just hold hands, talking about their day.

Jenny giggles, seeing how he lies on his back with his eyes closed, ready for another nap. She rolls over closer, kissing him passionately. She quickly straddles him when he gets fully erect, slowly swinging her large breasts about, taunting him. Slowly moving up and down on top of him, then she moans out loud. She is like a wild woman going at it nonstop and, worse, is extremely loud.

He looks up at her, so shocked that she wants to have sex again. He lets her indulge herself while lying on his back, not saying a word. Having sex out on the beach is fantastic, and it doesn't get any better than this. He can't believe she is doing this, especially after the long walk up onto the island.

Jenny finally collapses on top of him. They both lie together silently, letting the waves splash over their bodies. The sun is low on the horizon, changing the clouds to a burnt orange color. They both watch the beautiful sunset together until Ben slowly falls asleep, totally exhausted.

"That was great!" she yelled out, waking him up. "Come on, sleepyhead! We got chores to do. It's going to be dark soon. You need to get the fire going, and we need something to eat. I'm so hungry after that workout!" giving him a long kiss.

"I bet you are... We have plenty of oranges to eat. I'm so tired. If I close my eyes, and that will be it for me," ready for a long nap.

She puts her arms around him. "After great sex on the beach," she said in her sultry voice. "I think I deserve a little more than just an orange! Why don't you try to catch a fish or something? A few sliced oranges will bring out the flavor of a nice fresh cooked fish!" rubbing her breasts over his face, teasing him again.

That wakes him up. "I don't know if it's the fresh air or what, but I have a feeling you're going to be a handful!" seeing how sexy Jenny is.

She laughed, then helped him up. "It's got to be this place that's doing it to me. Maybe it's that tight little butt of yours that's driving me crazy," slapping his butt hard.

"Come on, girl… Let's get you something to eat," he said, taking her hand, walking back to the camp.

With the sun just above the horizon, Ben knows they have a lot to do to cook dinner. Luckily, he gets the campfire going in no time. Jenny gets everything ready for their first fish dinner. All they need now is the fish.

"So, what kind of fish do you want?" he asked, gathering up his fishing gear. "It's been a long time since I have been surf fishing."

She laughed at him. "You're telling me you can select certain types of fish you want to catch!"

"No, I was thinking about just keeping the ones we can eat. I don't have a clue about any of these fish except for trout and redfish. What's a good one? Give me a hint. You're the expert."

"Just bring me something you think that looks good!" realizing she is also a little out of her element with this area of the world.

"You don't have a clue either," he laughs, walking out to the beach.

* * *

Within fifteen minutes, Ben returns with a couple of fish and a big smile on his face. "This is a great place to fish!" he shouted out. "So, what do you think? These are kind of small, but I guess they'll do."

"Oh, my God! I know what those are. You caught some papio!" rushing up with the pan. "We'll be eating good tonight! Can you get some more firewood while I get these ready?" so thrilled with the catch.

"We're using up the firewood a lot faster than I thought. I figured we had enough for a few days, and it's already gone. I'll see if I can get enough for tonight, and hope the fire doesn't go out before you get those cooked."

"Well, we can have raw fish if you want," she said, getting ready to clean them. "It may not be that bad. You might like it."

"I don't think so... I'll be back shortly with as much firewood as you need," disgusted with the idea of eating raw fish, wondering if she was joking about it.

* * *

Sitting together by the roaring fire, they discuss the events of the day while eating their first fresh fish meal marinated with oranges. Even with another day with no signs of rescue, they feel better about discovering the fruit trees and the cave.

"It's getting close to eight o'clock," Ben said, looking at his watch. "I guess we better check the news on the radio. I'm curious to know why they're not around here. It's been several days now."

"How about some coffee?" Jenny asked, trying to change the subject, seeing him getting annoyed.

"That will be great! You're one great cook. Again, you've done wonders! You definitely got into the wrong business being a shrink. You'll make a fortune with your own restaurant."

"Oh, no, not me... That got a little old. It's nice to fix a meal like this just for two, but with a restaurant open twelve hours a day, seven days a week, it's not much fun. It doesn't mean I don't like to cook for myself or maybe a special person," leaning over, kissing his cheek.

He blushes. "I was planning to take you out to dinner at a fancy restaurant when we get out of here. But now, I think no matter where I take you, their food isn't going to be anything like how you cook! Do you even go to other restaurants?"

"Well, when you're in the business, you don't eat out much. We always ate at home or at the restaurant. Besides, it's not good to be seen eating at your competitor's. Most times, they don't like you there anyway because they think you're spying or trying to steal their signature dish!"

"You got to be kidding!"

"Nope, it's a dog-eat-dog world," she explained. "My dad didn't like them snooping around either. He had a spotlight set up, so when he saw one of our competitors eating at our restaurant, he would shine the spotlight on them. Then he'll get on the intercom telling everyone that our food is so good, even the other restaurant workers eat here! He made sure they'd never come back," laughing hysterically.

"So, I guess a date with you is either at your restaurant or pizza delivery at home!"

"You learn fast!" she said, still laughing.

They lie down next to the fire, listening to the news. The atmospheric conditions are just right to pick up Honolulu on the shortwave band. Hearing all the various crimes and traffic accidents in Honolulu is something they don't miss at all. The announcer mentions an update about the rescue mission after the commercials. They quickly sit up, staring at the small radio to hear about their fate.

"I bet it'll be tomorrow!" she said, turning to Ben. "Just think, we could be sleeping in a nice warm bed with no sand!" with a glint in her eye.

"I bet you'll be putting these babies away for good when we get out of here!" reaching over, cupping his hand under her breast.

"I can say the same for you!" she said, looking down at his lap. "This might be our last night to run around naked. We need to remember to put something on in the morning. I don't want to be caught out on the beach when a helicopter lands!"

He laughed. "It's a good thing they didn't show up this afternoon when you were so horny out on the beach! I've never known anyone to scream out like that! If there's anyone else on this side of the island, they'd sure know we're here!"

Her face turns red. "I got a little carried away. I mean... Oh, they're talking about the rescue now," getting flustered, wanting to change the subject.

The radio announcer talks about all the ongoing rescues. Four small boats were found with survivors. Two sailboats are still missing and feared lost at sea. Most of the islands in the area have wind and water damage.

Then, the announcer mentions the flight. "The search for Ace Flight 191 officially ended today. The small commuter aircraft from Honolulu to Kwajalein Island disappeared from radar screens as it approached the storm. There has been no contact with the aircraft. Rescue ships did not find any wreckage. The flight carrying twenty passengers and two crew members on board are presumed lost at sea. A memorial service will be held this Sunday at the chapel--"

Ben turns off the radio, absolutely stunned. He doesn't want to hear any more. Jenny is sitting motionless. Her face is so pale, staring at the radio in disbelief.

"I can't believe it," he mumbles, then turns to Jenny. "They stopped looking! We haven't seen a damn thing in days! Where the hell are they? I think the biggest question is, where are we? What island is this? What the hell is going on?"

"They can't do that! It hasn't been that long, and they are already giving up!" she shouted, crying hysterically.

He puts his arms around her, not knowing what to do or say. He just stares at the campfire. Being stuck on this island is something he was not expecting. Being rescued was always just a few days away. He doesn't understand how these people can give up after only one week.

"What are we going to do?" he asked, still staring at the fire. "How are we going to survive out here?"

"I don't know. I just want to go home," she sobbed.

"We'll keep looking around here for someone. They might have stopped looking for us, but we're not going to quit. We'll find a way out."

Jenny doesn't say a word. The idea of never seeing her family again is tearing her apart. What is worse, her family doesn't know she is alive. She can't believe this is happening. She just wants to go back home to her family, crying herself to sleep, giving up all hope.

Ben is feeling numb all over. He looks around at all their meager possessions. Now, they have to rely on all this for their survival. The past few days on the island were a struggle, but tolerable. Having to live like this for a long time will be a nightmare.

After thinking about their situation, Ben knows he needs to be strong and positive. He had been in bad situations before while camping up in the mountains, but he survived because he knew not to give up. He always lived with the attitude that there is always light at the end of the tunnel, and it's no different here. They just have to wait it out because it's just a matter of time before someone finds them here.

Ben tosses the last of the firewood onto the campfire, seeing it's about to go out. He checks the sleeping bag. After being out in the sun for several days, it's finally dry. The sleeping bag is the one thing they can use, especially on chilly nights. Since Jenny is already asleep, he carefully places her inside it.

He goes through all their possessions and takes an inventory of all the food, survival, and camping gear. For a few days of camping, it's adequate, but not knowing how long they'll be out here, he is now getting scared. He never paid much attention to the medical or survival kit from the airplane, but now he knows it's going to help keep them alive.

* * *

Chapter 20

The Phone Call

Now, it's official. The search and rescue operation has been canceled, and everyone on Flight 191 has been declared lost at sea. Paul Rutherford has been calling the families of the passengers every day since the aircraft vanished. For the past six days, he has provided them with all the latest information regarding air and sea rescue efforts. He has grown to know each family, but now he must make the heart-wrenching call that he has been dreading. One by one, he must break the hearts of those families.

Walter and Mary Hughes wait patiently by the phone for the daily call from Paul Rutherford. Usually from seven to nine at night, they waited for the call, hoping it would bring news that their son had been found. Since the airplane went down, it has been nothing but waiting around aimlessly to hear news about their son. The ordeal has put their lives on hold.

When the phone rings, Walter quickly answers it. Mary sits quietly, looking for any facial expressions that will indicate good or bad news. She knows right away that something isn't right. This call is different. Usually, her husband asks all sorts of questions, but this time, he is just listening and staring at the floor.

"Thank you for all your help," Walter quietly said, hanging up the phone, putting his hands over his face, and started crying.

Mary puts her hand over her mouth in shock. "What is it? What did they say?" fearing the worst.

After a few minutes, he composes himself. "They stopped searching for them! They said Ben had been listed as lost at sea. He's gone. We lost our son."

"No! It can't be! He's alive! I know he's alive! I just know it!" she screamed out, crying uncontrollably.

Walter calls the rest of the family to inform them that he has lost his youngest son. One by one, friends and family rush over to the house to be with Walter and Mary in their time of need. There are so many unanswered questions. Everyone felt it was just too soon to stop the search, especially since it's not even been a week.

The call to Jenny's parents is the worst, and are outraged. Losing their daughter is bad enough, but not giving her a proper burial is too much for them. They just hated the thought of their little girl sinking to the bottom of the ocean all alone. They are among the first to start legal procedures against the contracting agency, the airline company, and anyone else involved.

* * *

Chapter 21

No Hope

Jenny wakes up totally confused, trapped inside something in the complete darkness, unable to move. In a panic, she struggles to free herself, thinking she is back on the airplane again.

"Ben, help me!" frantically trying to get free.

"Good morning! It sounds like you had a bad dream?" unfastening the zipper, opening the sleeping bag for her.

"What a nightmare! I thought I was in a coffin or something," realizing she was in the sleeping bag.

"Sorry, I put you in it last night to keep you warm. I was kind of getting worried after all that bad news we had last night. Are you OK?"

"I guess... It seems like things are getting worse for us."

"I wouldn't say that... We got enough food and water here to last us a while. They might have stopped looking for us, but I think they're looking in the wrong place. They're still looking for other people. Eventually, someone is going to check this island. Also, we still don't know what else is here."

She smiled. "Yeah, you're right. So, what time is it?" shielding her eyes from the bright sunlight.

"It's about eight. I thought I'd let you sleep in late. What do you think about the sleeping bag?"

"Oh, this is great! I slept so good. So soft and warm, it feels like I'm back in my old bed again. It blocks out the light too. When I woke up, it was so dark. I thought it was the middle of the night," wrapping herself back up in the sleeping bag with just her head sticking out.

"I thought you'd like it. It's designed for all seasons. It keeps you warm in the winter and cool during the hot summer nights."

"That was the best night's sleep I had since we've been here. It's so comfortable, too. There's plenty of room, and best of all, no sand! So, you finally decided to wear clothes now?" seeing him in his swimming trunks.

"Well, after I lit the fire, there was a big popping noise. An ember shot out, getting a little too close to the boys! Then, when I was out fishing, I almost caught myself with a treble hook! That was more than enough signs to get me to wear my swimming trunks."

"You need to be more careful!" she said, laughing at him.

"I see you're really concerned," seeing her laughing hysterically.

"I'm sorry," she said, finally regaining her composure. "I can just see you hopping around with a hot ember on your thingy! So what are you cooking?" wanting to change the subject.

"What do you think?" he asked, showing her the fish fillets in the pan.

"You actually cooked fish for breakfast? I'm surprised! You even cleaned it, too."

He shakes his head. "Oh, it was so horrible... I don't know how you do it. It might not be as good as what you cooked last night, but it's a start," handing her a hot cup of coffee.

"Wow, breakfast in bed!" she said, really impressed with him.

"You cooked one hell of a meal last night, so I thought I'd make breakfast."

"You need some help?" she asked, seeing him struggling with the fish.

"No, thanks... I need to figure this out myself. I'm more used to eggs and bacon for breakfast. Cooking fish is a little new to me. Oh, by the way, happy anniversary!"

"It's already been a week, hasn't it?"

He nods his head. "Yep, a whole week since we were out on that beach in Hawaii. Here you go, fish for breakfast," handing her the fish fillet smothered with several chunks of oranges and grapefruit.

"Thank you... This looks great! What type of fish are these?"

He sits down next to her. "I think it's the same ones we had last night. Not bad for the first time," tasting the fish.

"This is great!" she said, leaning over to kiss his cheek. "I can't believe you cleaned them too," knowing how hard it is for him to clean a fish.

"It wasn't a pretty sight," he mumbled, trying not to think of it.

"I just can't imagine what my family is going through right now," she said, quietly sitting wrapped up in the sleeping bag, staring at the campfire.

"I know... But we're OK. There is still a chance of someone finding us here. It's just a matter of time," putting his arm around her.

"You're right! We need to look on the bright side. We have all those fruit trees, not to mention all the bananas, coconuts, and fish. Now, we also have a campfire to cook things. So far, we've been doing OK."

"Hell, we've been really lucky! Look at all this stuff we got, and we haven't even used the tent yet. There are still things getting washed up on the beach as well! No telling what else we're going to find that we can use here," looking around at the makeshift camp.

"Ben, we need to see what's on the other side of the island!"

"So, I guess you want to see where that other trail goes to, up by the cave?" he quietly asked, still feeling sore from the previous day.

She gives him a big smile. "After hearing that they've stopped looking for us, I just can't sit here doing nothing. This may be our home for a while, so we better know what else is here. We do know that people once lived here, so there should be a house or something. They had to live somewhere other than that cave."

"There still can be someone up on the island," he explained. "We need to keep an eye out for smoke from a campfire. I forgot to look last night."

"That is a good idea! Anyone on this side can see the smoke from our campfire. But if they can see ours, we should have seen theirs too," looking at the smoke slowly drifting up through the trees.

He nods his head, agreeing without saying a word, having a feeling that there is no one else on the island. He suspected it after the first day but doesn't want to say anything. The old, rusty cans and things they found probably confirmed it. He doesn't want to tell her any more bad news, but he can be wrong. The one thing he needs more than anything is a positive attitude and to keep his suspicions to himself.

* * *

After hearing the bad news about the search and rescue, they feel that there is no point in just sitting around and giving up hope. Exploring the rest of the island is now more important than ever. They clean the campsite, reorganizing things a little. The camp is now their home and not just a place to store their supplies.

With knowledge of the trail, they opted for minimal clothing. Ben wears only his swimming trunks and shirt. Jenny opts for her blouse and shoes. Walking to the cave will mean another long, strenuous day, but at least there is a trail to the top of the island. They also learned from experience that the fewer clothes they wear, the better.

Grabbing several water bottles for the trip, they make their way down the beach. The small pond is now their favorite place. They take turns washing each other, enjoying it immensely. An excellent way to start the day, and it gets their minds off all their problems.

Walking up the trail is a lot easier than going straight up the hill through all the trees as they did the day before. After taking plenty of breaks, in only a couple of hours, they reach the grassy lookout. The fruit trees are a big reward after the long, exhausting walk.

Taking a break at the edge of the cliff, they eat a few oranges, admiring the fantastic view. They are safe on this beautiful island. Knowing everyone at home is being told they had died in the crash makes them depressed and extremely frustrated. Unfortunately, there is nothing they can do about it.

* * *

They make their way up to the cave after a short break. Ben is also curious to see if anyone actually lived in it. He has his small flashlight just in case there are any spiders or snakes in it.

"There is nothing of value other than some old rusty cans," Ben said, searching around in the cold, dark cave. "From the looks of things, whoever was here really cleaned it out good. It might be a good place to store firewood. It should keep dry in here."

"It would be a great place to stay during a storm!" she suddenly blurted out. "We can have a fire to keep us warm and cook the food."

"Jenny, I think you're right! Look at that burn mark on the ground. That's where they had their campfire. It would never get wet, even when it rained! We can stock up on the firewood, so we'll always have dry wood. That will really help us out!"

"If there are more storms on the way, this is where we need to be! We can't let everything get wet again. It took days to dry it all out," thinking about her sleeping bag.

"You're right! We need to go through our supplies and put the extra stuff in here. Half down at the beach and the other half up here," so glad to see she is planning ahead.

* * *

After exploring the cave, they continued down the trail to the north side of the island. The path leads away from the peak to the northwest, downhill all the way. The trail is nothing special, just winding through the tall trees. After about a hundred yards, they come across a large opening, discovering another orchard.

Ben comes to a complete stop. "Look at all the orange and grapefruit trees. There's even more here than at the one by the cave. Check out the size of those bananas! Those things are huge!"

"I see some breadfruit and a lemon tree. Oh, there's a mango, and I think that's a papaya tree way over there. Hey, look at that! It must have been their house!" she shouts, discovering the remains of a small shack.

Ben walks over, pushing back the tall grass, revealing a pile of twisted corrugated tin and half-rotted timber. "At least we now know someone was living here. It explains all these orchards."

"Ben, maybe there's something we can use underneath it. Can we lift this up and check it out?"

He leans over, lifting one of the corrugated sheets. Jenny immediately screams out, then jumps back. A huge black scorpion runs into the long grass.

Ben quickly drops the corrugated roof. "Oh, hell! I didn't know scorpions got that big!"

"What! You mean to tell me those things are crawling around here?" she screamed, freaking out.

"I didn't think about that. I wonder what else is on this island!" looking in the long grass for more scorpions.

"That's all I need! Now I got damn scorpions and spiders to worry about!"

"Don't panic... Just watch where you step, and don't pick anything up without checking it first."

They don't want to be anywhere near the remains of the old shack. Carefully watching their step, they continue to explore the area. Now, it's so clear that this was more than someone's hobby. The orchard is more like a farm that produces a lot of fruit.

Ben finds two pieces of weathered wood in the grass. He kicks them with his foot to make sure nothing is hiding underneath. He cautiously picks up the wood, seeing that it used to be attached with old rusty nails. There is an inscription on the opposite side.

"Jenny, take a look at this!" holding it up for her.

"It's a grave marker. There's no date on it. I wonder when they died?" Jenny asked, examining the old wooden cross.

"It's hard to say. It could have been twenty or thirty years ago."

Looking over the old grave, he notices another small mound right next to it. "There's another one over there. I guess this is where they buried everyone."

"So, this must be a gravesite?" she asked, placing the marker back on the ground.

"Yeah, it's probably the people who used to live and work here. From the looks of things, I bet there are a few more graves around in that tall grass."

Jenny stares at the graves and then looks over at all the fruit trees. "This was probably a central depot for fresh fruit. In the old days, sailing ships had problems with scurvy because of the lack of vitamin C. They probably planted these years ago, leaving a few people behind to tend to the orchards. This might have been going on for a hundred years. Anyone sailing in the Pacific back in the old days probably used this island to replenish their stores."

"If that's true, then we're in the middle of an old shipping lane," he replied after thinking about it. "This must be a well-known island. I still can't figure out why we haven't seen any ships."

"This island might have been well-known years ago. Nowadays, people fly to get wherever they need to go. I wonder how long these people had been here? I can understand having something like this a hundred years ago, but not thirty years. They wouldn't have needed all this."

"You're right. It was probably phased out over time," Ben explained. "Maybe the people here didn't want to leave. They could have sold or traded some of the fruit to anyone who stopped on the island. The only people to stop here nowadays would be mostly tourists or people out sailing from one island to the next."

"You know what that means, don't you!" she said, giving him a big hug.

"Yep! If anyone knows this area, they would know the fruit trees are up here. We need to keep an eye out for sailboats anchored off the island!" hugging her again.

* * *

After eating a few more oranges and bananas, they continued down the trail to the north side of the island. Walking down this path is not too much of an effort. There are no spectacular views, nothing but dense forest.

After over an hour, there are no houses or any signs that someone is still living on the island. Hearing the crashing waves and feeling the humidity, they know the beach is nearby.

"Well, I don't see any ponds at the end of this trail," she said, walking out on the beach.

Ben turns around, trying to get his bearings. "Yeah, we might have to look around for one."

"We would have never known the ponds were there on the other side without the run-off on the beach," she explained. "We need to look around for one on this side."

He stares at her for a moment. "Wait a minute! We've already been on this beach. Those are our footprints over there. We didn't see any streams or dry creeks on this side of the island."

"You're saying there is no water on this side?" she asked.

He shakes his head. "I don't think so... Notice how the clouds are on the other side of the island. That's probably why all the water is on our side. There could be a little stream, but not enough water to reach down here."

"This side of the island does look a little different," she mentioned, looking down the beach. "There are no rocks or boulders here. The beach is altogether different, too. The grains of sand are bigger, and it's harder to walk on this beach, and the waves are huge and a lot louder. Our side is much better."

He looks at the waves crashing on the beach. "You can see it's a steeper drop off, and it must get deep real quick. We can walk quite a ways out on our beach. I think we made the right choice staying on the other side."

"You're right about that, from the looks of things. We must be on the opposite side from where our camp is," looking back up at the peak.

"Wow!" he shouted, a little surprised. "That's pretty good! So, you already figured out your bearings here?"

"It's simple... During the day, the shadows from the trees here point out to the ocean. On our side, the shadows always point to the island. So, we must be on the north side," nudging his shoulder.

"That also tells us we are still above the equator, but not by much. And if it's cloudy?" he asked, trying to test her.

"That tells us where we are!" she shouted, pointing up at the peak of the island.

"Good for you! I'm definitely taking you out camping when we get out of here."

She laughed. "Not another camping date! When we get out of here, you better start thinking of other places to take me," kissing his cheek. "Come on... Let's go for a swim. Then I want to rest for a while."

"Good idea!" stripping off his clothes, he ran into the water.

"Wait for me!" dropping out of her clothes, chasing after him.

* * *

So tired from the trip over the island and with more sex on the beach, they both are sound asleep. Taking a nap too close to the water was not a smart move. One thing they didn't think about was the tide coming in. The waves are getting closer and closer, but they never stir.

A massive wave crashes right on top of them. Ben is coughing like mad after breathing in the water. Jenny frantically holds on to Ben so she doesn't get washed away. The water rushes back into the ocean, dragging them with it. Another massive wave hits, and they roll end over end until they are back up on the beach.

"Are you OK?" seeing how he is still coughing and gagging.

He can't talk, just nods his head. He tries to crawl through the loose sand to get away from the crashing waves. The sand is so loose that his hands and knees go deep in the sand, unable to move up the beach.

"Let me help!" helping him out of the water. "Hurry, another wave is coming!"

Ben slowly gets up. "What a nightmare! I'm so glad we're not staying on this side. It's a little too rough," looking at the enormous waves crashing right on the beach.

"I know... I can barely walk on this sand. My feet sink in about six inches every time I take a step."

Ben looks around, seeing all the shadows. "Oh, no! It's really late... We screwed up this time. We need to get back fast," seeing how dark it is.

"Oh my God!" she screamed out. "I can't believe we slept so long!"

"This is not good," walking to the trees to collect their clothes. "It'll be dark soon. It's a big mistake being so far away from the camp with no water," seeing their water bottles are almost empty.

"How long do you think it'll take us to get back?" she asked, looking up at the island.

"I'm not sure... I don't think we have enough time. Getting back to the cave will take us a couple of hours. Then, we still have to go down the other side to get back to the camp. That's another two hours, and that's without stopping for breaks. Even if we start now, I don't think we'll even reach the cave. The last thing we need is to be stuck up there in the dark."

"So what are we going to do?" she frantically asked, dreading the thoughts of having to sleep out on the beach again.

"Well, we have a few options. Spend the night here, walk along the beach to get back, or up by the trail. I don't even want to try going up that trail in the dark. We could get lost, or worse, we'll be sleeping with the bugs," remembering the big black scorpion.

"Wait! We got the flashlight!"

"Oh, that's right! I forgot all about it. It's a good thing we brought it with us today," pulling the flashlight out of his pocket.

"Since we got the flashlight, do you think we can walk back on the trail?"

"I don't know," he said, looking up at the island. "We'll probably be walking up the hill for hours. I think the beach will be safer and less strenuous. If we try to get back by the trails, we'll have to stop once the batteries go dead."

"OK, let's walk on the beach then... When the batteries run out, what are we going to do?" Jenny asked, getting concerned.

He shrugs his shoulders. "All we can do is find a nice spot to sleep. The alternative is to keep going in the dark. It'll be a lot easier on the beach than up on the trails. I guess all we can do is go as far as we can until the batteries go out."

"Well, that's just great!" she shouted, so frustrated. "We're going to use up the batteries in one night. Now we're going to be stuck here without a flashlight. That could have come in handy during the night if I needed to go to the bathroom!"

"It's not a problem... The batteries are rechargeable. I thought you knew that?"

"What good are rechargeable batteries when we have no electricity to charge them?" getting so mad.

Ben laughed. "We didn't have electricity in the mountains either. I got a solar charger. It's the same with the radio. The batteries should charge fast with all the sunlight we have here."

"You got to be kidding!" she shouted, so relieved. "That means we can still keep using the radio and the flashlight forever!" hugging and kissing Ben.

"Like I told you... I'm always prepared! It's a good thing I bought brand-new batteries before I left. Anyway, I guess we better get started. It's going to be a long walk," remembering the first time they walked around the island.

"So, which way do we go?" she asked, looking up and down the beach.

"I think west towards the sun," looking up at the peak of the island. "We're probably more than halfway there. It's still going to take us a long time to get back. We need to hurry!"

Walking along the beach for hours in the dark. They use the flashlight sparingly, only turning it on for a few seconds to help see what is in front of them. Finding the camp in the dark is going to be a big problem. Having to go to sleep with nothing to eat is not a good way to end the day.

Jenny is so hungry, always thinking about food. "Ben, I'm thinking for breakfast, we can cook a big fish like we did this morning. I think we might have a couple of oranges left over. At least we can eat one when we get back. The other we'll use for breakfast with the fish. We just can't let this happen again."

"Yeah, but it's just like camping at home," he explained. "You always learn from your mistakes. We'll have to make sure we always have extra fruit. The biggest problem we have is storing away enough food before it goes bad. The fruit should last a couple of days in the shade. There's plenty of fish in the ocean, but we have to cook and eat them right away. What else can we do?"

"We'll have to think of something. We have to start playing it smart from now on. I'm not going through this again!" getting serious about the situation and worrying about their future here.

Ben thinks about the wealth of fish near the shore. He has only been out fishing twice and has lost several fishing lures. He has the snorkeling gear, but he needs some kind of spear or net to catch the fish.

Then he gets an idea. "Jenny! That cargo net that is on the raft. We can use it out here! I can't believe I didn't think about it before!"

"That netting on the raft where we keep all our things? What's that got to do with anything?"

"We can use it as a casting net!" he explained, putting his arm around her. "It's big enough, and it's not doing us any good now. Come to think about it, that's maybe why it's so big, and it's removable."

"You think it'll work? Can you catch a fish with it?"

"Sure, that's how we used to catch shrimp when we went fishing on the coast! We can use it to catch all sorts of fish around here."

"If it doesn't work, you still have your fishing rod. You've been catching plenty of fish with it so far."

"That's true, but we have a limited amount of fishing gear, and after this morning, I know it's not going to last long. You know, if we used our net to catch the fish, it wouldn't harm them. We can catch as many as we want, then dump them in that small tidal pool by that big rock on the beach! So, we can always have a little stash for those rainy days!"

"Sounds like a great idea!" realizing that will solve one of their biggest problems. "We'll try it out tomorrow!" leaning over to kiss Ben's cheek.

* * *

In the darkness, walking at a slow pace, it's taking a lot longer than they thought. Tired and hungry, Ben is now wondering if it's time to stop and find a place to sleep. The flashlight batteries are almost dead. Ben turns on the flashlight sparingly to make sure the beach is clear to walk on so they don't trip on any rocks or boulders.

Once in a while, Ben stops and looks up at the island. All he sees is a dark silhouette against the bright stars in the background. He stares for a long time, letting out a long sigh.

"What is it?" she asked. "Are you getting tired? You want to stop here for the night?"

"No, just looking up on the island... There are no campfires. I don't see any lights up there or even smell smoke," he quietly mumbles.

"Oh, that's right... We need to look for campfires or lights," she added, looking as well.

"There might be something on the east side," he said, getting depressed. "There is so much of this island we have not seen yet," wanting to keep things positive.

"Yeah, we have to remember to look in the morning for smoke on our side," she said, putting her arm around him.

They continue on in the darkness, walking at the edge of the water. Seeing the reflection of the stars in the water as the small waves rush up on the beach helps keep them on the right path. One of the benefits of being on an island in the middle of the Pacific is that the stars and even the Milky Way Galaxy can clearly be seen. It cast enough light over the island to help guide their way back to camp.

Ben looks at his watch, so shocked, seeing it's eleven at night. They have never been up this late. He is wondering if they walked by their campsite, not having a clue where they are. From his experience camping out in the wilderness, you do not make mistakes like this. From here on out, everything must be well planned in advance.

Jenny suddenly stops. "Does that sound unusual to you?" she asked, hearing something strange just in front of them.

"I hear it too! The waves do sound a little different," shining the flashlight ahead of them.

"Look!" she screamed out. "We're at the big pond! That's the water that leads up to it!"

"Jenny, you're getting good!" he said, turning off the flashlight to save the batteries. "That has to be more than fifty feet away, and you actually heard it."

"I know! It's so great how you can hear just the littlest things," wrapping her arms around Ben, giving him a big hug.

"When you're living outside long enough, you start to pick up on things like that," giving her a long kiss.

"Well, it's been one hell of a long day, but we made it! Only a little ways to go now."

"Yep! We finally made it!" giving her another long, passionate kiss.

* * *

The day was long and exhausting after the long walk around the island. Seeing the huge boulders out on the beach, they finally made it. Jenny goes up to the small tidal pool on the side of the boulder.

"You know," she said, shining the flashlight into the tidal pool. "I think it'll work. It's big enough to hold several good-sized fish. It's high tide now, and these fish still have no way of getting out."

"I think they're the same ones we saw the other day. It'll be a good holding place for any fish we catch."

"We'll worry about it tomorrow," she said, reaching over to put her arm around him. "Come on, let's go to bed," walking back to their camp.

"It's a good thing that we have the camp near that big boulder. We wouldn't have found it in the dark. We could have been sleeping out on the beach again."

"See, we did something right! We just got to remember not to fall asleep on the other side of the island."

"I can't believe we did that," he said, shaking his head. "Next time we go out, we need to make sure we have enough water and food for the whole day. I'll remember to charge the batteries the day before as well."

"Ben, you need to tell me about some of these things. I didn't even know these were rechargeable batteries. You even have a solar charger. Where do you get this stuff from, anyway? I didn't know they even made these things. In the morning, you're going to explain how all this works. I need to know everything about all these gadgets you have."

"We'll go through it all tomorrow," feeling too tired, having to explain it to her.

They walk into the camp, now too late to light the campfire. They are just too tired. The flashlight is almost dead. They hurry to get things organized before the batteries go out. Luckily, a bottle of drinking water is in the camp, and they both quickly finish it, sharing the orange.

He unzips the tent's door flap and looks around inside. After seeing the giant scorpion, he is so glad he kept it closed. He learned long ago to always keep the tent closed up, preventing the bugs from crawling in.

Jenny crawls into the tent, snuggling up to him. "This sleeping bag is so nice and cozy. There's plenty of room in here."

"You are wearing perfume?" he asked, taking in a deep whiff.

"Of course! It's called Passion Fruit! It's our first night sleeping in the tent together. I wanted to smell nice!"

"It's my favorite scent," he said, taking in another whiff. "Fresh tropical oranges!"

She laughed. "That's all I got, so you better like it," putting her face close to his.

"This is so nice," putting his arm around her, gently kissing her.

"I'm surprised at how comfortable it is. There's so much room in this sleeping bag. It's nothing like the ones we had back home. This is what we've needed for the last few days," snuggling up to Ben, quickly falling asleep.

Ben thinks about their day out on the island. Except for the big orchard, it's more of the same. The idea of someone else living on the island is not an issue anymore. He now knows they are alone, not seeing any campfires on the other side of the island, and that confirms it. The only chance of being rescued is when a boat comes to the island. With plenty of water, fruit, and fish, they'll be all right for a while. They just have to wait it out.

* * *

Chapter 22

Funerals

F unerals are being arranged for all those who lost their lives on Flight 191. Twenty-two people are never to be seen again, presumed to be in the depths of the Pacific Ocean.

Ben's mother is not accepting his death until they recover his body. In her mind, he is still away on a job far from home. Every night, she wakes up crying, still having dreams about her son being alive. She tries to convince everyone, but no one will listen anymore. She refuses to have a funeral. That will mean her son is not coming home and is gone forever. Instead of a funeral, Ben's family gathers for a wake to celebrate his life.

To many of Ben's friends and family, it was no surprise to hear that he lost his life in some exotic location in the Pacific Ocean. He always traveled the world, camping in the wilderness, climbing mountains, riding class five rapids, or flying gliders. Even though his life was cut short, he lived every day as if it were his last. Everyone he knew envied the life he lived, and they all knew he always lived life to the fullest.

* * *

Jenny's family is deeply distraught. They had a private ceremony at their country home. The family put her grave up on the hill under a large tree on the back of their 160-acre estate. That was her favorite place to be in her younger days. She would sit under the old tree, reading books, and playing games.

After the funeral, Jenny's mother was always at the grave, telling her how much she loved her and missed her dearly. She always ends up crying uncontrollably. Losing her daughter is just too much.

The stress on Jenny's father is taking its toll. He has not been in his restaurant since hearing the news that she was missing. Every night, he has the same nightmare of her slowly descending into the depths of the ocean. His anger grew as the days passed. All he thinks about is getting back at the people who had taken his daughter away from him.

Jenny's father initiated the lawsuit against everyone involved. When he received the envelope from the insurance company, it infuriated him so much that he ended up in the emergency room. The envelope contained a check for $40,000 for his daughter's death benefit. No letter explaining what caused the plane to go down or even a note saying they were sorry for losing his daughter. That put him over the edge. He promptly burned the check and swore he would make them all suffer for the grief they had caused him and his family.

* * *

Chapter 23

Island Life

After several months, Jenny and Ben have accepted the island as their new home. Living off the land is not an easy life, but it's never boring or mundane. With so many chores to do, there is not much time to sit on the beach looking for something not there. Never having seen any airplanes or ships, they just stopped looking.

Every day is a constant search for firewood and hiking up to the cave for fresh fruit. All the drinking water has to be carried from the ponds. The desalination pump broke long ago, so the water has to be boiled first to get rid of any bacteria or parasites. They learn from their mistakes, so life on the island is a little more comfortable and more like an extended vacation away from home.

When living off the land, nothing goes to waste. They even save the seeds from the oranges and grapefruits. After noticing all the discarded seeds are taking root and growing all over the campsite, Ben knows what he has to do. Once they have enough, they plant the seeds all over the island to help replenish the fruit orchards.

Ben stores his watch in the cave, realizing it's pointless to know the exact time or even the date. Living on an island, all they need is the sun and the shadows to get a general idea of the time. They learn to recognize all the main stars, constellations, and the moon's position on clear nights. The only important thing is keeping track of the tides. Other than that, there is no need to know the day or even the month.

There is no getting away from the brutal sun when living outside. They find it best to take a nap during the hottest part of the day. In front of their campsite, the old Milo tree is the best place to rest, being right out on the beach. Coconuts solve many of their problems with the sun. Not only is it used for food and cooking, but the oil is also an excellent skin moisturizer and hair conditioner. A small amount of oil goes a long way. The coconut shells also make good bowls, and the husks are great for starting the campfire.

Ben's skills with the casting net always kept them with an abundance of fresh fish to eat. They always make sure to store plenty of fish in the tidal pool for those rainy days. He also makes several long spears out of bamboo, using them for spearfishing while out snorkeling. Spearfishing is a lot easier than using his old fishing tackle. Now, he can select the fish he wants for their next meal.

Jenny quickly finds that living outside has some drawbacks. She is tired of the rain putting out the campfire while cooking their meals. She remembers how they cooked food by burying it in the sand at a luau when they were in Hawaii. The technique may help their situation. Since they live on the beach, there is plenty of sand around.

While boiling the drinking water, she tosses a few lava rocks into the campfire. An hour later, she pushes the hot lava rocks into a hole she dug in the sand. Then she puts wet banana leaves on top so as not to burn everything. She prepares a couple of fish to see how this will work, wrapping them up tightly with banana leaves. Covering everything again with more banana leaves, she then buries everything up with sand.

In just over an hour, she pushes away the sand, carefully pulling the leaves and rocks out, revealing a steaming hot meal. It is a wonderful discovery. Something as simple as a few hot lava rocks buried in the sand can cook a meal just as good as her oven did at home. A more convenient way to cook, and not having to watch it all the time. Also, it means more variety of meals, but mostly, no more cooking over an open flame with smoke blowing in her face.

Every morning, they have this ritual of walking down the beach, searching for any debris that is washed up. Not a day goes by without finding something they can use. They always alternate their paths, trying to cover as much of the beach as possible. Occasionally, they walk to the far side of the island to check out the beaches there. Unfortunately, any good finds on the north side are a long haul back up to the cave.

There is always an abundance of rope being washed up for some unknown reason, from little twines to one-inch thick anchor rope. Old fishing nets are being washed up as well. Most of it is nothing more than a huge mass tightly wrapped around some poor old shark. The old casting net will not last much longer, so Ben is glad to salvage as much of the fishing nets as possible.

The cave is convenient for storing not only their firewood but also everything else they are not using. There is no more worrying about anything getting wet or blown away by the wind. When the bad rainstorms hit the island, they spend the day in the cave. They quickly realize it's better than waiting out the storm in the small tent. At least in the cave, there is plenty of room, and the campfire helps keep them warm and dry on those cold, rainy nights.

* * *

Since the first day on the island, Ben had always wanted to climb to the top of the peak. That is the only place on the island they have not yet explored. He has always been curious to see what is up there. Most importantly, the view from up there will be spectacular. They will be able to see the entire island from one location.

One day, Jenny finally agrees to go but refuses to do any rock climbing. All they will do is explore the area to see if there is a way up. Unless there is a trail leading up to it, she is adamant she is not going, and neither is he. For Ben, that is good enough. He has been trying to convince her for months, but she always has the last word.

After a hearty breakfast of grapefruit and bananas, they fill the water bottles at the small pond and then hike up the trail. They stop at the small orchard, gathering fruit for the rest of the trip. Once they reach the cave, it's time for a quick break.

The cave is the best starting point since it's not far from the peak. A small trail leads from the cave directly to the peak. After about twenty yards, it disappears within the trees, probably washed away over time. On this trip, they will spend most of the day looking over the area more thoroughly.

Reaching the end of the trail, Ben used his walking stick to clear away the brush and ferns. He never understood why there was no trail leading to the top of the island. They found numerous trails to various points on the island but none to the top. One thing they discovered is that all paths lead to something important.

Jenny follows closely behind, carrying the water and fruit, while Ben thrashes away, trying to clear a path. She knows he always looks up at the peak, longing to climb it. He always talked fondly about climbing some big mountain in Colorado. This small volcanic island is not much of a challenge for him, but he has this thing about climbing and exploring. She knows the peak is constantly calling him, and hopefully, this one trip is enough to get it out of his system.

* * *

Once they reach the cliff face, Ben searches for the best way to go around it, then sees something strange. "Check out those trees!" pointing them out to her.

"I can't see anything... What am I supposed to be looking at?" Jenny asked, not seeing anything more than a group of trees.

He points again. "Look, if you stand here, you can see a small clearing along those trees. It's where the small shrubs are."

"Sorry, I just don't see it," not understanding what he is pointing out to her.

He walks a few more paces, then crouches down, pushing back the shrubs with his walking stick. "We found it! This is it! It's an old trail leading around the peak!"

"I don't know... It's not much to look at," a little dubious about it.

"It's a trail! It's small, but you can see it under the bushes here. Out of all the trails, this one was probably used the least. If people were on this island, you think someone would be at the top for a lookout or something. There is only one way to find out," making his way down the narrow trail.

While walking on the small trail in front of the southern base, the peak towers well over a hundred feet above them. Away from all the trees, the old trail is very narrow, making it extremely difficult to walk. One slip, and they will have a bad problem.

When they reach the east side, they are well above the trees. The view is spectacular. Being up so high and exposed, the wind is now an issue. The wind is whipping around the cliff face, almost blowing them off their feet.

"This makes sense now. It's all on the north side," Ben explained while walking along the rocky ledge on the north face of the island.

"I still don't see it. All I know is that we're really high up. How are we going to get up there?"

"This side is covered with natural ledges through years of wind and erosion. It will be an easy climb to the top. All we have to do is follow where others have traveled. Whoever had been here before spent a long time clearing a path to the top. You can clearly see the trail from here."

"I don't know... Looks kind of scary!" Jenny said, getting so nervous.

"They've carved out some good paths for us. It's a little steep, but if we take it slow, we'll be up there in no time."

"You lead the way, but if it gets too bad, I'm heading back, and so are you!"

Ben laughed. "You'll be OK... It's going to be an easy climb."

* * *

After struggling for an hour, they are so disappointed to see the trail end abruptly. With only thirty feet to the top, there are no signs of a way up. A dead-end, with nowhere else to go, there is nothing else to do but to go back.

Ben is so frustrated that they have come this far with the trail ending like this. "I can't believe it stops here!" desperately looking around for a way up.

"It's far enough for me!" she cried out. "Just look at the view! You can almost see the whole north side of the island from up here!"

"It's way better than the lookout. Just think what the view is like from the top. We'll be able to see everything!"

"Ben, from the looks of things, this is as far as we're going. I'm ready to go back now."

"Not yet," he said, so frustrated. "There's got to be a way up there," looking around for a clue to where the trail is.

"Looks like we don't have a choice," she said, so glad to be going back.

"Yeah, I guess you're right... At least we made it this far."

"Ben, look at that! It looks like some steps behind that rock," pointing behind a huge boulder.

"That's it! I knew there had to be something around here. Think you can make it?" he asked, surprised to find the trail to the top is hidden up behind a boulder.

The trail continues on just after getting past a huge boulder. Then it stops abruptly. Right at the end of the trail are small steps that have been chiseled out of the side of the cliff.

"Ben, are you sure you want to do this? It looks a little risky to me," seeing the narrow ledge.

"If we don't check it out, I'll go nuts wondering what's up there. We're almost there, only a few more steps!" wanting so much to continue on.

"OK, let's get this over with," she said, letting out a big sigh, "but I ain't going to do this ever again. This is the one and only trip I'm going to make up here!"

Ben takes the lead, having no fear of heights, slowly making his way up the narrow ledge. The trail is nothing more than a natural ridge on the north side of the cliff leading up to the peak. An easy path, but on the edge of a cliff face with a hundred-foot drop-off, going straight down, and is a nightmare for anyone scared of heights.

"You can do it!" trying to encourage Jenny, seeing how scared she is.

"Let's call it a day and turn back," she frantically said, standing on the small ledge.

"We're almost there," looking back to check on her. "Just a little more... Take small steps. Keep your eyes on your feet and don't keep looking down the cliff. That makes it worse!"

"I can't help it! When I look at my feet, it's hard not to look down there. I hate this! I wish I hadn't come up here. Never again!" getting so mad that he talked her into this.

"You're doing fine... Just a little more," he said, knowing that this is nothing compared to the trails back in Colorado.

Ben keeps his back to the cliff face, taking one step at a time, constantly looking back at Jenny. The last couple of steps are the worst. The ledge is very narrow at the top. He knows it will not be easy, and one slip, it will be fatal. Right at the end, he can see the top of the plateau. The trail comes to an abrupt end, only four feet from the top.

The last part is the worst. Several rectangular holes have been chiseled out of the rock. Whoever chipped these out of the solid rock did a good job and must have spent a long time doing it. Whatever reason these people had, he knows there must be something very important at the top of this plateau to do all that work.

He decides to go for it. The worst part is turning around to face the cliff. The wind is not helping either. He waits several minutes for the wind to die down, then carefully places his foot in the first one, lifting himself up. Then he sees another handhold on top of the plateau filled with water. Reaching up, he quickly grabs it, pulling himself to the top.

At the top of the plateau, he turns around and lies on his stomach to help Jenny. He wedges his hand into the top handhold then reaches down to help her up. She follows his instructions, slowly putting her hands and feet into the handholds. Once she is close enough, he grabs her hand, dragging her up. From the look on her face, he knows she won't be coming back up here ever again.

Standing on the top of their island, they quickly discover there is nothing here. It's only a flat, solid rock plateau about thirty feet wide and fifty feet long. The long trip was basically for nothing.

Ben is so disappointed. "Looks like the remnants of an old lava column from an extinct volcano that eroded away," expecting to see a permanent shelter or at least something man-made up here.

"Well, all that for nothing!" she blurted out, getting mad, knowing it was a waste of time coming up here.

A huge depression is on the east side, filled with rainwater. It's nothing more than a pear-shaped pond, about nine inches deep at the center. It appears to be a favorite drinking place for the seabirds, with all the white droppings surrounding it. Taking off their shoes, they wade through it, so relieved after their long, strenuous walk.

"Look at this! Now I know why they came up here," running his hand over the dark spots at the center of the plateau.

"Ben, it looks like an old campfire," glancing down at the blackened area.

"Oh, it's not just a campfire! Look how big it is. It must have been a signal fire. Can you imagine dragging wood all the way up here? I bet that was a big chore."

"Maybe that's how they used to signal other ships, letting them know they were here. Maybe it's something we should do?" she asked.

"I don't know... That climb is bad enough, but can you imagine hauling wood up here too!" he replied, looking at her so surprised.

She shakes her head. "There's no way I'm going to carry firewood up that trail. Especially that last part!"

"On a rainy day, this would be the last place I'd want to be. With nothing to block the wind or even to hold on to, we could be blown right off."

"Ben, it's already too windy up here now, and it's cold! It's not bad after the walk, but after a while, it'll be just too cold for me. I like the warm beach much better than this," she said, shivering.

Walking around the edge, they look down over their small island. From this one spot, they can see everything. There are some places they have not yet explored, but from up here, they can see it all. Now, he knows there are no signs of anyone else on the island.

"Look, Ben! There are islands over there!" pointing to the west.

Ben, too busy looking down on the island, doesn't even think about looking out on the ocean. "So, we're not alone after all!"

"You think someone is over there?" she asked, surprised to see three small islands just above the horizon.

"Hard to say," he said, holding his hand up over his eyes to block the sun. "I don't see any structures or smoke. Too far away to see anything. They don't look much bigger than the one we're on now. Of all times to forget my binoculars. We could have used them up here."

"Yeah, I wondered why you didn't bring them. You know, there might be people living on those islands. Maybe we can fix up the raft to get over there."

He looks at her in disbelief. "You got to be kidding! Those are miles away, and the raft is history. A small sailboat might do it, but we don't have one. From the looks of things, those islands don't look any different from this one."

"We have to do something. We need to build a raft to get over there."

"Maybe," he said, putting his arm around her. "That's a long way out there. You know anything about boats or sailing?"

"No, I don't! Do you?"

"Nope!" he said, shaking his head. "I don't have a clue. Even if we build a raft and head in that direction, the winds and the currents may take us somewhere else. Look at those whitecaps out there. That wind is blowing hard, and it's not going toward the islands. If we were out there on a raft, we would be blown along with the wind. And also in the wrong direction," pointing over to the south.

"I guess we're stuck until someone finds us here. At least we can light a big fire out on the west side. If anyone is living there, they might be able to see it! Maybe they'll come here and rescue us!"

"That is a good idea! Even better, if we go to the west side at night, I can use my binoculars. We might be able to see if there are any campfires or lights on those islands. So, I guess it wasn't a wasted trip up here then?"

"You got lucky!" she said, putting her arm around his waist. "There's a whole lot of nothing up here. Never again!" still staring at the neighboring islands.

They take a break, eating some oranges and drinking plenty of water. They keep staring at the neighboring islands, hoping to see smoke or at least a boat. Since they arrived on the island, it's the first good news they have had. At least now they know they are not alone.

So high on the island, the breeze is chilly, but the direct sunlight is still overbearing. Jenny takes off her clothes, rinsing them in the water, putting them out in the sun to dry. After the strenuous climb, the water looks so refreshing. Examining the water, she can see it's somewhat clean and sits in it to rinse off.

Jenny walks back, sitting next to Ben. "It's time you washed up too. You'll feel a lot better," she said, seeing how he is so fixated on the neighboring islands.

"Yeah, it's getting a little warm," he replied, knowing when she hinted about him having a wash, he must have been a little stinky after the long hike.

He takes off his clothes, rinsing them in the water, setting them on the warm rock to dry. The last thing he wants to do is wear wet clothes on the walk back. He is so tired from the long walk, but the cold water is invigorating. Lying in the water, he glances over at Jenny. Seeing her beautiful body makes him forget how tired he is, and it's enough to get him aroused again.

Ben walks back over to Jenny, lying down next to her. The warmth of the rock surprises him, especially compared to the cold water. He reaches over, holding her hand. She giggles, seeing he has another erection. She rolls over, lying on top of him, kissing him passionately. Obviously, he is not the only one getting aroused.

She gets up on her hands and knees, slowly running her breasts all over his body. She finally straddles him.

"I hope there's no satellite up there taking pictures," he said, looking up at her. "They'll be getting some great images right now!"

"Hello up there!" waving up at the sky, then leans back, shaking her breasts side to side.

He laughed. "Oh, they'll really like that! We'll probably have all the secret military satellites tracking us now."

"Sure... Like they can really see us."

"Oh yes, they can!" he jokingly said. "Wait till tomorrow, then you'll see... The entire Seventh Fleet might be out on the beach looking for the big booby girl who loves having sex outside! I bet those pictures of you will be all over the Internet!"

She quickly covers herself with her arms, getting a little concerned. "You never know... They can be taking pictures of you too!" realizing he is joking with her.

"Not when I got you around," he said, grabbing her breasts. "They wouldn't even know I exist. You know, it's a shame there is not an easier way to get up here. I love being on top of the world!"

"It's beautiful up here," she said, looking all around, seeing nothing but the blue ocean and small white clouds surrounding them.

"This is way better than the beach," rubbing his hands on her thighs.

She laughed. "Better enjoy it while you can. You're not getting me up here again, even if it is for sex!"

Jenny moves her hips up slightly, placing him inside her. He slowly massages her breasts while she is rhythmically gyrating on top of him. She is getting carried away and extremely loud. For some reason, she is a different person when they have sex, getting so wild.

He lies on his back in awe. Jenny is bouncing up and down, yelling and screaming out loud. She is in control when she is on top, so he just lets her do her thing. All he has to do is massage her breasts, enjoying every minute of it.

Utterly exhausted, she collapses on top of him. He put his arms around her, holding her tight for a long time without saying a word. They lie quietly together on top of their small island, basking in the sun.

* * *

In the middle of the day, the sun is too intense. The top of the island has one major flaw. There is no shade at all, and they both feel the fierce heat. They know they can't be out in the open much longer without getting sunburned. The top of the peak absorbs the heat from the sun, making it difficult to lie down on it for too long. Feeling the heat, they both walk over to the little pond. Sitting in the water, they playfully wash each other to help cool off.

"I'm sorry," she said, suddenly getting up, "but it's time for us to get back," placing all their clothes in the small bag.

"And what are we going to wear?" he asked, seeing her putting all their clothes away.

"They're all clean and somewhat dry, so I'll save them for tomorrow," holding up the bag.

"You mean we're walking all the way back with nothing on but our shoes!"

She laughed. "Yes, that's all we'll need. We'll be in the shade for most of the trip. It's really humid once we're in the trees, so walking back without anything on will be better for us, anyway."

He looks at her, a little confused. "Yeah, but going down the rocky trail. It might be a little harsh on the bare skin, don't you think?"

"It's not that bad! We already know where we're going. So, there aren't going to be any more surprises. We only need our shoes, anyway. Besides, it'll be nice to walk down the trail naked for a change," swinging her breasts about teasing him.

"OK," letting her have her way. "We'll save our clothes for tomorrow," seeing she was very adamant, not wanting to get their clothes dirty again.

He doesn't mind walking around naked on the beach, but climbing down off this rock and through the jungle is another matter. He knows she is getting to the point where she doesn't like to wear anything for most of the day. What makes matters worse, when she doesn't wear clothes, she won't let him wear anything either. Jenny is slowly taking charge of everything.

Getting off the plateau and back onto the small ledge is the worst part of the entire trip. Climbing down, Ben holds on for dear life, hoping to get his foot in the first foothold. He can't see a thing, wishing he had paid more attention to where they were. Lying down on his stomach, he slowly lowers his body until his foot finally slips into the first cutout.

Ben is so relieved to get back on the ledge. Jenny quickly hands him the bag, then carefully turns to lie down on her stomach. She slowly scoots down the edge of the cliff while he guides her feet into the cutouts. Standing right underneath her, Ben knows right then they should have worn their clothes. Not only is she getting scratched up by the rocks, but she is also in pain lying down on the hot rocks too.

After a long struggle, they both finally make it back onto the small ledge. Getting back on the trail is just the start. Ben leads the way, knowing it's going to be worse going down the narrow ledge than it was going up. On top of the peak, the view was great, but it was not worth it.

"I'm never coming up here again!" she cried out, so scared. "There is nothing up here anyway!" trying to keep her footing on the small ledge.

"Well, we needed to find out what's up here. At least we now know we have some other islands nearby."

"I don't care!" she blurted out. "I just want off this rock and back on the beach where we belong! You're never ever going to talk me into doing anything like this again!"

"Just get down on your hands and knees. Start crawling backwards. That usually helps," he added, knowing that Jenny is so scared to continue on.

"Never again!" she shouts, turning around, kneeling on the narrow ledge.

"It'll be OK... We're almost there now. We just got a little ways to go," trying to calm her down.

Ben knows she is terrified but can't help seeing the funny side of it. He tries to comfort her, slowly making their way down the cliff face. Trying to crawl down this ledge is bad enough, but doing it naked is another matter. She constantly yells out, complaining. For some reason, she is more scared of going down than climbing to the top.

* * *

"Well, that's the last time I'm going up there!" Jenny said, finally reaching the dirt trail.

"It wasn't that bad. Wait until I take you on some of the trails back in Colorado. Some of those have fifteen hundred feet drop-offs."

"I don't think so," she promptly replied. "I prefer the beach... You're not going back up there either. It's just too dangerous!" leaning over, rubbing her bruised knees after crawling on the ledge.

He can't help laughing, seeing this new side of her. "Well, you made it up there and back! I'm so proud of you. Most people would have given up halfway there. At least we discovered this new trail around the peak, and not to mention the other islands."

She sits down to rest. "Never again!" she shouted out, and she meant it.

"I'm sorry," he said, sitting down next to her. "I didn't tell you, but the trip down is always worse than going up. You're right, though...

There's no need to go back up there again. Unless you like having sex on top of a pedestal for the whole world to see!"

"That was good, wasn't it?" she asked, winking at him.

He let out a long sigh. "I've never done anything like that before. Talk about some wild sex! What's come over you? You've changed a lot since we've been here."

"Well, this place kind of brings out the salaciousness in a person," she explained, her face turning red, getting embarrassed. "I have never been like this before. I don't know what it is, but I just get so damn horny for some reason and I just can't help it."

He laughed. "I'm the same way. With you prancing around naked all the time, it doesn't help me either," reaching over, cupping her left breast in his hand.

"You don't need to tell me!" seeing he is getting aroused again. "You got it far worse than I do. I've never seen anyone get an erection so fast and as often as you do!"

"I'm not as bad as you," he jokingly said, massaging her breasts.

"That's enough for you!" she promptly said, standing up, seeing Ben getting a little carried away, constantly fondling her breasts. "Come on, let's get back to the beach. You can lead the way!" pointing down the trail through the trees.

"OK, let's get going then," he said, slowly getting up, reluctantly walking down the trail.

Ben keeps turning around, admiring Jenny's fantastic body. Seeing her breasts swinging about as she walks is driving him crazy. He doesn't like missing the view with her walking behind him. He knows he is being punished for taking her up there.

"Ben, you just turn around and keep on going. It's my turn to walk in the back. Now, I can look at that cute little butt of yours!" seeing how he is constantly turning around to gawk at her body.

"You talk about me staring. You're just as bad!" he said, wiggling his hips side to side.

Seeing him walking about naked is driving her crazy, especially now that he has a bronze tan and is getting very muscular. "We girls like to look as well. You just keep on shaking it!"

Walking through the trees, Ben looks back to see she is still staring at his butt with a big smirk on her face. He is getting a little frustrated. He always walked behind her whenever they were on the trails because she walked slower than he did. Things are changing. She is a lot more confident now. Climbing to the top of the island was a major achievement for both of them.

Jenny realizes how much she loves it here. She thinks it's so sensual to have sex anytime and anywhere she wants. The island is a paradise with tall palm trees, beautiful beaches, and warm crystal clear water. She finds it so romantic. It's more like being on their honeymoon and not stranded on this small island in the middle of nowhere.

* * *

Once they reach the camp, Ben drops the bag of oranges and the clothes. He is so tired after their long day out. All he can think about is getting into the ocean to cool off.

"Come on, Jenny... Let's go for a swim!" running back out on the beach.

"Wait for me!" chasing after him, still full of energy.

The sun is getting close to the horizon. The chilly breeze from the ocean makes this the best part of the day. Even the water is unusually calm, with small, gentle waves breaking on the beach. Although this day was an unusual one, it was one of their best. They also never spent the entire day running around naked. This day was a first in many ways.

"Ben, we need to have something special to eat tonight."

"What do you suggest?" he asked.

"How about lobster? You think you can catch one?"

"Are you serious? That might take a while. I caught a few so far, and I was lucky to get them."

"It'll give you an excuse to use your snorkeling gear," she said with a big smile on her face. "It'll be a nice way to finish off the day with a big lobster dinner!"

"That does sound nice... OK, I'll see if I can round up one. It might be a while, though," running back to the camp to get his things.

Hunting for lobsters is extremely frustrating. They are always hiding among the coral or lava rocks at the bottom. He floats on top of the water, waiting for one to make the wrong move. With the crystal clear water, he can see over twenty feet down. The lobsters don't have a chance once they are out in the open.

He finally sees two lobsters hiding in a small crevasse in the coral. Taking a deep breath, he dives into the water hovering just above the sand. Once close enough, he jabs one with his spear. The spear just nicks the end of the tail, and it's fighting like mad to get away. He drops the casting net over it, and it quickly tangles itself up in the net, trying to escape. That's all it takes to catch a lobster. He is so amazed at how easy it is, but that's when he is lucky to see one.

Ben swims to the shore, so thrilled with his catch. Looking around, he is so surprised to see how far down the beach he drifted. He runs back, finding Jenny sprawled out on the sand, sunning herself.

"Guess what we got for supper!" holding up the net with the lobster still thrashing around.

She gasped out loud. "I can't believe you caught one so quick!"

"I got lucky... I saw a couple out there. Look at the size of this thing! It's the biggest one so far."

She stands up, brushing off the sand. "My God! That's a huge one! We're going to be eating good tonight. I have an idea! Why don't we have a cookout on the beach tonight?"

"Like a beach party! Sounds good to me. We'll build a fire down here by the water and have a big luau!"

Cooking a simple meal is always a lot of hard work. They both grab bundles of firewood, carrying it all down to the edge of the beach. For cooking lobster, all that's needed is water to boil it in. Unfortunately, they are almost out, so it means another trip down to the pond.

* * *

The roaring campfire is ready for their first big lobster feast down on the beach. The sun is just over the horizon. With just a few clouds in the sky, it's going to be one glorious sunset, a perfect setting for their big feast.

"So what do we do now?" he asked, placing the cooking pot over the fire. "This is going to take a while."

"We can sit on the beach and watch the sunset. Once it starts to boil, all we have to do is toss him in! There is not much we can do until then," trying not to giggle, seeing he has another erection again.

He notices how she is staring at him with a big smirk on her face. "So, maybe we should have a little fun before we eat?" hoping Jenny is up for a little more sex out on the beach.

"What is it with you?" seeing how he is extremely excited again. "After hauling all that water down the beach, I thought that would be the last thing you'd be wanting. Are you sure you're up to the job?" giving him a big hug.

"You bet I am!" he boasted, wiggling his erection in front of her.

"You have to catch me first!" she yelled out, running down the beach laughing.

Ben can't believe his luck but doesn't expect to have to chase after her. He is so exhausted but tries to run as fast as he can. Seeing her cute little body running naked down the beach is enough to keep him going. He knows she can't keep up this pace much longer, seeing how she holds on to her breasts. Having big breasts and not wearing a bra, running about naked is one thing she just can't do.

Jenny runs as fast as she can. She knows he is tired but is going to make him run for it. She makes the mistake of running into the water, slowing her down, so Ben easily catches up with her. He puts her over his shoulder, carrying her back to the roaring campfire. She is laughing hysterically, kicking her legs, trying to get away. He holds on tight, occasionally smacking her butt hard. The last thing he wants is for her to escape, having to chase after her again.

Reaching the campfire, Ben carefully puts her down on the sand, lying down next to her. He is wondering how they are going to do this again. He is so exhausted from the long day, not to mention the trip carrying all that water from the pond.

Jenny gets up, straddling him. "OK, I'm ready! Just one more time before we eat!"

"My God! What has come over you?" he asked, a little astonished by the way she was acting.

"Me? What about you? I can't believe you're still horny after running all the way down the beach!"

"Hey, it's not my fault!" he explained. "You've been prancing around, taunting me all day long. Ain't no red-blooded man can go more than a minute without getting excited with you around!"

She laughed. "Actually, I'm just making you work for your supper," leaning over kissing him passionately.

* * *

After another wild sex session on the beach, Ben is ready to collapse. He does not know what is going on with Jenny. He is used to subtle little hints when she wants to have sex. Now, she jumps him every time she gets in the mood, which is getting more frequent during the day.

"Wow!" she shouted, quickly getting up. "That was great! You go wash up, and I'll prepare the lobster," trying to brush the sand off her legs.

"Yeah, that was the best!" Ben replied, ready for a nap.

"Just can't get away from this damn sand. That's why I don't like wearing clothes anymore!" Jenny explained, walking into the water. "With no clothes on, all we have to do is rinse off in the water. It makes life so simple!" splashing the water over her body.

"So that's your reason!" he jokingly said. "I thought you were just tormenting me with that beautiful body of yours!" watching Jenny rinsing off.

"I wouldn't talk!" she said, glancing over at him, still sitting on the beach. "You've been doing a good job at it as well. I don't know if you noticed it, but you've really buffed up since we've been here. You got a nice, well-tanned body as well. You are all muscle now!"

"I might have lost a little weight, but I look about the same," looking down at his abdomen.

"Like hell you do! Ben, were lily white and way out of shape. I know you sure didn't have a six-pack either! You may not see it, but I sure as hell do! You're like one of those Greek Adonises now," giving him a sheepish smile.

"Well, you ain't doing so bad yourself!" he said, somewhat surprised she said that. "To be honest, you're looking more like one of those Playboy Playmates with that perfect tight little body of yours!"

She smiles at him. "You think so? I thought I was a little on the thin side," looking at her abdomen.

"No! You look great! Especially that nice butt of yours!"

"You get cleaned up," getting a little self-conscious, "and tend to the fire while I get everything ready. Let me know when the water boils. We're going to have one hell of a feast tonight!" running back to the camp.

"OK!" lying down in the water, so the small waves wash over him.

Ben amorously watches her as Jenny runs off, shaking his head in disbelief. He knows it doesn't get any better than this. He has never met anyone like Jenny before and feels as if he has known her all his life. Being alone on this beautiful island with her is like a dream come true.

* * *

They sit next to the campfire, eating their big lobster dinner. With an enormous roaring fire out on the beach, it's more like a big Hawaiian luau. Ben gets out the old radio to listen to the music and ends the night dancing around the campfire. By far, this has been the best day since they arrived on the island.

For Ben, this is by far the best day he has ever had in his entire life. No more sitting in a cubicle all day long staring at a computer monitor and working on some worthless program, trying to get it to work. He doesn't miss his old life at all. Living on the island is more like one big camping trip than being stranded. The abundance of fresh food and water makes life easy. He knows this is the only way to live, but mostly, being able to share it with Jenny.

Jenny also loves her new life on the island, quickly adapting to the outdoor lifestyle. Before, she would always think about the day they would be rescued and return to civilization. Now, she knows it will be difficult to leave this beautiful island. Just living a simple life and enjoying her time on the beach with Ben means more than anything to her now.

* * *

Chapter 24

Surprise

Jenny and Ben live day to day without a care in the world on this island paradise, and they can't complain about anything. The weather is always perfect, and they have an unlimited supply of fresh food. Since arriving on the island, they had been in good health until one morning.

While on one of their early morning walks scavenging the beach, Jenny starts feeling ill. "I'm sorry," she mumbled, feeling weak. "I need to go back."

Ben is startled, seeing how pale she is. "What's wrong? You all right?" he asked, getting concerned.

She leans up against him. "I'm not feeling too good... A little weak," then lost consciousness, collapsing into his arms.

Ben, in an absolute panic, gently puts her down on the sand. "Jenny! Jenny, what's wrong!" tapping her face with his hand, trying to revive her.

She is only unconscious for a few seconds, then opens her eyes, seeing Ben hovering over her. The look on his face said it all. He is terrified. She has never seen him like this before.

"Ben, don't panic... I'm OK. Can you take me back? I'm so tired. I just need to lie down for a while."

He quickly picks her up. "OK, I'll get you back," carrying her to the camp.

After a few minutes, Jenny motions for him to let her down. Feeling so nauseous, she slumps to the ground and starts vomiting. Ben tries to help, but she pushes him away. He is so frightened, and does not know what to do. Neither one of them has ever been sick since arriving on the island. Seeing Jenny is in trouble, now he wants so much to get her off the island and back home.

Ben tries to think about what could make her sick. One thing they are always concerned about is spoiled food. They always cooked everything thoroughly and even boiled the water before drinking it. Anything questionable is always tossed out.

"I'm OK... Don't worry. Can you help me get down to the water so I can rinse off?" she said, seeing how Ben is pacing back and forth in a panic.

"Is there anything I can do?" he asked, taking her arm to help her up.

"No, it's just an upset stomach. I feel all hot for some reason. Maybe the water will cool me off a little."

"You think it was something we ate yesterday?" he asked, helping her walk down to the shoreline.

"You ate the same thing I did. How do you feel?"

"I feel fine... Maybe we better make sure we fully cook things from here on out. I'll check the pots and pans to see if they're OK. Maybe we didn't clean them thoroughly. It could be that cast-iron pot we boil water in."

"Ben, that would be the last place to have any mold or germs. We keep that in the fire all the time. That pot gets so hot there isn't anything that's going to live long on that thing. Maybe we'll let the water boil a little longer before we drink it."

Jenny kneels in the shallow water, splashing water on her face, unable to get up on her own. He finally carries her back to camp after letting her rest. He hopes it was just an upset stomach. Things are going to change. He knows they need to be more careful and make sure it's not food poisoning or bad water.

* * *

At the camp, Ben puts her inside the tent, giving her some water to drink. He goes through the medical kit to see what they can use. Luckily, they never had any need for medicine. The kit is still full and untouched.

"I have a few things from the medical kit," he said, handing her some pills. "I got what looks like Tums, which might help settle your stomach. Also, we have some ibuprofen that may help as well."

She slowly sits up. "I could use some ibuprofen."

"Here, we have plenty of those," he replied, handing her one. "I'm going to check out all the cooking things and give them a good cleaning. We'll have a day off and take it easy so you can rest up. I'm also going to check the medical kit. It has a lot of stuff in it that we never use. Maybe now we need to pay more attention to what's in it."

"We need to get that little medical book out and start reading it. If we do have an emergency, we'll be better prepared. If one of us gets hurt, we both need to know what to do."

"Good idea! I'll get right on it. You rest up. I'll get started with the cleanup first."

While Jenny is asleep, Ben goes through all the plates and cooking utensils, checking for something they might have missed. He inspects the old iron pot, making sure it's as clean as a whistle. He promptly starts a fire and runs down to the pond to get a full pot of water to boil. Everything needs to be boiled for hours to ensure this will not happen again.

He goes through the medical kit. The canister is full of everything that one can use in an emergency. He finds the medical booklet, looking for some answers. The booklet has so many symptoms and remedies for an upset stomach. He was worried before, but after reading the medical book, it's a miracle that they have gone this long without any problems. He learned that their best bet to ward off any illness is to take vitamins every day, and there are enough to last for six months.

* * *

After several hours, Jenny finally wakes up feeling much better, insisting on getting up. She is now hungry, wanting something to eat. At last, she is herself once again, cleaning up the camp as if nothing had happened.

"Has there been anything else bothering you?" he asked.

The question obviously annoyed her. "You know, we have no secrets... I know that I can talk to you about just about anything, but sharing my aches and pains is another matter. Besides, you're too squeamish to hear the details."

"Jenny, don't keep me in the dark. Maybe you should be telling me," he said, realizing she had been keeping things from him.

After Ben's persistence, she finally caves in. "OK... I had some headaches, and my stomach has been bothering me lately. Also, my breasts are a little sensitive, if you must know!"

"I think I might be the cause of that last one," glancing down at her breasts.

She laughed, knowing his enthusiasm for them. "I'm thinking it's because I'm not wearing a bra anymore. I have never gone this long without wearing one. Maybe not having any support after all this time, I'm now paying the price," cupping her breasts in her hands while she examines them.

He laughed. "They do look a little different. It looks like they're getting bigger."

"Yep, I think it's time to put these babies away," she jokingly said, with him staring at her breasts longingly. "I'm going to have to start wearing my bra again!"

Ben's mouth drops wide open, hearing how she is thinking about covering up those beautiful breasts. "Awe, you're not, are you? It'll be like taking candy away from a baby!"

"Sorry, playtime is over... Besides, if I don't, they'll get a little droopy. I might start wearing it on our walks up to the cave and back. That's when I need it the most, anyway. Where is my bra? I haven't seen it in a long time."

"I think we put it in the cave, or did I accidentally drop it in the fire last week?" he jokingly asked, wishing he had.

She glares at him. "You better not have. I'm going to be needing it now."

* * *

Ben watches her closely in the following days. She is doing OK, so the incident is quickly forgotten. They go back to their normal daily activities just as before. Although he noticed she had lost interest in sex and had been talking about cutting back on the amount of sex, anyway. After she was sick, she was definitely not in the mood.

Everything is back to normal until a few days later, when Jenny returns from her morning bath. She walks back into the camp, finding Ben still sound asleep.

"Come on, sleepyhead… Time to get up!" giving him a big kiss.

"Are you OK?" he asked, noticing the slight smell on her breath. "You've been sick again, haven't you?"

She quickly turns away. "It's nothing," walking over to the campfire, not wanting to talk about it.

"Jenny!" he called out, getting concerned.

She sits down by the campfire, staring at the ground. "It's been happening since that first day I got sick on the beach," putting her hands over her face, then started crying.

He looks at her so stunned, not knowing what to say. He puts his arm around her, trying to comfort her, but she just keeps crying, not saying a word.

"Are you feeling OK now?" he finally asked.

"It's just an upset stomach," she explained. "I don't know why, but I just don't feel good. I'm always tired and have no energy at all. Maybe it's something I'm eating that's not agreeing with me."

"It could be the fish. We need to keep track of what we're eating. Also, you need to take it easy for a while. I'll start making the run for the fruit and water on my own."

"That might help. I just don't understand. We always eat the same thing. Why aren't you having any problems?"

"Maybe you're getting tired of seafood. We'll put you on a solid fruit diet for a while. I'll keep track of what we eat from now on."

"That's a good idea... It's probably time for a change in what we eat."

They stay at the camp all day, taking it easy. Ben closely watches her, never letting her out of his sight. He doesn't like finding out that she had been keeping all this from him. He makes it clear that she needs to let him know if she is having any more problems.

Jenny's bout with stomach problems ends as quickly as it began. Since Ben never had any issues, they concluded it was just one of those things. That taught them to be more careful. They cook their food more thoroughly, making sure all the cooking utensils are boiled in water. With no soap, it's the only way to clean everything thoroughly. With the constant humidity, mold and bacteria are constant problems. They find the best way to sterilize all the cooking utensils is to toss them all into the fire. Once it glows red, no germs or mold will survive that.

* * *

The days turn into weeks, then months. Life on the island is good, with no major problems. They have perfected the daily chores, making life easy. With all the work and walking, Ben loses all his body fat and is extremely muscular, to Jenny's delight. She has also lost weight as well with a firm and slender figure.

The changes in their bodies are gradual, but they live a healthy, active life. They notice it the most when they wear their regular clothes, finding how loose and ill-fitting they are.

Jenny's bra is a big mystery. Since all of her clothes are now too big, her bra is too small. For some reason, her breasts have increased a few cup sizes, but she assumes that her bra just shrank after being in salt water for so long.

* * *

One day, lying out on the beach, Ben notices a slight change in her appearance. He looks again to make sure. They both have lost weight, but now she seems a little different.

"I think you've been eating too many coconuts and lobsters," he jokingly said, patting his hand on her stomach.

She is a little surprised at his comment, smacking the back of his head. "Ben, that's not the kind of thing a woman wants to hear!"

"I'm sorry," he mumbled, realizing his mistake. "I didn't mean it," seeing the mean look he was getting.

"Well, I have been eating a lot lately," looking down at her torso at the small but just noticeable bulge. "It's kind of funny how we've both been losing weight and now I'm putting it back on. What about you?" looking over at his stomach.

"I'm not!" he boasted, looking down at his abdomen, smacking it with his hand. "Check it out! I got me a six-pack down here now. I haven't had anything like this since high school. We're eating healthy food, probably burning more calories than we're taking in. We shouldn't be gaining any weight," glancing over at her stomach again.

He doesn't say anything, but thinks it's a little odd. It's hard not to notice when Jenny is lying on the beach with no clothes on. She does have a bulge down there, and he regrets joking about it.

Jenny has been quiet for a while and just stares down at her stomach, running her hand over it. She suddenly gasps, holding her hand up over her mouth. Her eyes are wide open as she turns to Ben, speechless.

"What is it? What's wrong?" he quickly asked, seeing the shocked look on her face.

"Ben! I can't believe it!" she shouted.

"What? You're not sick again, are you?" he asked, getting worried.

"Oh no," she said with a big smile. "I'm OK, so don't worry," putting her hand on Ben's shoulder.

"So, are you going to let me in on your little secret?" he asked, getting concerned, wondering what was going on.

She giggles. "I can't believe it! I think I just figured it all out, but I haven't told you, but I was late!"

"Late for what?" he asked, still confused.

She puts her arm around him, looking into his eyes. "Ben, I think you're going to be a daddy!"

"That's not funny!" he promptly said.

"No, I'm serious! It all makes sense now. I can't believe I didn't realize it earlier!"

"Jenny, you got to be kidding!" he said, in absolute shock. "Do you realize what you are saying?"

She laughed. "Yes!" giving Ben a big hug and kiss.

"Wait a minute! How do you know for sure?" looking down at her stomach.

"We'll definitely know for sure in the next few months!" she answered, running her hand over her belly, extremely thrilled with the notion that she might be pregnant.

* * *

With the prospect of Jenny being pregnant, Ben takes up all the heavy chores, just in case. They are not too sure about it but can do nothing more than wait and see what happens. They continue their daily walks up to the cave. Jenny always waits in the cave, with a small fire to keep warm, while Ben gathers firewood on the far side of the island.

Ben loves the island life, but now he regularly thinks about getting back home. He always keeps an eye out for any ships or planes, scanning the horizon with his binoculars. A huge stack of wood is out on the beach, ready to be lit if something comes by.

Seeing no ships always bothers him. By now, they should have seen something, even if it's miles away. Now, he feels the pressure. They have only nine months to be rescued. If Jenny is pregnant, he dreads having to go through all that alone on this island.

* * *

Chapter 25

Typhoon

T he consistent, calm weather is now a thing of the past. The weather pattern has changed. It has been nothing but overcast skies for days on end. Even the temperature is dropping, and it feels cold and damp, especially at night. They had already experienced a few tropical storms, which generally last less than a day. The storms are more of a nuisance with the torrential rain, causing them to wait it out in the tent or up at the cave.

The only good thing about the storms is the abundance of rainwater that runs down off the island. The waterfalls at the two ponds go from trickles to a massive flow of water. With all the rain, the waterfalls are so big that it's impossible to stand underneath without being knocked over. Luckily, the rain flushes out the ponds, leaving nothing but clean drinking water.

* * *

The next day, Ben is on the beach using the casting net, trying to catch a few more fish. With every break in the rain, he is out trying to catch as much as possible. They are down to just a couple of fish left in the tidal pool. If the storms don't let up, they will be eating fruit for days.

As Ben wades out into the surf, it's obvious they are in for another storm. Standing knee-deep in the water, he has knocked over several times by the enormous waves. The waves are breaking right up on the beach, and it's not even high tide for several more hours. After a while, he realizes it's a little too rough to be out fishing. He gives up sitting down by the trees, watching the massive waves crash down on the small beach.

He learned long ago to watch the weather for any drastic changes. This storm is entirely different. The wind has a chill to it. Severe turbulence is building up, and there is a definite darkening in the cloud base. The one thing he notices that is very odd is that the clouds are moving extremely fast, unlike anything he has seen before.

* * *

After an hour, the sky to the south is pitch black. A lot of rain is falling on the east side of the island. The wind is picking up dramatically, and the ocean is nothing but whitecaps. The waves are enormous, pushing the water way up on the beach. After seeing all the warning signs, he knows it's time to move to the cave.

"Did you get any good ones?" Jenny asked, wondering why he was back so soon.

"Nope, not a thing," Ben replied. "It's way too rough out there. We also lost the ones in the tidal pool. We're down to eating fruit for a while."

"How did that happen? I was hoping we could stock it up a little for the rainy days."

"The water is so far up on the beach, the fish in the tidal pool got washed away," he explained. "Looks like a big storm is brewing up. I think we should head up to the cave before it starts raining again."

"I don't know," she said, still trying to clean up the camp. "It's not that bad. The cool breeze feels great. We can wait it out in the tent until it blows over."

"I don't think so," he said, shaking his head. "You need to look out there and see what's coming. This one looks more than just a little rain. You should see the size of the waves, too!"

"Is it going to be bad?" she asked, looking up at him a little concerned.

"You need to see it for yourself," holding his hand out, motioning her to follow.

"My God!" she gasped out loud, walking out on the beach. "I don't like the looks of that!" seeing the dark black clouds and the massive waves.

"So, what do you think? Ready to move to the cave?"

She doesn't have time to answer as a massive wave crashes down on the beach. The water rushes up to where they are standing and has never been this close to the trees. They know right then that they have to leave and fast.

"We need to pack up everything and move out now," he said, seeing the water rushing over his feet, knowing it'll soon be up to the tree line.

"Ben, we don't have time! Just leave everything here! We need to go now!" she yells, panicking.

"Oh, no! These waves might run over the beach and into the camp. We can't afford to lose anything. It won't take long to pack."

They quickly return to their campsite to find leaves and branches are already blowing off the trees. Ben dismantles the tent while Jenny stores everything in the duffel bag. After a few minutes, they had gathered up all of their possessions. They have only the essentials here at the campsite, with the rest already stored away in the cave. They store all the heavy items far back among the trees, so it doesn't get washed away.

As they walk back out to the beach, they know it's going to be a severe storm. The ground shutters as the enormous waves break right up on the beach. In the short time while they were packing everything away, the waves are now rushing past the tree line and into the campsite.

They quickly make their way down to the pond, keeping as far from the beach as possible. Reaching the small pond, they see a flowing river instead of the dry creek bed. All the fresh rainwater is wasting away, flowing out to the ocean. They have no time to stop for a break, heading directly for the trail.

Ben struggles to keep his footing on the slippery, muddy trail. Jenny follows close behind, trying to keep up. As they make their way up the trail, the wind is getting worse. Lightning strikes nearby, followed by a horrific boom. They realize it's just too dangerous to be out in the open, especially now with the lightning, and pick up the pace, going as fast as possible.

* * *

Finally reaching the lookout, Jenny runs over, picking a few oranges and grapefruit. Ben walks over to the edge of the cliff. He is so shocked to see how dark and low the clouds are. Looking down at the ocean, dark bands of rain are racing towards the island. He rushes over to Jenny, opens the duffel bag, and fills it with oranges and grapefruit. Seeing the bands of rain coming up right behind them, it's a mad race for the cave.

Just as they reach the cave, the torrential rain finally catches up with them. The wind is howling, and the leaves and branches are flying by the entrance. After a few minutes, they have the fire lit, settling in for the night. The small fire illuminates the cave and provides some warmth.

There is not much room in the cave since it's already filled with all their supplies and firewood. Jenny quickly gets everything organized to give them a little more room. With not much else to do, they sit next to the fire, wondering how long the storm will last.

Ben remembers the radio being stored away somewhere in the cave. They have not used it lately, not wanting to hear all the bad news in the world. He finds it tucked away in the back. After swapping the batteries from the flashlight, he turns the dial to find a station to hear news about the storm. After a few minutes, they find out that it's a typhoon named Lisa, and it's a big one.

"Well, that explains all the clouds and the rain we've been having," Ben said.

"I was wondering what was going on. It's a good thing we moved when we did!"

"From the looks of the wind, it's probably south of the island. That's good news for us!" he said, standing at the entrance, looking in the direction the wind is coming.

"They said it's moving northwest. Is it going to hit us?"

"No, that means we're on the edge, and it's going to miss us."

"If this is the edge of the storm, I can't imagine what it's like near the eye. So, what are we going to do?"

He shrugs his shoulders. "Not much... All we can do is wait it out."

"Do you think the cave will take all this wind and rain?" she asked, looking around for any leaks in the ceiling.

"This cave has been here for thousands of years. Besides, the people who lived here probably used it during the storms as well. The ground is always dry, so I don't think any rain has seeped through it. You can even see some places where they chipped away at some of the rock to make it bigger. Luckily for us, they did. We are even luckier that it's here in the first place. Otherwise, we'd be out there in this mess, hiding behind a rock."

"You know... We need to look around for other caves. It would be nice to have a few more of these, especially on the north side."

"I never thought about that. If there's one, there should be more. We'll have to put that on the list of things to do."

"We only have enough food to last a couple of days. Since we lost the fish in the tidal pool, our meals will be oranges, coconuts, and banana fruit salad. I can mix up the meals so we can have a variety, but it's still nothing but fruit."

Ben sighed. "We might have to make a run for the fruit trees if the storm doesn't let up. At least it's not too far away. It's a shame we lost the fish."

"Well, next time we see a storm coming, we need to put some in the net to make sure they don't get washed away."

"I know," Ben reluctantly said, not believing he hadn't thought of that before. "We'll also put that on our list too."

* * *

Jenny is on her favorite cushion next to the fire. She pulls up her blouse, rubbing her lower abdomen, and is indeed very pregnant. On their own, with no doctors or any help, it will be a terrifying ordeal if the baby is born while on the island.

More effort is being made to search for help. Before, they wouldn't even bother looking for ships or airplanes, but now it's something they have to do all the time.

"I guess we weren't thinking of the consequences when we got here," he said, seeing her running her hands over her stomach.

She let out a long sigh. "I guess we got careless on that first few days."

"I think we were careless for the first couple of months!" he quickly replied.

She giggled. "Yes, we were a little on the wild side back then. You know. I never thought we would be out here this long. Now, we have to deal with it. I always thought someone would have found us by now!"

"It shouldn't be much longer," he said, lying down next to her and running his hand over her abdomen. "Maybe this storm will bring someone by to check the islands."

"So, are you going to marry me? Do the right thing?" she finally asked, winking at Ben.

He loved her with all his heart, and getting married was on his mind. "I thought we were married as soon as we got here!"

She laughed. "Oh no, you don't! I want a proper ceremony. We're going to have a big church wedding too!" wrapping her arms tightly around him, kissing him passionately.

"Hey, wait a minute!" he said, pulling away from her. "Isn't this how we got into trouble?"

"You just need to learn a little self-control," she jokingly said. "So, are you going to marry me?" still smiling at Ben.

"I guess so," he mumbled, a little hesitant. "But I thought I was supposed to be proposing to you," reaching over, taking Jenny's hand.

"I'm not waiting until our baby is born for you to ask. If we're going to get married, we need to do it soon," glancing down at her stomach.

He gets down on his knee, holding her hand. "Jenny Mason, would you marry me and be my companion for life?" feeling so awkward and nervous.

She tries to hold back the tears. "Yes! I'll marry you and spend the rest of my life with you. Provide you with a loving family. I always wanted children. I'm so happy! Oh, I love you so much!"

"I love you too," he whispered, leaning over to kiss her.

"So what do we do next?" she asked, wiping the tears from her face.

"I guess we need to start making plans. Hopefully, we'll be off the island by the time the baby is born. We can safely tell our families that we were married well before the little one arrived!"

The big debate is trying to figure out how far along she is. Neither of them has any clue how long they have been on the island. Ben stopped wearing his watch long ago, using the sun's position in the sky to figure out the approximate time of the day. He thinks it's time to start wearing it again, rummaging through the containers looking for his watch. Once he finds it, he is so glad to see it's still working but surprised to see the date.

"My God!" he shouted. "You're not going to believe this! How long do you think we've been out here?"

"Hard to say... It must be at least a month or two."

"You are not even close... Check it out," he said, handing Jenny the watch.

"That's over four months!" she said, so shocked, seeing how much time had passed.

"I guess what they say is true. Time flies when you're having fun. Maybe you should start wearing this."

"Why are you giving it to me?" she asked.

"I don't know... I guess we're going to have to keep track of the days and months now. Have you any idea how far along you are?"

"I don't have a clue... If we've been here for four months, then I'm probably two or three months at the most!"

"That gives us at least six months for someone to find us here."

"You know, it just doesn't make any sense... It's been four months, and we have not seen a single boat or plane."

He let out a long sigh. "Yeah, it's weird, isn't it? We haven't seen a thing since we got here. Not even the high-altitude jets, and you can see those from hundreds of miles away!"

"From what we hear on the radio, nothing serious has happened. It's not like there's been a big war or something. Since we've been out here, it's like the world has come to an end. Maybe we are all that's left."

"I know," he said, shaking his head. "I wonder where we are? What island is this? We can't be far from Kwajalein, although this would be a great tourist spot. You would think there would be no end of sailboats going all around these islands."

"Let's not worry about it anymore. Someone will be here someday. Let's just make the best of it."

Ben, getting frustrated, unrolls his sleeping pad lying down next to her. "Well, we got about six months to worry about it," running his hand over her belly.

The howling wind and the torrential rain are nonstop all night long. Jenny has no problem sleeping through a typhoon. Once she is in the sleeping bag, she can sleep through anything, but Ben can't sleep at all. With all the wind and rain, it's a lot colder than usual. He tends the fire all night long, giving him something to do.

* * *

Hearing the hourly chime from his old watch marks the beginning of another day. The morning finally arrives, but the winds and rain never let up. Still unable to sleep, Ben watches as all the leaves and branches fly by the cave entrance. He is so glad that he packed everything away at the camp. They could have lost it all, blown all over the island or washed away, probably lost forever.

Ben tends the fire, getting it ready for breakfast. The stash of bananas will come in handy that he put in the cave days earlier. He really misses his morning coffee. Now, he has to settle for fried bananas with orange juice for breakfast.

Jenny finally wakes up, smelling the aroma of cooked bananas. "Good morning, my new husband and father-to-be. I see you're up really early."

"Good morning," he said with a big smile. "You must have been exhausted. It's been a while since you slept in this late."

"It's ten in the morning!" she said, glancing at her watch. "It's so late! I always get up at sunrise every day."

"Not today... You might as well sleep in. There's not much else to do, anyway. We'll just have a lazy day until this weather blows over."

"It's so cold up here," she complained, sitting up still wrapped up in the sleeping bag. "Without that campfire, I think I'd freeze up here at night! Good thing we brought the sleeping bag."

"That sleeping bag is the only thing we have to keep warm," he said, handing her a plate of cooked bananas. "We need to make sure it doesn't get wet. The fire does a good job of keeping the cave warm, but all the heat is going right out the door with this wind. We're going to have to make some changes. Maybe move the fire back a little or block up the entrance with something. Although it's not too bad for our first typhoon."

"I know... I guess we can't complain. If we had waited any longer, we would have been caught in all this mess. We need to start using the radio more often, at least to check the weather."

"Well, we learn from our mistakes," he explained, sitting down next to her with his breakfast. "Being stuck in this cave is going to give us time to think about what we need to do for the next one."

"I already know what I'm going to do. I'm grabbing all the fish out of the tidal pool and dragging them up here. We're going to get tired of eating bananas and oranges real quick!"

"You're right... The only problem now is that the tidal pool is far out in the water. I hope this storm doesn't change the beach too much. It could be filled in with sand or permanently underwater."

"It better not be... That's our only place to keep our fish. We'll be hurting without that!"

"These storms can change the beach. They can bring in more sand or wash it away. Let's just hope for the best."

* * *

For the rest of the day, fierce winds and torrential rain slam into the small island. With not much else to do, they talk for hours, discussing some changes to their daily chores after seeing the mistakes they made with this storm. For the first time since arriving on the island, they sit around with nothing to do, a pleasant change from their never-ending daily chores.

Ben takes naps for most of the day after being awake all night. Jenny passes the time with her new basket-weaving hobby. She gathered many types of fauna and palm leaves to see which was best to use. Her goal is to make a sun hat or even a basket to carry the fruit. With a lot of trial and error, she makes a few things, but it keeps her busy and helps pass the time.

Jenny misses her daily activities, especially her morning walk along the beach. She can't wait to get back down there to check out the beach once the storm is over. After a storm, it's like having a big sale, and she is missing it. Scavenging the beach is her favorite activity, never knowing what she will find. For people living off the land, there is no such thing as garbage. Anything they find on the beach can be used for something.

* * *

By the end of the day, the rain finally stopped. Ben notices the cloud base is extremely low, almost touching the tops of the trees right outside the cave. The wind is still strong, but it's their first break in the storm. He makes a run down to the lookout to check on things and bring back some more fruit. Jenny is against it, but Ben knows they will spend the night and possibly another day in the cave, whether they like it or not.

He quickly makes his way down to the lookout. Leaves and branches cover the trail. The wind is blowing so badly that he is having a difficult time keeping on his feet. Water rushes down the path, making it extremely slippery.

Reaching the fruit trees, he is so disappointed. So many oranges and grapefruits cover the ground. He fights his way over to the edge, looking down on the island. The beach is gone, and the ocean is all the way up to the trees. Massive waves are still hitting the island. He can also hear the constant thumping of the waves crashing far below.

Looking up at the dark cloud base, Ben is so surprised to see how fast it's moving. The break in the rain will not last long as a dark gray band rushes toward him. With the top of the island still in the clouds, it will generate an abundance of drinking water. Unfortunately, it's all going straight into the ocean.

Standing next to the ledge, a gust of wind knocks him off his feet. Right then, he knows it's still too dangerous to be outside. Running back to the fruit trees, he takes off his shirt, using it to gather as much fruit as possible. Seeing most of the fruit on the ground, he knows it's all going to rot. The trees will take a long time to recover from this storm.

* * *

"It's a real mess out there," he said, running back into the cave. "No telling how long this is going to last."

"Oh, great! I was hoping to get out of here today!"

"There is nothing we can do about it. At least we got plenty to eat."

"Why did you pick so many?" she asked. "What about saving some for another day plan we had?" concerned with all the fruit he brought back.

Ben shrugs his shoulders. "These are all from the ground. Not much is left on the trees. I guess we'll be having lots of orange juice for the next couple of days. It will be the last of it for a while from the looks of things out there."

"So, how does it look?" she asked, gathering up the fruit and stacking it all up next to the wall. "You think the worst is over?"

"I think so," he said, tossing a few more logs on the fire, "but there's probably going to be a lot of wind and rain for a while. We might be here for another day. I'll tell you one thing. It's going to be cold tonight. You should have felt how cold that wind is. This storm must be dragging in the cold air from the Antarctic."

"At least we still have plenty of firewood, but we've better double up after the storm. You need to get your wet clothes off and sit next to the fire," seeing Ben is dripping wet and looks a little cold.

"We need to make sure this fire doesn't go out," he said, getting up close to the fire, trying to get warm. "Also, we need to get a good night's sleep. We'll have some heavy chores to do after this," regretting not getting any sleep the night before.

"Why?" she quickly asked. "All we have to do is set up the tent."

"It'll be a chore just getting down to the beach. We'll be clearing the trails first. The one just down to the lookout is covered with leaves and branches. It's also like a raging river down there. It's probably like that all the way down to the beach. At least we'll have plenty of firewood for a while from all the fallen trees. God knows what it's going to be like at the camp."

* * *

In the morning, the sun shines into the cave. Both run out to see the sunrise for the first time in days. The sky is nothing but small, white puffy clouds. They know it means the calm, typical weather has returned.

In a short time, they pack everything up. Ben carries the duffel bag while Jenny drags a bundle of dry firewood behind her. On the way down, they are overwhelmed with all the damage. The trees are bare, stripped of their leaves. The storm uprooted many trees, destined to become firewood.

The trail is intact, not eroded as much as they thought, but it just needs a little cleaning up. Many of the trees have been damaged, but they'll grow back. The trail is now so slippery, slowing them down to a crawl. Many fallen branches and even trees block their path. Most are just pushed down the hill, but some of the tall trees are dangling precariously by the roots. Those are the dangerous ones, not knowing when the roots will break and will be falling down the hill.

* * *

Reaching the end of the trail, they see that the small pond is now a huge lake. The small trickle of water is now a roaring waterfall, and the noise is so deafening. The dry riverbed leading down to the beach is now a river rushing out to the ocean. They walk through a foot of water where there used to be nothing but dry sand all the way out to the beach.

Ben is so shocked to see all the water spilling out into the ocean. "Look at all our drinking water. It's just wasting away!"

"At least I have fresh bathwater now! I can't wait to get under that waterfall for a good long shower!" having to shout to be heard over the thundering waterfall.

"You better wait for a while! Look at all that debris coming down with the water. I bet it's a lot deeper now, with all the sand getting washed away."

"You are right! I can't wait to see the Big Pond. I bet that waterfall is massive!"

"I have a feeling we're going to see a lot of changes when we get back."

"I hope for the better," seeing how her favorite bathing pond has changed.

Out on the beach, the waves are still larger than usual, but at least the shoreline is back where it should be. The typhoon churned up a lot from the ocean, dumping it all over the beach. They will have a field day with all the wealth of new things that they can use.

Jenny is already running from one find to the next. Ben can see she is so happy with all this junk. They are not even halfway to the camp, and she already has way too much to carry. She dumps the rest up by the trees to retrieve it later since it will take several trips to haul it all back to camp.

The big boulder is still in its place, marking the position of their campsite. They run over to see whether their tidal pool is still there. Luckily, nothing has changed. To their surprise, the original fish are gone, but about half a dozen new ones are now trapped in it.

"I can't believe this!" she shouted, so thrilled, seeing all the fish. "At least we got something to eat other than those damn bananas and oranges!"

"They all look a bit stunned, don't they?" seeing how sluggish they are.

She leans over for a closer look. "You'd be too if you went through what they did. I guess the big old boulder acts like a shelter. The waves must have slammed them up onto the rocks and then got stuck in here. Good for us, but bad for them!" seeing many of the fish with scars.

"Come on!" he said, looking towards the trees. "Let's check it out. I wonder how bad it is," already noticing a few trees are missing.

The campsite is in shambles, full of fallen trees and branches. The circle of rocks surrounding the campfire are long gone. It's obvious that a lot of water has gone through the camp. The soft, dry sand is also gone, replaced with hard sand saturated with water.

Ben is so stunned seeing their campsite. "Talk about a spring cleaning. It looks a lot like when we first got here," seeing no signs of anyone ever living here.

"Looks like we have more sunlight now! Half the leaves are gone, not to mention a few of the trees. Our camp is now a lot bigger," noticing the huge open area up above.

"It does brighten things up a little. I bet we'll get a little more breeze too," seeing the slight improvement to the campsite.

"Well, we might as well get started before it gets too hot," she said, looking around. "I'm glad we're not going to spend another night in the cave again!"

"You're right about that! I think I'll even sleep outside tonight so I can look up at the stars!" happy to be outside in the warm air.

They drop everything and start cleaning up, putting all the branches together in one big pile in the direct sunlight to dry it out. Now, they have enough firewood to last a week just from the fallen branches within the campsite. That will help considerably, not having to cut up any more wood for a while.

Ben searches all over for the rocks that surround the campfire. He finds them all in the back of the camp, a clear sign of how bad it was. At the base of the foothills is a big pile of rocks, leaves, and branches. There is one long pile of debris to the left and right as far as he can see. That marks how far back the water had reached. The water washed everything from the top of the hill, leaving one big mess.

He grabs the heavy cooking pot and the wok, carrying them back. One by one, he hauls all the rocks back to rebuild the campfire. To move 10 to 20-pound rocks that far, the waves must have been enormous. He is so glad that he packed everything, carrying it all up to the cave. They didn't lose anything in the storm. The worst of it is having to start over, building the campsite from scratch.

* * *

By the end of the day, they are exhausted and hungry. The only thing left to do is prepare for the big feast. After eating nothing but fruit for several days, Jenny is ready to cook most of the fish in the tidal pool. It also means another big bonfire and a party out on the beach. They are going to celebrate their return in style.

After surviving their first typhoon with no major problems, Ben knows they got lucky. He also has a feeling that it will not be their last one. The radio is now used more often to help keep track of the storms wandering through the Pacific. Knowing the location and direction of the storms will give them a good idea of how bad it will be. They learn to become very mobile, packing up everything within an hour and moving to the cave. Never again will they be caught by surprise as they did on their first typhoon.

* * *

Chapter 26

Wedding

While sitting by the campfire, Jenny is constantly talking about her wedding plans. She dreams of walking down the aisle in her white wedding gown in front of her friends and family, talking about it every day. In a way, she is planning out the wedding in such detail so they can get married as soon as possible when they get back home.

Ben always listens to Jenny's big dream wedding. Unfortunately, all the planning will be a big letdown if they don't get off the island.

"You know, we can always have it here," Ben suggested.

"I don't think so," she quickly replied, giving him a mean look.

"Why not? When we get back home, we'll have that big church wedding with our families. A lot of people have a small wedding on some exotic tropical island just like this place. Later on, they'll have a big ceremony back home."

Jenny gives him a long kiss, then sits back, looking up at the dark sky. "OK, that might be a way we can do this! In a way, we would be married. The only problem with having the wedding at home is the thought of walking down the aisle six months pregnant. That's not the type of wedding I had in mind!" imagining what she would look like pregnant and in a wedding dress.

"I wouldn't worry about it. Just tell everyone we've been married since the day we arrived. Besides, no one is going to think anything about it, anyway. I can tell you now. My parents would love the idea of more grandkids to spoil rotten. My brother dumps his kids on Mom and Dad all the time. They always complain, but they won't admit they really love it."

"That's true... My mom and dad will probably be the same. It will be their first grandbaby, so God knows what they'll be like around them. The big problem is they'll be wanting us to live near them."

He laughed. "Mine will, too… That's another thing we'll have to figure out. Where are we going to live? I sure don't want to live in Texas. It's just too hot and humid there."

"Is the weather that bad?" she asked. "I have never been to Texas before."

"Oh, it's horrible," he explained, shaking his head. "It'll be in the hundreds all summer. Then it'll be below freezing in the winter. That's the bad part about Texas. It'll go from one extreme to the other. You think this place is humid. This is nothing compared to the Gulf Coast. What about where you live?"

"Oh, the winters are just too cold, month after month, nothing but snow and ice. It would be nice to be around my family, but I don't think I can take the cold anymore after living out here. Even the cave is too cold for me now."

"Yeah, the weather here is perfect. We have a nice breeze all the time, and it's cool at night. It might get hot at noon, but in the shade, it's still not that bad. This would be a great place for a vacation. I'm so surprised there's nothing already here."

"I know! Just think of all the people who would come here to get married. This would be the perfect place. It's so romantic with all the palm-lined beaches, and it's got the best sunsets. The best place I can think of is out on the lookout by the fruit trees!" she suggested, glancing over to see his reaction.

"That would be a perfect place to have a wedding!" he said, reaching over to take her hand. "How about a sunset ceremony? We can even have our wedding night up there. We can bring the tent and have a big campfire. What do you think?"

She quickly puts her arms around him, giving him a big hug. "So, we're really going to do it? Get married here on the island?"

"Yep, if that's what you want?" he asked, giving her a big kiss.

"Yes!" she screamed out, so excited. "We're getting married! I'll start getting our clothes together!" jumping up and down, dancing around the campfire.

"Why do we need to wear clothes?" he asked, seeing Jenny dancing about naked. "What's wrong with the way we are? We'll be like Adam and Eve."

She gasped out loud. "There is no way I'm having a naked wedding. We're going to be wearing clothes, and you're not wearing those damn swimming trunks, either. You're going to wear your good shirt and pants, and even your shoes! I guess I can make my wedding dress from some of that sail we found."

"OK, I'll get my clothes out of the cave and get them cleaned up. I might be able to build a makeshift arbor. We can use the flowers out by the waterfall to decorate it. Oh, by the way, I can't wait until the big wedding night!" noticing how great she looks standing next to the campfire.

She laughed. "Every day we've been here has been like our wedding night with wild sex all over the island. I think that's one of the reasons why we have to get married," nudging him.

"I never really thought about it. Although it was a lot of fun!"

Jenny lies down, putting her head on his lap, looking up at the stars. "It has been great, hasn't it? I guess we still can have sex for a while. I'm not sure how much longer, but we'll just have to be a little more gentle," giving him subtle hints so not to disappoint him on the wedding night.

"So we're still good for a while?" he asked, reaching over to rub her belly. "I always thought once you are pregnant, that was it for the sex!"

"Afterwards, maybe for a while, but it'll be OK until the last month or two. My friend Barbara got so horny when she was pregnant. She'd be either craving weird food or sex, and sometimes at the same time. Her husband was a real mess for a long time after that."

"I have a feeling I'm going to be a basket case after all this. Let's hope we're out of here when the time comes."

* * *

The wedding is to take place on the edge of the lookout, their favorite spot on the whole island. It's also the best place to view the spectacular sunsets. They spent days preparing for the wedding. Ben works hard, constructing an arbor out of bamboo. Jenny is busy making her wedding dress from old remnants of nylon sail found on the beach. They have no particular date selected. Once they finish everything, they only need to wait for a beautiful day.

* * *

On one perfect afternoon, everything is ready. Ben finishes the arbor and puts it up on the lookout, facing west for the sunset. Jenny covers it with flowers. They moved their camp up to the lookout for their big wedding night. A campfire is waiting to be lit. The radio will be a big part in the ceremony. With the batteries fully charged, the radio will be their entertainment for a night of dancing.

Jenny spends hours in the cave getting ready. She has been working on the dress for weeks, hiding it up in the cave, not wanting Ben to see it before the wedding. The sails that washed up on the beach are coming in handy. Most are made of nylon or polyester so that they can be used for anything. She has more than enough material for not only a wedding dress but a few more blouses and a shirt for Ben.

Seeing the smoke from the campfire, Jenny slowly makes her way down the trail. Ben is in awe, seeing her for the first time wearing her wedding dress and carrying a bouquet of yellow hibiscus flowers. If he didn't know any better, her wedding dress looks as if she had bought it from a store.

Jenny, fighting hard to keep the tears back, takes her place next to Ben at the arbor. With the sun about to set, they stand silently and awkwardly together. They turn, facing each other. Ben reaches out, taking her hands, looking deeply into her eyes. As the sun touches the horizon, the clouds turn a burnt orange. It marks the beginning of their ceremony.

Ben takes in a deep breath. "I, Ben Hughes, take you, Jenny Mason, to be my wife, my partner in life, and my one true love. I will cherish our friendship and love you today, tomorrow, and forever. I will trust you and honor you. I will laugh with you and cry with you. I will love you faithfully. Through the best and the worst, through the difficult and the easy. What may come, I will always be there. As I have given you my hand to hold, so I give you my life to keep," so relieved he could say his vows on the first attempt.

She stands up straight, takes a deep breath, and looks into Ben's eyes. "I, Jenny Mason, take you, Ben Hughes, to be my husband, my partner in life, and my one true love. I will cherish our friendship and love you today, tomorrow, and forever. I will trust you and honor you. I will laugh with you and cry with you. I will love you faithfully. Through the best and the worst, through the difficult and the easy. What may come, I will always be there for you. As I have given you my hand to hold, so I give you my life to keep forever," her hands trembling.

Jenny completed her vow, and both announced in unison, "I pronounce us married!" smiling at each other.

Now they are married. The only witnesses are the sun, the sky, and God. They kiss each other for the first time as husband and wife. Holding each other, they watch the sun slowly drop below the horizon. It's one of the best sunsets they have ever witnessed.

Ben switches on the radio, and they dance on the ledge overlooking the island. The sun had set long ago as they danced the night away. Jenny doesn't want to admit it, but she is getting tired. Staying up late at night is a thing of the past, and she still has to cook the wedding dinner.

"You want to take a break?" he asked, noticing she is getting tired. "You ready for dinner?"

"That sounds great! I'll get the fish ready, and you set up the fruit tray."

They have everything ready for the big feast. The dinner is still swimming in the iron cooking pot to keep fresh. Jenny is preparing the fish while Ben gathers fresh oranges and grapefruit from the nearby orchard. It's a nice reception dinner with an abundance of fruit, bananas, coconuts, and fresh fish.

* * *

After the wedding dinner, Jenny hears a waltz playing on the radio and is ready for more dancing. Ben stumbles his way through, trying not to step on her feet. He is not good at dancing, constantly looking down at his feet, trying to keep up with the beat, counting his steps the entire time. Jenny, however, is a natural and glides along with the music without even thinking about it.

"It's our wedding night, you know," he said, noticing Jenny trying so hard to hide her yawns. "We can't keep dancing all night," knowing full well that she is ready to go to sleep.

"Just one more dance, then we'll go to bed," still trying to teach him a few more dance moves.

"It's a good thing we don't have an audience," he jokingly said. "They'd never let up kidding me about my dancing."

"Well, you got plenty of time to practice. When we get back home, we're going to do this all over again. We'll have all our families and friends there too."

"I like this much better than a church wedding."

"Oh no, you don't! We're still going to have a proper wedding when we get back home!"

They have their final slow dance, gazing into each other's eyes. Getting a little cold, they dance around the campfire to keep warm. The wedding was perfect, and they couldn't have planned it any better.

At the end of the song, Jenny gives him a long, passionate kiss. "Let's go to bed," taking his hand and leading him to the tent.

Standing next to the tent, they slowly undress each other. Ben passionately kisses his wife before crawling into the small tent they called home. They quickly slip into the sleeping bag to get warm. They leave the rain shield open to see the campfire from inside the tent. There is a long silence. Both are feeling a little uncomfortable with each other. Ben slowly leans over, kissing Jenny. Then, they make love for the first time, now as husband and wife, with so much caring and gentleness.

Staying up late in the night, they talk for hours about their future. They are making plans for when they do get back home. Life on the island is fantastic, but now, with the baby on the way, being here all alone is starting to be a big concern. With the baby due in less than six months, they have to make do with what they have and be extremely careful. They never give up hope of being rescued. Someday, someone will show up to take them home. Holding each other, they talk all night until they both fall asleep in each other's arms.

* * *

Chapter 27

New Family

As the months go by, Jenny is getting extremely big and is having a hard time getting around. She is now limited to short walks on the beach. Going up to the cave is now a thing of the past. She spends most of her time at the camp, making hats and baskets out of various leaves and vines. She becomes a master at repairing and altering their clothes.

After a big storm, the remains of a polyester sail got washed up on the beach, and it provided an endless supply of material for new clothing. The timing couldn't have been better since none of Jenny's original clothes fit anymore, and most are falling apart.

Every time she bathes in the small pond, Ben has to go with her. The walk is now too much for her to do on her own. Occasionally, he has to carry her back to the camp. She has not gained that much weight, but her stomach is huge. They wonder how big this baby is going to be. Not knowing how far along she is, it looks more like she is in her ninth month and is due any day.

Ben has been making the daily trips up to the cave alone for months. He strives to get it done as quickly as possible, jogging up the trail, not wanting to leave Jenny alone. The firewood is still the biggest chore, and every day they use a lot, so their supply has to be replenished continuously.

Once Ben returns from his chores, they walk out to the beach, spending time together. Occasionally, he goes out snorkeling to bring back a lobster, which has become one of Jenny's latest cravings. Sometimes, they get lucky and catch a few shrimp with the casting net. Shrimp is one thing Ben never liked. With all the prep work before cooking, it amounts to nothing more than a little bite-sized snack. The shrimp is a novelty item, but naturally, it's also another one of Jenny's cravings.

* * *

Jenny is finding it difficult to get up and move around. Getting in and out of the tent is a major chore. To help her out, Ben makes some rudimentary wooden chairs and benches. Learning through trial and error, he found which designs worked best. He lashes everything together with rope, and it's extremely sturdy. After months of sitting on the ground, it's a nice change to sit on a bench or a chair.

With his newfound talent, Ben is making all sorts of furniture. He surprises Jenny one day with an odd-looking contraption. He made her a small bench with a round hole at the top.

"Now, what's this thing supposed to be?" she asked, looking it over.

"I guess it's been a while since we've seen one of these," he said, so proud of his little invention, putting it down on the sand and sitting on top of it.

She figures it out, laughing hysterically. "It's a potty chair! Oh, this is great! I can't wait to try it out!"

"You've been having problems getting up, so this might help."

"In other words, now you don't have to stick around when I go to the bathroom and can't get up."

He smiles. "You got that right! If it works out, I'll make me one too."

"You don't want to share my potty chair?" she asked, laughing at him.

"No, we are a two-bathroom family. I'm going to keep mine on the other side of the camp," still insisting on separate bathroom areas for privacy.

With the popularity of some of his woodworking projects, Ben is thinking of bigger things to build. Still stuck on the island, they are now accepting the reality that the baby will be born here. He knows it's time to start thinking about a better shelter. The tent is not the place to bring up a newborn baby. They need a larger home to live in, one that is sturdier and is off the sand.

On the west side of the campsite, there are four palm trees about equal distances apart. The palm trees align up almost in a perfect square, about seven by eight feet. They had used these trees before, rigging up canopies to sit under during the rainy days, which never lasted longer than a few weeks before the wind tore them apart. Ben knows this can be the base for a more permanent structure.

After a lengthy discussion, they decide to build at least a wooden deck about a foot off the ground. This project will take a long time and will use a lot of resources. The worst part is getting all the wood, not wanting to use up their firewood supply. With bamboo all over the island, it's the best thing to use. Luckily, they have some small remnants of plywood they found on the beach to use for the flooring.

* * *

After a week, Ben gathers enough bamboo trees to start the project. Getting the rope to lash everything together is easy. They have been collecting rope for months and have more than enough. Constructing the base is the first part. He ties four large bamboo poles to the palm trees about a foot off the ground. Then, he adds the crossbeams about a foot apart, forming the base. The rest of the one-inch bamboo is packed tightly together to make the floor. The old plywood is on top, so it will be easy on the feet.

Ben is so surprised at how sturdy it is. The deck is lashed to the base of the palm trees, so it doesn't move at all when the wind hits the trees. Since it's high enough off the ground, there is plenty of room to store the firewood and anything else they want to keep out of the rain. If any big storms hit the island, the water will flow underneath it, and it won't get washed away.

After seeing how easy it was to construct the deck, they decided to add some walls. The walls don't have to be that sturdy. All they have to do is make four more frames using the small bamboo. It means going back out and gathering more bamboo trees, but now they know what they are doing, and constructing the walls should be a lot easier than the deck.

With the four walls completed, they added the roof to finish it. The vinyl from the old raft is put on top to ensure it's waterproof, then top it off with palm leaves to block out the heat from the sun. They quickly discover that their new home is well-designed. When the wind blows through the trees, the little hut doesn't move at all.

* * *

After a couple of weeks, the beach hut is now finished. Being only seven by eight feet wide and eight-foot-high, it's a major achievement. The hut is everything that they wanted it to be. With the doorway facing the campfire, they can keep an eye on the cooking from inside. A small window facing the beach allows the breeze to flow through. They add a shutter to seal up the window during the storms. Being cramped up in the tent on those rainy days is now a thing of the past.

The hut is not much to look at, but Ben knows it'll be a good shelter for a while, especially when the baby is born. He even made a small bed out of the leftover bamboo using a rope for the bedsprings. They move the little bench and table inside against the wall opposite the bed. With the bed, table, and chairs, it's a perfect place to live.

They put their new hut to use right away. Jenny promptly moves out of the tent, dragging all of her things into their new home. She finishes making the bed, adding the old cushions, and places the sleeping bag on top. Not having to sleep on the ground is a blessing. Now, she has a proper bed and can finally get in and out with no help.

The new hut is better than the cave, with plenty of room to move about, and it's not as cold. Jenny can now sit comfortably on the bed, making baby clothes or experimenting with different weaves for hats and baskets. Ben loves to sit up at the table to eat their meals on rainy days. He wishes they had built the hut months ago, seeing how easy it was, making their lives a lot easier.

The hut is a great place to store all their firewood, built a foot above the ground. Now, they can keep several days of wood at the camp without worrying about it getting wet. It also means fewer trips to haul wood from the cave. Little by little, life on the island is getting more and more comfortable.

Ben is non-stop with his woodworking projects. The next project is so simple that he is kicking himself for not thinking of it earlier. He makes a canopy with four bamboo poles two feet high, placing it over the campfire. Now, the campfire has a cover on it to protect it from the rain. Too many times, they start a campfire to cook their dinner only to have the rain put it out. Being one of the easiest things he made, it's the most rewarding one of all.

* * *

Ben goes about his daily chores. Now, with a baby on the way, he stocks up on everything. Once the baby is born, it might be days before making the run to the cave. In the last few weeks, he has been grabbing a bundle of firewood and a bag of fruit, running back as quickly as possible, not wanting to be away from Jenny. He is now at the point where he can run to the cave and back without stopping.

When Jenny experiences her first few contractions, everything comes to a complete stop. The baby is due at any time. They always thought they would have been rescued by now. The idea of having the baby on the island is making Ben a nervous wreck.

Jenny takes it all in stride, with her natural maternal instincts taking over. She instructs him on what he should do when the time comes. He is so scared of having to help with the delivery and never thought he would have to do this while still on the island. Being very squeamish, he is hoping not to pass out. Still having problems cleaning a fish but helping with the delivery is going to be far worse.

With a long list of new chores to do, he inventories everything they have. He has problems finding decent materials for baby clothes, diapers, and bedding. The only thing he knows about giving birth is having plenty of clean towels or sheets. The only thing they have is an old nylon sail. He promptly cuts it up into two-foot sections and boils them all for hours to make sure everything is clean and sterile.

Jenny had already been making little clothes for the new arrival. Her skills in making clothes are now at the level of a professional seamstress. She is always thrilled to show off her new outfits for the baby. Ben is always impressed by how she can put together a little outfit with no plans or guides. Even the shirts she made for him are the best-fitted clothes he has ever worn. Unfortunately, his days of getting new clothes are over. Now, it's all for the baby. He is down to his old trusty swimming trunks and one shirt, and he has to make them last.

* * *

After talking it over with Jenny, she thinks there is enough time for one last run for firewood and fruit. With the timing of the contractions, it can still be twelve hours or more. He is reluctant to go, but they need extra supplies. He already made a run this morning, but once the baby is born, it could be days before he can haul supplies from the cave.

Coming down the trail, Ben notices another storm is brewing up to the southwest. Looking at the cloud formation, he knows it will be a big tropical storm, and it's heading their way. They'll be getting some much-needed rain, but it will force them to stay in the hut for a day or two. With the baby on the way, a storm is the last thing they need right now.

Returning to the camp, he hears a faint cry then drops everything, running into the hut. "Are you OK?" he asked.

"Ben, I think it's time!" she cried out. "I have been having several bad cramps!" writhing in severe pain.

"When did they start?" he frantically asked.

"Just before you left."

"You had these before I went up to the cave?" he asked, so shocked.

"I didn't think it was anything at the time," she replied, rubbing her stomach. "Now, I do!" nodding her head.

"So what do I do?" he asked, starting to panic.

"Nothing right now," she explained, leaning back on the bed. "You might want to start getting everything ready. All we can do is wait until things start happening."

"OK, I'll get everything ready," he said, his hands trembling.

Jenny is strong and always looks on the bright side of things. She constantly lets Ben know everything will be all right and there will not be any problems. She knows Ben is dreading this moment and will have some serious problems helping deliver the baby since he is so squeamish.

Ben, however, can't think straight at all. He paces back and forth, his hands constantly shaking. He finally completed all of his tasks. The big cast iron cooking pot is full of water, simmering above the roaring flames. He keeps checking everything repeatedly. They have plenty of firewood on hand. Freshwater bottles are in various places in and around the hut. Stacks of clean sailcloth are on the table, ready for the big moment.

* * *

By the end of the day, the wind is picking up. The occasional flashes of lightning are in the distance. Ben knows this is the one time they don't need a storm. It might mess up all their plans. He walks out onto the beach to get a better view. The ocean is nothing but whitecaps, and the waves are enormous. The small tropical storm he saw earlier is brewing up into a massive one.

He runs back to the hut to check on Jenny's progress. "How are you doing?"

"I'm doing fine," she mumbled, hearing the thunder in the distance. "Although it's a bad time to have a storm."

"Well, at least we won't be going to the cave tonight," he jokingly said, but the idea was in the back of his mind.

She laughed. "I don't think I'm in any condition to make that trip at the moment. We've been really lucky so far. I guess I should have tried to make it up there well before now. Maybe it might have been better having the baby up in the cave?" having second thoughts about it.

He quickly shakes his head. "I don't think so... It's too far from the water and too cold up there, anyway. I think we'll be OK down here."

"Yeah, but up there, we wouldn't have to worry about the wind and rain. The hut made it through some of the storms, but we haven't had any big ones yet," getting worried.

"We'll do fine... The hut is strong, and the storm might miss us altogether," seeing Jenny is having second thoughts about staying at the beach.

Ben closes his eyes, quickly going over the plan for a last-minute move to the cave. He knows he can carry Jenny all the way, but if it starts raining, it's going to be a problem. Also, if they are halfway up the trail and she goes into labor, they'll be in big trouble.

The storm is now so close, and it's just too late to make a move. Everything is ready at the camp, but the rain is going to cause some big problems. The canopy he made for the campfire will help keep the rain off the fire, but it may not last long in a big storm. The conditions are getting worse for delivering a baby.

Ben holds Jenny's hand, trying to comfort her. "OK, Ben!" she screamed out, experiencing another contraction. "I think it's time for you to start earning your keep!"

"OK, I'm ready," he said, getting so scared.

Now is the moment he has been dreading. Jenny is struggling with so much pain. Her contractions are continuous, one after another. He can only watch, comforting her and giving her encouragement. He has never been so scared in his life. If something goes wrong, there is nothing he can do. Now, he wants so much to be off this island. The delivery should be in a hospital with doctors and nurses who know what they are doing and not on a beach in the middle of a storm.

* * *

Hours go by, and the darkness sets in. The storm finally hits the small island. All the beautiful calm nights they had in the past few weeks, and now of all times to have a big storm. The wind has blown away the cover of the campfire. Within minutes, the torrential rain quickly puts out the fire. The flashlight doesn't last long. The batteries are dead after a couple of hours. Now, the only light they have is from the occasional flashes of lightning.

The storm is getting worse. The hut shudders with the constant gusts of wind. Huge coconuts are dropping off the trees, hitting the top of the hut with a loud crashing sound. The rain is even seeping through the walls. The cave would have been a better choice. All they can do is pray that the hut will last through the night.

Ben feels so useless and so frightened as the hours pass by. He keeps wishing someone were here to help. Not being able to see anything is making the situation worse. He can only use his hands in the complete darkness to feel how far she is coming along. The occasional lightning lets him see it's getting close. He has no clue what to do. Even with all her instructions, things are not going as planned. Also, he never thought it would take over twelve hours.

"OK, I think this is it!" Jenny yelled out.

"That's good, that's good," he whispered, feeling the top of the head emerging. "You're doing OK... We're almost there."

He can feel the baby slowly slip into his hands, already kicking and crying. Tears flow from his eyes, so happy and relieved it's finally over. Lightning strikes not too far away. The quick flash of light illuminates the hut, finally seeing his baby for the first time.

"Congratulations, it's a girl!" handing her over to Jenny.

So exhausted, Jenny cradles her new baby. "Oh, Ben... We have a little girl," then cries.

"She's a wild one, too," he proudly said. "She's already kicking and screaming."

"Better get used to that sound. I think she is fine. Everything is going to be all right, so you can finally relax now!" cradling her little girl in her arms.

Ben gets up, stumbling across the room in the dark for the stack of sailcloth. He hands her a few, and together, they clean the baby. After a few minutes, Ben knows what his next task is. He reaches over to the small table for the fishing line and his pocketknife. He ties off the umbilical cord. Waiting for the next lightning strike, he wants to make sure to do this part right, hoping not to pass out.

It doesn't take long for the next lightning flash. "OK, it's finally over," he said, quickly cutting the cord.

"How are you guys doing?" he asked, wishing he could see them.

"I think we're both fine... Oh, sorry, but I can feel something stirring again. I think you may have to deal with the placenta now," feeling so uncomfortable.

He doesn't want to think about his next task. "OK, I'll get the things," stepping out of the hut, standing outside in the pouring rain, so relieved it's over.

Ben fills the metal wok with hot water from the big cooking pot. He brings it in, setting it on the table next to Jenny. He takes his position again, ready with one of the cooking pots waiting for the placenta to emerge. She is pushing hard, obviously in a lot of pain.

"I thought it's supposed to follow through real easy?" he asked, getting confused.

"I don't know," she screamed out. "It's just as bad as before!"

Again, he places his hand on her and feels something, but it's not what he expected. He is not sure what is happening. She struggles again, pushing repeatedly. Another lightning strike hits nearby, followed by a massive thunder blast, shaking the small hut and making everyone jump.

The lightning lights up the small hut, allowing him to see what is happening. "Oh, God!" he cried out.

"What is it?" she asked, starting to panic. "What's wrong?"

"It's OK! Nothing is wrong," then suddenly, the second baby slid into his hands and immediately cried just like the first one.

"What's happening?" she asked, so confused, hearing the crying.

He is a little stunned by this new event. "We have a late visitor here... It's another girl!"

"Twins! Oh, my God! We have twin girls!" she screamed out, so shocked by the news.

"Well, that explains a few things," he said, now knowing why she was so big.

Jenny is ecstatic as Ben hands her their second daughter. He holds the first one in his arms while Jenny cleans the recent arrival. Both babies came out crying and kicking their little arms and legs. They both sit in the dark, cradling their little girls. They are now a family of four on their small island in the middle of nowhere.

* * *

The night is finally over, and the storm is long gone. Jenny is still wide awake, feeding her little girls. Now, with an enough light in the small hut, Ben can finally see his two little girls for the first time. He has never seen such a beautiful sight and has never been so happy in his life.

"Look how beautiful they are!" Ben shouted. "How are you doing? Do you need anything?" seeing how tired Jenny is.

"Let's just say I'm glad it's over," she said, shaking her head. "I never thought for one moment I was going to have twins! What a surprise! Mom and Dad will not believe this!"

He gently strokes the back of one of his girls. "Yeah, I know! Mine will be on cloud nine when they find out I got twins!"

"Are they OK?" she asked, looking down again at her little girls, already suckling on her breasts.

"They look healthy to me," he said, looking them over. "Got all their fingers, and toes, and plenty of hair. Check out the way they're feeding. It looks like they're going to be a handful at dinnertime."

"I know... I think we're all going to be OK," leaning over, gently kissing each one of her girls.

Ben sits quietly on the edge of the bed, so proud to see his new family. After the most exhausting day of his life, it's all over, but in reality, it has just begun. He can rest for a minute or two before having to start the rest of the chores. He slowly falls asleep after not having had any sleep for days.

"Why don't you get cleaned up and take a nap?" she whispered, nudging him. "I'll be OK with the girls for a while."

"OK," he said, tripping over a pan on the floor.

"You might want to take that out and put it in the sand," pointing to the pan he just tripped over.

Ben nods, knowing his chores are not over. Now, it's time to clean up, disposing of the umbilical cords and placentas. Being a little on the squeamish side, he makes sure not to look in the pan. He walks out among the trees, finding a place to bury everything. After digging a hole in the sand, he dumps everything in and quickly covers it up. He dares not even look, closing his eyes the entire time.

He walks out onto the beach and kneels in the water, completely exhausted. The storm is now gone. The sky is clear. A yellow glow is emerging on the horizon as the sun is about to rise. He looks down, seeing his hands and arms covered with blood and other disgusting fluids. That's enough to put him over the edge, and he quickly passes out.

* * *

As a small wave splashes over his face, Ben finally regains consciousness. The sunlight blinds him. So exhausted, he slowly gets up, walking into the water to wash himself off. The cold water quickly revives him. He can't stay away from Jenny and his girls for too long. He still has a lot of chores to do, and the day has just begun.

When he stands up, a huge white object at the end of the beach catches his attention. He can't focus his eyes, being so tired. He rubs his eyes, trying to clear out the saltwater. His mouth drops wide open. A sailboat is at the far end of the beach. He is so excited and relieved that the day that they have been waiting for has finally arrived. They are going to be rescued and taken off this island. They are going home, and it couldn't have come at a better time.

He runs to the small sailboat as fast as he can but then notices something doesn't look right. The sailboat is on its side near the edge of the beach and not sitting out in the water. As he approaches the sailboat, he comes to a complete stop, so disappointed. Only the front half remains, and it looks as if something sheared it in half. He feels so sorry for the people who were on it, another victim of the massive storm and the cruel ocean.

He thought they were finally going home, and now it's a big letdown. Suddenly, it struck him. There may be people here. He runs around the sailboat looking for survivors, yelling out continuously, but there are no replies. There are no footprints on the sand, either. At least there are not any bodies washed up on the beach, but there might be some inside.

Ben examines the damaged end of the sailboat. He can see that something collided with it. To cut a ship in half, something really big must have hit it. The fiberglass-constructed sailboat didn't have a chance. He carefully walks into the huge opening and has a good look around. With debris scattered all over, it's one big mess. All the cabinets are hanging off the walls, and the contents are all over the floor.

He knows right away that this is a great find. Nothing this big had ever washed up on the beach since they had been on the island. The sailboat contains so many things that they can really use. He can't understand why people risk their lives in such small boats on this vast ocean. He has seen this ocean at its worst and has a lot of respect for it.

Rummaging deeper in the sailboat, he sees a door on the bulkhead at the far end of the room. It looks promising. Carefully stepping over all the debris, he reaches the door, still tightly sealed with several locks on it. One by one, he unlatches the locks, and with several more tugs, it finally opens. To his surprise, he discovers it's the main bedroom. He was expecting water to rush out. Looking around inside, he is astounded to find everything still dry.

He steps inside, so relieved there are no bodies. Everything smells somewhat clean, maybe a little musty. Opening one cabinet after another is a major find. The cabinets and drawers are full of sheets, blankets, and pillows, and they are all still dry and in excellent condition.

The sailboat shifts, rocking back and forth. Ben can hear the waves crashing against the side of the boat. Since it's low tide, it wouldn't be long before the big waves start coming in. The last thing he wants is for it to wash back out with the tide, especially while he is still in it.

Realizing how long he has been away, Ben grabs as much as he can carry. He can't wait to tell Jenny about his find running back to the camp. Finding out that they are not going home is a big letdown, but with all their new supplies, it makes up for it. Everything from the sailboat is really going to help, especially now with the babies.

* * *

Ben walks into the small hut with his arms behind his back. With the sun up over the horizon, there is now plenty of light. He has a big smile on his face, seeing Jenny and his two little girls. He is now a father, and this is his family. It's a feeling he has never had before, so overwhelmed with emotions.

"Where have you been?" she asked. "I was getting worried!"

He simply smiles. "I went for a little swim and cleaned up a bit."

"Well, what do you think of your little girls?"

"They're so beautiful!" he blurted out, not able to contain his excitement. "It's a shame they're sleeping. I was going to give them their birthday presents," holding out the blankets and towels.

She gasps out loud. "Where did you get those?" she asked.

He sits on the edge of the bed, staring at his little girls. "Jenny, you're not going to believe this... There's a sailboat washed up on the far end of the beach."

"What! There's a sailboat! Are there people here?" getting excited about being rescued.

He quickly shakes his head. "No, it's all busted up... It must have collided with another boat or something during the storm. There was no one on it. I looked around and didn't see anyone. At least one compartment was watertight. Everything inside is dry. It's one hell of a find!"

"This looks brand-new!" she said, feeling the towel. "It's a lot better than what we have now!"

"These are real towels, not from some old sail. It didn't look like it was drifting for long. It probably got hit during the storm yesterday. Let's get these girls wrapped up before they get cold," handing her the soft towels.

"What else is in it?" she asked, excited about the find.

"Plenty! I had a quick look around. There's stuff all over the place. Just think, a complete bedroom with everything in it, and it's all still dry! I went through some cabinets, and they're full of sheets, blankets, and pillows. There are even two good mattresses. I even saw some kitchen stuff, too!"

"I can't wait to check it out! It couldn't have happened at a better time. It's really going to help us out, especially with these two!"

"Well, you may not be able to see it for a while. You need to rest up a little. I'll make a few quick trips down there to get everything out. It's low tide now, but when the tide comes in, it'll probably be underwater or, worse, get dragged back out into the ocean."

She frowned. "Damn! The tide comes in this afternoon. You got to clean it out before then."

"We got plenty of time," not taking his eyes off the girls.

"Good! I guess it's time for you to get acquainted with your daughters," handing them both over to Ben.

"They're so tiny," he whispered, seeing how small and fragile they are.

"If I only had a camera," she proudly said, seeing how awkwardly he held the babies. "What a picture!"

"So, what are their names?" he asked, looking at his girls. "Have you come up with anything yet?"

She sits quietly for a while. "I have been thinking about it. I kind of like the ones we came up with the other day. We'll have to use the names that was on top our list for a girl."

He nods in agreement. "Well, I guess we'll call you two April and June," looking at each of them.

"You know... We're going to have problems telling them apart. I think they're identical twins."

"Yeah, I know... Wow, we got twins! They'll never believe this at home!" studying their little faces, seeing how they looked alike.

"I know," she mumbled, getting upset.

"Are you OK?" he asked, seeing Jenny crying.

"I'm OK," she said, wiping away the tears, reaching over to take one of the babies. "I was just thinking about Mom and Dad, wanting so much to show them our little girls. They'd be so thrilled!"

He looks down at his little girl cradled in his arms. "Yeah, my family would be the same. My mom would love to know I got twin girls. She would spoil them rotten."

"I wish we were back home now. I really miss my family, and I want so much to go home," Jenny said, crying again.

"Well, it shouldn't be much longer," he said, taking her hand. "Someone will find us out here. There's got to be a plane or boat showing up here one day. At least one showed up today. There might be another search and rescue for that sailboat out on the beach. It might bring someone here, and they'll find us. Then we can go home and show everyone our little girls!"

He always makes sure to be positive around Jenny. She has been through a lot, delivering twins with little help. He is so relieved that everything worked out fine. The nightmare is over, but it's the beginning of a new life. He is now very content with his life and his new family.

The worst is over. If they made it through the last 24 hours, then the rest will be easy. Ben doesn't want to spend his life wondering if they are going to be rescued or not. He wants to enjoy his life on their little island with his beautiful wife and two precious little girls. With that, he said goodbye to his family back home, hoping they don't worry about him anymore.

* * *

Chapter 28

Gone Forever

B en's mother, Mary, had another terrible night. She had more dreams of Ben again, far worse than any other dreams she had ever had before. She is tossing and turning all night long, yelling out for him. Finally, she wakes up sobbing uncontrollably.

Ben's brother and sister rush over early in the morning after getting a frantic call from their father. Many months had passed since she had those dreams. She had settled down, finally accepting the loss of her son. For some reason, she is having the dreams again.

Walter can't do this alone. The entire family is at the house to help. Mary slept in late since she had been up most of the night. Everyone sits in the living room, discussing their options for most of the morning. Counseling has not worked, and no one knows what else to do.

* * *

Finally, around noon, Mary slowly walks out of the bedroom. She sits on the couch surrounded by her family. She doesn't say a word, just stared at the floor, totally exhausted.

"Are you OK?" Walter asked. "You want something to eat?" hugging her.

She doesn't look up, staring at the floor. "I had another dream about Ben... I don't know why, but he was terrified. Something has happened. Everything was so dark, and he kept calling out to me."

"It's OK, Mom," Kelly whispered, reaching over to hold her mother's hand.

"I didn't know what was happening," Mary continued. "He was so scared and didn't know what to do. He wanted to come home more than ever," starting to cry again.

"Come on, let's not go into it," Walter said, gently hugging her. "You're just getting yourself upset over this again."

"No, I have to say this… I know you all think I'm going crazy, but Ben is still alive. He's out there somewhere, but he just can't get home. I didn't know what was happening because everything was so dark. I could feel that he's never been so frightened in his life, and he's never scared of anything. The strange thing about it all is that he went from being so scared, and for some reason, he was so happy. I don't understand why, but everything is OK now. In a way, I think he was telling me goodbye and that I should not worry anymore. I now know that wherever he is, he's very happy and has finally found peace. So, I know now... I have to let him go," she explained, and cried uncontrollably.

Everyone stares at her, not knowing what to say. It has been a problem ever since Ben was first reported missing. Mary has finally accepted that her son is gone forever. Now, the entire family feels the loss all over again. It's like the day when they first heard the news that Ben's plane was missing. Now, it's finally over, and they can move on with their lives. Ben will always be in their memories. The son and brother who went on an adventure of a lifetime, only to spend eternity roaming the heavens.

* * *

Chapter 29

Family Life

Ben's first chore of the day is to boil more water to sterilize all the new towels from the sailboat. He keeps checking in on Jenny and the babies, glad to see they are all sound asleep. Seeing his two strong, healthy little girls makes him so happy and proud.

Waiting for the water to boil, he can't help running the soft plush towel over his face. Their clothes are made of sailcloth, and they are a little rough on the skin. The sand is not helping much either. The storm was a blessing in disguise. After all the hardships they have endured, this couldn't have come at a better time.

Seeing Jenny sitting up, he brings in some warm water to help wash the babies. He helps the girls with their first bath, then wraps each one up in clean towels. He cradles them in his arms while Jenny washes. Having twins has changed their plans dramatically.

While holding both girls, he realizes he can't do anything else and can't put them down either. They need to think of something and fast. After all the planning, they never thought about this part. He needs to make a baby crib that's big enough to hold them both.

Ben is in awe of his little girls. They are so beautiful and so tiny. They don't cry at all, looking up at him, constantly kicking their little feet. Then it dawns on him. He is now a married man with two children. In less than a year, his life has changed so much. He never thought he would have a family out here in the middle of nowhere.

After being up all night, he is so tired and hungry. There will be some rough times ahead. Since the babies don't have a place to sleep, he quickly makes two small hammocks from the old cargo netting. Spending all his time helping Jenny with the babies, he is wondering how they will make it through all this.

* * *

The quiet days on the island are now over. Crying babies is something that they'll have to get used to hearing. Ben quickly sees that Jenny's maternal instincts are emerging. He is so intrigued to see her handling the babies as if she has been doing it for years. Unfortunately, while she feeds one, the other baby cries as he holds her. Jenny finds it's easier to feed them both together. The girls are a handful. Only a few hours old, they go after Jenny's breasts, trying to outdo each other.

Jenny cries when her two little girls hold each other's hands while they feed. They are acknowledging each other for the first time. Even Ben has a tear in his eye. He wishes he had his camera. He is so frustrated at missing all these great baby shots.

Ben still has all the chores to do, and now it's all his responsibility. For months, they planned everything, and now it's time to put it all into action. The campfire has to be going all day long and for most of the night. They need boiling water for most of the day. The tidal pool has enough fish for three or four days. The fresh fruit is the only thing that never lasts long enough. More than ever, the flashlight has to be fully charged so they can check on the girls at night. With so much to do, he is already exhausted, and this is only their first day.

* * *

Jenny finally gets up for a short walk. After being in the hut for several days, she is glad to get out. Ben follows closely behind, carrying the girls since Jenny is still uneasy on her feet. After a few minutes, she has had enough, lying next to the campfire with the twins. It gives Ben a chance to clean up the hut. He is so glad that he put a piece of plastic over everything to protect the sleeping bag and the cushions.

Ben cooks up a feast of fish and lobster to celebrate their new family members. It's the first time he has prepared lobster all on his own, and it will probably be the last. Just as they are about to eat, the girls are hungry again. They put everything on hold. The girls make sure they get their food first, crying out loud until they are fed. The quiet evenings sitting down to eat are now a thing of the past.

Jenny is so happy to sit next to the campfire, warming herself and watching over the twins. Ben is too tired to eat but knows this is probably the only hot meal he'll get for the rest of the day. His cooking is no match for Jenny's fabulous meals.

Ben doesn't even try any of the lobster. He feels so bad having to toss it in the boiling water, worse having to cut it up once it's cooked. If it weren't for Jenny's cooking, he could easily be a vegetarian.

* * *

With supper finished and everything cleaned up, Ben has no time to rest. The sailboat needs to be cleaned out before the tide comes in. Jenny wants to go so badly to see what is in it. Unfortunately, after giving birth to twins, she is not going anywhere. The sailboat is too far down the beach, and there is no way that she can make it on her own.

After kissing Jenny and the twins, Ben is on his way. He runs all the way down the beach to take everything out of the sailboat and get back quickly. The tide is coming in fast, and the sailboat is rocking back and forth with the waves. He knows it won't be long before the tide drags it back into the ocean.

As he walks up to the sailboat, the first thing he needs to do is stabilize it. With it constantly rocking back and forth with the waves, there is no way he can get inside it. He grabs the anchor and pulls it out as far as possible, then digs it deep into the sand way up on the beach. He then takes one of the rigging lines, tying it to the closest tree.

Once he is in the sailboat, he grabs everything that's not bolted down, tossing it all out on the beach. There are no photos or paperwork to see who owned the sailboat. He hoped whoever was in it had a chance to get out before it went down and called for help.

His next task when he gets back is to make a signal fire out on the beach. If any rescue ships or airplanes are nearby, he needs to be ready to light them at a moment's notice.

The one thing that he hopes to find is not there. All the radio and navigation gear are missing. He doesn't see any charts either. That would have given them a clue about what island they are on. He can't complain. The bedroom is sealed and undamaged. They now have a wealth of supplies that are worth their weight in gold.

* * *

After several hours, the sailboat is stripped clean, leaving nothing but the fiberglass hull. The rope and even the remains of the sails have been removed. From the rugs on the floor to the cabinet doors, they can all be used someday in the future.

On his last trip inside the sailboat, he finds a black leather organizer wedged between the bulkhead and the back of one cabinet. Opening it up, he discovers it's filled with paper, pens, and pencils. It might have been for the captain's log and had fallen behind the cabinet. No entries had been made, and it looks as if it's never been used. He recalls that Jenny always wrote notes while in Hawaii, so he knows she is going to like this.

Ben stacks the rest of the bounty up by the trees, making sure none of it gets washed away. Getting too dark inside the sailboat, he calls it quits. The biggest chore now is hauling it all back to the camp. He grabs the first pile of goods and makes his way back. With no sleep in the last couple of days, he is about to collapse, and this is the first of many trips hauling everything to the camp.

* * *

Ben quietly places the last load by the campfire, seeing that Jenny is asleep. He knows Jenny is so frustrated she can't go herself. Scavenging out on the beach is her favorite pastime, and she is missing the biggest find since they have been on the island.

"Oh, you're back already?" she asked.

"Yeah, it's the last one for today," he replied, trying to catch his breath. "This was the easy stuff. Tomorrow, I'll see if I can rip some of the cabinets off the walls."

"What are we going to do with all of this?" she shouted, seeing the huge pile of goods.

"There is still a lot down there I dumped in the trees," he added. "These are some of the bedroom things we can use now."

"This is amazing," she replied, rummaging through all the sheets and towels.

After showing her everything he found, Ben left the best for last. "Here is one that I know you'll love!"

"Oh, this is wonderful!" Jenny said, so pleased with the writing organizer.

"I don't think it was ever used. It was stuck behind one of the cabinets."

"This is so nice... I always wanted one of these but could never afford one like this. It must be an executive model for writers," she said, seeing it's complete with pens and pencils.

Ben sits down next to her. "I guess you can start a journal now and write down all our adventures here. I found another rim of extra paper. You got enough here to write a book!"

"You know... That's a good idea! We can keep track of our daily activities. Even better, I can keep track of the girls now! I need to record what and when they ate, plus their sleeping habits. I might even write about all the things we've done since we got here," looking over at the twins, who are sound asleep.

"You have plenty of paper, so you can put in whatever you want. You better get started, and you got nine or ten months of our lives here to catch up on," knowing Jenny is eager to start writing again.

She leans over, giving him a big hug and kiss. "Thank you! You really outdid yourself today. I'm going to write all about it. I want the girls to know what their father did on the day they were born," and starts writing her first entry.

"I didn't do much... You're the one who did all the work, giving birth to two girls."

She laughed. "Now I think about it... It's all one big blur. One day, you may have to help me remember all the details."

"Well, let's just say, luckily, it was dark."

She couldn't help laughing. "You've come a long way. Not only did you clean the fish, but you also cooked and prepared the lobster. Then, to top it off, you helped deliver your own two girls!"

Ben shuddered, trying not to think about it. "I'm going to have nightmares about that for the rest of my life."

"Which one? Cleaning the fish or delivering the babies?"

Again, he shuddered. "Both, if you must know!"

She laughed. "Well, at least we got all these new supplies to help us out. What a find!"

Ben is rummaging through everything. "Looks like I need a haircut and a shave!" he added, looking at himself in the mirror for the first time in months, seeing his stringy hair and a full beard.

He hands Jenny the mirror, but she refuses to take it. "Oh, no... I don't want to look after what I have been through in the last few days."

"Oh, come on... You're beautiful. There are a couple of items I found you might like," holding up an unopened bag of women's razors, soap, and a couple of deodorant sticks.

She laughed. "So, are you trying to tell me something?"

"Ah, no... It's just some of the things I found," realizing the big mistake he just made.

"We both can use a little cleaning up!" she said, pulling on his beard.

He is so relieved she is not mad at him. She is always good-natured, but her mood swings have kept him on edge ever since she has been pregnant. He still has a hard time knowing when she is joking or is downright mad at him.

Quickly getting up, he goes through all their new supplies. Feeling exhausted, he is ready for a nap but still has a lot of chores to do before it gets dark. He has never worked so hard in his life, and this is just the first day with the babies.

The campsite is overflowing with new supplies from the sailboat. They now have two single foam mattresses, four sets of sheets and blankets, two pillows, a stainless steel cutlery set for six, two lifejackets, a full-size hammock, a sewing kit, scissors, and various cookware. With still more down on the beach, it will take weeks to go through everything. The hardest part is having to haul half of it up to the cave. All the supplies from the sailboat are a great find, but it's way too much to handle in just one day.

* * *

Ben wakes up early after sleeping all night long. The hammock is the only thing from the sailboat that he loves the most. There is no more sleeping in the cramped little tent or on the hard ground. Realizing he had slept all night, he runs into the hut to check on Jenny. Luckily, they are still sound asleep. Seeing Jenny with the girls is a beautiful scene, but he is still not used to it.

Tossing the last few logs on the campfire, he can't believe how much they have used. Checking under the hut, he is surprised to find that most of the firewood is gone. Everything had been carefully planned for months, but now they are using more supplies than expected.

The first chore of the day is getting more water. The one-gallon water bottles from the sailboat are already coming in handy. Hauling all the water bottles and the big cooking pot down to the pond is a tremendous job. The worst is bringing it all back, filled with water. On their first day with the babies, they used more water than ever. He has a feeling he is going to be hauling water twice a day at the rate they are using it now.

Once he returns with the water, the campfire is already in full flame. After checking on the girls, he sets up the cast-iron pot over the fire. After seeing what he looked like in the mirror, it's time to clean up. Shaving off his beard is now easy with all the new soap, scissors, and razors. Cutting his hair is more difficult, but he gets it short enough, and he'll have Jenny help clean it up later.

After a while, Ben hears Jenny moving about in the hut. He peeks in, seeing that she is already feeding the girls.

"Good morning!" Jenny said with a big smile. "Now, that looks a lot better!" seeing him clean-shaven.

"It feels great without the beard," running his hand over his clean-shaven face. "Although I don't look forward to shaving every morning. Oh, I'm sorry I slept through the night. So how are they doing? Is everything OK with the girls?"

"Don't worry about it," she replied, proudly looking down at her little girls. "I think I'm getting the hang of this now. There's not much you can do, anyway. I thought I'd let you get a good night's sleep. Besides, we're down to our last fruit and don't have much water either. Do you think you can make the trip today?"

"Sure, I'll make a quick run. I already got the water, and the fire is already going. Will you be OK on your own?"

"We'll be all right... Just don't make it too long. Oh, we need some more firewood, too."

"I'll grab as much as I can. You need anything from the cave?" he asked.

She laughed. "You got to be kidding. We have more down here now than we have up at the cave. Maybe we should go through some of this and store the extra stuff up there."

"I think you're right," looking around at all the bounty from the sailboat. "There's even more piled up down the beach. It's going to take us a while to go through all this. I'll take some of the extra towels and things up there in case it rains."

"Before you go, I want to walk around a bit and get some fresh air," handing Ben one of the babies.

He is still a little nervous holding them since they are so tiny. Jenny has the babies wrapped up in towels like little cocoons. She then hands him a white cloth that is tied in a loop with a knot.

"What's this for?" he asked.

"It's a baby sling... Just put it over your neck and shoulder, then put the baby in it."

"Wow, how did you figure this out?" he asked, slinging it over his arm and gently putting the baby in it.

"It was one of those things I saw on TV years ago on one of those nature channels. It just came to me last night when I was feeding the girls. You know, it's funny the things you remember."

"It works great! She fits right in. Now, I don't have to worry about her slipping out of my hands."

"I noticed you were a little scared holding them. I made two, so now we can walk together carrying them," she explained, taking out the other sling, putting it on, placing the other baby into it.

"So, where are you going?" he asked, seeing her walking towards the beach.

"I need to go out for a short walk. I can really use a good bath, too."

"Oh no," he said, shaking his head. "It's too early for you to be walking around. Keep around here for a couple of days. You've been through a lot, and you need to rest up."

"No, I have been cooped up here for weeks. I need to get out and start exercising. I have been walking around the camp and feel OK. Besides, I can't wait to check out the sailboat. Of all the times for a wonderful find to wash up, and I can't get to it!"

"You think you can make it down there?" he asked, not liking this at all. "I don't think you can. It's too soon."

"Well, I do... I'll take it one step at a time. You might have to help carry the babies, but I think I can do it."

"OK, I'll take them both," he said, knowing that once she has her mind set on something, it's no good arguing. "Just don't overdo it. Remember, you have plenty of time to exercise," carefully taking the other baby.

Ben carries the babies as they stroll down to the beach. He is excited to show his girls the beach for the first time. He can feel them react to the warm breeze as well as the crashing waves. They always kick their legs and arms around as if they are ready to go out and play.

Jenny is so relieved to get out of the camp for a while. She wants to get on the beach again and has been looking for this day for a long time. The fresh air and the cool breeze are something that she misses the most.

"So, that's it," she said, seeing the sailboat way down the beach. "It's odd having a boat sitting on our beach. It's a lot farther down than I thought. That's going to be a long walk."

"She will be there for a while. I got it tied up. She made it through the high tide, so you can take your time getting down there," knowing the walk just down to the water is already too much for Jenny.

"Maybe tomorrow we can go down and check it out."

"Tomorrow will be better," he suggested. "Let's sit out here for a while with the girls. I'll take care of them so you can relax."

"OK, but I want to have a quick wash first," seeing how calm and clear the water is.

"Don't go out too far," he said, getting concerned about her.

He sits on the beach with his little girls, telling them all about the ocean and their new home. Jenny is so glad to see Ben with his babies. She disrobes and walks out into the surf with her new soap for her first bath in a long time. Eventually, she lies back, floating on the water like she always used to do.

The babies seem to be OK, but now Ben worries about Jenny. She has been through an ordeal having the twins and is still very weak. He is relieved to see her wanting to get out and walk around. The sailboat down on the beach is calling her. She is intent on making it all the way down the beach to check it out herself. He knows it might take a day or two, but she will do it.

After a long soak, Jenny is ready to get back. She is feeling so much better now. So full of energy, she longingly looks down the beach at the sailboat. Scavenging the beach and the sailboat will have to wait. Their first outing with the girls is short, but it's a good start for Jenny.

* * *

Ben gets ready for the trip up to the cave. He doesn't feel good about leaving Jenny and the babies all alone. He plans to make a fast run there and back. It will also be a good time to store away some of their new supplies. There will be enough supplies for the camp and the cave if another storm hits the island, so there will be no need to drag everything with them. The extra mattress will come in handy at the cave for Jenny and the girls.

"Are you sure you're going to be all right on your own?" he asked.

"Yes, just take your time… We're not going anywhere. You do your chores. We'll be fine right here."

Ben hates to leave them on their own, but they are getting short of everything. "I'll just make it a quick trip," giving them all a big kiss.

He grabs some water bottles and a stack of supplies to store in the cave. He slowly walks out, constantly waving at his little girls. Once he is out on the beach, he runs as fast as he can.

At the small pond, he doesn't even stop, dropping all the water containers. He races up the trail, worrying about Jenny and the girls being all alone.

* * *

Ben makes it to the cave in no time, storing everything away. Bundling up as much firewood as he can carry, he dashes back down to the fruit trees. He fills the bag with as many oranges and grapefruit as it can hold, making sure they have enough for several days.

Dragging the heavy load down the trail is exhausting. Ben is in absolute agony. Every muscle in his body ached. Thinking about Jenny being all alone with the babies keeps him going. He is not used to all this responsibility. He keeps thinking of his two little defenseless girls and how they are out here living in the wilderness. They lived a hard life, but now, with the babies, he is getting scared. The wrecked sailboat is now their only hope, and it might eventually draw in some rescue ships to their island.

Ben runs down the trail without stopping. Reaching the small pond, he quickly fills all the water containers. Without taking a drink, grabbing everything, he runs down the beach. Utterly exhausted, he drags himself into the camp, finding Jenny still sitting next to the campfire, holding the babies.

"Ben, do you know how long you have been!" she shouts, so surprised to see him back so soon.

"I'm sorry," he mumbled, dropping everything. "I went as fast as I could," still gasping for air.

"That's not what I meant!" she explained, getting annoyed with him. "You've only been forty minutes! You ran the whole way, didn't you? I told you I'd be all right here with the babies. You didn't need to run like that," concerned that he was going to collapse.

"I didn't want to be too long in case you needed something," he said, taking a swig of water.

"Well, you ain't in any condition to help out now anyway," she said, getting so mad. "Look at you! You're completely exhausted!"

"I'm OK... Just a little winded," sitting down, trying to catch his breath.

Jenny scolds him for a long time. Ben knows she is right, but this is his first time being a father. She explains to him that things are not going to change. Everything is gradually going to go back to the way they were when it was just the two of them. He has never seen this side of Jenny before. Now, as a mother, she is setting down a whole bunch of new rules.

* * *

In just a few days, they are back to their day-to-day routine. Jenny regains her strength and resumes her morning scavenging hunts. She can't wait to get down to the sailboat to go through it, seeing what else she can find of value.

While Jenny is running about on the beach, Ben's new chore is to carry the twins as they walk. The baby slings make it easy to carry the girls at the same time. He is still not used to being a father with so much responsibility. Every waking moment of his life is now spent thinking about Jenny and his girls. With two newborn babies who are so defenseless, relying on him for everything is by far the biggest challenge of his entire life.

The sailboat quietly disappeared one night. After being stripped clean, it doesn't take much for the tide to carry it back into the depths of the ocean. They are sad to see it go. The wealth of supplies from the sailboat will make life on the island a lot more comfortable. They saw it as a gift from above since it showed up on the day the twins were born.

* * *

Chapter 30

Odd Things

April and June can swim before they can crawl. Their love of the water is insatiable. The big pond is their favorite place to play. Every day for several hours, when all the chores are done, it's family time at the pond. Ben always uses this time to teach them how to swim or float on the water.

With the twins crawling about, always getting into things, Jenny eventually moves them out of the hut. The tent becomes their new home and their playpen. With an open campfire constantly being used, the tent provides a safe place to play and a bug-free environment.

The twins play in the tent for hours. Whenever they have enough, they sit together quietly, waiting for someone to release them. They don't scream or cry but patiently wait, watching their father's every move. He always thinks it's a little spooky when they do things like that. He notices how they are already learning how to make him feel guilty so they can get out of their playpen early.

Ben refurbishes the hut after much-needed repairs. After months of wear and tear, it served its purpose. Now, it's only used for storage and shelter on rainy days. With the mattresses and the hammock, sleeping outside is so nice, especially on warm nights.

* * *

When Jenny is preparing the food, that is the one time she doesn't want the girls to get into things. Once they smell the aroma of freshly cooked fish, they hover around the campfire, always getting in the way. They carefully watch everything their mother does. Their love of freshly cooked seafood is insatiable.

"Ben, can you put them in the tent while I finish this up?" Jenny asked, seeing the girls were getting in the way.

He picks them up, carrying them back to the tent. "OK, you two... It's playpen time!" with both fighting like mad, trying to get away.

"Make sure you seal up the tent. They learned how to open the door," she added.

"Yeah, I noticed that... I'll tie it up real good so they won't be getting out anymore," realizing the twins have been escaping lately.

"It looks like it might rain soon… Can you clean things up in the hut while I finish up with the food?" Jenny asked.

"I'll get it ready just in case," he said, putting the twins in the tent.

While Ben is tidying up in the hut, Jenny glances over at the girls, hearing them laughing out loud. She froze instantly, seeing a dark object inside the tent with them. She can't believe her eyes, having to blink several times. The twins are on the far side playing together, and they see it as well, pointing over to it. The dark object slowly moves closer to the girls.

"Ben!" she screamed. "Hurry! Get out here! There's something in the tent with the babies!"

"What is it?" he asked, frantically running out of the hut.

"Get them out!" she yelled out in absolute panic. "Get them out quick! Hurry!" pointing over at the tent.

He frantically runs over, looks in the tent, but sees nothing. The twins are scared by all the commotion. As he unties the zipper fastener, he looks around, trying to see what it is. They are always afraid of rats or scorpions crawling into the tent with the children.

"I think they're OK," he said, quickly pulling them out and checking for bites.

Jenny rushes over with a big knife, trying to pull everyone away. She is so scared, not taking her eyes off the tent.

"Don't panic! They're OK! No bites or anything. I didn't see anything either. What was it?" he asked, not understanding why she was panicking.

"I don't know, but it was big!" looking in the tent.

"What was it? A scorpion?" he asked again, handing the girls to her.

"No! Nothing like that! It looked like it was almost as big as the girls!" handing the knife to Ben.

He looks at her in disbelief. "You got to be kidding?" turning back to the tent for another look.

Again, he sees nothing, carefully pulling out the sleeping bag. Nothing else is in the tent. He holds up the sleeping bag, making sure nothing is in it, still thinking it's a rodent or scorpion. Opening the sleeping bag, he lays it out on the sand to make sure.

"So what was it? What did it look like?" he asked, not understanding how Jenny could think something was in the tent with the girls.

"I don't know! It wasn't a bug or anything like that! I could only see its shadow, but it was huge! Even the girls saw it," not taking her eyes off the tent.

He doesn't understand, walking back over to the tent. With the entire top of the tent made of netting, he can see everything inside it. With nowhere to hide, it will be easy to see whatever is inside it. He picks the tent up off the ground, but it's empty, and it's clear to him that nothing is inside.

"Look, there is nothing inside it!" he said, holding it up.

"No, I saw it! Maybe it got out!" she explained, still shaking her head.

He examines the tent, seeing that it's still sealed up. "There are no holes or anything for something to escape. The only opening is the zipper door, and I was there the entire time. I didn't see anything, nor did anything get out."

"I know what I saw, and it was big!"

He takes the tent apart, removing all the support poles. Then he lays it out flat, folding it up and rolling it up tight. The compact tent is now nothing but a ten by four-inch rolled-up nylon.

"See, there's nothing in it... The only way something could get out is through the door, and I was there with the girls."

"I don't know what it was, but I do know it was in there with them," sitting down next to the campfire, still a little shaken. "The girls saw it too. I saw them react to it. It was weird. I really couldn't see it clearly, but it was there."

"So, what do you think it was?"

"Like I said, it was more like a shadow. To be honest. It almost looked as if someone was sitting in there with them. At first, I thought it was one of the girls, but then I saw them both sitting together at the other end. Ben, it looked more like another child was in there with them."

"What? You got to be kidding! You saw another person in the tent?" so astonished.

She just nods her head. "Ben, I know what I saw."

"I didn't see anything," he said, looking at her a little confused. "There was nothing else in it when I got the girls out, and there's nothing in it now. I thought you were talking about bugs or a rat. Not a person, or a large animal!" pointing down to the tent, rolled up tightly on the ground.

She thinks about it for a while. "Maybe it was on the other side and not really in the tent. Maybe the fire cast a shadow on the tent, and it was really behind it!" trying to figure it out.

"That could be it, but look at my shadow," he explained, walking over to where the tent was set up. "It had to be in front to cast a shadow on the tent. It might have been behind it. Maybe that's why you couldn't see it clearly. You might have seen it through all the netting, but I didn't see anything run off. I don't see any footprints either," looking around the area.

"Ben, I'm so scared!" she said, holding the girls tight. "I don't feel safe if something is roaming around here, especially at night!"

"I know... We'll have to keep an eye on things. We haven't seen any animals since we've been here. Maybe something was washed up."

"That could be it! Maybe it smelled the food, and it's hungry!"

"I think you're right about that. We'll set a trap and put out some food. So, I guess we'll be sleeping in the hut tonight."

"I know I will, and the girls will be too! You need to put up the door! I don't want anything crawling in there while we're sleeping."

When living on the beach, bugs and little rodents are constant problems. One of the benefits of camping on the sand is that most animals always leave their tracks behind. Ben looks around the camp for footprints. Even small birds and the occasional rat or mouse leave footprints in the sand. He doesn't see anything and doesn't know what to make of it. It is a big mystery.

* * *

After a few days, it's all forgotten. No animals or any tracks have been seen around the camp or out on the beach. The scare taught them to be on the constant lookout for scorpions or bugs. They never take anything for granted. They always seal up the tent to make sure nothing ever crawls inside it. Even the campsite is always kept clean, making sure no food is left out. The last thing they want is some animal crawling about the camp in the middle of the night, looking for food.

* * *

Months later, in the afternoon, Jenny notices something odd when she walks on the beach to check on the girls. "Ben, will you come out here and look at this!"

"What's up? So, what mischief are they getting into this time?" seeing the girls running about on the beach.

"They've been out here playing for a while, and I noticed something odd," Jenny said.

"They look like they're having fun making sandcastles and playing games," he replied, wondering what the problem is.

"I told them not to go near the water. I can always tell where they've been by the footprints in the sand."

"So, what's the problem?" he asked. "They haven't been near the water. They're leaving their tracks everywhere but out there."

"That's just it," she said, walking over to a row of footprints. "I just happened to notice these near the wet sand."

"I don't get it?" he asked, looking down but doesn't see anything unusual.

"Ben, there are three sets of footprints!"

He pauses for a few seconds. "How are the little buggers doing that?"

"I don't know. I didn't think anything of it at first, but out here near the wet sand. You can clearly see it. Then I notice it's all over the place. Everywhere you look, there are three sets of footprints."

"They do have some palm leaves out here. One of them is covering their tracks, so we don't see where they've been. Maybe it's one of their new games."

"Did you teach them that?" giving Ben a stern look.

"No, I didn't... It's a pretty good trick, though. They are covering their tracks, so we don't know they've been in the water. They're getting real sneaky."

"Well, I don't like it, and I'm putting a stop to it," she said, walking over, picking up all the palm leaves, escorting the girls back to the camp for a nap.

Ben looks over the area in front of the camp. He knows the girls were running about, dragging palm leaves behind them. One of the good things about living on a beach is that everyone leaves tracks in the sand.

Then he notices something odd. Kneeling on the sand, he places his hand over one of the footprints. One set is a little bigger than the others. Both the girl's feet are the same size. Right away, he sees this was not a feeble attempt to cover their tracks. There is another set of footprints here.

He gets up, walking around retracing their steps. The twins were dragging palm leaves about, but it wasn't to cover up footprints. Following everywhere they went, it all started right in front of the campsite. The larger footprints are right next to a palm tree, looking like someone was waiting. From the size, it appears that whoever it was is not much older than the girls.

Jenny walks over, wondering why Ben is staring at the ground. "So, what are you doing?"

"How long have they been out here playing?" he quickly asked.

"Maybe five or ten minutes," she answered.

"You saw them when they were out on the beach?"

"Well, yeah... I was cleaning up when they ran out to play. I glanced out a few times to check on them and saw them running around. Why? What's going on?"

"Oh, it's nothing... I'm going to keep an eye on those girls to make sure they don't get into trouble," not wanting to tell Jenny anything to get her scared.

"Yeah, we can't have them out here alone. It's too dangerous. If the girls get near the water, one big wave will knock them over, and they'll be dragged out."

"That's what I was thinking," not letting on that someone else could be on the island.

The worst part about it all is that it happened around the girls. They were not afraid, but it looked like they were out playing on the beach at the time. At least the footprints are small, almost like a child's, but a child cannot survive out here on their own.

Ben doesn't want to tell Jenny about it, not wanting to scare her. He is going to keep a close eye on the girls for a while. Luckily, the tent is being used as a playpen to prevent them from roaming about, and they sleep in it at night. From now on, someone always has to be with them.

They had some odd things happen since they had been on the island. Even though it's been a long time, they have seen no one else here. One of the things he is going to do is keep an eye out for footprints that are not theirs and put out a few traps just in case. There might be someone else on the island, and they are hiding, but the footprints are small, from a child. What is so odd is how can anyone else be on the island without them knowing about it? From the shadows within the trees to the tent incident, it's all a little spooky and still a big mystery.

* * *

Chapter 31

Storm

On an ordinary, carefree day, the weather catches them off guard. Ben arrives at the cave from the far side of the island when he sees the large cumulus clouds building up to the south. He had no idea that the weather was changing. On the north side, it's clear and calm, with no signs of any impending weather. That is one of the problems of being on the far side of the island for too long.

He runs down to the lookout to get a better view of the storm. Seeing the massive black cloud just south of the island makes him stop dead in his tracks. These are not typical storm clouds that they have seen so many times before. The winds are already picking up, and the waves are enormous. They are about to be hit by a big storm, and it's approaching fast.

He doesn't bother carrying any supplies, running down the trail as fast as he can. By the time he reaches the beach, he is so shocked to see how massive the storm is. What was once a calm ocean is now enormous waves driving water up to the trees. Right away, he knows it's bad, and they need to get up to the cave.

* * *

Once he reaches the camp, it's already getting dark. The winds are blowing so hard that huge palm leaves are dropping around him. Luckily, Jenny packed everything and is ready to leave.

"Thank God you're here!" she cried out, so relieved to see him. "I didn't think you were going to make it back in time!"

"I headed straight back here as soon as I saw the clouds! It's coming in fast! You ready to go?"

She nods her head. "Everything is packed. We've been ready for the last thirty minutes. You get the duffel bag, and I'll get the girls!" running over to the hut, grabbing the twins.

"Where did you put the flashlight?" he asked. "I have a feeling we're going to need it from the looks of things."

"It's in the bag on top of everything else," knowing that would be the first thing they would need when they got to the cave.

"Good, I'll keep it in my pocket just in case," opening the bag and taking out the flashlight.

Ben picks up the old duffel bag, now heavier than usual, with all the extra supplies they acquired. He goes through the hut, making sure everything is safely stored away. The hut will go through its first test to see if it will survive a big storm. Luckily, it's been a quiet season since the girls were born. Now, their luck has suddenly run out.

"I think we got everything we need," he said, looking around one last time.

"Do you think we can take that as well?" she asked, pointing to her mattress in the hut.

"You got to be kidding! You already have one at the cave. We might not be up there that long. Remember, what we take up there, we'll have to bring back!"

"One is not enough... Remember, we got the girls too. They'll need something to sleep on."

"You guys are getting spoilt nowadays. In the good old days, a cushion was all we ever needed," folding up the mattress, stuffing it under his arm.

She laughed. "My days of sleeping on that cold hard floor are over. Let's get out of here before it gets any worse!" walking out to the beach.

The twins are so scared, not understanding what is happening. Everyone is panicking. Normally, on a rainy day, they will stay in the hut. For some reason, they are leaving the safety and shelter of their home. They keep pointing to the hut, screaming out loud, wanting to go back.

"It's OK... We're just going up to the cave," Jenny explained, trying to calm them down.

Both of the girls are screaming and pointing at the hut. They want to get out of the rain and know something is not right, constantly chattering to their mother, wanting to go back. Luckily, they are too young to remember all the other times waiting out the storms in the cave.

"No hut today!" Ben said, following right behind them. "We're going on an adventure. It'll be a lot of fun!" trying to make it sound like it's a good thing, seeing they don't like being out in the wind and rain.

The girls don't listen, screaming out loud. They keep pointing to the hut, wanting to get back to the safety of their home.

Out on the beach, they feel the full force of the wind. The rain is not that bad, but the wind is brutal, pelting them with blowing sand and the mist from the crashing waves. The waves are already running past the trees, and it's a mad rush to get off the beach. They are out in the open in a major storm, and they still have a long way to go to reach the cave.

* * *

Once they walk up the trail, Jenny is having a hard time carrying the twins. She has made the trip to the cave twice since the girls were born. In those times, Ben had to make multiple trips. First, he carried the twins, with Jenny following close behind. Then, he would make another trip for their supplies. This time, with no warning, they have to do it all in one trip with no time to stop and rest.

Halfway up the trail, they feel the full brunt of the storm. The small section of the trail that opens up with a spectacular view of the island is the last place to be during a storm. Having lost the protection of the trees and being at a higher elevation, they are at the mercy of the brutal wind.

The twins, wrapped in towels, have little protection from the pelting rain. Jenny tries to shield them with her body, but it makes walking even more difficult. With the trail being so slippery, she worries she might fall. This part of the path is very treacherous, being narrow and with a steep hill. One slip, and it's a long way down.

Darkness quickly falls over the island. In the middle of the afternoon, it looked more like the sun had just set, adding to their problems. The torrential rain turns the trail into a small river, making every step even more difficult. With the gusting winds and driving rain, visibility is down to just a few yards.

Getting to the cave takes forever. Jenny is having a difficult time carrying the girls. Ben slows down to a crawl so she wouldn't get too far behind. He is having problems as well with the duffel bag since it's way too heavy. The mattress is also getting heavier as it soaks up all the rainwater. He now knows it was a big mistake to take it with them to the cave.

As they struggle on, a huge palm leaf falls right in front of Jenny. She stumbles over it, almost dropping the twins. Luckily, it missed her by just a few inches.

"Are you OK?" he asked, hearing her scream.

"Ben, take the girls! I can't carry them anymore! You need to get them to the cave! It's too dangerous for them to be out here."

"OK, I'll take the girls!" quickly dropping the duffel bag and mattress. "I'll come back for these later. You can do it! I'll walk slower," taking the twins from her.

"No! You take them to the cave! Don't wait for me!" motioning for him to go alone.

"No! We need to keep together! You can do it!"

Just as Ben turns, lightning strikes nearby. They are almost knocked off their feet by the blast and blinded by the brilliant light. The smell of ozone fills their lungs. The twins are terrified and start crying, wanting to return home.

"Get the girls to the cave!" Jenny screams. "Do it now! Don't wait around for me! I'll be right behind you!"

"OK, I'll come back for you! Just stay there and rest up," knowing she is right.

"No, I'll make it on my own!" she said, sitting on the duffel bag. "I just need to rest for a minute!"

"OK, but make it quick! It's getting bad out here!" running up the trail, holding the twins tightly in his arms.

Ben runs as fast as he can, ignoring the pain in his legs. The twins are holding on for dear life, so scared and crying the entire time. Running at such a fast pace, it doesn't take long to reach the cave. He is so glad to get into the shelter away from the torrential wind and rain. He puts the girls down just inside the cave entrance. They are afraid, wanting to be held. Neither wants to leave the protection of their father's arms. They don't like the dark cave, and they are soaking wet and shivering in the cold air.

Ben makes his way to the back of the cave, looking for the extra towels. He is so glad that the flashlight is in his pocket. He finds a towel and quickly removes their wet clothes. The twins are shivering, not used to the cold, damp cave. He immediately wraps them both up with dry towels to keep them warm since all their clothes are still in the duffel bag down on the trail.

Ben waits for over ten minutes, but Jenny is nowhere in sight. He can't leave her out in this storm on her own. The twins have never been left alone, but Jenny is going to need help. At least the twins are safe in the cave, but he has to go back to get Jenny. Kneeling in front of his two girls, he contemplates what he is going to tell them. Both are so scared, constantly crying, wanting to be held.

"You guys have to stay here," he sternly said, looking right into their eyes. "Here is the flashlight, so you won't be scared. I have to go back and get Mommy. OK? Do you understand? You have to stay here and don't go outside," leaning forward, giving each one a big hug and a kiss.

"Stay here in the cave," he repeated. "I'll be back soon! You don't follow me! I'm going to get Mommy."

The twins are still crying, reaching out, wanting to be held. Seeing their father backing away, they step forward.

"No! You must stay here!" he repeated, pointing his finger at them.

"You're big girls now!" he said, backing away a few more steps, still facing them. "You watch each other and make sure you stay here. I'll be back soon with Mommy. You must not leave the cave!" so relieved they are not following him.

The twins suddenly stop crying, holding each other's hands. Ben is standing in the torrential rain for a few seconds to make sure they stay in the cave. He is so scared, not wanting to leave them, but he has to go back and get Jenny.

"You stay in the cave!" he repeated, pointing his finger at them again. "I'll be back soon!" then quickly turns, leaving his girls all alone.

Ben runs a few yards, then turns to make sure they stay in the cave. To his surprise, they are still standing at the entrance, holding each other's hands and waving at him. The scene he knows all too well. They would do the same when he left for his daily trips over the island to get fruit and firewood.

He is about to leave, then sees something else in the cave with the twins. The heavy rain blurs his vision. He can't make it out, but it looks as if something moved inside the cave. For a second, his vision cleared, seeing a dark figure walking up right behind them.

"Oh, my God! What the hell is that!" he yells out in absolute shock.

He panics, frantically running back. It's the worst time to have something hiding in the cave. When he approaches the girls, he discovers they are alone. Nothing else is in the cave with them. He takes the flashlight and works his way to the back, but nothing is there, and there is nowhere for anything to hide. He figures it's all the stress and the rain in his eyes causing him to see things.

After waiting a few minutes to check the cave, he knows he has to leave. "OK, now," he said again. "You be good. Stay here in the cave. I'll be back with Mom," handing them the flashlight and giving them one more hug and kiss.

He slowly walks out of the cave, again making sure they don't follow him. He is so proud of his little girls. They stay in the cave, waving at their father. They don't cry, standing just inside the cave, holding each other's hands. He slowly backs away, keeping an eye on them until the rain blocks his view. Then he turns to run back down the trail.

He is praying they'll stay in the cave. The vision of something else in the cave really spooked him. Even though he checked it out, making sure nothing else was there, it still bothered him. He figures his eyes are just playing tricks on him, or it's probably nothing more than a shadow cast from the flashlight.

He quickly catches up with Jenny. She has made little progress. She is walking so slowly, taking one step at a time, looking exhausted. He knows it will take her way too long to reach the cave at the pace she is going.

"You left the girls!" she screams out in a panic once she sees him. "Never leave them alone! You should have stayed with them! I can get there on my own!"

"They're OK! They're safe in the cave," he replied, quickly reaching down, picking her up in his arms.

"I could have made it on my own! You should have stayed with them!" so furious with him.

Ben ignores her and starts running back up the trail carrying her in his arms. Holding on to him in disbelief, she is so shocked to see how he can run at such a fast pace while carrying her. The entire time she never lets up, constantly scolding him about leaving the girls.

* * *

April and June eagerly wait for their mother and father. Standing quietly at the cave entrance, holding each other's hands, they look through the rain, looking for any signs of their parents to return. They are so scared, never being left all alone. The torrential rain and continuous lightning are not helping the situation at all.

Seeing a large dark figure moving towards them through the dense rain, they are so frightened. Thinking it's a big monster, they don't know what to do and have nowhere to hide. Pointing the flashlight at the dark figure, right away, they see it's their mother being carried by their father. The twins scream out loud, waving their hands up in the air, jumping up and down, so relieved it's finally over.

Ben rushes into the cave with Jenny, so glad to get everyone together again. She leaps out of his arms, hugging her girls, so proud of them. They stayed in the cave on their own, and they didn't even cry.

"You girls are so brave!" she said, hugging them again. "You did so good staying here on your own. I'm so proud of you!"

The twins are chattering nonstop. They keep pointing outside the cave, then up in the air. Then they put their hands over their ears, trying to describe all the rain, lightning, and thunder. They are acting out all their experiences of being all alone in the cave and the big storm.

"You did! Wow, that must have been scary. You both are so big now," she added, pretending to understand what they are saying.

Ben is in the back, looking around. The vision of something else in the cave is still bothering him. He is still trying to figure out what it could have been. So many things are scattered about on the floor. A loose piece of plastic blown up by the wind is about the only thing it could have been, or maybe a shadow, but it's still a mystery.

"What are you looking for?" Jenny asked, seeing him poking around with a piece of wood.

He shrugs. "It's nothing," not wanting to elaborate on what he is doing.

The twins run over, hugging their father, constantly chattering about something, pointing their fingers up in the air. They take his hand, escorting him from the back of the cave, trying to get him to sit down with their mother.

"I know!" he said, hugging and kissing the twins. "It's a bad storm out there. You guys did really good on your own, but I can't stay. I need to go back out again and get the rest of our things. I'll be back in a minute."

"Oh no, you don't!" Jenny shouted. "We'll get it when the storm eases up!"

"I have a feeling we're going to be up here for a while," he explained, staring at the heavy rain and wind. "We're going to need all our supplies. We don't want to lose the duffel bag. It won't take long," then quickly turns, running back down to retrieve everything they left on the trail.

Although it's mid-afternoon, it's so dark. The storm clouds are blocking out almost all the light. Jenny quickly starts a fire, preparing the cave for the long stay. Luckily, they keep half the towels, blankets, and other supplies in the cave just in case of emergencies. Their experiences with big storms and typhoons taught them to never leave anything at the camp. The cave is the only place on the island where their supplies will be safe and will not get wet or blown away.

Jenny tends to the girls, wrapping them up in a blanket to keep them warm. With the fire illuminating the cave, she rummages through their supplies. She brings out the old seat cushions, placing them next to the fire. The twins don't want to sit down. They insist on standing out by the cave entrance, wrapped in their blankets, waiting for their father to return. Sitting by the fire, Jenny is starting to worry since Ben is taking way too long.

* * *

After the torrential rain, the darkness sets in, Ben can hardly see anything. He doesn't dare run, worried he will slip and fall, or worse, step off the trail. Luckily, with all the constant lightning, it's the only way he can get his bearings.

Seeing a white object in the distance, he runs up, so disappointed. The mattress is still there, but the duffel bag is nowhere in sight. Filled with all their prized possessions and supplies that helped them survive on the island, it's the one thing they can't afford to lose. He wonders if the rain might have pushed it back down the trail.

Looking around for the duffel bag, he hopes it doesn't get washed all the way down to the beach, not wanting to make that trip again. With another lightning strike up on the island, he sees a white object about thirty feet down the side of the steep hill. The storm washed the duffel bag off the trail, and now it's stuck on a tree.

He knows it will be an enormous risk, but he has to go down and get it. Keeping hold of a nearby tree, Ben wedges his foot up against every rock on the way down. Everything is extremely slippery, covered with mud. Water flows down the hill, dislodging all the topsoil and any rocks that are not deeply embedded in the hillside. Even the small trees he is holding on to are being pulled right out of the ground. Seeing how slippery things are, he knows it will be a nightmare to get back up to the trail.

As Ben reaches the duffel bag, he takes hold of a nearby branch with his right hand to stabilize himself. Once he gets hold of the strap, he wraps it tightly around his wrist so it won't get away from him. Pulling hard on it, but it doesn't budge at all. The last thing he wants to do is empty it out, hauling everything back by hand.

With one last attempt, Ben pulls hard, then hears a loud cracking sound. The branch he is holding snaps off, sending him rolling down the hill. With the strap still tightly around his wrist, the duffel bag breaks free, sliding down the hill right behind him. He grabs at anything to stop his fall, but it either slips from his grasp or is pulled right out of the ground. While he is trying to slow down, the duffle bag passes him up and is now dragging him down the hill.

Finally, the bag slams up against a huge tree with a loud thump. Luckily, Ben hits the duffel bag, which cushions his fall. He rests against the bag, letting the rain wash the mud from his face, trying to figure out a way out of this mess. With no clue where he is or how far down the hill he has fallen, it's a dangerous situation to be in, especially stuck outside during a big storm.

After several attempts to crawl back up the hill, he knows he has no choice but to go all the way down to the beach. Resting for a few minutes, he sits down just above the duffel bag, digging his feet deep into the mud. With the strap securely wrapped around his wrist, he pushes the bag away from the tree. Slowly, it slides down the hill at a more controlled pace. He digs his feet into the mud, using it as a brake to make sure things don't get out of control.

Slowly but surely, he makes his way down the steep hill to a point where he finally comes to a stop. With the darkness and all the rain, he can barely see at all. If it were not for the constant lightning, he couldn't see much of anything. He walks straight into the wind, dragging the duffel bag behind. He has no choice but to try to make it out to the beach.

* * *

Ben knows he is getting close to the beach, hearing the crashing waves. The wind is brutal, whipping through the trees, stripping off huge palm leaves falling all around him. He is bombarded with everything from rain, leaves, and the occasional coconut. He makes his way from one tree to the next, using them for cover from the wind and debris.

Finally, reaching the beach, the wind and the rain are so fierce that he can barely keep on his feet. The ground shudders with every wave that crashes onto the beach. Holding tight to a palm tree for a few minutes, he is trying to think of a way to get out of this mess.

Another flash of lightning illuminates everything around him. The view is something that he is not expecting. The beach is almost gone, and the massive waves are all the way up to the trees. Breaking just a few yards away, the water is up to his knees. All he has to do is take a few steps in the wrong direction, and the waves will drag him out into the ocean.

Dragging the duffel bag is a hindrance but also a lifesaver. Since it's so heavy, it prevents him from being dragged out into the ocean after a wave knocks him off his feet. Being blasted by the wind and rain, he struggles from one palm tree to the next. He struggles on, trying to keep close to the tree line, feeling the full brunt of the storm.

Ben feels as if he has been out here for hours and has no clue where he is. Completely lost, the only thing he can do is try to find the camp to wait out the storm. He slowly moves on, going from one palm tree to the next. Looking into the trees, it's so dark there is no way he will be able to see the hut, and it may not be still standing.

A massive wave crashes close by, almost knocking him over. The water is over his knees, but luckily, he is holding onto a tree. While waiting for the waves to subside, he hears something odd coming from within the trees. The constant roaring sound is very unusual. As he walks towards the next tree, his foot drops into a depression filled with water. The water is cold, rushing out to the ocean. Right away, he knows it's the run-off from the small pond. The sound must be all the rainwater rushing off the island, making one huge waterfall.

He waits for more lightning strikes to illuminate the dense trees. Once it happens, he doesn't recognize any of his surroundings. It's more like a lake with water everywhere. With so many fallen trees covering the ground, if he hadn't found the small stream flowing from the pond, he would have never known where he was.

He finds it's easy to navigate in the dark by walking up the stream to reach the small pond. The water is getting deeper the closer he gets to the pond, almost up to his knees. The roaring sound of the waterfall is deafening, but it's a sign he is getting closer.

With the next lightning strike, accompanied by the massive thunder, everything comes into view. Right away, Ben spots the trail, heading straight for it. Although when the lightning hits, the sight of the massive waterfall is one he won't ever forget.

* * *

After struggling up the muddy trail, Ben finally reaches the mattress. Still lying out on the trail, he is so tempted to leave it. Saturated with water and covered with mud, it'll take weeks to dry out. He kneels on it to drain out the water, then picks it up, slinging it over his shoulder, and keeps walking.

Fighting the constant wind and rain, Ben is slowing down to a crawl. The weight of the waterlogged mattress and the duffel bag is taking its toll. The trail is slipperier than ever, covered with debris washed from above, causing him to fall several times. He makes sure not to let go of the duffel bag. The last thing he wants is to lose it and have it slide down the hill again.

Finally, he reaches the last part of the trail, up by the lookout. With no trees around, he feels the full force of the rain and wind, having to crawl on all fours, unable to keep on his feet. This part of the trail is the worst. The trail always turns to mud whenever it rains, making it extremely slippery and a constant problem.

He attempts to crawl up the trail, but the heavy duffel bag is holding him back. Whenever he pulls it up behind him, he slips right back down. Everything is either too slippery or too heavy. He finally figures out a way, tossing the mattress out in front of him and using it as a deadweight, where it just clings to the ground and doesn't move at all. He then crawls on top of it, pulling up the duffel bag behind him. Repeating this over and over again, he struggles to get up the last part of the trail.

Ben crawls up the last few feet on his hands and knees to the ridge that leads to the cave. Seeing a yellow glow in the distance, he knows he has made it. Covered with mud from head to toe, he picks up the mattress and duffel bag and walks the last few steps up to the cave.

Through the driving wind and rain, he sees two small silhouettes at the cave entrance. Never again will he risk everything for a few old trinkets. If anything had happened to him, Jenny and the girls would have to survive here on their own. That is his biggest fear of living on this island.

* * *

"Ben, where have you been?" Jenny frantically asked. "I thought you got lost! What happened to you?"

"The trail is slippery as hell," he explained, dropping the waterlogged mattress just outside the cave, dragging the duffel bag behind him. "It's also dark out there, and it took a little longer than I thought," making sure to leave out the part where he slid all the way down the hill to the beach.

"You shouldn't have gone!" she said, getting mad. "The storm is getting worse. There is nothing in that bag that's worth getting hurt. The girls have been going nuts ever since you left. They've been standing there waiting for you all this time. Even they know you shouldn't have gone out in the storm."

"Sorry," he said, kissing her. "Yeah, you're right... It was a mistake to go back out."

"Yep, you guys are right as well," he said, hugging and kissing both the girls. "I should have stayed in the cave," amused to see his girls still chattering away, probably telling him off.

Jenny notices the way that he is hugging the girls. Something went wrong while he was out in the storm. He looks as if he is terrified and is trying to hide it. Now is not the time to scold him. Later on, when things settle down, she is going to get to the bottom of this.

The twins are chattering about something, taking their father's hand, pulling him over to the campfire. He is trying to figure out what they are telling him. They keep on chattering in their baby talk. Both of them are pointing to the fire, then waving their fingers at him.

Jenny laughed. "I think they're trying to tell you to get those wet clothes off and warm up by the fire."

"I see they're taking after you, ordering me around."

"They know you shouldn't have gone out. You better dry off. It's going to be a long, cold night."

"I wonder what they're on about?" he asked, seeing the twins are really mad about something.

She sits down next to June, rubbing her back. "God only knows! They've been doing this ever since you left. I think you're getting told off for going out in the rain. At least they know when to come in during a storm!" giving him a stern look.

"Yeah, it wasn't such a good idea," he said, letting out a long sigh. "Although bringing that mattress up here wasn't a good idea either. It's saturated with water and weighs a ton. I don't know if we're going to be able to use it again."

"Sorry," she replied. "I should have left it in the hut. We should have been more prepared. We messed up this time, and it will not happen again! Once we're all in the cave, we're staying put!" giving him a mean look.

"Yeah, I learned my lesson... We just got caught by surprise this time. It's strange how this storm came up out of nowhere. No more going back for things we can live without."

"Also, you're never to leave the girls! Someone always has to be with them. I could have made it on my own."

Ben just nods, staring at the fire, knowing he has not heard the last of this. The twins are holding him tight, still chattering away. They always mimicked their mother. They are scolding their father for going back out into the storm in their own way.

* * *

With not much else to do, Jenny takes out a pan to fry up some bananas. Without any fish, it's all they have for a hot meal. Their meals are going to be nothing but fruit until they get back to the beach.

Once Jenny starts cooking, the twins can't wait to help out. They run over to get all the plates, knives, and forks. One by one, they place each plate next to the campfire, carefully putting each knife and fork together. Jenny made sure they knew the basics of being a good chef. Even the presentation is essential, especially when something as simple as setting up the plates.

"There they go again," he said, noticing the extra place setting. "Are they miss counting, or what?"

"I don't think so," she jokingly said, seeing the five plates laid out. "Maybe we got company coming for dinner."

As soon as Ben puts away one of the extra plates, the twins get mad. They start chattering up a storm, putting the plate back down with the others. They immediately begin waving their fingers at their father, telling him off.

"I think you're in trouble again," she said. "It's probably for their little invisible friend. It's so cute how they always do that."

"Yeah, but where do they get all this stuff? It's not like they see it on TV or get it from other kids. I never told them stories about invisible people or anything like it."

She laughed. "Who knows how they come up with all their little games? I used to do the same when I was little. My sister is a few years older, so she never wanted to play with me. So, I had an imaginary friend. I'd always go to the top of the hill behind the house and sit under the big old tree playing with my imaginary friend all day long."

"So, you're the one who has been teaching them this imaginary game thing. So, you used to set out an extra plate for her too?" he jokingly asked.

"Actually, I did! Mom used to bring our lunch up there. Even on my birthday, Mom and I would have a special party with just the three of us up on the hill. We'd have cupcakes with candles and even presents. It's funny how my mom was the one who made the extra effort with my imaginary friend and me. God, it's been a long time since I thought about those days. I even had a name for her. It was Amy," she explained, thinking about those good old days so long ago.

"Amy!" the twins both shouted in unison as soon as they heard the name, pointing to the extra plate.

Jenny gasped. "Oh! So your little friend's name is Amy, too!"

The twins are chattering again, pointing to the back of the cave and then down at the plate.

Ben is so shocked after hearing the girls repeating the name. "Oh, they can say Amy, but they still can't say dad yet!"

"Give them time... The twins only know a few words. At least they can say, Mom," teasing Ben a little more about the first word they spoke.

"I guess you're the one who's been telling them about imaginary friends and calling her Amy. That would explain where they got it."

"No!" she said, shaking her head. "I never said anything. It's been a long time since I even thought about it. From what I remember, they've been doing this for a long time. I never encouraged them at all, like my mom used to do with me. Although it's strange how they reacted to her name like that."

"Yeah, I noticed that," he said, looking at the girls. "It's a little strange how they do that. Where is Amy?" he asked, curious to see their reaction.

The twins lit up hearing the name, then looked around the cave. Again, they both are talking their gibberish, pointing their fingers at the extra plate.

"They do recognize the name... You must have told them stories about it and just don't remember."

Jenny shrugs her shoulders. "Maybe so... It doesn't matter, anyway. At least they're keeping up with the family tradition. I guess that means we got company tonight. Our little babies have a friend over for supper. Shame we haven't got something better to serve," placing fried bananas on all the plates.

Ben doesn't see the humor in this. Remembering the footprints on the beach and the shadow he saw with the girls, he looks around at the back of the cave. If he didn't know any better, he thought he had seen someone. There is nowhere to hide, and there is no way anything could have gotten out of the cave. He doesn't want to mention it to Jenny, especially now that they have to spend the night here.

* * *

Jenny puts two cushions end to end so the twins can sleep on them. Wrapped up in their blankets next to the campfire, it doesn't take long for them to fall asleep. Spending the night at the cave is a big treat, and just like everything else, the twins quickly adapt. They don't fully understand what is going on but see everything as a game.

Jenny sets out the remaining mattress next to the fire. "You must be tired... Come on, let's go to bed," she said, seeing Ben nodding off again.

"You got that right," he replied, half-asleep. "I'm going to sleep tonight," mumbling the last few words.

"From the looks of this storm, we'll probably get to sleep in late," motioning him over.

"You mean I get to sleep with you for a change!" he said, crawling on the mattress.

She giggled. "That's right! It's been a while since we slept together," snuggling up to him.

"Oh, this feels so nice," he said, lying on his back. "It's like the good old days."

"I remember those days," she whispered, resting her head on his shoulder. "That's how we got the girls."

"After all the fun we had, I'm surprised we don't have a few more."

"I'm not going through that again," she said, slapping his arm. "So don't get any ideas!" remembering the nine long months of being pregnant with the twins.

Ben doesn't respond. She looks over, seeing he is already sound asleep. Jenny knows something terrible happened, seeing how exhausted he is. One day, she'll find out, but he has learned his lesson and won't be going back out in a storm ever again. They had an exhausting day, and this is one they will never forget.

* * *

SECTION 3

Family

Chapter 32

Helping Hands

At four years old, April and June are eager to learn how to live off the land. Jenny enjoys her time with her daughters, teaching them everything from weaving hats to preparing meals. They take after their mother, and they love to cook. Seafood is their specialty. At times, even Jenny is amazed at some of the meals they prepare.

Ben makes daily trips to the other side of the island, chopping down trees for firewood and gathering fruit. Still taking at least four to five hours, it makes for a lonely day. He misses having someone to go with him. Unfortunately, the chores always have to be done, especially now with a family to support.

Somehow, the twins always know when it's time for their father to return from work. They wait on the beach, sitting on the little bench he made for them. When they see their father, they run down to greet him, screaming the entire way. They are always so eager to help out. He gives them each a small bag of fruit to help carry back. Once they are back at the camp, the twins help store it all away, then run out to the beach for family playtime.

* * *

Fishing is one of the things the twins love to do, and they quickly learn how to catch fish with the casting net. They are so thrilled to bring home a fish or two and can't wait to fry it up for supper.

One of Ben's biggest problems when fishing with his girls is that they are always on the loud side, constantly talking all the time. Unfortunately, every time they see a fish, they get so excited, screaming out loud, scaring all the fish away. Ben sees a lot of potential meals being chased away because of the constant chattering.

To solve the noise problem, he starts teaching them how to use hand signs. That was one of the things he learned while out camping with his old buddy, Kyle, a former Navy SEAL. The hand signs really do help while out fishing. He used it a lot while fishing in Colorado with his friends.

The twins quickly learn this new way of communicating, and it doesn't take long before they add more of their own hand signs, building their vocabulary. Just like everything else, it's a new game for them to play, and they excelled at this new hand sign game, using it all the time.

Jenny is not too happy with these new secret signals. Too many times, the twins will signal each other and start laughing out loud. She bans them from doing any more hand signs while they're in the camp. Jenny is now making all the rules, and she always has the last word.

* * *

April and June are becoming restless being at the camp all day. Jenny takes them on extended walks down the beach, scavenging for anything useful. Unfortunately, they want adventure and to explore the island with their father on his daily travels, gathering food and firewood.

Hearing all the stories, they long to go to the top of the island and walk among the clouds. Day after day, they sit out on the beach looking up at the peak of the island, wanting to go so badly. They don't want to talk about anything else.

Ben always told tall stories of his adventures while up on the island. He makes it sound exciting, and that makes them want to go even more. Unfortunately, the hike over the island was tedious and extremely hard work. The twins had not been to the cave for a long time, and they always had to be carried.

He wants to start taking the girls on his daily trips, but Jenny is reluctant. She thinks they're too young, and the hike is more than they can handle. Jenny and Ben constantly debate about letting the girls go, but she doesn't think they are ready for such a long trip.

* * *

One morning, Jenny surprised everyone. After discussing it all night long, she finally decides to let the girls go with their father to help with the chores. The only condition is that only one can go at a time. She thinks it will be too difficult to watch them both and do all the chores up at the cave. There are still plenty of chores to do at the camp, and she doesn't want to be left alone doing them all herself. There are times for fun and games, but the chores always have to be done. That's the number one rule of life on the island.

Naturally, both April and June want to be the first to go with their father. Ben knows it's going to be difficult to choose one over the other. They both have that puppy dog look on their faces, wanting so much to be first. It's a terrible position to be in, not wanting to show favorites. He has a good idea to solve the problem. Let them draw straws to see who gets to go.

"OK, here's how we're going to do this," Ben said, picking up two small twigs. "I have two sticks here, and the one who selects the biggest gets to go," holding the twigs in his hand in front of his girls.

April is so excited to be going with her father. "Is this the big one?" she asked, holding it up.

He laughed. "I don't know... June has to pick the other one. Then we compare them to see who gets to go with me."

June slowly approaches, pulling the last twig from her father's hand. "This one is mine!" holding it up for everyone to see.

"OK, let's see who has the biggest stick. That will be the one who gets to go today," getting ready for the big disappointment from one of the girls.

"June is the lucky one," he said, comparing the twigs.

April is already pouting. "I'm not going?" she asked, trying not to cry.

"Sorry, June gets to go with me today. You'll get your turn tomorrow!"

June is so thrilled but sees how sad her sister is. "It's OK, April! You get to go tomorrow. I'll tell you all about it when I get back!" giving April a big hug trying to cheer her up.

"It's not all fun and games," Jenny added. "There's a lot of hard work to do at the cave. The worst part is having to walk up there. It's not going to be easy," seeing how sad April looks.

"I know," April replied, trying not to cry. "But I want to go too… Can I go with you?" looking up at her father.

"Mom is right," he said. "We all can't go. Someone has to help out here, too. There's plenty of work to do down here at the camp. We can't let Mom do all the chores by herself, can we?"

"I know. I got my chores with Mom," April said, looking dejected.

"We'll have a good time while they're gone," Jenny said, giving April a big hug trying to cheer her up. "Don't worry. You'll have your day out with your father tomorrow!"

* * *

Jenny is getting very emotional as she helps June get dressed for her first trip over the island. June wears her long dress and her big-rimmed hat to protect her from the sun. She also wears her favorite handmade shoes. Going up to the cave will be a very long and grueling trip for her, but it's an essential part of life on the island.

Jenny goes into the hut and comes out, hiding something behind her back. "I knew this day was coming, so I made something to help you out. I was going to wait until I finished both of them, but I guess you can have yours now."

"Is it a surprise?" June asked.

"It sure is... It will help you carry things when you're out with your father," handing the present to her.

"Wow! I got my own carry bag!" seeing her mother holding out a bag with two ropes attached to it.

"No, this is way better!" Jenny explained. "It's a backpack! You can take it with you on long trips like today. I'm still working on the other one, so you two may have to share for a while," making sure to let April know she has not been left out.

Jenny is so proud, showing everyone the new backpack she made. She is getting good at making things they can use from old, discarded materials. The small bag is constructed from an old rubber mat and nylon rope that she found on the beach.

"See, now you can carry your lunch and water with you," Jenny explained. "So you won't have to worry about dropping anything. There's still room in there for other things too."

"Wow! This is nice!" walking around, showing off her new backpack with an ear-to-ear smile.

"April, are you OK?" Ben asked, seeing her pouting, and gave her a big hug.

A little tear runs down her face. "I'm OK... It's June's turn today. I'm trying to be happy for her," wiping away the tears.

"It's going to be rough on your sister, and it's a long trip. It's going to be the longest walk she has ever done, and it's uphill all the way. This time tomorrow, you'll be doing the same thing. I guess you'll be taking turns."

That brings a smile to her face, although she is so disappointed that she is not going on the first trip. April walks up to her sister, giving her another big hug.

The twins never fought or argued about anything. It will be the first time in their entire lives that they are going to be apart. For June, it'll also be the first time being away from her mother.

* * *

Finally, it's time for them to leave. Standing out on the beach, the small family hugs each other. The time has come for Ben and June to start their journey. It was an emotional time for Jenny. Her little babies are growing up.

"You be good now and listen to your father," Jenny said. "You stay close to him and no wandering off," with tears running down her face, hugging June again.

June starts weeping. "I will, Momma. We be back with lots of food and wood for the fire!" so scared, having to leave her mother for the first time.

"June, are you ready to go?" wondering if she is going to change her mind.

June smiles, nodding her head. "I'm ready!" reaching up, taking her father's hand.

"I'll do a quick trip to the cave. We'll probably be back at the usual time," he explained, seeing Jenny is getting worried.

"Have a good time together, but don't overdo it! If it's too much for her, just come on back. We have plenty of supplies down here to last a few days," Jenny replied, wiping away the tears.

"We'll see how things go... Don't worry, she'll be OK!" seeing Jenny is falling apart.

"Tomorrow is going to be your day! Better be ready!" he said, noticing April was so quiet.

She gets a big smile on her face after hearing that. "I know! I can't wait!" waving to her father.

Ben turns, slowly walking down the beach, holding June's hand. June is so thrilled with her first big day out with her father. She keeps turning around to wave at her mother and sister. It's a big day for the family and a big step for the little girls to learn how to survive on the island.

Being away from his family every day is getting old. He has hiked to the cave on his own since Jenny was pregnant. Now, after over four years, he is so thrilled that the girls are old enough to join him. He is so proud of his little girl and glad to have someone to talk to on the long trip up to the cave.

Jenny can't help crying. She holds April's hand, watching as they walk down the beach until they're out of sight. Even April is concerned about her sister going far away up on the island. She already feels lonely, having never been away from her sister since they were born.

Ben knows it's going to be a really quick trip. They'll be lucky to make it up to the lookout. It will be stressful for anyone who's never made this trip before, especially for a little girl. He'll probably be carrying her most of the way up and back down the trail as well.

June leads the way as Ben points out all the various trees and plants along the trail. He walks slowly and stops numerous times for water breaks. He remembers what it was like the first time he made this trip and how exhausting it was. She is already panting and out of breath. Not even at the halfway point on the trail, and it looks as if she has had enough. No matter how many times he offers to carry her, she refuses, wanting to do it on her own. She has her mind set on walking the entire way.

Once they reach the halfway point on the trail, June is yelling and screaming out loud, seeing the spectacular view for the first time. She is so excited, being up so high on the island, seeing the beach far below.

As they continue, June is exhausted. Her pace is slowing down to an excruciating slow walk. She doesn't even want to take off her backpack. She insists on making it on her own. He is so shocked at how stubborn she can be. She had her mind set on it, and that was it. She definitely takes after her mother.

* * *

After several long, grueling hours, they arrive at the lookout. June is so tired, struggling to keep on her feet. For Ben, it's the longest it's ever taken to walk up the trail, but it doesn't matter. He is so surprised and proud that she has done it on her own. Once she sees the view from the lookout, it gives her a second wind.

Ben holds her hand as they walk out onto the grass towards the orchard. "See there... That's where we get all the oranges and grapefruit. They grow all over the trees, and we only pick what we need."

All the stories she heard were true. She is so amazed at all the enormous trees filled with fruit. Seeing it for the first time, she is almost speechless. The top of the island is a whole new world for her.

With so many new things, she can't wait to get back home to tell her sister all about it.

"I never saw so many! Can we get some?" she asked.

"Sure! That's why we're here… We'll pick a few for now, then take a break out by the bench. Don't you remember this?" seeing the surprised look on her face.

"No!" she said, shaking her head. "I never ever been here. April and Mom will want to see this too!" not remembering the times they were here when they were young.

"You guys have been here plenty of times. The last time was probably over a year ago when we had the big storm. We stayed in the cave for days. You remember that, don't you?" walking her over to the fruit trees.

"No, I would have remembered that."

He picks her up so that she can get her own oranges. "OK, pick some big ones. We'll have a long break here before we head to the cave."

"This is fun!" so thrilled to be pulling oranges off the tree.

"Come on… Let's sit on the bench and rest up. You're going to see the best part of being up here!" he added, walking her over to the edge of the lookout.

"Wow!" June screamed out, so astounded by the view and seeing the trees and the beach far below.

"So, what do you think?" he asked.

"Wow, look how high up we are!"

"You can see everything from up here," he explained. "It's the top of the world. We're up so high. Sometimes you can even touch the clouds," putting his arms up in the air.

"I want to touch the clouds too! Can we do that next?" looking up at the sky.

He laughed. "Not today… They're too far away. When it gets cloudy, and you can't see the top of the peak, that's when you can touch the clouds."

"I can't wait to tell April about this! I wish she were here with us," feeling a little sad being away from her sister.

"Well, she'll see it all for herself tomorrow."

"Mom will like this too! She going to come up here too?"

He laughed again. "Your mother used to come up here with me all the time before you guys showed up."

"I want to come up here every day! This is way fun! Why doesn't Mom want to walk up here?"

"Well, for a start, someone has to stay home and look after you two. Mom has chores to do down there as well. I have to come up here to get the fruit and cut up the firewood. There are always chores to be done, and it's not all fun and games."

"Good! I can help with the chores," nodding her head.

"That's good to hear," he said, hugging her. "I can really use the help. I've been doing this all by myself since you were born."

They sit together on the small wooden bench at the edge of the lookout, admiring the spectacular view. June is so thrilled with it all. Seeing their home from so high up, she can now see that their home is indeed a small island. The small section of the beach in front of the camp is all the twins have ever known. She feels as if she is on top of the world.

June sees smoke emanating from the treetops. "Is that our home?" she asked, pointing it out to her father.

"Yes, it is!" Ben replied, looking down at the beach. "Mom is probably boiling some water. You can see the smoke from all the way up here. Sometimes when the tide is out, I can see you guys playing out on the beach."

"I can't see them!"

"It'll be a while before Mom goes out for her walk. They're probably starting the chores now. We have a lot of work to do as well. We don't have time to sit around. You ready to go to work?"

"Yes! So, what do we do first?" she asked, jumping off the bench, eager to help.

"Well, we got to collect some fruit. We're probably going to need a whole bag full. Then, if you're up to it, we can go to the cave."

"I want to go to the cave!" she shouted, jumping up and down.

"It's not far from here, but it's a steep climb. Think you can make it?"

"Hurry!" taking her father's hand. "Let's get the food, and then I want to go to the cave!" pulling him over to the orchard.

He holds her up again, letting her pick the oranges and grapefruit off the trees. She promptly stores them away in her new backpack. Once it's full, she puts the rest into the small sack.

They continue walking up to the cave, dropping off the bag of fruit at the foot of the trail to pick up on the way back. The short section between the orchard and the cave is the worst part. He wonders if she is going to make it. She doesn't complain, taking one step at a time. Even with her backpack filled with oranges weighing her down, she is adamant about walking the entire way with no help at all.

Ben, noticing the shadows from the trees, is so surprised how late it is. Taking a lot longer, he knows Jenny will get worried. They should have been halfway back by now. He doesn't say anything. She has wanted to do this for such a long time. It is her big day, and he wants her to enjoy it.

"We're almost there, just a few more steps. So, you ready for a little nap?" noticing June is dragging her feet.

"No, I don't want a nap… Can we eat when we get to the cave?"

"Sure, we'll take a long lunch break and rest up. Once you make it to the cave, that's as far as we go, and no more uphill climbs. Going back is easy. It's all downhill, but it's still a long way. Just think, I have to do this every day."

"This is hard work! We almost there?" she asked, gasping for breath.

"Yes, but let's take another water break. Just a few more steps to go," stopping again to let June rest, seeing how she is struggling.

She finishes up the last of her water. Her hands are shaking. Ben is about ready to pick her up, whether she likes it or not. To his surprise, she hands the empty bottle back and turns, walking the last few steps. Even on the steepest part of the trail, June is intent on doing it all on her own.

* * *

After almost twenty minutes, they finally reach the top of the ridge. Too tired to talk, June still has the biggest smile on her face. Ben takes her hand, slowly walking her to the cave. Once they reach the cave, she is exhausted, covered with sweat. He hands her his water bottle, letting her drink as much as she can take. He has a feeling that she will probably sleep for the rest of the day.

"This is it!" Ben said, standing out in front of the cave. "You finally made it! Don't you remember this? We spent many nights up here."

She cautiously looks into the dark cave. "No, don't remember this… It's dark in there. Looks spooky."

"It just looks that way from out here. Once your eyes get used to the dark, you can pretty much see your way around in there. Wait out here while I go in and get something for us to sit on," walking into the cave, rummaging around.

"Daddy!" June shouts, nervously waiting outside the cave. "What are you doing?" getting scared of being on her own.

"I have something for you to lie on while we're up here," he said, walking out of the cave, putting two cushions on the ground.

"It's time to take off your backpack," he added. "You need to take a long break and get something to eat and drink. That was a long walk you just did."

She quickly drops the heavy backpack, sitting on the soft cushion. "Can we stay here a while?" taking another drink of water.

"Yep, it's break time! It's as far as we go today. Sit back and enjoy the nice cool breeze we got up here," sitting on the other cushion next to her.

"It's cold up here!" looking in the direction of the wind.

"I know! That's why it's a nice place to take a break. It gets even colder up here at night. When we spend the night in the cave, we need to have the campfire lit all night long to keep us warm. We need the blankets, too."

"I'm not sleeping in that cave!" she quickly blurted out. "Things could be in there!" glancing into the dark cave.

"You and April spent many days and nights there. You just don't remember because you were really little. It's been a quiet season this year. We haven't spent a night in the cave for a long time. The storm season is coming up soon, so you might get to spend a few nights up here. Won't that be fun?"

"No," she said, shaking her head. "I like sleeping on the beach. Too dark in there," glancing in the cave, not too sure about it.

After all the years of doing this hike on his own, Ben loves having someone to talk to while walking the trails. They share one of the oranges as he points out all the features and paths to the peak of the island. They sit together for a long time, enjoying each other's company. June is full of never-ending questions, always wanting to know more. For every question answered, there are still several more questions to follow.

* * *

Jenny is going through her daily chores, taking care of the campsite. She is busy making new clothes for the twins or repairing the old ones. She tries to keep April amused with new things to do, but all she is interested in is talking about going with her father on tomorrow's trip.

Now a little older, the twins want to explore the island and do more things, just like their father. They are always curious about what their father does when he is away. He doesn't help by always telling them tall tales of his times up on the island. It's a big adventure for the twins, which sounds more fun than staying around the camp doing chores.

Jenny knows from experience that change is always a good thing when living on such a small island. Also, from here on out, things are going to be different. The days of having both of her daughters with her all day long are coming to an end. Tomorrow, April will have her turn with her father, then on the next day, June will want to have her turn again.

She knows Ben is getting tired of being on his own, making the never-ending trips over the island. Ever since she was pregnant with the girls, he had never complained about making the trips on his own. She made the trip so many times in the early days, but now, with the twins, it's not feasible for them all to go. With so much work to be done at the camp, someone has to stay behind. They all have their share of chores to do, and it's the way it has to be.

Jenny is concerned that this might have an impact on his daily chores. Just walking up to the cave and back takes several hours. Ben shortens the time by jogging up and down the trail when he is on his own. She knows it's hard work cutting up firewood and stacking it all away in the cave, not to mention the trip hauling everything back down to the beach.

In the next couple of days, the walk to the cave will be nothing more than bringing back firewood and fruit. She will put a stop to it real quick if the girls slow things down too much. They will have to stay at the camp, whether they like it or not.

* * *

While June sleeps, Ben finishes cutting up some of the wood from the previous day. He is relieved that she is asleep. The trip was hard for her. Although it'll be a short stay at the cave, she needs a nap before heading back. At least the worst of it is over, but if she can make it up to the cave, going back down will not be a problem.

June finally wakes from her nap. "Daddy, can we go back now? I'm cold!" starting to shiver.

"Anytime you're ready... Oh, by the way, look what I found," handing her a small four-foot-long wooden stick.

"Wow, this is great! What does it do?" she asked, curiously looking at the wooden stick.

"It's a walking stick!" he explained. "Just like the one I have. It helps you keep your balance, and it's good for pushing back the long grass or leaves when you're out walking. It'll probably come in handy, knocking off some oranges from the trees!"

June is so thrilled, giving her father a big hug. "This is nice! I can't wait to show Mom and April! I got my own walking stick! Thank you, Daddy!" waving it around in the air.

"You're welcome... You deserve it after walking all the way up here on your own like that. Not too many people can do that on the first day," he said, so amazed how such simple things pleased his little girls so much.

"It's getting late," he said, seeing how low the sun was getting. "It's time we headed back. Let's clean up and get ready for the long walk back."

June quickly gets up, picking up the cushions. She slowly approaches the cave, cautiously looking in, not wanting to get too close. She tosses the cushions in, then runs back, standing next to her father.

"You're not scared of the cave, are you?" he asked.

"It's spooky!" she said, grabbing her backpack, and putting it on. "I don't like it. Too dark in there."

He laughed. "You'll like it when a storm shows up. That's our other home, and it doesn't leak like the hut does. You might be spending a few nights there in the next couple of months."

"No way!" she shouted, shaking her head. "I'm not going in there."

"It's not dark when we have a campfire going, and it's nice and cozy in there. It's a lot better than the hut when it rains. You'll see someday during a storm. We'll all be in there anyway, so don't worry about it. We better get back before Mom starts worrying about us being out too long."

"Can you put some more oranges in my backpack?" she asked. "I want to carry back as many as I can. Then we can have lots and lots to eat!"

"I think that's enough for you. It's a long way, and your backpack will get heavy after a while," surprised that she noticed he removed a few while she was asleep.

"It ain't heavy! I got my walking stick to help out," waving it around.

"Wait till we get halfway down the trail, then you might think twice about carrying a full backpack."

"No, I can do it... I want to show Mom I can help out just like you do."

He puts a few more oranges in her backpack. "I know you can do it," so proud of his little girl.

"OK, June, let's go! Lead the way. Time to go home!" he shouted, picking up a small bundle of firewood, looking around, making sure everything was stored away.

"Let's go!" June shouts, eager to get back.

June proudly leads the way as they walk down the trail. Going downhill is a lot easier, but it's still a long way carrying firewood and food. They sing songs, having a good time. He is so proud of his little girl as she leads the way, her backpack filled with fruit. He hopes she'll be able to make it back on her own. That will be one big accomplishment.

It is a turning point in their lives on the island. April will be next, and Ben knows this will probably start a trend with them coming along to help. He wasn't sure how the day would go, but now, he feels a lot better knowing June made it to the cave without any problems. On the next trip, Ben is thinking about teaching her how to cut up the firewood. He now knows that if anything happens to him or Jenny, the girls will be able to survive on their own.

On the way back, Ben walks behind, letting her set her own pace. They sing songs and tell jokes all the way down to the small pond.

The freshwater pond is always a sight for sore eyes. They both drink a lot of water, then refill their water bottles before having a good wash in the pond. Ben makes sure to take a long break before the walk on the beach. Walking on the loose sand is not easy, especially after the long walk to the top of the island and back.

* * *

As they walk on the beach, June is exhausted. The heat and humidity is too much for her. Walking on the loose sand is not helping either. She still doesn't want to be carried. He holds her hand to help keep her up on her feet. She wants everyone to see her walking back on her own and bringing plenty of fruit, just like her father.

"Why don't I carry you on the last part?" Ben asked, walking at such a slow pace. "You made it to the beach. That's pretty good for your first time."

"No! I'm a big girl now!" she sternly said, looking up at him. "I want to show Momma I can walk all the way! I walk right up to the hut just like you do!"

"OK, you'll do it just like I always do," he said with a big smile. "We're almost there, anyway. So how was your first day at work?"

"It was fun!" June said, looking up at her father. "I can't wait to go again! Next time, I want to do the firewood."

"Good! That will really help me out. Just think, one day, you and April will be able to make this trip all on your own. Mom and I can stay home and relax for a change," thinking it might scare her a little.

"Wow! You mean it! Me and April can go by ourselves? Can we go tomorrow?"

"Well, maybe after a while when you get a little older," a little surprised by her response, now regretting he mentioned it.

* * *

Getting so late, Jenny is starting to worry. She is already regretting her decision to let June go with her father. She knows it's too much for her little girl. Anything can happen on the long walk up the trail. She is trying to think of a way to tell April that she might not be going tomorrow.

"They're back!" April screamed out, running down the beach to greet them.

"Oh, thank God it's over," Jenny mumbled to herself, so relieved.

June sees her sister running towards them and starts waving. She tries to run as well, but after a few steps, she just can't do it, coming to a complete stop, gasping for air. So exhausted from the long trip, she can barely stand up.

"What was it like?" April asked, giving her sister a big hug. "Was it fun? Did you see the cave?"

"Yeah," June nods. "It was fun... We were way up high in the clouds!" waving her hands up in the air.

"Was it a long walk?" April asked, noticing how exhausted her sister looked and all the sweat running down her face.

June nods her head up and down. "It's a long way up there... It took a long time," she mumbles, struggling to get the words out.

"So, how was your day?" Ben asked, picking up April and hugging her.

"I can't wait for my turn tomorrow! Daddy, I want to see the cave too!"

"I hope you're ready for it! You're going to have just as much fun as June did. Let's get back home. Mom is waiting for us," he explained, seeing June is still having a hard time trying to walk in the soft sand.

June is a very stubborn little girl. She intends to walk back to the camp on her own. She doesn't let her father carry her or have anyone help with the backpack. Both Ben and April take her hands, encouraging her to keep going. Slowly, step by step, they reach the camp where Jenny is patiently waiting.

Jenny kneels in the sand, giving June a long hug and kiss. "So, how was your day? It wasn't too much, was it?" seeing how exhausted she looked.

"It was great!" June replied with a big smile. "We picked oranges right from the tree! Then we looked out over this big flat place with grass on it, and it was way up in the air! Then we had a picnic at the cave! We did good, didn't we, Daddy?" looking up at her father with a big smile.

"You did so good! You're a good helper. It's going to make my job a little easier now, having help like that."

"I can't wait to go! I want to pick oranges, too!" April shouted.

"You'll get to do the same things as June did. It'll be lots of fun!" Ben explained, glad to see April is still excited about going after seeing how tired June is.

"Sounds like you had a nice day... Let's get back home so we can hear all about it!" holding June's hand as they walk the last few steps into the camp.

June is dead tired and can barely keep on her feet, but she still will not let anyone carry her. She wants to walk the last steps to the camp on her own. She doesn't even let anyone take her backpack.

"So, how did it go?" Jenny quietly asked Ben.

Ben nods his head. "It was OK... She had a little nap at the cave. Can you believe she walked the entire way? I didn't have to carry her at all."

"No wonder she's so tired!" Jenny blurted out, so shocked. "You should have carried her."

"Yeah, right!" he added. "June takes after you. She had her mind set on doing it all on her own. I was so impressed. She walked all the way up there and back! Even had a full backpack coming down the trail."

Jenny helps June take off the backpack. She is so shocked to see how heavy it is.

"I can't believe she hauled all these oranges down with her. You know how heavy this is?" Jenny asked, getting a little mad.

Ben just nods. "She wanted to do it."

"Look at all the oranges I got!" June shouted, pouring them all out. "We're going to have plenty to eat for days!"

"Wow!" April replied, seeing the pile of oranges. "I'm going to bring back that many when I go!"

"No, we only take what we need," Jenny explained. "We have more than enough to last us for a few days."

"Mom, but I got to bring back some food too!" April said, getting upset.

"Mom is right... We only take what we need. We'll be needing more firewood, so that's what you'll be hauling back when it's your turn," Ben explained, seeing this coming.

"OK, Daddy!" April replied with a big smile, then turned to her mother. "I'm going to bring back wood for the fire tomorrow! Lots of firewood!"

Jenny hugs her. "That sounds like a good idea to me. I'm glad you two are helping us out with the chores like this."

June is about ready to collapse. Ben helps her in the hammock, giving her some water and several orange wedges. Being so tired, it doesn't take long before she is sound asleep.

"It's your turn tomorrow," Ben whispered to April. "You better rest up because it's going to be a long day. We'll be cutting up a lot of firewood, and that's hard work. You can see what it's done to June. She'll probably sleep the rest of the day."

"OK! I'll take a nap," seeing her sister is sleeping. "I'm going to be ready for my turn tomorrow!" then quickly pulls out two cushions from the tent, placing them next to the hammock lying down for her nap.

While the twins sleep, Ben tells Jenny all about his day with June. He is one proud father, having his girls helping out, especially being able to achieve the strenuous walk up to the cave and back.

Jenny is not too thrilled about another trip up to the cave with the girls. She thinks that it's too much for them, especially after seeing how exhausted June is. Jenny knows there is no way to prevent it now that April has her heart set on going with her father. At least April is not so stubborn and probably wouldn't mind being carried if she gets too tired.

***

The next morning, April is up early. She can't wait for her big adventure with her father. Ben knows April wants to experience the very same things her sister has done. She wants to pick oranges and sit on the bench looking over the island. She even wants to take a nap at the cave. Just like the day before, it's a big event, but this time it's all for April.

Jenny is helping April get ready for her big day. April is getting nervous, having a good idea of what is in store for her. Even June helps with the backpack, explaining everything to her sister. With a couple of oranges and an extra water bottle tucked away in the bag, it's time to leave.

June grabs her walking stick. "Don't forget this... You'll need it for the walk—"

"No, that one is yours," Ben whispered. "Only those who walk the trail get to have a walking stick. She'll get hers later while she is at the cave. Don't let her see it."

June quickly hides the walking stick behind the tent. "Oh, OK... It's a surprise!" knowing that her father is going to give April her own walking stick once they reach the cave.

Ben wants it to be a rite of passage. He has been planning this for a long time. Once his girls made it up to the cave, only then will they get their very own walking stick.

April never catches on about the walking stick. She is too scared and nervous about the trip after hearing all the tales from her sister. Knowing that this will not be easy, she is now a little hesitant about the whole thing.

Jenny and June walk out to the beach to see them off. Just as they have done on the previous day, but this time June is glad to be staying at the camp. She is still tired and so sore from the long walk.

"You be good now, and have a nice day," Jenny said, getting emotional seeing her little girl all dressed up for her big day out.

"I will, Momma," April replied, trying to hold back the tears, taking her father's hand as they walked down the beach.

"Bye, April! Bye, Daddy! We'll be here waiting!" June said, waving her hands up in the air.

"OK!" Ben said, waving back. "Don't worry... We'll be back about the same time as yesterday, or maybe a little longer."

As they walk down the beach, April keeps turning around to wave at her mother and sister. She is quiet and not as talkative as she usually is. Ben knows April is terrified of this trip. He keeps telling her how much fun it's going to be to help motivate her.

On this trip, he'll probably help carry her if she gets too tired. Deep down, he has a feeling that if June walked the entire trip, April will probably do the same.

Walking the trail is no different from the day before. The pace is extremely slow. Ben makes sure this time to take more and longer breaks to let her rest. She is doing just as well as her sister and wants to walk to the cave on her own.

At the halfway point, it's a big inspiration for her. The view is spectacular, just as June described. That gives her a second wind and the motivation to continue to the cave. From all the stories she has heard, the lookout is the best, and she will get to see the entire island. She can't wait to see it for herself.

* * *

Reaching the lookout is not as difficult as April expected. They take a little longer, but it makes a difference with the additional breaks on the trail. She is so full of energy, jumping up and down, so thrilled she made it. All she can do is yell out with excitement, seeing the spectacular view.

Again, Ben makes sure to repeat everything he had done with June the previous day. April even waits next to the trees to be picked up to get her own fruit. Picking a few oranges, they walk over to the wooden bench for a break. She stands in awe, looking over the island for the first time. The view is not even close to what she was expecting.

April can't wait to get to the cave. After a quick break, they are off again for the worst part of the trip. With just a few oranges in her backpack, she is doing far better than June. Ben makes sure not to overload it this time. Also, on the steepest part of the trail, he makes sure to hold her hand, helping her along. A lesson learned, and poor June had to pay the price.

April is just as nervous about the dark cave as her sister and will not even go near it. Ben walks into the cave and brings out the cushions. They take their lunch break and talk together for a long time.

After a while, he notices April is anticipating something. He doesn't catch on until he sees how she is constantly glancing at his walking stick. She must have heard about it from June and is eager to get her own. He doesn't say anything and will wait until she has her nap.

Ben has plenty to do since this is the second day of limited chores. Firewood is a necessity since they use so much of it. Now, with the girls helping out, he has less time to do his chores. The trip takes three times longer, so he has to make up time by doing as much as possible while at the cave. He is glad to make the adjustment because now he has someone to talk to, and not to be alone at the cave.

April is so thrilled to help with the firewood. She carefully places it all in a neat stack next to the cave. She still doesn't dare go near it. At least having the wood in a neat pile is one less chore he has to do. That's a good start for her. Any little help goes a long way.

Ben knows it's going to be a slow process, but eventually, he will teach the girls how to do it all. Picking out a good firewood tree, cutting it up, and storing it away for those rainy days is extremely important. The first step is getting them used to the walk up to the cave. Eventually, they will walk the trail with no effort and help with some of the chores.

The long walk is taking its toll. April eventually falls asleep on the cushions. Ben is so amazed at how she can help with the chores before getting too tired. He lets her sleep so she can rest up. This time, he is going to take his time and not rush back. There is no fixed plan. Jenny knows they might be late, but she is still going to worry.

* * *

By the time he finishes cutting up the firewood, April wakes up from her nap. He is glad that she had slept a long time, resting up for the long walk back. She jumps up, puts on her backpack, and is ready to go. She can't wait to tell everyone about her day, standing quietly while her father stores everything away in the cave.

Ben knows she has been waiting for her big moment. While he is putting the last of the firewood into the cave, he can see her anxiously peering in from a distance. Just like June, she doesn't go near the cave. Once everything is packed away, he walks out with one hand behind his back.

"April, you did real good today," he said, not wanting to make her wait any longer. "I'm so proud of you!" handing her the walking stick.

"My own walking stick! Wow! Thank you, Daddy!" jumping up and down so excited, hugging her father.

"You deserve it! You've done a good job and really helped out. It's been a good day."

She looks down at her feet, a little sad. "But I didn't get to help much with the wood. I fell asleep."

"Oh, you did plenty! It's not over yet. We still have to carry the firewood back. That's the hardest part. We have a whole lot of wood to haul back today!" pointing to the huge stack of firewood.

"Yeah! I get to help carry the wood!" so thrilled to have more chores to do.

He already has several small logs cut real short for her to carry back. He places a few into her backpack. Carrying those few logs makes her day. Another great day for Ben, and he has enjoyed his time with his little girl.

The trip back is just as exhausting for April as it was for June. Ben secretly takes out a few pieces of firewood from her backpack to help her out. Luckily, she is too tired to notice. Once they reach the small pond, he quickly puts them back when she goes into the water to cool off.

That was the longest trip up to the cave and back that he had ever done. He took his time and made sure not to get April overexerted. He can see it made a difference, seeing how she is not as tired as June was.

* * *

Jenny is getting so worried since they have been gone way too long. Walking down the beach with June, she is wondering if something has happened. Jenny is already planning to walk up to the cave if necessary. Reaching the small pond, she is so relieved to see them playing in the water.

"Oh, you're here!" Jenny said, so relieved. "I have been so worried! I thought something had gone wrong. You two were up there a lot longer than yesterday!"

"Oh, we took our time," Ben explained. "We had a lot of wood to cut up, so I spent a little longer up there. She did really good! Walked all the way up and back on her own, and she even helped carry the firewood, too," rubbing April's back as she played in the water.

"Mom, it was fun! I want to go again!"

"I think you need to rest for a while before going up there again," Jenny suggested.

"I get my turn tomorrow!" June said, quickly taking off her dress, running into the water. "Then April gets another turn. Then it's mine again."

"Hey, wait! When is it Mom's turn?" Ben jokingly asked. "Maybe she can go tomorrow."

Jenny quickly shakes her head. "My days of going up to the cave are long gone. I don't miss that walk one bit!"

"You never go!" April said. "Only Daddy does. We like going up to the cave! I even got my own walking stick, too," proudly showing everyone.

"That's a real nice one!" Jenny said. "You can walk a long way when you have one of those. Maybe in a few days, I'll finish up the other backpack so both of you will have one."

"If me and April have one, then we can carry lots of things!" June added.

"That's right... You can use them on the beach too!" Jenny explained. "When we go collecting, they'll really come in handy."

"Oh, so that's why you made them!" Ben said with a big smile. "They're for scavenging!"

"Well, they can use them for the trips up to the cave as well. They've been having problems carrying things on the beach. The sacks we have are too big for them, and they always drag them in the sand," she said, embarrassed that Ben had just figured it out.

"They worked out really good. It holds the water bottle, lunch, and a few other things. Maybe now we can go on a long hike around the island. It would be like a vacation away from home."

"That sounds like a good idea! So, how would you two like to go on a day trip to the other side of the island?" Jenny asked the girls.

"Yeah! We want to go!" they both yelled out, jumping up and down.

"Looks like we better start making plans," Ben said. "I think we got a vacation coming up," trying to think of the last time they made that trip together.

Both the girls are so thrilled with all the new possibilities with their new backpacks and walking sticks. They can't wait to get back up to the cave, although neither will go near it. Now, they have proven they can get to the cave and back. It opens up much more. The twins had always heard about a trip around the island, and now they get to go. They are so excited about it all.

* * *

After a quick break at the pond, it's time to return to the camp. Just like her sister, April has to walk all the way back, carrying the firewood. They slowly walk together, encouraging April on every step. Both Jenny and June hold her hand, helping as she walks down the beach. They all know this is the worst part of the entire trip. The sand is not as easy as the trail to walk on, especially after a long day.

Jenny doesn't like seeing her little girls struggling like this, but they want to be like their father. She knows the trip up on the island is just too much, but they insist on going. Unfortunately, they are slowing Ben down considerably. She hopes they will get tired of going after a while, letting things get back to normal.

Once they reach the camp, April ends up being just like her sister. She is totally exhausted. After a long drink and a quick snack, she is on the hammock resting. Everything has to be the same. April doesn't take long to fall sound asleep, still holding her new walking stick even as she sleeps.

All June wants to talk about is being able to go back to the cave in the morning. She is so excited about it. Ben notices it's bothering Jenny that the twins don't want to stay with her. He also thinks it's just a passing phase, and after several days, they'll gladly want to stay home. Until then, he will teach them all the chores he does on a day's outing up on the island.

* * *

Chapter 33

New Family & New Chores

As time passes by, Ben notices Jenny is acting a little odd. Even the twins see it too. She keeps to herself, always letting the girls go with their father to help with the chores. Her eating habits also change. She is always hungry, constantly talking about food. When she prepares some strange meals, especially for breakfast, Ben knows something is wrong.

"Oh, I think I'm pregnant again," Jenny blurted out as they sat down to supper, handing him his plate.

"You're joking, aren't you?" Ben quickly asked, his mouth dropping wide open.

"I don't think so," shaking her head and giving him a big smile.

"I thought we've been careful after the girls."

She stares at the campfire. "Well, I guess it's no use crying over spilled milk. What's done is done."

"How far along?" he quickly asked, looking at her stomach.

"Maybe two or three months. You're going to be a father of three now! So, how do you feel about another mouth to feed?" putting her hand on her belly.

He just stares at her, not knowing what to say. He doesn't expect this at all. The image of that night when the twins were born flashes through his mind, making him shudder.

"It's a surprise," he mumbled. "Another one on the way. Wow! It's hard to believe, and you haven't said anything. How do you feel about it?"

"I think it's great!" she blurted out with a big smile. "I don't know why, but this one kind of surprised me. It's definitely different from when I had the girls. I always thought I was just tired, but then the reality hit me. There is another baby on the way!"

"That means a lot of changes around here. We're going to have to start taking over all of your chores. It's going to be light duties for you for the next six months or more."

"What's Daddy going to do?" June asked, overhearing the conversation.

"He's going to be doing some extra chores from now on," Jenny explained. "We're going to have another family member in the near future."

"We are?" April asked, a little confused. "But we are all here! Momma, Daddy, June, and me," pointing to everyone.

"Well, it means you might get another sister or even a brother."

"A brother?" April asked, still confused. "What's a brother?"

Jenny continues to explain, but to no avail. Their questions are never-ending. The twins can't comprehend what a brother is, but also it's growing inside her. Ben sits quietly, so stunned by the news.

All the daily chores have to change with Jenny being pregnant. The twins take up more responsibilities, to their delight. They never complain and are always eager to help and take over many of the chores around the camp. Also, they help their father with the fishing and the hikes over the island.

Again, the twins are taking turns staying with their mother. While Ben is away, someone always has to be with Jenny to help and look out for her. Neither of them complained about staying behind. Although they still don't understand why. They only know their mother is not feeling good and has to be looked after.

* * *

As the months pass by, it's obvious Jenny is pregnant but is not as big as she was with the twins. Deep down, she knows it's only one this time, which is a big relief. A single birth is not as risky as having two. That is one ordeal that they don't want to experience again. At least this time, they are more prepared. With the twins helping with the chores, it might not be as bad as when they were born.

The hut is in dire need of repairs, and some of the wood is weak or loose. They added more palm leaves to stop the leaks. The hut is good enough for storage and a temporary shelter, but Jenny now wants to move back into it again.

With help from the twins, Ben fixes up the hut and cleans it out. They have done such a good job, and Jenny is so impressed, she moves in right away. Her old bed is better than ever. Sleeping in the tent with the twins is getting too crowded. Naturally, the twins are so thrilled to get to sleep in the tent on their own.

April and June are getting so curious about their mother's tummy getting bigger and bigger. Jenny tries to explain it to them, but it prompts a barrage of never-ending questions. They always yell at their mother's tummy, asking their sister to come out and play. They still don't understand why their new sister is inside their mother, but mostly how it got in there.

* * *

Nine months go by so fast. Jenny's days are now restricted to the camp, and someone always has to be with her. Everyone is waiting for the big moment. Again, they have no clue when the baby is due. They can only guess from her size that she might be in her eighth or ninth month.

Ben stocks up on firewood and food. The tidal pool is full of fish. There is enough firewood stored in the cave and under the hut to last for months. New clothes are being made. They boil the towels for hours to sterilize them and then store away. At least now they are better prepared.

Ben makes quick trips to the cave. Only quick runs for firewood and fresh fruit, then he runs back as quickly as possible. Occasionally, he takes one of the girls with him while the other stays with her mother. The twins are very helpful with all the daily chores, especially at the camp. Jenny doesn't have to worry about cooking or tending to the fire. All she has to do now is sit back and relax.

* * *

One morning, it's apparent that Jenny's belly has dropped. A sign that the baby is due at any time. They all stayed at the camp for several days, but nothing happened. Another false alarm, but she is doing OK. She is not having any contractions, but she knows it will be soon.

Spending several days at the camp waiting for the baby to be born creates a problem. They are running short of everything. When the baby arrives, they'll need plenty of fresh fruit and water. Ben stocks up on everything because it might be the last trip for days.

Running out of fruit, they have no choice but to make a quick run to the cave. It means a heavy load of firewood and fruit to bring back. Ben decides to take April with him so she can help. He doesn't want to leave Jenny, but after waiting around for several days, they can't put it off any longer.

Ben and April make a quick dash for the cave. They plan everything out in detail. They are going to make it a fast run. He knows there is no way that April can keep up, so he carries her. She thinks it's so much fun wanting him to go faster and faster.

The only stop is at the small pond to fill all the water containers. Once that's done, they leave everything on the ground to pick up on the way back. Then, a fast run up the trail with Ben carrying her the entire way. For April, it's going to be the quickest run to the cave she has ever done.

* * *

Reaching the lookout, Ben drops April off so she can gather the fruit on her own. He runs to the cave for the firewood. April's job is to head straight for the fruit trees to fill her backpack and the sack with as much fruit as she can carry. Once she is done, she is to run back alone. Then he will catch up with her on the way down.

Luckily for Ben, the stacks of firewood in the cave are ready to go. All he has to do is tie as much up as possible and carry it back. With several large bundles lashed together, he races back down the trail as fast as he can go. It's the most firewood that he has ever carried at one time, and he is already feeling the strain on his back.

Reaching the lookout, he is so relieved to see April is not there. With both bundles of firewood under his arms, he jogs down the trail. His arms strain from the weight, but it will be worth carrying double the amount as it means one less trip. Occasionally, he sees an orange on the trail. He is happy to see his girls helping like this. They always give a hundred and ten percent and never complain.

Ben quickly catches up with April. She is running down the trail, dragging the big bag of fruit behind her. Even with a full backpack overflowing with fruit, it doesn't slow her down. With just a few stops for water, they reach the beach in record time. He is so proud of his girls like never before.

Walking along the beach, they are exhausted. Carrying all the supplies and the water makes it worse. The deep sand slows them down to a crawl. April is having a hard time dragging the heavy bag behind her. They are close enough to the camp, so they can always drop a few things and come back later if it's too much.

Halfway down the beach, June is running towards them at a frantic pace. Right away, Ben knows something is wrong. He always told the twins never to leave their mother alone for any reason.

"Mom says it's time! Hurry!" June cried out as she approached them.

Ben immediately drops everything. "You guys carry this back! I'll check on Mom!" running back to the camp.

"OK, Daddy!" April replied.

All Ben can think about is Jenny being all alone, having the baby with no one to help. Within minutes, he reaches the camp. Rushing to the hut, he looks inside, expecting the worst. To his surprise, Jenny is sitting up on the bed, writing in her journal.

"It's OK, Ben! Don't panic. I have been timing the contractions. We have plenty of time," so startled, seeing him panting hard, trying to catch his breath.

"Thank God!" he said, so relieved. "I thought you were having it now. Oh boy, here we go again! It's going to be another night delivery," realizing it's about the same time she went into labor with the girls.

"I bet it'll be about nine to maybe midnight," looking at her watch.

He let out a long sigh. "Oh, great! I better get everything ready then."

"Where are the girls?" she asked, looking out the doorway.

"I left them down the beach... They should be here shortly."

"Oh, Ben... You're going to frighten them. Just act naturally around them, and don't panic! They sense it when you're scared. I explained everything to them, so they'll have a good idea of what's going to happen."

"Good... I'll probably need some help. I remember the last time when they were born. What a nightmare!" sitting down in the doorway to rest.

Ben takes out the flashlight batteries and hooks them up to the solar charger, placing them in the direct sunlight. The old batteries are showing their age, not lasting as long as they used to. At least there are no storms around, and it looks like it's going to be a calm night. He doesn't want a repeat of the night when the twins were born. That is one of the worst and most frightening nights of his life.

* * *

"We're here!" April and June said, walking in carrying all the fruit and firewood.

"Sorry!" Ben said. "I forgot about the supplies. You should have left some of that on the beach. I could have got it later," seeing how tired they are, dragging in everything.

"No, Daddy!" April said. "We got it all! We big girls now and do all the chores!"

"So, what happened? Is the baby here?" June asked, looking about the camp.

"No, it might be later on tonight," Ben explained, shaking his head.

"Hi, Mom!" April said, looking into the hut. "We did real good! Me and June got all this stuff on our own!" emptying the sack of fruit on the floor.

"That's great!" Jenny said so proudly. "We're going to have plenty of food and firewood for days! You two are really helping out."

"OK, guys! Better rest up," Ben told them. "Get something to eat and drink. We have a lot of work ahead of us tonight. The fire will be going all night long, so we'll be needing all the firewood stacked up out here. We're also going to need plenty of water because we're going to be boiling that up all night long."

"OK, Daddy," the twins replied in unison, untying the firewood.

"I'll get more water, and you two get the fire going. I'll be back shortly," Ben said, picking up the big iron pot, tossing all the empty water bottles into it.

June nods her head. "OK! We make a good fire for the baby. You go get the water."

Ben walks up to the hut, looking in the door. "Jenny, I'll be back soon... I'm going to top off our water supply. Is there anything else you need while I'm out?"

"No, I'm OK... I'll get the girls to make me some orange juice. Take your time and don't rush. The girls are here if I need anything else."

"OK, I'll be back real quick," he nervously replied.

"Watch your mother," he whispered to the girls, rushing to the pond.

* * *

When Ben returns, the campfire is already going strong. So exhausted from carrying over a hundred pounds of water, he places the heavy iron pot on the raging fire. A stack of towels and washcloths are ready to be boiled. The girls have done a good job with that. Jenny is keeping them busy, knowing that they are getting a little nervous.

"Let's store these away for later," Ben said, handing out the water bottles. "How is Mom doing?"

"She's OK… She still in there doing her writing," June replied, storing away all the bottles.

"We all ready now!" April added. "Got a big fire, plenty of water… Now, we can have something to eat."

"Let me check on Mom," he said, "and see how she's doing first. You two are doing really good! That fire should last all night."

Ben is so amazed, seeing Jenny as he enters the hut. Not even childbirth will prevent her from writing in her journal. Everything they have done or said is written down for the children. She is so fixated on her writing that she never even notices Ben sitting down next to her.

"I see you've forgotten all about the baby," he jokingly said, seeing her jotting down something important in the journal.

"Oh, no!" she said, leaning over and kissing him. "I get reminded once in a while. It's getting close!" putting down her journal.

"So, how much longer do you think it'll be?" he asked, trying to hide his nervousness.

She thinks for a while, placing her hand on her belly. "Maybe a few hours. This one is different. I know it's not twins, but this is a really lively one. I feel a lot of kicking going on down there," then her face grimaces as she feels another contraction.

He gives her some water, trying to comfort her. After several minutes, it's over, but it's a sign of things to come. He wishes these things would happen during the day. He is dreading having to help deliver another baby at night.

"You still fancy something to eat?" he asked. "I think the girls are ready to cook something."

"Oh yeah! I'm starving!" she quickly replied.

"I can't see how you can eat at a time like this!" he said, shaking his head in disbelief.

"I'm eating for two now. This one has gotten a hankering for some fresh seafood!" patting her hands on her belly.

He laughed. "There ain't nothing else here to eat but seafood, so she better get used to it!"

He gets up, goes over to the doorway. "Mom wants a nice fish for supper. Can you two catch us a good one for tonight?" he asked.

"OK, we'll catch a real big one!" June quickly replied, holding her hands out wide.

"We'll bring back a good one!" April shouted, grabbing their sticks and casting net, and ran out to the beach with her sister.

"If you need any help, let me know," Ben said, knowing they could handle it all on their own.

"What would we do without those two?" Jenny asked.

"Probably starve... I don't know how we did it before."

"I don't either," she added, lying back in the bed. "Just think what it's going to be like with one more."

"We won't have to do anything after a while, from the way things are going now. Those two don't even let me go fishing anymore. They're catching all the fish now. Last time I was out there, I was just getting things ready, and they caught a big fish. I hate to say this, but they make me look like an amateur nowadays."

"Tell me about it," she said, so proud of her little girls. "I haven't cooked a meal in months."

He laughed. "Yeah, it's like they've taken over."

The twins make life so much easier by helping with all the chores. Ben remembers what it used to be like years ago, where he had to do everything himself, especially after they were born. Now, he doesn't have to go out fishing or even light the campfire. With another baby on the way, the twins are now getting more and more responsibilities, and they love every minute of it.

* * *

April and June catch one of their favorite fish, dragging it back to camp. Ben sits down, watching as they prepare it for supper. Since Jenny is pregnant, the twins have been catching, cleaning, and cooking supper every night. They love to cook, and some of their new dishes even surprise their mother. Jenny passed on her family secrets of preparing seafood. It's now so evident how quickly they have moved far beyond what she taught them.

Jenny doesn't eat much, and her contractions are getting closer together. Ben ushers the twins out of the hut, seeing how scared they are whenever their mother yells out in pain. He wants to send them out to the beach, getting them far away until it's over, but Jenny wouldn't hear of it. She knows it'll be best to keep them busy and act normal around them.

"OK, it's going to be a long night," he explained while sitting with his girls by the campfire. "Your job is to help me with the towels and warm water. I'll be with Mom in the hut, helping her out. You guys stay out here until I ask you for something. She might be in a little pain, and you might hear her cry or scream out, but she'll be OK. You understand?"

"OK, Daddy," June nervously said. "We'll be out here to help with the fire and things."

"Is Mommy hurt? She going to be OK?" April asked, hearing another scream.

"She's all right," he explained, hugging her. "This is normal for when babies are born, so don't be scared. I'll be helping Mom, so don't worry."

June leans over, peeking in the hut at her mother lying on the bed. "I don't like this," she whispered to her father. "Can you make that baby go away?"

"No," he said, putting his arms around his girls. "This is your little brother or sister. Your mother went through the same thing when you two were born. She'll be fine, but she might not be feeling too good for a while. She'll be in bed for a few days. You guys need to think of the new baby's name when he or she arrives. So when I'm in there with Mom, you two sit out here and think really hard about a name."

"We get to make up a name for her?" April asked.

"Yep!" he said, nodding his head. "You need to think of a name for a boy or a girl."

"Can we play on the beach with her tomorrow?" June asked. "Will she be helping with the chores?"

"Yeah, will she be taking turns going up to the cave?" April added.

He smiles. "No, it'll be a while before Mom or the baby will be doing any chores. You can help take care of the baby, but it'll be a long time before you can play out on the beach. Remember when you saw the baby birds and how their mothers had to help feed them? It'll be like that for a long, long time."

"We going to feed her up in the trees?" June asked, really confused. "The momma birds only feed the baby birdies when they are in the nest. We going to make her a nest? Is it going to be like that?"

"You'll understand by tomorrow," he added, seeing they were still confused. "You better get ready for a long night. We're going to be up really late. Remember, this fire has to keep going all night long. Keep the water hot too. Use your sticks to take out the towels from the hot water. Then put them in the cooking wok until I need them. Don't let anything drop in the sand."

They never said a word, nodding that they understood. Jenny has been practicing with them for weeks, boiling the water and sterilizing the towels. They don't want the girls getting hurt by the campfire and the hot water. At an early age, they were taught to be extremely careful around the campfire. With children running about and a fire in the middle of the camp, it's part of the island life, and they learn to live with it.

* * *

The sun has set, and darkness soon follows. The big moment is here. Already, it's too much for the twins to hear their mother yelling out in pain. They are getting too scared and start to panic. They also can see their father is scared as well. Just from the looks on their faces, Ben knows it's not a good idea for them to be right next to the hut, having to hear all this.

"OK, I think I can handle this on my own," Ben finally said. "Why don't you two go out and sit on the bench out by the beach? I'll help Mom, and if I need anything, I'll yell out for you," knowing it's not far enough away, but at least the sounds from the waves might block some of the screams.

They don't argue or say a word. Both quickly walk out to the small bench out by the edge of the trees. So scared, they can't handle the screams from their mother. Sitting on the bench, they hold each other, crying.

Once the twins are out of sight, Ben quickly goes back to the hut to help as best as he can. He had been through this before. It is still terrifying, just like the first time. At least now he is better prepared. They have plenty of light to see by with the roaring campfire. The one thing that's helping is that they have a cool, clear night and a full moon.

* * *

To their surprise, it's over so quickly. The baby is already crying, just like April and June. Jenny can't believe how easy this one was

LANI MOKU

compared to the twins. Ben proudly holds his new baby in his arms as the tears flow from his eyes. The ordeal is finally over. They are now a family of five.

"Congratulations!" Ben proudly said, handing the baby to Jenny. "We have a little boy!"

"It's a boy!" she said, then started crying. "That doesn't surprise me one bit after carrying him for nine months," wrapping him up in one of the towels.

"He looks healthy. He's really loud, too," Ben added.

"That's boys for you!" she explained, kissing her new baby. "He's going to be a wild one," seeing how he is kicking his legs.

Ben is so thrilled with his little boy and ever so proud of Jenny and his two little girls. After they wash him and cut the umbilical cord, it's all over. Now, they can relax.

"Where are the girls?" she asked. "I want them to meet their little brother," looking out the door.

"I sent them out to the beach. They were a little scared."

"You shouldn't have made them wait out there. They'll be scared being out there all alone," feeling sorry for the girls having to endure it all.

"Not as scared as they were sitting out by the campfire. It was a little too much, and I think they're a little squeamish like me about these things."

"Poor things... Go get them and tell them everything is OK."

Ben steps out of the hut and has a quick wash before getting the twins. This one was a lot easier, but at least it's over, and everything is OK. From the glow of the campfire, he sees his two little girls sitting out on the bench together. They are both quietly singing one of their favorite songs when he walks up behind them.

"Is Mom OK?" they both asked.

"Yes, Mom is doing fine!" he said, putting his arms around his girls, giving them a big hug. "You guys ready to meet our new family member?"

They both jump up, clapping their hands, yelling out with delight. Ben holds their hands, walking them back to the hut. He is going to let Jenny have the honor of telling them about their little brother.

As the twins approach the hut, they are very hesitant. "I don't want to go in there... I'm scared!" April cried out, trying to hide behind her father.

"Me too!" June said. "You sure Momma is OK?"

"Of course she is... She's in their waiting. She has a big surprise for you."

The twins peek into the darkness as they cautiously approach the hut. They can see their mother sitting up in bed, holding something, but it's too dark to see. They slowly walk up to the bed, not sure what to expect.

"April, June," Jenny quietly said, so pleased to see her little girls. "I'd like you to meet your little brother."

"It's a boy!" April shouted.

"Shh, you need to be quiet around the baby. He's not used to loud noises," Ben whispers, then turns on the flashlight so that the girls can see.

"Here he is," Jenny whispered, pulling the towel from his face. "This is your little brother."

"He's so tiny," June said.

"He won't be able to carry much," April added. "How come boys are so small?"

"He is just like you when you were born," Jenny explains. "You two were much smaller. He'll grow up fast and will be as big as you in a few years."

"I'll clean up out here while you guys get acquainted," Ben whispers, seeing everything is all right, then quickly leaves the hut to finish his duties.

The twins are so taken and curious about the new baby. They are so thrilled when they put their finger next to his little hand, then he grabs it and holds on. They watch as their mother feeds him, asking all sorts of questions. She has already explained everything to the twins about newborn babies, especially about the breastfeeding part. Seeing it firsthand makes it easier for them to understand.

"It's late, and it's been a long day," Ben whispered, sticking his head in the hut. "Get washed up. It's time for bed. You'll have plenty of time tomorrow to see the baby," handing them each a warm washcloth.

"You did tell the girls that they can select the name for their baby brother?" Jenny asked, looking up at Ben.

"Oh yeah," Ben said. "I forgot all about it… So, what's his name going to be? Have you decided on one?"

"Baby!" April and June yelled out with big smiles on their faces.

"You want his name to be Baby?" Ben asked, a little confused.

"Yeah! We going to name him Baby! That's the one we like," they both said, nodding their heads up and down.

Jenny laughed. "OK, girls, bedtime... You can see your brother tomorrow."

They both kiss their mother goodnight, waving at their little brother. After the long day, they are so tired. Now, it's all over. They can't wait to get to bed.

"Get cleaned up," Ben said. "I'll tuck you in bed in a few minutes."

"OK, Daddy!" they both said, running to their tent.

"Baby?" Ben asked, turning back to Jenny, confused by the name.

She chuckled. "I know... They're tired. Maybe they need a little more time to think of a name."

"I hope so," he whispers, leaning over to kiss Jenny, seeing his son is already sleeping. "The poor boy will hate that name when he gets older. I'll get the girls to bed, then come back and help you with the little one. Wow, I have a son!" so astonished by it all.

* * *

The next morning, the twins are the first ones up. Both are hovering over their little brother while he is sleeping. All wrapped in his towel in the small hammock next to their mother's bed. The baby stirs, then wakes up and starts crying. The twins are scared, slowly backing away, looking at each other, not knowing what to do. Jenny immediately wakes up, hearing the crying and seeing the twins standing by the door, looking guilty.

"What are you two up to?" Jenny promptly asked them.

"We didn't do nothing… He started crying on his own!" June explained, pointing to the baby.

"That's right!" April added. "We just looking."

"Come on over," Jenny said, taking the baby out of the hammock, cradling him in her arms. "It's OK… He's just hungry," then starts feeding him.

The twins are a little hesitant about the crying baby. They slowly walk up, curiously looking at him. They are not used to all of this. Their mother is now too busy for them, and all the attention is going to someone else.

"Hi, Baby!" June said, carefully examining her brother. "You remember me? My name is June, and this is April," pointing over to her sister.

They wait for a reply, but nothing happens. The baby continues suckling his mother's breasts, ignoring everything else.

"Mom, how come he don't talk back?" June asked, a little disappointed.

"He's just a baby," Jenny explained. "It'll be a while before he learns to talk. All he can do now is cry to let me know when he's hungry."

"Is that all!" April added. "What about helping with the chores? What chores will he be doing? We all have to help out. That's the rules."

"He won't be doing any chores for a long time," Jenny explained, shaking her head. "We're going to have to do everything for him until he grows up a little. He'll need plenty of help learning everything. You two will need to teach him all those things we taught you."

The baby cries again. April and June shake their heads, a little disappointed with their new little brother. It is not what they were expecting.

"I don't know," June said, putting her hands on her hips, looking up at her mother. "He's really loud and can't be doing that when we out fishing. He going to scare all the fish away. Why can't he do signs like we do?"

Jenny smiles. "I don't think he'll be doing any hand signs. Crying is all he's going to be doing for a long time. Just think, we had to put up with both of you girls crying, and at the same time as well!"

"No, I don't remember that!" April said, shaking her head. "We always do signs."

"We don't cry anyway," June added. "We big girls! Daddy isn't going to like this. Can't you tell him to stop?"

Jenny laughed. "No, and I don't think your father is going to mind either. This is the way babies are for the first couple of months, so get used to it."

"I don't know," April said. "Daddy not going to be happy about this."

"He will," Jenny said. "One of you, go wake your father up. Better get things ready for breakfast."

June turns, running outside to the hammock where her father is sound asleep. "Get up, Daddy! Mom said you have to get up!" pulling on his arm.

"Nope!" Ben replied, still tired from being up all night. "Today's my day off."

"He's not getting up!" June shouted, running back to the hut. "He said he got the day off!"

"We got the day off today?" April quickly asked, wondering about all the chores.

Jenny giggled. "Yes, we do, but tell him he has to get up. We still got some chores that need to be done."

"Get up!" June shouted, standing in the doorway with her hands on her hips. "Mom said you need to get up! We got chores to do!"

Ben groans as he rolls out of the hammock. He notices how bossy his little girls can be. He knows he is not wearing the pants in this family. Now, with a son, things are going to be a little different. He is not the only one in this group of girls.

* * *

The morning goes well. April and June help their mother and the baby, spending the rest of the day at the camp. This time, they have everything planned out. They have enough food and firewood for several days, so there is no need to go up on the island. With the twins helping out, they can now take it easy for a couple of days without having to do any major chores.

Jenny and Ben discuss their little problem with the name that the twins have chosen. He finds out that Jenny also had the same talk that he had earlier. The girls insist on calling their little brother Baby. So, Jenny and Ben decide to name their son August, keeping with the month naming tradition they have used with the girls.

They don't have the heart to tell the twins and decide to explain it to them later. The name Baby will not be a problem until he grows up. If they get rescued, they will have to use his real name, August. Until then, Baby will be his name.

They spend the day out on the beach celebrating the new arrival. Ben is creating all sorts of games for the girls to keep them amused.

Jenny sits in the shade under the palm trees with her son. They all enjoy having a lazy day without any chores to do. For everyone, it's such a rarity to spend the entire day at the camp just having fun.

* * *

At the end of the day, Ben lights an enormous bonfire out on the beach. The twins catch a few more fish, planning to have a big fish fry. They are having a great time cooking up as much as they want. It gives the girls a chance to try new ways of preparing the fish.

With everyone sitting around the huge bonfire, Ben gets the old radio out. The twins dance about and sing their songs for hours. Now, everyone can sit back and relax. The worst is all over, and now things can get back to normal.

April and June are having the time of their lives. Now, they are like little girls playing out on the beach. They love building sandcastles and playing all sorts of games without a care in the world. No more worrying about how many fish are in the tidal pool or how much firewood they have in storage.

"Can we do this again?" June asked, running up to her mother.

"What do you mean? You want another one?" Jenny asked, wondering if she was referring to having another baby.

"We all stay home and play all day and have lots of fun!" June explained.

"Yeah, it's a fun day!" April added.

"I think they're right," Ben said, listening in on the conversation. "We do need to start having a day off occasionally. Just lie back and do nothing, spending more time together. We can call it fun day, like April, suggested."

"Sounds like a good idea to me," Jenny said, nodding her head. "I think once a week, we should have a fun day, just like today!"

"So, what do you two think about doing this every week?" he asked the twins.

April jumps up and down, clapping her hands. "Yeah! We want to do this again!"

"Me too!" June said. "I want a fun day!"

He looks over at Jenny and smiles. "I guess that's a vote for a fun day!"

"OK, from here on out, we're going to have a fun day once a week, just like today," Jenny said. "We're going to sleep in late. There will be no chores to do, and we'll have a big party out on the beach."

* * *

Within a few days, Jenny is back up on her feet again. Delivering one baby is nothing compared to twins. In no time, she is up, walking the beach again for exercise and scavenging. So much has washed up on the beach in the last few months. Now, she has so much catching up to do.

Ben stays in the camp, taking care of his son while the girls are out on what he called their early morning shopping spree. He loves spending time with his new son but has to learn again how to handle a small baby and change diapers. He can't wait to take his son out to the beach showing him how to fish and explore the island.

Ben continues his daily hikes up over the island. The twins take turns going with their father. Now, they want to stay at the camp with Baby instead of trudging over the island. They enjoy helping with their new brother and are so curious about everything. To Jenny's delight, the twins are becoming little girls again with the never-ending feeding, diaper changes, and baths.

* * *

Chapter 34

Problem Child

Baby is growing up fast, constantly getting into everything. When he discovers he can crawl about, the calm, quiet days have been replaced with constant turmoil. He does whatever he wants and doesn't listen to anyone. Everything has to be stored away or placed up high in the hut out of his reach. Someone always has to watch over him, especially around the campfire. He is drawn to it like a moth, tossing everything he gets his hands on into the fire, and it's a major problem. He is far more active than his sisters were at that age.

While eating supper, Jenny gets tired of her son constantly tearing up the camp. She has had enough, and it's time for a little help.

"OK, girls... I got some new chores for you," explaining all their new responsibilities in detail.

The twins take on their new assignment without question.

"So, what's this all about?" Ben asked, surprised at all the new chores for the girls.

"I think it's time for them to learn how to take care of their little brother," she explained. "I can really use the help and can't seem to get anything done nowadays. He's getting into everything, and I can't turn my back on him for a minute. Maybe they might be able to teach him how to behave."

"Yeah, he's a little rambunctious," Ben said.

"A little? I had an easier time looking after two girls. Your son is a wild one! I think the girls will set him straight."

Ben looks over at the twins. "I guess you guys will be spending more time with Mom and your little brother. She's going to teach you some new chores. Sounds like it'll be a lot of fun!"

"So, what do we get to do, Mom?" June asked, always eager to learn new things.

"Everything! Just like your father taught you how to fish and bring home the firewood. So now you get to learn how to take care of your little brother."

"Everything, including the dirty diapers!" Ben jokingly said, so glad to get out of that nasty chore.

"That too?" April asked, not liking the idea of changing his diapers.

"Everything," Jenny repeated. "You'll be in charge!"

"Yeah!" the twins yelled out, jumping up and down with excitement.

"OK, calm down," Jenny said, a little surprised by their reaction. "We can start tomorrow morning."

Ben can't help laughing. He knows his girls are in for a big shock having to help take care of their little brother. With so many chores to do, it's challenging having to stop everything because Baby is in one of his destructive moods. Now, the twins will get to spend even more time at the camp, but their enthusiasm may change after a few days of chasing after their little brother. Change is always a good thing.

* * *

The following day, Jenny is teaching the twins how to take care of their little brother. First, she shows them how to prepare his food. Mashing up his food and checking for any bones in the fish is so important. Then she teaches them how to change his diapers, putting the dirty ones in the pot to clean later. She is so pleased to see how attentive they are.

When Jenny shows the twins how to change Baby, they always mimic their father, constantly coughing and gagging. She can't help laughing, seeing how well the twins can copy their father's antics.

Ben doesn't care. He is so relieved they are going to take over the diaper department. He will make sure that the girls get plenty of practice, hoping he'll never have to change another stinky diaper.

Bath time is another chore assigned to the twins. They have always helped bathe their little brother since he was born, so it's nothing new. The small pond is Baby's favorite place to play, but getting him cleaned up is another matter. Now, it takes two to bathe him, one to hold him down while the other washes him. The twins do this job better than anyone else.

Jenny can't emphasize enough how important it is to never let him out of their sight. Whenever they are at the pond or near the campfire, they always have to watch over him. Baby is a handful, especially down by the beach. He loves playing out in the water but is oblivious to the waves, always getting knocked over. Never turn your back on the waves is the most important rule when being out in the water.

Ben also teaches his son a few basic signals. A clicking sound is the signal for Baby to keep close and to stand behind him. That was the first signal he taught the girls when they were little. For the children, it's all a big game. Even the twins are trying to show their brother a few hand signs as well. The little boy is bombarded from all sides with hand signals and birdcalls. When he is fed up with it, he just lets out a loud scream, putting his hands over his eyes. That is the first sign he made up, letting his sisters know to leave him alone.

* * *

Chapter 35

Amazon Girls

N ow that the children are getting older, life on the island is getting back to normal. With everyone helping out, there is more time to relax. Once a week, they have a fun day where everyone sleeps in late, plays games on the beach, swimming in the water at the big pond. At the end of the day, they all celebrate by having lobster for supper, sitting around the bonfire, singing songs, and telling stories. They dance to the music from the old radio late into the night.

The radio is now an important part of the children's entertainment. Every day after supper, they sit around the campfire listening to music. Jenny teaches the twins how to dance. As usual, the twins' ability to learn new things never fails to astonish everyone. Not only do they learn all the new dances, but they can make every little move together in unison. At times, it's like a mirror image, seeing them dancing with all the steps identically together. They also learn to lip-sync to all the songs.

The twin's favorite radio program is the afternoon children's hour from some distant island. They love the classic children's stories and have endless questions about them. The old stories had them going at times, having problems telling the difference between real and make-believe. The story of 'Jack and the Bean Stalk' had them constantly looking up into the clouds for the big giant. When they listened to 'Little Red Riding Hood,' it had them on edge for days, looking around for the big bad wolf.

Right before bedtime, Ben always tells the children a story. He has a great imagination, telling the children tall Texan tales, using one of the children as the main character. He always starts every story with the words 'Once upon a time' and then makes it up as he goes along.

One story really stuck with the twins. Ben made up a story that they were from another island far away, full of Amazon warriors.

Their job was to chase away any sharks from their island. They ride upon the backs of dolphins, holding the harness in one hand while holding their sticks in the other. One day, they chased a big shark all the way over to our island and cornered him on the beach. As they got close to the shark, it turned around and scared the dolphins, throwing them off into the water. The shark chased off the dolphins, leaving poor April and June stranded with no way to get back home. Jenny found them on the beach one morning and took them home. That is the story of how the twins arrived on the island, and they believed every word of it.

The twins always carry their walking sticks, thinking they are little Amazon girls. Ben edges them on by telling them more tall tales. It motivates them to use more birdcalls and hand signs while out exploring the island. Walking on some of the rarely used trails, the twins pretend they are on an Amazon warrior mission. They move silently through the jungle without saying a word, only communicating with each other with hand signs and whistles.

Ben also knows some basic Korean martial arts using cane poles. He teaches them how to use their sticks for self-defense. Jenny is not too keen on the idea, but he wants them to be able to defend themselves in case they meet up with any wild animals on the island.

Day after day, Ben goes out on the beach with them to practice the basic stances and falls. Learning self-defense is a nice change of pace from the never-ending chores. As usual, the twins learn fast, like everything else they are taught. Nothing is ever a game to them for long, taking everything way too seriously.

Ben teaches them more hand signs and birdcalls. It really helps when someone is way down the beach. A simple hand gesture is all it takes to communicate with each other. Unfortunately, Jenny can't keep up with it all. At times, she can't tell the difference between a real bird squawking and the girls playing their Amazon games.

Jenny is concerned that Ben is overdoing it, teaching her little girls to be like Navy SEALs. She agrees that they should learn the basics so they will be self-sufficient. Living off the land is a rough life, but now Ben and the girls are overdoing it with all the martial arts and missions on the island, looking for land sharks or monsters.

She knows Ben's distrust of people made him teach the twins to be wary of any strangers. One of their biggest fears of being discovered on the island is by drug runners or, worse, modern-day pirates. Together, they explain to the children that they should hide if they see someone else on the island. Then, they should let their father know about it so he can check to see who the strangers are. They probably never see other people on the island, but they wanted to be prepared just in case.

One of the things Ben teaches the twins that Jenny doesn't have any problems with is how to use their sticks as spears to catch fish. Since most of the old fishing gear is long gone, it's the only sure way to bring in a fish. With an abundance of bamboo on the island, they have a lifetime supply of fishing spears.

The twins love spearfishing more than anything. Standing on a lava rock waiting for a fish, they never say a word, constantly communicating with each other using hand signs. They never go after the first one that swims by, always shopping around for the biggest fish or one that they fancy eating for supper.

For Ben, it always takes several attempts to spear a fish, and that was at a close range. It is a skill that took him a long time to master. He always had a bundle of spears ready. Once he spots a fish, he throws one after another until one hits the target. He thought he was good at it until the twins took over. Once the twins learn something, they usually surpass what they were taught within just a month or two, catching any fish they want on the first throw. It makes life a little easier now, with the twins always bringing in a wealth of fish for supper.

* * *

Chapter 36

Christmas

As winter gets near, preparation for Christmas is well on the way. Christmas is now a big event since the children are a little older. The small Travelers palm tree near the entrance of the campsite is the Christmas tree. Everyone helps decorate the small tree with flowers, scraps of tinfoil, and red ribbon they found. With the radio blaring out Christmas songs, this will be their first proper Christmas with all the decorations.

Every night, they all sit around the campfire listening to the children's Christmas programs. The twins are always asking about Santa and his reindeer. When they find out what a reindeer is, the only thing they want to talk about is how to prepare it for supper. Food is their only interest, and anything moving about the camp is in danger of being the next meal, especially a reindeer.

The Christmas gifts are handmade from things that they found on the beach. Even the wrapping paper is made from various leaves tied with twine. They all secretly worked on their gifts for weeks. Jenny made everyone new clothes or weaved hats from the various leaves she collected. Ben always made his gifts from wood. He is very secretive, doing all his work in the cave so no one knows what he is making.

With the constant stories about Christmas presents, the twins are always snooping around. Hiding the gifts is a simple task. The one place they don't think to look is right under their feet. Jenny buried them in the sand right behind the hut. It was all planned out well in advance. On Christmas morning, when all the children are asleep, she will dig up the presents, putting them under their Christmas tree. They'll be amazed to see what is in store for them on Christmas morning.

Hearing how this Santa Claus man is supposed to show up at night and leave presents doesn't go too well. April and June know the big day is coming and are always on the lookout for him. They don't appreciate anyone showing up at night wandering around in their camp, and it's a big conflict with one of the things their father always taught them. They consider any other people a threat and always refer to them as land sharks. Having a land shark wandering about in their home is something the girls don't like at all.

* * *

On Christmas Eve, the twins sleep with their father on the hammock. They are so scared that a stranger is coming to their island and don't want to sleep in their tent alone. What makes it worse is knowing it's supposed to be at night. They are not too sure what to make of it all. Both are peering out from under the blanket, waiting for the Santa Claus man to show up. With a long night ahead, they both fight hard to stay awake.

The twins wake up early on Christmas morning. To their surprise, under the Christmas tree is a big stack of presents. They immediately jump off the hammock, grabbing their sticks. A barrage of hand signs and whistles goes out as they signal each other on what they should do. They keep close to their father, making sure the Santa Claus man is not around anymore. They are so shocked and don't understand how someone could walk into their camp undetected.

"So, did we get a visitor last night?" Jenny asked, seeing the twins acting as if they were on guard duty.

"Mom!" June shouted. "The Santa Claus man snuck in! We didn't see him at all. Look, he left all those presents too!" pointing under the tree.

"That's good! That means you've been good girls."

April is so mad. "No! We didn't catch him. Dad is going to be mad!"

"Yeah," June added. "We should have caught him. We was watching all night too!" frantically waving her stick around.

"Better wake Baby!" April said. "He'll want to see this."

"No, he's still sleeping," Jenny said. "It's going to be a long day, and he was up late. Let him rest."

"We need to check the beach!" June tells her sister. "That Santa Claus man can still be here!"

"We need to make sure he's not around," April said, nodding her head. "We'll check the beach to make sure there are no more land sharks!"

Jenny wakes up Ben. "You need to explain how Santa is not one of your land sharks. Look at the way they're acting!"

"OK, you two!" he shouted out, seeing them holding their sticks, nervously looking about the camp. "There is no one else around. He came last night while you were sleeping and left you your presents. He's long gone and far away."

"Why didn't you wake us?" June asked. "We could have got him!" getting overexcited.

"He didn't come here to hurt anyone," Jenny explained. "He shows up at everyone's home to hand out presents, so calm down! Ben, would you tell them!" getting frustrated with the girls seeing how they are still cautiously peering into the trees for intruders.

"It's OK... He left long ago," Ben said, still lying in the hammock. "He comes every year. You just don't remember. I gave him a few oranges and a banana, then told him how good you've been. So, put your sticks down. We need to get everything ready for a big, fun day!"

"We going to have a fun day!" the twins shouted out, jumping up and down with excitement.

"Oh no, this is a Christmas Day," Jenny explained. "It's much better! Christmas comes only once a year, and it's one of the biggest fun days ever."

"Wow!" the twins shouted. "We going to have a Christmas fun day!" dancing about in circles.

"I see someone doesn't care about Christmas," Ben said, motioning over at Baby standing at the door of the hut, looking as if he is still half-asleep.

April runs over to her brother. "Look! We got presents!" pointing over to the tree.

He just yawns, leaning up against the door, trying to go back to sleep. He is not a morning person like his sisters and takes forever to wake up. Unfortunately, once he is up, he is full of energy, running about all day long.

"I have a lot of things to do today," Jenny said, "so you guys got your hands full looking after him. Just keep him away from the presents until we have something to eat."

Ben is going to have a problem keeping his son occupied. On the previous day, he stumbled upon the presents, unwrapping them all. Luckily, the twins have not found out about that. Jenny quickly re-wrapped everything, burying them all in another location. Baby has been running around frantically trying to find them again. The twins don't understand why their brother is constantly tearing up the hut and digging holes in the sand. They just think he is in one of his destructive moods.

* * *

After a quick wash at the small pond, a big breakfast, everyone sits around the Christmas tree, waiting for the big moment. Their first real Christmas, with presents and a tree adorned with flowers and pieces of foil. The twins are now old enough to understand what Christmas is. Baby thinks it's a game, wanting to open anything that's wrapped up.

"OK, I guess it's time to open the presents. Let's see what Santa got for us," Ben said, seeing how eager the children are.

"June, this one is for you," Jenny said, handing out the first of the leaf-wrapped gifts.

"Wow! This is nice!" June shouted, showing everyone her new dress with red flowers painted on it.

"I think this one is for you," Jenny added, handing April her present.

"Thank you, Mom!" April said, opening her present, getting a dress with yellow flowers.

"Go ahead, put them on. Let's see how you look in them."

They quickly put on their new dresses, parading around the camp, showing them off. Jenny's skill in making clothes is outstanding. Making clothes is a never-ending task, especially with the children constantly outgrowing them or wearing them out.

"It looks like a good fit," Jenny said. "I wonder how Santa knew your sizes?"

"Thank you, Santa!" April said, looking up at the sky, waving at him. "I like my new dress!"

"Thank you!" June added, looking up, trying to see if he was still flying around with his reindeer.

"OK, this one is yours!" Jenny said, handing Baby his present, which he quickly grabbed, ripping it open.

"That's my boy," Ben proudly said. "Look at him go!" seeing his son trying so hard to rip open his present.

"So, what do you think?" Jenny asked, seeing her son holding up his little blue shirt.

"Now, that's a really nice shirt! Let's see how it fits," she said, helping Baby put it on so that he can copy his sisters parading around the camp showing it off.

"I think you got some more here," Ben said, holding up three small packages.

They all scream out loud, running over to their father. Quickly unwrapping their presents, they each get the same round doughnut-shaped wooden toy. The first thing Baby does is start chewing on his.

"What is it?" April asked her father, examining her toy.

"It's a roly-poly," he explained. "Let me show you how it works."

Ben takes one and rolls it on the sand across the camp. "See how it goes... It'll be better on the beach. You can even put it on your stick and sling it a long way out. You can make up all sorts of games with these!"

"Wow, look at that, Mom!" April said, rolling the wooden toy across the sand.

"Those are nice toys!" Jenny said. "You'll have lots of fun with those."

Baby runs back for more. Jenny hands him his other present. He promptly rips it open, so thrilled to get his very own hat. There are no more hand-me-downs for him anymore. He quickly puts it on and walks around, showing it off to everyone.

"I think we got one more for Baby!" Ben said, pulling a big package from behind his back.

Baby runs over, yelling and screaming out loud. Ben hands his son the big leaf-wrapped gift.

"Look at him ripping it open!" Ben said, trying to help him unwrap it. "I wonder what Santa got you?"

Baby holds up his new toy, wondering what it is. He has never seen anything like it before. April and June are also confused, carefully examining their brother's gift.

"What is it, Daddy?" April asked.

"It's a guitar! It's for playing music. He'll be able to play this while you sing your songs with the radio."

Jenny laughed. "That's a wonderful gift! He'll really have fun with that. You'll have to teach him how to play it."

"OK, this is how it works," Ben explained, strumming the little two-string guitar.

It doesn't take Baby long to figure it out. He grabs the guitar and starts plucking the strings. The guitar Ben made is nothing more than a little wooden box attached to a foot-long PVC pipe with two strings.

"Did you teach him how to play already?" Jenny asked, seeing him holding it correctly and strumming the strings.

"No, I had it up in the cave... It's the first time he's seen it. Look at him go… My boy is a natural!"

"Where did he learn that? It's not like he's seen it on TV. You must have taught him how to play it."

Ben shakes his head. "Nope, I never said or showed him anything about playing guitars. Like I said, he's a natural. I think he has found his calling. We got a musician in the family now."

"Baby, make sure you move your head up and down while you play," Ben explained, showing him how it's done. "You got to be a headbanger and do all the proper moves."

Jenny laughed again. "Oh, my God! Look at him go! He's sure got all the right moves," so amused with her son dancing about, moving his head up and down while he plucks on the strings.

"I can't wait to see what he does tonight when they listen to the radio. We're going to have him do some guitar solos like Lynyrd Skynyrd's Freebird. My boy is going to be a rock and roller!" Ben said, seeing how Baby has taken to his new guitar.

While the children are playing, Jenny and Ben hand each other their gifts. Ben opens his present. He has a new shirt, then leans over, giving her a big kiss.

"Thanks! This is great! Perfect fit, too! You really outdid yourself this time," trying it on.

Jenny is curious about her gift, a big bulky object resembling a box. She knew he had been working on a secret project for a long time. She carefully pulls off the leaves, so excited to see it's a writing board with small folding legs.

"This is fantastic!" she said, with a big smile on her face. "I can't believe you made this. I can really use this when I write in my journals," reaching over, giving Ben a big hug and a long kiss.

"I know you were having problems trying to find something firm to write on. It took me a while to put it together. I think it worked out pretty good."

"Is it Formica?" she asked, running her hand over the smooth surface. "This is perfect for my writing."

"I believe it is... I think it was part of a cabinet door. It took a long time to get those legs to fold up like that. You won't have any problems storing it away. It looks like it's going to work out fine."

"Thank you!" she said, hugging him again. "This is a wonderful present!" kissing his cheek.

"You know... We can even use it for a dinner tray when we eat!"

"Oh no, you're not! I want one thing to be able to write on that doesn't smell like fish. This is only going to be used for my writing, and it's not for anything else."

"I know... That's why I made it. Let's hope we can get the fish smell out of your papers. Years from now, we'll know what we had for supper when reading your journals."

"Tell me about it... The only flat thing I can use to write on is also what we clean the fish. No matter how many times I clean that board, it still smells like fish. Oh, I got one more present in the hut," remembering one of the presents she made for the girls.

"I only had time to make one, so you all can share it," she explained to the girls, bringing out a small wrapped package from the hut.

They both eagerly run to their mother, so excited about getting another present. Jenny sits down in the doorway, handing it to them. April and June sit down together, opening their gift. Baby runs over, making sure not to be left out. Jenny puts him on her lap to keep him out of trouble. She can't wait to see their reaction.

Both April and June are confused when they see the gift. "It's real nice, Mom! But what is it?" June asked.

"It's a little doll. I had one of those when I was a little girl. I would play with her every day."

"What is a doll?" June asked, still confused.

"It's a doll or a dolly. You can play with it like a little friend," seeing they still do not understand what it is.

Jenny is so talented at making things for the children. She made the doll from a small piece of cloth tightly wrapped around a few leaves with two small buttons for the eyes and stitches for a smile. Around the neck is a little ribbon, leaving the rest of the cloth for the dress.

"We got a dolly!" April shouted out, holding it up for all to see. "Thank you, Mom!" hugging the small doll.

She then hands it over to June. She closely examines it, then hugs the little doll and thanks her mother. Naturally, Baby doesn't want to be left out, wanting to hug the little doll as well, copying his sisters.

"So, what's her name going to be?" Ben asked.

Jenny smiles. "Oh, that's right! You get to name her. So what do you think would be a good name for her?"

"How about Casper?" Ben jokingly suggested. "Kind of looks like it with the round head and the white cloth for the body."

The twins look down at their doll. "Booboo!" they shouted out in unison.

"Booboo! How did you two come up with that name? That's a strange name for a doll, isn't it?" Ben asked, a little disturbed when they do things like that.

June turns to her father. "It's a nice name! We're going to call her Booboo!" nodding her head up and down.

"Then that's what we're going to call her. Welcome to our little family, Booboo!" Jenny said, kissing the doll.

"Hi, Booboo! You want to play with us?" April asked, walking over to show the doll their new wooden toys.

Jenny is so thrilled to see her girls playing with the doll. Seeing the girls acting their age means so much to her. With the never-ending chores of cutting up firewood and catching fish, this is what the girls should be doing. She wants them to do this more often. Just sitting around together playing games without a care in the world is the way it should be. Unfortunately, she knows all too well the twins loved to help with the chores and run about being little Amazon warriors.

Ben has one last surprise gift for Jenny. A small package wrapped in white sailcloth with a red hibiscus flower tied to the top.

She gasped, seeing it. "Good things come in little packages. I wonder what it can be?" then shakes it.

"You will never guess in a million years. Go on, open it!" Ben said, with a big smile.

She carefully opens the gift, placing the hibiscus flower just above her left ear. Slowly, she pulls back the wrapping, gasping out loud.

"My God!" she cried out. "Where did you get this?" looking at the large black pearl mounted on a gold chain.

"Oh, I went out shopping the other day," he jokingly said. "I just happened to come across this quaint little jewelry store on the other side of the island."

"No, really! Where did you get this?" she asked, hugging and kissing him. "Look at the size of it! It's so beautiful!" putting it around her neck.

"The girls were playing with an oyster they found out in the water. I opened it up, finding the pearl inside. I have been keeping it for a special occasion. The gold chain I found in the back of the cave when I was cleaning up. No telling how long it's been in there. It took a while to figure out how to get the pearl mounted on the chain. I think it worked out fine for my first attempt at making jewelry."

Tears run down her face as she stares at the enormous black pearl. "This is so wonderful! I'm going to keep this forever!" kissing him again.

The twins quickly notice something is going on, running over to see what they are missing. They rave over the pearl necklace. Naturally, they both want one as well. Each one has a turn, prancing around the camp wearing Jenny's necklace.

* * *

They all go out to the beach to play later in the afternoon. Jenny and Ben are so surprised to see how three small wooden doughnut-shaped toys keep the children occupied for hours. They roll the wooden toys up and down the beach, making all sorts of games with them. Even the little doll Jenny made is also a big hit with the children. At least it proves that they know how to share their toys.

Christmas dinner is fish and lobster with fruit for dessert. Missing his big Christmas dinner with his family back home, Ben plays the food game with the girls. He always pretends that their fish and lobster is a big roasted turkey dinner with all the fixings.

Jenny is so amused by Ben's attempts to pretend their food is something else. He always tells them about his mother's Sunday dinners or the big Thanksgiving turkey. The twins can't comprehend most of what their father is telling them. They always thought the strange meals he would describe to them were tall stories. They just can't believe those types of meals are real.

At night, they have a big bonfire out on the beach. The radio plays Christmas songs all night long. Baby is now the center of attention, constantly plucking his guitar. He is indeed a natural headbanger with all the right moves. Singing songs and dancing around the campfire, this is by far the biggest fun day they have ever had. Jenny and Ben's first big Christmas with the children is one they will never forget.

* * *

Chapter 37

Rite of Passage

O ne morning after breakfast, Ben gets ready to go on the daily trip up to the island. He thinks it's time for a change and has a good idea for his girls. They have been making the trip to the cave for a long time with no problems. The girls know what needs to be done and when to do it. They always look for new adventures, and he will give them one that will make their day.

As April and June are getting ready for the hike, Ben calls them over. "Today will be a special day for you guys. You've been going up to the cave for a long time now, so I think you should be able to handle it all on your own. You don't need me to go with you anymore."

They quickly look at each other. "You not coming, Dad?" June asked, looking a little nervous.

"No, you're big girls now. I think it's time to see if you can handle it all by yourself."

Jenny shakes her head. "Ah, Ben... I don't think so," wondering what he is doing.

"It'll be OK," he said, knowing Jenny was concerned, winking at her.

"Ben, are you sure?" knowing he is up to something.

"They'll be all right. I know they can do it," Ben said, winking at her again.

"If your father thinks you can handle it," Jenny said, looking over at Ben, getting concerned. "Then you can go on your own. Just go up to the orchard near the cave and get some fruit. That's all we need for today."

"If you are up to it," he added, "you can finish that big branch we got yesterday. Just cut it up, and store it away. Then come back home just like we always do," glancing over at Jenny, hoping she'll agree with his plan.

"If it's too much, just come on back… I don't want you to overdo it," Jenny added, not liking the idea that Ben is making them do all the work.

The twins are caught off guard, not expecting this at all, and are so nervous. They have never gone to the cave by themselves before, wondering what is going on.

Ben helps with their backpacks, putting in the drinking water and a banana for lunch. What surprises him the most is that they never questioned it, although they look a little nervous.

"It'll be OK," Ben said, handing April her little doll. "You can bring Booboo with you, just in case."

April takes the little doll, hugging it. "OK, Dad!" then hands it over to June.

June also hugs the small doll and looks down at it. "You get to come with us today! We'll look after you. You can ride with April," placing the doll in her sister's backpack.

"You're not going with us?" April asked, having second thoughts, looking up at her father, wanting him to go.

"Not today," he said, shaking his head. "You're a big girl now. You've done this many times before. Just keep on the trail. We'll be here waiting for you when you get back."

"OK, Daddy," April replied, holding back the tears.

Ben gives them a big hug. They run over to their mother, hugging her as well. Even Baby knows something is up when his sisters are hugging him. They are apprehensive about it, but everyone must help with the chores and do their share. Now, it's their job to go up to the cave on their own.

Jenny glances over at Ben, giving him a mean look. She doesn't like this at all. He always jokes around, but this is no joke. If this is, he will be in big trouble. Usually, they discuss everything about the children together, but this time, she is in the dark. She is getting ready to put an end to this real quick.

They all walk out to the beach together. Ben, Jenny, and Baby stand silently, watching the twins walk down the beach all by themselves. Holding each other's hands, April and June occasionally turn to wave back at their parents and little brother.

"It's like watching them go off for their first day of school, isn't it?" Ben asked.

"So what's going on?" she asked, giving him a mean look. "You're not letting my babies go all by themselves, are you?"

"No way, I'm going to follow them and stay far enough away but keep them in sight. I want them to think they're doing this on their own. I thought about it last night and was curious to see how they'd do. They're at the stage now where they can do everything I can. It'll be a good test. Hopefully, they'll never have to go on their own."

"You better keep close to them!" Jenny said, getting a little concerned. "I don't want my girls to go all the way up there on their own. They might get lost, or worse, get hurt!"

"They'll do just fine... In the last couple of weeks, they've been doing everything, anyway. I just been tagging along. It'll be good for them. This will be a day they won't forget!" so proud of his girls.

Jenny cries as she watches her girls walk down the beach all by themselves. "Awe, look how brave they are... You noticed they didn't question it either. I think they deserve something special when they get back. We should have a big party out on the beach tonight."

"That sounds like a great idea! OK, I'm off!" he shouts, seeing the twins walking behind the trees at the far end of the beach, running after them.

"Keep close to them! Don't let them get scared! If they can't handle it, bring them back with you!"

"I won't let them out of my sight!" running as fast as he could to catch up with them.

Reaching the small pond, he hides behind the trees to see where they are. He hears their voices singing one of their favorite songs. He can't believe they are already up on the trail.

He hides behind a tree, waiting for them to get out of sight. Then, secretly, he follows them up the trail. He keeps close, always hiding within the trees, making sure that they don't see him. The twins are not worried at all about being on their own. They are singing songs and discussing their big day out all alone.

As they approach the lookout, Ben runs ahead, keeping just within the trees. He finds a spot where he can watch them without being seen. Right away, they knock down the fruit from the trees using their sticks. After filling their sacks with fruit, he is so shocked to see them both go over to the small bench to have their lunch break.

He thought they would have hurried back home, but instead, are enjoying their day out together like they always do. They sit together, looking down at the island, pointing out the landmarks, and looking out over the ocean just like any other day.

At one point, they both stand up, pointing down at the beach, waving frantically. "Hi, Mom!"

He knows Jenny has probably been down there waiting since they left, using the binoculars to check on them. He knows it makes them happy to see their mother down on the beach, constantly yelling out and waving to her.

* * *

After their lunch break, the girls are getting ready to leave. This is the big moment he has been waiting for, to see what they will do. Seeing them heading for the cave, he gets a tear in his eye. He has never been so proud of his girls. They could have picked some fruit and headed straight back home, but they wanted to do it all. The big test is to see if they can handle the firewood. If they can do this, then he knows they can survive on their own.

Again, he hides among the trees, trying to keep out of sight. He finds a good spot far across from the cave to watch them. He is so surprised to see them getting the cushions from the cave. At first, it looks as if they are going to take a break or even a nap. To his amazement, they put their doll Booboo down on the cushion. They place a small cloth over her, telling her to take a nap. He did the same thing when they made their first trip up to the cave.

Right away, they cut up the branch he had left the previous day. They store some in the cave, tying up the rest with rope. He is so shocked to see them planning to bring some of the firewood back. He taught them well, and they have done everything right. They have no problems being out on their own. On just this one trip, he is confident that they can handle anything.

The twins have another brief break, sharing an orange and having plenty to drink. Then they set their doll, Booboo, on the cushion, explaining all the rules to her. They are copying their father word for word. In a few years, they will teach their little brother all the rules of living on the island and eventually walk him up to the cave as well.

Then he sees something that makes him cry. The twins walk out of the cave, looking somewhat suspicious. They both stand together in front of their little doll. Then June holds out a small wooden stick about six inches long. She gently places it next to their little doll. They are carrying on the family tradition. They awarded Booboo her very own walking stick for making it up to the cave.

They quickly pack up everything and head back to camp. April carries the fruit while June takes the firewood, both singing their songs as they walk. Ben is so proud, knowing his little girls can take care of themselves. He follows them back down the trail. It's a glorious day, and he is planning one big celebration when they return home.

* * *

When April and June reach the small pond, Ben slides down the side of the hill through all the trees, making sure they don't see him. The pond is the one part he is not sure of. Will they stop there to rest or not? So, he runs straight for the camp, going through the trees right next to the beach. He had made it this far, and the last thing he wants is to be caught on the beach.

Ben finally reaches the camp. "They're on their way back!"

"How did it go? Are they all right? Where are they now?" she frantically asked.

"They did fine! No problems at all. They should be walking down the beach now," trying to catch his breath.

Jenny motions to Baby that the girls are coming back. He rushes out to the small bench to sit and wait for his sisters.

"I saw them up at the lookout," Jenny said. "So, they weren't scared?"

"Oh, no! It was like any other day. I'm so proud of them, and they're even bringing back some firewood! There is nothing they can't do. They were having a great time out on their own and even teaching Booboo a few things."

"That's so sweet... Our babies are growing up," then cries.

"I know... It's like the first day at school," giving her a big hug and kiss.

Baby starts screaming out loud, seeing his sisters walking down the beach. Jenny and Ben rush out. Seeing the big smiles on the twins' faces said it all.

Jenny is crying, watching her babies walking back home. Ben puts his arm around her, giving her a big hug. They are both very proud parents.

Baby runs down the beach to greet his sisters, stumbling now and then. He gives both of them a big hug. He is always happy to see his sisters when they return from their hike. June gives him an orange to help carry back, just like their father did with them.

Jenny can't wait any longer, running up to her little girls. She is so glad that it's finally over. She kneels in the sand, hugging and kissing each one of them, constantly crying.

"Did you see me waving at you?" she asked, wiping the tears from her eyes.

"Yeah! We saw you all the way down here. We waved, yelling at you too! You see us?" April asked.

"Yes, I did!" Jenny said, slowly getting up. "I'm so proud of you two. It's a big day for all of us," holding their hands, walking them back to camp.

"Nice job!" Ben said, hugging his girls. "You did it with plenty of time to spare."

"No, Daddy!" June said when he reached down to help with the firewood. "I get to do it all. You get to help Mom this time. These are our chores now."

"OK, you did a good job with the firewood. How come you brought some back?"

"So we have some for the rainy days," June explained. "We can store this under the hut with all the rest."

"Oh, we can always use extra firewood," Jenny said, hugging her again.

"I see you got plenty of fruit," he said.

"Sure did! We got big ones!" April said, holding up the bag.

"You two did such a good job today," Jenny said. "Let's get you back home and get something to eat."

* * *

June stores all the firewood under the hut. Even April stores away all the fruit. They want to do all the chores without any help. Once they put everything away, the twins can't wait to tell everyone about their day.

"So, how does it feel to go up on the island all by yourselves?" Jenny asked.

The girls look at each other, frowning. "It was fun," June explained, "but next time, we don't want Daddy following us. We want to go all by ourselves! We big girls now."

"I was here all the time!" Ben said, so shocked that he got caught.

"No, we saw you halfway up the trail," June said, looking up at her father, pointing her tiny finger at him. "We saw you watching us! That's not fair!"

"Yeah, Daddy!" April added. "You tricked us! We want to go all by ourselves! You have to stay home with Mom and Baby."

"Mom, the next time, make Daddy stay home," June said. "No more sneaking up with us anymore. He has to help with the chores here. Everyone has to help out," waving her finger at her father.

Jenny laughed out loud. "Well, he was worried about you and wanted to make sure you were OK."

Ben hides his smile, knowing that Jenny redirected all the worrying over to him. He doesn't say anything, letting Jenny gloat over her little girls. They forget all about their father watching over them after hearing about the big party to celebrate their first trip up to the cave. Although Jenny will never, ever let the twins make that trip all by themselves.

* * *

Chapter 38

Change

One afternoon, Jenny takes April down to the beach for a scavenging walk. June is in one of her bad moods, staying behind at the camp. Ben is changing Baby while June looks on. When she is in a bad mood, Baby doesn't want her to change his diaper. It's one of the few times Ben has to change him, and he is so glad it's not a stinker.

"How come we don't have a tallywhacker like you and Baby?" June asked, watching her little brother being changed.

"Well, only boys have those," he explained.

That doesn't sit well with June. "How come boys get everything!" she shouted, having a tantrum, jumping up and down.

"Well, where did you put yours?" he jokingly asked, getting a little annoyed with her. "I hope you didn't lose it on the beach?"

"I don't know," she said, frantically looking around on the ground.

He gives her a discerning frown. "I told you about being careful where you put things. Well, you better go out with your mother, and see if you can find it! I hope she doesn't get mad at you for losing it. You know how she gets with you guys when you are not putting things away," seeing how she still hasn't figured out that he is joking with her.

"OK, I'll go look!" then quickly turns, running down the beach to catch up with her mother and sister.

He can't help laughing, seeing June running down the beach. She is in a bad mood and probably not going to appreciate his little joke. She is getting restless and needs a long nap. He walks out to the beach with Baby to see how his joke will play out. They sit in the shade under the trees, playing in the sand, waiting for the big moment.

Ben watches as June is frantically running all over the beach. Jenny walks over to see what her problem is. He watches from a distance as June explains what she is looking for to her mother. Even from a distance, Ben can see that Jenny is extremely confused. He can't help laughing, seeing June lift her dress, pointing down at where her tallywhacker should be. Then she points back towards her father and starts searching in the sand again.

The gag is up. Jenny stands there with her hands on her hips, glaring at Ben. He knows he is in big trouble but can't help laughing out loud. Jenny sits on the beach with the girls, having a very long and drawn-out discussion. Occasionally, June turns to look back at her father. With her arms folded across her chest, she keeps giving him a very scornful look. She is so mad at being the target of one of his little jokes.

Jenny and the twins finally get up and continue walking down the beach. They are still discussing something together and are probably planning to get him back. No joke goes by without retaliation. June was in a bad mood, and now she is furious. She keeps turning to her father, yelling out something, and waving her finger at him.

Baby is mocking his sisters, yelling out and pointing his finger back at them. He thinks it's a great game but doesn't know how mad his sisters are and is just making things worse.

Ben carries Baby back to the camp for his nap. He wonders what the girls are scheming up for him and will need to keep his eyes open and be ready for any retaliation.

* * *

Jenny and the twins finally walk back into the camp. They approach Ben while he is lying on his hammock with Baby. He knows he is in trouble from the looks on their faces.

"That wasn't funny at all," Jenny sternly said, waving her finger at him. "We had a little talk, and we decided that we girls are going to stick together."

"Yeah, we girls stick together!" the twins yelled out, putting their arms around each other.

"Tell your father what little girls are made of?" Jenny asked them.

"Girls are made of sugar and spice and everything nice!" June promptly said.

"And what are boys made of?" Jenny asked April.

"Yeah, boys are made of snails and puppy dog tails too!" April shouted. "All bad things!"

Baby sits up, blowing a raspberry at the girls.

"He said it all!" Ben said with a big smile. "And by the way, we boys stick together too!" followed by another big raspberry from Baby.

"I see you're teaching him a few bad things as well," Jenny blurted out.

"Oh, I taught him well," he said, trying to provoke them a little more. "Show them what else you know."

Baby promptly puts his hand under his armpit. Then he moves his arm up and down real quick, making little farting noises. Ben can't help but laugh. His son found his calling, learning new ways to torment his sisters, and is very good at it.

"Well, from here on out, things will be different," Jenny said, seeing enough of this. "You can take care of Baby while I stay with the girls. I'm going to start teaching them how to be young ladies."

"Yeah, we going to be ladies now!" June explained. "No more boys anymore! It's just us girls!"

"Yeah!" April shouted, copying her little brother with her hand in her armpit, trying to make the farting noises.

"Come on, girls!" Jenny said, seeing she was quickly losing April. "Let's go play on the beach by ourselves. We don't need boys to have fun!" she then walks them away.

The war has started. Now, it's the boys against the girls. Ben knows this will be interesting and doesn't mind the change, wanting to spend more time with his son. The one thing he didn't think about was having to cook for himself. April and June's cooking is something that he will really miss. His little joke might cost him to be eating fruit for the next couple of days.

* * *

At night, everything is in turmoil. Ben and Baby stay in the camp, eating an orange and a banana. Ben tries to make the most of it, but it's hard to keep Baby amused since he wants to go out on the beach and play with his sisters.

The girls are having a big fish fry out on the beach, and the aroma from the big feast is making things worse. None of this is by accident. Jenny intentionally positions the campfire so that the breeze blows right through the campsite. Ben never realized how mean she could be, tormenting him like this.

The sleeping arrangements have changed as well. Jenny is now sleeping on the hammock with the twins. So, that means Ben has to sleep in the tent with Baby. He hasn't slept in the tent for years, and it's a drastic change. Having to be cooped up all night long in the small tent is something he is not used to, and the ground is hard and cold. Baby is constantly fidgeting about, wanting to play. Ben knows it's going to be a long, uncomfortable night with no sleep.

* * *

The next morning is no different. Jenny announces she will be taking the girls out over the island. She wants to spend more time with them. Ben is happy that she wants to do this since he has been hiking over the island almost every day. Now he gets to take care of Baby and stay at the camp. Change is always a good thing.

The twins are so excited about the first all-day girls' outing. Everything is being turned around. Now, they get to go to the cave with their mother. The only time their mother goes is during the storms. It's a big event, and the twins are looking forward to it.

While Jenny is getting ready, Ben takes the twins aside. "You guys need to watch out for Mom. She hasn't done the hike in a long time, so take your time. You know what to do. Just keep it simple," winking at them.

"OK, Daddy!" June said. "We make sure she doesn't get lost. We make her take plenty of breaks and give her lots of water."

"Good... I'll see you when you get back. Have a good time," hugging his girls.

They all quietly walk out to the beach together. Ben can see Jenny is having second thoughts about it. She hasn't done this in years. The twins are already taking charge of things and making one last check of all their gear. After one last hug, Jenny and the girls make their way down the beach.

Ben feels so odd being left behind, never really being alone at the camp. He sits on the bench with his son, waving at the girls as they walk away. Everything is so quiet, reminding him of the old days before all the children.

"Well, I guess it's party time for us," Ben said, glancing down at his son.

Baby yells out loud, jumping off the bench, running back to camp. Ben chases after him and has a feeling this is going to be an interesting day. With plenty of chores to do, he doesn't waste any time cleaning up the camp. The next thing on the list is boiling up the water to clean the dishes and wash all the clothes. That is the one chore that takes the longest.

Ben notices right away how helpful Baby is. His mother has been teaching him the ways of the island. He is getting to be just like his sisters. He is growing up fast, always wanting to help with the chores.

After washing all the clothes, Ben decides it's time for a break. He is enjoying the day, spending time with his son. He takes Baby down to the beach for a swim and a little fishing, netting a few good-sized fish.

Ben decides it's time to teach his son how to fish with the casting net. He takes one corner of the fishing net, placing it in Baby's hand, showing him how to throw it correctly. With a little help, he tosses it into the tidal pool. Once the net hits the water, all the fish frantically swim about, trying to escape. Baby quickly pulls in the net. His first cast is a winner, pulling in three fish.

That is the best way to teach him, so he will always catch something on every cast. Ben carefully places the fish back in the water so he can catch them again. Repeatedly, Baby keeps tossing the net in the tidal pool, catching fish, putting them back into the water.

Once Baby gets the hang of it, Ben takes him out in the water for the real thing. They walk out to the best spot near the rocks, where there are always plenty of fish. Baby stands up on one of the rocks holding the net. Ben kneels behind him, holding on so he won't fall, having him practice tossing the net in the water repeatedly. Baby gets so frustrated not seeing anything on the net when he drags it back in. The tidal pool is more fun, where he always catches something.

After many attempts, Baby finally catches his first fish. A tiny blue surgeonfish, not big enough to eat but is a trophy fish for a first catch. Baby is so thrilled carrying it over to the tidal pool, releasing it with the other fish. He doesn't want to do anything else but sit and watch his very own fish swim about with all the others. It is a good day, and it makes Ben a very proud father.

* * *

Jenny already feels exhausted trying to keep up with the girls. The pace is way too fast than what she used to do years ago. Even with the breaks, she is just too tired. Once they reach the lookout, the twins gather fruit for lunch. To Jenny's surprise, they head straight for the cave. They don't have time to sit around with all the work to be done. The twins now prefer taking their lunch breaks at the cave since it has plenty of shade and a gentle, cool breeze.

Jenny sits down to catch her breath at the cave, not wanting the girls to know she is exhausted, feeling so out of place. The twins prepare lunch, making their favorite fruit salad of bananas, oranges, coconuts, lemons, and grapefruits with a splash of water. Jenny is so impressed with how they handle themselves. She doesn't have to do anything. Before she can do anything, the girls are already handing out the food.

After a brief break, they set out for the far orchard. April and June don't even do any chores at the cave. Jenny doesn't question it, following the girls, wondering what they are going to do next.

Jenny can't believe how they are always signaling each other with hand signs. Instead of a walk to gather food and firewood, this is more like a Navy Seal mission, always looking for land sharks or monsters. Things are getting out of hand, and it's not a game anymore. She is going to talk to Ben about this and put a stop to it.

Jenny has forgotten how hard it is to walk to the other side of the island. In the past few years, she has only gone to the cave. Going down the steep trail on the far side is extremely difficult. She is wondering how fast they can go on their own, seeing how the girls are constantly slowing down to let her catch up.

* * *

Reaching the big orchard, Jenny is so shocked. "Where did all these trees come from?"

"They have always been here," June explained. "This is where we get our fruit from," pointing to all the trees.

"There is a lot more here than what I remembered," Jenny said, seeing all the new trees.

"This one is mine!" April explained, walking up to a small tree. "That one is June's, and that little one is Baby's tree. It be a long time before they start growing fruit," pointing them out to her mother.

"Oh, your father has been planting some of the seedlings out here. It explains why there are so many more trees than when I was out here last time," trying to count how many years since being up here.

"Yep!" April said. "We always plant new trees. One day, we'll have lots more lemon trees! We got only one, so we have to be careful not to pick too many. Those are the special ones. We always plant the lemon seeds, so we'll get more. Then the lemon tree won't be all by herself. She'll have other lemon trees to talk to."

"That's nice," seeing how Ben is teaching them his philosophy that plants can talk to each other.

Jenny watches as the twins pick fruit off the trees using their sticks. They are careful not to damage the trees, choosing only the best ones. Jenny helps collect the fruit in the bag. Once the bag is full, April and June walk back to the trail.

"So, is that it?" Jenny asked. "Are we heading back home now?" looking forward to a long nap.

"Oh, no! We got to get the firewood now," June explained, leaving the bag of fruit in the shade next to the trail.

"Yeah, we go down there for the firewood," April added, pointing down the trail leading to the beach. "Then, we have to pick up the fruit bag on the way back."

"OK, lead the way," Jenny said, feeling a little out of place.

They continue down the trail to the far side of the island. Jenny doesn't understand what they are doing and just follows along. She did not know that they went this far for firewood. All she can think about is the long walk back up to the cave.

"Now, girls, you know you're not supposed to leave the trail!" Jenny said, seeing them walking into the deep forest. "You might get lost!"

"Mom, this is where we get the firewood," April explained. "It's over there," pointing over to a group of trees.

"Your father brings you all the way out here for firewood?" Jenny asked, seeing a small trail leading to a large cypress tree that had fallen.

"Sure, it's our firewood tree!" April said.

"We always get firewood from here," June replied. "Dad says this one will last us for a long time."

"Yeah, it's a good one!" April explained. "Nice and dry... Easy to cut and burns really good."

"Oh, OK... So what do I do? How can I help?" Jenny asked.

"You sit over there and rest up. This is our chore. We always do the firewood."

Jenny doesn't argue, sitting down in the shade to rest. She watches as they take out the small wire saw, going to work on one of the smaller branches. They don't waste any time, quickly cutting off the branch, then tying rope onto the end. She now knows why they picked this tree, since it doesn't take long to cut it up.

"Let me help with the tree branch," Jenny said, feeling so guilty for not doing anything.

"OK! You hold this and drag it behind you," April explained, handing her the rope.

"I know how to do this. I dragged a lot of firewood in my time before you two were born. Lead the way!" dragging the tree branch back to the trail.

"Mom, where are you going?" April asked. "We not done yet!" so embarrassed that their mother is going back up to the cave.

"What else is there to do? Aren't we done?"

"No, Mom!" June said. "You have to put that down and go with us," motioning for her to follow.

"OK, so what do we do now?" dropping the rope, wondering what is in store for her.

"You follow us, Mom!" June boasted, with a big smile on her face. "We'll show you!" taking her mother's hand.

The twins are giggling, not letting on to what is coming up next. They continue down the trail to the beach. The twins race out onto the sand, pulling off their backpacks, stripping out of their clothes.

"Come on, Mom!" June yells. "It's break time!"

"Thank God!" realizing Ben had taught them well, slipping out of her clothes, running into the surf with the girls.

They play in the water for a while to cool off. Jenny looks around, remembering the first time that she was here. She has not ventured to the far side of the island in such a long time. Having children kept her at the camp for years. Now, she wishes she had done this more often.

"How come you look so sad?" April asked, seeing the look on her mother's face.

"It's nothing," Jenny said, daydreaming about the past. "I was just thinking about the first time I was out here with your father. That was a long time ago when it was just the two of us here."

"Where were we at?" April asked, a little confused.

"Oh, you two weren't even born then. It was just your father and me."

"That must have been when me and June were living on the other island," April replied. "The one with the dolphins, remember!" pointing out to the ocean.

"That's right!" June shouted, nodding her head up and down. "We were on the other island, way far away," coming to the same conclusion.

Jenny can't help giggling. The twins still believe their father's tall Texan tales and now have become a part of the children's lives. No matter how wild the stories are, the children always believe every word. One day, when they are older, it'll be a big shock when they learn the truth.

"It's getting late," June said, looking up at the sun's position. "We need to start back now."

They rush back to the beach. Jenny stops, picking up all the clothes. The twins keep on running to the trees, grabbing a towel draped over one of the branches.

"So, that's what happened to one of my good towels?" Jenny asked.

The girls laugh while they dry themselves. Their mother has just discovered one of their little secrets.

"So what other things don't I know about?" she asked.

"I'm not telling!" then April laughs.

"You have to ask Dad!" June added, laughing as well.

"Oh, I will!" she said, getting a little frustrated. "I'm going to have a long talk with your father after today. Too much is going on that I don't know about," realizing she has been out of the loop.

The girls are already motioning to their mother to hurry. Jenny quickly gets dressed, dreading the trip back. She is so tired but now realizes she has to walk all the way back up to the cave.

After a short walk, they reach the place where they left the tree branch. Jenny grabs the rope, dragging the tree branch up the trail.

"Mom, what are you doing?" June asked.

"I'm helping out... It's way too heavy for you."

"We don't drag the wood up the trail. We'll show you how it's done," June explained, getting frustrated that her mother doesn't know how to do any of this.

June pulls out some rope from her backpack, tying it to the opposite end of the branch. April grabs the rope on the other side, putting it over her shoulder. They both lift the branch off the ground, then walk up the trail.

Jenny watches in awe at her two little girls. She thought they were going to drag the tree branch, but instead, they carried it. It all makes sense now. Dragging the large branch up the hill will be harder to do. She can't believe how self-sufficient they are. She follows them up the trail, knowing that they have everything under control.

"Mom, you want to help carry the bag?" June asked once they reached the big orchard.

"Why don't I help you since it's so heavy? You two can carry the fruit bag."

"No, we do the firewood," April said. "It's our job!"

Jenny doesn't argue, reaching down, picking up the bag. "Does your father make you do all this when you're with him?"

"Sometimes he helps," June said, "but we like to do everything. It's our job!"

"Yeah, we Amazon girls!" April added. "Daddy says this will get us real big and strong!"

"I'm going to have a little talk with him when I get back," Jenny quietly mumbled.

A tear runs down her cheek as she watches her two little girls walking up the trail ahead of her. They have grown up so fast. None of this is easy. She knows how Ben always teaches them how to do everything, but not to this extent. Having the girls do all the chores is probably his way of making sure that they can survive on their own.

* * *

Once they reach the cave, Jenny is exhausted. All she did was carry the bag of fruit. She feels so useless. The twins are not even out of breath, and they are carrying the heavy branch up the steep trail. She can now see why Ben is so muscular after doing this almost every day on his own. She knows it's time for her to get back in shape and is not doing her share of the work.

"It's break time!" April shouted. "You look tired, Mom!" bringing out some water bottles from the cave.

"I can really use a break!" Jenny said, sitting down. "That was so tiring."

They sit down with their mother, giving her an orange and more water to drink. Even though they took it slow, the trip was too hard for her. She is going to need a long break before heading back to camp.

April runs into the cave, bringing out two cushions, placing them together. "You can lie down here and take a nap while we cut up the firewood."

June pulls out their little doll Booboo from her backpack, handing it over to her mother. "You get to watch over Booboo. Eat your orange. It makes you big and strong. You need to drink plenty of water, too. That's the rules!" waving her finger at her mother.

"OK, I'll help you in a few minutes," Jenny said, taking the little doll. "I just need a little rest. You two need to take a break as well. That was a long trip."

"We OK!" April said. "You rest while we do the firewood."

Jenny is too tired to argue. She lies down on the cushions and is soon sound asleep. April walks into the cave, bringing out a towel, placing it over her mother to keep her warm. Their father told them to watch their mother. They know it means they need to keep an eye on her, making sure she drinks plenty of water, but they didn't expect things to be this bad.

April and June cut up the branch, keeping an eye on their mother while she sleeps. They know their mother is not ready to help with all the chores. She always stays at the camp, taking care of Baby, but needs to learn all the rules. In time, they know their mother can do it.

* * *

After cutting up the firewood and storing it all away, the twins pull out two bundles of dry wood from the cave, tying up with rope. Once all the work is done, they store everything away, and now it's time to return home.

Jenny has been asleep the entire time. The twins are taking their time so their mother can rest, but it's getting late. They need to return home soon so their father won't worry.

"Wake up, Mom!" April said, gently nudging her mother. "Time to go home!" trying to wake her up.

"Oh, did I fall asleep?" Jenny asked, surprised to see the girls standing over her. "Are you two ready to head back now? I thought you were going to cut up the firewood?" seeing them already wearing their backpacks.

"We did that already!" June blurted out, giggling. "You slept a long time. It's time to go home now!"

"I must have fallen asleep," Jenny mumbled, slowly getting up on her feet.

"You need to drink some before we leave," April said, handing her mother a water bottle.

"Thank you, but I don't need a drink... I feel fine," Jenny politely said, shaking her head.

"No, you have to drink some before we leave," April said.

"It's the rules!" June added, nodding in agreement.

"I see your father has taught you well," Jenny said, taking a good long drink.

The twins know they have to slow down, making sure their mother doesn't get too worn out. The hardest part is over, and it's downhill the rest of the way. They spent way too much time at the cave than they usually do. Both are glancing up at the sun, getting concerned about the time.

When Jenny hands the water bottle to June, she notices her necklace is missing. "Oh, no! It's gone!" looking at the ground.

"What's gone?" June asked.

"My pearl necklace!" she frantically explained. "It must have dropped off!" searching all over for it.

"Maybe you put it down on the beach!" June said, not seeing it anywhere.

"When was the last time you saw it on me?" she asked, getting so frustrated. "I don't remember taking it off."

"Maybe at the orchard way on the other side," June said. "You want to go back and look for it?"

"I don't know if I can do that trip twice in one day," walking over to the trail leading to the far side. "Maybe we should look up here first."

They looked all over for the pearl necklace. Jenny doesn't have the strength to go back to the far side to search for it. Since it's already getting too late, they'll have to look for the pearl necklace another day. All they can do is hope it's somewhere on the trail leading back to the camp.

"OK, girls," Jenny reluctantly said. "We can't spend any more time looking for it. It's been a long day! Let's go home."

"We can look tomorrow," June said. "Then, we show you how to cut up the firewood!"

"Oh, that's nice," Jenny replied, wondering how to get out of this.

"We need to go!" April shouted, looking up at the sun. "Dad is going to worry! It's really late!"

Jenny smiles. "We better get back home then. I'll carry the bag. Lead the way. Keep your eye out for my necklace. Hopefully, it's out on the trail somewhere."

The twins walk down the trail, carrying huge bundles of firewood on their backs. Jenny can see how much they emulate their father. What is supposed to be a backbreaking chore is nothing more than a leisurely day out for the girls, singing their favorite songs all the way down the trail.

* * *

Jenny is totally exhausted by the time they reach the bottom of the trail. She aches all over, ready for a nice, long soak in the pond. Just the walk alone wears her out, and it's a lot more work than what she is used to doing. To make things worse, she doesn't find her necklace.

Ben surprises them all. He has been getting worried and meets them at the pond. Jenny hasn't done this in years and knows they will be gone a long time, but not this long. He was getting ready to go up the trail to check on them. He remembers what it was like on their first days going over the island and knows she will be tired.

"Mom! Mom!" Baby screamed out loud, running up to his mother.

"Hi, Dad! Hi, Baby!" April said, so relieved to see them.

"You get worried?" June asked.

"Naw," Ben said, shaking his head. "You guys know what you're doing. So, was it a good trip?"

"It was OK," June said, glancing over at her mother, not wanting to say anything bad.

After one look at Jenny, he knows right away that she is exhausted. She is rather quiet and doesn't even have the strength to pick up Baby. Walking straight for the pond, she drops out of her sweat-laden clothes, sitting in the water to cool off. She doesn't say much at all, being so exhausted from the trip.

Ben makes a quiet whistle sound to get the twins' attention. He taps his finger on his wrist to indicate how late it is. The girls signaled to their father, waving their fingers on their right hand. That is the sign for being too tired, glancing over at their mother. Without a word being said, they let their father know the trip was too much for her. Ben just nodded, letting them know he understands the problem.

Baby is so happy that everyone is at the pond. He is ready to play, running over to his sisters, splashing water on them, starting a big water fight. The twins are still full of energy and ready to play.

"So, how was your day?" Jenny asked Ben.

"It went well... I took care of the camp. Did a little fishing. Then, Baby and I had a nap. How about your day?" he asked, having a good idea of how it went.

She let out a long sigh. "Well, I don't think I'll be ready to make another run for a while. I can't believe you did all that on your own."

"It's not so bad... You'll get used to it after a while. At least I have the girls to help out now. You'd be surprised at what they can do."

"Oh, I have seen what they're capable of doing," she quickly replied. "I never felt so useless. I didn't realize how out of shape I had gotten over the years."

He smiles at her. "After a few trips, you'll do OK... It's been a long time. Maybe we should get you started by just jogging up to the cave and back."

She laughed at the idea. "I don't think so," realizing Ben is not joking.

"OK, maybe a slow walk then."

"Ben, I got some bad news... Sorry, but I lost the pearl necklace you gave me. I don't know how, but I noticed it was missing when we were up at the cave."

"Did you put it down somewhere? Maybe it's at the camp?"

"No, I had it on when I went up the trail. I remember it was hitting my chest as we walked. The chain must have come loose. It's probably out on the beach on the far side."

"We'll look for it tomorrow... Don't worry, we'll find it."

"I hope so... I should have left it at home," she sighed, closing her eyes, almost falling asleep.

Ben gathers up her clothes, rinsing them off in the pond. She is a little out of shape, but walking up to the cave will fix that in no time. Jenny still has a great voluptuous body, but her muscles need some work. After having three children, she sure can't complain about her body.

* * *

Jenny wakes up after Baby splashes water on her. "OK, I'm awake... Ben, I'm ready to go back now," picking up Baby.

"OK, let's move out," picking up all their clothes and the bundles of wood.

They all make their way back home. The twins run naked down the beach, dragging the bag of fruit. Baby hobbles along, trying to keep up with his sisters.

"Where do they get all the energy?" Jenny asked, watching them running off.

"They never get tired," he explained. "It's all a big game to them."

"If I only had my camera," he said, looking over at Jenny's naked body as they walked.

She smiles and hugs him tightly. "I'm so glad you still think of me in that way. I still need to get back in shape. Now, I can see why you are all muscles and no fat!" pinching his side.

"Oh, come on!" he replied, with a big smirk on his face. "I look about the same as when we first got here. Maybe lost a little weight," looking down at his waist.

"Bull!" she quickly blurted out. "I love to show you a before and after picture. I think I'll start calling you Conan with all those throbbing muscles of yours," running her hand over his chest.

"Yeah, right," he said, not noticing any change except for a bit of weight loss.

Once they reach the camp, Jenny goes straight to bed for a long nap. The twins are so happy to have a day out with their mother. They are looking forward to going back out tomorrow to do it all again. They still have much more to teach their mother about all the chores that need to be done.

After a big supper, they settle in for the night. Jenny tries to remember when she last saw her necklace. She can't believe she lost it after all this time, wanting to go back and retrace her steps to find it. With every muscle in her body aching, she is determined to walk the trail again in the morning to get back in shape.

Walking up to the cave every day will do the job. It will be a pleasant change to have the family together for most of the day. She can stay with Baby at the cave while the others are on the far side. That's her new plan, and in the morning, she will put it into place.

* * *

The next morning, she tells Ben about her new plan. He is so glad to hear she likes the idea of changing things up a little. Change in their daily lives is a good thing. Being stuck in the same old rut gets boring day after day. He enjoyed his day alone with Baby and can see more days like this to come. Even having the whole family up at the cave will be nice. He likes the idea and is looking forward to spending more time with his family.

After a hearty breakfast, they all make their way up to the cave for a family day outing. The most important chore of the day is looking for the pearl necklace. All eyes are on the ground for the entire day, tracing their steps from the camp to the cave. Jenny even ventures to the other side of the island hoping to find it. They spend hours on the beach sifting through the sand. Ben also uses his snorkeling gear, trying to find it out in the water.

* * *

By the end of the day, Jenny is so depressed. With everyone helping, she thought someone would have found it. She never forgave herself for not putting it away in a safe place, only wearing it on special occasions.

For days, everyone has been looking for the necklace. They search near the trail, going through the thick grass at the lookout and the far orchard. It could be lost in the sand on the far side or lying just off the trail under a leaf. Eventually, they stop looking. The necklace is lost somewhere on the island, but one day, someone will find it. It's just a matter of time.

* * *

Chapter 39

The Visitors

S pring arrives on the small island, and the flowers are in full bloom. As usual, the twins are out on their favorite pastime, spearfishing. With spears in hand, they quietly wait on one of the lava rocks, searching for a nice-sized fish. Not making any movements or noise, they wait patiently for a fish to swim by them. They are so fixated on what they are doing that they don't even hear the splashing sounds coming from behind.

"What are you guys doing?" a strange voice yelled out.

April and June are so startled hearing the strange voice. They quickly turn in absolute shock. They are standing face to face with not just one but two land sharks standing only a few feet away. One is an older girl, and the other is a boy.

April and June quickly remember their training. Taking a defensive stance, they point their spears directly at the land sharks. Slowly moving off the rocks, they never lose eye contact. Out in the water, they are in a bad position. The twins quickly walk towards the beach, trying to get some distance, always pointing their spears at the land sharks just in case they attack.

"Hey, what's the matter?" the boy asked.

Carol and her brother Mike looked at each other, a little puzzled. The response is not what they were expecting. These two little girls are acting strangely, always waving those sticks around. They follow the strange little girls back to the beach, wondering what is wrong.

"You shouldn't be pointing those sticks at people," Carol said, a little perturbed. "You can hurt someone!"

"Hey, we just came over to see what you're doing! What's wrong with you two?" Mike asked, seeing how odd these girls were acting.

April and June don't say a word. They signal each other with a barrage of hand signs and whistles, trying to figure out what to do.

The two land sharks are bigger than they are, but at least they don't have any spears or knives. Slowly backing off, the twins try to keep a distance from the approaching land sharks.

Carol gets annoyed with these two little girls. Since these girls don't talk at all, she thought maybe they don't speak English. All they are doing is making weird noises and hand signs. The one thing that irritates her the most is how they keep pointing those sharp sticks at her. She decides to put a stop to this, walking up to take the sticks away.

Seeing the land shark approaching, June signals April to attack. June swings her spear hard, striking the side of the girl's head. April runs forward towards the boy, jabbing her spear into the sand, using it to lift herself up, slamming her feet into his chest. The blow knocks the boy down flat on his back, and he gasps for air.

The twins now have the advantage, slowly approaching the land sharks, ready to attack again. Carol and Mike are so scared, not understanding why these two little girls attacked them. Carol pulls her brother up, trying to get as far as possible from these two wild girls.

April and June are so relieved to see the two land sharks running away. Luckily, they are the only two on the beach. With no clue where these land sharks came from, they quickly scan the ocean, thinking more might come out of the water. Not seeing anything else around, and with the land sharks far enough down the beach, they rush back to camp to warn everyone.

* * *

Hearing the girls screaming out loud, Jenny knows something is wrong. These are not typical screams when they are out having fun on the beach. She rushes out to see what is going on.

"Land sharks!" the twins shouted, running up to their mother, so frightened. "We got land sharks! Two of them on the beach!"

"What do you mean, land sharks? What are you two talking about?" Jenny asked, thinking it's some sort of game.

"Mom! Two land sharks snuck up on us!" June cried out, still trying to catch her breath, pointing down the beach.

"Yeah!" April added. "We were out fishing, and they came up real close to us! They real sneaky, too. Didn't even hear them coming!"

"Oh, my God! There are people here!" Jenny yelled out, seeing two small figures running away.

"No, Mom! Those are land sharks!" June explained.

"Yeah, we whacked them good too!" April added. "Better tell Daddy we got land sharks!"

"You didn't hurt them, did you?" she asked.

"I don't know," June replied, shrugging her shoulders. "We better get Daddy!" so proud to have taken on the two land sharks. "We go back after them, right, Momma!"

"Oh no, you don't!" Jenny blurted out, trying to think what she should do.

"We got land sharks! We need to go finish them off!" June shouted, ready to go back after them.

"Where is your father?" she asked, trembling, looking around for him.

"I think he's on the potty!" June replied, pointing over to the trees.

"Ben! Ben!" Jenny yelled out. "Get out here quick! Hurry!"

Seeing the two people running down the beach, Jenny picks up Baby and starts chasing after them. April and June are so shocked to see their mother running after the land sharks. She doesn't have any sticks or knives, and worse, she is carrying Baby with her. They quickly chase after her, not understanding why she is not hiding in the camp like they are supposed to do.

"Mom, what are you doing?" April asked after catching up with her. "You not supposed to bring Baby! Those are land sharks!"

"We need to wait for Daddy!" June shouted. "He's going to get real mad you bringing Baby! We need to go back!"

"Mom!" April frantically yelled out. "You not doing the rules! We supposed to hide!"

Jenny is not listening, still in shock, seeing people on the beach. The twins are behind her, trying to get her to turn back and wait for their father.

Reaching the bend, Jenny comes to a complete stop, seeing a large sailboat anchored just off the beach. Not only is there a camp set up with bright-colored tents and picnic tables, but there are also several families here with children.

The two children that the twins attacked finally arrive back at their camp. They are apparently telling their parents about their ordeal, pointing back down the beach towards Jenny. Everyone starts strutting down the beach, and none of them look too happy.

The twins are so shocked to see there are more than two land sharks on their island. Many are much bigger than the first two that they saw. To make matters worse, they are all coming towards them.

"No, Mom! There are too many! We need to go back and get Daddy!" June said, pulling on her mother's arm.

"Yeah, Mom!" April yelled, getting scared. "We need to hide in the trees and wait for Daddy!"

Seeing how close the land sharks are getting, June decides it's time to take charge. "Mom, you protect Baby! We'll hold them off!" making warning signals that Baby understands.

"Hush and be still!" Jenny said, seeing the two families approaching.

As the land sharks get within ten feet, the twins immediately run in front, taking an offensive stance and pointing their spears at the group. They dig their feet deep into the sand, getting ready to lunge their spears at the land sharks.

"What the hell's going on!" the woman yelled out, obviously very angry. "Why did you attack my kids!"

Jenny panics, seeing that the boy is still crying, and the girl has a big welt on the side of her head. "I'm so sorry!" she said, so embarrassed. "The girls have never seen anyone else before. They were just frightened. I hope they didn't hurt them."

"You mean to tell me that these little girls are the ones who attacked you?" the father asked his son.

The poor boy is so scared. He just nods his head, still sobbing, hiding behind his mother.

"I thought you said they were a bunch of big bullies going after you?" the mother asked her children.

"That girl hit me with that stick!" Carol yelled out, pointing at June. "All we did was go see what they were doing?"

"Look, we're not going to harm you," the man explained, seeing the two little girls waving their sticks at him. "We're just out having a beach party with our family."

"Bad land sharks!" June yelled out, not letting up at all. "You go back in the water! Go away!" waving her spear back and forth.

"This is our home! Go away!" April yelled, then lets out a loud screeching birdcall that startles everyone.

They all look at the two girls in disbelief. The little girls are making all sorts of birdcalls, and it sounds like the real thing. Every time one of the girls makes a birdcall, it prompts the birds in the trees to reply. No one knows what is going on, and it's a little bizarre.

"It's OK!" Jenny said, knowing the twins were so scared. "It'll be best if you don't get too close to them. They're just protecting their little brother."

One man steps forward to introduce himself. "Hello, I'm George —"

Seeing the land shark getting too close, April and June quickly point their spears right at his throat. Baby let out a loud screeching birdcall, holding on tight to his mother. That prompts more birds to start squawking from the trees.

The man stops dead in his tracks. The two little girls stare right at him, not even flinching. He looks down at them, realizing they mean business. Seeing the sharp points on the sticks, he knows this is a dangerous situation and that he should not get too close to the girls.

"Oh, sorry," the man said, stepping back. "I'm George, and this is my wife, Sally… My son Mike and daughter Carol," pointing over to them.

"I'm Jenny," she mumbled after a long pause. "This is June, April, and Baby."

"Over there is Bob," George said, pointing over at the others behind him, "and his wife Margaret, and their kids John, Peter, and Heather. That's our captain, Wayne Peterson."

"Hi," Jenny said, waving awkwardly at them, finding it so difficult to speak.

"We didn't know anyone else was on the island," George explained. "We didn't see your boat."

"We don't have a boat," Jenny responded, still in shock.

"How long have you been here?" Margaret asked, noticing the rags Jenny was wearing.

"I'm not sure anymore," Jenny mumbled, unable to think straight, then cried, so overwhelmed. "We were on a flight to Kwajalein. It went down. We ended up here."

"Your plane went down?" George asked, seeing Jenny was babbling and not making much sense. "I never heard any reports of a plane going down around here. Was it in the last couple of days?

There have been no reports on the radio," turning to Captain Peterson to see if he knew about it.

"It's news to me," Wayne said. "We would have heard something and been on the lookout for it."

"It was long ago," Jenny mumbled.

"That can't be right," Wayne explained. "This entire area just opened up to the public. No one has been allowed near these islands for years."

"That's one of the reasons we've come out here," George added, also a little confused. "This is uncharted territory. We thought it would be nice to be the first ones here before all the tourists find out about it."

"Like I said," Jenny replied, overwhelmed with emotions. "It was so long ago... We gave up hope. This is our home now."

Everyone is curious about this strange woman, wondering how she got here, especially with three children. They can see that she is a little apprehensive. What is so odd are the two little girls. They are a bit on the wild side, always pointing their sticks at everyone, making strange clicking noises, hand signs, and birdcalls. They are not letting anyone get near their mother and the baby boy.

Seeing the clothing the two little girls have on, and especially what Jenny is wearing, Margaret guesses they might have been here for a long time. It would explain their reaction when seeing other people on the beach.

"Are you hungry?" Margaret asked, trying to make them feel more at ease. "We have plenty of food and drink here. Why don't you all come and join us at our camp?" wondering when they had their last decent meal.

"Thank you," Jenny reluctantly said, looking back down the beach for Ben. "Maybe just for a little while," wondering what is keeping him.

Jenny feels so awkward. She lost all of her social skills, not used to being around other people. Having people here on the island is too much of a shock for her. She doesn't know what to do, and being on her own is not helping. She keeps wondering where Ben is.

Everyone can see something is wrong here. Maybe this woman and her children have been alone on this island for a long time. Margaret makes everyone else walk ahead of them back to their camp. Seeing how apprehensive Jenny is and how the little girls are acting, it is apparent they don't feel comfortable being around other people.

As they are walking, Margaret keeps a distance from Jenny. The two little girls are making sure no one gets too close. They are very adamant about protecting their mother and little brother. She can't help smiling, seeing these little girls doing all those weird hand signals to each other. The constant whistling and birdcalls are so bizarre. She can see that they are definitely a little on the wild side.

"So, what sort of game are they playing with those sticks and the sounds they are making?" Margaret asked on the walk back to their camp.

"It's no game... They were taught to protect their little brother," Jenny replied, not elaborating on any more than that.

"Oh, really," Margaret said, looking down at the little girls. "Well, we are all friends here. We're just here to help," smiling at the little girls.

She thinks it's odd that the little girls don't even reply. They just keep staring at her, looking as if they are ready to pounce. The girls are pointing those sticks at her the entire time, making sure she doesn't get too close. She knows it might be best for everyone to keep a distance from these two wild ones.

* * *

Once they reach the campsite, Captain Wayne Peterson gathers everyone around to discuss the situation. "OK, we got a problem here."

"Yeah, I don't remember hearing about any plane crash," George quietly mentioned to the others. "Have any of you?"

"No, I haven't... Maybe they're a little confused," Wayne explained, looking over at Jenny and her children just behind them. "They're probably some of those people who drop out of society to live on a tropical island. Maybe they just couldn't handle it. They couldn't have been out here too long. Remember, this entire area just opened up to the public. I figure they've been here a couple of days, maybe a week at most."

"I can't believe anyone would bring those little babies out here to live under these conditions!" Sally blurted out.

"There's a lot of that going on out here," Wayne added, shrugging his shoulders. "People see that Disney movie 'Swiss Family Robinson' and think they can do it too. It's so sad... Many of them don't make it out alive, and that's after only a few weeks."

"We need to do something about this," Sally said, so outraged. "We can't just leave them here."

"I'll make some calls," Wayne said. "We need to find out who they are. Maybe we can persuade them to come back with us."

"I don't know about those two little girls," George quickly added.

Sally laughed. "Talk about some wild little Indians. We need to keep all the kids from those two. Someone needs to take those sharp sticks away before they hurt someone."

They warn everyone to keep their distance from the two girls. They all notice how the little girls are always out in front of their mother, constantly eyeing them all. Also, the odd clicking noises the girls make are so strange. The birdcalls are very odd as well. They look as if they are communicating with each other. It is definitely a wild family that they discovered on this small island.

* * *

Margaret and Jenny arrive at the camp, sitting down at one of the picnic tables. The twins never let up, standing on both sides of their mother while Baby is on her lap. Jenny is obviously upset and overwhelmed, being discovered here on the island. Everyone else gathers around on the opposite side of the table, trying to find out what is going on with this family.

"So, did you or your kids get hurt when your plane went down?" Margaret asked.

"Oh, no!" Jenny answered, looking down at Baby. "It was just Ben and me at the time. The children came along later."

Everyone just stares at her in dead silence. It is getting to be one wild story. They are all looking at each other, wondering if she is crazy.

"You mean to tell me that all three were born here?" George asked, looking down at the children, trying to guess how old they were.

"I don't understand? So when exactly did your plane go down? Was it a few days or a week ago?" Wayne asked, getting concerned, wanting to get to the bottom of this mystery.

"I can't remember exactly," Jenny replied, pausing a few moments trying to recall the date. "I think it was the winter of ninety-seven."

"That can't be right!" Margaret shouted out. "That's over six years ago!"

"Oh, God... Has it been that long?" Jenny asked, not realizing how long they had been on the island.

"Wait a minute! I remember a plane going down about that time," Wayne added.

"You were there?" Jenny asked.

"Yeah, I was working at Kwajalein back then. There was a plane lost, but that was years ago! It was all over the news, but there were no survivors! Everyone knows about that. They even have a memorial with a plaque on it at the main entrance. Come on now! Who exactly are you, and how long have you been here?" Wayne asked, approaching Jenny, pointing his finger at her.

The twins quickly pick up on the growing tension. Seeing the land shark getting too close, they slowly move in, ready to attack. There is a barrage of whistles and hand signals. Baby screeches out a loud birdcall, a sign to his sisters to protect him, holding on tight to his mother. June takes the lead and is about to sling her spear at the land shark.

"It's OK!" Jenny shouts, seeing the twins are about to attack. "Back off! We're just talking. Keep calm, and put those sticks down!"

April sends out the signal to pull back. Slowly, they back away, never taking their eyes off the land shark. Returning to their mother, they are still ready to pounce at a moment's notice.

"I'm sorry," Wayne said, stepping back, seeing things getting out of hand. "I shouldn't have raised my voice. It's OK... We are all here to help you."

"Wait a minute!" Margaret said, still trying to get to the bottom of this. "You're telling us that you were on that plane that Wayne was talking about all those years ago?"

Jenny doesn't reply. The memory of it flashes through her mind. She just nods her head, not wanting to remember that horrible day.

"So, you're telling me that you are Jenny Mason from Kwajalein Island?" Wayne asked, looking at her closely, remembering the name on the plaque.

"Yes," she simply replied, so shocked, hearing her full name after all those years.

"You said you were here with another person?" Wayne asked. "His name was Ben? What happened to him? Is he here?"

"He should be here by now," Jenny said, looking around for him. "Where is your father?" glancing over at the girls.

They both turn, looking over at the trees, not saying a word. They don't want the land sharks to know where he is. June flashes a sign to her mother to let her know where their father is.

"Tell him it's OK," Jenny said, now that she knows he is hiding in the trees. "We're all fine… These are friendly people."

June makes a loud bird call sound. Seconds later, a strange birdsong emanates from within the trees. The twins immediately look at each other. More hand signals go between the two girls. June then turns to Baby, giving him a hand signal. He smiles, signaling back that he understands. He then screeches out a loud birdcall. Right away, more birds are squawking from the trees. He turns to his sisters, and with a big smile, starts laughing.

June screeches out another loud birdcall. Everyone is amazed but mostly confused about what is going on. The little girls are squawking like tropical birds and doing all these strange hand signals. Something is happening. All the attention moves toward the trees.

Seconds later, without any sound, Ben emerges from the trees. He stands in clear view of all these people, carrying a seven-foot-long pointed spear with a twelve-inch cooking knife at his side. He just stares at all these strangers, not feeling comfortable with his family being so close to them.

Ben makes a clicking sound. That is the signal to Baby, but also to the twins. Baby quickly jumps off his mother's lap, running as fast as he can toward his father. April and June immediately follow, still pointing their sticks at the land sharks protecting their little brother while he is out in the open.

Baby quickly hides behind his father. April and June stand next to their father, still pointing their sticks at the land sharks. They are so relieved he is with them now. Things are now in their control.

* * *

Ben had heard Jenny screaming and came out to see her running down the beach with the girls. He knew something was wrong, chasing after them. Seeing the sailboat, Ben ran back to get his weapons. He followed along, keeping out of sight, hiding just within the trees to evaluate the situation.

Constantly signaling the twins with various birdcalls, he let them know he was there and what they should do. The twins were always between Baby and the strangers to protect him, just like he had taught them. He is so proud of his little girls for not being scared at all. They did everything right that he taught them if a land shark showed up on the island. Even Baby was in on it, signaling to his father with the few birdcalls he knew.

* * *

Everyone is so stunned, seeing Ben walking out of the trees, looking extremely intimidating. They quickly backed away with this six-foot-tall bronze muscular man glaring at them. Wearing only shorts and a tattered Australian hat on his head, Ben is well-armed and makes sure they all know it.

"Wow, talk about Conan the Barbarian," Margaret quietly whispered to Sally, seeing this tall, bare-chested man with a short beard.

"Looks more like Tarzan to me," Sally quietly said, admiring his bulging muscles and well-tanned body.

Both Sally and Margaret are so amazed to see the two little girls at his side, especially with the little boy peeking out from behind his father's legs blowing raspberries. It is indeed a sight to see.

"Daddy, they look kind of scrawny," June said, looking over the land sharks. "We can take them all!"

"This is our home!" April added, also getting a little feisty. "Make them go away!" swinging her spear back and forth.

"I don't know... Might be nice to have some company. They look kind of friendly. Mom seems to like them," Ben added.

"April is right!" June shouted, not comfortable with all the land sharks looking at her. "Make them go away! This is our home, and they be eating all our food!"

"Let's not jump to conclusions," Ben said. "Let's wait and see what they want and what they're doing here."

"This is my husband, Ben!" Jenny spoke out, trying to be civilized, gesturing over to him.

Bob cautiously walks up to Ben. "Glad to meet you... My name is Bob," then holds out his hand.

Ben is hesitant at first, making sure this man is not carrying any weapons. After an awkward pause, he swaps his spear from his right hand to his left, jabbing the spear in the sand, holding it upright. He takes one step forward, keeping himself between this stranger and his children.

The twins imitate their father's every move. They move their spears to their left hand, jabbing the ends into the sand, holding them upright. Although they make sure Baby is always behind them.

Ben slowly reaches out, shaking the man's hand firmly without saying a word. He is awkward but guarded since it has been too long since meeting anyone else. He still doesn't trust other people, especially when they are standing too close to his family.

"So, you were on that plane that went down?" Bob asked, cringing as he felt his hand being crushed by Ben's excessively firm handshake. "So, where are all the others?"

Everyone else is looking around, expecting to see more people emerging from the trees.

"There are no others," Ben said, keeping the conversation short.

"My God! You've been here all this time by yourselves?"

Ben nods his head up and down, not saying a word. He then realizes his mistake. He has let on that they are alone. They still don't know who these people are and why they are here on their island. Although it makes him feel a little better knowing that they have children with them.

"Why don't you join us?" Bob asked, feeling uneasy with Ben and the two little girls glaring at him. "Meet the rest of my friends and family."

Ben glances over at Jenny, seeing her motioning him to come over. Again, he is not much for words and only nods. He cautiously walks over to the picnic table with Jenny. The twins still keep by their father's side, closely followed by Baby.

Ben stands at the end of the table with his spear in hand, looking as intimidating as possible. He promptly signals to Baby, who jumps back on his mother's lap. He whistles another signal to the twins. They quickly stand on each side of their mother, keeping close to their little brother. They never let up, still pointing their spears at the land sharks.

Ben feels uneasy among all these people. He is still very wary of them, eyeing each one and every little move they make. It is not the way that Ben wanted it to be. He would rather watch them from a distance before making any contact.

"Can you tell the girls it's OK?" Jenny asked, seeing the mean looks on the twin's faces, still pointing their spears at everyone. "We don't want anyone to get hurt."

Ben reluctantly signals the twins with a hand sign. Immediately, they step back, jabbing the ends of the spears in the sand, holding them upright as if on guard duty.

"Why don't you go play with him?" Jenny said, taking Baby off her lap. "Go sit in the shade while we talk to our visitors," knowing he is the reason they are overprotective.

Ben whistles several signals, telling Baby and the twins what to do. Baby bolts for the trees to play in the shade. The twins quickly follow without saying a word. They sit down with their little brother but always keep an eye on the land sharks.

"Your girls make nice babysitters, don't they?" Sally remarked, watching the three little children playing together, trying to keep the conversation going.

"Oh, yes!" Jenny replied, glancing over at her children. "We always felt that it was important to teach them how to take care of and watch over Baby. Unfortunately, my husband went overboard and taught them to be little Amazon warriors, or like Navy SEALs."

"So, that's what they've been doing all this time with all those hand gestures?" Margaret asked. "They've been signaling to each other?"

"Oh, yes... Ben taught them how to do that at an early age. They could communicate with each other with hand signals long before they started talking. Since they are twins, there are times I wonder if they can read each other's minds."

"I thought they were twins!" Margaret said. "They look so much alike. They're so sweet!" seeing how they play together.

"They've been making all those sounds, too," Sally mentioned. "Those are birdcalls they been doing? Even your little boy was doing it?"

"Yes, the children know how to imitate the local birds. They also use birdcalls to communicate with each other."

"So, what were they saying to each other?" Sally asked.

"I'm not sure anymore," Jenny explained. "I can never keep up with it. That's my husband's department," looking over at Ben.

They all look over at Ben, expecting him to elaborate. He is silent, not wanting to let on to their ways of communicating with each other. The one thing he will not do is let these people know what he has been telling the twins. He just glares back at Jenny, letting her know she is divulging way too much information.

Wayne is curious about the family they found on this island. For a family who are supposed to be stranded for years, they appear to be very healthy. He is wondering if these people are who they claim to be.

"Are you sure you were going to Kwajalein?" Wayne asked. "This place is so far out of the way. How did you all get out here, anyway?" trying to get more answers about how they arrived on this island.

"From what I remember," Jenny answered, seeing Ben is not too talkative, "we were drifting in the raft for days. The storm that brought the plane down never let up until we arrived here. Ben can tell you more about the plane. He was talking to the pilots when they started having problems."

"We had a direct lightning hit or something," Ben reluctantly replied. "They lost almost all their instruments. We were flying blind for a long time, and things kept getting worse. They ended up ditching the plane before it got too dark. With no communications, they hope someone saw us on the radar and send help. No one ever showed up."

"You've been here all this time?" Margaret asked, still in total disbelief, listening to the story. "Didn't they search for you?"

"We had a radio," Jenny explained, "and heard they were searching, but we never saw anything. They stopped looking after a week. Since we've been here, we haven't seen any planes or boats until now."

Wayne remains unconvinced but continues to play along until he can make some calls. Surviving alone on this island is one thing, but bringing up a family here is another. It just doesn't make sense to him. They all look too healthy. He still has a feeling that these people are not who they say they are.

Jenny cries, thinking about all those people on the plane with them. That was so long ago, but now it feels as if it were yesterday. Ben walks over, standing next to her, putting his hand on her shoulder, trying to comfort her. He also remembers all the friends they lost on that day.

"We're about to get something to eat," Margaret said, seeing Jenny getting upset, trying to change the subject. "You're welcome to join us."

"No thanks," Ben quickly replied. "Had something to eat not too long ago," not wanting to stay any longer.

"Please stay!" Margaret insisted. "We have plenty of food here."

"We don't want to impose on you," Ben quickly added, wanting to return to their camp to talk this over with Jenny alone.

"You do look as if you've been eating well," Sally said, getting all flustered, noticing Ben's physique up close.

"Oh, yes," Jenny replied, regaining her composure. "There's plenty of fruit and banana trees here, plus a bounty of fish and lobsters," wiping the tears from her eyes.

"You have lobsters here?" Bob quickly asked.

Ben simply nods, still not being very talkative.

"I can sure go for one of those... Fresh lobsters! I hadn't had that in years!"

"Same here!" George shouted out.

"We have a couple in the tidal pool," Jenny explained. "You're welcome to them. We can always get more."

"If you don't mind, I'd love one of those," Bob said with an ear-to-ear smile. "We have everything else here. We can have a big cookout to celebrate!"

"Not just yet!" Sally blurted out. "I want to hear how they have been able to survive out here. You can wait a little longer before you eat again!" glancing over at his beer belly.

"That's right!" Margaret added. "You bunch have been eating too much, anyway. I want to hear this as well!"

All the attention is on Jenny again. Everyone gathers around the table while Jenny tells how they survived on the island and the arrival of the children. She explained all of their triumphs and failures, from the early days with nothing to do but wait around to be rescued. Then how they raised a family on an island paradise without a care in the world.

* * *

The entire time Jenny and Ben are with these people, they don't realize what it means to them. They think this is just an oddity in their everyday life. Having someone else in their home makes them feel awkward and uneasy. Never having entertained anyone before, they are trying to be sociable. Maybe have a little barbecue and share some food. They can even make a fun day out of it.

"We're scheduled to leave tomorrow," Wayne said. "We can take you back to Kwajalein with us."

"What do you mean?" Jenny asked, so confused.

"Well, we can't leave you here... We have plenty of room on the ship. We're leaving tomorrow, anyway. So we can take you all back with us."

"We're leaving? We're going home!" Jenny cried out, just sitting there with a stunned look on her face.

Margaret smiles, nodding her head. "Of course you are! You mean to tell me after all this time you've been with us, and you didn't realize you've been rescued?"

"Ben, we're going home! We're finally going home! Oh, my God, I can't believe it!" taking his hand, then cries.

"I guess we are," he said, the news catching him off guard as well.

For some reason, it never occurred to them that they had been rescued. Still in shock, just seeing other people, but hearing that they are leaving the island makes them numb all over.

"How far away is Kwajalein from here?" Ben asked, looking over at the catamaran anchored just off the beach.

"Maybe a few days if the wind holds up," Wayne explained.

"Oh, we don't want to ruin your vacation," Jenny said.

"We are scheduled to go back tomorrow anyway," Wayne replied, shaking his head. "It's been a week of hopping around all the islands in this area. We're going in your direction, so it's not putting us out."

"So, where exactly are we?" Ben asked, still staring out at the catamaran.

"I believe this is Mocker Island," Wayne explained, "but these islands have several names. It depends on what charts you use, and some of them don't even show these islands. All this used to be in a restricted area for the military for various missile or satellite testing. They reduced the restricted area a while back because of cutbacks in some of the programs. So, we took advantage of it and decided to check it out before everyone else does."

"This is a military area?" Ben asked, a little confused. "That's news to me... I have never seen any missiles or even a plane out here. It's always been real quiet except for the occasional high altitude flights going over," glancing up at the clouds.

"I'm surprised you haven't seen anything," Wayne said, looking out at the ocean. "I guess all the testing is done miles from here on the western islands. This island is now just outside the new restricted area. If we venture too far west, they'd be hauling us off to jail!"

"It's hard to believe they can do that," Bob said. "They think they own the world!"

"Yeah, I know," Wayne explained. "They just made a big circle and said everything inside is forbidden to the public. That includes these islands around here. It's a shame. These would have made some great tourist spots over the years! Lucky for us, they opened it up not too long ago, and lucky for you too."

"Maybe that's why you never saw anyone," Bob explained. "No one has been allowed in this entire area for years. That's why we're so surprised to find you here."

Ben stands quietly, looking out at the ocean with a terrible feeling in his stomach. His life here in paradise has just ended. For some reason that he can't explain, he is not looking forward to returning to society and leaving his home.

"Well, I'm going to start the barbecue," Bob said, getting a little hungry. "Why don't you join us?" glancing over at Jenny and Ben.

"Please stay and help us eat the rest of this food. We don't want to have to pack it all back with us. We'll have a big feast. It's our last day, so we might as well enjoy it," Sally added.

"I guess we can stay… We do have plenty of food. Do you need anything?" Jenny asked, looking over at Margaret and Sally.

Everyone is speechless at being offered food from people who have been stranded here on this small island.

"Oh no," Sally said. "We have more than enough for everyone."

"We do have two lobsters in the tidal pool," Jenny added. "We also have plenty of oranges, bananas, and grapefruit. They're all fresh."

"Lobsters!" Bob blurted out, with a big smile on his face upon hearing that. "Sure, if you can spare them. That sounds good to me."

"Oh, no," Margaret said, feeling guilty. "We can't take your food! We have plenty of hamburgers, hot dogs, and steaks."

"It's no problem… I guess it doesn't matter since we won't be here after tomorrow," Jenny said, realizing this is going to be their last day.

"I guess this will be our last meal here," Ben said, still in shock. "Might as well cook up the lobsters then," turning to the twins, and nods.

The twins quickly jump up, so excited to hear they are going to have lobster for supper. Before running off down the beach, June looks Baby in the eye, then points over to their mother. Baby quickly gets up, running over to his mother, crawling up on her lap.

Ben feels so numb. Knowing that this is their last meal on the island doesn't sit well. They had always planned everything in advance, and within a few minutes, their entire world had turned over. They are leaving the home that they loved so much. There is not enough time to talk about it. It is all happening way too fast. He wants to discuss it alone with Jenny before they do anything.

"He really minds his big sisters, doesn't he?" Margaret asked, seeing the little boy was so happy.

"He better if he knows what's good for him," Jenny said, giving her son a big hug.

"So, how old are the girls?" Margaret asked.

"I guess they're about five now," Jenny answered, having to think about it for a moment. "Baby must be a little over a year old. Not too sure about his age now that I think about it."

"They're identical twins, aren't they?" Sally asked, just as curious about the little girls.

"Oh, yes! At first, we really couldn't tell them apart. It wasn't until they were a little older that we could see the differences between them, mostly in their personalities. April is the calm and curious one. June takes after her father and gets a little grumpy and moody at times. Baby, on the other hand, is so mellow and carefree. All he wants to do is play and have fun."

"Baby?" Margaret asked. "Is that his name?"

Jenny laughed. "Oh no, August is his real name. The girls gave him the name Baby, and it kind of stuck."

While Jenny is talking with the women, Ben is checking out all the fancy camping gear. He can't believe there is so much here just for a simple day out on the beach. These people have far more camping gear than what they have been living with for over six years.

"Come on, we'll show you around after we get this barbecue going," Bob said, noticing Ben was checking out all the camping gear.

"Yeah, you're going to appreciate this cooker we got," Wayne boasted.

Ben is still a little cautious but follows them to the large stainless steel gas barbecue set up in the middle of the camp. Bob turns on the gas and pushes the ignition button. Within a second, flames shot up, heating the lava briquettes.

Ben can't help laughing, seeing how quickly it lights up. "That's way too easy," wishing the twins were here to see this.

"Oh, it'll still take a few minutes to heat up," he said, closing the lid. "So, what have you been using out here to cook things?"

"We do things the old-fashioned way," Ben explained. "You find a tree, then you chop it down. You stack the wood up in a nice little pile and use a flint starter to get it going. Then you have to wait thirty minutes or more for it to heat up and pray it doesn't rain."

They both look at Ben, a little shocked, and can't tell if he is joking or not.

"You're not serious, are you?" Bob asked.

Ben nods his head. "That's also what we have to do to heat the water and keep warm at night."

"Damn… I wouldn't last long out here," Wayne said.

"Well, welcome back to the modern world. Let me show you some of my new camping and fishing gear I picked up for this trip. We've had some great fishing out here!" Bob said, seeing Ben is eyeing the fishing rods.

Ben is loosening up a little. He follows Bob, George, and Wayne around as they show him all their new fancy camping gear. None of it looks more than a week old. Although he thinks it's all a little odd. These people go out and buy all this expensive camping gear just to sleep on the beach while a million-dollar catamaran is anchored a hundred feet away.

"These are really nice," Ben said, so impressed by all the large tents. "This makes our tent look pathetic."

"You have a tent here?" Wayne asked.

"It's not much of a tent... It's only a small one-man tent I used on my camping trips in Colorado."

"How did you get a tent out here?" George asked, surprised to hear that.

"I brought some of my camping gear with me, thinking I could use it while on Kwajalein," Ben explained. "Luckily, it's one of the few things that got washed up on the beach from the plane. It helped us survive out here in those first few months."

"Damn, we've been camping out on the beaches around here for a week," George said. "I don't know how you guys put up with it for so long. I'm glad this is our last night here, and I can't wait to get back to my own bed and air conditioning too!"

"I feel the same way," Bob said, shaking his head. "The heat and humidity out here is just unbelievable. How do you live with it?"

"You get used to it after a while. It's really nice most days with the breeze off the ocean," looking down the beach where their campsite is.

Ben stares at the beach, remembering all the great times he has had out here. Feeling sick to his stomach, he doesn't want to talk anymore. The reality is setting in that they are leaving their home. Everything is happening too quickly. There is no time to think about it. On their last night on the island, there is so much to do. Knowing that they'll be off the island this time tomorrow, he is not even happy about it at all. He just blanks it out of his mind, not wanting to think about it. It is like a bad dream, or worse, a nightmare.

* * *

April and June soon return, carrying two huge lobsters in the casting net. They also bring extra fish and a bag full of fresh fruit. They are so happy to have two lobsters for supper. For them, it's starting to look like a fun day.

"Mom, we couldn't bring the cooking pot," June explained, tossing the net on the table.

"Yeah!" April shouted. "It's too heavy. We got a big fish too, cause there are lots of people here. Do you want us to cook these over a campfire? We can dig a hole in the sand for an imu?"

Bob is drooling, seeing the huge lobsters. "My God! Look at the size of those things. Let's throw those babies on the gas grill. I'll get my cooking utensils," running back to his tent.

"Girls, why don't you show our guests how you prepare lobster? Let your father show you how to use their grill," Jenny boasted.

"OK, Mom!" the twins said in unison.

"You mean you're going to let the girls cook those lobsters?" Margaret asked, thinking it was a joke.

"Sure, they always do," Jenny proudly said. "It's their favorite thing to cook."

Bob returns with a box filled with all the cooking utensils one will ever need. The twins are so excited to see all the shiny knives. They climb onto the picnic table seat, untangling the lobsters from the net. June reaches into the box, pulling out two large knives, handing one to April. They stand silently, watching the lobsters, waiting for the right moment. Without warning, they both plunge the knives deep into the lobsters' heads, killing them instantly.

Everyone is so shocked. No one expected to see these two little girls killing the lobsters with one blow. They all stand utterly speechless, watching them prepare the meal. Seeing how well they handled the knives, it's more like a famous chef at work instead of these five-year-old girls.

"It's amazing seeing them helping out like this. Just look at my kids over there just waiting to be fed. They never help out at all," Sally said, so disappointed with them.

"My kids are the same," Margaret added. "All they do is sit there with their noses in those damn video games."

"Well, around here, everyone has to help out, or you go to bed hungry," Jenny explained, trying to be polite.

"I can't believe they know how to prepare lobster and everything else that goes with it," Sally said, shaking her head.

"Oh, that's their signature dish! They basically can do everything we can do. If something happened to us, we always wanted to make sure they could survive on their own. I taught them how to cook. Ben taught them how to fish and to live off the land, including how to protect themselves."

"I was wondering about that, seeing how they kept pointing those sticks at us," Margaret said. "I thought they were just playing a game."

Jenny pauses before telling them. "Well, no... They were really serious. When it comes to protecting Baby, they don't play around. It's their job to watch and protect their little brother. Ben taught them how to live in the wild, but mostly to fear people. Being on our own, we were prepared for the worst."

"You mean they would really harm someone?" Margaret asked.

"I hope not," Jenny said, looking over at her two little girls. "This has never come up before. You kind of caught us off guard."

"I don't know," Wayne said, overhearing the conversation. "That one looked as if she was ready to take me on a while back. I was coming close to taking those sticks away from them."

Ben cringes. "That wouldn't have been a smart move."

"You're a little overconfident in their abilities," Wayne said, chuckling at the idea these little girls can harm an adult.

Ben picks up a water bottle from the table. "May I demonstrate?"

"Sure," Wayne answered, curious to see his little demonstration.

Ben tosses the plastic water bottle about twenty feet away, then whistles a signal to June. She promptly jumps off the picnic table, walks over to her spear, pulling it out of the sand. Ben just points to the water bottle, not saying a word.

June takes her spear, getting into her throwing stance. She stands silently, eyeing the water bottle, estimating its range, and noting the direction of the wind. With a quick lunge, she throws the spear with little effort. The spear hit its target right through the center. She runs out, pulls the spear from the bottle, and comes back to help with the cooking without saying a word.

Wayne stands with his mouth wide open, not believing what he has just seen. "That was just a fluke. A little lucky, I'd say."

Ben smiles, signaling April to do the same. He throws the bottle back out onto the beach. She also jumps down, fetching her spear. Again with little effort, she tosses her spear, piercing the water bottle.

"Damn, that's a little scary… So, when they came at me, it was you that signaled them to attack?" Wayne asked, a little disturbed seeing this.

"No, they signaled me to which one of you they were going for," Ben explained, shaking his head. "You have to understand… We had no idea who you were. Normally, we would have watched you from a distance until we're sure you were friendly."

"Are you serious?" George asked, so scared after hearing this. "They would have harmed us?"

Ben simply nods. "They're protecting Baby... It's not wise getting too close to him," giving them a stern look.

Right then, George knows this guy is very serious. Seeing how these little girls can throw spears and handle a knife with the lobsters, he thinks it will be best to keep a distance not only from the girls but especially from the boy.

"Do they always carry those sticks around with them?" Margaret asked, not too thrilled hearing all this.

"Oh, yes!" Jenny said. "They're really walking sticks. Most of the time, they use them to knock down fruit from the trees or for spearfishing. Fishing is their second favorite pastime when they're not cooking."

"You mean to tell me that they can catch a fish with those sticks as well?"

"Sure, I have seen them get a fish on the first throw. Even Ben can't do that. When they saw their father spearfishing, naturally, they wanted to do the same. If you haven't noticed, they imitate their father's every move."

"Oh, yes… I'm starting to realize that now," Margaret said, looking over at Ben, wondering how dangerous he could be if he is threatened.

"I can now see why you all look so well-fed," Sally mentioned. "I think you got everything you'd ever need out here. All the fish and lobster, plus all the fresh fruit, and it's all free. It must be nice living out here if you like the outdoor life."

Jenny looks around and nods. "It's been great! I can't complain… It wasn't easy at first, but we learned how to live with just the basics. There was an adjustment when the children came along, but now they're a little older, they really help out. It's made life here so wonderful."

* * *

When the food is ready, everyone quickly sits down at the picnic tables. The twins carry the fish and lobsters on a big plate, carefully garnished with orange slices. They know how to cook but also understand how important presentation is. They are so excited to cook for all these people but also enjoy all the attention. Also, being able to use all these new, fancy cooking utensils makes their day.

Everyone drools over the fresh fruit, fish, and lobster. This is more like eating at an expensive gourmet restaurant instead of a beach barbecue. None of them would have believed that little five-year-old girls cooked all this if they hadn't seen it with their own eyes. Now, they all know why this family is so well-fed if they eat like this every day.

For the twins, this is one of the biggest and best fun days they have ever had. Also, it's the most food they have ever seen. There is more than enough food here to last them for a month, and it's all for one meal. Although the smell of freshly cooked beef is something they are not used to, and don't even want to try it.

"Would you girls like a cold drink?" Sally asked the twins, handing out the cups.

The twins look over at their mother to see if it's OK. Jenny nods, curious to see their reaction. Sally hands them two drinks filled with ice cubes. The twins are so puzzled by the brown fluid and the square things floating in the cups.

"Oh, this will be a big treat for you!" Jenny said, seeing her girls experiencing ice-cold soft drinks for the first time.

April takes a whiff of the drink. "I don't think this is good water. Smells funny, and it's a funny color, too. You should always boil the water before you drink it!" handing it back.

"It's not water," Sally explained. "It's a soft drink. You'll like it. Give it a try."

June sticks her finger in it. "Wow, that's cold!" smiling at her mother.

"That is ice," Jenny explained. "It keeps the drinks cold."

April touches one of the ice cubes. "Mine's hot!" so confused touching something that cold for the first time.

"Well, mine is really cold!" June said, taking a small sip of the drink.

"That's really tasty! Try it, April!" June shouted.

April follows suit, taking a sip as well. "Wow! It's good! It tingles in my mouth!" sticking her tongue out.

Ben can't help from laughing, seeing his two little girls drinking ice-cold Pepsi for the first time. Naturally, Baby doesn't want to be left out, babbling loudly, wanting his drink too. He always waits for his sister's approval before trying anything new. He guzzles it down so fast, screaming out loud, experiencing his first brain freeze.

This is by far the biggest feast that they have ever had since being on the island. Jenny, Ben, and the children never tried the hamburgers, hot dogs, or steaks. After so many years of fresh fruit and seafood, they have no desire for meat, turned off by the smell. Although they can't get enough of all the bread, sweet jams, apple pie, and vanilla ice cream. The children have their first ice cream cones, and it's not long before it's all over their faces. Ice cream is definitely their favorite, with the Pepsi coming in a close second.

After the big feast, one of Margaret's boys brings out his CD player and turns it on. The music fills the air with a quality and clarity they have never heard before. Right away, the twins and Baby are out dancing. It makes everyone feel a little more at ease watching the children dancing and having fun. At least now, they act more like little girls and not Amazon warriors walking about with spears ready to pounce.

Everyone is so amazed at these little girls. Not only do they help protect their family, but they can catch and cook their own food. Seeing how their children are lazing about and constantly complaining about everything makes them so disappointed and embarrassed.

* * *

Chapter 40

The Call Home

Wayne makes a quick trip back to the ship to make some calls. He contacts the people at Kwajalein to let them know what they have found and asks what he should do about it. Bringing unauthorized people back without permission will get him arrested. All he has is their word of who they are. With this family not having any forms of identification, it may cause some problems on a military-controlled island.

When Wayne returns to the beach, he pulls Ben aside. "I contacted the people at Kwajalein. They are questioning your story. I don't think they are buying that you're who you say you are. Without any identification, you can be anyone," wondering how he is going to take the news.

"Sorry, I lost my driver's license," Ben jokingly said, knowing they don't have any identification at all. "So, what do you do when you have absolutely nothing to prove who you are?"

"I guess they'll figure it out when we get there. Fingerprints are the only thing they might use. They probably have that on file somewhere. Until then, you're Jane and John Doe. They were also asking a lot of questions about you guys. When I told them how long you've been out here, they were concerned you might be spies!"

Ben laughed. "Well, they're in for a shock!" remembering the mentality of these types of people who worked in the military.

"When I told them it's a family with kids, it made them a little less suspicious. But at least we got the OK to bring you in. You will go through some intense questioning. Just don't worry about it. You got to remember the nature of these people."

"Well, at least they know we're here," Ben replied, shrugging his shoulders, not concerned about it.

"Until then, I thought you might want to call home," handing Ben a portable satellite phone. "There's not much battery left, but it'll be good for maybe one quick call. Jenny already tried but got a disconnected number. I hope you have better luck!"

Ben is stunned. The thought had never occurred to him. He is still having problems realizing that they have been rescued. He had not thought about his family at home for a while and didn't think he would ever see them again.

"It's been a long time," Ben mumbled, shaking his head in disbelief. "No telling where my family is. It's going to be hard. What do you say?" looking at Wayne.

"I really don't know... Maybe you should think about it for a few minutes before you call," he said, glad to see Ben is letting his guard down.

Wayne is glad to see that Ben wants to call his family. He is coming around to the idea that this could be Ben Hughes and Jenny Mason. The people at Kwajalein don't believe their story at all. They are ready to arrest this family for trespassing on federal land. If this is Ben Hughes, contacting his family will prove his case. He knows the shit is going to hit the fan at Kwajalein when they find out there are survivors, and they have been here all along.

Ben takes the phone, sitting down in the shade on an old fallen tree trunk for a little privacy. April, June, and Baby rush over, curious to see what he is doing with the little box, not wanting to be left out of anything.

He dials his parents' number, hoping it's still the same. With so much static on the phone, he can barely hear the ringing. He is wondering how the world has changed. Reality is sinking in that they are going to leave their island home. He doesn't have a good feeling about it. The last few years were more like a big vacation in a tropical paradise. Then to find out it's your last day, and worse, having to go back to work.

* * *

On a warm Sunday evening, Mary and Walter are home with the family. Kelly, her brother Sam, his wife Vanessa, and their kids are all there. Every Sunday, Walter always has everyone over for the weekend for the big barbecue, Texas-style.

Ben's mother, Mary, is alone in the living room when the phone rings. She is not too surprised since their extended family usually makes all the calls to them on Sundays. She sits on the couch, picking up the phone. At first, all she can hear is static, thinking it's a bad line.

"Hello! Hello!" she keeps repeating, not hearing much of anything.

In the background, among all the static, she finally hears a faint voice. "Hello, Mom... Mom, can you hear me?"

She is so shocked, recognizing the voice. The voice was so faint, but she heard it. A voice she thought she would never ever hear again.

"Ben! Ben, is that you? Ben! Ben!" she frantically yelled out, trying to hear his voice through the static.

Mary presses the phone against her ear, trying to hear his voice, but then there's nothing but silence. She frantically keeps calling his name, yelling on the phone. She knows what she has heard. Her long-lost son is trying to contact her after all this time.

* * *

Ben is so frustrated with all the static but then hears a faint, 'Hello...'

Right away, he recognized his mother's voice. "Hello! Mom... Mom, can you hear me? It's Ben! Hello, Mom!"

Ben hears nothing but static. Then the phone goes dead. Glancing at the screen, he notices the weak satellite signal. He is so frustrated, seeing not much has changed with these portable telephones. Bad connections and dropped calls are all you get out of them. At least he got to hear his mother's voice after all this time.

* * *

Sam's daughter, Shelly, hears all the commotion coming from the living room. She walks in and sees her grandmother crying and yelling on the phone.

"What is it, Granny?" she asked, so scared, seeing her grandmother was upset. "What's wrong?"

"It's Ben! He just called me! I could hear his voice!" yelling on the phone again for her son.

Shelly runs out to the backyard. "Granny is crying! She's trying to talk to Ben on the phone!"

Everyone runs into the house. The last thing they want to see is Mary crying uncontrollably. Hearing how she is talking about Ben again, it's not a good sign.

Walter sits beside her. "What's wrong? What's got you all upset?" he asked.

Vanessa ushers the children out of the room, knowing her mother-in-law might be having another breakdown. Kelly doesn't know what to do. Her mother had been doing so well for years, accepting Ben was gone. She doesn't have a clue what set her off again.

"What is it, Mom?" Sam asked, sitting in the chair next to his mother. "Are you OK?"

Mary finally regains her composure. "It was Ben! On the phone! I heard him. I really heard him! He's trying to contact me," she shouted, still holding the phone in her hand.

They are all so sad. After all this time, Mary had let Ben go. She had been doing so well, but for some reason, it started up again. They try to console her, but they know it's going to take time since they have been through this before.

* * *

Ben tries calling again, but now the line is busy, making him even more frustrated. All this new technology is already frustrating him. These cell phones are something he has always hated, and now it's coming back to him why he hated them so much. They were always so unreliable.

He redials the number. Finally, he is getting through with a clear ringing tone. Looking down at the meter, it's a good strong signal, and he can really hear the difference.

Ben gathers the children around. "I think we're going to get through this time! We're going to get to call home."

They clap their hands, cheering out loud, but they still have no clue about what is happening. All they hear are these strange beeping sounds coming from this talking device.

* * *

As the family is consoling Mary, the phone rings again. Everyone just stares at it. No one said a word. They all look at each other, waiting for someone else to answer it. Mary is trembling, motioning over to Sam since he is the closest one to the phone.

Finally, Sam picks up the phone. "Hello..."

Sam doesn't say a word, listening to whoever is calling. His mouth drops wide open, sitting there utterly speechless. He looks up at his family in utter disbelief. Everyone can see the stunned expression on his face, wondering what is going on.

"It's me, Sam!" he finally uttered, finding it difficult to speak. "Sorry, who am I speaking to?" looking over at his parents sitting on the couch.

"Please be him… Let it be him. God, please let it be my baby," Mary keeps praying as she watches her son talking on the phone.

"My God!" Sam yelled out, jumping up out of the chair. "Ben! Where the hell have you been!" the tears running down his face, realizing he was talking to his long-lost brother.

"We're all here!" he continued. "Hold on. I'm putting you on the speaker!" pressing the button so everyone can hear.

They all stare at each other, completely lost for words, hearing Ben's voice for the first time in years.

"Hello! So what's everyone doing?" Ben casually asked.

"Ben! It's you! Are you OK?" Mary asked, so shocked.

"Hi, Mom! Yeah, I'm fine... So how is everyone there?" he asked, as the tears ran down his face, hearing his mother's voice for the first time in years.

"We're fine... Where have you been?" Walter asked, so shocked, hearing his son's voice. "They said you were lost with all the others!" then he cries.

"Yeah, we had a few problems a while back," Ben explained, "but two of us made it out and ended up on this island. It just so happens we had some people show up today. They're going to take us off the island tomorrow morning."

"You're coming home?" Mary cried out, fighting to get the words out.

"Soon as we can," Ben simply replied. "I'm not too sure about all the details, but we're coming home."

They are all stunned and so elated at what they are hearing. No one knows what to say. This is like a dream.

Ben hears a couple of beeps, glances down, seeing the battery is getting low. "I may not have much time to talk," he blurted out. "This portable phone I'm using is about to go out. They're taking us to Kwajalein Island. I'll contact you from there. Also, can you get in touch with the people at Kwajalein? They don't believe it's really us, and I don't have any ID or anything."

"Oh, I'll contact them all right," Walter said. "I'll give them a piece of my mind! Those damn bastards!"

"There's someone else here, too," Ben continued. "She needs to get in touch with her family as well. Her name is Jenny Mason. Can you look up her parents and let them know she's OK?"

"OK, Ben!" Walter said. "We'll do what we can on this end."

Static on the phone is drowning out Ben's voice. They can barely hear him.

"Oh yeah, I better mention you're a grandpa and granny three times more!" Ben mentioned.

Ben holds the phone down to the children. "Better say something to Granny, hurry!"

"Hi, Granny!" the twins shouted on the phone. "We are coming to see you!"

Ben puts the phone back to his ear. "Did you get all that?" he asked, hearing nothing but static, then the phone went dead.

* * *

Sam finally hangs up the phone after hearing nothing but static, and the line goes dead. No one can believe this is actually happening. They are speechless, staring at each other. They don't know what to make of the high, squeaky voices on the phone before it went dead. This is all so surreal.

"You all heard him, didn't you?" Mary asked, looking around at her family. "I'm not dreaming this, am I?"

"We all heard it! I can't believe this! After all this time!" then Sam laughs.

"Thank God, it's all over!" Walter cried out, so elated. "He's coming home! My son is finally coming home! I thought I would never live to see this day!" wiping away the tears from his eyes.

Mary is jumping up and down. "I told you he was alive! I knew it all along and kept telling everyone, but no one would listen to me!" pointing her finger at each one of them.

"Yes, you were right all along," Walter said. "Those bastards! I can't wait to get them on the phone! I can't believe they left them out there like that!"

"Come on, we need to clean the house… Ben is coming home! We have a lot of work to do!" Mary said, so full of energy, and started cleaning up the living room.

Walter, his son, and his daughter all look at each other, not knowing what to make of all this. That was the last thing they expected her to do.

"Well, Mom is back to normal," Sam jokingly said, seeing his mother going around dusting everything.

"Wait a minute!" Kelly said, putting it all together. "He said only two of them made it to the island, right?"

"Well, yes," Sam said, looking at her, confused. "That's what I heard him say."

"Don't you get it?" Kelly asked.

"What are you trying to say?" Mary asked. "Ben is coming home, ain't nothing else matters! My baby is finally coming home!" putting her hands together with a prayer, thanking God for returning her son.

Kelly laughs. "Mom, he wasn't alone on the island... He's with another person."

They all stare at her, so confused. She doesn't make any sense.

"I don't get it... What are you trying to say?" Sam asked.

"It's a woman he was with, this Jenny Mason," she added. "The one he wants us to help contact her family."

Sam thinks about it for a few seconds. "Wait a minute... Ben was stranded on an island with a woman?" and starts laughing out loud.

"Yes!" Kelly shouted out. "You're a grandpa and granny three times more! You heard it! Those little voices you heard at the end saying they're coming to visit! Who do you think they are? He said only two of them made it. From the sounds of those voices, those are young little kids. That means only one thing!"

"He has kids?" Walter asked, figuring it all out. "Wait, three times more. That means he has three of them!"

"What!" Mary blurted out, so surprised. "My baby has three little ones... Oh, my God! We have three more grandchildren!" so excited about the notion of having more grandchildren.

Walter shakes his head in disbelief. "He's got his hands full now," then laughs out loud.

"I can't wait to see this," Sam said, sitting back in the chair. "Ben is a father, and I'm finally an uncle!" glancing over at his sister.

"Oh, great!" she said, catching on to what her brother was implying. "I'm the odd one out again."

"There is that nice boy where you work," Mary added, quickly jumping at the opportunity. "Maybe you should invite him over for dinner sometime?"

"Mom," Kelly said, getting so frustrated. "Let's not get into that again. Keep on the subject. Ben is coming home!" so glad to change the subject away from her not being married.

"Well, this is going to be a day I'll never forget!" Walter yelled out. "Come on, let's get the Champagne out. We're going to celebrate the best day in our lives!" grabbing his wife, dancing around the room.

What started as a typical Sunday barbecue with the family ended up being a day no one will ever forget. They are on the phone calling everyone, telling them the good news. When they put down the phone, it rings again. Someone who's just heard the news is calling to congratulate them. The phone calls are nonstop late in the night, and the party continues until the early hours of the morning.

* * *

Ben looks over at his children with a big smile on his face. "Now, that was nice! You got to talk to your granny and granddad! I bet they can't wait to see you. I know Granny is going to make you a big Sunday dinner with all the fixings!"

"We going to have shepherd's pie, treacle pudding, and lots of things!" the twins said, so thrilled to get the big Sunday dinner they always heard about from their father.

He nods his head. "And lots more! Just like all the things we had today! Apple pie, bread, jams, and lots of ice cream. It's going to be fun!"

"We going to have some Pepsi too?" June asked.

He hugs them all. "Yes, everything you ever wanted and more."

Jenny walks up. "Did you have any luck?"

"Oh, yes! I got lucky... They were all at the house. I didn't have much time, but at least I got to talk to them."

"I can't wait to talk to my mom and dad," Jenny explained. "It's going to be strange having to tell them about our three little ones and you. Maybe I should give it another try."

"Oh, sorry... I think I used up the battery. Do they have another or a charger?" he asked, feeling bad that the phone went out, and she didn't get to talk to her family.

"No, that's all they have... I have already tried and couldn't get through. Wayne told me he'd call someone at the base on the radio to get them to contact my family. I think I'll wait until we get to Kwajalein so I can have time to figure out what to say."

"I know... It was hard to think of what to say. My mom just fell apart. I guess it was a big shock to her. My dad is going to contact someone at Kwajalein to explain things to them. It's a shame I only got to talk to them for a few minutes. I also asked them to contact your family, too."

She smiles. "That's good... At least they'll know. That's the most important thing. I can't wait for them to meet the girls, and especially Baby! They're going to spoil them rotten," picking up Baby and dancing around with him.

"Yeah, I was just thinking of that. My mom and dad are going to do the same. I wonder if they're going to be able to handle the girls."

She laughed. "You got no one to blame but yourself!" knowing Ben is referring to them being a little on the wild side.

"Well, so far, they're doing good... The girls haven't hurt anyone yet."

"Yet!" she repeated. "We still have a long way home. You need to have a little talk with them and explain a few things before we leave. We're going to be on that boat for a few days, and we don't need anything bad happening."

* * *

Chapter 41

The Last Sunset

J enny and Ben thank everyone and walk back to their own camp. Jenny is so exhausted. All she wants to do is go straight to bed to let this sink in. Ben is so sad to be leaving like this. The island is their home, and it's just too quick to get up and leave so soon. They still have not told the twins that they are going, probably never to return.

The twins are so excited about all the new food and drinks. They are more interested in all the tents and camping gear than talking to these land sharks. They were taking inventory of everything that they saw. The visitor's camp is filled with prime stuff, and the girls can't wait to haul it all back to their camp.

Baby doesn't care about the visitors, either. He spends the entire time running around the beach, kicking his new beach ball all over the place. Even Ben is having a good time kicking the ball around with the children.

One of the things Jenny and Ben noticed was how antisocial the other children were. They were so rude and extremely lazy, spending the entire day with their faces glued to their small video games, constantly clicking on the buttons. None of them even helped. All they did was sit around, waiting for someone to cook and clean up after them.

"So, what did you girls think of our new friends?" Jenny asked on the walk back.

"You mean those land sharks back there?" April replied.

"No, those are our friends, and they're not land sharks," Jenny quickly replied. "Didn't you like meeting them?"

"Mom, are they going to stay long?" April asked. "This is our home and our beach. They need to go away, right, Daddy?"

"No, they don't," Ben explained, seeing the evil look he was getting from Jenny. "Those are nice, friendly people. They even shared their food with us. It was the best fun day in a long time, don't you think?"

June nods her head. "Yeah, that was the best one ever! I liked all those desserts. That was the best!"

"Mom, where did they get all those things?" April asked. "Shouldn't that be ours since it washed up on our beach? We supposed to have all those things. It's our home and our beach, too!" getting a little frustrated.

"Yeah, they can't have things that wash up on our beach," June added. "We need to go back and get our stuff!" getting a little irritated that they missed out on a great find.

"No, they brought it all here with them on that boat," Jenny explained. "It's like when we pack up everything to go to the cave, bringing everything with us. They do the same but put it all in that boat out in the water."

"You mean we got a storm coming?" June asked, getting a little concerned. "We going up to the cave, Daddy?" looking out over the ocean.

"No, those people pack everything up to go on a big adventure," he explained. "They ride around in that big boat going to other islands."

"So when they leave, are they going to take it all with them?" April asked.

"Of course they are," Jenny said. "It all belongs to them."

"We need to go back and take that ball," June said. "Baby really likes playing with it!"

"We need to go back and get a few other things too," April added. "Mom, wouldn't you like a new tent? They got too many, and they're nice big ones too! We got only one, and it's tiny," looking up at her mother with a big smile.

"Oh no, you don't!" Jenny shouted, not believing what the girls were telling her. "There won't be anyone going over there, taking things that don't belong to us. We don't do that around here."

"But we share things, and so do they!" April said, still smiling at her mother.

"That's right!" June added. "We can go back and share their things. Be nice to share one of those big tents, won't it, Daddy?" nodding her head up and down.

Jenny doesn't say a word to the girls, turning to Ben, giving him a stern look. "You need to explain a few things to them. We don't need any secret scavenging missions in the middle of the night," seeing the girls signaling each other, already planning something.

"I'm not the one who taught them how to scavenge for things out on the beach," he jokingly said.

"You know what I mean," she fired back.

Ben glances down at the twins. "You know, I think they're going to let us have a ride on that boat. Would you like that?" trying to change the subject.

"Yeah!" the twins yelled out. "I want to ride the boat! That be lots of fun!" jumping up and down, clapping their hands.

"Then they're going away, right, Daddy?" April quickly added.

"Well, we'll see about that in the morning," not wanting to tell them they'll be leaving the island as well.

"Ben, you got your work cut out for you in the next couple of days," Jenny quietly said, looking over at him. "I'll be taking care of Baby. Those two are your responsibility."

* * *

When they walk into their camp, it strikes them how simple their lives have been. After seeing how luxurious the visitor's campsite is, they see their home in a different light. For the first time, they wonder how they survived this long.

Jenny lies on the hammock, staring up at the evening sky. This is one day that she will never forget. She is still having a hard time realizing that it's all over. They are finally going home after all those years.

The twins are getting washed up and ready for bed. None of this bothers them one bit. They are ready to get back to their island life without a care in the world.

With Baby already asleep, Ben hands him over to Jenny. "I guess I better start going through our things. It's going to be hard trying to figure out what to bring back with us."

Jenny laughed. "We don't have that much here if you think about it. We only showed up with the clothes on our backs!"

"Well, we do have three little ones to bring back with us," glancing over at the girls, so proud of them.

"Just think what we've been through over the years," she said, looking down at Baby, who was snoring away, then over at her two little girls. "I don't think I have ever been so happy in my whole life. It feels so strange. I'm glad we're going home, but deep down, I don't want to leave."

"I know! I have been thinking the same. The past few years have been the best in my life. I couldn't have asked for a better life than this. We don't have much here, but we're happy," he explained, getting depressed.

"It's not fair to them... They can't spend the rest of their lives here. We've been really lucky so far. If one of us got sick or something, what would have happened to them? Remember, we have our families at home as well. I can't wait for the children to meet my mom and dad. I know they'll be proud when they meet our little girls and boy, not to mention my husband!" winking at him.

"That's right," Ben jokingly said, dreading the thought of having to meet his new in-laws. "I finally get to meet your parents. I hope they like me."

"They will, but don't forget," she said, seeing the scared look on his face. "I get to meet yours as well!"

"Oh, so I guess we both have something to look forward to," noticing how she is getting worried about meeting his family.

* * *

Ben drags out all of their possessions, separating everything into two piles. One is for what they're going to bring home with them, and the other is to be stored away in the cave. After seeing it all sprawled out on the ground, he finds it so odd that most of their possessions are someone else's trash that got washed up on the beach.

He is thinking about all that fancy camping gear. He wishes they had found things like that instead of all the garbage they have now. That would have made life a little easier, especially with those nice tents and lounge chairs.

"Daddy, how come you packing everything away?" June asked, noticing something was odd. "We're not going to have a storm, are we?"

"You think those land sharks down there are going to take our things?" April asked.

"No, we're going on a big adventure in the morning. We need to pack everything away in the cave for a while."

"We going on a trip around the island?" June asked, getting excited.

"Better than that... It's going to be a big surprise. You'll see it in the morning. Watch out for Mom and Baby. I'll be back shortly."

The twins are really excited now. They have no clue what is going on, but they know they are in for a big treat. A big adventure is always something special. Trekking around the island is their favorite, spending several days setting up camp on different beaches for the night. Other times, they explore up on the island, camping out in the dense forest. The big adventures were their vacation and always helped them get away from the day-to-day chores and the hard life of living off the land.

* * *

Ben soon reaches the cave. He unloads the duffel bag, storing everything on top of the firewood, rummaging through the cave, searching for things to take back with them. Everything he picks up is something that they can get back home. Most of their keepsakes are things made for each other for Christmas or birthdays, and they are in the camp. He decides to leave everything in the cave. If anyone else gets stuck here as he and Jenny did, all of their old supplies will help them survive here.

Stacking everything up on the woodpile, Ben picks up the old seat cushion from the plane. The memories of that fateful day flash through his mind as he runs his hands over the woven cloth. So long ago, but now remembers it so clearly as if it were yesterday. He can still see the faces of all those people who were on the plane. So many had lost their lives on that day. He always wondered why he had been so lucky in life.

Ben walks down to the lookout, grabbing a few oranges to bring back for breakfast. He sits on the old bench for a few minutes, watching the sky turn to a burnt orange color as the sun touches the horizon. Ben always enjoyed this spot, looking out over the ocean, the island, and their home. Deep down, he doesn't want to leave, but he knows he has to, for the children.

While watching the sunset, it then occurs to him. This is going to be his last one. The last sunset on their island, and it's such a beautiful one too. He wishes so much that Jenny and his children were here with him to see this. Now, he is getting so depressed.

He stands up, looking at the sunset. "I'll be back!" he shouted out loud, with tears running down his face. "One day, I'll be back!" running down the trail.

* * *

Ben walks into the camp just as the darkness sets in. He is so startled to see someone else there. Sally and Margaret are sitting around the campfire, visiting with Jenny. Seeing the twins and Baby sleeping in the tent puts him at ease. He is still not used to having other people at the camp.

Jenny is having a great time with her new friends, telling them all the stories of their adventures on the island. Ben is so glad to see she is getting along with these people. He joins them, sitting around the campfire listening to all the latest gossip. They have so much catching up to do since being isolated from the rest of the world. So much has changed in the last six years, but for Ben, it's more reasons to stay on the island.

Late in the night, the camp is now so quiet after Sally and Margaret had left. The gentle waves of the ocean are now the only sound anyone can hear. The children sleep together in the tent while Jenny and Ben hold each other in the hammock. They don't want to sleep at all on their last night in paradise. Even though it's been a long day, neither of them wants it to end. In the past few years, they have been through a lot. Deep down, they know if they had to do it all again, they wouldn't change one thing.

* * *

Chapter 42

Last Day in Paradise

J enny is up early, rushing the children to the small pond to get cleaned up for the big trip. She has no idea what is in store for them. In just one day, their lives have turned into chaos. She is having second thoughts about leaving the safety and solitude of their small island home. A few days out on the open ocean in a small boat might be fun for some people, but for her, it's an absolute nightmare.

Ben stays behind to pack away the last of the camping gear. He has done this so many times during the storms. Today is different, and everything is being stored away for the last time. He places everything in the big cooking pot, keeping the duffel bag for their clothes and things they are taking back with them. He looks through the hut and finds that Jenny has already cleaned it out. Gathering up the last few things, he looks over the camp, seeing how bare it is. The only things left are the hut and the campfire. He is so depressed, knowing this is their last day in paradise.

Jenny returns with the children, all are dressed up in their best clothes. The twins are so shocked to see that everything is gone. With their father holding the duffel bag and everything else packed away, they know what it means.

"Daddy, you sure we not going to the cave?" June asked.

April looks up at the sky, confused. "It's a good day! No dark clouds anywhere. Don't even smell the rain. How come we going to the cave?"

"Oh, no... I'm just storing everything away while we're gone. Remember, we're going on a big adventure. We're going to get a ride on that boat, and then we're going to see Granny!"

Their eyes lit up, all excited hearing that. Baby is jumping up and down, screaming out loud. Even he knows something good is going to happen. Unfortunately, Ben does not have the heart to tell them that this is a one-way trip.

"Jenny, I'm ready to make the last run to the cave. Is there anything you want me to bring back?"

She thinks about it for a few seconds. "All we need are our clothes and the gifts we made for each other. My journal is the one thing I want to make sure we bring with us."

"It's already packed in the bag. I guess this is it. It's not much when you think about it," glancing down at the old duffel bag and looking around to see if there is anything else they might have forgotten.

The big cooking pot is the only thing left. The old pot has been at the camp since they found it in the cave. He filled it with the last of their supplies. Now the camp is bare. The hut is also empty, leaving only the old bed frame, table, chairs, and a few woven bowls Jenny made long ago. The campfire is the only thing left. Still warm from the last of their many campfires.

He rolls up the mattress and sleeping bag for the last time, then grabs the heavy pot. "I'll be back shortly," walking out to the beach.

Jenny and the children sit in the doorway of the hut, talking about their big adventure. The twins are excited, but deep down, they can sense something is wrong. Jenny is fighting back the tears, trying to keep up the appearance that this is a happy occasion.

"Mom, what's wrong?" June finally asked. "You look so sad."

"Oh, there's nothing wrong... I was just thinking about the big trip we're going on. We might be gone for a long time."

"How long? A couple of days?" April asked, getting concerned.

She hesitates before answering. "Maybe a little longer than that... Where we are going is far away. You're going to meet my family and your father's too. We'll probably get to stay with them in their home for a while. It'll be a lot of fun. You'll be seeing a whole lot of new things like you did at our visitor's camp."

"So, does Granny got a big tent, like they do?" June asked.

Jenny smiles. "Even bigger! And they have big cookouts every day! I can't wait for you to show my mom and dad how well you can cook. They'll be so proud of you," wiping away the tears from her cheek.

* * *

Ben feels so strange having to make the trip to the cave for the last time. He struggles to carry it all, but this is the last run, so he doesn't mind taking his time. Everything they removed from the cave is being put back. The old cast iron cooking pot is going back to its resting place. Everything that was originally in his duffel bag is going to be left behind. Much of it is well used and needs repair, but it will still be helpful for anyone stranded on the island.

He stands inside the cave, looking at all the things that helped them survive. He knows that whoever gets stuck here will not have to worry about firewood for a few months. The last thing in his hand is his trusty walking stick. Reluctantly, he places it on top of the stack of firewood.

Ben slowly walks out of the cave. He pauses, having one last look around. Everything is so quiet, and even the birds are not singing their songs. A strange feeling runs through him. The place looks so barren and cold. Looking back at the cave, he wonders how long it will be before someone else finds shelter here. It is the one place on the island that helped them survive. He is so sad to see it for the last time. Deep down, he knows this is going to be a bad day.

He jogs down the trail to the big orchard on the far side. Collecting the last of the oranges, grapefruit, and lemons, he is glad he brought the biggest sack they have. It will be the last of the fruit he'll be hauling down the trail. He is so sad knowing that all this fruit will fall to the ground, wasting away.

Ben kneels at the foot of the young trees he planted many years ago. "I see you're all grown up, big and strong. It won't be long before you'll be as big as the others and bear lots of fruit. It's a shame... I won't be here to see it," clearing away the leaves.

He carefully fixes the three little markers in front of the trees named April, June, and Baby. On the day his children were born, he planted a tree for them. Every day, he tended these special trees, hoping they would have long, fruitful lives here on the island. When the children were older, he taught them how to take care of the trees and how to plant their own. He taught them well since the area was covered with little seedlings. Now, he has to leave them all on their own.

Finally, he walks over to the old gravesite to bid them farewell. Over the years, Ben fixed up the old graves, made permanent crosses, and placed rocks around the entire site. No one will ever know the names of the former inhabitants. He always wondered if this would have been their destiny. A lone grave up here on the hill next to the orchard. He feels so sorry for these people, not knowing if they chose to live out their lives here or were stranded.

Ben stands at the end of the gravesite. "Well, I guess this is goodbye... We are leaving this beautiful island and our home. We had a wonderful time here, but we have to leave for the children. I'm not sure what brought you here, but I'm hoping you felt the same as we did living on this beautiful island. I know I'm going to miss the sunsets and the walks out on the beach, but mostly, sharing it with my family. One day, I'll learn about your lives and who you were and let your families know. You have a beautiful resting place, a piece of heaven. May you rest in peace," then said a silent prayer for them.

He takes one last look around at the old orchard with its abundance of fruit. He hopes that one day someone else will live here and maintain the fruit trees. Then jogs back up the hill carrying the last haul of fruit.

* * *

As Ben reaches the lookout, he walks over to the edge, sitting on the bench, his favorite spot on the whole island. He feels a lot better sitting here alone, looking over his little world while eating fresh oranges. He can clear his mind by staring out over the ocean. The ship is still anchored just off the beach. His heart sinks low. Deep down, he wishes they had left and is not looking forward to this at all.

After eating the oranges, he slowly stands up. He remembers the old gravesite of the previous inhabitants of the island. There was no record of who they were. He wants people to know that for a short time, the island was their home. He stares at the old bench he made so long ago, knowing that it will be here forever. Taking out his pocketknife, he inscribes 'Home sweet home' into the wood, then adds their names, the date of their arrival, and their last day on the island. The bench will be their plaque, a record of their life on the island that they loved so much.

Ben looks down, seeing the beach far below, feeling so depressed. On such a beautiful day, it makes leaving even worse. This is by far the worst day he has ever had on the island. He has been so happy to live here with his family, but deep down, he knows they have to do it for the children. He closes his eyes to block out the view that he loves so much. His emotions are in such turmoil.

"Oh God, I don't want to leave!" he cried out, then quickly turned, running down the trail.

* * *

Once Ben reaches the pond, he kneels in the shallow water for a quick wash. The small pond had never looked so pristine, with flowers growing all over the cliff face. The morning birds are singing their songs, and the wind gently blows through the trees high above. He smiles, seeing all the little footprints that his children have left in the sand. Running his hand over one of the footprints, wishing they will be permanent, never to fade away. So it will be here forever, on the island he loves so much.

He never thought this day would ever come. Every day on the island, he was happy to be alive. His emotions finally catch up with him, crying uncontrollably on the saddest day of his life. He is having a difficult time trying to regain his composure, splashing water on his face. There is no way he can face his family like this. He wants to be strong and set a good example for the children, not letting them know how he really feels.

* * *

Ben walks into the campsite and sees Jenny and the children patiently waiting. The twins are wearing their nice dresses and big floppy sun hats, their mother made them. With their sticks in hand, backpacks filled with fresh fruit, and a full water bottle, they are ready for their big adventure. Even Baby is ready for the big trip, holding his sack filled with an orange, a water bottle, and all his toys.

"I see you're ready to go," Ben said.

"We're all packed," Jenny replied. "Not much else is here," looking at the empty camp.

Ben rummages around the camp, having one last look around for anything that they might have missed. "It looks so strange with everything gone."

Jenny puts her hand on his shoulder, seeing he is reluctant to leave. "It's time for us to go."

He just nods without saying a word. He can't speak. All he can do is think about the good times they had here.

"It's for the children," she whispers, holding his hand, knowing how difficult this is for him.

"I know," he replied, holding back the tears. "It was such a wonderful place to live. The best six years of my life."

She hugs and kisses him. "It was mine, too."

Standing in the middle of the camp, they all said goodbye to their home. For the small family, it's such a somber moment. Everyone is so sad.

"We going to take the Christmas tree with us?" June asked.

"I'm sorry, but we can't take everything," Jenny explained. "I think he's going to be happy here. He'll grow up big, like all the others. Besides, someone has to watch over the camp while we're gone."

The twins walk up, hugging the little tree. "Goodbye, Christmas tree! We'll be back to see you later."

"We have to go now," Jenny said, picking up Baby, slowly leading everyone out to the beach for the last time.

Ben slings the duffel bag over his shoulder. Filled with all their possessions, it's not even full. He picks up the last bag of fruit, slowly following Jenny out to the beach.

April is the last one to leave. She stops, then turns to look at her home. She feels so sad seeing everything is gone. None of this feels right. For some reason, deep down, she knows they are not coming back.

"Goodbye, home... I'm going to miss you," she whispered with one last wave, running out to the beach crying.

"What's wrong, April?" Jenny asked.

"I don't know," she replied, wiping away the tears. "I'm just sad."

"You shouldn't be sad... You're going to have lots of fun in the next couple of days and see all sorts of new things. We are all going to have a fun time!"

"I know... Something doesn't feel right. It makes me sad."

June turns to her mother. "Maybe we should stay here. Those land sharks should go away. Then we all can be happy again!" feeling the same sadness as her sister.

"No, this is a happy day for all of us," Jenny explained. "We've been waiting for this for many years. Remember one of our golden rules. Change is always a good thing."

"Yes, Momma," the twins quietly replied in unison.

Deep down, the twins know it is a sad day for everyone. Stopping at the tidal pool, Ben smiles, seeing all the fish still swimming around. He thought about all the good times they had out fishing and all the great meals they had.

"We need to free all the fish," Ben mumbled. "We won't be needing them now."

"Why, Daddy?" June asked. "They'll be here when we get back."

"No, let them go," Jenny said. "We can catch more later."

One by one, the twins toss them all into the ocean. "Go, free fishies! Go free!"

"Good thing we had the lobsters for fun day!" April shouted.

"That was a nice meal you guys cooked up yesterday," Ben replied. "I think it was by far the best you two ever did. I'm going to remember that meal for a long time."

"Thank you, Daddy!" June said, hugging her father.

After setting all the fish free, they stroll down the beach for the last time. Jenny can't hold back the tears any longer. Ben puts his arm around her, trying to console her.

The twins don't understand any of this. Their mother and father are acting so odd. Usually, everyone is happy when they go on an adventure, but this time is different. Everyone is so sad.

Jenny and Ben take their time strolling down the beach, wanting this to last as long as possible. Early in the morning is always the best time of the day for a walk. The water is so calm and clear. Palm trees along the beach gently sway in the slight breeze. The tropical paradise that they called home never looked so good.

The twins can't resist scavenging on the beach. Luckily, they found nothing worth keeping. They collect the occasional coconuts that had rolled down the beach. Already thinking of their next meal, they want to add coconut to the desserts the land sharks had made.

Reaching the big pond, they have one last look. They walk along the shallow water that leads into the dense trees. The big pond is their favorite place on the island. The small waterfall trickled off the cliff from high above. Topical flowers and ferns still cover the cliff face. Baby and the girls wanted so much to jump and play in the water. They spent so many hours here learning how to swim and jumping off the cliff.

No one said a word. All are standing quietly and looking at the beautiful scenery, thinking of all the good times they had here. Now, everyone is so sad. One by one, they slowly turn, walking back out to the beach.

* * *

As they reach the visitor's camp, they find everyone is already busy packing everything away.

"How would you like your coffee?" Wayne asked Ben.

Ben's eyes lit up, hearing that. "Now, that's the one thing I really missed. I'll have mine with plenty of milk and one sugar, please!"

Wayne turns to Jenny, seeing she has been crying. "Are you OK? Would you like anything?"

"No, thank you," Jenny said, wiping away the tears.

"Do you have any more luggage?" Wayne asked, seeing Ben was only carrying two bags. "I can run down to your camp and help carry the rest."

"Sorry, this is all we have," Ben explained, dropping the old duffel bag on the sand. "The other bag is filled with fruit, so we don't have much to carry. Most of the things we had, I stored in the cave. I thought it would be best to leave it for anyone else who might get stranded here."

Wayne just nods. "That sounds like a good idea. Come on over and have a seat. I'll fix you up with some coffee. We got some breakfast out on the table, so help yourself."

"Thank you," Jenny said, leading the children to the picnic table.

"Looks like you got some nice coconuts there. Want me to help open them up for you?" Wayne asked April and June.

"No, it's OK," June replied. "We open these all the time."

"You can have one of these," April said. "They good eaten. You just chop up the coconut and put it all over your food. That makes it real tasty!" handing him one of her coconuts.

"Well, thank you!" Wayne replied. "I'll give it a try," surprised to see how polite the girls are.

There are so many choices of breakfast food on the table. There is plenty of fresh bread, bagels, pancakes, and all kinds of jams. The children, still so amazed at the abundance of food, make sure to try one of everything, except for the milk. The smell and taste is something none of them like at all, and the white color doesn't help. Fresh orange juice is still their favorite breakfast drink.

Jenny and Ben savor their first cup of coffee in years. The bagels are also their favorite, and can't get enough of the strawberry jam. With not much else to do, they enjoy their first real breakfast. Just to sit down and eat is such a novelty, especially not having to do any work for all this food.

Baby doesn't take long to find the beach ball again. He and his sisters are running about kicking the ball all over the beach. Something as simple as a beach ball keeps them amused for a long time. They don't have a care in the world, and that's the way it should be. No more living off the land and worrying if they have enough firewood or food for their next meal. Now they can act like children for the first time.

Margaret walks over, noticing how sad Jenny and Ben look. "What's wrong? I thought you'd be happy about leaving."

"Oh, we are," Jenny said, trying to hold back the tears. "You have to understand... This has been our home, and we've had a good life here. Our children were born here, and this is all they've ever known," watching them playing out on the beach.

Margaret looks around and sees that this is indeed a paradise. "It's so beautiful out here. You've been so lucky, but what if one of you got sick?"

"That was one of my biggest fears. You are right... No matter how we feel, we must go home for the children's sake."

"You were lucky. Real lucky. Nevertheless, you have to move on. Your kids are going to grow up fast, and they need to experience the real world. You also have families at home who thought you were gone. Maybe in a few years, you can always move back if things don't work out. You need to remember one thing. This beautiful island will always be here."

After hearing what Margaret had said, it cheered Jenny up a little. Margaret is right about the island. It will always be here, and they can come back one day. Once they get settled, they can return for a vacation and even bring their families here on a big sailboat like these people had done.

* * *

With everything finally packed away, Wayne makes several trips in the motorized dinghy, carrying it all back to the catamaran. Once all the camping gear is gone, it's time to ferry everyone off the island. Jenny and Ben want to be the last ones to leave the island, savoring every minute on their island home.

Sitting on the beach, Jenny keeps digging her hand in the sand, letting it flow through her fingers. The warmth of the fine sand never felt so good. She wants so much to take off her clothes and lie out on the beach for one last time. She closes her eyes, listening to the gentle waves, not wanting this to end.

There are so many things she wants to do before they leave. Not even a day has gone by since being rescued, and here they are already about to leave. She wants so much to tell these people to go without them. Maybe in a month or two, someone can come back, giving them a little more time. It's all happening way too fast. They are just not ready to leave their island and the home they love so much.

Ben feels so numb, looking up at the island and then down at the beach. All the trees, the hills, rocks, sand, and the sounds of the surf are going to be with him forever. He wishes they could stay just a little longer for one more sunset and one more walk on the beach with his family. If they only had one more day, but it was not to be. Life on their island is finally over.

Wayne makes his last trip back to the beach. Watching the children running up and down the beach playing, he wonders how much their lives will change in the real world. Seeing how Jenny and Ben hold each other, looking so depressed, Wayne feels sorry for them. There is no way that he can leave them here, especially with the children. He has no choice but to take them off the island, knowing that this family is so lucky they have been able to survive this long on their own.

Wayne beaches the dinghy one last time. "Sorry, but it's time to go!" knowing how hard it is for them to leave their home.

The twins eagerly jump in, followed by Baby. Seeing the other people riding in the dinghy, they can't wait for their turn. In just one day, they have experienced so many new things they could have never imagined. Now, they can't wait to ride the dinghy and see the big boat.

Jenny and Ben hold each other, standing all alone on the beach. They slowly turned to have one last look at their home. Wayne patiently waits so they can have their last moments together on the island.

"I never did find my necklace," Jenny whispered, putting her hand up to her chest. "It was so beautiful, and it would have made a great keepsake of our home here."

"It's OK... I'll get you another one."

"No, it won't be the same... My pearl necklace came from this island, our home. You spent so much time making it. It was so special, and it meant a lot to me."

"I take it that you don't want a store-bought one to replace it," he jokingly said.

"No jewelry store will ever have anything that nice. I like handmade things, like we do for all our gifts. That's what made it so special," Jenny said, putting her arms around him, giving him one big hug and kiss.

Jenny looks deeply into Ben's eyes. "These have been the best years of my life. I never thought I could ever be so happy. Living here with you and the children, it can never get any better than this. Ben, I love you so much!"

Ben gives her a long kiss. "I love you too, Jenny. We'll be back one day. When the children are older, we can always come back and spend the rest of our days here together. We can have those long walks on the beach and watch all those sunsets that you love so much."

She holds him tight. "I'm going to miss our walks on the beach. It's for the children," crying uncontrollably.

"It's time for us to go," he whispered, trying so hard to keep his composure.

On the catamaran, everyone is so shocked to see how these people are so reluctant to leave. One would have thought this family would be happy to be rescued after six long years. Instead, it's a tearful goodbye. Everyone on the catamaran is getting emotional. Many have tears in their eyes as they watch the sad event taking place on the beach.

With one last hug, Jenny and Ben slowly walk off the beach, joining the children in the dinghy. Wayne pushes the dinghy out into the deeper water and jumps in. With the motor started, they quickly head towards the catamaran. The children sit in the front seats of the dinghy, so thrilled with their first boat ride. They hold on tight to the ropes when the first wave hits, knowing what is coming next. Watching the small boat carrying the others to the catamaran, they can't wait for the big waves, seeing how much fun it is bouncing up and down and going fast.

"Do it again! Do it again!" the twins shouted every time a wave hit them.

"Hold on! Here comes another one!" glad to see the children are having fun.

* * *

They reach the catamaran in just a few minutes. George is at the stern, helping everyone get on board. Jenny is the first on the ship, carrying Baby, and Ben follows, taking April and June. They all follow George down into the ship, so amazed at how big and luxurious it is.

"You have a cabin to yourselves," George explained. "It's small, but if you need more room, we can make other arrangements."

They enter the cabin, surprised that it's bigger than the cave. There are two single beds on each side of the room, separated by a small bedside table with a lamp on it. Their duffel bag is already on the bed. The twins are already looking around the cabin in awe.

Jenny is so amazed by the cabin. "Oh, this is so nice! It'll do just fine."

Ben is so impressed. "You slept on the beach instead of this?"

George nods his head. "When we're out sailing, it's OK, but nothing compared to a night out on a beach!"

Ben agreed. "You got that right," remembering all those nights sleeping outside on his hammock.

George points down the hall. "We have the bathroom a few doors down and a galley on the other side."

"You have a fabulous ship," Jenny said. "I didn't realize it'd be so big and roomy inside."

"Yep, she's a beauty... I wish she were mine, but Wayne is good enough to invite us on a few trips. He does a lot of charters, but now and then, he'll take her out for fun, and we get to tag along. This has been the best so far, spending an entire week exploring the islands out here. I dread having to go back to work after this."

Ben cringes. "I don't even want to think about that. I don't like the idea of having to go back to the five-day workweek with only two days off."

Margaret stops by to check on them. "So, how is your cabin?"

"It's great," Jenny said, "but we don't want to put anyone out," wondering who had been sleeping in the room.

"Don't worry about it," George explained. "The kids were playing around all night, making too much noise, keeping everyone else up. So, we're going to make them sleep in our cabin."

"Do you want to come up on deck?" Margaret asked. "We're about to leave. There is a fantastic view of your island from up there."

"Oh yes, we'd like that," Jenny quickly replied.

They walk back up on the deck, sitting on the bench at the stern of the ship. Jenny holds Baby on her lap, and Ben has both the girls sitting next to him. They quickly realize how small their island is after seeing it for the first time from a distance.

"We're going to circle the island before we head out," Wayne announces over the intercom. "I thought you might like one last look."

"Thank you!" Jenny replied. "That would mean a lot to us."

"It's so strange seeing our home like this," Ben said. "Looks altogether different, doesn't it?"

Jenny nods. "It's so beautiful," still trying to hold back the tears.

"It looks small from here, don't it, Daddy," June said.

"I know... I always thought it was bigger."

"Daddy, are we going for a ride in this boat too?" April asked.

"Yes, we are... They're going to take us way out on the ocean. It'll be a lot of fun!"

"Yeah! Make it go real fast so we can go up and down on the waves!" she yelled, getting excited.

"Oh no! I think this one goes nice and slow," he quickly said, dreading the thoughts of the rolling waves out on the open ocean.

A strange mechanical sound emanates from the ship as the anchor is slowly pulled up. Within seconds, the sails open up, catching the slight breeze. The catamaran slowly moves away from the island.

Baby is getting scared by all the noise, holding his mother and hiding his face. On the other hand, the twins are like a sponge absorbing every new sound and sight around them.

The catamaran moves farther out from the beach and turns to the west to circle the island. Jenny and Ben are silent, watching the beach and all the palm trees slowly go by. April and June are so excited, pointing out all the features they know. After six years, they know every little detail of their island, remembering all the good times at various locations.

On the north side of the island, he can easily see the big orchard on top of the hill. It is full of bright orange colors, acting as a beacon to let weary travelers know the abundance of fruit is here waiting for them.

The ship slowly circles the small island. Ben can't believe how quickly it takes to go around the island, knowing that it would take most of the day to walk around it. After only 20 minutes, they are back on the south side, in front of their campsite.

"Look! That's the rock in front of our home! It's so small!" April said, pointing it out.

"Yep, that's our home!" Ben said. "I can't believe you can see it from out here," wishing that he was still there.

"I can see the lookout!" June shouted. "Look, there's the bench! That's where we sit and have lunch! Can you see it, Mom?" pointing up at the island.

Jenny is so surprised to see the bench and even the orange trees from the sailboat. She starts weeping again, seeing the place where they were married and all those beautiful days looking out over the island.

Ben is not feeling any better about leaving, especially after seeing the island from a distance. He imagines what it would be like to sit up there now and see the catamaran sailing away. He looks back at the area where the camp is located. The huge boulder out in front makes it easy to spot. He is so surprised that he can't see the hut or even the entrance to their camp. He wonders how many ships might have sailed by never knowing anyone was on the island.

After circling the island, the catamaran slowly turns to the south, heading out to sea. After over six years, it's finally over. They are going home. Being rescued happened so quickly that they didn't have time to think about it. They are oblivious to what is in store for them when they return to the civilized world. The one thing they know is that their days of living in paradise are finally over.

"Goodbye, home sweet home," Ben whispered, the tears running down his face, staring at the island and their home.

Seeing a tear running down Jenny's cheek, he put his hand on her shoulder. "We had some good times, but the children will need a little more in life. Don't forget... We also have our families waiting for us back home," trying to cheer her up.

"I know... It's not fair to the children to live out here."

"Daddy, can we go back home now?" April asked. "We're too far away!"

"Yeah, let's go back!" June added. "I don't like it out here. I want to go back home," wiping away the tears from her eyes.

"You want to go back already? We just started our journey. Remember, we're going to see Granny and Granddad. They live far away, and it might take a while to get there."

"How we going to find our way back?" April asked.

"Wayne is the captain. He drives the boat and knows where all the islands are. He can go from one island to another without getting lost."

"Are you sure?" April asked, getting worried.

"It's just like how we know where everything is on our island. When you've been somewhere once, you can always find your way back."

Jenny and Ben hold each other as they watch the island getting smaller and smaller. The children wave goodbye to their home as it eventually disappears below the horizon. Now, there is nothing but the ocean surrounding them. They all are so sad and depressed.

An eerie silence falls onboard the catamaran when the small island disappears. The only sound is the wind rushing through the sails. Everyone notices how sad this family is. No one understands why, thinking they would be elated being rescued, but it's the exact opposite.

For Jenny, this has been such an emotional day. She is so depressed, leaving the home that she loves so much. Looking out over the vast empty ocean brings back so many terrible memories. Now, she is so concerned about her children being out on this cruel ocean so far from their home. She can't take it anymore, crying uncontrollably. Ben tries to console her, but it doesn't do any good. He knows this has been building up all day.

Margaret and Sally walk over, trying to help. "Maybe it would be better if I took her below to your cabin."

"I think that might be best," Ben said. "I don't think she slept at all last night."

"I'm OK," Jenny explained. "I just need to lie down for a while. I'll take Baby with me for a nap," seeing he is already nodding off.

Margaret leads Jenny back down to the cabin. Ben gets up to follow, bringing the girls.

"Daddy, can we stay up here?" June quietly asked, pulling on his shirt.

"I'll be OK," Jenny said. "I'm just tired… Why don't you stay up here with the girls?"

Ben knew right away that she wanted to be alone. "OK, we'll stay up here."

As Jenny walks back down to the cabin, Ben sits on the bench with his girls.

"Why is Mom crying?" April asked. "Is something wrong?"

"No, Mom is just sad because we're leaving our home."

"Daddy, we coming back home after we see Granny, right?" April asked, getting a little concerned.

Ben paused, wondering what he should tell his little girls. "It might be a while before we come back. Granny and Granddad might want us to stay with them. We also got your mother's family to visit as well. You're going to meet lots of people in the next couple of weeks or even months. It's going to be one big adventure, and we might be gone for a long time."

"OK, Daddy," the twins said in unison.

"As long as we get back before the storms," April added. "We need to check on the fruit trees and stock up on the firewood!"

"That's right!" June said. "We can't be too long! We can't get behind on the chores!"

Ben smiles. "Don't worry about it... Things will work out just fine. You're going to see a lot of new things while we're away, like the ice cream, apple pie, and Pepsi we had yesterday. You really liked all that, didn't you?" hugging his two girls.

They both nod their heads. "Sure did!"

"Daddy, you think they got some more?" April asked, getting hungry again.

He smiles. "I bet they do... That's just a small sample of all the new things you're going to see."

Sally overheard them. "Would you like anything to eat or drink?"

"Can we have Pepsi with that ice in it?" the twins excitedly asked.

"Some of that apple pie too?" June added.

"Sure! I'll be back with your drinks and pie," she said with a big smile, promptly leaving for the galley.

"See... It's going to be a fun trip!" Ben said, glad to see they are perking up a little.

Hearing about all the new food and drinks gets the twin's attention away from leaving their home. Ben knows they are not only getting scared of being so far out on the ocean but also seeing civilization for the first time. The catamaran is an experience in itself, but it's so much to absorb in one day. Even he feels a little out of place, not being in control of their surroundings.

The twins are not used to being waited on like this. Hot apple pie with vanilla ice cream fills the spot and makes their day. They still can't get enough of the Pepsi. Ben needs to make sure they don't overdo it. The children grew up with nothing but good, healthy food, so all this sugary junk food will be an issue.

* * *

With no shade on the top deck, it's too hot in the direct sunlight. Ben knows it's time to get out of the heat, but he also needs to check on Jenny. He carefully escorts the twins down to the cabins. With the ship rocking back and forth, walking is almost impossible. All they can do is hold on to the handrails to keep from falling.

"I don't like this!" April said, trying to keep her footing.

"It keeps moving around! Can you get them to keep it still, Daddy?" June asked, crawling on her hands and knees.

Ben is having the same problem. "Sorry, this is the way it is on a boat!" he explained, starting to feel a little nauseous.

George walks out of his cabin and starts laughing, seeing their guests struggling. "Now, you see why we spent the nights out on the beach. Don't worry… You'll get used to it. Just think, this is a calm day."

"Thank God for that!" Ben said. "How is the weather for the next couple of days?" remembering those days in the storms so long ago.

"Clear and calm! So, don't worry… It's going to be a nice smooth ride all the way there."

"You call this a smooth ride?"

George keeps on laughing. "You bet! It doesn't get any better than this. Oh, by the way. The captain wants to talk to you."

Ben just shakes his head. "Oh, great! I just came down from there. Tell him I'll be there in a few minutes. Let me get the girls to the cabin first."

They finally reach their cabin, finding both Jenny and Baby sound asleep. They stumble into the room, quickly sitting on the other bed to rest. If this is a calm day on a sailboat, it's going to make for a very long trip.

"You two stay here," Ben whispered, "watch Mom and Baby. I'm going to talk to the captain to check a few things."

"OK, Daddy," they replied, a little scared.

"Remember, you stay here," he repeated. "No wandering about, and keep this door closed while I'm gone."

They nod their heads, knowing it's their job to protect their mother and brother, especially while they are asleep. Ben leaves them, making sure to close the door. Now he can have a good look around. The ship is the utmost in luxury, seeing the other rooms and the galley. The one luxury he is so glad to see is the bathroom, and he can't wait to try it out.

Reaching the bridge deck, Ben finds everyone else already there. The bridge deck is the highest point on the ship, with an unobstructed 360-degree view. Captain Wayne Peterson is sitting quietly, watching all the instruments. Everything on the ship is computerized and automated. Wayne can't wait to show Ben how it all works. The ship is GPS driven with various satellite links getting all the latest weather images of the area.

Ben is so impressed with all the gadgets but is a little nervous, knowing that a computer is steering the ship. He knows too much about software engineering to trust them for something important like this.

After showing off all his latest gadgets, Wayne explained that the people at Kwajalein wanted to talk to him as soon as possible. Ben knew this was coming and ended up being on the radio talking to them for a long time. They are asking questions about his life, trying to figure out if he is Ben Hughes. He knows these people are very suspicious of him. Anyone with a computer can get the same information from the Internet if they want to steal someone's identification.

Ben is so frustrated in trying to answer all the questions. He knows right away that these people are unprepared. Most of the questions are probably from his resume or a simple employment application that he filled out for the job at Kwajalein. His biggest problem is trying to remember it all after being away for over six years.

He knows these people are not convinced. They are still concerned that he and Jenny might be impostors. The military type hadn't changed at all. They are still suspicious of things they don't understand. The only real test is the fingerprints. Until then, they are still John and Jane Doe.

* * *

Chapter 43

A Peace of Mind

W alter is frantically rummaging through all the insurance papers, looking for phone numbers. Paul Rutherford is the one who kept them up-to-date every day about the rescue mission and is the only one he wants to talk to about his son.

Finding the number on one of the old forms, he quickly makes the call. He doesn't care what time it is in Kwajalein and will wake them all up.

A woman answers the phone. "Human resources, Jane speaking. May I help you?"

"Yes, this is Walter Hughes... I would like to speak with Mr. Paul Rutherford. Is he still working there?" Walter asked.

"Yes, he does, but he's in a meeting right now," the woman on the phone quickly replied. "Would you like to leave a message?"

"No, I need to talk to him. It's about my son! You get him on the phone right now!"

He is not going to wait around for these people to call him back like before. Times have changed. He will give these people a piece of his mind for leaving his son out on some island for six long years.

Jane is caught off guard, already knowing who this person is. "Mr. Hughes, hold on. I'll see if I can put you through."

Walter is relieved to hear that. Usually, he was always told that they would call back but ended up waiting for hours. This time it's different. He is the one who is now in control.

Jane can't believe Walter Hughes is calling. Everyone is in an emergency meeting concerning a call from a ship finding two people on an island who claimed to be Jenny Mason and Ben Hughes. With Walter Hughes on the phone, somehow, the news has already leaked out. Most likely, the other families will call as well.

When Paul Rutherford was notified about these people on the island, he was absolutely appalled. They all think it's a scam or a bad joke. He immediately calls in his staff to find out what is going on. He wants to put an end to it real quick before it gets out to the public.

Jane runs into Paul's office, knowing this is too important to wait. She interrupts him while he is talking to his staff. This is not a good way to start the day. After being up all night, they are all tired and irritable, and it will not get any better.

Paul is angry, seeing his secretary bolting into his office. "Jane! We're busy... I don't want to be interrupted for any reason at all!"

Jane, ignoring her boss, looks him right in the eye. "Sorry, but Walter Hughes is on the phone. He wants to talk to you about his son!"

Paul stares at his secretary in shock. "Oh, shit... Does he know?"

She shrugs her shoulders. "Mr. Hughes didn't say... He just wants to talk to you, and he sounds pretty mad about something."

"Why the hell would he be calling me after all this time? Damn! The news media may have gotten hold of this. Do any of you know about this?" glancing over at everyone in the room.

They all quickly look at each other, wondering if someone might have carelessly said something. Even though it's only been a day, that's more than enough time for the news media to jump on it. With all these twenty-four-hour news channels eager for an exclusive, they can broadcast it all over the world.

"Maybe his wife had another one of those dreams again," someone mentioned, recalling all the times he had talked to her on the phone.

Paul gets mad. "Bob, that's not funny at all!"

"It wasn't meant to be... Mrs. Hughes called me so often, telling me all about her dreams. Shit! It will be something if it is them. After all this time, and she was right, it's going to make us look real bad!"

"Put him through," Paul said to his secretary. "Let's see what he knows," sitting down at his desk.

He doesn't want to give false hope to anyone. He just figures these two people are probably pulling a scam for insurance or publicity. They don't want anyone to know about this until they can check it out thoroughly first. Maybe it's just a coincidence that Walter Hughes called.

Paul quickly picks up the phone. "Hello, Mr. Hughes. It's been a long time. How may I help you?" not wanting to give out any information.

Paul Rutherford's mouth drops wide open upon hearing about the phone call. It's far worse than he initially thought. Whoever these people are, called the Hughes family, and claiming to be their son. The last thing he wants is to open up old wounds and have these people suffer again with false hopes.

"Yes, we did receive a message," Paul explained, "about two people who were found on Mocker Island. We're still investigating, but we wanted to confirm who they are before we contacted anyone. You say they contacted you directly? You have talked to this person who claims to be your son?"

"Yes, I have!" Walter replied. "It's Ben! I have no doubt about it! They were using one of those satellite phones and called me right from that island!"

"You have to understand our position here, Mr. Hughes. We want to identify these people, but it could take time. But, are you absolutely sure the person you talked to is your son?"

"I'm one hundred percent positive. He is my son! There is no doubt whatsoever! He has been out there all this time! What the hell is wrong with you people? Why didn't you look for him there? Do you know the hell you put us through?"

Paul puts his hand on his forehead, staring down at his desk. "I know... I'm so sorry. Walter, if you're that positive that he's your son, I'll take your word for it. However, until we check their fingerprints against our files, our official position is that their identities are in question. It just doesn't make any sense. How could they survive out there after all this time?"

"I don't know, but they did," Walter answered.

"Anyway, we are preparing things here for their arrival. We will keep you updated on any new information we get. Let me be the first to say I'm sorry. I'm so sorry… We failed so miserably in not finding your son."

Walter doesn't want to argue the point. "I got my son back, and that's all that matters now. You just make sure he gets home safely!"

"I assure you, we will... It's a shock to us all. I can't believe that after all those years, then to find out they've been stranded on some small island in the middle of nowhere. How they got out there, we just don't know."

"How come no one checked the area he was in?"

Paul looks up at the map. "The island they were on is so far west from their flight path, but it's also in a restricted area. The security around those islands is massive. No one can even get near there without setting off some sort of alarm. Hell, they wouldn't even let us search near those islands. We were told that they had no radar contacts out there and that we shouldn't bother to look. We are definitely going to investigate this. They should have known someone was living on that island after six years."

"You would think so!" Walter blurted out. "Especially after their plane went down! I can't believe no one checked."

"I know... I assure you there will be an investigation. Nevertheless, we'll be here waiting for them. They will be admitted directly to the infirmary for a full checkup and positive identification."

"Do you know anything about the children?"

"Yes, we heard there are twin girls and a baby boy. We don't have any more details than that. That's why we questioned it when we first heard the report. It made their story even harder to believe. Anyway, we'll know more when they arrive."

* * *

Mary sits quietly, listening while her husband talks to the people at Kwajalein. As Walter hangs up the phone, he looks over at his wife with an astonished look on his face.

"So what did they say?" she frantically asked.

"Can you believe it? They don't know much about anything. They still doubt that it's really Ben. They're supposed to arrive at Kwajalein in a couple of days. Then they'll know for sure."

"So, what about the kids?"

He can't help smiling. "Oh, apparently, they have twin girls and a baby boy!"

She is so elated. "Ben has three little ones! Twin girls too! My God. I can't believe it!"

"Now, that's going to be a sight to see," and starts laughing.

"I need to go to the store and get some baby things," she said, quickly getting up. "We got to some beds for our little babies! We also have to redo the bedroom. There's a lot of work to be done!"

"Now? It'll be a few days before they get to Kwajalein. They're going to check them in at the hospital at the base first. It might be a few more days or even a week before they get here."

"Oh, no!" she said, pulling him up out of the chair. "We're going now... I have a lot to do! We might have to paint the bedroom first. We can't have them staying here with those dirty walls. The carpet needs replacing too. Can't have my little babies crawling about on those old dirty carpets!"

Walter shakes his head. He knows he has already lost the argument. For the next few days, it's going to be a mad rush getting everything ready for the big reunion. The entire house is going to get a complete work-over with fresh paint and new carpets. He doesn't mind since his one wish in life came true. His long-lost son is finally coming home and bringing his family with him.

* * *

SECTION 4

The Civilized World

Chapter 44

Return to Civilization

Jenny and Ben find their first day on the catamaran so restrictive and way too crowded. They are grateful to their hosts, but it's difficult to be around so many people all the time.

Ben still feels uneasy with all these people around his children. He is an overprotective father out of his element. On the island, he was always in charge and in control of his surroundings, but here, he is so out of place and doesn't like it one bit.

Jenny finds it difficult to keep up with all the conversations. She feels like these people are from another world, discussing strange topics she has never heard before. One thing that she noticed is that everyone is so interested in reading her journals. Pages are being handed around, and everyone is so enthralled reading their story.

Baby is so frightened by all the new surroundings and doesn't like being around all these people. He always wants to be carried. Jenny is glad that her son slept most of the time. He is not as active as he was on the island. She doesn't trust him running about, and it's worse being up on the deck. She is so scared that he will slip, falling off the ship into the deep ocean.

Ben is in charge of the twins, always having to keep track of them. They are going through the ship scavenging, taking whatever they can get their hands on. The ship contains a wealth of fabulous finds, more than they ever had on the beach. They are always wandering around, filling their backpacks with their newfound bounty and bringing it all back to their cabin. The trash cans are the biggest find. So many empty boxes and bottles, all neatly packed away in a huge plastic sack. All they have to do is drag it all back to their room and sort through it all.

April, June, and Baby are discovering so many new things. They even get to watch television for the first time. Baby is so enthralled, always laughing out loud, watching his first Tom and Jerry cartoon. April and June stand right in front of the television, trying to figure it all out, and don't know what to make of it. At times, they think the cartoon characters are really inside the television, constantly yelling for them to come out and play.

* * *

With one bathroom and so many people, the captain has a shower schedule. Luckily, Jenny is at the top of the list since she kept raving over how luxurious the bathroom is. Getting to have her first hot shower with real soap and shampoo is a big event. She is so depressed having to leave her home, but having a bathroom is the one thing that makes her feel better. She is already seeing some of the benefits of living in the modern world.

Margaret and Sally give her a few basic toiletries. The thick cotton bathrobe is the nicest thing she has worn in years, and she has never been so pampered in her life. Things like soft towels are a luxury that she thought she would never see again.

After her first hot shower, Jenny leaves the bathroom, feeling a little better about herself. She walks into the galley and finds Ben reading a 'Sleeping Beauty' book to the children. Seeing her husband with Baby on his lap and the girls sitting on each side is a wonderful sight. They are now acting like children instead of running about with spears, hunting down their next meal.

Jenny sits down with Ben while he reads the story to the children. The twins are so thrilled to show their mother their new book, telling her all about the prince and princess, pointing out all the pictures.

"Daddy, we have to go back!" June frantically yelled out. "I forgot something!"

"What did we forget? I thought I got everything in the bag," trying to think of what they might have left behind.

"The potty chair," June whispered. "I have to go."

"Oh, they have one here on the boat," Ben explained.

"I'm not going to use their potty! That's disgusting! I only use my own potty chair!"

"It's a nice one. You'll really like it."

"So, how can we go potty?" April asked, looking around. "They got no sand in here!"

"Oh, you guys have to see this! I'm surprised you haven't discovered the bathroom yet. You two have been exploring all over the boat, scavenging, and you don't know about it?" he asked, really eager to show them.

He rushes down to the bathroom with his girls. He explains how the toilet works, flushing it a few times, showing them the sink, and how the hot and cold running water taps work. They are stunned, seeing all this for the first time. Fresh water on demand is something even Ben is amazed to see.

The twins let out a long "Wow!" as their father points out all the modern conveniences.

"But Daddy! There is only one!" April said, getting frustrated.

"One what?" he asked.

The twins quickly point to the toilet. "The potty! We always go together!" getting a little fidgety, needing to go.

Potty time was something the twins always did together, sitting under the trees and singing their songs. Ben didn't think about it when they got on the ship. Having to be here for days, he knows it's going to be a big problem.

Jenny walks up just in time with Baby. "I think this is my department... You can take him for a while," handing him over to Ben.

"Good... I'll leave it up to you to explain why they can only go one at a time. I'll take Baby back out to the galley," Ben said, so relieved.

"What's wrong with those two boys?" she quietly asked. "They keep hovering around me all the time. That's why I came in here with you. It's a little unnerving."

"Maybe you should wear that T-shirt they gave you," looking down at Jenny's robe, noticing she is showing a lot of cleavage.

She looks down. "You think it's a little too showy?"

"Have a look in the mirror and see for yourself," knowing why the boys were gawking at her.

Jenny looks at herself in the bathroom mirror. "If just a little cleavage gets all this attention, it's a good thing they were not on the island with us. I guess I better start getting used to wearing clothes again."

Both April and June are frantically jumping up and down. "Mom, we got to go!"

"OK, hurry up," Jenny said. "But one of you has to wait!"

She then turns to Ben. "Let me handle this before they have an accident," shutting the bathroom door behind her.

Wayne walks up. "Ben, is everything all right?"

"Everything is great! We now realize all the nice things we've been missing over the years. A real toilet and hot and cold running water! It makes life too easy."

Wayne laughed. "Yeah, we take so much for granted. Oh, there is one thing... The news media has gotten hold of your story. Several news crews are already on Kwajalein."

"I thought it was a secure military base? How did the news people get there?" Ben asked, remembering all the security clearances they needed to work on the island.

Wayne shrugs his shoulders. "Things have changed... It all depends on what's happening in the rest of the world. Right now, things have kind of slowed down, so there is less security. In the good old days, when you were stationed out here, you could bring your family with you. Now, they have big problems because of budget cutbacks. The families were the first to go. The morale got so bad the company had to bring in families or friends to visit. It's a lonely place for a family man."

"But these are the news people. You think they'd be the last ones you want on a military base snooping around," Ben added, getting frustrated.

"I know... It's more of a public relations thing. We also have civilians occasionally visiting the island. There's not much to see on Kwajalein, anyway. There were a lot of conservationists crying about how we were destroying all the wildlife and the coral reefs. They let them come out to see for themselves. Most of the island is still restricted, so the military police had to keep an eye on all the civilians while they were there. The military boys don't like it, but what can you do?"

Ben let out a long sigh. "Well, it would be nice to keep our arrival simple and quiet. The children have not been around other people. We were hoping to get them up to speed gradually."

"Oh, yes... I informed them about that. They will escort you directly to the infirmary and keep everyone away until you have time to get adjusted," Wayne said, putting it mildly.

Wayne had warned the officials on the base about this wild bunch. Especially with Ben being a very overprotective father who doesn't trust anyone near his family. Seeing all the bulging muscles, he needs to keep on Ben's good side. To make matters worse, the two little girls are extremely dangerous. He never forgot his first encounter with them and how they could handle knives and throw spears. He knows to keep his distance from those two, warning everyone on the ship not to mess around with them.

Ben returns to the galley with Baby. Since there is not much else to do, he feels so useless just sitting around. The children's books are great, keeping Baby occupied for hours. He always wants someone to read to him and see all the colorful pictures in the book. Baby is so amazed at seeing all the animals for the first time.

* * *

April and June run back to the galley. "Dad! You should see the potty! It was great! All you do is sit on it and do your poops. Then you push the handle, and it goes whoosh away with water. Then all the poops are gone, and you don't have to use leaves! They have real soft paper to wipe your bum. It's really nice!"

"Yeah, it's great!" April added. "You don't have to cover it with sand or nothing. But they only got one, so you have to wait your turn. Can you make one of those for us?"

Ben laughed. "I'll see what I can do."

"Mom, Daddy is going to make us one of those potties when we get back!" April boasted, jumping up and down with excitement.

Jenny is amused by the joke. "That will be nice. I'll be wanting one of those too."

"Mom, how come they have only one?" June asked. "Everyone should have their own potty chair."

"Yeah, I don't want people using my potty!" April added. "That's not nice!"

"Well, there is not much room here on the boat. We'll have to make do until we get to your granny's house. They probably got enough for each one of us."

With the discovery of the flushing toilet and the hot and cold running water, April and June spend all their time in the bathroom. The toilet is the only thing they are most impressed with on the catamaran. They keep flushing the toilet repeatedly, tossing in things to see them being washed away. Jenny finally hauls them out for playing around too much. With one bathroom and with all the people on the ship, it's not the best place for them to be playing.

* * *

Dinner time is an ordeal with the ship being overcrowded. Everyone can't fit in the galley with all the tables set up. Bob and Margaret opted to eat up on the deck with their children. That makes enough room for Jenny and Ben to sit at the table on their own. The galley is no different from staying up in the cave. Everyone is all cramped up trying to cook and eat in one little room.

Wayne and George land a couple of good-sized fish, which means fresh seafood for dinner. It's a first for April and June, not having to catch and cook their meals. George is in charge of the cooking, wanting to show off his culinary skills to his guests. The twins are always hovering around him, constantly asking questions about how he will prepare the fish. He quickly discovers that these two little girls know more about cooking seafood than he does.

The twins are so curious about all the strange devices in the kitchen. The propane stove is still a big mystery. Again, seeing someone just turn a knob and have an instant fire is hard for them to comprehend. The microwave oven is the one thing that they can't figure out. With no fire, smoke, or even heat, somehow, the food is still being cooked.

As for a meal, it's a feast for Jenny, Ben, and their children. The twins are not only impressed with the abundance of food but also with how well it's prepared. They are discovering so many new things, always asking what that particular taste or ingredient is. It is indeed a new and exciting world for them.

Sally can't wait to serve up the strawberry cheesecake that she made for dessert. She watches intensely, seeing the girls' reaction after taking their first bite, and it's a big hit too. This family loves food, and dinnertime is an important part of the day for them. The twins are a little on the wild side, but at the dinner table, they are role models for their children. Even the little boy is attentive and well-behaved.

George and Sally love all the appreciation for their hard work in the kitchen, especially when the twins want to help clean up and do the dishes. They get depressed and embarrassed seeing how their own children act. Their children are very unsociable, taking their meals straight to their cabins to play video games while they eat. They never helped with the cooking or cleaned up afterward. Most of the time, someone even has to go to the cabins to collect all their dirty dishes.

* * *

Late in the night, everyone settles into the cabins. Jenny and Ben's first night from the island is a little unnerving. They can't believe how late it is, and they also missed the sunset. With the lights on in the galley, no one noticed it was dark outside. Sitting on the beach to watch the sunset is something they always do after supper. The sunset marked the end of a day on their small island home, and time for them to go to bed.

Ben has the chore of helping the children get washed up before bedtime. Life was a lot easier at their camp, where they had plenty of warm water left over to wash with, and headed straight to bed. Now, they have to wait for the bathroom to be available. Once it's clear, all three children run naked down the hall, yelling and screaming. They had heard all the stories about the shower and can't wait to get their turn.

"Hold on," he said, making them wait to get everything ready. "Let me adjust the water so it's just right. We don't want it to be too hot," trying to get the right temperature.

"Hurry, Dad! It's getting cold!" June shouts, shivering in the cold air.

Baby doesn't care about anything. He is having a good time playing with the toilet, constantly flushing it. Then he starts unrolling all the toilet paper. He is a handful, always getting into everything.

"OK, I think it's warm enough," seeing Baby is getting out of control.

The twins can't wait to use the shower after hearing all the stories. Standing under the waterfall at the pond is all they have ever known, and it only had cold water. This one is much better with warm water, and there is no sand anywhere.

"I really like this!" June said. "It's like having our very own waterfall!"

"It's lots better!" April added. "They got nice warm water here! Daddy, how come we don't have warm water in our waterfall? Can you make ours warm when we get back?"

Ben hands them the soap and a couple of washcloths. "We'll see about it... Here you go. Wash up real good, and wash Baby while you're at it!" knowing the twins will make sure their little brother is squeaky clean.

He leans up against the sink, keeping an eye on them through the frosted shower curtain. At least now, he can keep them all occupied for a while and not worry about what they'll get into next. The lack of sleep is finally catching up with him. Now he can sit back and relax for a change.

Ben looks around, wishing they had something like this on the island. It is indeed an easy life in the real world. Never having to haul water and wait for it to warm up over the fire. Never having to gather firewood and carry it down a narrow trail. It is all way too easy.

June peeks out from behind the curtain. "We finished!"

"You got Baby all cleaned up?" he asked.

June nods. "Sure did! He's cleaner than ever!"

"Good, it's time to get out," turning off the water.

He drags them out of the bathroom. They are having too much fun, wanting to do it all over again. Running back to their cabin yelling and screaming, they can't wait to tell their mother every little detail of their first real shower.

* * *

They are all up at sunrise. Ben finds it so odd to wake up and not have any chores to do. He makes his way down to the galley to see what everyone is doing about breakfast. Jenny ushers the children into the bathroom for the morning wash. The twins can't wait to get back in the shower again. Luckily, being so early, no one is in line for the bathroom.

Jenny looks down the hallway, not seeing anyone else. "OK, it's a quick wash, and we'll need to get out so someone else can use the bathroom."

"Can we have a shower again?" April asked, stripping off her clothes.

Baby is already in the shower screaming out loud. He keeps pointing up at the showerhead, wanting the water to come out again.

"OK, we'll make it a quick one," Jenny said, so eager to have another shower as well.

"Wow!" June shouted. "It's already warm! We don't even have to start a fire to heat it up!"

"It's just like a little waterfall, isn't it?" April asked, so excited.

Jenny takes off her robe, getting in the shower with them. "Oh, this is wonderful! You're right. It's so nice not to have to wait for the fire, and it's all so easy. Hot water whenever we want it!"

"This is lots better than the pond, right, Momma?" June asked, seeing how easy it was to turn on the tap for all the water they wanted.

"There's going to be a lot of new things you'll be seeing in the next few days."

"Better than this?" April asked.

"Oh, yeah!" Jenny said. "Lots better than this. A whole bunch of things you never dreamed of!"

"Daddy is going to make us one of these when we get back home," June said. "We going to have hot and cold taps too!"

"He's going to put one of those fancy potties in the cave and the hut!" April added. "We going to have hot water taps in the pond too!"

"Oh, that will be nice," remembering all those days at the little pond.

Again, she feels depressed. These modern conveniences are great, but she misses the pond with all the flowers and the birds. She is already thinking about returning and having Ben build them a little house. Hot and cold running water and a real bathroom would make the island life so much better.

* * *

After a quick shower, Jenny ushers the children to the galley, worrying about being late for breakfast. She is surprised to find they are the only ones up. Ben is all alone, rummaging through the cabinets. He makes the coffee and is looking around for something for the children. Deep in the cabinet, Ben finds the bag of fresh fruit they brought with them. He quickly hands out an orange to each of the children.

Ben sips his coffee while sitting at the table. "It feels great having it all to ourselves. There's plenty of room now. I don't mind it when it's like this," glancing around the luxurious galley.

Jenny nods. "Oh, this is nice... I don't know why, but I still feel awkward being around all these people. I guess it's more noticeable being cramped up on this boat, which makes it worse."

"Tell me about it… It's kind of like being in the cave during a storm with nowhere else to go. Unfortunately, we got a lot more people stuck here with us."

She sighed. "It's going to take a long time to get used to this. I guess once we get off this boat, it should be better. At least we can get away and be on our own for a while."

"Sorry, but it's not going to get any better," he explained. "Yesterday, Wayne mentioned that the news people found out about us. They're already at Kwajalein."

"Oh, great!" dreading the thoughts of being pounced on by reporters.

"I'm not interested in doing any interviews, so they made the trip for nothing. From what I hear, the people at Kwajalein are going to take us directly to the hospital. I guess after a day or two, we'll be flying back home."

She smiles. "That will be great! The sooner, the better. I can't wait to see my family again."

"No word from your mom and dad?"

She slowly shakes her head. "Nothing yet... I thought by now we would get a message on the radio from the people at Kwajalein."

He hugs her. "From what I understand, they still don't think it's us. So maybe that's why you haven't heard from them. I don't think they're talking to anybody right now until we get there. Once they verify who we are, then they'll contact your family."

She frowned. "That's so stupid! Once we get to Kwajalein, I'll call them myself! I'm not going to wait for those idiots to see it's really me before they contact my parents."

Ben laughed. "I know... These military people just don't think, do they? I have a feeling I'll be having some problems dealing with those type of people again."

"Talk about some early birds," Wayne said, walking into the galley. "I'm usually the first one up. So how was your night?"

"Fine, thank you," Jenny replied. "I didn't think I could ever sleep on a boat again. After lying on that bed, I think we all fell asleep so fast! You do have a wonderful boat. It's so nice!"

"Thank you... It was my lifelong dream to own a ship like this and sail the South Pacific. I sold everything when I retired, then went out and bought her."

"So, you just sail around out here on your own?" she asked.

"Oh, no... I have a contract with the people on Kwajalein. I spent about six months there, taking people out on cruises. It's hard to believe they pay me to sail the high seas."

"How long have you been there?" Ben asked.

"About eight years now. I was there when your plane went down. That was a sad day. They changed a lot of procedures after that. It should never have happened in the first place."

"We were in bad weather," Jenny said. "They did the best they could."

"It's not just that," Wayne explained. "You shouldn't have been on that flight. That plane was just too small. From what I heard, some generals and politicians took the regular shuttle flight, bumping your crew. There was an extensive investigation. They were supposed to be on an inspection tour but ended up deep-sea fishing and playing a lot of golf. There were a lot of early retirements and resignations after that."

"And a lot of people lost their lives," Jenny said, glaring back at Wayne. "So, all they got was a little slap on the wrist for it."

He just nods. "I'll start breakfast," trying to change the subject.

Wayne is making eggs, sausage, and toast for breakfast. April and June stand up on a chair next to the stove, watching his every move. The strange unfamiliar smells are enough to get their interest and ask never-ending questions. They want to know everything. Wayne makes the girls' day by giving them samples to try. The strawberry jam on toast is still their favorite.

* * *

Most people would love to sail around the Pacific Ocean on a huge ship that has everything that anyone wants, but it's not for Jenny and Ben. They feel so out of place with nothing to do. Everything close at hand makes for a very long and boring day. All the food and water they want, and not having to work for anything. It is a lifestyle they are not used to after all the years of living on their island.

For the rest of the day, everyone is out on the top deck, basking in the sun. Jenny, Ben, and the children sit in the shade of the mainsail. They think it's so odd how everyone is lying out in the scorching sun on purpose. Even with all the suntan lotion, it's the worst time of the day to be in the direct sunlight. They know from experience that this is not a smart thing to do, but these people have no clue about the basic rules.

Whenever the twins have a chance, they explore every part of the ship. Wayne always keeps an eye on them, knowing they are up to no good when they walk around with backpacks on and carrying those spears.

Things started disappearing as soon as the girls boarded the ship. If anything is missing, he knows where to find it. He has already retrieved dozens of items from their cabin. What the twins refer to as scavenging, he sees as nothing more than two little thieves hauling away anything that's not bolted down.

* * *

By the end of the day, Kwajalein Island appears just over the horizon. A small flat island with no impressive features. As they slowly approach the island, a few buildings and the flight tower are all that can be seen. The twins are not impressed at all. This island is nothing like their home. They are used to seeing their island towering so high into the clouds and the beaches lined with palm trees.

"We're home!" the captain announced. "We should be there in about an hour."

"Come on... We better go below and start packing!" Ben said, so relieved it was finally over. "Get all your things together. We're going to leave the boat in a while."

"We going to see Granny on that island?" April asked, getting so excited.

"Oh, no... She lives far from here. We're only going to stay here for a day or two. Then we're going to see your granny and granddad. They have a really big house. You're going to like it there. Oh, make sure you pack everything in the bag. Don't forget your book."

"You mean we get to keep it?" June asked.

Ben nods. "Sure! The captain said, you can have it."

The twins are so happy to get to keep their first book. They quickly store it in the bag with all their other things.

Jenny turns to Ben. "How long do you think we'll be staying?" getting a little concerned.

"Probably not too long... Maybe get the next flight out, which might be tomorrow or the next day. I'm not too sure how many flights they have here. They didn't say anything about it when I talked with them on the radio. But anyway, we'll be stopping by the hospital for a quick checkup. I think that's mostly for the children."

"That's not necessary. They are all healthy. Actually, we all are."

"Well, maybe they're concerned about the kids not being immunized," he explained. "They haven't had any of those kiddy diseases yet. Might be a little susceptible to colds and the flu as well.

Come to think of it, none of us has ever had a cold. Since we've been on the island, I have never been sick at all."

"Oh, that's right. None of us had ever been sick. I guess that's because of all the fresh food and the healthy environment."

He laughed. "We also haven't gone through one of those cold winters either!"

"That's one thing I haven't missed," she shudders, just thinking about the cold winter weather she used to live through.

Jenny and Ben are so glad to have reached Kwajalein Island with no problems. They first thought the catamaran had plenty of room, but it ended up being extremely confining, far worse than the cave. With so many people on board, they felt claustrophobic most of the time. Having to deal with so many different personalities didn't help their situation. They realize it will take a long time to get used to being around other people again. It's a sign of things to come.

* * *

Chapter 45

Kwajalein Island

At Walter and Mary's house, everyone is there to watch the big event on television. All are waiting with anticipation to see the live coverage of their son's arrival at Kwajalein. The news of Jenny and Ben coming home is in all the papers, on every news station, and it's a worldwide event. Even Ben's aunts, uncles, and cousins living in England are all watching it live as well.

Mary is in a tizzy, waiting to see her son for the first time in years. The 24-hour news channels have been covering it live for hours with nothing new to say. As they flip from one channel to another, Walter and Mary are astounded to hear how many different stories the news media has about their son and the island. Most of it is speculation, with all the so-called experts talking about what it takes to live on a small island in the middle of the Pacific.

The moment they have been waiting for is finally here. The first sight of the catamaran appears just above the horizon. Jumping up and down, the Hughes family are so excited to see the ship, even though it's far away. As the camera zooms in, showing the small ship, miles out to sea in full sail.

* * *

As the catamaran approaches the island, Ben is so shocked to see a vast crowd waiting for them. They were told there might be a few people out to greet them, but it looks as if everyone on the island is there. Things are bad enough having to deal with all these people on the ship, but this is far worse and something they don't need.

"OK, guys... Keep on my side. There are a lot of people here. Remember to keep an eye on Mom and Baby," Ben said, getting concerned.

"OK, Daddy!" they both said, grabbing their sticks, getting scared, seeing all the people on the pier.

"I don't know if I'm ready for this," Jenny said. "It's a shame we didn't arrive at night," getting nervous seeing all the people, especially the reporters.

He shakes his head, getting frustrated. "Too late now... We'll just keep together. Wayne told me that the military police are going to escort us through the crowd and straight to the hospital."

"What about all the news people? They're not going to be interviewing us, are they?" she asked.

"I'm not going to talk with them. It'll be best if we just ignore them."

"I hope the children don't get too scared, especially the girls," looking up at Ben, a little concerned.

"I'll keep them next to me. You hold Baby," knowing that she is getting scared about the girls attacking someone.

While the catamaran slowly approaches, several of the news crews run down the pier. The captain is concerned with all the chaos. He doesn't like the idea of all those people rushing up while he is trying to put the ship in. He radios the security to clear the area. Within a few minutes, the military police are pulling everyone behind the security rope. From the looks of things, everyone on the island is here, and it's going to be a big problem for the Hughes family to walk through the crowd.

* * *

Walter and Mary get excited as they watch the camera zoom in on all the people standing on the catamaran. Mary stares at the television, trying to get a glimpse of Ben and his family. Several people are moving about on the ship, but they can't make out who they are. Even the commentators talk among themselves, trying to figure out which ones are Ben, Jenny, and their children.

The reporters do not know how many people are on the catamaran. Since several do work on Kwajalein, no information has been released about the crew and the passengers. The security on the island is tight, but no one can control the live broadcasts. The only thing the people at Kwajalein can control is information, which is disseminated very sparingly.

The first ones off the catamaran are Bob and Margaret, closely followed by their children. Since no one knows who else is on the ship, the crowd goes into a frenzy. Many assume this is the family. The news commentators announce that this is Ben and Jenny walking off the ship.

"No, that can't be them!" Mary shouted, leaning forward to get a closer look.

Walter is shaking his head. "Those damn bastards don't know anything! Those kids must be at least twelve or thirteen! Our babies are only five years old."

Another family gets off the boat, but it's not Ben. Mary feels a little uneasy, thinking that maybe it's all a big mistake. Maybe it's not him. Minutes go by, and nothing is happening. Both Mary and Walter feel sick to their stomachs, and it's just too much to bear. Two men walk on the deck of the catamaran. The commentators are now at a loss as to what is happening. Now, they are guessing that this might be the lost family on the deck of the ship.

All eyes are glued to the television. Several people are talking together at the far end of the catamaran. Then, a woman wearing a large sun hat is carrying a baby and walks off the ship. A big applause comes from the crowd as the woman stands on the pier. Photographers and camera crews are jostling for better positions trying to get a clear shot of her from behind the security rope. The commentator is now indicating that this is indeed Jenny Mason.

"I wish they get it right!" Mary angrily shouted. "Everyone who gets off the boat is either Ben or that girl! Why don't they know anything?"

"Oh, these TV people don't know what the hell they're talking about!" Walter shouts, getting so frustrated. "Looks like there are a lot of people on that boat. He's got to be on there. That could be her," pointing to the television.

Sam leans forward. "My God! He's been stranded on that island with that woman! Man, what I'd give to be on a deserted island with her!"

"Sam... We're going to have a little talk when we get home," Vanessa said, glaring at her husband.

Sam cringes. "Oh, sorry... I was just... You know, thrilled for Ben," regretting that he was thinking out loud.

"That's probably your new sister-in-law you're gawking at!" Kelly added, also a little annoyed with her brother's comment, giving him a mean look.

"Hush up, you two!" Mary blurted out, and started crying. "If that is her, then that must be my little grandson! Oh, my God! Look at my little baby boy!"

Two little girls wearing big sun hats walk off the ship. They quickly stand behind their mother, both carrying their sticks. Another loud applause comes from the crowd. Right away, it's clear to everyone that these are the two little girls. All the cameras zoom in on the small family.

Mary cries again, seeing her little granddaughters for the first time. "That's got to be them! I know it is! Those are my little babies!" pointing to the television.

"I think it's them!" Walter said, trying to clear his eyes. "Look how tiny they are!"

"Awe, they're so cute!" Kelly yelled, the tears running down her cheek. "I can't wait to meet them! It's funny how they're all wearing those big sun hats! Look how the girls are standing at attention, holding those sticks. I wonder why they're doing that?"

All the cameras quickly turn back to the catamaran to several men talking together. The commentators are still guessing and have no idea who is who.

"Where is Ben?" Mary frantically asked, starting to panic. "Why is he taking so long? Where is my baby?"

"He's got to be there!" Walter said, trying to figure out which one was Ben.

"He can't be one of those guys," Sam added. "Maybe he's still on the boat?"

Two men walk off the catamaran. Everyone leans forward, staring closely at the television, but something is not right. Ben should be there.

"Check out that big, beautiful hunk!" Kelly said, pointing to the television. "Look at all the muscles on him! Oh, those skimpy shorts he's wearing too! I bet he's been sailing around the South Pacific for a few years to get a tan like that."

Sam looks a little closer. "That must be the crew. Why doesn't anyone say who these people are?" getting so frustrated.

"I don't think they know either," Walter explained.

No one knows who any of these men are that just stepped off the ship. Everyone intensely watches, trying to see which one is Ben. The man wearing an old beat-up Australian hat bends over, picking up the white duffel bag, throwing it over his shoulder. He almost knocks one of the other men off the pier, swinging the heavy bag around.

The camera keeps going back to the ship, looking for someone else. The newscasters are not even sure which one, or if any, is Ben Hughes. Everyone is still guessing, but no one can tell which one is Ben or if he is on the catamaran.

Suddenly, the man carrying the duffel bag walks down the pier with the woman holding the baby. The little girls quickly rush out in front, leading the way. A loud cheer comes from the crowd. The news crews are going mad trying to get closer. The commentators finally announce that this is indeed Ben Hughes.

"Oh, my God!" Mary yelled out. "That is Ben! It's Ben!" crying profusely, pointing at the television.

"It is Ben!" Sam shouted, so shocked, seeing how different he looked.

"I can't believe it!" Kelly shouted. "My God, he has changed so much! I didn't even recognize him!" realizing the big, beautiful hunk was her brother.

"Welcome home, son," Walter whispered, burying his face in his hands, weeping.

"It's time to celebrate!" Sam boasted, grabbing the Champaign bottle from the ice bucket.

* * *

After thanking the captain, Ben is ready to leave. Seeing the vast crowd yelling and screaming out loud, he is a little hesitant. It's the one thing they don't need. Unfortunately, they have no choice in the matter. As they slowly approach the crowd, the twins are getting scared. Already in their protective mode, they walk in front, taking their defensive stances, and waving their sticks. Ben is trying to explain that these are friendly people, but it doesn't help. He is also so overwhelmed by all these people, especially with everyone yelling out loud.

The photographers and camera crews are scrambling to get the best shot. Reporters hold out their microphones, yelling out questions. Ben knows this is a big mistake, seeing all the chaos. He wanted to arrive anonymously without all the commotion, at least for the children's sake.

As Jenny and Ben approach the crowd, the military police push their way into the crowd. The police take control, pushing everyone back to make a clear path to walk through. Ben hesitates at first, but they wave him on to follow.

Instead of making things better, the police make it worse by having them walk through the middle of this huge crowd. On both sides are reporters and curious onlookers from the base. Since there is not enough room to walk together, reluctantly, Ben and his family have to walk right behind each other. He is now having second thoughts about all of this.

Jenny takes the lead, carrying Baby. Ben thinks it best to be in the middle so he can keep his eye on both Jenny and the twins right behind him. They cautiously and slowly walk down the middle of the huge crowd.

The reporters are yelling out questions, trying to get this family to look at the cameras. Ben ignores all the questions but keeps his eyes on each one of these strangers.

The twins walk with their backs to each other, constantly waving their sticks back and forth at all the land sharks. They keep as close as possible to their father, always signaling to each other.

One photographer kneels right next to June to take a photo. He makes the mistake of grabbing her arm to get her to face the camera. She immediately lets out a high-pitched scream. She swings her stick around, whacking him on the side of his head. The man is almost knocked unconscious, falling flat on his back. Both the girls quickly pounce on him, hitting him with their sticks. The man cowards away, trying to block the blows with his arm.

Ben quickly turns, hearing all the commotion. Before he can do anything, the twins attack the poor man. He whistles a signal for them to back off. The twins stop, standing next to their father. They point their sticks at the frightened photographer, waiting for the next signal.

June is furious. "Daddy, that land shark grabbed my arm!" ready to pounce on the man.

April starts waving her stick at him. "Bad land shark! You go back in the water! Bad land shark!"

"He sure looks scrawny!" June shouted, looking up at her father. "Let's throw him back in the water! Let the fish have him for supper!"

Ben laughed. "I'll take care of him. You two go and protect Baby."

"Bad land shark! You bad!" the twins constantly yelled out, slowly backing away from the man on the ground, waving their sticks at him.

Seeing all the land sharks getting too close, the twins swing their sticks at them. They stand back to back, moving in a circle, signaling each other. Slowly, they push back the crowd, waving their sticks aggressively as they make their way back to their mother.

"You OK?" Ben asked the photographer, still sprawled on the ground. "They didn't hurt you, did they?"

"You should keep those brats on a leash!" the man yelled, trying to get up on his feet.

Ben grabs the photographer by the neck with one hand. With no effort, Ben picks him up off the ground, holding him up high. Gasping for air, the man struggles to get free, his feet dangling in midair.

Ben looks him right in the eye. "That's not a nice thing to say about my babies, now was it?" glaring at the man.

The photographer is scared to death, gasping for air. Ben's hand is so tight around the man's neck that his face is turning blue. The man panics, about to faint from the lack of oxygen. Ben quickly drops him to the ground after seeing his face turning blue. The military police rush over, grab the photographer by the arms, and promptly pull him away.

"I guess next time you'll think twice about messing with my babies," Ben said in a slow, calm voice.

The photographer is terrified. He keeps apologizing as the military police quickly haul him away. It's what the police feared the most. They knew the press would be a problem. Even after telling all the reporters not to disturb the Hughes family, they still do it anyway, constantly yelling out questions, all wanting interviews.

* * *

Ben's family is stunned, watching it all on television. Seeing the little girls beating the photographer with their sticks is something they don't expect to see from little five-year-old girls.

"I'm glad they'll be staying here with you guys," Sam jokingly said, looking over at his mother.

"They do look like they're a little on the wild side," Mary said, a little shocked, glancing over at her husband.

"I would have done the same," Walter replied. "It's about time someone put those damn reporters in their place!"

"Did you see the way Ben just picked that man up off the ground like it was nothing?" Kelly blurted out. "Jesus, the size of his arms! They're huge! I bet you ain't going to be picking on him anymore," looking over at her brother.

"No shit!" Sam jokingly said. "He's changed a lot... Damn, he looks like Hercules with all those muscles," shaking his head in disbelief.

Sam stares at the television in shock, seeing a totally different person than what he once knew long ago. The out-of-shape brother, who never exercised a day in his life, now looks like a professional wrestler with massive muscles.

He cringes, thinking about all those days as kids teasing and tormenting his little brother. They always used to wrestle around when they were young. He was really big on wrestling, and Ben always got the worst of it since he was really skinny. Now that the tides had turned, Sam hoped his brother had forgotten all about those days so long ago.

* * *

Jenny stops, looking back through the crowd for Ben. Seeing the twins back-to-back circling each other, she knows it's not good. Something is wrong, and she tries to decipher all the signs to see what is going on. All she can read is land shark, attack, and protect Baby. She knows right away that they are not making a good first impression.

"Where is your father?" she asked the twins.

"That bad land shark grabbed me!" June yelled out, pointing back towards the crowd.

"This is not a good situation, Momma! Can we go home now?" April asked, waiting for their father.

"It's OK... They're not bad people. They're just happy to see you," Jenny explained, seeing they are a little overwhelmed with all the commotion going on around them.

When Ben walks through the crowd, everyone quickly gets out of the way. Seeing how he handled the photographer, now no one wants to get too close to him. The military police are right behind, making sure nothing else goes wrong.

"Ready to go?" Ben asked as he caught up with Jenny and the children.

"What's going on back there?" Jenny asked.

"Someone made a mistake touching June's arm," he simply explained.

June is looking back through the crowd. "Yeah! Daddy going to feed him to the fishies! Bad land shark! Bad land shark!"

Ben knows the girls are getting terrified. "You two take the lead! Protect Baby!" hoping it will keep them busy getting their minds off things.

The twins don't question their father. They quickly move to the other side of their mother, swinging their sticks back and forth at the crowd. They slowly push everyone back out of the way as they make their way forward. Even the military police are keeping their distance from the two girls.

The twins suddenly notice a man kneeling down, holding a video camera. Curiosity gets the best of them. This strange gadget the man has on his shoulder is something they have never seen before. The little flashing lights and the big glass lens in front are a big mystery as well.

"What's that thing, Daddy?" April asked, pointing to the camera.

He looks down at the big video camera with CNN on the side. "It's like one of those telephone things you saw back home. Your granny will probably be able to hear you and see you, too. It'll be like you being on that TV thing they had on the boat."

The twins slowly approach the camera, look into the lens, and start waving. "Hi, Granny! We coming to visit!"

"Daddy, I don't hear her," June said after a few seconds.

"Is this live?" Ben asked the cameraman. "Are they seeing this at home now?"

The cameraman nods. "Yes, sir... It's live."

"Oh, that's even better," Ben explained. "You can tell Granny what you want," hoping his family at home is watching.

"Granny!" the twins shouted. "We coming to visit and have Sunday dinner too. We want shepherd's pie, gravy, baked potatoes, batter pudding, green peas, strawberry jam, and treacle pudding for afters. Then we have a cup of tea!"

"Yep, and a cup of tea!" April added, nodding her head up and down.

"Aren't you two forgetting something?" Ben asked them.

"Oh yeah, Pepsi!" April added after thinking about it for a few seconds.

"Yeah, we need plenty of Pepsi! We like the Pepsi drink a lot!" June boasted, with a big smile on her face.

* * *

"Hello, my babies!" Mary said, waving back at the television, so glad to see them now as inquisitive little girls.

"Oh, look at them!" Walter blurted out, seeing the faces right up close to the camera.

"They're my babies!" Mary proudly said, so stunned, hearing how they described the Sunday dinner she used to make Ben years ago. "I'm going to cook you the best Sunday dinner ever!" talking to the girls as if they were in the room with her.

"You better cook a big meal," Walter jokingly said. "I bet Ben can really eat from the looks of him now!"

"You're right!" Mary replied, not catching on that he was joking. "We need to get to the store and get some more food. I got a lot of cooking to do!"

The phone rings. Mary quickly answers, knowing it's her sister who is calling again. Her family in England is also watching the big event live on television. They were also surprised to hear what the girls wanted for their first supper. Everyone feels better knowing that Ben still has his sense of humor, since it's typical for Ben to teach them something like that. They are already making plans to come over to America to meet Ben and his new family.

* * *

One of the military police approaches Jenny. "Excuse me, mam, but we need to keep moving," waving them on.

"Sorry... Come on, girls. We have to go," Jenny said, ushering them on, wanting to get away from this crowd.

The twins had one last wave to the camera. They immediately take their positions in front of their mother, waving their sticks back and forth, keeping everyone at a distance. The military police are now surrounding the family. By blocking everyone else from leaving the pier, they now have control of the situation.

At the end of the pier, the medics are patiently waiting. They are not too sure about the health status of this family. Many were expecting to have to carry these people off the ship on stretchers. From past experiences, most people found drifting out on the ocean or washed up on some small island were always in the same condition, extremely weak from exposure to the elements, and malnourished. This family is neither. All look extremely healthy and well-fed. Many still doubt that these are actually the people whom they are claiming to be.

After the episode with one photographer, more military police are called in, and Ben is now their major concern. Seeing how he could pick up a grown man by the throat with little effort is making them nervous. They don't want anything else to happen before they get this family to the infirmary.

The military police can finally separate the press and onlookers from the family. The military police and even the medics are smart enough to keep their distance. They had been warned that this family might be a little on the wild side, and now they had seen it with their own eyes. With the little girls not hesitating to attack an adult, they now believe all the stories they heard. No one wants to see what Ben is capable of doing if things get out of hand.

Once separated from the crowds and noise, Jenny and Ben are so relieved. The twins keep to their mother's side to help protect their brother, always swinging their sticks, keeping everyone at bay. It is such an alien world to them with so many strange things they have never seen before. If it were not for all the land sharks, they would love to explore this new world.

At the end of the pier, four people wearing white coats wait next to the ambulance. The military police stop, forming a large circle around the family. Ben doesn't like this at all. He keeps an eye on everyone of them. The military police are irritating him, but at least they are smart enough to keep their distance.

A tall man wearing a white coat with medical insignias on his lapels walks cautiously forward. When he approaches, the two little girls immediately point their sticks at him, ready to attack. Seeing this firsthand, he knows right away he is going to have problems with this family. Obviously, they don't trust other people and have been isolated for far too long.

"Are there any immediate medical needs that you or your family have?" the man in the white coat asked, making sure not to get too close to the girls and their pointed sticks.

"No, we're fine," Jenny replied.

"We have an ambulance waiting to take you and your family to the infirmary," keeping a close eye on Ben, seeing he is definitely an overprotective father.

"Ah, we don't mind walking," Jenny said, thinking twice about getting the children in an ambulance.

"Yeah, we'll walk," Ben added.

"We already have it here. So we might as well use it. The infirmary is quite a distance from here anyway," a man said, standing next to the ambulance, noticing how this family does not like to be told what to do.

"I don't know... What do you think?" Jenny asked, looking over at Ben, a little concerned.

"I'll keep an eye on the girls," Ben said, knowing what that look meant.

"Is this really necessary?" Jenny asked, walking up to the big ambulance. "We don't really need this. We're all fine. You shouldn't waste it on us."

"It's just for the ride," the nurse explained, waiting by the ambulance door. "We weren't too sure about your condition, so we thought we should be prepared just in case."

"You should wear a hat when you're out in the sun," June bluntly said, looking up at the nurse, puzzled. "You got a bad sunburn!"

Even April is staring at the nurse as well. "Daddy, how come she so dark?" April asked, tugging on her father's shirt. "Does she got a bad sunburn?"

Ben realizes it's the first time they have seen an African American. "Oh, no, I don't think so... She's from another island," keeping the explanation simple.

"I guess you two haven't seen any Black people before?" the nurse asked, with a big smile on her face.

"No, we only see Mommy, and Daddy, and Baby!" the twins replied.

The nurse laughed out loud. "Wow, stereo!" hearing the girls talk simultaneously.

"You talk funny, too!" April shouted, hearing the southern drawl.

"April, be nice," Jenny quickly said.

"Oh, it's all right, mam," the nurse explained. "Well, you see... In Alabama, we all talk this way. My name is Nurse Able. I'll be taking care of you while you're staying with us," holding out her hand.

Seeing how the little girls are so confused, the nurse leans over, shaking their tiny hands. "It's so nice to meet you all! Welcome to our island!"

The twins don't know what to make of this land shark. They had never seen anything like her before. Not only is she really dark, but she is also the biggest one they have ever seen.

"Does it hurt?" April asked. "You want some coconut oil?" still really curious, examining the nurse's hand.

"Does what hurt?" the nurse asked.

"Your hand!" April said, pointing to it.

"Oh no, it doesn't hurt," she replied, seeing the two girls examining the top of her hand. "I was born this way. I have dark-colored skin, and so does everyone else where we live. This is the way we are."

Both Jenny and Ben are glad to see the girls being friendly with this nurse. Not only are they not scared, but both are so enthralled with this new discovery that people look different.

They all step into the ambulance with Nurse Able. The twins immediately take to the nurse, wanting to sit right next to her, talking with her all the way to the hospital. They are so busy asking the nurse all sorts of questions that the twins don't even notice that this is their first ride in a car.

Jenny is so glad to see the girls making friends and not seeing everyone as land sharks. Their curiosity is a good thing, getting their minds off all the commotion that is going on around them. At least it's almost over, and they only had one bad incident so far. Now, she can start thinking about getting home to see her family and Ben's family as well.

* * *

Chapter 46

Hospital

The trip to the hospital is a short one, lasting only a few minutes. As soon as the ambulance stops, the rear door quickly opens. Ben is the first to jump out, a little surprised but also glad to see only one hospital attendant holding the door open. He is expecting more of what was out at the pier packed with people and reporters, but luckily, no one else is here.

Nurse Able steps out, helping with the twins. The twins gasp out loud, seeing the huge building, wondering how it all got here. Jenny is the last one out of the ambulance. She is holding Baby, who does not care about any of this. He is too tired, ready for a nap. Once everyone is out of the ambulance, the rest of the military police arrives, including the medics. They are all watching this family closely, not knowing what to expect.

Ben quickly realizes these people do not have a clue about their condition. Seeing all the orderlies standing next to the stretchers and wheelchairs, he knows it's all for them. He always hates hospitals and doctors and wants to get this over with as quickly as possible so they can get back home. The children are the only ones needing a good checkup. As far as Ben is concerned, he is in the best shape ever.

Even Jenny doesn't care for the hospital visit. They are all in great shape and ready to move on to see their families. She doesn't like the way everyone keeps circling them. What makes it worse is all the armed military police. It's not a pleasant welcome, and she knows it's agitating Ben and the girls.

"OK, this way," Nurse Able said. "We're almost there… We got a private room for your family. So, you won't be bothered by anyone while y'all be staying with us," escorting the family to the main lobby.

"Oh, thank you! That will be nice, but wouldn't it be better if we stayed in a hotel?" Jenny quickly replied, not used to hearing the Southern accent.

The nurse laughed. "From what I hear, you've been through a horrible ordeal out there. That's why you're checking in here first. Besides, the hotel is all booked up with all the news media. At least here, they won't be bothering you."

"I didn't think about that... That's the last thing we need right now. There were way too many people out there waiting for us. All we want now is to sit back and relax after two days out on the ocean in that boat."

Upon entering the hospital, the family gets their first taste of the civilized world, air conditioning.

April is the first to complain. "It's cold, Daddy! I don't like it here!"

"Awe, this feels great!" Nurse Able said. "I'm so glad to get out of the heat. It's so nice and cool in here. Don't you think?"

"It does feel a bit cold," Ben said, so uncomfortable in the cold, dry building.

"Well, no wonder," the nurse replied. "Look at what you're wearing! Don't worry... I'll get y'all some new clothes once we get you checked in," noticing how everyone is shivering.

"Thank you!" Jenny replied, so glad to be getting new clothes. "That will be nice. We can use some extra things to wear since this is all we got," feeling a little awkward with everyone else wearing regular clothes.

Except for three men, the lobby is deserted. One is apparently a doctor, but the other two are large, burly orderlies wearing blue medical smocks. Nurse Able escorts the family over to the three men.

One of the men walks up, introducing himself. "Welcome! I'm Dr. White. I'll be your physician during your stay here," holding his hand out to Ben.

"Hello," Ben replied, a little hesitant, reaching up, shaking the man's hand, but keeping a close eye on the two orderlies standing right behind the doctor.

Dr. White can see right away all the antisocial signs of living in total isolation. Especially for Ben, who is always standing between his family and anyone else. Even the little girls are wild, always wielding sticks around at people. From the communications with the captain bringing them in, this is what they were expecting.

What makes the situation worse is Ben and his obvious overprotective stance. After viewing the incident with the cameraman on the surveillance video, they cleared all the personnel and other patients from the lobby and corridors. They don't want any more problems or anyone getting hurt.

Dr. White turns to Jenny. "Is there anything that you or the children need?" making sure not to get too close.

"No, not really," she said, shaking her head. "Maybe a blanket for Baby. It's a little cold in here, and it's time for his nap," still shivering from the cold.

"Oh, sorry," Dr. White said. "Let's get things moving then," motioning them down the long corridor.

"Our first stop will be the exam room. We'll get everyone a full physical—"

"Why?" Ben interrupts the doctor, giving him a stern look.

Dr. White is a little shocked by his abrupt response. "Well, we would like to get you and your family checked out first. We got the full staff here ready in the ER, and they are in there waiting. You've been out there for a long time. You're going to need some medical attention. That's why you're here and not at the hotel."

"We are OK," Ben said, shaking his head. "Just a little tired from the trip."

"We would like to settle in first," Jenny added. "It would be nice for the children to take a nap and rest up. It's a little too much for one day. Maybe a change of clothes is our only priority right now."

Dr. White stops and gives them a quick look over. "Sorry, we were expecting you to be a little malnourished. You do look as if you've all eaten well. We were ready to carry you all in on stretchers. I got the staff ready to put you in the emergency room as soon as you arrived."

"No thanks," Ben replied. "No need to bother with all that. We're just cold and tired!"

"It's up to you," the doctor said, seeing they're not that eager for any medical treatment.

"Oh, we don't need to be in an emergency room," Jenny said. "It's a little too much for all of us at the moment. Maybe we can have the children looked at after we settle in."

Nurse Able turns to Dr. White. "Shall I take them to their room?"

Continuing down the hall, Dr. White agreed. "That's fine... We'll let you get settled in first. You can get freshened up. We'll set you up with some new clothes," noticing the rags everyone is wearing, and all are shivering, not used to the cold air conditioning.

"That will be great!" Jenny said, feeling worn out from the trip.

The twins are so amazed by all the lights and the pictures covering the walls. "This is lots bigger than our cave! But it's too cold in here! I don't like it!" June shouted.

"Daddy, can we start a fire?" April asked. "We'll need to make a real big one to warm this cave!"

Nurse Able is shocked to hear that. "Oh no, you don't! Fires aren't allowed in the infirmary."

"You need a fire to warm up!" April shouted out, a little confused. "We always have a fire in our cave, right, Daddy!"

"I'll adjust the temperature in your room to make it more comfortable for you," the nurse explained.

April wouldn't let up about starting a fire. "We always have a campfire. You got to have a fire to cook food and to warm up the water," waving her hands up in the air, getting a little agitated.

"Let's wait until we get to the room," Jenny said. "It might be a little warmer in there."

"Mom, what's a room?" June asked.

"It's like a cave... Like the one we had on the boat," Ben explained, knowing full well, the questions were going to be nonstop.

"How come they got all those lights on?" June excitedly asked. "They wasting the batteries!" looking down the long hallway.

"Yeah! Where do they get all those lights from, anyway? They got way too many. We need to take some and put them in our cave! They need to share some of these lights, right, Daddy?" April added, looking forward to a little scavenging trip to bring it all back home.

"You're missing all the pretty pictures on the wall," Jenny said, knowing all these questions would not end. "Look, there's one with a big pink flower," pointing to one of the many paintings.

April and June are in their element with a new place to explore. The long hallway echoes their voices as they continue with their never-ending questions. Their little squeaky voices are getting louder and louder.

Seeing they are getting out of control, Ben gives the hand sign to be quiet and listen. Right away, the twins are silent, slowly moving their heads from side to side, trying to pick up any sounds of intruders. In their stealth mode, they are on the search for monsters, or worse, land sharks. With spears in hand, they are ready to pounce.

Dr. White quickly notices the change in the girl's behavior. He didn't believe all the stories from the captain. Now, he sees it firsthand. The subtle hand signal from the father and the little girl's personality changed so quickly. Instead of talkative, inquisitive little girls, now they are stealthy Amazon warriors on a mission. He knows right then that there is no way he can let this family out in public until they have time to acclimate. This family definitely needs some counseling sessions before they can leave the base.

The cold is not the only thing Ben doesn't feel comfortable with in this place. While walking with Nurse Able and Dr. White, two orderlies are right behind them. He makes sure that Jenny and the twins walk ahead, keeping himself between them and the orderlies.

The two orderlies are really bothering him. These two never speak and always keep their eyes on Ben the entire time. From looking at their posture and mannerisms, they are a threat, and he is their target. He makes sure these two don't get too close to his family.

At the end of the hallway, Dr. White motions them to an open door. "Here we are... You'll be in room 105 during your stay here. We thought it would be better to keep you down here away from all the other patients, to give you a little privacy."

"Thank you! This will be great," Jenny said, seeing the huge room.

The room is a little more than what they were expecting. It looks more like a hotel room than a hospital room with two full-size beds, a small table, chairs, a chest of drawers, and even a baby crib. The twins are so excited to see it filled with so many new things, and it's better than the one they had on the catamaran.

"We'll leave you alone for a while," Nurse Able said, "so you can unpack and settle in. There is some fruit on the table if you get hungry."

The twins run to the big bowl on the table. They are astounded by all the strange new fruit and the biggest bananas they have ever seen.

"Nurse Able will be your nurse during your stay here," Dr. White explained. "So, if you need anything, just let her know. Nurse, they're all yours," then promptly leaves the room.

The nurse stands at the door holding up a tape measure. "Oh, before I leave, I need to get your measurements so I can get you all some new clothes," noticing that she is being ignored.

"Thank you, but no... We're fine," Ben mumbled, too busy looking over the room with the girls.

The nurse gives Ben a mean look. "I have been told to get you and your family suited up with some clothes. You can't go around in all those old rags you are wearing. Besides, like you said, it's cold! I'm going to get y'all some nice new warm clothes."

Jenny hands Baby over to Ben, holding out her arms. "OK, you can start with me."

Nurse Able is not the kind of person to be pushed around and always gets her way. That is one of the reasons she is assigned to this family. Ben notices she is not intimidated at all. She stands her ground and lets it be known who is in charge around here. The twins pick up on that right away and really like this land shark.

After all the measuring is done, the nurse leaves the room, leaving them alone for the first time. The twins immediately start snooping around. They methodically inspect everything, seeing how it's made, feeling all the new textures with their hands. The chest of drawers is a big discovery, such a convenient place to store away all their things.

"Look!" the twins yelled out, discovering the bathroom. "They got one of those potties, and it's got that nice bum paper, too," pointing to the toilet paper roll.

They rush over, standing next to the toilet, constantly flushing it to see the water rush away, then slowly fill up again. Something that no one else would have noticed is a really big event. Even for Jenny and Ben, it's a novelty, but most of all, for the first time, they have their very own bathroom.

Jenny gasps, seeing the bathtub. "Oh, finally! It's going to be so nice to soak in a bathtub after all this time!"

Ben stands at the bathroom door, so impressed with it all. "I guess you're first!" turning on the water.

The novelty of water on demand is just extraordinary. The children all stand watching in astonishment as the clear, hot water fills the bathtub. Having so many places to get water without having to walk all the way down the beach, it's almost like magic.

"OK, listen up," Jenny quickly explained, with June constantly flushing the toilet. "No more wasting water, so stop playing with the potty. We're going to have some new rules here. Just like at home, there are things here that can hurt you. Here, we don't have to boil the water. It just comes out of those taps. All you have to do is turn this, and hot water comes out. So you need to be careful and let us do it because you can burn yourselves. Don't let Baby touch these either, and especially do not let him in here by himself. That's very important!"

"OK, Mom!" the twins replied.

"Come on, guys!" Ben said. "Let Mom have her bath alone."

"Thanks! I won't be long," Jenny said, quickly stripping off her clothes, slipping into the water for her first hot bath in years.

"No!" June cried out, seeing her mother getting into the bathtub. "We want a bath too! Can't we all get in? Plenty of room in there."

"No, it's Mom's turn first... You guys will have your turn later. Come on... We still have to look around. There are so many things we haven't seen yet," dragging them all out of the bathroom.

He walks over to the window, opens the blinds, feeling a little claustrophobic. Their room is at the end of the hospital, with a small garden area just outside. It's a typical military-designed structure from the Cold War days, or maybe from World War Two.

"Now, this feels more like it!" Ben said, opening the door, stepping outside into the warm air.

Baby can't wait, running out onto the manicured green grass and rolling on it. He waves to his sisters to come out and play with him.

June runs outside. "This is way better out here! I don't like that cold place. Let's make camp out here, Daddy."

"I don't know... That room has some nice soft beds, just like the ones on the boat. Shame the view isn't much to look at," Ben mentioned, looking at the two-story building that surrounds them on three sides.

"They got no beach here," April said, a little disappointed. "Can't even hear the waves. Can we find a better place to camp?"

He chuckled. "Baby seems to like it out here. Maybe we'll let Mom rest up for a day or two. What do you think?"

June nods. "Yeah, maybe a day or two. We can explore around and look for a better place on the beach."

"Sounds like a good idea to me," he replied, not wanting to tell them the truth.

They walk around the area, exploring the well-kept formal garden. Small trees are scattered about the area and provide little shade.

Flower gardens surround the entire area, filled with an abundance of tropical flowers.

The soft grass is another new experience for the girls. The twins are having fun running about, out chasing their little brother, rolling around on the grass, wrestling with each other.

"This is so nice and soft!" June said. "Can we sleep out here?"

"Maybe a little later... Let's go back in and put Baby to bed. Looks like he's ready for a nap," seeing he is already lying on his back, sucking his thumb, looking up at the sky.

April frowned. "No! We want to stay out and look around!"

"We like it out here," June said, not wanting to go back to the room either. "We want to explore!"

"We'll have plenty of time for that later. We don't know what else is around here. It's been a long trip, and we need to rest up. Remember, that nurse is going to get us some new clothes, and we haven't checked out the room yet," surprised by their outburst and the first time they have ever disobeyed him.

"What about the chores!" April said, getting mad. "We haven't got any firewood yet! We still have to get the fruit. There are no big trees around here! Where are all the fruit trees?" looking about the small garden.

"Yeah, we got lots of work to do," June said. "We need to get some food for supper. Where do they keep their trees, and where do we catch some fish?" getting a little concerned.

"It'll be like on the boat where they had all the food stored away. I bet you this place has one of those cooking stoves, too. So don't worry about the food. I think they got that all under control. Anyway, we're on a big adventure, so we don't worry about things like that. Besides, we already got a bowl of fruit in the room. We didn't even have to walk up over the island to get it!"

"OK, Daddy," they replied, a little confused, but then started chasing each other around in the garden again.

The twins are so excited about all their new surroundings but love being outside the most. They reluctantly return to the room to explore and see what other new things they can find.

Ben puts Baby in the crib, covering him with a soft yellow blanket. "This is Baby's new bed. He won't be able to climb out of this one."

"This wood is so smooth," April said, examining the crib to see how it's made. "Feel how soft the blanket is!"

"This is really soft!" June added, running her hands over the blanket.

"Now, keep it down... Baby needs a nap. It's been a long day," Ben said, seeing how the girls are still so excited about everything.

"Hey, what about your book?" he asked. "Why don't you sit down on the bed and read it," trying to keep them occupied.

"Yeah! We can look at our book again!" they both yelled out, rummaging through the duffel bag.

"Shh, let's keep it down," seeing how their voices echo throughout the room.

The twins jump up on the bed, so happy with their book. Ben wishes they had a few more, knowing it'll keep them quiet and occupied for a long time.

Back home, they had plenty to do to keep busy. Now, the twins have so much time on their hands, but unfortunately, there's not enough time for them to adjust. He wishes they could have stayed on the island a little longer to prepare them for all of this.

* * *

Chapter 47

Old Friend

Ben finally gets the children to calm down. He lies on the bed, ready for a nap, so tired since he couldn't sleep on the catamaran. Baby is sound asleep. The twins are so enthralled with their book. Everything is so quiet, just like the days back on the island.

Just as Ben closes his eyes, there is a knock at the door. He doesn't like the idea of not being able to see or hear other people approaching. He knows it's probably the doctor or nurse wanting to drag them off for some medical exams.

"Stay with Baby," he promptly told the twins.

Slowly opening the door, a strange man and a woman stand in the hallway. "Yes?" Ben abruptly asked.

The man at the door holds out his hand. "Hello, Mr. Hughes. I'm Dr. Miles, the administrator here at the infirmary."

Ben doesn't say a word, just stares at the man. He is already irritated with these hospital people but eventually shakes his hand.

"May we come in?" the doctor asked.

"Sure," Ben said, feeling awkward, not used to having guests dropping by.

"Oh, sorry, may I introduce Mrs. Burns," Dr. Miles said. "I don't know if you remember her."

Ben looks at her closely. "Well, hi! It's been a long time," recognizing her from their days in Hawaii.

"I'm so sorry... I'm so sorry," Mrs. Burns cried out, then burst into tears, hugging Ben.

The twins abruptly come from behind the door, pointing their sticks at the two land sharks. Seeing this woman grabbing their father, they are not too sure if she is attacking him or what.

"It's OK... Sit on the bed and read your book. Just keep an eye on Baby."

April and June know what the term means. They are to keep close to their little brother and watch these two who just entered the room. This is their cave, and no one else is supposed to be here. There are too many land sharks around, and the twins don't like it at all. They slowly back off, always keeping eye contact with these two. Once they climb onto the far bed, they look through the book again without a care in the world.

Dr. Miles is so amazed at these two little girls. He had heard all the stories but wanted to see it for himself. He already knows he is going to have a big problem with this family.

"They're so precious!" Mrs. Burns said, looking over at the girls. "I can't believe you had a family out there!"

"We couldn't either at first, but it worked out OK... I wouldn't have had it any other way."

"I want to personally welcome you here," Dr. Miles said. "We're in the process of getting all your paperwork started. As you probably know, we're going to start the physicals in the morning for you, Jenny, and the kids. Are there any immediate issues that we need to know about?"

"No, actually, I think we're all fine," Ben said after thinking about it. "For myself, I have never been healthier."

"I can see that! As you know, we were ready to put you all in intensive care when we got the call. So it'll be just a basic checkup, but the kids will probably need a good exam and all the standard inoculations."

"That's one of the things we were concerned about," Ben explained. "I can tell you now... The kids won't like it one bit. Oh, the captain mentioned that you guys don't believe that we are actually Jenny and Ben, plus a few extra ones. Are you going to be checking our fingerprints or something?"

"That's why I'm here!" Mrs. Burns said. "I told them that I would know right away if I met you myself!"

The doctor nods. "That's right... It was quicker to fly her out here to speed things up. Once she heard about you two, she was already packed anyway. It can take a couple of days just to dig up all the paperwork for your fingerprints, so at least now we have verified your identities. It'll help with the security issues, plus we can get the process started right away."

Mrs. Burns hugs him again. "Oh, Ben... I'm so glad you're here. It's so sad everyone else is gone," then she cries again.

"It's OK... It's OK," he replied, not knowing what to say.

* * *

Hearing strange voices and someone crying, Jenny quickly gets out of the bathtub, grabbing a towel. "I see we have company," she said, seeing two people talking with Ben.

"Oh, Jenny," Ben said. "This is Dr. Miles. He's the administrator here."

"It's a pleasure to meet you," Dr. Miles said, a little startled seeing Jenny walking out of the bathroom, drying her hair with nothing on. "I'd like to welcome you here, and I hope you find everything to your liking," trying hard to keep eye contact with her.

"Oops, let me put something on," Jenny blurted out, quickly rushing back into the bathroom for her T-shirt.

"We're not used to having visitors," Ben explained, getting frustrated.

Jenny comes back out. "Sorry, it's so nice to meet you," waving at their guests.

"You don't remember me?" Mrs. Burns asked, surprised to see how much Jenny had changed.

Jenny takes a second look at the woman. "I'm so sorry! I didn't recognize you. Mrs. Burns, what are you doing way out here?"

Mrs. Burns cautiously walks over to Jenny, seeing she is still a little apprehensive. She cries again and gives Jenny a big hug.

"I had to see you again... It was such a horrible ordeal. I always thought it was my fault for getting you on that flight," Mrs. Burns whispered.

"No, it's not your fault... It's just something that happened, but we all made it OK. We're here now and doing fine," trying to console her.

With Mrs. Burns hugging their mother, it gets the twins' attention again. They both grab their sticks, looking over to their father for a sign.

Ben notices the twins getting ready to pounce. He quickly gives the hand sign that everything is OK. They go back to their book but keep a constant eye on these land sharks just in case.

While Mrs. Burns talks with Jenny, Dr. Miles hands Ben some papers. "This is some of the information about the infirmary. Here are some maps of the base. Also, there are some things you can and can not do while on the island. It might be best to stay here for now, but once we get through all the exams, feel free to look around the island. If there is anything you need, just let us know."

"Oh, there is one thing. How do we use this phone?" Ben asked. "I promised to call home as soon as we got here."

"It's a little complicated from the rooms here," Dr. Miles replied. "You'll have to go through all the switchboards to get through to the mainland. Just follow the instructions in the folder. Talk as long as you want, and don't worry about the bill. It's all taken care of."

Ben laughed. "Well, that's good to know since I lost my wallet."

"Out here, you don't need to worry about money. Although it might take a while to get you back in the system again when you get back home. The two of you have been deceased for more than six years. That's going to take a while to fix."

Nurse Able knocks on the door, slowly entering the room with a handful of clothes. The twins lit up, waving at the nurse.

"Look! We have a picture book," June holds it up to show her.

"That looks like a really nice book you have there," Nurse Able said. "I also got y'all something nice too. New clothes for everyone!" placing everything on the bed.

"Well, it was nice to meet you all," Dr. Miles said. "We'll leave you with the nurse so she can get you set up."

"It was nice meeting you," Jenny said as the doctor left the room.

"I'll talk to you later once you are settled in," Mrs. Burns said. "There is so much I want to hear about how you were able to live there for so long."

"We'll get together later," Ben said. "It's good to see you again," then Nurse Able ushers them out of the room.

Before leaving the room, Mrs. Burns stands at the door, looking at the twins still sitting on the bed. They are so cute, and she wanted so much to go over and hug them. She saw how they acted when she entered the room and knew they were not used to being around other people. The staff also warned her not to approach the children and to ignore them.

Right away, she noticed that neither Jenny nor Ben had introduced her to the children. She also saw how Ben was always between her and the children the entire time they were in the room, and he was not comfortable around other people. She feels so sad knowing it's all her fault because she was the one who got them on that fateful flight.

"OK, there are two sets of everything here," the nurse said once everyone else was out of the room. "We do have a couple of stores here, so if you need anything else, this will get you started."

"Oh, this one looks nice," Jenny said, picking up one of the colorful flower shirts. "It's silk, isn't it?"

"I think it is, but that's a man's shirt," Nurse Able explained. "I picked that one out myself just for you," glancing over at Ben.

Jenny laughed. "You got to put this on! You'll look great wearing a Hawaiian shirt!" teasing him.

He takes the shirt, thinking twice about it. "I kind of like the one you made me."

"Nope... We're going to be wearing nice new clothes from here on out. Try it on," Jenny said, knowing how stubborn he can be about his clothes.

"That's all the craze nowadays," Nurse Able said, giggling. "Big flowery Hawaiian shirts!"

Even the twins are teasing their father, seeing the gaudy shirt. "Looks real pretty, Daddy!" knowing he doesn't care for it too much.

Ben knows there is no fighting it. They are all against him. He takes off his shirt to try on his new clothes. Right away, the nurse notices the knife handle sticking out of his shorts. He also has a rope over his shoulder going around his back.

She has a bad feeling about this. "I hope that isn't what I think it is," the nurse said.

He looks down, realizing he has forgotten about the knife. "It's nothing... We just use it for sharpening our fishing spears."

"Ben, put it in the drawer over there," Jenny said, "so the children don't mess with it," knowing the nurse was getting concerned.

"OK," he mumbled, seeing the nurse meant business, then pulled out the knife from the sheath sewn into his pants.

Now, the nurse understands what the rope over his shoulder is for when he turns around. She is so stunned, seeing he has another extremely large knife tied to his back, also stored in a protective sheath. He is heavily armed, and no one knew anything about it. She is so glad that the security people didn't search him.

Jenny let out a long sigh, seeing the big knife. "Better put the other one away as well. He just uses that to chop up the firewood," glancing over at the nurse, who is now getting nervous.

"No, it's not!" April explained, correcting her mother. "That's our fighting knife for the land sharks or monsters! Right, Daddy?"

Ben puts the knives away, knowing he is in trouble with Jenny. He puts on the Hawaiian shirt, hoping to change the subject, and it does the trick. The twins laugh, seeing their father in his new colorful flower shirt.

Jenny isn't fooled by any of this. She knows something is up. The twins look a little guilty of something.

"OK, you two!" she said, looking over at the girls. "If your father has to put his knives away, so do you!"

They both look up at their father, not knowing what to do. Ben just nods. They don't like this at all. Both pull up their little dresses, revealing they are also armed with knives. They untie the protected sheaths from their thighs, handing their knives over to their mother.

"Mom!" June said, getting annoyed. "You giving away all our secrets!"

"They will not allow you to keep those in here," the nurse quickly said. "It might be best if I take them away?" turning to Jenny.

"It's not a problem," she said, handing all the knives over to the nurse.

"You can't give our knives away!" April yelled out. "We might be needing them!"

"Daddy! What's Mom doing?" June asked, not understanding any of this.

Ben knows they are in trouble, seeing the look on Jenny's face. "I think the nurse is going to have them cleaned and sharpened for us."

June thinks about it for a few seconds. "Oh, that's good... Don't take too long, and be careful! We might be needing those later."

"Oh, I'll take real good care of them," the nurse said, smiling at the girls.

"Thank you so much… Is there a place where we can get some food?" Jenny asked, feeling a little hungry.

"We do have a nice cafeteria here. Luckily, they built it next to the infirmary, so you don't have to go far. At least you don't have to worry about eating hospital food. It's the same food they serve everyone else on the base. Dinner starts at six o'clock, but if you're hungry now, they can still fix you up with something. The directions and menu are in the pamphlet. If you feel you would like to have dinner in your room, we can do that, too."

Jenny looks over at Ben to see what he wants to do. He just shrugs his shoulders, not interested.

"I guess we can eat at the cafeteria later on. It'll be nice to eat out for a change. Ben never takes me out to eat," Jenny said, giving him a sheepish smile.

He smiles back. "Better talk to the girls about that. They may not like us eating out, especially eating someone else's cooking," already missing the freshly cooked meals they would serve up every day.

"Well, I'll leave you all alone," Nurse Able said. "If you need me, just push the call button on the nightstand," closing the door behind her.

The girls think this is another Christmas seeing all the new brightly colored clothes, quickly going through it all, trying to find out who gets what. They are so excited about all these new clothes, ready to try them on.

"Oh no, you don't!" Jenny said. "You're going to need a bath first!"

"We get to go in that bathtub!" the girls excitedly shouted out, immediately dropping everything, running into the bathroom.

"Ben, can you watch them while I go through all this?" Jenny asked.

"Sure," he replied, following April and June into the bathroom.

"Don't be too long… They are in there to wash and not to be playing around. That goes for you, too!"

The twins quickly jump in, splashing water all over the floor. They immediately clap their hands, sending soap bubbles all over the bathroom. Having a bath in warm water is a big treat, and the girls really love it.

He tosses them a bar of soap and a sponge. "Make sure you wash behind your ears. I'll be back in a few minutes to help wash your hair."

"Do we get to use that shampoo again?" April asked with a big smile on her face.

"Yep, we're all going to be squeaky clean from now on," Ben added.

He keeps the door open as he leaves the bathroom to keep an eye on them. Seeing Jenny standing in the middle of the room wearing her new panties and bra gets his attention.

He can't help but stare. "Damn, you look nice!" seeing how great Jenny looks.

"You think so? I can't believe I have gone so long without wearing any underwear. You'll feel better with some new clothes."

"No, I like these better."

"I don't ever want to see you in those damn shorts again," she said, tossing him his new clothes. "You've been wearing them way too long!"

"What! These are my favorites!" he jokingly said. "I was going to keep wearing these. They're so comfortable and still good for a few more years," looking down at his tattered shorts.

She just stares at him in disbelief. "You ain't going to wear those ever again. I have patched those shorts for the last time. They're falling apart!"

Jenny realizes he is pulling her leg. "Get those off! You're going to start wearing some decent clothes from now on."

Ben reluctantly puts on his new outfit. They both look at each other and start laughing. He looks so much like a cheesy tourist with tan shorts and a Hawaiian flower shirt. Jenny has black shorts and a pink blouse. The socks and sneakers are the best of it all since they have not worn shoes in years. They think it all looks a little odd, but getting to wear new cotton and silk clothes makes up for it. The harsh, weathered, worn clothing is now a thing of the past.

"I don't see any diapers for Baby," Jenny said. "He's going to need some now we're here," dreading the thought of him having an accident.

"I know, Baby will need to learn not to poop wherever he wants," then points under the crib at the full box of diapers.

"They thought of everything, haven't they?" she said, so pleased to see the big diaper box.

"Yeah, we have everything we would ever need here!"

"After only two days, we're already getting spoilt. How did we ever do it?"

He just let out a long sigh. "I don't have a clue… This is just too easy. We don't have to work for anything!"

* * *

Jenny and Ben help the children get dressed. After years of wearing just a dress and a sunhat, it takes a long time to put on all the new underwear, socks, shirts, and pants. The twins are already confused about having to wear it all at the same time.

"Wow, these are so nice and soft," April said, so thrilled with her first pair of shoes.

"Yeah, these are nice!" June added. "You did a good job on these ones. Thanks, Mom!" giving her mother a big hug.

"Oh no, I didn't make these," Jenny explained. "You better thank Nurse Able for all these new clothes."

"Mom, you think she can show us how she made these?" June asked. "She really knows how to make nice things."

"I don't think she made these. She must have gotten them from the store."

"Mom, what's a store?" June asked, totally confused.

Ben laughs, listening to the conversation. The children only wore handmade clothes and don't know anything else. Having new clothes will be a pleasant change for Jenny. Too often, they would always complain that their dresses were making their skin sore, or that they were falling apart. The soft, clean cotton clothes are already a big hit.

April, June, and Baby are all running around, jumping up and down, testing out their new shoes. With all the yelling and screaming with excitement, it's more like a Christmas morning. They are all so thrilled with the abundance of new clothes to wear.

Ben forgot he was supposed to call home. "Oh, we need to make a few phone calls. You want to go first?"

Jenny gasped. "I can't believe I forgot! Oh yes, let me call first. I hope I can get through this time," getting all excited.

"Let's see how we're supposed to do this," Ben said, sitting down, looking over the pamphlet with all the instructions on how to make a long-distance call.

He finally figures it out and dials all the numbers. "OK, now you dial your number with the area code, and that should be it."

Jenny dials her parent's phone number. She waits for the dial tone but gets the same recorded message indicating a disconnected number. The look on her face said it all. After all the waiting, it's all for nothing. She is so disappointed.

She hangs up the phone, looking over at Ben. "It's the only number I can remember. They might have moved, but I can't see them doing that. They have been in that house since I was born. Why would they change their number?"

He sits down, putting his arm around her. "I don't know... We need to get the people here to see if they can find out where your parents are. They should be able to track them down. We're supposed to be on the news, so they'll probably be calling here as soon as they see it. Just give it a little time."

"You need to call your family," she said, wiping away the tears. "They're probably waiting."

Ben calls home, and Jenny is right. They are literally waiting by the phone for the call. He speaks to his family at length. He explains everything that had happened to them in the past six years. After that, he hears all the gossip about what he missed while living on the island.

* * *

The girls notice their father sitting alone on the bed, talking to himself. They walk up a little curious, realizing he has one of those talking things they saw on the island. Right away, they want to speak to their granny, jumping up and down, getting overexcited again.

It's a side of the girls that he has never seen before. They were always very reserved, taking things seriously. Now, after being in the civilized world for less than a day, they are more like little girls for the first time.

"OK, you guys... Gather around the phone so we can all talk to Granny and Granddad," then turns on the speakerphone.

With that, Ben cannot get another word in. April, June, and Baby stand around the phone, telling all their tales. He is so impressed with how quickly the twins adapted to something new. They act as if they have been using a phone all their lives. Even Baby caught on, constantly babbling to the telephone, imitating his sisters.

Ben sits quietly, listening to the conversation. Then he notices Jenny is on the other side of the room, folding up the rest of the clothes, looking a little uncomfortable. He then realizes his big mistake. Neither of them had to go through the awkwardness of meeting each other's families. Jenny still has not talked to her new in-laws, feeling a little left out of the conversation.

Ben gets up, walks over, and takes Jenny's hand. "I'm sorry... I guess I better introduce you to my mom and dad."

She blushes. "It's OK, let the children talk," a little hesitant.

"Nope, come on," he said, shaking his head. "Don't be shy," pulling her over by the phone.

She sits on the bed, looking scared. Not saying a word, she listens to the children talking.

"OK, guys! Better give Mom a chance to talk," Ben said, noticing Jenny was a little apprehensive.

Jenny doesn't know what to say. She feels so awkward.

"It's easy, Mom!" June said, pointing to the phone. "You just talk, and they talk back to you!"

"Yeah, Mom!" April added. "You say something!"

"Hello," Jenny mumbled, feeling a little uncomfortable, not knowing what to say to her new in-laws.

Ben sits on the other bed, putting Baby on his lap, watching his wife talk to his parents for the first time. The thought of having to do the same is making him nervous. He quickly thinks of a few opening lines that he can use on his new in-laws. At least he has a little more time to think about it. Poor Jenny is thrown right into the middle of it. No wonder she looked so scared, cowering on the other side of the room while everyone else was talking on the phone.

* * *

After over an hour of talking on the phone, Jenny feels a little better. "Now, that wasn't too bad, was it?" Ben asked when she hung up the phone. "I think they have really taken to you. Why don't you try calling your parents again? Maybe you should call information in the city where they live?"

Jenny's mouth drops wide open. "Why didn't I think of that? You girls ready to talk to my mom and dad?" she asked the twins.

"Yeah! We want to talk on the phone again!" they both yelled out, jumping up and down.

"What's with these girls and the phone?" Ben asked, looking at them so confused.

"Welcome to the civilized world! They'll be wanting their own phones next. They'll be talking all day long, just like I used to do!"

"Oh, great... Well, I won't be looking forward to that. No more phones for me."

She looks over at Ben and smiles. "Your turn next! Better be ready. Dad will want to talk to you."

He cringes. "Oh, no! Do I really have to?" hoping to put it off a little longer.

"I can't wait to tell him I married a man with no job or money, and we have three kids!" she jokingly said.

Ben has a stunned look on his face, realizing it was so true. "Oh God! That's right! I don't have a job, and we have nowhere to live either. Better ask if we can stay with them since we'll be needing a place to sleep!" joking with her.

She laughed. "Oh, knowing Dad, he'll put you to work. You'll be busing tables and cleaning fish!"

They are joking with each other, but deep down, they know it's so true. A job and money is something that neither one of them has. Jenny doesn't like the idea of going back to work at a restaurant. Ben sure doesn't want to sit in an office from eight to five every day either.

After getting the operator for information, she has several numbers to try, but it's not much help. She keeps getting disconnected or gets wrong numbers. Even their restaurant is not listed anymore. She is so frustrated and upset, not able to talk to anyone in her family. After six years, she can't remember any of her friend's phone numbers or even the neighbors. To make things worse, she can't remember anyone's address or even the street names.

For some reason, it's as if her family just disappeared from the face of the earth. Their rescue is all over the news, so someone should have seen it. The restaurants had been there for years, but they have disappeared as well. She doesn't understand any of this. All she can do is wait for a phone call. Deep down, she knows something is not right.

* * *

Nearing six o'clock, everyone is getting hungry and a little curious about the cafeteria food. Jenny and Ben want to be positive, but after years of nothing but freshly cooked seafood, deep down, they are not looking forward to it. With everyone dressed up in their new clothes, they are ready to head out.

"No, you don't!" Jenny quickly said, seeing April and June grabbing their sticks. "They stay here. We're going out to dinner, and we won't be needing any sticks," taking them away.

"Mom, we need our sticks!" June shouted, getting mad. "We Amazon girls! We always bring our sticks for protection. Lots of land sharks around here."

Jenny turns to Ben. "You need to talk to your girls!"

"Oh, they're my girls now," he jokingly said, turning to June. "Mom is right... We're just going out to eat, so leave your sticks here. It's only down the hall, so we're not going far."

"What!" April shouted and didn't like the idea either. "We never go anywhere without our sticks."

"I'm going to cut off the points from your sticks, too," Ben added. "We don't want anyone getting hurt."

"We need sharp sticks to catch fish," June said, so shocked, hearing all this. "How are we going to get food?"

He gives them a stern look. "They have plenty of food here. There are no sticks at dinnertime. That's the rules here. Let's go!" pointing to the door.

The girls start pouting, stomping their feet as they leave the room. Both are getting mad and irritated.

Jenny is confused by the way the girls are acting. "Ben, what's with them? I had never seen them act like this before. They never question us like that," picking up Baby.

"You noticed that... They were like that when I took them outside while you were in the bath. I told them to come back to the room, and they basically said no. They wanted to stay outside and play."

She cringes. "I think it's all the new surroundings and being around all these people. The long trip in that boat didn't help. I hope they'll settle down before we get back home. You also need to wean them off the Amazon Warrior thing. Everyone here is scared of them."

He laughed. "Yeah, I noticed that too," so proud of his little girls standing up to all these people.

They walk down the corridor and find Nurse Able waiting for them. The main arboretum of the hospital has various plants, small trees scattered about, with a little gift and flower shop. At the center of the arboretum, there is a small sandbox with several children's toys surrounded by wooden benches.

The twins have a keen sense of smell. Once they catch their first whiff of food, their noses go up, drawing in deep breaths. They can't make out any of these new aromas. With so many strange smells, it gets them curious.

As they enter the cafeteria, Nurse Able hands Ben a hospital badge with a string attached. "Give this to the cashier and don't worry about a thing. Get anything you want. It's open twenty-four hours a day, seven days a week. The main dinners are at six in the evening, breakfast is at seven, and lunch at noon. Any other times, you can still get something, but it's a limited choice."

"Oh, thank you!" Jenny said. "The girls will love this."

The nurse ushers them to the counter. "Take your time and enjoy. I'll be back at my station if you need anything," leaving them on their own.

With no one else in line, it's obvious that someone asked everyone to get out of line at the food counter just before they arrived. Ben is even shocked to see all the food. There is enough food here to last for weeks or even months back on the island.

Being too short to look over the counter, Ben picks up the girls to let them see it all for themselves. This is a sight to see. So much food, and most of it, they do not have a clue what it is.

"You cooked too much!" June commented. "It's all going to spoil!" giving the man behind the counter a mean look.

"Yeah, we can't eat all this," April added. "You didn't leave nothing for tomorrow, or even the next day!" waving her finger at the man.

Jenny is so embarrassed. "Hush, girls! Don't be yelling out like that. They cook for everyone here. Just like we did back home."

"Do you have any fish?" Ben asked.

The man nods, pointing down the counter. "Sure, we have baked cod and tuna today. The commander made sure we always had fish for every meal during your stay here."

Jenny smiles. "That sounds nice... We'll have five of the baked cod and that fruit salad over there."

Everything looks good, but Jenny knows they better stick with seafood. Ben makes sure he gets Pepsi for the children. It's even better not having to worry about money, especially since they have none. All he has to do is show them the card.

Their first meal is a little different from what they are used to eating. Not having to do anything but just select what you want and sit down to eat is a novelty. With no blowing sand or wind to worry about, it's a pleasant change, and indeed, it's an easy life.

They quickly notice people at the other tables are watching them. They are drawing a lot of attention. A long line forms at the counter in just a few minutes, and most are looking over in their direction. A lot of whispering is going on. Jenny feels so conspicuous in the cafeteria, wishing they had their meals back in the room.

Right away, the twins criticize how the meals were prepared. Being overcooked and not having enough seasoning, it's not going over too well. The entire meal ended up being one big discussion of how they would have prepared it.

Jenny and Ben know the fish is probably frozen. The girls can tell something is a little odd about the fish. They have been spoilt eating fresh seafood their entire lives and know of nothing else. The dessert is a huge success. The fruit salad contains many new things like apples, pineapple, grapes, and the obvious favorite, strawberries.

Ben noticed right away that the people on the base still don't trust them. Three men sit nearby, each eating alone at their own table. Even though they are wearing blue medical smocks, he knows these are military police. Luckily, the twins are too busy deconstructing their meals to notice them.

* * *

On the way out of the cafeteria, they met up with the administrator. "So, how was your first meal?" Dr. Miles asked. "Did you all enjoy it? We have an excellent chef here."

"It was really nice... Thank you," Jenny replied with a big smile.

"Glad to hear it," Dr. Miles said.

"It was nice to have something different," Ben added. "Although it was a little strange not having to do anything, just sit down and eat."

"Well, you're going to have to get used to that. We do have some barbecues out here occasionally. It's nice to get outside with an open fire and cook up a big steak."

He looks down at the twins. "So what did you girls think? I heard you had the baked cod. That's my favorite. I bet you haven't tasted fish like that before, have you?"

"No, we haven't!" April and June said, looking at each other, frowning.

"It was rubbery and not enough seasoning," June explained. "If you had cooked it a little lower over the fire and basted it more, it would have been better."

"June! You know what I told you," Jenny said, so embarrassed.

"It was very nice," June mumbled. "Thank you," averting her eyes away from the man.

"OK, I'll talk to the chef about that," Dr. Miles replied, a little surprised by her comment.

"We liked the strawberries!" April said, smiling at him.

"Yeah!" June added. "That was a good dessert! The Pepsi was good, too!"

"Well, I'm glad you enjoyed it," the doctor promptly said.

* * *

Walking back to the arboretum in the hospital, they are a little lost, looking for something to do. They are not used to having so much free time. Baby sees the big sandbox running over to play in it, closely followed by his sisters. Finding little shovels and plastic buckets in the sandbox makes their day. Jenny and Ben sit on the bench, watching the children play.

"You would think they'd be tired of playing in the sand," Ben said jokingly.

"I don't think they know anything else. I already miss the beach myself. It's been almost two days now. I feel so restless not being able to walk out on the beach."

He agreed. "Yeah, I know... I don't know if I can get used to this. A couple of days ago, if you had told me we'd be sitting here in a cafeteria eating dinner, I wouldn't have ever believed it. It's like a big dream."

"It's been one hell of a ride. Well, at least the children are taking it well. They've been really good so far."

He let out a long sigh, putting his arm around her. "But they think this is a big adventure and that we'll be going home soon. I don't have the heart to tell them that they'll probably never see their home again."

A tear runs down her cheek. "I know, but it's for the best. In time, they'll understand."

"OK, let's go back to the room," Jenny said, seeing the girls yawning several times. "Time for bed!"

"No, not yet!" June replied. "We still have to go down the beach looking for stuff."

"Well, we do that at home, but I don't think they do that here."

"Sure they do!" June abruptly said. "That's where they get all these nice things."

"Yes, but I think they have people to do that here," Ben explained. "We don't want to go around picking up stuff from their beach, do we? They might get mad at us."

"We share like we do at home," April said. "We'll go with Nurse Able when she goes scavenging on the beach."

"Looks like you two really like Nurse Able, don't you?" Jenny asked.

"She's our friend," the twins said in unison. "She's really nice!"

April has that curious look on her face. "Daddy, if Nurse Able is African, then what are we?"

Ben doesn't know what to say at first. "I think we're just good old country folk."

April nods her head up and down. "Good... I'll tell Nurse Able that we are good old country folk when we see her."

Jenny is glad to see the girls are accepting the nurse as a friend. She hopes they will accept the rest of their family at home that way.

"Come on," Jenny said, seeing they were so exhausted. "It's time for bed."

The twins collect everything that's not bolted down. They are not cleaning up but taking everything with them.

"Let's leave all this here for next time," Ben said, since they were ready to walk off with everything that they could get their hands on.

June looks around. "We got to take it so it doesn't get washed away," knowing never to leave anything on the beach.

"I hope the waves don't get up this high," Ben said, so amused, seeing how they think they are still living on a beach. "I think they store it all here. That might be why it was here in the first place. So, better leave it all where you found it."

They reluctantly put everything neatly in one corner of the sandbox before running back down to their room. The long hallway is like a giant echo chamber. All three are running about, yelling and screaming out loud. Jenny and Ben now realize how loud their children are. Out on the beach, with the wind and sounds of the surf, they could yell and scream all they wanted, but here it's really noticeable. Not only are they loud, but they are also running around, stomping their feet, trying out their new shoes.

* * *

When they enter the room, a big bouquet of flowers is on the table. "I think you might have a secret admirer, or maybe it's from your family," Ben said.

Jenny is excited as she reads the card but then cringes. "Oh, it's from your family... It's so nice of them to send this," getting so frustrated, wondering why no one could find anyone from her family.

"They might be out of town," he explained, knowing she was getting upset. "It's only been a couple of days. They'll be calling as soon as they hear about it."

"It'll be my luck that they're out on a three-week vacation. I wish they would hurry up. I have so much to tell them."

Ben reads the card and laughs out loud. "Mom is already fixing up the rooms. They want to know when they can expect us."

"I guess we'll stay at your parent's house first. Then we can stay at mine."

"It's going to feel funny coming back home with a wife and three kids."

She laughed. "Same here! I know my dad is going to make them head chefs at the restaurant when he sees how they can cook. I know you're going to love it there, too," reaching over to kiss his cheek.

Feeling so tired, Ben lies down on the bed, finds the remote, turning on the television. "Hey, check this out! We got our very own TV! I wonder if they have cable here?"

"Let's watch the Tom and Jerry!" April shouted. "We like that one!"

Baby screams out loud when he sees the television, ready to watch more cartoons.

Ben flips through the channels and stops at the CNN news. "Hey, look! We're on TV!" seeing the close-up of the twins rattling off what they wanted for dinner after they just got off the ship.

"Look, Momma, we on the TV!" June cried out.

Jenny rushes out of the bathroom. "Oh, my God! Look at you two! You're famous now!"

They are surprised to see it's already on the news, and it's only been a few hours. They had no idea that their story was being told to the entire world live. Scenes from the old footage of the rescue planes searching for them years ago are making them feel uncomfortable. When they show all the photos of the others who were lost, it's just too much for them.

Jenny turns off the television. "That's enough of that. You girls can have your bath now and take Baby with you."

The children are so shocked to see that the television has been turned off. Although after hearing how it's bath time, the twins soon forget about the cartoons. All three quickly run to the bathroom, so thrilled to be able to play in the bathtub again.

"Give it another try," Ben said. "Just call the operator and see if they can help find your parent's new number. I'll give them their bath while you're on the phone. Oh, it's probably the middle of the night where your family lives. The time difference between here and the East Coast is about eight or nine hours," picking up the phone handing it to her.

"Oh, I didn't think of that... Maybe I'll wait until tomorrow."

"No need to wait... This place has operators working twenty-four hours a day, so it doesn't matter. But it also means once you do get their number, they'll be at home. Your mom and dad might not be too thrilled about getting woken up in the middle of the night, but it'll be a call they won't forget."

She smiles. "That's right! They'll be home sleeping unless they're on vacation somewhere. So, where do I start?"

"Try the operators here," he suggested. "Maybe they'll help you find some numbers you can call."

"Yeah, they'll know who to call."

"I'll be with the kids while you call home," he said, walking into the bathroom.

"Don't let them mess things up in there!"

He laughs, seeing three naked children waiting patiently next to the bathtub. "All right! Get those naked bottoms in the tub! It's bath time!"

All three scream out loud, jumping into the empty bathtub. What surprises Ben the most is all the new clothes in neat little piles with their shoes carefully placed on top. For Ben, it's a big mystery where they learn this. He figures it must be from Jenny's side of the family. When he was their age, he was not as neat and would have thrown his clothes all over the floor.

* * *

Chapter 48

Worst Patient

U p at sunrise, and with no chores, is getting everyone so frustrated. Since leaving the island, they have not done anything. Waiting in their room is almost as bad as being stuck in the cave waiting during a big storm. There is no breakfast because of the upcoming physicals. They have nothing to do but wait and fill out never-ending medical forms.

Ben stays with Baby while the girls have their first medical exams. The doctors decide to keep Ben out of the exam room, still a little wary of the overprotective father. Ben doesn't mind. It gives him another opportunity to read the 'Sleeping Beauty' book to his son one more time. He wonders how his girls are going to handle it. Never having had to endure a physical, he knows they are in for a big shock.

* * *

Jenny soon returns to the room, looking exhausted but mostly embarrassed. She keeps apologizing to Nurse Able. The twins stomp into the room, looking mad as hell.

"So, how did it go?" Ben asked, knowing it didn't look good.

Jenny sighed. "Don't ask!" glaring at the girls.

"They poked me with those sharp things, and it hurt! I'm not going back in there again!" June starts kicking the wall, so frustrated.

"Me too!" April shouted. "They're bad! I whacked him big time!"

In a panic, he looks over at Jenny. "They didn't hurt anyone, did they?"

She sits on the bed with Baby nodding her head up and down. "The doctor is going to need a few stitches. Your girls tore up the place. They said the girls need to be separated before they see them again. I have never been so embarrassed in my life," giving the girls another stern look.

"He poked me!" June yelled again, still rubbing her bottom after getting her first shot.

Nurse Able can't help laughing. "Well, Ben... I guess you're next," she said, motioning him to follow.

June grabs her father's hand. "Don't go, Daddy! They bad land sharks, and it stinks in there too!"

"We got to do it," he said, also dreading the physical. "They're going to make sure we're all healthy, and big, and strong!"

Jenny stays in the room with the children, planning on having a long talk with the girls. She can't believe how much trouble they can be. Their ability to strike out at people without warning caught her off guard. She is dreading to think about what is going to happen when they get back home with her family.

* * *

Nurse Able escorts Ben down the winding halls. Upon entering the exam room, it's clear they are not taking any chances with him. Two huge orderlies are standing on each side of the doctor, and he looks as if he has been through hell. June was right about the smell. The room reeks of bleach, and it's overwhelming.

Ben is being poked and prodded, then x-rayed from head to toe. One of the most extensive physicals he has ever had included everything that one could imagine, plus a few he will like to forget.

Once the physical is over, Ben is being ushered straight to the dentist. The two burly orderlies shadow him the entire time. He thought the dental exam was going to be a quick checkup and cleaning. After prodding around his teeth and a few more X-rays, they start working on his fillings. Usually, it would have been several visits, but out here, they do everything right away. After the most horrendous physical ever in his life, now he has to endure even more torture, having several fillings done.

* * *

After several hours, Ben is so glad it's over. It is the worst that he has ever felt in years. Dragging himself back into the room, he tries to put on a smile. He doesn't want to let on what is in store for them.

Jenny takes one look and busts out laughing. "You look like hell!" she cried out.

"Thanks," he mumbled.

"He did just fine," the nurse said. "It's nothing but a little checkup. Mrs. Hughes, you are next," motioning her to follow.

Ben doesn't let on to what he went through. He can't say anything since his mouth is still so numb, and all he can do is groan. Ben knows she'll probably get it worse. Now, he knows why the girls attacked the doctors, not blaming them one bit.

* * *

After an hour, Ben is feeling a little better. He can't stand being stuck in the room any longer, feeling so confined being indoors all the time. Since it'll be a while before Jenny returns, he decides to look around with the children.

"How about exploring this place while Mom has a checkup?" he asked.

"Yeah!" the twins yelled out. "Let's go exploring!" quickly, putting on their shoes.

"Let's go check out that gift shop. You're going to see a lot of new things here," picking up Baby, then heads out to show everyone this new world.

Standing in front of the gift shop, April and June gasped out loud, seeing all the strange and colorful things stacked up on the shelves. Ben carries Baby, seeing all the fragile stuff he can break.

"Now remember, just look, and don't touch," he said.

"OK, Daddy!" they both replied.

The little gift shop has everything one would want. It is mostly for the occasional tourist. Filled with various souvenirs and clothing with Kwajalein Island imprinted on it. The candy section quickly attracts the twins. They hover around the chocolates on all the shelves without a clue what they are looking at.

"Daddy! What's that smell?" June excitedly asked.

"It's from those things," April replied, pointing at the shelves full of candy.

"Oh, you'll love this... It's chocolate!"

"What's that?" June asked.

"It's way better than strawberries!" he explained.

"Can we have some?" they asked, with big smiles on their faces.

Realizing they don't have any money, he is frantically wondering what to do. Taking his children to a candy store with no money is not a good idea. Then, he remembers the card they used at the cafeteria.

"Excuse me, can we use this badge here?" he asked the lady behind the counter. "They said we can use it to get a few things while we're here, but I'm not sure if it includes this store," handing her the card.

"Oh, yes! It's the same as money, just like a credit card," reading the security code on the back.

"Great, I guess we'll hit the junk food first," then rushes back over to the girls who are still checking out all the candy.

With so much to choose from, he thinks it's best to start with something simple. He grabs three packages of plain M&M's.

"These are great!" he said. "You'll love these. You get one each," handing them out.

Looking around the shop, June sees the cooler filled with soft drinks. Right away, she recognizes the Pepsi bottle.

"Look! That's that Pepsi drink! Can we have some?" getting so excited, jumping up and down.

Pulling out a sixteen-ounce bottle, he hands it to June. He was going to let them share but noticed April is already pouting. He quickly reaches in, pulling out another bottle for April. This is a new world for Ben, having to take them shopping.

April gets a big smile on her face. "Thanks, Daddy!" glad to get a bottle to herself.

"I guess there's plenty to go around!" pulling out another for Baby.

"What about Mom?" April asked.

"No, we need to get Mom something nice. I have a feeling she won't be in the mood for cold drinks when she gets back," knowing she will not be feeling too good after her physical.

"Let's get her a present!" April shouted.

They walk around looking for the perfect gift. There are so many things to get for their mother. Not only is there food, but plenty of shirts, posters, books, and all the souvenir trinkets.

"Look! It's home!" April said.

Ben laughs seeing the ceramic souvenir of a tropical volcanic island with three tiny palm trees. Not resembling Kwajalein at all, but it looks similar to their island. He takes it off the shelf, letting the girls have a closer look.

"I think Mom will really like this," he said. "It looks just like our home."

The girls nod in agreement. "Can we get it for her?"

"I think this will be a wonderful gift for Mom. It'll remind her of our home and all the good times we had there. Come on, let's go pay for all this and sit by the sandbox."

"Excuse me," the clerk asked while ringing up the items. "You're that family they found on that island?"

"Oh, yes!" he awkwardly replied. "We got here yesterday."

"Welcome to our little island! My name is Margery," waving at the girls.

"Hi!" the twins shouted out, waving back.

"You're famous around here," she continued. "Real celebrities! I even saw you on TV!" handing them the sack.

He feels a little uncomfortable being called a celebrity. "Naw, we just everyday country folk. It's nice meeting you."

"Well, you come back now, you hear," she said with a deep southern drawl.

"We probably will... Come on, girls. Let's go play in the sand," then walks back to the arboretum to let the children play in the sandbox.

They all sit next to the sandbox, enjoying their first chocolate candy and favorite drink. Even after all the pain from the dental work, Ben savors the wonderful taste of chocolate again. He enjoys being out with his family, but this is a far cry from the picnics they used to have. Unfortunately, the arboretum at the hospital entrance is not much to look at compared to their pristine beach.

After several minutes, Ben notices someone is suspicious. The hospital staff always wears white or blue uniforms, all busy doing something. Wearing jeans and a long sleeve dress shirt, this man doesn't belong here at all. Carrying a small black bag with a shoulder strap, Ben has a feeling he is a reporter.

"Stay here," Ben whispered to the twins. "Watch Baby."

April and June know something is wrong but continue to play in the sandbox. Ben gets up, walking over to the huge framed photographs that covered the far wall. While pretending to admire the photos, he keeps an eye on the children through the reflection in the glass.

Seeing Ben step away, the photographer removes a camera from his bag and slowly walks up to the children. Ben is so furious at seeing this guy taking photos. Without making a sound, he quickly sneaks up behind the photographer, grabbing him by the back of his neck with one hand. With little effort, Ben quickly drags the man away from the children.

Ben slams the man against the wall. "I don't think I gave you permission to take any pictures of us!"

The photographer doesn't have a chance to respond, screaming out in pain. Ben lifts him off the ground with one hand, tightening his grip around the man's neck. Two military police and several huge orderlies come out of nowhere. They quickly run over, pulling the photographer away. Ben takes the camera, rips out the film, then snaps off the lens from the camera, tossing it to the floor.

"I thought this was supposed to be a secure location?" Ben asked one of the military police. "Why is he in here bothering us?"

"I'm sorry, he must have snuck in," one of the military police replied, looking very agitated. "There are still a few news crews on the island. They have been snooping around all over the place."

"So why is he in here?" Ben asked again.

"He won't be here for long," he explained, so furious with the situation. "He'll be arrested and kicked off the island. Hopefully, with the rest of them! It's all we've been doing all day long is chasing these idiots around. They should have never let them on the base in the first place. If they're not trying to get photos of you and your family, they're out trying to get photos of the classified areas. They think it's all a big game out here, and they can do whatever they want."

"I wonder who he's working for?" Ben asked, opening the camera bag to find several used rolls of film, destroying them all.

He sees a badge at the bottom of the bag. A press badge from the Globe. This paper is one of the worst of the bunch.

Dr. Miles, the administrator, races down the hall after hearing all the commotion. Seeing the military police hauling off someone, he knows it's trouble.

"I thought you said we weren't going to be bothered by the news people in here?" Ben asked.

Dr. Miles is so flustered. "It's OK... We'll handle it. Who is that guy?" he asked one of the orderlies.

"He's part of the news media they brought in," the orderly answered.

Dr. Miles turned to Ben. "I'm so sorry... I'll put an end to this. These people have been a big nuisance since they arrived. That idiot doesn't realize he just committed a federal offense by breaking in here."

"I hope this doesn't happen again," Ben said, handing the ID badge over to the administrator.

Dr. Miles looks over the badge and hands it to the remaining MP. "Round up these guys. Make sure they're on the next flight out. They overstayed their welcome."

"Yes, sir! I'll inform my men," then quickly turns and is on the radio, giving orders to start picking up the rest of the reporters.

Having reporters on the island was not their idea, and the security detail doesn't like it one bit. The press is only here as a public relations stunt from some general at the Pentagon. After just one day, there are so many security breaches to warrant throwing them all out.

Ben walks back to the children, who are still playing in the sand. He wishes he were back home again, where they are in control of their lives.

"Wow, you caught another one of them land sharks. Right, Daddy?" April asked.

"He's a bad man, and they are going to take him away. Probably spank his bottom too!" he added, trying to humor the children.

June sees the military police through the window, putting the photographer in the car. "Bad land shark! Bad!"

"Calm down. There's nothing to worry about now."

"He's like that one who grabbed my arm! I don't like it here! Can we go home now?" June asked.

"Yeah, Daddy!" April added. "When we going home?"

"We'll be here just a little longer," he said, putting Baby on his lap. "Then we're going to see your granny and granddad. You don't want to miss that. She's going to cook up a big Sunday dinner for all of us!" trying to change the subject.

"Yeah, we want a big Sunday dinner at Grannies!" June shouted.

"Let's go see if Mom is back. You can give her that gift you bought her and show her all the new candies you have!"

"Let's go show Mom!" they both yelled out, running down the hall.

Returning to their room, they discover Jenny is not there. The girls are getting tired of this. They are not used to their mother being away and not knowing where she is. Ben is also getting worried. She has been gone far longer than he had been.

Ben puts Baby in the crib. "I'll go check to see how Mom is doing. You two sit on the bed and look at your book. Watch Baby while I'm gone. I'll be a few minutes," closing the door behind him, walking down to the examination room to check on Jenny.

* * *

Dr. Miles is concerned about the Hughes family. Their initial suspicions were correct. After only one day, they have seen enough to know it's a big problem. Living in isolation away from people for so many years made Ben and Jenny distrust anyone and see other people as a threat. He knows Ben is an overprotective father looking after his family. The biggest problem is Ben's size and strength, and he can really hurt someone or worse.

Also, he can see that the little girls are on the wild side, and they don't think twice about hitting anyone with their sticks. After just one day, one of their physicians needed stitches after being struck by one of the girls, and they almost destroyed one of the exam rooms. He knows it will not be safe to let them back in public so soon.

With the incident with the photographer on the pier and the one in the hospital, it's not going well. Even in a controlled environment, the family is having problems. They are so glad that they kept this family separate from the rest of the patients and most of the staff in the hospital.

Luckily, the little girls accepted Nurse Able as a friend. The nurse is the only one who can get near them. No one has been able to get close to the little boy. He is the one who is protected the most and is the root of many of the problems. He knows the girls were taught to protect their brother and do so with a vengeance.

* * *

Dr. Miles walks into the psychologist's office, assigned to work with the Hughes family. Dr. Karen Martinez's job is to help them return to civilization and deal with other people.

Dr. Miles doesn't beat around the bush. "Karen, I think we'll start the sessions with the Hughes family."

Dr. Martinez nods her head in agreement. "I told you this would happen! I had already heard about the incident at the arboretum. Dr. Larson has a bad laceration and probably a concussion. And all that is from one of the little girls. I'd be scared to see what Ben is capable of doing. We should have started the sessions with them as soon as they arrived!"

"I wanted to give them a little time to settle in. They've been through a lot in the last few years."

"Well, they haven't been here twenty-four hours, and look what's happened. You need to keep everyone far away from this family until I have time to talk with them to see what we're dealing with here. It's just too dangerous for them to be walking around. We need to get things under control before it gets worse."

"I know… Let's get started before someone else gets hurt," Dr. Miles said, not wanting to argue the point anymore.

"So, where are they now?" she asked.

"Jenny is still in the exam room with Dr. Kearsley. Ben and the kids are back in their room."

"Good! Let's go talk with him now," she said, and both left the office, heading down the hall.

Finding the door shut, Dr. Miles gently knocks. "Anyone home?" slowly opening the door, not hearing anything.

The next thing they hear is a scream from the room. "No one home! Go away!"

He peeks in, seeing the twins standing on the far bed, already swinging their sticks in an offensive stance. With the mean looks on the little girl's faces, he knows they are not playing around.

"Is your daddy here?" Dr. Miles asked. "We'd like to talk to him."

They get no response. The girls are even more agitated.

Dr. Martinez walks into the room. "All right, you two! Put those sticks down before you hurt someone," trying to get control of the situation.

She approaches the girls, trying to grab their sticks. With a swift flick, June promptly smacks the woman upside her head, knocking her to the floor.

"Call the orderlies," Dr. Martinez orders, quickly crawling away, "and get Nurse Able in here right now!" a little dazed from being struck so hard.

"You're off to a good start," Dr. Miles said, getting furious with her. "You are not making a good first impression, are you?"

Things are already out of control. He can only imagine what havoc these two girls would create out in the real world, especially around other children.

"You go away!" June yelled out to the intruders. "This is our cave!"

"We're not here to harm you," Dr. Miles explained to the girls, trying to calm things down. "We are only here to see your daddy."

"Go away!" the girls waved their sticks back and forth.

Just then, two orderlies rush into the room, seeing the standoff. Dr. Miles knows it's going to make the situation worse. He motions for them to stand by the door.

Dr. Martinez is concerned about the baby in the crib. At first, she thought these two wild girls might harm their brother. Trying to get closer to see if the baby is all right, but it makes things worse. The girls are more agitated the closer she gets, constantly pointing the sticks at her, trying to fend her off.

"I just want to check on your brother to see if he's OK," she said, making sure not to get within striking distance of those sticks.

"Baby, OK!" June said. "You back off! Go away! Bad land shark!"

"My lord, what's going on here?" Nurse Able asked, entering the room. "You girls put those sticks down. You might hurt somebody."

"Bad land sharks here!" April explained, so relieved to see a friendly face. "They want to hurt Baby!"

"OK, everyone, calm down," Nurse Able said. "They're just watching out for their little brother. Y'all need to move back. You're just scaring the girls," motioning to the doctors and orderlies to move away, seeing the situation is out of control.

Nurse Able knows the girls have been trained to watch and protect the baby when their parents are gone. She moves a little closer to see he is still sleeping in the crib. April quickly points her stick at the nurse, seeing she is getting too close.

"I'm just checking on your brother," Nurse Able said, knowing April was so scared.

"Baby is OK!" June shouted out nervously. "We checked already. No bugs or spiders around!"

"I got to go potty," April whispered to June.

"We need Daddy!" June shouted, so scared, never having to face so many land sharks before, wishing they were back home, away from all of this.

April looks over at Nurse Able and jumps off the bed. "You help watch Baby," then hands her the stick.

Dr. Martinez is so relieved. She sees it as a significant breakthrough for the two little girls. They now trust the nurse enough to help them protect their baby brother.

"Now, what am I supposed to do with this?" she asked, taking the stick.

"You point the stick at them," April promptly replied, "and if they get too close, you jab them!" pointing over to the intruders.

Everyone in the room cringes upon hearing that, knowing it's not an idle threat. These two little girls can hurt someone. Nurse Able points the stick at the doctors, still standing by the door, while April runs to the bathroom.

"OK, see if you can get the other stick," Dr. Miles said, motioning to the nurse.

Nurse Able immediately points the stick at him. "Now, now... You know better than that. It will be best if you keep your distance. We don't want anyone getting hurt, now do we?"

"Yeah, you tell them, Nurse Able!" June shouted out, glad for the help, swinging her stick back and forth, jumping up and down on the bed.

Dr. Miles is not amused. "OK, maybe it's best if we all go back to the hallway. Let's leave the nurse to keep an eye on things here until Mr. Hughes comes back."

"I think that might be the best thing to do," Nurse Able said. "You're just scaring the girls."

April rushes out of the bathroom, taking her stick from the nurse. "Thank you! We handle it now!" and jumps back up on the bed with June.

Nurse Able starts shooing everyone out of the room and then closes the door. The twins are cheering her on.

"You girls sit on the bed and read your book. I'll make sure they don't come back," sitting down in the chair next to the door.

"OK, we watch things over here," June said. "You watch the door, and if you hear anyone coming, do this," showing her a hand sign.

"So what does that mean?" she asked, trying to copy the hand sign.

"It means land sharks might be around," April explained, repeating the sign. "Everybody has to be quiet and listen. Then you supposed to be ready for any land sharks."

The nurse nods. "I'll remember that… I'll be watching out for any of those bad land sharks. They won't be coming in here. I'll make sure of that."

With the door closed, the twins sit on the bed, looking at their book. April takes it all in stride, but June is still a little shaken and keeps glancing over at the door.

"I see you got some chocolates," Nurse Able said.

April holds the book up to show the nurse. "No, this is a book. It's got pretty pictures in it!"

"Oh, that's a nice one," Nurse Able explained, "but I meant those M&M's you have."

"These are candies!" June said, holding up the bag. "They're real good. Baby got some, too," pointing over to his crib.

"You try some," April said, jumping off the bed, carefully pouring a few into the nurse's hand. "They're real good! We don't have any of these at home. They only have these in the store."

Nurse Able pops the candies in her mouth. "They are good, aren't they? I know my kids used to love these too."

"You have babies too?"

"I have six! Four boys and two girls."

"Wow! That's lots of babies. Can we play with them?"

"Oh, they're all grown up now and live far away," she explained. "I really miss them. I don't get to see them too often since I'm working out here."

"Are they on the other side of the island?" April asked.

The nurse laughed. "Oh, no! They are a lot farther away than that. It'll take days to get there, and that's on a plane."

"Daddy says Granny lives far away too," April said, "but we going to visit. You can come too! We going to have a big supper and cook lots of things for her."

She smiles. "That sounds like fun. I wish I could go too, but I have to stay and take care of all the people who don't feel good. That's my job here."

"Why don't they feel good?" April asked. "They got a tummy ache?"

The nurse smiles. "Yes, that and a few other things."

* * *

Walking down the hall, Jenny and Ben notice the doctors and orderlies standing outside the room. Right away, Ben can see they are not too happy and knows something has happened.

"We've had a few problems here," Dr. Miles explained, "You need to take those sticks away from those girls before they hurt someone."

Ben doesn't say a word, quickly entering the room. Nurse Able is sitting quietly by the door. The girls are on the bed, looking at their book.

He turns to the two doctors, a little confused. "I don't see any problems."

"Hi, Daddy! Hi, Mom!" the twins shouted, waving at them as if nothing had gone on.

"Nurse Able came to visit us! She tells us lots of stories!" April said, pointing to the nurse.

The two doctors enter the room to have a long talk with Jenny and Ben. Jenny is so embarrassed. She knows it's getting out of hand with the girls always protecting their brother.

Jenny looks over at Ben. "You know what you have to do. Those sticks aren't necessary anymore, and yes, they might hurt someone."

She then turns to the twins. "You two shouldn't be threatening anyone with those sticks. All these people here are friends."

"They getting too close to Baby," June mumbled. "We watch Baby. It's our job!"

Jenny turns to Ben, giving him a stern look. "You need to stop telling the girls that. It gets them all worked up."

He glances over at his two little girls, so proud of them. "Yeah, you're right."

None of this bothers the twins. They both sit on the bed without a care in the world, going through their book and eating M&M's. They know their job is to take care of their little brother. It's more important than ever with all these new people around, even though their little brother had slept through it all.

Dr. Martinez informs them about the sessions they will have with her. Ben is not interested but quickly finds out it's not an option.

Getting back home to see his family is the only thing he wants. Having a physical and getting the children their shots is one thing, but having sessions with a shrink, he thinks it's so ridiculous.

Jenny doesn't like it at all. Being a psychologist, she doesn't like being on the other end of a session and can read this doctor like a book. Jenny knows they have some issues. Being stuck here going through counseling is the last thing she wants. She wants to go home, but mostly to find out where her family is so she can finally talk to them.

* * *

After a long hour, the doctors finally leave the room. Jenny and Ben are so glad to have the room to themselves. Surrounded by so many people and the endless medical tests, paperwork to be filled out, the pressure and frustration are finally taking its toll. Life on the island was so carefree, without any problems other than the occasional storms.

After a quick snack of fresh fruit, Ben remembers the gift the twins got for their mother. "What about that surprise you got Mom today!"

"We got you a present!" they shouted, jumping off the bed, running over to retrieve the small bag.

"You'll like it too," April added. "You not going to guess what it is!"

Jenny takes the small bag. "Well, thank you... I wonder what it can be?" cheering her up a little.

She reaches in, pulling out a leaf-wrapped gift. Ben is confused, knowing that it was wrapped in tissue paper and in a little box when they bought it. Looking over at the plant in the corner with one leaf missing is the answer to that question.

"Oh, thank you! This is so nice!" Jenny cried out, so pleased with the ceramic island with little palm trees.

"Look! It's our home!" June explained.

"You like it?" April asked.

"I love it!" Jenny said, getting all flustered. "It does look like our island! It is the best present ever. I'll always cherish it! Now, this has made my day," giving the girls a big, long hug.

The twins point out all the places on the small souvenir island where they thought the campsite and the cave should be. It is a remarkable likeness to their island, but not anything like the flat, featureless Kwajalein Island it was supposed to portray.

Ben is so proud of his little girls. They love the simple things in life. That was the life he loved so much. Just being with his family is all he wants, without all the troubles of the modern world. Now, their days are nothing but meetings, paperwork, and endless medical tests. He thought things were bad, but now they are expected to start sessions with a psychologist. The last thing he wants is a psychologist trying to analyze him with all his little quirks.

* * *

After the episode with the children, the doctors postponed the rest of the medical exams. Dr. Martinez schedules counseling sessions for the entire family. With all the problems on their first day, counseling is now more important. They don't want any more injuries, especially from the two girls. Things have to change before they let this family leave the island.

Dr. Martinez is relieved to see how April, June, and Baby likes Nurse Able. That's a good start. The girls need to be deprogrammed from their constant overprotective stance with their little brother. The little girls won't let anyone near their brother, protecting him at all costs, and it's a big problem. Also, Nurse Able is the only one allowed to enter the room while the children are alone.

While Jenny and Ben attend their first counseling session, Nurse Able stays in the room with the children. April and June don't know it, but this was their counseling session as well. The nurse has been instructed to start teaching them how to trust other people and how land sharks don't exist.

Nurse Able knows all children like watching cartoons and decides to give them a treat. For their first session, she brings them a Disney movie, bottles of Pepsi, and M&M's. Luckily, the room has a television with a VCR. The nurse puts the tape in, and everyone sits down, ready to watch their first Disney movie.

* * *

Hearing the maintenance call for room 105 over the intercom, the administrator thinks nothing of it. He figures with the three kids, it's probably spilled milk or something similar. After a minute or two, he remembers that Jenny and Ben are with Dr. Martinez, and Nurse Able is watching the children. Immediately, he jumps up, running down the hall to see what the problem is.

At the end of the corridor, Nurse Able and the two little girls are standing over a pile of rubble. In the middle of the hallway are the remains of the television. The maintenance man is sweeping up the broken glass and plastic, tossing it all into a large garbage can.

The administrator cannot believe what he is seeing. The two little girls are waving their sticks at the smashed television, shouting something about monsters.

"Sir, I'm so sorry!" Nurse Able said, so flustered. "It's all my fault!"

"What the hell happened here?" the administrator asked.

"Well, I thought it would be nice to let the children watch a Disney movie," the nurse explained.

He is so confused. "A cartoon caused all this?"

"It was Beauty and the Beast!" the nurse continued, a little flustered. "It's my favorite movie. I wanted the children to see it, but I didn't expect they would react that way when they saw the beast on the TV."

June points to the smashed television. "That had a bad monster in it! We don't like monsters!"

"We don't like monsters in our cave!" April added. "We throw it out!" smacking the remains of the television with her stick.

The twins walk back to their room, slamming the door behind them. Nurse Able is lost for words and didn't expect this at all. She thought she had things under control.

"So, how did the TV get out here?" the administrator asked.

"Apparently, they thought it was a real monster. The girls yanked the TV off the wall before I could stop them. Then they tossed it out here like it was nothing. I didn't realize how strong and resourceful they are," the nurse explained.

"Is the boy OK?" getting concerned if he is scared, or worse, hurt.

She smiles. "Oh, he's fine! He is hiding under his blanket in the crib. You know, they have their own special sign language. Even the little boy knows the hand signs. That's what caught me off guard. They all knew what was going on before I did. I can tell you one thing. There is a lot of communication going on between those three. I don't think anyone else has a clue to what they're saying to each other."

The administrator lets out a long sigh. "Dr. Martinez and her staff will have a field day with those two girls. Maybe it'd be best not to replace the TV until they understand the difference between the real world and a cartoon! Better get back in there and watch them like a hawk," then turns, stomping down the hallway back to his office.

Nurse Able lightly taps on the door. "Hi, it's me... May I come in?" she asked, worrying what was going to happen next.

"You monsters, stay out!" one of the girls yells out.

Nurse Able chuckled. "It's me! All the monsters have run away. They're all gone. Can I come in now?" slowly opening the door.

"Hurry! Get in, and shut the door!" June yelled.

"You shouldn't have done that," the nurse said. "Your mother and father are going to be mad. You're not supposed to break things. That TV costs a lot of money," promptly, closing the door behind her.

"But it had a bad monster in it!"

The nurse sits down and tries to explain the difference between what they see on television and what is real, but to no avail. They still live in their own little world, just too young to understand.

* * *

Returning to their room, Jenny and Ben are glad to see everything is quiet. The nurse is reading to the children. Everything appears to be OK.

"Look, Mom! We got another storybook," April and June said in unison, pointing to the book the nurse was reading them.

"That's great! You got two books now. You guys are so lucky to get all these nice books to read."

"So, how is everything?" Jenny asked the nurse. "Were they good?"

Nurse Able smiles. "Oh, everything is fine. I was just reading to them. So how was your session?" wondering if she should tell them about the television.

"These shrinks are full of it," Ben grunted, shaking his head.

Jenny glares at Ben. "He's still having issues. I thought it was very helpful."

"That's good... Dr. Martinez is one of the best. It'll do you a world of good. You've been through a lot in the past few years. She can really help you out," the nurse explained, pointing her finger at Ben.

"Well, it's been fun, but I need to get back to work," the nurse added.

The twins run over, hugging the nurse. "Thanks for the storybook. You come back and read us another one!"

"I'll do that... I'll see what I can find in the library tomorrow. OK, I'll see you later," she said, closing the door behind her.

Ben is so relieved to get back to the room. Sitting down in the chair, he notices the girls look guilty of something. Seeing Baby on the bed with a blanket over his head, he knows something is up. When Baby hides up like that, it's not a good sign.

"OK, guys, what did you do?" Jenny asked, noticing it too.

The girls sheepishly look about the room without saying a word. Baby starts babbling out loud, still hiding under the blanket, pointing his hands up in the air. No one can understand most of his babbling, but the one birdcall he keeps repeating gives them a clue. That is the one for a monster.

"What monster?" Ben quickly asked, looking over at the girls.

"There was a monster in the TV!" pointing up to where it used to be.

Ben notices the television is missing. "What happened? Did they take our TV away?"

"We don't like monsters!" April shouted. "We tossed him out!"

"Yeah!" June added. "We throw it out!" pointing to the door to the hall.

"You didn't break it, did you?" Jenny quickly asked.

April shrugs her shoulders. "I don't know. It did make a big noise. That man put it in that real big bucket."

"What man, and what big bucket?" Jenny asked.

Ben let out a long sigh. "I think she meant a big trash can."

Ben calls the front desk and discovers that the television was smashed and hauled away. The staff offered them a new replacement, but both Jenny and Ben thought better of it. Since the girls are still having problems, he opted not to have a television in the room. They all have better things to do than sit around watching television, anyway.

Jenny had enough, promptly taking the sticks away from the girls. She insists that April and June are going to start acting like little girls from here on out. The girls protest, not liking this at all. They always had their sticks, and this is the one time they'll need them with all these land sharks around. They look at their father for support, but unfortunately, their mother always had the last word, no more sticks.

* * *

Chapter 49

Resourceful

Rumors are spreading fast about the twins being a little wild and very resourceful. Only a few of the hospital staff have been able to get close to the family, but now they are gossiping with everyone else on the base.

Now that the reporters have been kicked off the island, the military press is handling all the information. The press is demanding more information about the two little Amazon girls after seeing them strike the photographer. The hospital administrator is the only one who can do interviews, and he is not releasing any information at all.

Dr. Martinez is so enthralled with these children. Unfortunately, the counseling sessions she had with them did not go too well. She tried talking to the girls, but all she got was a mean look. They saw her as a land shark and nothing more. The biggest problem is that they watch over their little brother like a hawk.

She discovers that their ability to communicate with each other is far more advanced than anyone thought. Not only are there all the various hand signs, but endless birdcalls and whistles. The only normal one is the little boy. Being so young, he doesn't have any issues being around other people.

The only thing Dr. Martinez knows about the children is from the sessions with the parents. Hearing how the two girls have been taught to survive on their own at an early age, she is interested in seeing how they interact with each other in an outdoor environment.

She asks Jenny if she can monitor the children while they are outside in the garden. The garden has a variety of trees, flowers, and a large fish pond in the center, so it will be a nice place to let them play. The event is to be supervised and in a non-intrusive environment.

Jenny quickly agrees to Dr. Martinez's plan. She is proud of her children and wants the people here to see that her girls are indeed just little girls. She also wants to show everyone how they play together, just like any other girls their age.

Ben agrees with the cameras, mostly because his family at home wants to see more of the children. They are not the only ones. The entire world wants to see more of the little Amazon girls.

Once Dr. Martinez gets all the permissions, she quickly sets everything up. They will record the event, but release only selected portions to the press. Various cameras are hidden around the garden, so the girls will not know they are being recorded.

One of Dr. Martinez's staff, Debbie Smith, is the only person who will be nearby. She'll sit on the bench near the pond to make sure they don't leave the area. With an earpiece and a hidden microphone, she will be in constant communication with Dr. Martinez the entire time. The security is extremely tight, so no one will accidentally walk in on the girls.

Jenny and Ben will stay in the room while the girls play outside. The twins don't know that this is a staged event. All they know is that they will be able to go out on their own, which is something they have wanted to do since arriving. Ben will keep an eye on things. The girls can't do much damage anyway since their sticks have been taken away.

* * *

Once everyone is in place, April and June are let out to the garden to explore. Ben leaves the door open to keep an eye on them. Walking around with their backpacks on and wearing their big-rimmed sun hats, they are having a great time exploring the garden. Baby is not too interested, and after a few minutes of running around, he is back in the room.

April and June systematically walk around the garden, carefully examining everything. The pond is their main interest, filled with a variety of fish, but mostly huge koi. They repeatedly walk around the pond, discussing how to prepare some of these strange-looking fish.

The twins start gathering rocks from the garden, placing them in a circle near the pond. Two huge boulders are put at opposing ends of the circle. Then they walk over to a small circular garden, sectioned off with a little-arched metal fencing. Pulling up the fence, they take a three-foot section, carrying it back to the circle of rocks. Walking over to the far side of the garden, they start pulling large leaves off the banana trees, carrying them all back to the pond.

Debbie sits on the bench, watching the two little girls. She knows the gardeners will be furious seeing their well-maintained gardens being torn up. Debbie is not to say anything or approach them, only make sure the girls don't leave the area. If the girls attempt to leave, she doesn't have a clue what she is supposed to do to stop them, hoping their father will help if things get out of control.

April and June are wandering around, going from one tree to another, pulling on the branches, testing them for strength. Hovering around a small group of bamboo trees, they select the one they want. Within a few minutes, they have it pulled out of the ground, ripping off the leaves. June then uses the wire saw to cut it to the proper size and is rather pleased with their new six-foot-long bamboo stick.

Walking back to the pond, April places one end of the stick on a large boulder. June strikes the end of the bamboo stick with a small rock. She then scrapes the end of the stick on top of the boulder.

Everyone watching soon realizes what they are doing. These girls are sharpening the end of the bamboo stick, making a spear.

The twins walk back out to the garden, gathering small dead branches, leaves, and dried grass bringing it all back to the pond. They gather up all the little ornamental driftwood that's scattered around.

Debbie knows right away that the girls are trying to make a campfire. "Are you watching this?" she whispers over the radio.

"Of course we are!" Dr. Martinez shouts. "It's fantastic! We first thought they were just a couple of little vandals, but it looks like they are making a campfire!"

"You know they made a spear with a sharp point on it," Debbie explained, getting concerned. "What do I do if they come at me?"

Dr. Martinez's answer is short and to the point. "Run as fast as you can!" knowing Ben will have to handle it.

All eyes are glued to the monitors watching the two little girls. Most of the hospital staff are peeking through the windows. Very few had seen the little Amazon girls since they arrived but had heard all the stories. The security is tight, and now everyone can see why.

April and June take off their hats, helping each other with their long hair, putting it underneath the back of their dresses. June rolls up one of the large banana leaves while April reaches into the backpack, removing an object. Both of them kneel on the ground, putting the dry grass in a small pile.

While April strikes the fire starter next to the dry grass, June blows through the rolled-up leaf. In less than a minute, a small flame emerges. Slowly and methodically, they add more dry grass and wood to the campfire until the flames reach two feet into the air.

June quickly places the metal fencing on top of the two larger rocks, using it as a grill over the flames. The twins sit back on the grass, watching the flames of their campfire grow and grow.

Ben is watching it all from their room. None of this is new to him. The twins have been always good at lighting a campfire and have been doing it for years.

Jenny can't be bothered with it all. She is too busy reading to Baby, showing him all the pictures. All she wants to do is sit back and relax without any more meetings and paperwork to be filled out.

The phone rings, startling everyone. Ben is already annoyed with all these interruptions.

"Hello," Ben said, hoping it was a call from his family.

"Ben, this is Dr. Miles... Do you know what your girls are doing out in the garden?"

"Sure, it looks like they're setting up camp," Ben said, looking out the window, seeing the girls sitting around a small campfire.

"I'm sorry, but we're not used to having campfires that close to the building," Dr. Miles explained. "Aren't they a little young to be playing with fire?"

"Don't worry… Looks like we're in for a barbecue. They've been doing this for a long time. It's no big deal," Ben proudly said, then hung up the phone.

Jenny glances out the window, hearing the conversation. "They're getting their money's worth with those two."

He laughed. "It's a shame these people weren't with us on the island for just one day. It would be enough for them to write an entire book on how to live off the land. They can all learn a thing or two from our babies out there."

"Are we boasting about our little Amazon warriors?" she asked.

"You damn right I am! I'm mighty proud of my little girls!"

Once the campfire has taken, the twins hover around the pond again. Both keep pointing down in the water, discussing something among themselves. June picks up the spear, and both stand motionless, staring down at the pond.

Everyone is trying to figure out what game they're playing. They watch June holding the stick up high with one hand and pointing it at the water. Without warning, she hurls the stick into the pond, spearing one of the fish.

Debbie is shocked and quickly gets on the radio again with Dr. Martinez. "You got to do something about this! I don't feel safe out here all alone!"

"I know!" Dr. Martinez responded. "We called Ben, and he is aware of what is going on with the girls. Just keep a close eye on things, and don't let anything get out of control."

"What do you mean, don't let things get out of control?" she frantically replied. "What do you call this? She's made a damn spear! They're tearing up the place, they lit a fire, and now they're killing the fish! They're not playing games out here. I might be next!"

"Don't worry... Just let them play. As long as the boy is not out there, they won't bother you."

"Easy for you to say!" she said, so scared to be close to these two girls. "You ain't out here… If this is how they play, I hate to see what they do if they get mad at someone!"

April takes one of the banana leaves, washes it off in the water, and places it on the grass. June plops the large Koi fish onto the leaf, letting it flop around. She then pulls a couple of oranges from her backpack, cutting them into small slices with a very sharp knife.

Once the fish is dead, the twins promptly clean it, tossing the head and guts back into the pond. April places tin foil on the ground, carefully laying out the fish fillets on top of it. She drags a few more things out of her backpack. Promptly adding the seasoning to the fish fillets, and placing slices of oranges on top of it all.

Once they are done, they carefully pick it all up, placing it on the wire fencing they set up over the campfire. Just another day for the girls, but for everyone watching, they are absolutely astonished. These two little girls are very resourceful.

Ben walks out to the garden with Baby to check on them. "So, what are you cooking?"

"We caught a nice fish," April said, pointing over to the small pond. "Don't know what it is, but I bet it's tasty!"

"I bet it is, too! It's been a while since we had a decent meal," smelling the aroma of the large fillets covered with orange slices.

"Yep!" June said, so thrilled with their campfire. "It's going to be some good eaten tonight! Just like at home!"

"Yeah, we can all use a nice fresh-cooked meal for a change. You've done a good job out here. Well, we'll be in the room, so let us know when everything is ready," Ben added, quickly returning to the room, not wanting to be on camera.

* * *

After fifteen minutes, April waves at everyone. "Supper is ready! Come and get it!"

Baby dashes across the garden to be the first one in line. He loves his sister's cooking more than anything. Jenny and Ben slowly walk out, feeling a little conspicuous, not liking the idea of being on public display. They all sit down in front of the small campfire while April and June serve the fish dinner.

Debbie is frightened, seeing one girl approaching her. April walks up, holding a banana leaf with a huge portion of fish with one of the many forks borrowed from the cafeteria.

"Here you go," April said. "This is yours!"

Debbie is a little apprehensive about being served fish on the leaf. "Thank you, but—" trying to think how to say no politely.

"Go on, eat up before it gets cold!" April said, waiting for her to take it.

"Thank you," Debbie replies, carefully taking the food, noticing the little girl is not leaving.

"No, you have to eat it!" April said, still waiting. "You try it!"

She takes a small bite, surprised by how good it tastes. "This is really good! Thank you!"

April smiles. "See, it's a tasty one... We had never cooked one of those before. Plenty more when you finish that," then she joins her family by the campfire.

Debbie can now see how wonderful it must have been to eat like this every day. Although she is a little apprehensive about eating Koi from the pond, but discovers that it tastes delicious. Now, it's obvious why this family was not malnourished when they first arrived at the hospital.

* * *

Watching from the administrator's office, Dr. Martinez can't take her eyes off the two little girls. She knows this will not be an easy job with these two. Just watching what they have been doing out in the garden, she will need more time with them.

Dr. Miles is getting weary of this entire ordeal. "How are these people going to survive in the real world? I can imagine the turmoil when those girls go to school. I bet everyone will be thrilled to see those two cooking up the school mascot out on the playground for their lunch!"

"Well, at least now we can see how they survived," Dr. Martinez said. "I'm glad we're getting this on tape! No one would believe this! They're only five years old, too!"

"Just think, a big cafeteria a hundred feet away, and they are out there with a campfire cooking up a fish from the pond. I don't envy your job. At least Ben taught them well. They do know how to take care of themselves."

"A little too well," Dr. Martinez blurted out. "It's one thing to teach them how to cook, but their ability to defend themselves is our biggest problem. I wouldn't trust them around other children. Those two will need more time to assimilate," watching out the window at the little barbecue, trying to figure out how they are going to handle this.

"I have seen enough... Let's wrap this up," Dr. Miles said, grabbing the phone, making a quick call.

After several minutes on the phone, Dr. Miles hangs up the receiver, turning to Dr. Martinez. "I'm keeping them here for a week or more."

"They won't like it," Dr. Martinez said, looking a little concerned. "I don't know whether the staff can handle it either. You better have a good excuse or something to persuade them to stay here."

"We don't need an excuse... I saw her test results. Jenny needs some minor surgery."

"Is it bad?" Dr. Martinez asked, so shocked upon hearing the news.

"No, it's nothing serious, but we can do it here right away. The sooner, the better. We have some serious legal problems, so the brass wants to take care of them. We're going to give them whatever they need. It'll give you some more time to get them acclimated back to the real world, especially for Ben and those girls!"

Dr. Martinez stares out the window. "That's true... They're somewhat isolated here and have limited contact with just a few of the staff, but they're already having problems. I'm going to need a week or two just with Ben. I can handle the girls, but he is still too much of an overprotective father. He controls them when he feels uncomfortable around other people. Those kids can sense his emotions, and there are a lot of secret hand signals going on between them."

Dr. Miles nods. "Nurse Able noticed that too. The head of security is interested in this as well. He is an old Navy SEAL, and he told me that Ben and the girls are probably stealthy hunters and gatherers. He also enlightened me about how those types of people also don't trust anyone else."

"That's the way you get when you live in the wild. The first thing we need to do is have minimum contact with the kids until Ben feels that we are not a threat. He has already accepted Nurse Able, so that's a good sign. The girls like her, too, but she still has to be cautious around the boy. The little boy is the key issue here. He is the most vulnerable, so they protect him, especially the girls. Don't let anyone ever get near him, or someone will get hurt. I got Jenny to hide the girl's sticks, but as you can see, they have already made a new one."

"You got one hell of a job out there. So don't screw it up! The whole world is watching us on this one," he said, staring at the barbecue going on in the garden.

"I feel better knowing we got a couple of weeks with them," Dr. Martinez said. "At least we can release some of this footage. The press will go nuts over it."

"Good, just release a little at a time. That will keep the public relations people and the damn politicians off my back."

The video of April and June out in the garden is all over the news throughout the world. Now, it's no secret that Ben and the girls are a little on the wild side. The news frenzy never lets up. Every day, there are news reports about the Hughes family. All the experts give their opinions on how this family survived for so long. The news media has nothing but opinions and speculation since Kwajalein Island is now locked down. The doctors control the only information being released, and that is the way they like it.

* * *

Chapter 50

Operation

Ben is in a state of shock after hearing about Jenny's operation. She isn't very thrilled about it but is glad to get it over with. The doctors don't waste any time scheduling the operation first thing in the morning. The good part about having the surgery at Kwajalein is that it will be at no cost and have it done right away. Ben is not in the clear either, with plenty of dental work still to be done.

Having to stay for two weeks does not go well at all. They want to get back to their families. Having the operation means waiting a little longer, but it will give them more time for much-needed counseling. The biggest problem is not having passports or any forms of identification. Even worse, they are still legally deceased, and to undo all the death records will take time.

The children are now the doctor's primary concern. Although they are extremely healthy, they have had no inoculations and can't be around other children. Since the incident with June, they will postpone the medical exams for a while. With the extra time, they will now get special counseling. It will give the girls time to settle down before they try to do another exam, and more orderlies will be present.

* * *

Dr. Miles finally receives confirmation about Jenny's parents. After being on the phone for days trying to find anyone in her immediate family, he suspected something was wrong. On the first day, not only did Ben's family contact them, but all the other families from the flight also inquired about their loved ones.

Initially, it was thought that Jenny's family was on vacation, as she mentioned. Since the news about Jenny and Ben has been all over the television, newspapers, and the radio every day, no one understands how anyone could not know about it.

The timing couldn't have been worse. Jenny is due for surgery, and the doctors do not want to delay it. She is already prepped and waiting to be taken to the operating room.

Dr. Miles walks into the room, trying to look cheerful. "So, Jenny, how are you doing?"

"Not bad... I'm looking forward to getting this over with as quickly as possible."

"You'll do fine… In a couple of hours, you'll be back here resting up. You'll be off your feet for a few days, but it'll be OK. We have the best doctors and nurses here. You'll be well taken care of while you're here."

"Better tell that to Ben. He has been pacing all morning."

The doctor smiles, seeing Ben is indeed pacing back and forth. "Can I have a quick word with you out in the hall?"

"Sure," Ben said, wondering if the doctor wanted to discuss something about the upcoming surgery.

Ben follows the doctor into one of the adjacent rooms. Right away, he gets suspicious. He knows something is up with the way the doctor is staring at him.

"What is it?" Ben asked, thinking it was about the operation.

"I didn't want to say this in front of your wife, but I have some bad news. We finally got a call from one of Jenny's aunts on the East Coast."

Ben is so relieved. "Oh, you finally tracked them down. So, how is this bad news? She'll be so glad to hear that!"

"No, I'm sorry," Dr. Miles said, getting a little apprehensive. "We found out from her aunt. Jenny's mother and father were killed in a car accident about six months after your plane went down. Her sister is still alive but lives in Paris. We don't know why she hasn't contacted anyone. Maybe she just hasn't seen the news or read about it."

Ben is lost for words. It is a horrible blow. Jenny couldn't wait to see her parents and have them meet her new family. Now, it's never going to happen.

"She will be in surgery in a few minutes," Dr. Miles added, putting his hand on Ben's shoulder. "Maybe it would be best to wait a couple of days to tell her. It might be a little too much for her now."

Ben agrees. "You're right... Now is not a good time. I'll need a couple of days trying to find a way to tell her."

"We do have counselors here to help. Also, the Padre can give you some guidance. If you need anything, just let us know."

"Thanks, I'll probably need some help with this."

Returning to the room, Jenny is already in a wheelchair and ready to leave. She looks a little nervous.

"She'll be back in no time," Nurse Able said, knowing Ben is a nervous wreck.

Ben leans over, kissing Jenny. "Don't worry... We'll be here waiting."

Jenny smiles. "Go out and do something with the children. Don't sit around here all day long waiting in the room. I think it's time for them to get outside and have a little fun."

She reaches over, hugging and kissing the children before being taken away by the nurse. Ben and the children stand in the hallway waving. The twins are not sure what is going on, being told it's just another exam like all the others. They don't fully understand and know something is not normal.

Ben knows it's hard to hide anything from the children. They have a sixth sense and can read people's expressions. He always joked about how they could smell fear, but now he can see it's no joke. They keep staring at him, knowing something is wrong. With the constant questions, he knows he is not doing a good job of hiding his emotions.

* * *

Dr. Martinez stops by the room after hearing the news about Jenny's parents. Again, Ben steps into the other room so the girls can't hear him talking. The doctor agrees it'll be best to wait a couple of days after Jenny gets over the surgery to tell her. Ben also finds out a few more details that really disturbed him. Jenny's sister knew all about them and never tried to contact her at all. Even the doctors can't figure this one out.

Nurse Able comes into the room to help watch the children. The twins are on the prowl in their silent and listen mode. Seeing a lot of whispering going on, they know something is up. It gives Ben a chance to call Jenny's aunt and talk to her personally to find out what the hell is going on.

After talking with Jenny's aunt, Ben is so upset after hearing about her family. He found out that shortly after the death of her parents, her sister sold up everything and moved to Paris with all the inheritance. What was once a close-knit family is now very dysfunctional. He doesn't want to tell Jenny any of this. He knows she wants so much to see her family again, especially for them to meet April, June, and Baby. At least she has her aunt, uncle, and a few cousins and is not alone.

Returning to the room, Ben lies on the bed. The twins sit on the other bed, reading their book to Baby. Everyone feels so restless just sitting around for hours with nothing to do. Eventually, they all fall asleep.

* * *

Finally, the phone rings. "How is Jenny doing?" Ben frantically asked.

"Jenny is in Post Op and doing well," the nurse said.

"Oh, thank you!" Ben shouted, hanging up the phone. "Stay here and take care of Baby. I'm going to check on Mom!"

He runs down the hall to the nurse's station. "Which room is Jenny in?"

"She's doing fine," the nurse said. "Follow me," then escorts him over to the window where he can see her lying in the hospital bed, still unconscious.

"She'll be out for a while until the anesthesia wears off," the nurse explained. "We'll be monitoring her for the next couple of hours."

"Can I go in with her?" Ben asked, so nervous, seeing her lying there with all those tubes on her arms.

"I'm sorry, but that's against the rules. Jenny is doing fine, so don't worry. She'll be awake in a while. There is not much you can do until then."

"How long will it be?" he asked.

"Oh, she'll be here for several hours. Why don't you go out for a walk? It'll get your mind off of things. We'll be keeping an eye on her. She'll be back in your room after a couple of hours, so you have plenty of time."

Ben sighed. "Yeah, that's a good idea... I need to get out in the clean air and the sun for a while. We haven't done that since we arrived here."

He reluctantly returns to the room. The girls are on the bed, showing Baby the new book that Nurse Able gave them.

"Where is Mom?" April quickly asked.

"Mom is still in the doctor's room down the hall. She'll be back in a few hours. You guys want to go for a walk and look around?" he said, getting tired of being cooped up.

"We going to explore?" April excitedly asked.

"Yep! Get your things on. Let's go!"

Getting the children dressed is now more difficult with all the extra clothes. The girls put on their backpacks and filled their drinking bottles with water from the sink. He takes some fruit from the bowl on the table, dropping them in their backpacks. Grabbing a small sack, he puts in a towel, and an extra diaper, just in case.

Ben picks up Baby. "Let's check this place out and see what they got around here."

"Daddy, we going to the beach?" April asked.

"Yep! Let's check out their beach. I bet it's nothing compared to ours," remembering how beautiful their beach was.

"Our beach is nice," June added. "Plenty of good things wash up on ours, right, Daddy!"

"I know... I bet it's slim pickings on the beach they got here," holding open the door leading to the garden, ushering them all out.

It is the first time they have been outside since arriving, except for the small garden area outside their room, and they are not too impressed. So many old buildings are in decay, with trash scattered along the streets and in the grass. The hospital is located right across the street from the beach. Unfortunately, it's nothing but coral that has been piled up to protect the island.

Ben looks at the map and heads north to the only beach with sand. And that's on the opposite side of the island. Not a far walk, but it lets them see the rest of the island. Walking along the road, Ben sees all the houses surrounded by tall palm trees. A nice little community with plenty of green grass for the children to run and play.

The one thing he does notice is the absence of cars on the road. There are not too many people about, but the ones they see are riding bicycles. Seeing a bike for the first time gets the twins' attention and starts a barrage of never-ending questions.

Walking through the small community of houses, it's obvious no one is living in these anymore. Ben is wondering what happened to this island. He remembered many years ago about a shortage of housing when he and Jenny were supposed to be here. They assigned all the single people to the barracks, having to share a room with someone else. Only families could live in these houses, and now they are all empty.

Finally, they found the beach. Luckily, they have the whole place to themselves. The clean, warm air and the sounds of the surf are like a sanctuary to them. As they walk on the beach, they are a little disappointed. The beach is nice, but it's not the same as the ones they have back home. Big, rusty garbage cans line the beach, overflowing with trash. The palm trees look as if they were planted not too long ago in unnatural groups.

The children quickly strip off their clothes, running into the water. With so much garbage blowing all over the beach and into the water, it's not too appealing. With the children picking up trash out of the water, Ben has had enough. He looks at the map to see what else is around.

The harbor is not far away, and the downtown area is right next to it. There is a Macy's store, which will be the first thing on the list to check out. He knows the twins will love to go shopping there. He is also curious to see how much the world has changed since they have been gone.

After getting the children dressed, they walk to their next destination. Once they leave the beach, it doesn't take long for Ben to notice they are not alone anymore. Two military blue trucks are always in sight. The military police are still watching them with binoculars. He is curious if they are keeping an eye on them or making sure that he and the children don't walk into any classified areas.

After showing the children the large ship unloading cargo and the harbor filled with sailboats, they walk to the downtown area. When they walk into the Macy's store, they are absolutely stunned. The store has everything that anyone would want on this island. He notices there are no toys. That is the first thing that he wants to show them. Being a father now, he can't wait to buy them all the toys they want.

"Is there a toy section here or a toy shop on the base?" he asked the woman behind the counter.

"I'm sorry," the woman said, shaking her head. "We don't carry toys anymore. Since the cutbacks, there are no families stationed here, so we cleared out all the toys. I think your three are the only ones staying on the island now."

"Oh, I didn't know about that. I guess that explains all those empty houses we saw." Ben said.

"Yes, it's a shame... We lost over half of the people here last year. The families were the first to go. A lot of my friends are gone. Unfortunately, that's the way it goes around here. So, is there anything I can help you with?"

"Yes, I was wondering if you accept this card here?" he asked, realizing they still had no money.

"Let me check it," the woman behind the counter said. "Let's see if it runs through," taking the card swiping it through the machine.

"We've been using it at the little gift shop and the cafeteria. They didn't tell us if it worked outside the hospital."

"Oh, it will work here!" the woman said, looking a little startled. "Don't lose that one. It has no limit on it. You can buy everything in the store with plenty of money left over."

Ben is a little surprised. "They didn't tell us about that. Is this some kind of credit or debit card?"

"Oh yes, we all use them here. It's easier than dealing with cash. You just buy what you need, and they'll take it out of your paycheck. They do have a limit, so you don't spend more than you get paid, but yours doesn't. That's one of the good ones!"

"It's a good thing I brought it here," he said, looking at the small plastic card. "I think we'll put this one to work then. OK, guys, let's go shopping!"

They wander about the store, trying to think of what to buy. The first thing Ben finds is a small portable CD player. The old radio is the children's prized possession, and he knows they will love a new one. Walking over to the CD section, he picks out a few for the twins and Baby. They have no clue what a CD is, no matter how many times he explains it to them.

They look around for something for Jenny. Trying to think of what she will like is difficult for Ben. He has never had to shop for her before. He is so surprised at how the twins can spot things so quickly. April finds a stack of leather organizers like the one her mother has. After years out in the elements, the old one she has been using is falling apart. It will be an excellent gift for her, and they also added a fancy writing set to go with it.

They are having a great time looking around the store. Most people take all this for granted, but it's an absolute gold mine after living off the land and scavenging the beaches. Even for Ben, it's hard to get used to all of this. Just going out and picking up whatever you want without any effort is so easy.

With an entire store filled with everything a person would ever need, the twins see the one and only thing they want. A shopping bag, and it only cost $1. They are so impressed with the canvas shopping bag with a big red star and "Macy's" painted on the side. It can carry a lot of things and has nice, big handles. They can even put it over their shoulder so it doesn't drag on the ground. They place all the things they bought into it and can't wait to get back to show their mother.

* * *

Walking out of the store, Ben notices the MPs are still watching their every move. He doesn't like the idea of being watched, but there is nowhere to hide. Luckily, they can keep their distance from the MP trucks by walking across the baseball fields.

Plenty of people are walking about or riding bicycles, but luckily, no one approaches them. Ben realizes everyone on the island must know who they are. Being the only one with children is a dead giveaway. Apparently, they are the center of attention, with people always pointing them out and watching their every move.

Ben doesn't like being out on a walk with other people around. He still doesn't trust anyone, so glad they are keeping their distance. Even the children are wary of being out in the open in full view of these land sharks. Having no sticks with them makes it even worse.

On the way back to the infirmary, they see the golf course. Seeing people whacking a ball with a golf club gets the twins' attention. Ben tries to explain the game to them with not much success. The notion of hitting a little ball around doesn't make much sense to the twins. Although they think the golf clubs will make a great weapon.

Walking by the golf pro shop, Ben notices a shaved ice booth. He knows the children will love those. As they enter the shop, the twins go straight to the golf club rack. They both grab one of the clubs and start swinging them wildly around. They quickly discover that these are even better than their sticks.

The people sitting inside the pro shop are startled to see Ben walking in. At first, no one knows what to do. They thought this family was still in the infirmary and not wandering about the island. They are all scared, especially seeing the twins swinging the golf clubs around.

"Can I help you with something?" the woman at the counter asked.

"I noticed the snow cone booth outside," Ben said. "I'd like to treat the children to their first snow cones."

"Sure, it's the best thing out here to keep you cool!"

"I don't have any cash, but I have this ID card thing they gave me. Do you use this here?" hoping they'll take the card.

She picks up a towel, cleaning her hands. "We don't do money here! It's all free anyway, so don't worry about it. Come on, let's get you some snow cones!" waving at the children to follow her outside.

The woman steps into the booth, leaning out the small window. "So, what kind of snow cones would you like? We got all the flavors up here to choose from!" pointing it out to the children.

Looking over all the flavors painted on the window, it takes a while for them to decide. June finally decides to get banana-flavored, while April wants watermelon. Ben and Baby choose strawberries. The twins quickly discover this is even better than ice cream.

Getting a little too hot out in the sun, and with not much shade around, they stay inside the golf pro shop to eat their snow cones. Ben is having a hard time holding Baby on his lap, trying to keep him from dropping everything on the floor. He is one big sticky mess, grabbing a huge mouth full of the strawberry ice, ending up shivering from the cold.

The twins enjoy their snow cones until getting their first brain freeze. That doesn't stop them from digging in for more and trying to figure out how it's made. They still have problems comprehending food that's not cooked or doesn't come from a tree or the ocean.

Everyone in the pro shop is watching the spectacle. Finally, someone gets brave and starts up a conversation. Again, it's more questions about how they survived on the island. Ben is so surprised to see the twins answering all the questions being asked of them. When it comes to the subject of food and catching fish, the twins won't stop talking.

Ben feels a little better being out of the infirmary. The pro shop is a small building, but has plenty of windows that overlook the golf course. The store is not as cramped and confining as the infirmary with its dark rooms and hallways. He is so happy to get away from all those doctors and nurses but mostly the smell of the hospital.

Right in the middle of June's lobster cooking story, one of the military police cautiously walks into the pro shop.

"Excuse me, Mr. Hughes," the MP said, keeping his distance from Ben. "We received a call. Your wife will be returning to your room."

"Oh, thank you… Kids, we got to go! Let's go see Mom!"

"I'll give you a ride back to the hospital," the MP said.

"Bye, peoples! Thank you for the ice drinks!" June said, holding it up in the air.

"You come by our home," April added. "We'll show you how to catch some really big fish. We can have a fun day out on the beach too, and cook lots of lobsters, won't we, Daddy!"

Ben smiles. "Sounds like a good idea to me... Thanks for the snow cones!" waving at everyone, following the MP out to the waiting car.

Ben helps the girls get in the back seat. He put Baby on his lap then the car quickly sped off towards the infirmary. He notices the girls are so quiet. They both sit with their mouths wide open as they look out the windows. They are awestruck at seeing everything going by so fast.

"So, what do you two think of this?" Ben asked.

"Wow!" they both shouted out. "We got to take one of these back with us!" not taking their eyes from the windows.

The short outing ended up being a great day for the children. Staying inside the hospital is getting them depressed. Back in their element again, they all enjoyed being outside. The car ride is astounding, and the twins can't wait to get back to tell their mother.

* * *

The children run down the hallway yelling and screaming, going back to their old ways, so full of energy. They burst into their room to find their mother lying in bed talking with Nurse Able.

"Mom!" the girls yelled out. "We went exploring, and we got you a present!"

Jenny is so thrilled. "Oh, thank you! Did you have a nice day?" still feeling tired.

April and June tell their mother about their long walk and all the shops. The car ride and snow cones were also a big event of the day. Even better, they got presents from a big store.

"Look Mom! We got a new carry bag!" they both shouted, holding it up to show her.

"That is a nice one! You can put a lot into that!" Jenny replied, seeing the Macy's bag.

"They have a Macy's here?" she asked, looking over at Ben.

"Oh, yeah! Nice one too!" he replied.

"We got some more!" April added, pulling out everything.

Jenny opens her present. "This is wonderful! I can really use this," surprised to see she got a new organizer.

"See!" April said. "You got plenty to write on now. They got a whole bunch more at that store!"

"Thanks for the gifts!" Jenny said, hugging the girls. "I have a lot more to write about now."

Ben puts Baby on the bed beside her. "He's got one for you too!"

"What have you been doing?" she asked, so shocked, seeing her son covered with red stains all over his face and clothes. "You're all sticky, and you messed up all of your new clothes!"

"They had their first snow cones today," Ben proudly explained. "He's wearing most of his, as you can see."

Jenny laughed. "I can see that! Looks like he's still hungry," seeing Baby is still chewing on the wrapping paper.

"You got me a present!" she said, gently taking the small package from his sticky hands.

She opens it, so surprised to see a fancy pen and pencil set. "Wow! This is great! Thank you for these wonderful gifts, and it's not even Christmas yet. You guys had a great day," glad they were having a good time.

"Look! We got some ice drinks too! Want some?" June asked, holding up the Styrofoam cup.

"Yeah, it's good!" April said. "But it hurts your head when you eat too much. You try some," handing over the half-empty sticky snow cone.

"Maybe a little later," Jenny said, looking up at Nurse Able, seeing her shaking her head no.

"Your mother can try that later on," Nurse Able said. "It might be a little too much for her right now."

"Show her what else you got," Ben mentioned.

"We got something too!" pulling out the small CD player.

"That's a nice radio!" Jenny said. "Now, you can listen to all your music."

"OK, you guys," Ben said, seeing Jenny getting tired. "Let's give Mom a break. Why don't you sit on the other bed so I can talk to her?"

All three quickly jump up on the other bed, examining their new CD player. With so many new things that they have never seen before, it's even better than Christmas.

Ben sits on the edge of the bed, talking with Jenny and Nurse Able. He is so relieved to hear that everything is fine. Jenny will be back on her feet again after a day or two, although she will take it slow for the next two weeks. She is more interested in hearing about their first day out than having to talk about the details of her surgery. She also can't wait to get out in the sun, not wanting to be cooped up in bed for several days.

* * *

"Well, I'm off duty now," Nurse Able said. "Jenny, if there is anything you need, just press the button. They'll be checking on you most of the night, so don't be surprised when someone comes into your room," giving Ben that look.

Ben knows all too well that comment is meant for him. None of the hospital staff are to barge into the room without calling in advance. Nurse Able is their only main contact. The others won't even go near the room.

"Thanks for everything," Jenny said.

"You're welcome... I'll be around first thing in the morning. Goodbye, girls, Baby! I'll see you later," waving to them as she left the room.

"Bye!" April, June, and Baby shout out, waving back at her.

"Daddy, can you get the radio to work?" April asked, holding up the new CD player.

"What did you get them?" Jenny asked, seeing all the new things on the bed.

"It's a portable CD player with a built-in radio and lots of CDs."

"How did you get all this with no money?" she asked, looking up at Ben, concerned.

"Apparently, this is like money here," he said, holding up the small ID card. "For some reason, we got a big bank account here too! Maybe it's all our paychecks for the last six years, all on this one little card!"

"That would be nice... So what did you get for yourself?"

He shrugs. "Nothing, I don't need anything. I have these new clothes and shoes the nurse gave us. That's about all I need for now."

"I bet you looked at all the cameras," she mumbled, having a hard time keeping her eyes open.

He thinks about it for a few seconds. "Yeah, they did look nice, but that's all in the past."

"You should have gotten one. We'll need one to take pictures of the children to send home," then slowly closes her eyes, falling asleep.

He gets up, putting the blanket over her. She fell asleep so quickly. As Jenny sleeps, Ben sits on the bed with the children, helping with their new radio. After putting in the batteries, then tunes the radio to one of the local stations. They are all shocked, hearing the clear sound.

"Wow! That sounds nice! But what do these do?" April asked, holding up the CD.

"Oh, these have all the music on them," Ben explained, forgetting they had never seen a CD before. "Just put one in, and it plays them for you. This one has over 100 children's sing-a-longs. You'll really like these."

"What's a sing long?" April asked.

Ben smiles. "These are songs that you can all sing with each other. Just like the ones we sing back home from the radio. You can even teach Baby to sing these."

"Can we do one now?" June asked, trying to get the CD player to work.

"OK, guys, you better sit outside on the grass so you don't wake Mom."

"Yeah, Mom is taking a nap," April whispered. "Let's go outside and sing some songs."

They all run outside, sitting in a circle, so excited about their new present. One of the things they love to do is listen to the radio, sing, and dance. They don't take long to figure out how to operate the CD player and are already learning all the new songs.

* * *

Chapter 51

Bad News

After several days, Jenny is already up and walking about but stays in the room most of the time. She is back to writing in her journals again, trying to catch up since leaving their home. With an endless supply of paper and pens, she is so glad to write again without using the entire page with small print.

Returning from the dentist, Ben is not surprised to see the twins talking to his mother on the phone. Speaking on the telephone is now their favorite pastime. Baby is up on the bed, dancing about to his music from the CD player. Ben doesn't like seeing his children cooped up in the room and not enjoying themselves outside.

Ben knows Jenny is getting more frustrated as the days pass. She never says anything but gets agitated whenever the girls talk to his parents on the phone. The people at the hospital give her the runaround every time she asks about her family. He dreads having to tell her but can't put it off any longer.

After talking to his mother for a while, Ben keeps the conversation short so he can talk to Jenny. Hanging up the phone, he sends the children out to the garden to listen to their music so he can be alone. Sitting on the bed, he looks up at the ceiling, dreading this moment.

"What's up?" Jenny asked, seeing Ben was deep in thought about something.

"Oh, nothing," trying to think how to do this.

"Your teeth still bothering you? Don't tell me there are more forms to fill out," seeing the stack of paperwork in his hand.

He doesn't say a word. Getting up, he shuts the door leading out to the garden, then pulls up a chair sitting next to Jenny. He keeps looking away, trying to figure out the best way to tell her.

She knows this is not good news. "It's about my mom and dad, isn't it?"

He takes in a deep breath and looks her in the eye. "Jenny, I have been trying to find the right moment to tell you... No, it's not good. They were in a car accident not long after we were on the island. I'm so sorry. They didn't make it."

She puts her writing pen down and just stares at him without saying a word. The news is devastating. Somehow, she knew something was wrong when she couldn't contact her family. So lost for words, she buries her face in her hands, crying hysterically. Helping her up, Ben walks her over to the bed. She doesn't want to talk or be around anyone. It is just too much for her. She never imagined that the news could be this bad.

"What about my sister? Was she with them? Are they all gone?" Jenny asked after regaining her composure.

"No, she wasn't with them at the time. After the funeral, she apparently sold everything and moved to Paris."

She is so confused. "What? Why would she do that? How come she never called? Does she know?"

He slowly shakes his head. "I really don't know... No one's heard from her. They did get a call from your aunt. That's how we found out. I talked to her a couple of days ago."

"A couple of days ago! You knew about this and didn't tell me!"

"They found out right before your operation. The doctors thought it would be best to wait until you recovered a little."

She closes her eyes, trying to calm down. "You're right... I couldn't have gone through all that knowing this. What a nightmare!" crying again.

"I have been keeping your aunt up-to-date with everything. She's waiting for you to call. Here are their numbers and the one for your sister. I tried calling her, but I kept getting an answering machine. I left a message, but no one has called back. Maybe she is away from home or something," handing her all the phone numbers.

"I don't understand why my sister hasn't called if she knew we were here?" she asked, looking down at the paper so confused.

"Maybe she has a reason for it. She thought she lost you, then her mom and dad not long after. You might try calling her."

"I knew something was wrong! I just knew it! They would have called me on the first day," thinking about her parents again.

"I know... It's only about nine or ten at night in France now. Why don't you call your sister and find out what's going on? Maybe she doesn't know?"

"I like to be alone for a while. I need time to think about all this."

"I'll go out and sit with the kids and keep them busy. If you need anything, I'll be right outside," Ben said, then hugged and kissed her.

Ben walks outside, sits on the grass with the children. They are having a good time singing all their new songs. Seeing the look on their father's face, they know something is wrong.

"What is it, Daddy?" June asked, looking up at her father.

He knows they can sense when something is wrong. He tries to explain how their mother's parents had gone to heaven. They don't understand, but Ben lets them know their mother will be sad for the next couple of days.

Ben feels so sorry for Jenny. After all they have been through, she finds out she has lost her family. He has his whole family waiting for him at home, but now she has no one. He keeps an eye on her through the window. She is on the phone talking to someone, but her reaction is not what he expected. She is distraught and angry. He knows it's most likely her sister. After talking with her aunt, he knew something was up between Jenny and her sister Kim.

* * *

Ben sits out in the garden with the children, listening to the music for a long time. For some strange reason, the children's favorite CD is the 'Best of Elvis.' All three are dancing wildly to the old Elvis songs. They are missing the big parties with the bonfires out on the beach and going out fishing every day. Even going up on the island for food and firewood is now just a memory. This island has plenty of new things and luxuries, but it's not their home.

Jenny finally walks out to the garden with a stunned look on her face. She doesn't say a word sitting next to Ben, putting her arms around him. They sit quietly together, watching the children singing and dancing.

"You talked to your sister?" Ben finally asked.

"I don't have a sister anymore," she whispered. "I don't have anyone now."

"What happened? Is she still in France?"

"Yes, she is... I can't believe she sold everything we had. Our home, the restaurant, everything is gone! All those years building up the restaurants, and now it's all thrown away. Dad would have wanted us to keep it in the family. But now, she's sold it all to live a life of luxury in Paris. All she talked about was money and all the expensive things she had. She didn't even want to talk about Mom and Dad. I just can't believe it. It's like she doesn't even care that I'm alive!"

"What's wrong with her?" he asked, not understanding any of this.

"I don't have a clue!" she said, wiping the tears from her eyes. "I tried making arrangements for when we can meet. She told me that she is real busy and will get back to me in a couple of months!"

"A couple of months!" Ben blurted out, so stunned.

"I didn't know what to say... All I wanted was to see her again and to meet you and the children. I can't believe that I don't have a family anymore. I have no one."

"You still have all of us now, plus the twenty or thirty I got back home. You're part of our family now," he said, putting his arm around her, holding her tight.

"You have a loving family, all eagerly waiting for you to return. Mine is worried about losing half of her money!"

"Just don't worry about it. It'll all work out in the end. Maybe we'll show up one day and surprise her. We'll let the children loose in her fancy house."

"Oh, she'll love that!" she said, being sarcastic.

"I can just see the girls tearing up some of her antique chairs for firewood so they can cook up one of her pets. Then Baby will be running around, squatting down, pooping on all her expensive Persian carpets."

She laughs. "They'll probably be doing that at your parent's house as well."

He cringes, realizing she might be right. "Yeah, I know... I better warn them about that!" and starts laughing.

"Well, you do have your aunt and uncle," he said. "She seems really nice. You need to call her."

"I did, but they're not home. Maybe I'll try a little later. I can't believe this… I'll never see Mom and Dad," then cries again.

After thinking about her parents and all the good times they had together, Jenny is overcome with emotions. Ben takes her to the room so she can lie down for a while. All he can do is to be by her side and help as much as he can. He finally calls the front desk and asks the Padre to help.

The hospital is making Jenny so depressed. Padre William Fisher and Dr. Martinez walk her to the small chapel to help her deal with the loss of her family. Ben takes the children out for a long walk to keep them busy.

* * *

After several days, things are getting back to normal. They scheduled another physical for April and June. After the last incident, the girls are separated. Both are apprehensive about their physical. No matter how much it is explained to them and how there is nothing to worry about, they don't like it one bit.

April is the first. After talking with her sister, she is reluctant to go. Jenny walks her down to the exam room, while Ben stays in the room with June and Baby.

April tries to be brave. After walking into the exam room, seeing all the people and strange medical instruments, she knows it's not going to be good.

June is pacing back and forth in the room. She doesn't like this at all. She keeps talking about going back home, where they don't have to go through all these horrible exams and where life was simple and easy. Ben feels the same, but he knows it's for their own good.

Things are quiet until June jumps up. "Daddy! Something's wrong! It's April!"

"What do you mean?" he asked, startled by her outburst, glancing around the room.

"She's in trouble! You watch, Baby!" reaching under the bed, pulling out two newly made sticks, running out of the room.

"No, no! You stay here!" chasing after her, but June was already too far down the hallway.

Baby starts screaming, being left alone. Ben runs back to the room to get him. He quickly grabs Baby and races back down the hallway. He knows there will be some serious problems if he doesn't catch up with June.

June runs as fast as she can. She follows the screams of her sister echoing through the long hallway. She reaches the exam room, finding the door closed. With a swift kick, the door slams open, knocking over the nurse. April is screaming out loud, fighting to get away from the doctor and the immunization shot.

"April, I got your stick!" June said, tossing it to her sister.

April grabs the stick in midair and strikes one nurse on the back of her head.

Complete chaos fills the room. Before anyone can do anything, June smacks the doctor upside his head with her stick. Trays are knocked over, scattering everything on the floor. Everyone is scrambling to get far away from the two little girls.

"June, no! You put that down!" Jenny grabs her stick before she can strike again.

"You bad peoples!" June shouted.

"Mom! You're not helping! These bad peoples!" April cries out, trying to strike the doctor with her stick.

Nurse Able grabs hold of June before she can hit anyone else. "You calm down! They're not going to hurt April! They are here to help!"

Once Ben reaches the room carrying Baby, everything is in turmoil. Alarms are sounding, and red lights are flashing. To make matters worse, three huge orderlies show up at the door.

"Ben, you're supposed to keep her in the room!" Jenny said, getting so furious with him.

"Sorry!" he said, handing Baby over to her. "She knew something was wrong and just ran out. I didn't have a chance to stop her."

June lunges at the doctor again. "Daddy! They are hurting April!"

"Ben, I told you no more sticks!" Jenny blurted out.

"I hid them up," he said, quickly grabbing the sticks. "I guess they made some new ones."

"Yeah, why is everyone taking our sticks?" June asked, getting so mad. "We keep having to make more! We need our sticks!"

"You're the one who trained them," Jenny said, "so you're going to have to fix this. They can't keep attacking people."

"Sorry," he said, looking over at the girls. "OK, guys... It's time for your shots."

April is so mad. "We don't like shots! They hurt!"

"You are Amazon warriors, aren't you?" he asked, giving them a stern look.

Both girls nod. "Yeah, we Amazon girls! We ain't scared of nothing!" lunging at the doctor again.

"That's right! So, show these nice people how you can take a shot and not be scared. Ain't no crying, either. Amazon girls are so brave, and they don't cry over nothing!"

"OK, Daddy," April said, a little hesitant.

Ben motions to the doctor. "They won't give you any more problems. You can give them both all their shots. Let's get this over with now."

The doctor is hesitant, but he knows this is the only chance he has got. He gets Nurse Able to help. They quickly give both the girls all their shots right then and there. The twins don't even flinch.

"See, that's all it is," Jenny explained. "It's just a little shot. All that fuss over nothing," a little perturbed, seeing how they stand there getting one shot after another.

"So, are you finished with April?" Ben asked the doctor.

"That's it for her... She's as healthy as an Amazon warrior! But I still need to check June, though," glancing over at her, a little reluctant after the last attempt.

Ben turns to June. "You're next, and I don't want to hear about any problems. You're going to get a checkup just like April did. Mom is going to be in here with you. I'll wait outside with April and Baby."

"Thanks," Jenny said. "I think I can handle her now."

"Come on," he said, taking April's hand. "We'll wait in the hallway until June is done."

April turns to her sister. "Don't worry! We'll be out there just in case," pointing to the door.

In the hallway, Ben finds even more orderlies waiting. The administrator and Dr. Martinez are standing with stunned looks on their faces.

"You just need to know how to handle them," Ben explains, seeing the look he is getting.

"We're going to talk about this later," Dr. Martinez said, pointing her finger at Ben.

"April just got a little scared. They watch out for each other. June knew she was in trouble."

"How did she know?" the doctor asked, looking a little puzzled about it all. "I thought you were in your room with her?"

"Yeah, we were... The girls have always been like that. Like you said, they're identical twins. They don't talk in stereo for nothing," Ben explained.

The doctor smiles. "Needless to say, we still need to discuss this," realizing that the girls can almost read each other's minds.

* * *

The last days on Kwajalein are quiet and peaceful. All the medical exams and the never-ending paperwork are finally over. Jenny has accepted that her parents are gone. She attended daily counseling to help her with her loss. Jenny has also accepted the fact that her sister Kim is more concerned about losing half of her money and possessions. At least she has her aunts and uncles back home eagerly waiting to see her again.

Ben's counseling is far more difficult. His trust in people is still not as they hoped when it comes to the children. He still watches people like a hawk whenever someone is near the children. The subtle signals to the twins always keep them on guard.

The twins, however, are just as wild as on the first day they arrived. They are just as resourceful and a threat to anyone who comes within reach of their sticks. Time after time, their sticks are always being taken away only to be replaced with others that are stashed away. When they found out where Nurse Able was hiding them, they secretly snuck out to retrieve them in the middle of the night, hiding them somewhere else.

The only one who showed the most progress is Baby, who is really friendly, always wanting to play. Although the doctors had learned that if he feels threatened, he will signal his sisters to protect him. That was the root of many of the problems with the twins. Being so young, he didn't know what he was doing, thinking it was all a game. At times, he would point to some orderly walking down the hall, then signal his sisters to attack. He always thought it was funny seeing his sisters chasing off a grown man with their sticks.

* * *

Chapter 52

Return Home

After returning from their morning walk on the beach, they are so surprised to see Dr. Miles waiting for them. He is so glad to see the Hughes family is getting out more. They are back to their old ways, getting up at sunrise, going out walking on the beach.

"Good morning! I got some good news. There are no more sessions, and it's all over. There is a flight heading for Hawaii tomorrow, and you're going to be on it!"

"We're going home!" Jenny blurted out.

"Yes, indeed!" Dr. Miles continued. "You're not going to believe this, but we just got word that they have confirmed that you are Ben Hughes and Jenny Mason by your fingerprints. They'll be issuing temporary passports for you and the kids in Honolulu."

"Why so long?" she asked. "They should have had that straightened out after a few days."

"It's nothing but bureaucracy at its worst," the doctor explained. "The biggest problem we had is with the contracting company that hired you. They went bankrupt with all the insurance claims and lawsuits, dumping all their employment records in the trash. They found it easiest to pack up and walk away. Those people did everything they could to cover their tracks."

"So, basically, what you're saying is that we're on our own?" Ben asked.

"No, the plane was under contract by Kwajalein, and the cause of the accident was pilot error. The personnel department here took over when they found you. Responsibility for dealing with you is bouncing from one federal department to another. With the new information you gave us about the accident, the FAA has reopened the case. It's now making a few people really nervous about who may be responsible for this mess."

"I can tell you now it was not pilot error!" Ben said adamantly. "They shouldn't take the fall for it."

He quickly retracted his remark. "I'm sorry... They'll most likely be cleared, but you know how things work. They'll look for something else like faulty maintenance."

"Welcome back to civilization," Jenny remarked. "Everyone's pointing their fingers at someone else to take the blame," remembering that fateful day.

"Don't worry about it," the doctor said. "Things will work out. Just remember… You're finally going back home."

"You're right," Ben said. "I guess we can't complain. We're going home."

Ben is lucky that his family is waiting for him. His mother is very adamant that they will stay with them. With all the hassles, getting new Social Security numbers and driver's licenses can take months. Until then, they have no money or ability to get a job. Removing their deaths from all the databases will take forever, with an endless number of forms to fill out. They will literally be aliens in their own country with no forms of identification.

The insurance companies are now taking legal action to refund the money awarded to Ben and Jenny's parents. Jenny's sister Kim, who lives in a foreign country, doesn't have to bother with any of the American lawyers. Ben's family is not wealthy, and most of Ben's life insurance was used to pay off their bills or fix up the house. The press is having a field day with the insurance companies, calling them evil and heartless as they harass the family trying to refund all their money.

Jenny makes good use of the money card before they leave. She goes to all the shops to get a new suitcase and more clothes for her and the children. Ben insists on keeping his old white duffel bag. He wants to have a big spend up with the card, getting one of those new digital cameras, and a laptop computer. After thinking about it, he realizes those days are long gone. Now, as a father with three children and a wife to support. The days of buying expensive toys for himself are over.

That night, they join the hospital staff for a final barbecue. Japanese lanterns are strung all around the beach. With plenty of food and a live band, it's the last of the fun days. The children really love it, dancing and singing late into the night until they all fall asleep.

* * *

Early in the morning, a transport van arrives at the infirmary, and all the doctors and nurses are at the main entrance to say goodbye. Life on the island will not be the same without the Hughes family. Jenny and Ben thanked everyone for all they had done for them and apologized for all the problems they had caused.

"I hope you're not going to give us the bill?" Ben jokingly asked, shaking Dr. Miles' hand with a very firm grip.

Dr. Miles laughed. "Don't tempt me... Although it'll be hard to bill someone when they are still legally deceased."

Ben smiles. "That's true... That'll be our first big hurdle when we get back home. Oh well, thanks for everything anyway."

"Remember, you have some hard times ahead, but you all are healthy. Just take it one day at a time. Oh, and remember, not everyone is a land shark."

Ben nods. "Thanks... I'll try to remember that."

"Thank you," Jenny said, hugging the doctor. "I hope we weren't too much trouble."

He laughed. "Oh, no... It's been great since you've been here. It's going to be so boring now that you're leaving."

Nurse Able gives Jenny and Ben a big hug. "I'm so glad to have met you. You have a pleasant trip home," wiping away the tears from her face.

"I'm going to miss you," Jenny said. "You've been such a great help with the children. I'm glad that they made a friend here."

"Well, I'm going to really miss them. It's been so nice having the children here on the island. Now, don't worry about anything. I think y'all will do just fine when you get back home."

The nurse then turns to Ben. "Now, you take care of the babies, you hear," giving him a big bear hug.

"I always do," he said.

Nurse Able cries, saying goodbye to April, June, and Baby. The twins are sad to be leaving Nurse Able, giving her one last hug before getting into the van. She is the children's first real friend, and they are going to miss her.

"How much time do we have?" Ben asked the driver.

"Your flight leaves in about thirty minutes. It'll only take a couple of minutes to get there, so you have plenty of time. They won't take off until everyone is on the plane, anyway."

"Can we stop at the memorial?" Ben asked. "We would like to see it before we leave."

The driver nods. "Sure, it's on the way."

The van pulls off the road near the main gate of the air terminal. Ben steps out, carrying Baby, followed by Jenny and the twins. Standing silently, they stare at the polished granite monument. Surrounded by flowers, it contains all the names of the twenty-two people lost on the flight.

Jenny reads out aloud all the names of those who lost their lives so long ago. They try to visualize the faces of their old friends. Seeing their own names, they realize how lucky they are. A very somber moment as they thought about those few days together in Hawaii.

After a few minutes at the memorial, they continue to the airport. The van drives right up to the 737, waiting on the tarmac. A small group of people is waiting by the ramp. Several are in full-blue dress military uniforms, plus a few military police.

When the van stops, two airmen open the back doors, taking out the bags, putting them in the cargo hold. Two men in full uniform stand by the ramp next to the plane. Ben recognizes one as the base commander but not the other.

Colonel Jones walks over. "I hope you had a pleasant stay while you were here."

"Oh, yes!" Jenny said, shaking his hand. "Thank you very much. Thank you for everything!"

"Thanks for all your help," Ben said, shaking the Colonel's hand.

"My pleasure! Have a safe trip!"

The other man holds out his hand to Ben. "Hello, sorry we have not met... I'm Paul Rutherford."

"I heard some fine things about you from home," Ben said, shaking his hand.

"Thank you," Paul replied. "Tell your mother she was right about everything."

"Yeah, I heard about that... Can't wait to hear the whole story when I get home," knowing he is talking about his mother's premonitions.

Paul then turns to Jenny. "I'm so sorry about your parents. I have spent many hours on the phone with them, and I even met with them in DC. They really loved you and were deeply saddened to hear of your loss."

Jenny hugs him. "Thank you! Thank you for all you have done," wiping away the tears.

An airman approaches. "Excuse me, sir, we're behind schedule," he said, looking a little impatient.

Jenny and Ben are apprehensive about getting on the airplane. They slowly walk up the ramp, taking one last look at the island. A stewardess waits at the top of the ramp, prompting them to hurry. Everyone must have been eager to get off the island and back to Hawaii for a vacation. The plane is only half-full, with most of the passengers going on their two-week vacation off the island.

The stewardess escorts them to the back of the plane. Although there are plenty of seats available, she keeps motioning them to the rear. Jenny wonders if they are being kept far away from the other passengers because of the children.

"The best seats on the plane," the stewardess jokingly said when they reached the very last row of seats.

"OK, I get it," Ben said, finally figuring out why they are being escorted all the way to the back.

"Well, I don't!" Jenny said, a little confused. "What's going on?"

"Remember, we sat in the back the last time."

"I'm sorry," the stewardess said, so embarrassed. "They figured you'd prefer these seats again. You can sit anywhere else if you prefer. As you can see, there are plenty of seats available."

Jenny shuddered. "Oh no, this is fine," remembering the last flight where they sat in the very last row of seats.

They feel so uncomfortable helping the children into their seats. Sitting at the back of the plane years ago was the only reason they survived the last flight. That is one memory that they are not too fond of, and they are not looking forward to this flight.

With three seats on each side of the aisle, they have to split up. Ben sits with the twins on one side, letting them sit next to the window. Right across the aisle, Jenny is with Baby.

The twins are so excited, pressing their faces up against the window looking outside. "Daddy, is this a boat?" June asked, still confused about airplanes.

"Oh, no, remember, this one is an airplane. It flies high up in the air, just like the birds do, but this one goes fast. It's going to be better than the car ride!"

"What's that noise?" April asked, hearing the engines starting up, getting scared.

"That don't sound good!" June added. "I don't like this at all!" feeling the plane moving.

"That's the engines... See those big things hanging from the wings. Just wait and see. It's going to be fun! Remember, you wanted to go fast in that car? Well, this one goes even faster!"

Jenny doesn't have any problems with Baby. He is already sound asleep.

"Are you OK?" Ben asked.

She simply nods. "I can't wait until we get there. At least Baby is already sleeping."

Ben laughed. "He can sleep through anything. I thought he would want to see this."

"Oh no, you don't! Let him sleep… I'm planning to sleep all the way to Hawaii as well."

Jenny and Ben look deep into each other's eyes, not saying a word. Like on their original flight, they hold each other's hands as the plane prepares to take off. Both are trembling. Knowing that they have their children with them this time makes it far worse. They can't stop thinking about that last flight all those years ago. Flying from Kwajalein Island to Hawaii and then to Texas will probably mean a whole day of traveling, and they are not looking forward to it.

The engines are so loud when the pilot gives it full throttle that the plane vibrates and jostles as it speeds down the runway. The girls are so thrilled to see how fast they are going. Once up in the air, they both are yelling out loud.

"We're really far up, aren't we, Daddy!" June said.

"It's like we are on the lookout!" April added. "Everything is way down there!" with her face pressed up against the window.

"That sure looks like it," Ben said, seeing the small island far below.

"Look! We are already up in the clouds!" June points to the small cumulus clouds in the distance.

"We're going to be even higher than that. You'll get to see what it looks like as if we're up on the clouds looking down at the ocean."

"Daddy, what's those things way out there?" April asked, pointing out to the horizon.

"Those are islands just like our home. See how small they look from way up here."

"Is one of those our home?" June excitedly asked.

"No, ours is way on the other side," Ben explained, shaking his head. "I don't think we can see it from here. It's a shame, though. It will be nice to see what it looks like from up in the air."

In just a few minutes, all they can see is the dark blue ocean far below. Seeing the clouds from this high up is still a treat for the twins. They know how to read the clouds to determine how the weather is going to be. Seeing everything from so high up prompts so many endless questions.

The girls are getting a lot of attention from the flight attendants. Luckily, the galley and the bathrooms are right behind them. The flight attendant serves them drinks and snacks right away. The twins get little coloring books and crayons, which keep them busy. For Jenny and Ben, this is almost like first-class, being pampered so much with the flight attendant always coming back and forth, checking on them, bringing them more drinks and magazines.

The doctors gave Jenny something to help her sleep since she had been apprehensive about the flight. She takes the pills, and it's not long before she is sound asleep. The twins fall asleep as well, having been up so late at the party. Baby is still sleeping without a care in the world.

Ben can never sleep on a plane. He spends hours thinking about the life that he left behind. Every day on their island was an absolute paradise. He feels like he is returning from a long vacation, having to go back to an eight-to-five job, working five days a week. The worst part of a job is spending all day sitting in a small cubicle with no windows. He is ready to go back home to their island to live the life that he loved so much.

* * *

Ben wakes the girls so they can see the famous Hawaiian Islands. As they approach Oahu, it's a spectacular view, especially with the sun just above the horizon. They both quickly have their noses pressed against the window, so excited with the view.

"Is that one our home?" April promptly asked, pointing down at the island.

"Oh, no, we're a long way from our home. That is the place where your mother and I were before we arrived on our island. It's way bigger than ours, and there are lots of people here too."

"It's bigger than the hospital place?" April asked.

"This island is a lot bigger!" Ben explained. "I bet you it'll take us a week or more to walk around this one."

"Look at that beach! I bet there's some good stuff getting washed up there. Can we go there first?" June asked.

"No, I don't think we'll have time," wishing they could stay in Hawaii for a few days.

"Can we go out on the beach just for a while?" June asked.

"Sorry, we'll have to get on another plane once we get off this one. It's going to be a long trip. Granny and Granddad live a long way from our home. They'll be so happy to meet you," he said, trying to encourage them, knowing that this is going to be a long, grueling flight.

"Daddy, we going to come back here to the beach after we see Granny?" April asked.

He sighed. "Maybe someday," feeling bad knowing how much they loved the beach.

As the plane comes in for its final approach, Ben checks on Jenny and Baby, who are still asleep. He is hoping to let them sleep until they reach the terminal. The plane lands with a hard bump, and it's finally over. The roar of the full-throttle engines to slow the plane is so loud it wakes everyone up right away.

"Thank God!" Jenny said, so glad they had landed. "It's nice to wake up and find it's already over. Just think, we finally made it! It took six years, but we're finally here!"

"Yeah, we made it," Ben said. "Unfortunately, we still have two more flights after this. Twelve more hours to Dallas, and then another hour to Austin," reaching over, taking her hand.

"I'm going to make use of these little babies. They knock you out real good," pulling out the little white medicine bottle from her pocket.

"I can't believe you slept the entire flight," he said. "Even Baby was asleep the whole time, too."

"Don't tell me you didn't sleep at all?" she asked, looking concerned.

"I can never sleep on a plane... The bad thing about these flights, there is nothing to look at but blue water! At least the next flight is at night. I might be able to sleep a little on that one."

* * *

They had wanted to spend several days in Hawaii, but their flights had been booked without their knowledge. They have only an hour at the airport before boarding the next nonstop flight to Dallas. Since they don't have any money or any forms of identification, it will be impossible for them to stay in Hawaii. Ben wonders how they will get on the other flight, knowing most require a photo ID before boarding.

The Boeing 737 goes to the same terminal as their original flight. As they departed the plane, following everyone into a small room. Being at the end of the line, it's a little unnerving seeing everyone getting their passports stamped by immigration officials. With no identification at all, they wonder what the immigration people are going to do with them.

Ben knows this is the beginning of the bureaucracy. Luckily, Mrs. Burns is waiting at the counter, waving at them and holding up their passports. Seeing that she is here to help is a big relief.

Mrs. Burns and Jenny talk with each other while the immigration officials are going over the documents. Luckily, they are the last ones in line, not creating a problem for anyone else.

While they wait, Ben notices two armed police officers hovering around. He knows right away that they are keeping an eye on him. His reputation has already preceded him, and probably the twins as well.

No one approaches Jenny or Ben, and especially the children. The entire area is cleared out except for the immigration officials. He is so glad that there is no welcoming committee or any reporters. This is the way he liked it. Quiet, with no special treatment.

Several important-looking people wearing suits walk up. They go through all the paperwork. Mrs. Burns is definitely in charge, telling everyone what to do. The immigration officials are scurrying about, looking confused. All they do is stamp every document two or three times while others sign the witness forms. Apparently, they have never done this before, and no one really knows what to do.

Ben carries Baby to keep him from running off and getting in trouble. April and June are a little unnerved with all the ruckus going on. The two armed police also get their attention, and the twins are staring them down. Standing next to their father, the girls are keeping an eye on things. With their sticks in hand, they secretly start communicating with each other with hand signals, ready to pounce.

* * *

After thirty minutes of waiting around, Mrs. Burns hands them their temporary passports. They completed the first step. They don't have to sign anything or talk to anyone. Mrs. Burns handled everything, and it's all done. After all those years, they are back on American soil again.

Mrs. Burns escorts them out to the terminal on an electric cart. The immigration officials instruct her to take them directly to the American Airlines terminal with no stops. Since they only have a few minutes before their next flight, there is no choice in the matter.

Security is an issue, but the press is also a big concern. All done in secret, only a handful of people know what is going on. Although it won't take long before the news media discovers that the Hughes family is now in Hawaii.

Jenny and Ben are concerned about Mrs. Burns driving the cart to their next flight. They are hoping she doesn't drive as wildly as she did on the trip to the airport.

The children love the ride through the terminal. Seeing all the people bustling about wearing such colorful clothes is a sight to see. The large walkway with all its windows, stores, and lights really intrigues them.

The police closely follow behind. The two men wearing suits are also riding with the police, constantly talking into their radios. Ben can see the suits are definitely government since they stand out from everyone else. The clean, short haircuts are a dead giveaway. They are also way too serious, looking as if they are escorting dangerous criminals through the terminal.

Mrs. Burns takes them straight to their next flight, stopping right in front of the gate. The gate is almost empty except for two airline attendants waiting by the door leading to the plane. She informs Ben that she has been in contact with his family several times and will make the next call as soon as the plane takes off. Jenny and Ben thanked her as attendants quickly ushered them straight onto the huge Boeing 777 flight to Dallas.

* * *

The flight to Dallas is a little different. They are now among civilians once again and on their own for the first time. Their seats are in the center row up front, right next to the first-class section. Facing the bulkhead, at least they have a huge flat-screen television to stare at for the rest of the flight. Unfortunately, they are in the coach section, able to see the luxurious first-class seating and pampering. With only four seats, someone will have Baby on their lap for a long time. In a way, that's good because it will keep him from running around.

Just like on their last flight, the plane moves away from the terminal once they are in their seats. Jenny and Ben sit on the aisle seats, keeping the children in the middle so they can't get up and roam around. They are now wide awake and ready to explore, wanting to look out the windows like on the last flight. Luckily, it's already dark, so Ben gives them their coloring books and crayons to keep them busy.

The flight is long and boring. They are stuck in small, cramped seats with nothing to do. They can either watch the movie or stare at the wall. Knowing that this is a twelve-hour flight doesn't help, and worse, they still have a connecting flight to Austin. By the time they arrive at their final destination, they will have traveled for almost 24 hours. At least it will finally be over.

Jenny has the first bathroom break with the girls. The years of going together were convenient on the island, but now it's a problem. Luckily, there are two opposing toilets vacant. She has both the doors half-closed while standing outside, waiting. As usual, April and June are singing songs out loud to the amusement of the nearby passengers.

Ben walks up, and down the aisle, taking turns with Baby and the twins. A few other people are doing the same, trying to stretch their legs. The one thing he does like about this flight is that no one recognizes them and leaves them alone. They are just like all the other passengers, anonymous.

The airline food makes the trip even longer. The choice between lasagna or baked chicken doesn't help. Not having any fresh fish or fruit is a big disappointment. The chicken is their safest choice. They pick over the food, finding it has absolutely no taste at all. The salad and bread rolls with strawberry jam are the only things that the twins can eat. The applesauce for dessert does put smiles on their faces.

* * *

After a while, it becomes difficult to keep the twins from exploring. They are so intrigued by the first-class section, always wandering in to look around.

The steward approaches Jenny. "Excuse me, but would you mind keeping your girls out of the first-class section?" he said, trying to be polite.

Jenny is startled, not realizing they are gone. She rushes into the first-class section to see the twins eyeing all the food being served.

"Come on, you two," she said, getting annoyed with them. "You know you're not supposed to go through that curtain," seeing both have helped themselves to the freshly baked cookies.

"Mom, how come they have all that food, and we don't have anything? Why don't they share?" June asked.

"Yeah! How come we didn't get any of these!" April shouted, holding up the cookie.

Jenny is so appalled as she looks around the plush settings. Seeing the abundance of food and wine irritates her. After seeing how nice the first-class seats are, it's going to make it worse having to go back to the small, cramped seats in the coach section.

"I think we have to wait our turn," she said, knowing they had already had their meal.

As Jenny ushers the girls back, a woman sitting next to the aisle stops her.

"Excuse me, but aren't you Jenny Mason?" the woman asked, with an astonished look on her face.

Jenny is a little startled, being recognized. "Why yes," she said, looking over at the woman, vaguely recognizing her.

"Oh, my God!" the woman blurted out. "I can't believe you're on my flight! We have been trying for weeks to meet you and your family. I don't know if you know me, but I'm Rachel Cook. I have a talk show in New York," so flabbergasted to meet the famous Jenny Mason.

"Oh yes, I do remember you!" Jenny replied, surprised when she finally recognized this woman. "I used to watch your show all the time."

"It's so nice to meet you!" Rachel said with a big smile. "I can't believe after all we've been through, and here you are on my flight! We've been in Hawaii for a week trying to write a story about you. We got absolutely nothing. They wouldn't give us any information at all or let us go to Kwajalein. Everyone we talked to said no or made no comment. We finally had to give up and go home with nothing, and here you are," shaking her head so astonished.

"Yes, we're finally going home."

"So, what have you been doing since you've been rescued?" she asked. "It's all a big mystery. No one knows anything."

"Well, things had been kind of hectic for the last few weeks. They wanted us to rest up before we went home. It's been a lot of medical exams. They wanted to make sure we were OK before we left the hospital," Jenny explained, not wanting to elaborate on all the issues they were having.

"So, these are the famous Amazon warriors! They're so cute!" looking over at the twins with their long flowing blonde hair.

"Oh, yes... But we're trying to leave the Amazon warriors behind us now. Say hello to the nice lady," trying to get the girls to be more sociable.

"Hello, nice lady," the twins said, still munching on their cookies.

"Oh, my God! Do they talk together like that all the time?" Rachel asked, amused with the girls' talking in unison.

"Oh, yes, all the time. Once in a while, one starts a sentence, and the other will finish it."

Rachel is so taken with the twins. "I saw you two on TV... You know, you're so famous now."

The twins just nod, not saying a word. They are getting a little fidgety being away from Baby and their father.

Rachel turns to Jenny. "You know you have one fantastic story to tell. The press has gone nuts over it. You're on every magazine and all the news shows. People just can't get enough of it. No one has been able to get through to you. We tried and kept coming up with nothing," knowing she had just stumbled on the most exclusive story of the year.

"Well, we've been at the hospital on Kwajalein and have not watched any TV or much of anything. It's a military base somewhat isolated out in the middle of nowhere, so we have not kept up with the news."

"We've been trying to get out there, but the military is in control of everything. They won't let anyone near that island. Worst of it all, they only release press statements or small video clips, denying any requests for interviews."

"Sorry, we didn't know anything about that," Jenny said, a little surprised.

"Have you thought about doing any talk shows?"

Jenny is shocked. "Well, no... We haven't really thought much of anything. It's all been like a big dream ever since we left the island. In the last couple of weeks, it's been nothing but medical exams and filling out paperwork."

"So, you don't have a public relations person yet?" Rachel asked.

"Oh, no! Right now, we just want to get back with our families again," she added, not wanting to mention the issues she is having with her sister.

The steward walks up. "I'm sorry... This is for first-class only. You must return to your seats."

"Oh, I'm so sorry," she quickly replied, startled, being told to leave.

"You do know who I am, don't you?" Rachel asked the steward.

"Yes, Mrs. Cook, but—" the steward said.

"We are talking!" Rachel barked out, cutting him off in mid-sentence. "Don't interrupt us again. While you're here, we'd like some Champaign."

"Yes, mam," the steward replied, promptly walking to the galley.

"I don't want to cause a scene. We'll go back to our seats," Jenny quickly said, so embarrassed.

"Oh, don't worry about him… Have a seat. I would love to hear about your experiences on that island," motioning her to sit in the empty seat across the aisle from her.

"Girls, I might be a while... Why don't you go back and sit with your father while I talk with my friend?" seeing that they are getting fidgety.

"OK!" they both quickly replied, running back to the coach section.

"Where is Mom, and where did you get all those big cookies?" Ben quickly asked, seeing the girls coming back on their own.

April sits down next to her father. "She is talking to a lady up there. They got these nice cookies too," handing them out to her father and brother.

"How come they have those nice big chairs in there?" June asked, pointing down the aisle.

Ben tries to explain the difference between coach and first-class. "Well, you see... They are special people up there. So, they get treated better, plus they paid more money for those nice big soft chairs to sit in."

"You mean they are special like Baby?" April asked.

"Well, some people have lots of money, and they like to be treated special. We're not like that. We're just good old common country people, and we make our own clothes, catch and cook our own food," he explained, confused with how she is comparing Baby to the people in the first-class section.

"Yeah, we good old country people," the girls replied, going back to their coloring books, content with their father's explanation of the first-class section.

* * *

Jenny is so thrilled talking with Rachel Cook, telling her all about what they have been through living on the island. She is happy to know that no matter who she talks to, everyone is always interested in hearing about their adventures. What makes it even better is getting to sit in first class, drinking champagne, and being served hors d'oeuvres.

When Jenny mentions she has been writing a journal almost every day for the past five years, Rachel is stunned. "Would you consider publishing it?" she quickly asked.

Jenny hesitated. "The thought had gone through my mind after we were rescued. I originally kept a journal, so if something happened to us, at least our family back home would have a record of our time on the island."

Rachel gives Jenny one of her cards. "When you are settled in, give me a call. I can set you up with a publisher. Also, I would love to have you on my show. You have a great story to tell, and people will be really interested. Right now, you and your family are the hottest tickets in town."

"I'm not too sure about that," she said, getting frustrated seeing June peeking through the curtains. "Oh, I better get back to the children. Thanks for everything. I'll give you a call in a week or two after we get settled in."

"We'll be waiting... I'll talk to a few people to get things moving."

"Thanks again," Jenny said, so excited knowing that her journal might be published.

Jenny is telling Ben all about her meeting with Rachel Cook. He has never heard of Rachel or even seen her talk show, but he is glad to see Jenny is excited about it. He knows this is what she needs to get out of her depression. Since hearing about the loss of her parents, she has been very quiet and somber. At least he has his family to go back to, but for Jenny, it is one bad turn after another.

June is getting interested in the first-class section again, always standing in the aisle peeking through the curtain. The steward notices her, then walks up and rudely snaps the curtain closed. That is all it takes to get her mad. She rips open the curtain, leering at the steward.

"Leave that alone and sit down!" Jenny said, seeing her messing with the curtain.

June pouted, putting her hands on her hips. "That man is bad! He keeps closing that curtain, and I can't see in! Why can't we go in there?"

"Because you're not supposed to go in there. Those are the rules. This is your seat, and you need to sit down and be quiet."

The steward comes back, standing at the door, giving Jenny a mean look, then snaps the curtain closed again. June's face turns red with rage. She pulls open the curtain again, stomping into the first-class section, so frustrated at not being allowed to explore this area of the plane.

An elderly woman notices June walking around. "Awe, isn't she special," she said to her husband with a big smile.

"No, I'm not special!" June replied, hearing the comment. "I'm just good old country people!" frowning at the woman.

Jenny runs up, grabbing June's hand. "I'm sorry she won't bother you again."

"Oh, she's all right," the woman said. "She's not bothering us. She looks just like my granddaughter."

"Mom, how come all these big people can't wipe their bottoms?" June asked.

Jenny is a little surprised and embarrassed by her comment. "Keep your voice down. What are you talking about?" walking her back to their seats.

"Daddy said these people up here are special, like Baby," June explained.

"I guess they are special," Jenny said, still a little confused, thinking that she meant being in first class.

"Special people can't feed themselves, and someone has to change their diapers and wipe their bottoms too. Right, Mom!" June said so loud that everyone on the plane heard it.

"I don't think he meant it that way," Jenny said, quickly pulling her out of the first-class section before any more embarrassing remarks.

"Yes, he did, Mom!" June argued.

"This is the first-class section. You must return to your seats, please!" the steward said, walking up behind them, pointing to the door.

"I'm so sorry," Jenny keeps apologizing, trying to escort June back to her seat.

"You bad! You bad people!" June points at the steward as she gets dragged out by her mother.

Everyone nearby is staring, wondering what is going on. Not one of Jenny's finest moments, and she is so shocked by it all. She blushes, making a quick exit back to their seats.

"So, what did she do this time?" Ben asked, seeing Jenny was not in a good mood.

"You don't want to know," she said, getting so flustered. "Ben, would you deal with her?" sitting back in her seat.

Ben gives June a mean look, and she knows she is in trouble. Then he signals for her to be quiet and still.

"They won't let me in there," she mumbled, standing with her arms across her chest, pouting.

He points his finger right at her face. "You will be sitting next to me, and you will not be going in there anymore, understand? Sit down and be quiet."

Without a word, she sits down in the seat next to her father. She is so frustrated at not being able to explore.

"There are rules here too that you must obey just like at home," he explained.

June listens with her arms crossed and is still fuming.

"Is this a sign of things to come?" Jenny asked.

Ben shrugs his shoulders. "I hope not... We have a long flight, and it's hard for everyone. They're just tired and don't like being confined. It'll soon be over, and they'll be back to normal once they get outside and run around," knowing the girls are getting bored.

"No wonder!" Jenny said, noticing the time. "They should have been in bed hours ago. You two get to sleep. It's so late," putting the blankets over them.

"Where do we sleep?" June asked. "There are no beds here!"

"You have to sleep on the seats," Jenny explained.

"We want to go home," April said, not happy being confined to the chair.

"We will someday," Ben whispered. "Remember, your granny and granddad are waiting for us. Just go to sleep, and when you wake up, we'll be there."

The cabin lights are finally turned off. There are no more problems with the children once they are asleep. Ben is up all night long, unable to sleep. He has to stay awake in case the girls wake up and start wandering around.

* * *

As the hours go by, Ben can't stand it any longer and can't blame the girls for acting up. Being stuck on this flight for hours is far worse than the cave. He is so uncomfortable and feels claustrophobic. He keeps getting up and walking the aisle to stretch his legs. In the darkness, he makes his way to the galley, hoping to get some freshly brewed coffee.

When the stewardess recognizes Ben, she gasps out loud. "Oh, my God! You're him!" getting all excited.

He quickly turns around to see if someone is behind him. "You mean me?" realizing he is on his own.

"You're Ben Hughes! That famous family from the island!" the stewardess blurted out.

"I guess that's me, but I'm not famous. I just need a cup of coffee, if it's OK?" Ben asked, feeling awkward with all the attention.

"Sure, Mr. Hughes... I'm Angela, and this is Kay," promptly pouring out a cup for him.

"Nice to meet you," he said, awkwardly smiling, seeing they were a little too friendly.

"My God!" Kay blurted out, looking him over. "You are a hunk. Look at the size of your arms! I'd give anything to be stranded on an island with you."

"We read all about you," Angela said. "I even saw you on TV. I can't believe you're on our flight. No one said anything about any VIPs on board."

He laughed. "We're in coach, so that tells you a lot about us. Although I hear there is a famous talk show woman up in first-class."

"Oh, we're not allowed to go up there," Angela replied. "They also don't tell us back here about who is in first class, anyway. Why aren't you in first class?"

"Well, first of all, we're broke. We don't even have the money for this flight, especially first-class. I don't have a clue who's paying for all this."

"If that were me," Kay said. "I'd make them put me in first-class everywhere I went."

"That doesn't bother us... We're just simple people living the simple life," remembering how he explained it to June.

"Is there anything else we can get you?" Angela asked, also staring at his biceps. "We have some cinnamon rolls or little chocolates."

"The chocolates sound good... I like to take some back for the children. It'll keep them quiet when they wake up."

She quickly gives him a handful. "Take all you want. If there is anything you need, just let us know," giving him a big smile.

"Thank you... I will. It's been nice meeting you both," then makes a quick exit.

Ben finds it odd the way those women acted around him. Walking back to his seat, he keeps turning around to see them both standing out in the aisle, staring at him and giggling. Ben is not used to this type of attention. As far as he is concerned, he hasn't changed at all since leaving Colorado. That is the first time anyone has said he is famous and wonders what is in store for them when they are back in the real world.

* * *

Chapter 53

The Big Reunion

W alter, Mary, and the rest of the family are already waiting at the airport an hour before the flight. The gate is empty, and the attendants are not at the booth. Mary is so nervous, pacing back and forth. She is getting loud and crying, going on and on about her son coming home. Everyone is concerned that this might attract unwanted attention. Luckily, no one else is around, but a few people at the next gate are looking over in their direction, wondering why the woman is crying and getting very loud.

The gate has televisions mounted on all the walls, and they all have the CNN twenty-four-hour news channel on. Once the news reports rumors of the Hughes family at the Honolulu airport, the cat is out of the bag. Close-up images of Ben, Jenny, and the children are on every television at the gate. Now, they are worried. They have been lucky so far. Having the whole family waiting at the Austin airport will be a dead giveaway that Ben is coming home.

* * *

After only 20 minutes, their luck had run out. Several news crews are scurrying about the terminal, setting up lights and video cameras.

Sam doesn't like the look of this. He doesn't want the family exposed to all the reporters. They have been lucky to avoid it so far, but now they are stuck right out in the open. He knows it won't be long before the reporters spot them, especially when Ben and his family get here.

Sam walks over to the ticket agent behind the counter. "Excuse me, but our family is arriving on this flight. Is there a way to keep the camera people away?"

"It looks like there might be some celebrities showing up on one of the flights," the ticket agent said, looking around. "I wouldn't worry about it. They won't bother anyone else."

"That's the problem," Sam explained. "I think they might be here for us."

"What makes you think they're here for you?"

"It's not for us, but more for my brother and his family."

"Well, we can't make them leave, but there are other methods," looking over at the bustling news crews.

"Such as?" Sam asked.

The ticket agent looks down at his clipboard. "May I have your name, and I need to see some ID? Also, what's the name of the party that's arriving?"

"I'm Sam Hughes... My brother is Ben Hughes, and his family is on this flight," showing him his driver's license.

"Ah! Mr. Hughes," the ticket agent said, nodding his head. "We were just informed about them being on the flight. Just one minute, please," then picks up the phone to call the security office.

Sam is getting worried. The reporters are already checking out the people waiting for their flight, searching for a familiar face. He is wondering if it's already too late.

"Mr. Hughes, everything has already been arranged," the ticket agent said after a brief conversation on the phone. "Your family can wait in the VIP lounge, away from the reporters."

"That will be great! Is there a way we can keep these news people away from my brother and his family when they arrive? We don't want them to walk through all this mess."

"Let me see what the plans are," the ticket agent replied, picking up the phone, calling the security office again.

"OK, here's the procedure," the ticket agent explains after a brief conversation on the phone. "They'll be the last ones off the aircraft, and they'll use the external gate and won't even go through here at all. They'll be escorted straight to the VIP lounge. Since the reporters are already here, you and your family might want to get up, just a few at a time, then walk over to the VIP lounge. If you all get up at once, they'll know it's you. Also, don't make eye contact with them, and act normal. If you try to avoid them, they'll spot you real quick. We already have two security guards waiting at the VIP lounge, and they know you're on the way."

Sam thanked the ticket agent and explained the plan to the rest of his family. Luckily, more people arrive at the gate, so they can blend in a little easier. One by one, they slowly get up and walk away. The reporters are too busy talking among themselves and miss their opportunity.

Mrs. Burns had arranged everything. The reason for not booking them on the direct flight from Honolulu to Austin is that the reporters can easily guess which flight they are on. By having a stopover in Dallas, no one will know which flight is to Austin or even the airline that they are on.

She also notifies airport security to expect a media frenzy when they arrive. In these situations, they have a room set aside for VIP arrivals and departures. After all the chaos, when they arrived in Kwajalein, the VIP room was her idea so Ben and his family would not be bothered by all the news media.

* * *

Ben's family waits in the plush VIP lounge. Two tables have been set up with a wealth of food. There is plenty of coffee, soft drinks, and even several bottles of wine, looking more like a wedding reception than the simple brunch that it's supposed to be.

"Don't touch that!" Mary shouted, seeing all the grandkids running for the food. "That is not for us!"

"It's compliments of Mrs. Burns, so enjoy!" the attendant explained. "We'll let you know when they arrive. We'll bring them directly here through the exit over there. If you need anything, just ask the security guards. They will be right outside the door here."

"Oh, thank you very much!" Mary said, so elated.

Upon hearing that, the rest of the family heads straight for the food and drinks.

"Well, if I'd known this was all here," Walter said. "I wouldn't have paid $4.50 for that small cup of day-old coffee!"

"She shouldn't have done all this," Mary said, looking over the table. "I bet this cost a lot of money."

"For what Ben had gone through, this is nothing. Not to mention what they put us through over the years."

"Let's not talk about that," she said, giving him a mean look. "This is a good day. My baby is coming home. We're only going to talk about happy things today. Oh, maybe we should wait for Ben before we eat?"

"We might be here a while, so let's enjoy ourselves," Sam said, helping himself to the fancy finger sandwiches. "Besides, you better get something before the kids eat it all."

"Excuse me!" Walter announced, seeing everyone had made it to the VIP room. "Can I have everyone's attention?"

"I want to thank you all for being here for this glorious occasion… Our son is finally coming home," he said, as the room got quiet, putting his arm around his wife.

A big applause interrupts him. Mary can't contain herself and starts crying again.

"I just want to remind everyone," he continued. "Ben might not be the same as you once remembered and may not even recognize some of you. I talked to the doctors, and they said he'll need our help. He has been through a lot in the last few years and needs time to adjust to being around people again. You need to be calm when they arrive. Don't make any fast or threatening moves around him, and especially around his family."

"Yeah, or those little girls will pop you upside the head," Sam jokingly said.

"This is serious!" Mary said, getting angry. "There's going to be no joking about while they're here," pointing her finger at her son.

"Sorry, Mom," Sam murmured, regretting his remark.

"She is right," Walter continued. "He sounds normal on the phone, but the doctors say he is still wary of being around other people and is extremely overprotective when it comes to his kids. It will be best to keep your distance from the little ones until he has been here a while and gets used to us again. But mostly, don't even get near baby August. The girls have been taught to protect him. They don't understand jokes either, so don't be messing around with them. Just be calm and don't make any loud noises. You might want to make sure all the little ones here understand that," looking over at his grandchildren.

"We're not too sure how they will react to all of us. They don't like crowds and noise. Let's be calm and welcome Ben and his family home. My baby is coming home," Mary added as the tears started flowing again.

There is complete silence in the VIP room, hearing all the warnings from Walter. Many with children are starting to worry. They have all seen the news broadcasts and saw how the girls will even attack an adult. They are all wondering how they are going to handle this.

"Maybe we should make all the kids stand by the table when Ben shows up," Sam suggested.

"That's a good idea... Let's put all the little ones behind the food tables. Make sure they leave some food for Ben and his family," Walter said, seeing how they are eating everything.

Everyone likes the idea and starts moving the children to the far side of the table, just in case. The children don't care. Most of them don't understand what is going on. Many are too young to remember Ben. Some have never met him since he always lived far away from home.

* * *

The flight finally arrives in Austin, to everyone's relief. Ben is getting excited to see his family again after all those years. It's going to be a little awkward having to introduce his wife and children to his parents.

Jenny is getting a little nervous about having to meet her new in-laws for the first time. Deep down, she wants so much for her family to be here too.

As the plane approaches the terminal, a stewardess approaches Ben. "Excuse me, sir... You and your family will be using a different exit. You need to stay seated until the plane is empty. Then a security guard will escort you to the VIP waiting room."

"Why do we have to do this?" Ben asked, confused that a guard was escorting them off the flight.

"Apparently, the reporters are already waiting for you at the gate," the stewardess explained. "We have been informed that you'll be using the exit at the rear of the plane."

"Thank you! We appreciate that!" so glad not to have to go through the fiasco like when they arrived at Kwajalein Island.

As the plane comes to a stop, the other passengers quickly jump up, getting their bags from the overhead bins. Ben and his family quietly wait in their seats while everyone else pushes their way to the front. They have a long wait for everyone to get off the plane. The extra time gives them a chance to get the children ready and pack everything away.

After most of the passengers leave the plane, the stewardess walks up. "Whenever you're ready. We'll take you through the galley exit at the rear."

"OK, girls," Ben said. "Get your things. It's time to go!" grabbing their bags.

The twins promptly put on their backpacks, sun hats, and their favorite sunglasses.

"We need our sticks!" June tells her father.

Jenny frowned. "I was hoping they forgotten about those things."

Ben reaches up, taking the two bamboo sticks from the storage bin. "Here you go... Be careful, and don't be swinging them around at other people."

"You never know... Always be prepared," April said, making sure her stick is not damaged.

Jenny let out a long sigh. "You keep those by your side. Don't be hitting anyone, or I'll take them away."

The twins frown, knowing that she would. They lost several good sticks while on Kwajalein, and that's after just pointing them at one of the hospital workers. They both longed for the good old days, using their sticks to catch fish and get fruit off the trees.

A security guard walks up. "Are these the ones?" he asked the stewardess.

"Yes, they're all yours."

The security guard promptly looks over at Ben. "If you're ready, we'll make our way to the rear exit."

"Jenny, are you ready?" Ben asked, knowing she might be a little apprehensive.

"I think so," she said, nodding her head. "At least there are no more flights. I don't know if I ever want to get on another plane again."

"Yeah, I don't like these planes!" June shouted. "Too many peoples and takes way too long. Next time we walk, right, Daddy?"

"Yep, next time we're going to walk," feeling how stiff his legs are after sitting down for so long.

With one last look around, making sure they have everything, they all slowly follow the security guard to the back of the plane. The warm air rushes through the aircraft as the galley door opens. They follow the man down the ramp outside, finally setting foot on the ground since leaving Kwajalein Island so long ago.

They follow the security guard through the maintenance door, then up two flights of stairs. No different from when they arrived in Honolulu, going through the back entrance. Nothing fancy at all, mostly used by the people working at the airport.

"This is our VIP waiting room... Welcome home," the security guard said, opening the door, motioning them to enter.

"Thank you," Jenny said, cautiously peeking into the room.

"Thank God we're finally here," Ben said, so tired from the long flight.

The room is so quiet. A large group of people is standing around several tables, stuffing themselves. Ben recognizes his family at the far end of the large room. No one has even noticed them since they entered through the rear door.

"Well, this is it," he whispered to Jenny. "There they all are. We're finally home."

"You go first," Jenny whispered, feeling a little shy, cowering behind him, nudging him forward.

"Is that them?" June quietly asked, pointing over to the group.

Ben nods. "Yep, that's all your family... You see Granny over there," pointing to his mother, sitting in a chair.

"Is that Granny?" April excitedly whispered.

"It sure is," he said, getting a little emotional seeing his mother again.

Ben thinks it's so funny that none of his family even knows they are here. Everyone of them is standing around the table, eating.

"Well, I can see nothing has changed here! You're all stuffing yourselves as usual!" Ben said really loud.

Everyone turns around, surprised to see Ben, Jenny, and the three children standing together at the far end of the room. They all start screaming and crying, rushing across the room. The twins are frightened, and Baby starts crying, seeing the huge crowd rushing up. Even Ben is a little startled, seeing everyone running towards him.

"Daddy, we don't like it here!" the twins shouted, standing behind their father, pointing their sticks at the crowd.

Everyone immediately stops dead in their tracks, seeing how frightened the children are. What Walter had warned them about is indeed true. They all stand at a distance from Ben and his family, wanting so much to hug them.

Walter and Mary slowly walk up to their son. Hesitant at first, they rush towards him, hugging and kissing him. The twins are cautious standing in front of their mother, protecting her and Baby. They keep an eye on these two land sharks that are hugging their father.

"I always knew you were alive," Mary whispers, hugging and kissing him. "I always knew it. Deep down, I never let you go."

"I know, Mom... I know."

"Welcome home, son," Walter whispered, giving his son another big hug.

Everyone stands around watching the very emotional reunion. There is not a dry eye in the room. After six long years, it's finally over.

After a long hug with his parents, Ben finally steps back. "Mom, Dad... This is Jenny and Baby," reaching out to Jenny, taking her hand.

"Hi, it's so nice to meet you," Jenny said, feeling so awkward.

The twins are still standing in front of their mother with their sticks in hand. They are not letting anyone get too close. Ben quickly signals that everything is OK. They both step back but still are a little wary of all these people.

Mary slowly approaches Jenny to hug and kiss her. Both are getting very emotional. Even though this is their granny, the twins are concerned that she is getting too close to their brother.

"Welcome to our family," Mary said and started crying, hugging her again.

"This is our little boy," Jenny said, still holding Baby. "His name is really August, but we call him Baby."

"Aren't you a big boy," Mary said, so excited to see her new grandson. "We're going to have a good time playing together," cautiously holding his tiny hand.

Baby, getting a little scared, buries his face into his mother's chest. It doesn't go unnoticed by his sisters. They are already signaling each other, wondering what to do.

"He is a little shy around new people," Jenny said, praying he does not scream out a warning call for the girls to attack.

Ben looks down at the twins, seeing they are worried about his mother getting too close to Baby. "It's OK... This is your granny and granddad," pushing them up front.

Mary cries, seeing her little grandchildren. "Awe, are these my little babies?" holding out her arms.

"Girls, this is your granny," Ben repeated, nudging them towards his mother.

The twins cautiously walk up, looking her over. They are not too sure about this person.

"Don't you want to give your granny a hug?" Mary asked, seeing how timid they were.

"You are Granny!" the girls shout out, recognizing her voice. "We talk to you on the phone!" giving her a big hug.

Walter reaches down and holds out his hand. "Howdy girls, remember me? We talked on the phone, too."

They both look him over, then slowly reach up, shaking his hand.

"Are you Granddad?" April asked.

"Yes, that's me... Mighty fine sticks you got there," he said.

"They bamboo sticks," June replied. "Made these ourselves," slowly swinging it around.

"Careful with those in here," Ben mentioned.

"They are OK," Walter said. "Actually, I'd like you to show me how to make one of those when we get back home."

"We show you how to make a good stick," April said, nodding her head up and down.

"Yeah," June added. "Not like these ones. We always put points on ours. Mom cuts off the points now, so we don't hurt people. We make you one that's really sharp so you can catch lots of fish!"

"Good, I'll be looking forward to getting myself one of those," Walter replied, amused by their candor.

Sam and his sister, Kelly, slowly walk up to greet their brother. Kelly is very emotional, but Sam can't wait to tease his longtime bachelor brother about being a dad.

Kelly leans over, hugging her new sister-in-law. "I'm so glad to meet you. We're going to have a great time together."

"I'm glad to meet you too," Jenny said. "Ben told me so much about you."

As Sam hugs his brother, he notices right away how much weight he has lost. He is now nothing but muscle.

"Man, you look good! What happened to that old potbelly?" Sam remarked, slapping Ben's stomach.

"Looks like it's over here!" slapping Sam's stomach hard.

"Welcome home, brother!" Sam said, seeing his brother had not changed a bit, giving him a big bear hug, then started crying.

* * *

One by one, everyone comes over to meet Ben and his family. Ben hugs each one and introduces them to Jenny, April, June, and Baby. The twins stand next to their mother. They hold their sticks in their left hand while shaking everyone's hands with the other, just as their father had taught them.

Ben is so proud of his little girls. They stand at attention as if they are guarding their mother and their little brother. Everyone sees how cute they are wearing their sunglasses and sun hats. Deep down, Ben knows they are indeed guarding their mother and protecting Baby.

Getting tired, Jenny and Mary sit down together on the plush sofas and chairs. Mary is in her glory. Baby is on her lap, and April and June are telling her all about their long journey. Ben stands close by, keeping an eye on things while he is talking with the others. He is so surprised at how everyone wants to hear the same old story over and over again.

Ben is so glad to see his mother with Baby on her lap, surrounded by the girls. She has really taken with the children. The girls are eager to show her their coloring books and all the pictures they did. They constantly ask about the big Sunday dinners and all those cups of tea their father used to tell them when they were back on the island.

Sitting next to Kelly, Jenny is having a great time talking and laughing it up. Ben is worried that they have been talking about him, especially when they keep glancing over at him and giggling. He is so glad to see Jenny smile and laugh like she used to when they lived on the island.

Uncle Mark comes over to Ben, hugging him again. Having had a little too much to drink, he holds on to Ben, trying to keep his balance.

Uncle Mark twists Ben around, pointing over at Jenny. "You are one lucky guy being out on an island with a girl as beautiful as she is!" he cries, hugging Ben again.

"I know," Ben replied. "She's really something."

"You got a family, too," Uncle Mark added. "A beautiful family," slurring his words.

Sam walks over to help Ben with Uncle Mark. They both help him to a chair, seeing he is about to collapse.

Aunt Sue brings over a cup of black coffee to help sober up her husband. "I'm so sorry, Ben... He was so upset when he heard your plane went down. Ever since he heard the news that you were alive, he's been celebrating every day."

Sam laughed. "We've been putting a few back ourselves too!"

"I have got plenty to celebrate, and it's only just started!" Uncle Mark slurred, raising his coffee cup.

"Well, I'm glad to see you all made it here," Ben said, putting his hand on his uncle's shoulder. "I can't wait to show the children your pool. You still do those famous barbecues?"

"Oh, yes!" Aunt Sue said. "Make sure you come on down. We'll get the rest of the family together and have a big homecoming party for you," helping her husband up.

Ben's cousin, Paul, seeing his dad is a little tipsy, walks over to help. "Welcome back to the real world, Ben. I think we better get Dad back home."

Ben helps walk his uncle to the exit. "You let us know about the barbecue. We'll all be there!"

"Your mother was right all along," Uncle Mark mumbled. "We should have listened. We could have come and got you."

"It's OK... We had a nice time out there, anyway. Everything worked out fine. We'll see you at the barbecue," helping them out the door.

Ben is so touched knowing how much his family had missed him. He never realized the pain everyone was in while they were on the island, thinking he was gone.

Ben walks over to Jenny and Kelly. They are both smiling and laughing as he approaches them.

"Jenny has told me some great stories about you," Kelly said, still giggling.

"Such as?" Ben asked, a little concerned, staring at Jenny.

Jenny quickly averts her eyes, turning away. Right then, Ben knows he is in trouble. He forgot to tell her that he doesn't like talking about his personal life with any of his family. He knows how much his family loves to gossip, but he can see it's already too late.

* * *

Sam's oldest boy, Steve, has a strange sense of humor. Being 18 years old, he is already bored and thinks it will be fun to play a little joke on the twins. He slowly approaches the girls from behind while they are talking with their grandmother. Then he gets on all fours, crawling right up behind them.

"I'm a land shark, and I'm coming to get you!" lunging at the twins.

April and June scream out loud. Baby immediately screeches out a loud sign for his sisters to protect him. June quickly leaps forward, smashing Steve's nose with her fist as hard as she can. April swings her stick around, striking his head so hard, knocking him to the ground. Steve rolls onto his back in pain, with blood running from his nose. Ben rushes over, grabbing the twins, seeing how they are ready to finish him off.

"What the hell are you doing?" Sam asked, picking up his son, handing him a paper towel. "You know you're not supposed to tease the girls!"

"I was only having a little fun," Steve said, still in pain. "They're a couple of out-of-control brats! I can't believe they hit me like that!"

"He said he was a land shark, Daddy!" April yelled. "Go get him!"

Ben signals the girls to back off and to protect Baby. They immediately run over to their brother, still sitting on his grandmother's lap. They stand in front of their brother, swinging their sticks back and forth to keep everyone away.

"It's OK!" Jenny shouted. "He was only joking," dreading that they are acting up so soon.

"No, he said he's a land shark!" April shouted, swinging her stick back and forth.

"Stay with Granny," Ben said, walking up to his nephew.

Ben is mad as hell when he hears Steve's comment. "They don't understand things like that! Why are you teasing them? You do that again, and I'll come after you, and you'll regret it! Don't be messing with them again! You understand me!" pointing his finger right at Steve's face.

Walter rushes over. "Ben, it's OK... He didn't mean it. Calm down."

"Ben, he was just playing!" Jenny yelled out, so shocked.

Steve has never been so scared in his life. Having Ben standing over him, threatening him, doesn't help. The look in Ben's eyes scared him more than anything.

Sam keeps apologizing for his son's stupid mistake. What is worse, he couldn't have stopped his brother if he had tried. Sam drags his son to the other side of the room to scold him in private.

The entire family can't believe that after all the warnings, someone teased the little girls like that. Eventually, Ben finally calms down. Walter takes Ben aside, having a long talk.

Sam, so embarrassed by the whole ordeal, keeps apologizing for his son's stupidity. After a few minutes, it's soon forgotten.

Although the twins, still with their grandmother, are keeping an eye out for any more trouble. All they do is stare at Steve, making sure he stays on the other side of the room.

"Bad land shark!" the girls yelled out.

"No, he's not a land shark," Mary explained, seeing the girls were still upset. "He's a naughty boy, and I'm going to spank his bottom for that!" a little annoyed with her grandson.

June waves her stick at him. "You a naughty boy! Granny is going to spank your bottom!"

April is getting worked up as well. "Granny, let's go over and spank his bottom!"

"Oh no, you're not," Jenny said. "You two settle down."

"They're not even scared of him, are they?" Mary asked, a little concerned. "He's more than twice their size."

Jenny cringes. "No, they'll go after anyone to protect their brother."

"Where did they learn that?" Mary asked, so shocked at hearing this.

Jenny points over at Ben without saying a word.

"Well, I'll have a long talk with him later about that," Mary promptly said.

Baby is making birdcalls, pointing over at Steve on the other side of the room. The girls look over at Steve, then walk towards him, signaling each other.

"Oh, no, you don't!" Jenny said, grabbing the twins. "You let him be! You stay here with us!" knowing he is telling them to attack.

"Why is he doing that? It sounds like a real bird," Mary mentioned, seeing how he is constantly repeating it.

"The girls got him worked up, too," Jenny explained. "They always signal each other," not wanting to elaborate on what the birdcall really meant.

"No, he's a naughty boy," April explained to her brother. "Not a land shark!" giving him various hand signs.

Right away, Baby laughs, blowing raspberries at Steve.

"Oh, what did they just tell him?" Kelly asked, seeing all the hand signals.

Jenny shrugs her shoulders. "I'm not sure... I can't keep up with all the hand signs anymore. That's Ben's department. He's taught them a lot of signs, whistles, and birdcalls. They also made up a few of their own. Now, they're teaching Baby. April, what did you just tell him?"

"I told him Granny is going to spank his bottom!" April said, pointing over at Steve.

"You mean he understands all of that?" Mary asked, so astounded.

"Oh, yes! He learns more and more every day. The girls make sure he knows the signs. He gets mad when they do signs he doesn't understand. What's worse, they're always doing their little secret signals between themselves, and they know I don't understand most of it."

"It's like they are whispering among themselves," Mary remarked. "I don't know if I'd like that."

"I don't either," Jenny agreed. "We have rules about that. No more secret signs in front of other people. It's mostly a game to them unless they are in their protective mode. That's when they turn into little Navy SEALs. Even the security guards at the base were impressed."

"So, when Ben whistled to the girls," Kelly asked, "they immediately came over here swinging their sticks around at everyone. Is that one of those protect ones?"

"Oh, yes! I know that one well. There are two basic ones that Ben taught them. One is to watch Baby, making sure he doesn't get in trouble. The other is to protect Baby."

April hears the phrase. She quickly grabs her stick, staring right at Kelly.

"Oh, no!" Jenny said, realizing her mistake. "I was just explaining the signs and what they mean. You just calm down. Everyone here is our friend."

"I see you have to watch what you say around them," Kelly said, seeing how quickly the girls can turn on someone, slowly backing away from April. "It's like having a lion ready to pounce on you!"

"I know... There's a big difference between the words watch and protect. I have been on to Ben about that. Back home, it wasn't a problem, but now it is. That was one of the reasons they kept us at Kwajalein for a few extra counseling sessions. I think Ben and the girls need a few more."

The little event with Steve showed everyone that Ben is indeed overprotective. Walter's warning is apparent to everyone that his son needs more time to adjust. The twins, however, are definitely on the wild side. Seeing it firsthand how the little girls will not hesitate to attack an adult makes them all a little cautious.

* * *

Chapter 54

Home

After over thirty hours of traveling, Ben and his family finally arrive back home. The old house hadn't changed at all, except the trees had grown a little. Maybe a different shade of brown paint, but it still looks the same as Ben remembered so long ago.

"Granny, what's this place?" June asked, seeing the big house, and the cars parked out in front.

"This is our home," Mary explained. "We live here. You'll be staying here too."

"Wow, this is your hut? Granddad, did you make this all by yourself?" April asked, so impressed with the big house.

"No, it was already here when we bought it, but I did add some paint over the years," Walter replied, confused by her comment.

"Daddy, can you make us one of these when we get back home?" April asked.

He laughed. "I'll think about it."

"Who stays in those ones over there?" June asked, pointing over at the other houses. "Does everyone have their own hut?"

"That's our neighbors," Mary answered. "Other people are living in all these houses you see around here."

"They way too close!" June said, shaking her head. "It's too crowded here! You should have told them to make their hut on their own beach!"

"Granny, where is your beach at?" April asked, not hearing the waves.

"We have plenty of time for questions later," Jenny said, seeing the girls are in that thousand-and-one question mode. "Let's get inside.

It's been a long trip. It's getting close to your bedtime," ushering them into the house.

Ben follows his father, dragging all the luggage to his old room. Everything in the bedroom is brand new. He dumps everything on the bed, so glad to see a real bed to sleep on.

The twins are very quiet, having a good look around. The house is filled with antiques and trinkets. They have never seen anything like this before, and it's so different from the hospital. This place has plenty of strange things scattered about, far more than what was at the gift shop at Kwajalein.

Everyone settles down in the living room while Mary is in the kitchen, making tea. Ben can't help laughing. After all they have been through, the very first thing when they get home is to have a cup of tea. Even in the middle of the summer, it doesn't matter. There is always a hot cup of tea waiting for you.

Jenny and Kelly really hit it off, always together gossiping. Kelly is a romantic, wanting to hear all the details of their wedding. Jenny doesn't leave out anything, able to recall every little detail of their lives on the island.

"It's teatime!" Mary shouted, walking in with a large tray.

April, June, and Baby kneel next to the coffee table for their first cup of tea. Mary makes them a special cup, mostly of milk. She even brings out some homemade cookies for them. Something so simple is a big thrill for the children.

Jenny loves the old English family traditions. She is still not used to her mother-in-law's strong English accent. After all the years of hearing Ben's old stories about this, now she is actually sitting here experiencing it all. Seeing her children sipping a cup of tea for the first time makes it even more special.

"Look at that big rat!" June said, jumping up on the couch.

"Oh, don't be scared of her," Mary said, quickly picking up her cat. "She is harmless. Come on over and say hello to Kitty."

April, June, and Baby are a little reluctant, closely eyeing the strange creature.

"It's OK... You'll like Kitty," Ben said, seeing the old cat for the first time in years.

The children cautiously walk over, staring at the cat. They have never seen anything like it before.

"You pet her like this, real slow and gentle," Mary explained, gently petting her. "You don't want to scare her. She doesn't know you yet."

Naturally, Baby is the first to run his hands all over the cat. The twins quickly follow suit. They are so amazed at how soft her coat is. They all laugh when hearing the cat purring away.

"Daddy, can we have it?" June asked, turning to her father.

"Well, she lives here with us," Mary explained. "You can play with her anytime you want," not understanding what she meant.

Ben cringes, not saying a word. He knows what his little girls are really asking.

"Can we have it for tonight, then?" June asked her grandmother with a big smile on her face.

"What do you mean, can you have her tonight?" Mary asked, still confused. "You mean you want to play with her? She loves to play with a string. She will chase it around, but only if she is in the mood and is really temperamental."

"No, we don't want to play," June added. "We want it for supper. We'll clean and cook it up for you. I bet you it's real tasty!"

Mary is shocked at what she just heard. She quickly turns to Ben, absolutely speechless.

Ben just smiled and slowly shook his head. "Girls, remember the rules... We don't eat anything that is a pet and has a name."

Mary takes the cat away. "No, we don't! Kitty is part of the family. If you want something to eat, you get something from the fridge!"

"Is that its name, Kitty?" April asked, pointing to the cat.

"Yes, it is!" Ben said. "The birds in the cage up there also have names," pointing to the birds they had not yet noticed.

"That's not fair!" June disappointedly shouted, looking up at the small birdcage. "Everything has a name!" getting frustrated.

"That's the way it is," Ben explained. "Everything here has a name and is a pet. So, don't be messing with anything."

"But Daddy, if everything here has a name, then what do we eat?" June asked, putting her hands on her hips.

"Granny, where do you keep all your fish?" April asked, looking around. "Do you have any orange trees? You got to have all your food ready when the sun goes down. After it gets dark, it's too late. Then, you have to wait until morning. You can't go out for food when it's dark, right, Daddy?"

"We have plenty of food here," Mary explained. "Come with me, and I'll show you," handing the cat to her husband before taking the girls out to the kitchen.

Jenny just closes her eyes, not believing that the girls still want to cook up anything that moves. That is her biggest fear. They just arrived, and the girls are already eyeing the family cat for something to eat.

Mary walks the twins into the kitchen, showing them the refrigerator and all the cabinets full of food. "See, we have plenty of food for all of us. We don't have to catch anything. When we need more, we just go down to the supermarket. That's where we get all our food."

"Granny, where do you put all your fish?" June asked. "You have a tidal pool?" still confused, not recognizing anything in the refrigerator that resembles food.

"You go to the cafeteria to eat?" April asked. "We go there for food at the hospital. At home, we don't have a cafeteria. We catch our food and then we cook it!"

She is a little surprised. "Oh, so you know about cafeterias then. We do have a few around here, but nothing is better than a home-cooked meal."

April nods. "We know... It wasn't nice. Mom said we supposed to be nice and say it was good. We didn't like it much," looking around to make sure her mother didn't hear her.

Ben walks into the kitchen, seeing the concerned look on the girls' faces as they stare in the refrigerator. "You don't happen to have any fruit salad? That was their favorite meal at Kwajalein."

"Yeah! We really liked that!" the girls yelled out, jumping up and down getting excited.

"Good, I have plenty of fruit," Mary said. "You girls sit at the table while I get everything out."

Ben sits at the table with Baby and the girls. Mary is in her glory, cutting up oranges, bananas, apples, grapes, strawberries, and huge slices of watermelon, placing it all on a big plate. The twins are watching her every move. Baby even stands up on one of the chairs, screaming out loud when he sees the grapes. Ben gets up and grabs a few for Baby, where he promptly stuffs them into his mouth.

"I never seen kids so excited over fruit before," Mary remarked.

"It's one of their favorites. They loved the fruit salad in the cafeteria. Once they discovered all the other fruits, they couldn't get enough of them. It got a little old just having oranges, bananas, and grapefruit every day back home."

"You'll have plenty of different types of fruit now," Mary said, carrying over the large plate. "Will this do?" placing it on the table with several spoons and forks.

"It's more than enough," Ben promptly said. "Look at all this! There's some here we hadn't had before," watching all three helping themselves to the feast.

"Ben, is that all they ever eat?" Mary asked, seeing her grandchildren stuffing themselves.

"Fruit, coconut, fish, or lobster. That was about it."

"We like lobster!" June shouted out. "That's our favorite, right, Daddy!"

"Yep, fresh lobster out on the beach with a big bonfire. That's the way we like it, right, girls?"

"Fun day! We going to have one here?" waving their hands in the air.

"No, not today... It's already too late. Maybe in a day or two."

"Let's join the others in the living room," Mary said. "Let's put this on the coffee table so you can eat in there."

Ben carries the plate, placing it on the coffee table in the living room. The twins and Baby quickly kneel on the floor, eating as if it's their last meal.

"It looks like they haven't eaten in a long time," Walter blurted out, watching the feast.

"When was the last time they ate?" Mary asked. "The poor things are starving."

"Hard to say," Ben answered. "We had a meal on the plane, but they mostly had bread, cookies, and salad. They don't like anything that they don't cook themselves, other than fruit."

"I saw them catch and cook that fish on the news," Kelly said. "Do they do that all the time?"

"That was great!" Sam said. "Can't wait to take them fishing with me!"

"Oh, yes!" Jenny replied. "They are pretty good at fishing. We also taught them to cook at an early age. It wasn't long before they were teaching me a thing or two. They have a gift for cooking. They are like little chefs. Unfortunately, they are very critical of any meals that they don't prepare themselves."

Ben laughs out loud. "You should have heard the comments about the airplane food we had. That's why they're so hungry."

"If you don't mind," Jenny said, feeling exhausted from the long trip. "I like to have a hot bath so I can freshen up a bit. It's been such a long day, and I have been wearing these clothes forever."

"Come with me," Mary said. "I'll show you where everything is."

Before she left the room, Jenny pointed at the girls. "You two be on your best behavior while I'm gone."

"OK, Mom!" April and June both replied, still stuffing themselves.

Once Mary and Jenny have left the room, Walter leans over. "Ben, you mean to tell me they would actually eat the cat?" Walter quietly asked.

Ben slowly nods. "If they can catch her, they'd fry her up in no time. We had that problem once before. I'll never bring home a pet for these two anymore. Coming home with a pet is like bringing them a bucket of chicken. These two always love to try new things to cook up. It's from Jenny's side of the family. They're all gourmet chefs with big fancy restaurants."

Mary walks in, overhearing the conversation. "I hope I don't find my cat being cooked up for supper!" giving Ben a stern look.

"We have this rule. You can't cook anything that has a name, right, girls?"

"No cooking things with names," June said. "We never cook those ones."

"We did cook Birdie!" April quickly added.

"Who is Birdie?" Mary asked.

The girls quickly drop their heads, realizing it's a bad subject to bring up.

"What happened to Birdie?" Mary asked, giving Ben that look.

"I made the mistake of bringing home a bird I found on the beach. It had a broken wing, but it was really tame. I figured the kids would like a pet. Unfortunately, after a couple of days, it mysteriously disappeared. The next thing I knew, we had bird stew," remembering that bad day on the island.

The children don't like it when their father talks about that fateful day. They keep eating the fruit salad, hoping for someone to change the subject. He never forgave them, or even Jenny. That was done behind his back, thinking that he wouldn't notice. Then, to make it worse, they served him the bird for supper as a special surprise.

"We're not having any of that around here," Mary explained. "The only food we eat here is from the store. No more hunting for food. If you want something to eat, it's all in the kitchen," pointing her finger at the girls.

"OK, Granny!" the twins said, seeing the mean look they were getting.

* * *

Sitting in the big recliner, Ben dozes off. The last time he had any sleep was on Kwajalein Island.

"Go lie down for a while," Mary said. "We'll watch the kids."

"Yeah, you're right," Ben said, feeling so tired. "I can't stay awake any longer."

Ben turns to the girls. "I'm going to take a little nap, so you mind Granny and Granddad. I'll be in the other room. Mom is taking a bath, so she'll be out in a few minutes."

"OK, Daddy! We'll watch Baby," June said.

"You lie down for a while," Mary said, walking Ben to his bedroom. "Don't worry about the kids. We'll watch over them."

"Watch the babies," he mumbled, getting on the bed, and was sound asleep as soon as he hit the pillow.

"Don't worry," she whispered, putting the blanket over him. "I'll watch your babies," wiping away the tears from her cheek.

* * *

Mary and Walter are so relieved it's all over. Now, they can enjoy being around their whole family once again. They are so proud watching over their new grandchildren, quietly sitting around the coffee table, still eating their fruit salad and drinking their tea.

"Can we have some more tea, please, Granny?" June asked with a big smile, holding up her empty teacup.

Mary is so thrilled that they love her tea. "You all want another cup?"

"Yeah!" all three yelled out as Mary dashed to the kitchen for a refill.

Mary is so proud of her grandchildren, seeing how well-behaved they are sharing the fruit salad. It is such a dramatic change from the Amazon warrior's reputation that she had heard.

Walter wants to show them something special. He turns on the television, switching to the cartoon channel. All three look up in amazement, seeing the cartoons. Baby yells out, pointing to his favorite one.

"Walter, don't put that on!" Mary said. "I don't think they're allowed to watch TV."

"It's only a cartoon... All kids watch these!"

"We saw this on the boat! That's a cartoon! Baby really likes these ones," June said, pointing to the television.

"Yeah, we watched the TV with Nurse Able," April explained, "but Daddy don't like it. He says it's too noisy. He doesn't like noise!"

"Did your daddy let you watch TV at the hospital?" Mary asked.

"We watch it a little," June blurted out. "There was a monster in ours, so they took it away."

"Well, no one is going to take away our TV," Walter said, confused by her statement. "Especially when Tom and Jerry is on!"

He looks over at Baby, who is so fixated by the television. "August! Ah, Baby! I got to get the names right… You want to sit on your granddad's lap and watch the cartoons together?"

Baby looks around, not seeing his mom and dad, glancing over at June for approval. As June nods, he quickly climbs onto the chair with his grandfather.

Kelly looks over at her mother. "Did you see that?"

"They sure take care of each other," Mary said.

"The girls really watch over their little brother," Walter remarked. "No doubt about that. He knows who the boss is," pulling Baby up on his lap.

It is the first time that Walter has been able to get close to his grandson. He is so surprised that the little boy is not scared at all. He just accepts everyone as a friend.

"He is just like his father," Mary said, with tears running down her cheek. "Ben always used to sit on his dad's lap watching the Tom and Jerry cartoons."

"I see Dad now has someone else to watch cartoons with," Sam said, also remembering those days.

"The tradition carries on," Kelly jokingly added, seeing how content her father is with his new grandson.

* * *

Steve walks in from the den. "Where is everyone?" not seeing Jenny and Ben.

"Jenny is having a bath," Sam answered, "and Ben is taking a nap. So, we're entertaining the kids."

Seeing Baby glued to the television watching cartoons, Steve is ready to play a little joke on him. He slowly walks up, putting his arms out in a threatening motion towards Baby.

"I'm coming to get you!" Steve yelled out, lunging at him.

Baby is terrified. He screams out loud, desperately trying to get away. Then, he signals to his sisters to protect him and to attack this monster.

April, being the closest, jumps up and grabs Baby, pulling him off the chair. She tries so hard to carry him back to June, who is holding out her fork, pointing it at Steve. Right away, they know this is not good. They are all alone with no sticks.

Walter is so furious with Steve for doing something so stupid again. "You know better than that! I can't believe you scared him! They're only little babies!"

"What's wrong with you?" Sam asked, grabbing his son's arm. "You've done it again. Ben is going to kick your ass for this one."

"I was just playing with him," Steve said, realizing his mistake.

"They only just met us," Mary said. "They don't understand such things."

April and June stand together behind the coffee table with Baby, not knowing what to do. Everyone stands in the living room, trying to console them, explaining that Steve was just joking.

June doesn't listen to any of it, pointing her fork at anyone who comes too close. "I want to go home!" she yells, then cries.

April, still struggling to carry Baby, gives out a series of clicking sounds. That is a signal to June for them to retreat and find their mom or dad. Slowly, they make their way to the hallway. June keeps her guard up, waving her fork at everyone, making sure she is between Baby and the others. Both of them regret leaving their sticks in the bedroom.

"Oh, look how they're protecting their little brother," Kelly said, crying.

"OK, everyone keep back," Walter said. "They're just scared."

Mary slowly approaches the twins. "It's OK, don't worry... No one is going to hurt you."

April, standing in the hallway, desperately looks around. Realizing she has no idea where her parents are, she signals June, letting her know they are on their own.

June backs off even more, still waving the fork at everyone. She knows they are in a bad situation with no way out.

"OK, everyone go to the den, so they don't get more frightened," Mary said, seeing the girls were so scared.

Everyone leaves the room. Sam quickly drags his son out to the backyard to have a few words with him.

"It's OK," Mary said once everyone left the room. "He's gone now, and he will get a big spanking from his father," cautiously walking up to June.

"I want my daddy!" June said, still sobbing. "I want to go home!" pointing the fork at her grandmother.

Mary realizes that they don't know where he is. "He is taking a nap back there in the bedroom, and your mommy is in the bathroom. Just go down there, and you'll see him lying on the bed," pointing down the hallway.

* * *

Ben wakes up with Baby crawling up on top of him, quickly followed by April and June. Still so tired, he looks up, seeing June holding a fork at his mother, who is standing by the bedroom door sobbing.

"What's going on here?" he asked.

"There's a monster out there, and he said he's going to get Baby!" June shouted.

Baby, pulling on his father's shirt, is waving his other hand up in the air, yelling out a long line of gibberish.

"Dad, it's a real monster!" April shouted out.

"I'm so sorry... Steve scared little August this time," Mary explained, finally getting a word in. "He was just playing and didn't realize what he was doing."

Ben sits up. "Why is he doing that? What's wrong with that boy?"

"He's a teenager," Mary said, shaking her head. "God knows why he does things. He didn't mean nothing by it."

"He's a monster, Daddy! Go get him!" June points at the door.

"Give Granny that fork. You know you're not supposed to be pointing things at people."

"You go get him, Granny!" June said, reluctantly handing over the fork.

"Yeah! Go get that monster!" April added.

"We'll spank his bottom later," Mary said. "Why don't you come back in and finish eating your fruit dinner?"

"We need our sticks!" April tells her father. "Not safe around here anymore! They got monsters!"

"You don't need your sticks! There are no monsters here, anyway. Remember what Mom said," Ben added, seeing they're getting worked up again.

"There are no monsters in our home," Mary explained. "Just one naughty boy who will get a big spanking."

Ben, still so tired, escorts them back to the living room. Sitting with them on the couch, he helps them eat the fruit and drink the rest of their tea.

Sam walks in with Steve. "Ben, Steve has something to say."

Baby immediately crawls onto his father's lap, seeing Steve again. He let out the monster birdcall, pointing at him.

June is so mad. "You bad! My daddy going to spank your bottom!"

"Yeah, you bad!" April joins in. "We don't like you!"

"I'm sorry, I didn't mean it," Steve said, holding his head down. "I was just playing," giving everyone a look of contempt.

"We better get going," Sam said. "It's been a long day."

"Thanks for everything," Ben said. "I'm sorry, but we're all a little tired. Maybe we'll get together in a day or two."

"You betcha!" Sam replied, hugging his brother.

Ben looks over at Kelly. "When did he get so touchy? He's always hugging people all the time."

"Come on, kids," Sam said, getting a little emotional. "Let's get home, so they can get settled in," giving his brother another hug.

As Sam and his kids are leaving, Steve walks by, giving Ben a mean look. Since everyone is already outside, Ben motions him over, stepping back into the hallway. He wanted to apologize to his nephew for yelling at him at the airport.

"You need to do something with those brats of yours!" Steve said, being so arrogant.

Ben doesn't see that coming, and it really pisses him off. He reaches over, grabbing Steve by his shirt, and lifting him off the ground.

"You better watch yourself," Ben whispered, looking him right in the eye. "Don't ever mess with my babies again. Do you understand?"

"OK, I'm sorry," Steve mumbled, so scared, regretting he ever said anything.

"Good... I'm glad we had this little talk. It's been nice seeing you again," hearing a strange sound coming from his nephew.

Ben smells a horrible odor, then realizes he may have scared him a little too much. The poor boy soiled himself. Steve quickly turns and bolts out the door, realizing it as well.

Ben walks out to the front yard to see his brother off. He shakes his head, knowing he is going to be in trouble for this one. So tired, he just can't think straight after several days with no sleep, but mostly having to deal with a teenager.

* * *

Sam drives his family home, so embarrassed about his son causing so much trouble. On the entire trip back, Steve is getting yelled at for the way he acted, ruining Ben's homecoming.

"Hey, I'm sorry!" Steve yelled out, still staring out the window. "What more do you want!"

"We're invited to Uncle Mark and Mary's this weekend for a big pool party. Somehow, I don't think you'll be going."

"Good! I'd rather be out with my friends!" Steve quickly replied.

"What the hell is that smell?" Sam asked, taking in a few whiffs. "Everyone check your feet. Did someone step in something?"

Steve turns red, so humiliated by the ordeal. He just stares out the window, hoping this day will soon be over.

* * *

Jenny comes out of the bathroom, seeing the empty room. "Did everyone leave already?"

"Oh, Sam and the kids left for home," Mary replied.

"Well, I'm staying," Kelly said, sitting down next to Jenny. "I want to hear more of the stories."

"No, we want to hear what you've been doing while we were gone," Ben jokingly said to his sister.

"I can do that in one sentence," Kelly quickly replied. "I get up to go to work, come home, eat dinner, go shopping, or stay home watching TV. That's how exciting things are around here. No, we want to hear all about it, and don't leave out any details."

"We've done that already," Ben said. "Let's move on," trying to stay awake.

"I'm confused about the baby's name?" Mary finally asked. "I keep hearing everyone calling him Baby, but then it's August. Which one is it?"

"We let the girls help with the name," Jenny explained, "and they came up with Baby. His real name is August."

"How come they keep calling him Baby after all this time?" Walter asked.

Jenny shrugs. "We just gave up, but I guess we need to start using the name August."

"No, he's Baby!" April said, listening to the conversation, pointing over to her little brother.

"Can't we call him by his real name?" Mary asked the girls. "I think August is the perfect name for him."

Both of the girls shook their heads. "No, we give him his name... It's Baby!"

"Give them a little time," Ben said. "Once he gets older, he won't want that name."

Again, they are telling all the tales about their experiences. Getting so late, no one wants to go to bed. Jenny is having a great time with her new family. The twins are content with their coloring books. Baby eventually falls asleep on Mary's lap. Ben is also nodding off.

After over six years, their long journey and adventure have come to an end. No more living off the land, but most of all, no more traveling to remote places far away. They are finally back with their loving family once again.

* * *

Chapter 55

The Civilized World

Mary is up early in the morning, as usual. She closes the bedroom door to let Jenny and Ben sleep since they are exhausted from the trip. The twins, however, are awake and snooping around in their new bedroom.

"Good morning," Mary said, seeing the girls were awake. "How was your night?"

"Went by real quick," June replied, still a little sleepy. "That bed is so nice and soft. Real warm, too!" pointing over to her new bed.

"It's late! Better get everyone up! We got chores to do!" April said, running for the bedroom door where her mother and father were still sleeping.

"Oh no, we better let them sleep in," Mary said.

"No, we got to get the fire going and wash up before breakfast," April said, shaking her head. "We always have a wash in the morning."

"I'll help you get washed up."

"We not supposed to touch the taps," April explained. "That's the rules… Momma does that for us."

"It's OK… I'll turn the water on for you," ushering them into the bathroom.

She is in her element again, with little grandkids running around the house. These two are a little different. They never argue and do what they are told.

"So, what do you want to do first?" Mary asked, walking the twins into the living room.

"Well, we can walk down the beach and pick up things we can use," June replied. "We can make sandcastles, then go swimming in the pond."

"Yeah, we'll show you how we jump way up high and make a big splash in the water! It's lots of fun!" April added.

"Well, that sounds nice, but we don't have a beach around here," Mary explained, surprised how they still think that everyone lives on an island.

"You don't have a beach!" June said, so shocked to hear that. "You always have your home next to the beach. Then you don't have to walk far to catch fish and play in the water."

"So, are we up high like at the cave?" April asked. "We can walk down to the beach where your camp is."

"Yeah, let's go down the trail to your camp," June added. "You have a big tent? Those people who came to our beach had some really nice big tents!"

"Well, let's have something to eat first," Mary said, seeing they didn't understand things here. "So, what do you normally have for breakfast?"

"We always have oranges or bananas," they both said in unison.

"Wow, stereo!" Walter said, reading the paper in his favorite chair. "I can't get over how they do that," seeing how the girls say the same thing simultaneously.

"No teasing the girls," Mary quickly said to her husband. "Let's watch what we say around them," hoping no one says something that will get the girls upset again.

"So, where are your trees?" June asked, looking around.

"Yeah, we help you get breakfast!" April added.

"We have plenty of trees in the backyard," Mary said, not understanding the girl's questions. "Oh, you didn't see them yesterday. You want to go out and see our backyard?"

"Granny, what's a backyard?" April asked.

Walter chuckled. "It's where we keep our trees."

"Don't mind him," Mary said. "He's always joking around. I'll show you all the trees we got. I have some pretty flowers, too," walking them both out to the backyard.

The small fenced area filled with trees and flower gardens shocks April and June. Walking around the small yard, looking up at the trees, not liking what they are seeing.

June puts her hands on her hips, turning to her grandmother. "This is not good!"

"Yeah, we better go tell Daddy," April agreed.

"What's wrong? Don't you like our yard?"

June points up at the trees. "Someone picked all the fruit! It's all gone! You not supposed to pick them all."

April nods her head. "Yep, that's the rules... You always leave some for tomorrow! Daddy is going to be mad. Now, we have to go all the way to the other side to get fruit from the other trees! That takes a long time!"

"We can start a fire for you to boil the water," June added. "Where do you keep the firewood?"

"Let's go back in the house and tell your granddad about it," Mary said, concerned about the girls wanting to start a fire.

"What's up?" Walter asked, seeing the shocked look on her face.

"They were expecting to get fruit from the trees in the backyard. They also want to start a fire," Mary explained.

"We always start the fire," June blurted out. "That's our job!"

"Well, we might not need a campfire just yet," she suggested, getting concerned about the girls.

Walter laughed. "Better not let them out of our sight. I don't want them to make a campfire in the backyard. They'll probably burn down all the trees since we've hadn't had any rain in months."

"But, Daddy is going to be so mad," April said to her grandfather. "No food in the trees. No stack of firewood. You always keep some for a rainy day. Now, we don't have any food," getting frustrated, waving her hands up in the air.

Walter can't help laughing. "We have plenty of food, so don't worry about it. It's all out in the kitchen."

"That's right!" Mary said. "Remember last night I showed you where we keep all our food. Come on, let's get you something to eat," ushering them into the kitchen and sitting them down at the table.

The twins are adamant about telling their father all the bad news. Seeing the bare trees and no stack of firewood shakes them up. The small backyard has nothing for them to use for food or to start a campfire.

"We still have plenty of fruit left, so don't worry... I'll get you something to eat before we cook breakfast," Mary explained, quickly putting the rest of the fruit on the table.

"What's this one, Granny?" June asked, holding up a small fruit she had never seen before.

"That's a tangerine... It's like a small orange. That one is my favorite!"

"What kind of tree do you get that one from?" June asked.

"Oh no, we don't pick them. We buy them at the store. We'll take you there later on to show you."

"You have a store here?" April asked.

"Yep, it has everything we need. That's why we don't need any fruit trees. We just go to the store to get whatever we need. It's real easy that way."

"We had a store at the hospital," June added. "They got lots and lots of things there, too, but you need money!"

"Yeah, Mom won't let us get anything," April explained. "We have to take everything back. You need one of those money cards to take things from the store."

"Oh, you already know about credit cards. Don't worry, we'll take you to the store, and you can help me with the shopping."

Both the girls scream in excitement, hearing that they are going out with their grandmother to gather food. Mary gets things ready for breakfast. The twins patiently sit at the table, waiting, not eating any of the fruit.

"You're not hungry?" Mary asked, setting the orange juice on the table for them.

"We always eat with Mom and Dad and Baby," April explained.

Mary thinks it's so cute. "You can have something first. We'll let them sleep in."

"No, we wait," June promptly said. "We always eat together," sitting quietly at the table.

Mary is still a little perturbed about her new granddaughters. They act a lot older than their age and are so polite. She can see how much her son had taught them to be so self-sufficient. Only after one day with the girls, she is so proud of them.

* * *

The first day at home is a nice, refreshing break. There is nothing to do but sit out in the backyard under the trees, relaxing. Jenny sits in the shade with her journal, eager to finish it. Ben is taking another nap, still so tired from the long trip. He is so relieved, being able to sleep outside once again.

The girls are not used to sitting around all day long with nothing to do. Even worse, they don't like being confined in the small backyard.

Mary notices the twins are always inspecting everything in the backyard and gets them to help take care of all the plants and flowers. She has never seen kids who are so thrilled to work in the garden, always wanting to do chores.

Mary sees them hovering around the pond, eyeing the goldfish. "Now, you remember these fish are pets, and they all have names," recounting her son's warning.

"Yes, Granny!" the twins reluctantly said, somewhat depressed, not being able to catch one of the small fish.

April looks up at her grandmother. "So when are we going to the beach? We can look for things we can use. We always find good stuff on our beach."

"I don't know about going to the beach. That's a long way from here."

"That's OK, we walk," April said. "The hospital had a beach, and it was a long way too. That wasn't a nice one. Our beach is lots better and more fun! We always play on our beach. We catch fish, make sandcastles, and even have a fun day with a big campfire!"

"We'll catch you a big fish and cook it up for supper!" June said.

"I don't know about going out fishing. Let's check with your mother and father to see if you can come with us to the store. You can help us get some food for tonight!" she said, surprised at how the girls still think they are on an island.

"Mom, Daddy! Can we go to the store with Granny? Please! Please!" jumping up and down.

Ben looks over at Jenny. "So, what do you think?"

Jenny shrugs her shoulders. "It's OK with me, but they might be a little too much."

"Do you think you can handle them?" Ben asked his mother.

"Oh, come on, Ben!" Mary smugly said. "I brought up you three plus all the other grandkids. I think I can handle these two," putting her arms around the girls hugging them.

Ben laughed. "Yeah, but we didn't go out to catch and kill our lunch. With these two, anything that moves is fair game for them. They really haven't seen the real world yet."

"You boys were far more trouble than you think. All those slingshots and bows and arrows you had. Little girls, I can handle."

Ben looks over at his girls. "I guess you can go, but you have to listen to Granny. It's a little different from back home. She is in charge, and she'll show you how to do the chores here."

The girls are so thrilled to get to help with the chores, jumping up and down and yelling out loud.

Walter laughed. "It sure beats dragging screaming kids to the store like the old days," seeing how excited they are.

* * *

Walter and Mary are getting ready for their first outing with the grandkids. Jenny helps the girls get dressed for the big event. Mary thinks the girls are so cute when they walk into the living room with their backpacks and wearing big-rimmed hats, carrying their sticks.

Ben sits down with his parents to explain some of the basic things to do and not to do with the girls. Right away, they can see he is still overdoing it with the kids.

"This is just a quick trip down to the store," Mary said. "And not a scouting party to gather food in the wild jungles."

"That's right!" Walter added. "Don't worry about it. We are just going down to the store for a few minutes. It'll do them good to see how the real world works."

Ben just shakes his head. "They're kind of used to the outdoor life. You know, like hunting and fishing. They have no clue what's in store for them," glancing over at his girls, wearing all their hiking gear.

June hands her grandmother two empty water bottles. "Can you put some water in these? We not supposed to touch the water taps."

Mary smiles. "That's right! You can get burnt if you don't know which one is the hot one. Let's go into the kitchen to fill these up."

"Granny, do you have something we can bring for a snack?" June asked, following her into the kitchen.

"What would you like?"

"We like bananas or oranges," April answered.

"So, why do you need all this?" she asked, handing them a banana and a bottle of water.

"We always have a lunch break at the lookout," June explained. "We sit on the bench, looking at the clouds. You can see all the way down to the beach. It's lots of fun up there. You'll really like it!" putting everything in her backpack.

"Yeah, it's so high up, and you can see real far!" April added, pointing up in the air.

"I don't think we have that here," Mary said, feeling bad for them. "Where we're going is just down the street. Just a short drive in the car."

"We going in the car?" June asked, getting so excited.

Mary nods. "Yep! That's how we do it here. We even got you your own car seats too!" glad to see that they are so excited to go out shopping.

Jenny and Ben feel a little strange walking out to see them off. It is the first time having the girls go out with someone else. Ben's parents are well prepared, and the car seats are already in the back seat. The girls jump in the car as if they have been doing it for years.

"I hope they know what they are doing," Jenny said, seeing them driving off down the road.

"You notice how they couldn't wait to take them out and show them off," he jokingly said.

"I noticed that... How far away are they going?"

"Not far... About the same distance as the small pond."

Jenny looked at him, so shocked. "And they are driving there?"

He smiled. "Yeah, I know... It's going to take a while to get used to this easy life."

"They do have a cell phone, don't they?" she quickly asked.

"Oh yeah! I made sure of that."

"Maybe we better sit by the phone and wait, just in case," she said, not liking the idea that the girls are going out on their own so soon.

"Luckily, it's just down the road… Nevertheless, we'll wait by the phone," Ben replied, already getting worried.

* * *

The local grocery superstore is less than a mile away. Mary can't wait to take the girls out shopping. She knows it will make their day when they see the huge grocery store. She makes sure to hold the girls' hands as they walk through the parking lot since they have never been around cars.

"Where are all the trees?" June asked, walking through the parking lot. "I thought we going to get some fruit," looking around in disgust.

"Not out here," Mary explained. "It's all in the store. Someone picks the fruit and things we need, and they put them in the store here for us to buy."

"Like the store at the hospital?" April asked.

"I think so," Mary replied. "Everything we need is in that big building over there."

April gasped. "That's a food store? It's a real big one!" seeing it's even bigger than the ones at Kwajalein.

"You haven't seen nothing yet. Wait until you get inside. You're going to be impressed with this place."

As they reach the entrance, Mary waits, holding the girls' hands while Walter walks over to get one of the shopping carts.

June looks around, then up at the sun. "Granny, where does the sun come up in the morning?"

"I think it comes up over there," Mary said, pointing over to the eastern horizon, wondering what prompted the strange question.

"What about when it goes down?" June again asked, looking in the other direction.

"Maybe over that way," Mary said, vaguely remembering, then pointed over to the west by a group of trees.

Both June and April turn their backs to the sun. Then they hold their arms out, pointing their right hand towards the east and the other towards the west, looking down at their shadows.

"Look how my shadow is following me," Mary said, thinking they were playing a game, then started kicking up her feet.

"Granny," June mumbled, rolling her eyes so embarrassed.

"So, what are they doing now?" Walter asked, walking up with the cart, seeing the girls standing with their arms out, looking down at the ground.

"We're playing a game! Look at our shadows following us!" Mary said, trying to get the girls to join in.

"No, we checking to see what time it is," April finally explained. "We need to get back by four. That's when Mom and Dad be expecting us. Then we'll go out to the beach and play and stuff. We always do that after we get food and firewood."

"How can you tell what time it is?" Mary asked.

"The shadows!" June explained, pointing to the ground. "We always tell time that way. See, you point one hand where the sun comes up and the other where the sun goes down. Then you look at the shadow."

"So, what time is it then?" Walter curiously asked, playing along with their game.

"It's about eleven," April promptly said. "It's kind of late for chores. We'll have to make this a quick run."

Walter looks at his watch, a little shocked. "How about that! It's fifteen past eleven!"

Mary's mouth drops wide open. "You're kidding," stunned by their ability to tell time by the sun.

"No, I'm not," Walter replied, shaking his head. "We need to talk to that boy of ours," pushing the cart into the store.

"What is that?" April asked, pointing to the shopping basket.

"This is what we use to gather food with!" Walter explained. "All we do is push it around and toss in what we want. I bet you didn't have one of these back on that island of yours."

April closely examines the cart, shaking her head. "No, we didn't! Wow, this is really nice. Got those wheels, too, just like a car!"

"Why don't you two get up in the cart, and we'll push you around," Mary said, not wanting the girls to run around.

"That be fun!" April shouted. "Can you push us really fast?"

"Oh no," Mary said, helping them into the cart. "We're going to go real slow because we don't want to hit anyone else, and we got plenty of shopping to do."

"Does it work like a car?" April excitedly asked. "Can we take it home?"

"We'll see," Walter said, seeing the endless questions are starting up again. "Why don't you think about what you want for supper?" which gets them talking endlessly about their next feast.

The twins are so thrilled riding in the shopping cart. They are even more astounded at the size of the store. It is bigger than anything that they have ever seen before. Row after row of shelves filled with all sorts of boxes and things, most they don't recognize.

"That way, Granny!" they both yelled out, seeing the produce section, pointing their sticks in the direction they wanted to go.

"I figured you might like this part," Mary said.

"Wow! Look at all that food!" June points to all the shelves laden with food.

Walter can't help laughing at their reaction. "See, we don't have to worry about running out of food here. I bet you girls didn't have anything like this where you lived."

"No, we didn't!" June said, so impressed with all the food.

They point out all the fruit they recognize, but many they have never seen before. That starts another barrage of questions, pointing to some strange-looking fruit or vegetable.

"Do you know what type of fruit you want?" Mary asked.

"Sure we do!" June said. "We always help with the chores, so we know what to get. Push us over there, and we'll load up," pointing over to the enormous stack of oranges.

"OK, but only take what you need," Mary explained.

Mary pushes the cart up and down the aisles in the produce section. April and June stand up in the cart, filling it up with all the fruit. They are having a great day out shopping. They fill the cart with oranges, apples, bananas, grapefruit, pineapple, lemons, and their favorite, strawberries.

They stop at the lettuce section. Mary is a little curious, watching the girls feeling all the different lettuce leaves. Then, they select one and start loading up the cart.

"Well, I see you like eating salads," Walter said, seeing all the heads of lettuce they were getting. "Those will make you big and strong."

"We don't eat these ones!" April replied, looking at him strangely. "You wipe your bottoms with it. We going to need lots of this with all the peoples here."

"These are good ones too!" June said with a big smile on her face. "Nice and soft!"

"No, this is lettuce for salads," Mary explained to the girls. "We have toilet paper at home… If you're not going to eat this, then we need to put it back," now knowing why her son kept telling them they might not be ready for the girls.

"OK!" April reluctantly said, tossing back all the lettuce except for one, just in case.

Walter chuckles. "It makes sense if you think about it."

Mary doesn't say a word. She is so shocked by the girl's knowledge of how to live off the land.

* * *

After loading up the cart with fruit, Walter and Mary walk around the store to finish up the rest of their shopping. The twins are carefully examining every item that is put in the cart. They are so curious about everything, and they ask never-ending questions. The rest of the store is an alien world with nothing but boxes and strange containers.

"I smell fish!" June said, looking over at April.

"Yeah!" April notices it, too. "It's lots of fish!" looking around, trying to find where the smell was coming from in this big store.

Walter points over to the fish counter. "That's what you smell. You'll like what they have over there."

"That way, Granddad!" the twins pointed their sticks at the glass counter.

Mary knows they eat only two things, fruit and fish. So, they will need to stop at the seafood section. She pushes the shopping cart up to the glass counter, letting them have a good look at all the fish. The twins scream out loud, jumping up and down when they see the enormous pile of shrimp.

"Wow, look at all that! We never caught that many before!"

"Those are big giant shrimps!" June remarked.

"Those are Texas-size!" Walter smugly replied. "I bet you have never seen shrimp like that."

"No, we only had small ones. Why they so big?"

"Everything in Texas is big!" Walter boasted.

"How come?" April asked.

Walter continued to tease them. "Don't know why... That's the way it is in Texas!"

The twins let out a long "Wow!" in awe, seeing all the shrimp.

"We'll take two pounds, please," Mary said to the man behind the counter, pointing to the shrimp.

"You catch all these?" April asked the man. "You must be really good at fishing!"

He smiles back, not knowing what to say, as he shovels the shrimp up on the scale.

"Can't wait to tell Daddy about this!" June shouted, so amazed at all the different types of fish. "I bet he won't believe this, right, Granny?"

"Oh, your daddy has been here plenty of times," Mary said. "He has seen all this before."

April and June look at each other, confused. "No, he's not been here, cause he would have told us."

"Sure he has," Mary said. "They have these in all big cities."

"No, I don't think so," April mentioned, shaking her head. "He tells us everything. Daddy never said anything about this!"

"Is there anything else, mam?" the man asked, handing Mary the shrimp wrapped in paper.

"Do you girls want something else while we're here?" Mary asked.

"I want to look at those ones down there!" June said, pointing to the end of the glass case, wanting to see the rest of the fish.

Mary pushes the cart slowly along the fish counter, letting them look everything over. "Take your time. They have plenty here."

"Look at those two!" Walter remarked. "It's like they're in a candy store with so much to choose from, they can't even decide what they want."

"I know... They grew up eating seafood every day. They don't know anything else."

The twins know what they want. They eagerly point at it with their sticks, jumping up and down in the cart, so excited.

"Lobster! I don't think so," Walter said, so shocked seeing what the girls wanted to eat.

"We always have lobster," June fired back. "It's our favorite!"

Mary, also a little shocked, turns to her husband. "Better let them have it. It's their first day, and I don't think they eat anything else."

"It's up to you!" Walter said, finding it odd buying expensive lobster for the grandkids when he doesn't buy it for himself.

"How many do you want, mam?" the man behind the counter asked.

"We want four!" June quickly said. "Big ones, too!"

Mary nods her head, agreeing. Walter rolls his eyes as he sees the price of the lobster being weighed on the scale.

"Do you think we need more?" April asked her grandfather. "Are we going to have a fun day? Those other peoples going to be there too?"

"Oh no," Walter quickly replied. "We're not having everyone over for lobster. It's just going to be us or mostly you two."

"We going to have some good eating tonight!" April shouted, looking back at her grandmother with a big smile.

Mary awkwardly smiles back. "Oh yeah! We're going to have a big feast!" wondering if they are expecting to be eating lobster every day.

* * *

This is by far the best shopping day they have ever had. As they wait in line at the cashier, the twins are so excited, constantly chattering with each other. They are getting loud, sounding more like two chipmunks with their never-ending chattering. Mary and Walter get concerned when all the people around them start looking in their direction.

Mary puts her finger up to her lips. "Shh! Keep it down, you two, and keep still."

The twins are shocked by the hand sign their granny had just given them. They don't say a word, slowly picking up their sticks. Both have mean looks on their faces, standing back-to-back, looking around.

"Oh God, what did you do?" Walter asked, seeing the girls were ready to pounce.

Mary steps back, so shocked. "I don't know! What do we do?" she asked, seeing the girls slowly swinging their sticks around.

The woman working at the next cash register is curious, seeing everyone looking in her direction. As she turns, she is shocked to see a little girl giving her a mean look, pointing a stick in her direction. Slowly, everyone backs away from the two girls standing up in the grocery cart.

"You two put down those sticks," Mary said. "You better not hit anyone!"

Both the girls hold their fingers to their mouths. "Granny, shh!" repeated the sign she gave them, looking around for something or someone.

"What are you two doing?" Mary asked, getting annoyed.

"Granny, you gotta be quiet," April whispered. "Bogeyman around," looking over the crowds waiting in line at the cashiers.

"Where did you get that notion from?" Mary asked, so confused. "There is no bogeyman here."

"Granny, you gave the bogeyman sign! You saw a bogeyman, didn't you?"

"What bogeyman?" Mary asked. "What sign? I didn't give you any sign."

June repeats the sign, putting her finger to her mouth. "That's the bogeyman sign. Don't you know that one?" not understanding why they don't know all the danger signals.

"No! That meant for you two to be quiet. There is no bogeyman here, so put down those sticks before I take them away!"

"Granny! If you want everyone to be quiet, you do this sign," April explained, putting her hand over her mouth, showing her, and is so frustrated that no one knows any of the basic hand signs.

"See, Granny! That the sign for quiet!" June shows her the sign.

Walter laughed, shaking his head. "We need to have a long talk with that boy of ours when we get home."

Now she sees why her son was warning her. She repeats the sign that June showed her to be quiet. Right away, the twins are silent, looking a little frustrated. Mary knows she better learn some of these hand signs when they get back home.

The twins are getting loud again. The people nearby are pointing at them, recognizing that these are the famous Amazon girls. It's a dead giveaway with their long blonde hair, large-rimmed hats, backpacks, and both holding sticks.

The cashier keeps his distance from the two girls while Mary and Walter quickly put all the food on the checkout counter. The girls help by tossing everything out. They soon recognized this part from the small gift shop, seeing the big cash register.

"We need that card to buy the food!" June explained. "We can't take this home without the card!"

"You two learn quickly," Mary said. "We'll pay for all this with our credit card, so don't worry about it."

June nods. "Yep, we had one at the hospital. You take what you want and give them that card. Dad says that's money."

"That's right!" April added. "Mom says you can't take things without the money," nodding her head up and down.

As Mary pushes the cart forward, June notices one magazine near the register with their picture on the cover. "Look, April! It's us! See, that is you, and this is me!" pointing to the magazine.

"Oh my God!" Mary gasped, seeing the People magazine with her two grandchildren on the front cover.

She picks up one, flipping through the pages, seeing an entire article about Ben, Jenny, and the grandkids. She quickly picks up five more copies giving them to the cashier.

"Ben never told us about this," Mary said. "Look, it's even got pictures of them at that hospital!"

He flips through the pages, amazed at all the photos. "They even have a few photos from the island they were on as well!" showing the twins.

"That's our home!" so excited to see their beach.

"Where was this one taken?" Mary asked, seeing one photo of them standing on the beach together.

"That's our beach!" April shouted out. "Our home is just over there," pointing to the page.

"You sure had a beautiful home," Mary said, looking at the photos.

"You can come back with us. We'll let you sleep in the tent. We'll sleep outside with Mom and Daddy."

Mary just smiles. "That sounds like a nice idea," not letting on that they are never going back.

The magazine has only a few group photos taken when they were on the island, but the majority are from Kwajalein. With all the restrictions at Kwajalein, there are no photos other than when they first arrived on the pier. Someone from the ship that rescued them made a good bundle selling the photos they took on the island.

Since the girls are on the front cover of the magazine, it's easy to see how people recognize them. Walter quickly pays the cashier, hoping to make a fast exit. A hush goes over the crowd as they walk by the checkout registers. Everyone stops what they are doing to see the famous Amazon girls being pushed away in the shopping cart. For the first time, the twins are so fixated on the magazine that they are oblivious to what is happening.

"Hi, Mary! Are these your new grandkids?" a woman asked as she approached them.

Mary looks up, seeing her friend. "Oh, hello, Jane! Oh, yes! These are the girls. They got in last night. They're helping us out with the shopping today."

"Aren't they the cutest?" Jane said, slowly approaching the twins. "Awe, look at their little hats, and they even got their backpacks on too!"

"Better not get too close," Walter warned. "They're still a little on the wild side," seeing how both June and April are staring at the woman slowly reaching for their sticks.

"Are you going to say hello to my friend Jane?" Mary asked the girls.

"Hi!" they both said together in unison as usual.

Walter laughed. "They talk in stereo a lot too."

"Oh, you must be so proud!" Jane said.

"Oh yes, my dream came true!" Mary said. "Not only is Ben back home, but he brought his family as well. I got three new grandchildren, too!"

As Mary talks with her friend, a crowd gathers around them. Walter notices the girls are getting a little nervous. They are silent and start signaling each other. He knows that's not a good thing. Seeing the girls grabbing their sticks is a sign that they need to leave and fast. They said a quick goodbye to Jane before leaving. As they walk out, they feel so strange being the center of attention.

They panic, seeing several people following them into the parking lot. To make matters worse, some are talking on their cell phones. After putting everything in the car, Walter makes a fast exit. The last thing they need is for the press to show up with cameras parked in front of the house.

Walter keeps looking in the rearview mirror to make sure no one is following them. "I think that was a mistake. I didn't think about them getting noticed in the store like that. Maybe we should get them to wear something different and not carry those sticks."

"Oh, that was nothing," Mary replied. "Everyone was just curious about the girls. They're big-time celebrities now. They've been on TV, and now they're in all the magazines!"

"Unfortunately, I don't want them to find out where we live and have those damn news people waiting outside the house! Ben will have a fit if that happens."

"Oh, I didn't think about that," Mary said.

"Ben doesn't want any of those people around. He wants to relax and not be bothered while they're here. I hope we didn't mess things up on their first day."

"It'll be OK... The girls were great! They really helped out!" so thrilled to take them out shopping.

Walter shakes his head. "I don't know... I have a feeling that every time we take them out shopping, they will be expecting lobster for supper. We better drive around the neighborhood to make sure no one is following us. We better be more careful next time," getting nervous.

* * *

April and June can't wait to tell everyone about their big adventure. They rush into the house yelling and screaming, telling everyone what they saw and showing off the new watches their grandmother bought them.

"So, how were they?" Jenny quickly asked. "Did everything go OK?" so relieved they were back.

Mary nods. "It went fine... They were no trouble at all. I think they really enjoyed it."

"So, how did you like the ride in the car?" Jenny asked the girls. "Was it fun?"

"It was nice, but those damn Yankees were getting in the way! They don't know how to drive!" waving her arms up and down.

"Yeah!" April blurted out. "Hell, if you can't drive, then get off the damn road! Those damn Yankees need to go back home!" getting all flustered.

"Ah, you're not supposed to talk like that," Jenny said, so shocked by what they were saying.

"But Mom, they drive real slow," June added, "and don't know where the hell they're going! You have to yell at them to get them out of the way! Those damn Yankees need to go back where they come from!"

Ben is a little surprised as well by their outburst. "Where did you hear all that?"

"Granddad told us!" April replied. "We can't go fast cause them damn Yankees are in the way! They just keep blocking the road!"

Mary's face turned red, so embarrassed. "I'm so sorry... He gets that way in the car nowadays. I'm going to have a long talk with him about that potty mouth of his!"

Ben just smiles. "Oh, don't worry about it," trying not to laugh.

"Daddy, what's a damn Yankee?" April asked.

"Ah, it's those people who live up on the East Coast, like your mother. She is from Connecticut, so I guess she is a Yankee too," glancing over at Jenny, knowing she hates that term.

"Mom, are you a damn Yankee?" April asked her mother. "How come you don't drive the car fast like Granddad?"

Jenny shakes her head, trying not to laugh. "I'll explain it to you later. Let's see what you brought back from the store," trying to change the subject.

When Walter comes out of the kitchen, everything is quiet. Seeing his wife glaring at him, he knows something is up.

"What's wrong? What I do?" seeing the mean look he is getting.

"That potty mouth of yours! We have little children around us now, so you need to watch what you say in front of them!" getting mad.

"I guess we forgot to tell you," Ben explained. "They repeat everything they hear."

"So, what's wrong with that?" he asked, wondering what was up with everyone.

"Granddad, tell them how all those damn Yankees kept getting in the way!" June yelled out.

His mouth drops wide open. "Oh, sorry about that."

"No more talk about the Yankees," Ben said, signaling the girls to be quiet. "Let's check out all the food you got!"

April and June drag out all the food. They were so impressed with the big food store. The girls go on forever, talking about all the new things they saw. They go into such detail about everything in the huge supermarket.

"It's hard to believe they can remember all that," Walter commented. "I have been in there for years and still can't remember where things are," amazed by their ability to recall everything they saw.

"It's one of the things Ben taught them," Jenny explained. "Wherever they go, they take inventory of everything. So, if they see a good firewood tree or a new plant that we can use, they will remember where it is. They memorized everything on the island. If there was anything we needed, they knew exactly where to get it."

"They're better than one of those Palm Pilot computer things," Ben proudly remarked, "and they never need batteries. I bet they can walk the island in their sleep and see everything as if they were there."

"Well, the girls were great," Mary mentioned, "but we did have a minor incident at the cash register."

Ben looks over at the girls. "What did you do?"

"We didn't do anything," they replied, shrugging their shoulders.

"They were really good, but they were getting a little loud," Mary explained. "I just tried to get them to be a little quieter."

Walter laughed. "Yeah, she did some kind of sign or something, and the girls hushed up all right. They looked like they were about ready to skin somebody alive!"

"Which one was it?" Ben asked his mother.

Mary looks over at the girls. "OK, this is just to show your daddy, so don't panic," showing him the sign.

That doesn't make a difference. When they see her do the bogeyman sign, they still look around, just in case. Baby screams out loud, knowing what the sign means, crawling onto his father's lap. He quickly signals his sisters to protect him.

Ben quickly signals to the twins and Baby that everything is OK. "Granny's just showing us the signs she is learning."

Jenny cringes. "That's the bogeyman one... It's one of the worst ones, too. After all this time, I just can't keep up with all their hand signs. I get to the point where I'm scared to scratch my nose. I just keep my hands behind my back when I'm around them nowadays."

Ben laughed. "Granny and Granddad don't know all the signs. So, don't get panicky when they get mixed up and do the warning signs by mistake."

"But Daddy, that's the bogeyman one!" April said. "Everyone knows the signs!" waving her arms up in the air, getting all frustrated.

"Well, your granny and granddad don't... You're going to have to teach them."

"OK, we teach you all the signs," April said, nodding her head up and down. "We teach Baby too. He knows the important ones. You can sit down with us, and we can teach you all the signs, too!"

"Now, that sounds like fun," Mary said.

"We do birdcalls too!" June added.

"Yeah, I heard a few of those, too," Walter jokingly said. "I thought we had a wild bird in the house this morning."

"Yep!" June proudly replied. "We real good at birdcalls!" nodding her head up and down.

"Oh, you'll like this... I found these at the register," Mary said, remembering the magazine with the girls' photos on the front.

Ben looks at the magazine, so surprised. "They're on the front page! Where did they get all these pictures?" flipping through all the pages.

"Oh my God!" Jenny cried out. "I forgot all about it. One of them did have a small camera," going through the magazine and seeing all the photos of them standing on the beach.

Ben's mouth drops wide open, seeing their old home. "That's right! They don't waste time getting these out. At least we got some good pictures of our beach. I don't know why I didn't think about borrowing it. I could have taken a few more photos before we left," he mentioned, going through the magazine.

"I was in a daze on that day," Jenny remarked. "It's still like a big dream. It's hard to believe it's all over now."

"I know... How many did you get?" Ben asked, seeing the stack of magazines.

"I got plenty more," Mary said, pulling out the rest. "I'll send these to my sister. They'll be thrilled to see these. It's got a big article about you and the kids!"

"Looks more like Tarzan and Jane," Walter commented, looking at all the photos. "Little skimpy outfits you guys are wearing," seeing the rags they had on.

"Just think," Ben said. "That was our Sunday best!"

"You are joking, aren't you?" Mary asked, so shocked, seeing the photo.

"We didn't have much of a choice," Ben explained. "We were getting low on clothes out there. My old swimming trunks were the last of our original clothes. All the rest just basically fell apart. We ended up using mostly old sails we found on the beach. If it weren't for that, we'd be wearing a lot less!"

Jenny laughed. "That's one thing I'm not going to miss. I never realized how nice cotton feels after all those years."

"It sure looks hot out there," Mary said. "It must have been horrible living out there with no air conditioning."

"That wasn't the worst of it," Jenny said. "The sand was everywhere. You could never get away from it. It was always on our clothes. Even after washing everything and hanging it all out in the sun to dry, they always ended up covered with sand. Most of the time, we found it best just not to wear anything unless we were out in the midday sun."

Mary laughs. "I bet he loved that! When he was young, he'd freak out if someone saw him in his underwear!" glancing over at her son.

Jenny smiles, looking over at Ben, seeing he is getting embarrassed. "Well, we kind of got used to it," not wanting to add any more details.

* * *

They spend the rest of the day relaxing in the backyard and having a big barbecue. The twins are so excited to cook shrimp and lobsters on the gas grill. They can't get over how easy it is to push the button to start the fire.

April and June are in their element testing out new recipes for the shrimp. The coconut and lime grilled shrimp is everyone's favorite. Mary and Walter are so amazed at how well their grandkids can cook. The lobster is one of the best meals they have had in years. It's nothing like the typical backyard barbecue they are used to, but more like eating at a five-star restaurant.

Ben is going through the magazine, looking at their old home. These are the only photos taken of their island, and they are so glad to have them. Ben regrets not borrowing the camera and taking a few more while he had the chance. Staring at the photos of their old home, he already misses the beach and the simple life.

Jenny notices Ben is spending way too much time staring at one photo in the magazine of the last sunset on the beach. She knows he is getting homesick. She misses the island too, but now with all the modern conveniences in the civilized world, it will be difficult to live on the beach again. This is their new life, and there is no going back.

* * *

Chapter 56

Pool Barbecue Party

The next day, Uncle Mark and Aunt Sue are having a big family reunion. Since all of Walter's family lives in Texas, everyone is already in town to see Ben. It's going to be the party of all parties, Texas-style.

Arriving in the old Buick, Walter pulls up to his sister's house. With nowhere to park the car, that's all it takes to get him grumpy and start complaining. Jenny sees how Ben takes after his father. June is the same, being a little grumpy at times.

"Don't tell me all these cars are here for the reunion?" Ben asked.

Walter nods. "Yep! From the looks of things, I think everyone is already here! We should have left a little earlier so we could have parked in front of the house. I bet all the neighbors will be complaining."

Ben cringes. "I was hoping for a smaller reunion. It's going to be a little crowded."

"Better get used to it!" Mary added. "Everyone's been waiting for this party ever since they heard you were coming back. You need to get used to being around people again. No time better than now. They're all your family, so there's no need to worry about it!" waving her finger at him.

Ben looks around. "You sure this is just the family?" getting a little wary of news crews or reporters.

"Yep, everyone is here. That's the way it should be," Walter said, knowing what his son is thinking.

"I don't know... Might be a little too much, too soon," Ben said, worrying about the children being around such a big crowd.

Walter puts his hand on his son's shoulder. "Your mother has been planning this for weeks, so don't let her down. She can't wait to show off her new grandbabies."

"OK, let's all have a good time!" knowing his mother would get her way.

Walter rings the doorbell several times. No one answers the door. After a minute, he hits the doorbell again. The twins are already in their constant question mode, not understanding what is going on. They were expecting a big party out on the beach and not going to another house.

"Maybe we got the wrong house," Ben jokingly said.

"They are probably all out back," Walter said. "I think we're a little late."

"Hello!" Mary said out loud, opening the door. "Anyone home? We're here!"

"Look at the size of this place!" June remarked, walking through the huge house.

"This is big… A lot bigger than I remember. You guys will love what they got out back," Ben added.

"Is it a surprise?" April asked.

"Oh, yeah! You're going to like this place!" he said, remembering the fancy pool in the backyard.

Looking out the large French doors, they see everyone in the backyard already in the pool. An enormous cheer goes up when Ben walks out. He is awestruck at seeing all the people here, a lot more than he expected. All of his aunts, uncles, and cousins are here, plus all of their families. There are way more people here than what was at the airport.

"This is all your family?" Jenny asked, also shocked to see the big crowd.

"I think so! I didn't think they'd all show up. There's a few I haven't seen before," seeing all the little ones running around.

Everyone rushes over, hugging Ben and patting him on the back. Most just got out of the pool, and it's not long before he is wringing wet.

Everyone is so amazed to see how much Ben has changed. He is now slim and trim, bulging with muscles, looking more like a bodybuilder. Ben is not used to having people feel his biceps. Some of his younger female cousins are getting a little carried away, running their hands all over his chest while hugging him.

Jenny is a little uncomfortable with all these people. Holding on to Baby, she hides behind Mary while Ben is meeting his over jubilant extended family. April and June are a little uneasy holding Mary's hand as they watch everyone greeting their father.

"They're a rowdy bunch, aren't they?" Mary said, noticing Jenny was a little wary. "They came from all over to be here today. Just think, this is just Walter's family. You still got my family in England to meet next. I think we got just as many over there."

"Oh, I'd love to go to England... Unfortunately, it's a far reach for us now. We still have a long ways to go to get used to being around other people."

"Don't worry... Just take one step at a time. With all the people here, you'll be used to it by the end of the day."

Jenny sighed. "It's going to take me a lot longer than that. I still feel so awkward being around other people. I hope the children can handle it!" worrying about another incident with the girls.

"They'll do fine," Mary said, hugging her. "Don't worry about the girls. They're going to have a lot of fun out here today."

"Being around other children might help. I think that's what they really need," Jenny said, seeing all the other children running around.

"There are plenty of kids here for them to play with," Mary said, pointing to the shallow end of the pool where all the children were playing together. "They're going to make a lot of new friends and have a good time."

One by one, Ben introduces everyone to his new family. Jenny is trying hard to remember all their names, but there are just too many. She is so happy to see such a close-knit family. After meeting everyone, she longed for her own family and missed them so much.

* * *

They all sit next to the pool, telling the same old stories of their lives on the island. Again, it is nothing but the same questions they have heard since they were first rescued. Jenny does most of the talking since Ben is rather quiet. He is at the point where he gives simple, short answers. Jenny, being a writer, always tells a better story.

Ben feels claustrophobic surrounded by all these people. Everyone is having a good time, and many are already a little drunk. He wishes they would have waited for a while before being thrown into the middle of all this. Jenny feels the same holding Baby, knowing he is scared, too. She doesn't want him to start sending out any bad signals to his sisters.

While everyone is talking, April and June hover around the large pool. They have little interest in these people who ask way too many questions, basically ignoring them. Their main interest is the big pool in the middle of the yard. The swimming pool is such an oddity, not having a river or waterfall to feed it. After seeing the other children playing in the water, the twins can't wait to jump in.

June runs back to her mother, tugging her arm. "Can we go play in the water, Mom?"

"You think it's OK if they can play in the pool?" Jenny asked, looking over at Ben.

"Sure, that's why we're all here!" Aunt Sue mentioned, overhearing the conversation. "Why don't you all go in? It's a great day for a swim!"

"Let's go, guys! We're going swimming!" Ben quickly takes the opportunity to get away from the endless questions and all the attention.

April and June yell out in delight, then start removing their clothes.

Jenny reaches over, grabbing them. "Oh, no, we have to wear those new bathing suits Granny got you."

"We don't wear things in the water," April said. "It'll get all wet!"

"Everyone else is wearing them. Your daddy and I are going to wear ours too!"

"Come on into the house," Aunt Sue said. "I'll show you where you can change."

They quickly follow Aunt Sue into the house. Jenny is so relieved to get away from all the questions. Since they left the island, they tell the same story so many times, and it's getting a little old. Even Ben feels awkward being the center of attention. He liked the old days when he was just one of the crowd and blended in with the rest of them.

* * *

While Ben and his family are in the house, the gossiping starts. They all notice how quiet and reserved Ben is. He is an entirely different person from who they used to know.

One of Ben's cousins is a little shocked. "Man, he has changed big time. He is almost a different person! The way he sits there and his eyes go back and forth, constantly looking over everyone. It's a little spooky."

"Well, he has been through a lot," Sam explained. "You got to remember they haven't been around people in years. The little ones have never even seen another person other than their mother and father."

"Yeah, I can see the difference in him too," Uncle Mark said. "I also noticed those two girls were eyeing everyone as well. I can't blame them. It's going to take time to get used to being around other people."

"The whole family does act a little odd. It's like they are all on edge, not trusting us," Jack mentioned, noticing it as well.

"If you had been through all they've experienced," Sam added, "you would be a little different too. Think about it. They survived a plane crash and were out on the ocean for days with no food. Yeah, they'll need some time to get over that. Even I can see a substantial difference in Ben. He is a lot quieter and more relaxed than he used to be, but don't let that fool you. After living in the wild for six years, he is very aware of everything around him. That's why you see him constantly looking everyone over. Whatever you do, don't make any fast or threatening moves around him, especially around his kids! I'll tell you right now, don't even get near the little boy. Those girls are trained to protect him, and they won't hesitate to attack. My oldest boy found out the hard way, and that's why he ain't here today!"

Everyone snickers, knowing about the little incident at the airport.

"I heard about that," someone commented. "I wouldn't show up in public either after getting a busted nose from a little five-year-old girl."

Mary is furious. "That is not funny! He was told not to mess around with the kids, and he found out the hard way. I don't want anyone here teasing my babies, or you'll have me to answer to!"

"She is right!" Walter shouted, putting his arm around his wife. "No joking around. Just act normal, but don't crowd them. Whatever you do, don't be teasing the girls. It would be best for now to keep a distance from them. Just ignore them and let them play on their own. Remember, Ben is an overprotective father. He's not used to having other people around his kids and needs a little time to get used to us again."

A hush goes over the crowd as everyone silently agrees with Walter. This is a special homecoming. They all want to celebrate, but many know Ben as the big prankster in the family. They were all so tempted to grab him and toss him in the pool to welcome him back home. Now, they are so glad they didn't do it. After seeing his size and all those muscles, they know it's best not to mess around with him at all.

* * *

Jenny and Ben put on their new bathing suits. They think it's a joke, having to put on clothes just to go swimming. Not like in the good old days when they didn't have to worry about such things. All they had to do was walk out to the beach and enjoy a swim.

"What kind of swimming trunks are these?" Ben asked. "Not only are they baggy as hell, but they come down to my knees! These are way bigger than my old swimming trunks. I think they're even bigger than my shorts. This has got to be a joke!"

Jenny can't help laughing. "They're the latest style, from what your sister tells me!"

"How can anyone feel comfortable wearing these things in the water?" he asked, shaking his head. "These are so ridiculous! Who picked these out?"

She laughed. "Your sister did!"

"I guess I should have told you about her strange sense of humor and fashion! I can't believe I have to wear this. They're all going to laugh."

"Well, it's all you got for now… If you think that's bad, look at what I have to wear," opening up her shirt, posing for Ben in her new bikini.

He is almost speechless, seeing how great she looks wearing a tiny two-piece yellow bikini. With all that cleavage, he knows she is going to draw a lot of attention. The bottom piece is even worse. The tiny thong doesn't cover much at all, showing almost all of her well-tanned bottom.

"So, what do you think?" Jenny asked, looking at herself in the mirror. "I thought you'd like it!" seeing how he is just staring at her with his mouth wide open.

"Oh, yeah!" he replied with a big ear-to-ear smile.

They grab their towels and walk back out to the pool. When Ben walks out with the twins, he gets plenty of attention. No one can believe how great he looks. All the women yell out catcalls, seeing Ben's broad shoulders, huge biceps, and that washboard stomach. All the men feel a little self-conscious about their potbellies and love handles, wishing Ben had kept his shirt on.

Sam stands next to Ben, looking him over. "Damn! What the hell? You look like Arnold Schwarzenegger! You've been working out?"

Ben just shrugs. "Not really... I'm no different than before."

"Like hell! We need to get out the old photo albums. I remember when you were lily white and way out of shape."

"You haven't changed at all either. Talk about me being lily white. When was the last time you were outside?" Ben asked, putting his arm next to his brother's.

"Hey, I just got a normal tan... Check out my biceps, too!" Sam boasted, showing off to his brother.

Ben laughs, then quickly makes his way to the pool with the twins, feeling a little awkward being the center of attention. All the women and a few of the teenage girls are drooling over him, constantly making remarks. He quickly jumps into the water, glad to get away from all the attention. The twins don't care. All they want to do is jump into the water and have fun.

Once Jenny walks out with Baby, she quickly attracts all the attention. Everyone is stunned, seeing the tiny yellow bikini. They all think it's a little revealing until they see the back. A loud gasp comes from the crowd seeing the thong she is wearing.

"I picked that one out for her," Kelly whispered to her mother. "What do you think?"

"How could you?" Mary blurted out, so startled, seeing how revealing it was. "She is a little overexposed in that thing. I bet she's embarrassed having to wear that in front of all these people. You should have gotten her one that's a little more modest."

Kelly gives her mother one of those looks. "Mom, you don't understand... You should have seen the ones she was picking out. They were even smaller than that. Talk about a nature girl. She kept walking out of the dressing room to see what I thought when she was trying things on. The biggest problem was that she only tried on the bottom part of the bikini! She kept walking about topless most of the time!"

"What! She was walking around topless?"

Kelly nods. "Yep! It didn't bother her one bit. I had a hard time keeping her in the dressing room. It was weird how she wasn't even interested in getting the top. Apparently, she doesn't like wearing any clothes when she goes for a swim."

"You got to be joking?" Mary asked, looking at her daughter in disbelief.

"Nope!" Kelly said, shaking her head. "At least she's wearing the top. You should be grateful for that!"

Jenny quickly walks up to the shallow end of the pool with Baby, stepping down into the cool water. She thinks it's so ridiculous having to wear a bathing suit in the first place. Now, being around other people, Jenny knows it will take time to get used to wearing clothes again. The looks she is getting from all the men will probably be nothing compared to if she went topless like she wanted to do.

While they are in the pool, everyone is gossiping again. All the boys, and eventually, all the men, work their way over to the pool, gawking at Jenny. They all acted like a bunch of school kids seeing a woman in a bikini for the first time.

Ben notices all the attention Jenny is getting, but it doesn't bother him. It's probably the most that she has ever worn going out for a swim. He can't blame them, anyway. She looks so nice in that tiny bikini. He knows she will not hesitate to bare it all in front of everyone. He is surprised that she has not already suggested everyone should go skinny-dipping.

Jenny is getting way too much attention, and it's very obvious to all the women. One by one, the women drag their husbands and boyfriends back into the house for a good scolding. Eventually, the only ones in the pool are Kelly, Ben, and Jenny, plus all the little kids.

Ben sits on the inflatable lounge, floating about, enjoying the day out in the sun. The twins play games with the abundance of water toys. Jenny and Kelly sit with Baby in the shallow end. Jenny can't believe how everyone reacted because of her bikini. She never thought it was going to cause so much turmoil.

Back in the house, it's nothing but 'Did you see the size of him!' or 'Wow! She is really built! You see that tiny bikini she has on!' and everyone is gossiping again.

All the men and boys are clambering over each other, trying to peek out the window. "That lucky son of a bitch," Jack said. "Can you imagine being stuck on a deserted island with a beautiful woman who has a body like that?"

"Oh, you ought to hear what happened at the mall," Sam said. "Kelly was telling me that she kept walking about with nothing on while trying on some of those bathing suits. Apparently, she has one perfect body. No tan lines at all!"

"Man, the thought of her walking down the beach naked," Jack boasted, still smiling. "I would give anything to see that! You think they're real?"

"Oh yes, I bet you those babies are real!" Sam replied, peeking out the window again. "The sad thing is, she's not going to notice any of us old potbelly boys. She is used to seeing Hercules out there. I can't get over how he looks. He's all muscle and strong as hell, too!"

"I couldn't believe it when I saw him," Jack said, shaking his head. "Looks like he's been working out every day. It makes all of us look pretty bad. You notice how all the girls dragged us in here because she's out there in that tiny bikini."

"Yeah!" Sam said. "Look how they're all checking him out, peeking through the windows! Well, I ain't scared. I'm going in the pool!"

Jack laughed. "You ain't scared cause your wife isn't here yet!"

"Damn right! She'll be here shortly, though. She's coming straight from the airport. I better get out there while I still have a chance!" running out to the pool.

Barbra grabs her husband's arm. "Jack, you ain't going out there!"

"Why not? Sam is going… Why aren't you going out?" Jack asked, wondering why his wife was hiding in the house.

"I'm not going out there… I can't believe how great Jenny looks. How does she have a flat stomach like that after having three kids?" feeling self-conscious.

"She looks like a damn supermodel. Ben doesn't help, either. I have never seen so many muscles," Jack added, now thinking twice about going outside and having to stand next to Ben.

* * *

Sam notices Ben looks way too comfortable lying on the inflatable lounge. He can't resist pulling a prank on his brother, quietly slipping into the pool, letting the twins know what he is about to do. He doesn't want any trouble from those two. They start giggling, knowing a prank on their father is about to happen.

Sam slowly submerges under the water and swims underneath his brother. With one massive heave, he flips Ben off the lounge and into the water. Ben knows right away that his brother is around and up to mischief. They always pulled pranks on each other as kids. He emerges from the water to see Sam on the far side of the pool, sitting with Kelly and Jenny, all laughing at him.

"So you think you're going to get the best of me, huh?" he asked his brother, slowly working his way over to him.

The twins know that no one pulls a prank on their dad without him getting you back. "Go get him, Daddy!" knowing what is coming up.

Sam just smiles. "It wasn't me! I'm not the only one in the pool," pointing over to the twins.

"We didn't do it! It was you! You in big trouble now!" April shouts, quickly pointing over to Sam.

Ben slowly approaches his brother. Sam is scared and tries to run, but it's too late. Ben grabs his brother by the waist just as he tries to climb out of the pool. Then he lifts Sam right out of the water, holding him high above his head.

Sam is so scared. "Put me down! Put me down! I was only joking!"

Jenny laughs. "Ben, he was only playing!" not knowing if he was mad or just playing around.

Ben starts laughing, seeing the look on his brother's face. With one massive heave, he tosses him into the deep end of the pool. Sam hits the water hard, about six feet away. He pops out of the water, gagging and gasping for air.

"Do it again! Do it again!" the twins shouted out, clapping their hands, jumping up and down.

Sam swims to the edge of the pool, gasping for air. He is so surprised to be picked up like a little child and tossed across the pool like that. He got the wind knocked out of him, slamming down hard on his stomach.

"You giving up already?" Ben asked, slowly moving towards his brother.

"That hurt like hell!" Sam quickly replied.

"Awe, it wasn't that bad," Ben said, knowing he hit the water hard. "I do that with the girls all the time. They love it! You just got to know how to hit the water right."

"Yeah, sure!" swimming to the shallow end of the pool, hoping his brother would not be doing that again.

"Who wants to go first?" Ben asked, looking over at the girls.

"Me first!" they shouted out, swimming over to their father.

June reaches him first. He picks her up, holding her high above the water. Usually at the beach, he would toss them as high as he could and as far out into the ocean. There were no boundaries in the open ocean, and it was never a problem with the soft sand. In the pool, there is limited space and a lot of hard concrete.

He makes some quick calculations, so he doesn't toss her too far out. But mostly, keep her from the edge of the pool. With one big push, June flies through the air, does a complete flip, then straightens out just before she hits the water, coming down feet first.

Everyone is shocked at how high she goes into the air. June quickly comes up to the surface, swimming back for more. April is next, and Ben does it again. He tosses her high above the water, where she comes down like an Olympic diver.

All the children in the pool applaud, seeing April and June diving into the water. The other children quickly rush over, wanting their turn. The twins have been doing this since they were babies, so Ben doesn't have to worry about them. He knows to keep it easy with the other children, not tossing them too high.

One after another, Ben tosses them all up in the air to the deep end of the pool. It makes his day just being outside playing with the children. Although the twins are not used to waiting in such a long line for their turn again.

"Is there anything those girls can't do?" Kelly asked, seeing all the flips they were doing while being tossed in the air.

"Nope," Jenny replied, so proud of her little girls. "We always taught them things to keep them busy. They'd always excelled in everything they did and always come back for more. As you can see, even playtime is something that they'll keep doing until it's perfect."

"If he tossed me in like that, I'd probably look like old Sam, doing a big belly flop."

Jenny laughed. "You and me both. He tried that on me once. I hit the water so hard, and it hurt like hell. That was the first and last time I did that."

"You think he would get tired after a while," Kelly said, seeing all the kids coming back for another turn.

"No, it's their diving game. They would do this for hours back home. Normally, the girls will get tired before he does. He has got so much energy. I don't know how he does it!"

"I can't believe how strong he is!" Sam said, still feeling the pain. "He picked me up like it was nothing. How did he get that way?"

"Having to lug around a huge iron pot filled with water every day," Jenny explained, "and carrying huge loads of firewood as well. I didn't notice it at first. We both got in shape with all the hard work, but he turned into a muscle man. Every day, he was running up and down the trails like it was nothing."

"He was always like that," Sam said. "Always hiking up in the mountains back when he lived in Colorado. We went up to visit for a week, and he wore us out on the first couple of days. A small hike ended up being ten miles to the top of some mountain. It took us the rest of the week to get over it."

"Yeah, he was always an outdoor nut," Kelly said. "He must have been in his glory out there on that island."

"You got that right... I was scared to death at first. We were stuck out in the middle of nowhere. Having to survive out in the wilderness, he acted like it was just another camping trip."

"You know... I can't wait to read your journal! I don't think you realize what you have there. If you get it published, I'll bet it'll be a bestseller!"

"I don't know," Jenny replied. "It's like publishing your diary. It was just meant for the children. I still have some catching up to do anyway, but I think it might be in the works."

"Hey, kids! I think they got the hamburgers and hot dogs ready in the house!" Sam shouted out, annoyed with all the splashing and the kids screaming.

"Hurry!" Kelly added, also getting a little annoyed. "Better get in there before it's all gone! I think everyone is already eating!" pointing over to the house.

That is all it takes, hearing the food might be gone to get them all out of the pool. One by one, the children climb out of the pool, screaming so loud, running into the house, except for April and June. They don't care about anything else, and nothing will get them out of the pool. They are having way too much fun.

Jenny motions to the girls. "Come over here with us. You can sit with Baby. You two need to take it easy and relax. We're going to eat in a little while."

"Let's take a break and rest up," Ben added.

Reluctantly, the twins swim over to the shallow end of the pool. They sit next to Baby, who is ready to play. He is happy to be in the water but finds it odd that there is no sand. All the water toys in the pool make up for having no sand to play in.

Ben sits down next to Jenny. "So, what happened to everyone? Why are they all in the house? It's really nice out here," so surprised that they are the only ones in the pool.

"I think you scared them all off," Sam jokingly said. "They're all in the house hiding."

Kelly slaps his arm. "Sam, be nice! Ben, don't listen to him. They're getting the food ready. They've all been out here most of the morning, anyway. Those kids needed a break and were getting way too noisy. Let's enjoy the peace and quiet while we have the backyard and the pool to ourselves!"

"You ought to see how they are all gossiping in there!" Sam mentioned, seeing how everyone in the house was still peeking out the windows.

"About what?" Jenny asked.

"Well, for starters, Hercules over there. All the women are drooling over him," pointing over to his brother.

Jenny laughs, nudging Ben. "See, I told you! The nurses were drooling over him as well while we were at the hospital!"

"I can't believe my brother turned into a hunk!" Kelly said, laughing. "I bet they'll be gossiping about that for a long time!"

"That ain't all that they are gossiping about," Sam added. "There is also the matter of this itty-bitty yellow bikini someone is wearing!" glancing over at Jenny.

"So, what's wrong with it?" Ben asked. "I think she looks nice."

"Thank you, dear!" Jenny said, leaning over to kiss him.

"They all act like they never saw anyone in a bikini before," Kelly said, so disgusted with them all. "If I filled it out like she does, I would wear one of those too!"

Sam chuckled. "Well, some of the women here are concerned that their husbands are a little distracted."

"He is right!" Jenny said, seeing a few peeking through the window. "Check it out! More peeping toms!"

Ben just shakes his head. "What's wrong with them? If they think this is bad, it's a good thing they weren't on the island with us. They'd be getting an eye full and plenty to gossip about!"

* * *

The rest of the family finally walk out to help set up the picnic tables with plates of food. Uncle Mark is going all out for this barbecue, along with all the hamburgers, hot dogs, and chicken. He makes sure to have plenty of fresh trout with massive amounts of shrimp for Ben and his family.

Uncle Mark makes sure to let everyone know that he is the cook in this family. He sure doesn't want two little five-year-olds telling him how to barbecue.

Sam's wife, Vanessa, finally shows up, sitting down next to Jenny and Kelly, hearing all the latest gossip. She has heard about her oldest son's episode with the twins. She keeps apologizing to Jenny and Ben, feeling so bad about it.

Jenny is having a great time with Kelly and Vanessa. Since her sister Kim was always distant, never really close, this is something Jenny has always wanted but never had. Now, she feels as if she has two new sisters. She can now start her new life and a lifelong friendship with her new in-laws.

* * *

Chapter 57

Book Day

Jenny's brief contact with Rachel Cook on the flight from Hawaii opened many doors. After submitting a copy of her journal to the company Rachel recommended, she has been on edge. Within a week, she receives a letter from the publishing company. Jenny is too scared to open the letter, so she hands it over to Ben and crosses her fingers.

Opening the envelope, Ben reads the letter to himself. The letter is simple and to the point. He looks up at her, so stunned.

Jenny can't contain herself. "What did they say!" she shouted out, jumping up and down.

"Well done!" he said, handing the letter to her. "They love the manuscript, and they're going to publish it! They also want you to call them right away!"

Jenny quickly reads the letter and then dances around the living room. Ben notices something else in the envelope. He pulls out a check, so stunned, seeing the amount.

"You'll want to see this!" he tells Jenny, waving it at her.

"You got to be kidding?" not believing her eyes when she sees the amount.

"I guess our money problems are over for a while," Ben said, so relieved.

"I can't believe it!" she screamed out, dancing around the room again.

"Everyone who's read your journal said you should get it published. Sounds like this company thinks the same, and they're saying it's the best they have seen in years. Having that Rachel Cook on your side is not a bad thing either, from the looks of that check."

She runs up to Ben, giving him a big hug and a kiss. "I know! I figured it would be rejected and be waiting around for months trying to persuade someone to publish it. Rachel really set me up good. Oh, I need to call them!" quickly, running to the bedroom.

Mary comes out of the kitchen, hearing all the noise. "What's going on?"

"Jenny is going to have her journal published," Ben explained with an ear-to-ear smile on his face. "She's already got a check for $50,000!"

"They pay that much for a book?"

"I think that's like a bonus check or an advance. The royalty checks are what counts. Jenny should get a percentage for every book that's sold."

"Well, that's nice," she said, sitting down a little shaken, hearing the news. "I guess you'll be getting a job soon. Then you can get a house and settle down," wondering if he is going to move away again.

"A job! I don't know… After six years, I'm already out of touch with all this new computer stuff. I might have to do something else. Maybe she can make all the money, and I'll stay home taking care of the kiddies!"

"Oh, you can't do that... You need to get a job to keep busy. Don't worry about the kids. I'll help take care of them," so thrilled to have the grandkids at the house.

* * *

Jenny has been talking on the phone for hours. Everyone patiently sits in the living room, waiting to hear the rest of the news. When she walks out, she can't contain herself, dancing around the room, giggling like a little girl.

"So, it must be good news!" Ben said, seeing how she was acting. "What did they say?"

She sits on Ben's lap, and it takes a few minutes for her to compose herself. "Not only do they want a book deal, and it's a big one! That's not all! They also want to do a movie as well. Several Hollywood companies are fighting for the movie rights," hugging and kissing him.

"You got to be kidding?"

"Nope! This is way better than I have ever dreamed! I need to go to New York to meet with them and sign all the papers! They even have meetings set up with several producers to talk about the movie."

"You mean they're really going to make a movie about you two on that island?" Mary asked.

"Yes!" Jenny excitedly replied. "I just can't believe it. They want to do the story from when we left to even when we got back here. They might have someone playing your part in the movie as well!" pointing at Mary.

Mary is stunned. "Oh, I don't know about that," getting all flustered.

"If you don't mind. They're interested in all the things that have gone on since we've been here!"

Ben laughed. "Maybe Meryl Streep might be playing Mom's part," teasing his mother.

"Don't be silly," Mary blurted out, starting to blush, thinking about some famous actress playing her in a movie.

"Can you imagine our whole family being up on the big screen?" Ben jokingly said. "I hope we don't have any skeletons in the closet."

Mary is almost panicking, then jumps up. "I better start cleaning up the house. We can't have everyone seeing this mess. Oh, I better go fix my hair first!" running to the bedroom.

"I only read a few pages of what you wrote," Walter said, a little concerned about the movie. "How much of us do you have in there?"

"Not much," Jenny explained. "I have been writing every night since we've been here, but I have been catching up on everything since we left the hospital. I haven't submitted that part yet, but you can read what I have so far, just to make sure it's OK with you and Mary."

"Don't worry, Dad," Ben said. "I made her promise to keep out the juicy parts and make us look like a normal family. Just like that Dallas show where we're all rich and live on a big cattle ranch."

Walter laughed. "That's about right! Put me down as that JR character. I'll have to start wearing my boots and a white cowboy hat again!"

Mary comes back into the living room. "Walter, you need to put on some decent clothes!" still trying to fix up her hair.

"What the hell are you doing?" he blurted out, not believing what he was seeing. "Why are you getting all dressed up? Are you going to church or a fancy dinner?" wondering why she had changed her clothes.

"Oh, this is nothing... I always dress like this when we have guests. I think we need to get some decent furniture. Look at all that mess on the coffee table! We can't have people seeing that. Walter, put away all those newspapers."

"What?" Walter shouted out. "I ain't finished reading those yet. What's gotten into you?"

Mary puts her hands on her hips. "Things are going to change around here. You need to start wearing some nice clothes. Look at what you're wearing. I'm going to toss those damn blue shorts of yours in the trash. You've been wearing them almost every day. I bet those things are over ten years old! Look how ratty they are!"

"These suit me just fine. They're the best shorts I have ever had and just got them broken in. I'm sure not putting on airs for anyone. I'm not going to be walking around the house wearing a suit and tie! People are going to see me as I am."

"That goes for me too!" Ben added. "I'm going back to wearing my swimming trunks again!"

"Oh, hush up, you two!" Mary said. "Everyone should start wearing some nice clothes. You two are famous now, being in all those magazines and on TV. We all need to be ready when they bring in all those cameras for the movie. We don't want them thinking we're all a bunch of country bumpkins."

Ben can't help from laughing, seeing his mother all dressed up in her Sunday clothes, getting all flustered. "Mom, I don't think they'll be filming in here. They'll just make that part up in the studio. I bet you they'll make it look like you live in a big mansion. You know this is Texas. Most people think that's how we all live, anyway."

Walter starts chuckling. "That's right! I need to go out and check on the oil wells. Probably ride out there on one of my horses, too! Better gather up the ranch hands. We need to check on the cattle as well!"

Ben laughs again. "Jenny will make sure not to add that part where Dad sits around in his underwear all day long while he's watching TV. Especially what happens after he's eaten Mexican food."

Walter laughs out loud. "Oh, yeah! That will be great seeing that on the big screen!"

Mary is furious, pointing her finger at her husband. "No more of that nonsense!"

Walter picks up the newspaper, pretending to read it, knowing he is in big trouble.

"So, Jenny, you write every day?" Mary asked, trying to change the subject from her embarrassing husband.

Jenny nods, trying so hard not to laugh. "Sure... It's like a diary. I have been doing it almost every day for years, ever since the girls were born."

"Yeah, she's always at it," Ben explained. "Just before the sun sets, she'll be writing everything down that happened during the day. Even at the hospital, she was always writing about something."

"I bet she has a lot of things about you in there you don't want people to read!" Walter jokingly said.

Ben laughed. "I made sure that if I did anything stupid, it wasn't around for her to see and write down in her journal. If she asked about my day, I would always tell her the good bits!"

Jenny turns, looking at Ben. "Oh, no! It's all in there. You forgot the girls love to talk, and they told me everything!" teasing him.

"So, when do you have to be in New York?" Ben asked, trying to change the subject.

"Unfortunately, right away. They already have my flight booked for this weekend. Ben, is that OK with you?"

"They don't waste time, do they? Of course, it's all right with me. How long will you be there?"

"Just a few days. I don't feel right taking the kids on another trip. It might be a little too much for them. They're still trying to adjust. You'll be all right watching them?"

"Sure, I guess we can't get into too much trouble in just a couple of days," Ben jokingly said.

"You're not taking my babies away!" Mary blurted out. "We're still getting to know each other. They can stay here, so don't worry about it! They've been through so much with all the traveling and hospitals, and they don't need any more commotion in their lives right now."

"That means Mom still wants them to help with the garden," Ben jokingly added.

Mary nods. "Oh, they have done wonders out there. They really do help out."

"That's what I thought, if it's OK?" Jenny asked. "I need a little time to deal with my sister too. I have to get in touch with our lawyer to see what's going to happen with all this."

"Just don't bother with her," Ben said. "She hasn't called you in all this time and doesn't return your calls."

"No, I need to resolve this now, so we can get it behind us," kissing him.

Ben is so happy that her journal is going to be published. Now, everyone is going to read about their lives in detail. He is having second thoughts about it all. It's happening way too fast. He likes his privacy, but now it's going to be made public. He wishes he had time to read it thoroughly before she sent it out.

* * *

The next day, Jenny and Ben have an appointment at the Social Security office. It will probably take most of the day and be nothing but endless meetings and more paperwork to fill out.

Mary quickly offers to babysit the children. She is already making plans for their day together and can't wait to take them shopping again.

"Don't worry, they'll be OK with us," Mary said. "You two just go out and take care of the things you need to get done."

"They'll be fine," Walter said. "We got plenty of chores for them out in the backyard to keep them busy."

"That will work," Ben said. "Just keep them busy."

"Don't let them make any more sticks," Jenny quickly added. "I want to start getting them off that phase. Maybe let them plant some flowers."

"Oh, that's a good idea," Mary said. "We can take them to the garden shop. I can't wait to show them all the flowers there, and I'll let them pick some new ones for my garden. I have wanted to do that for a long time. Now, I got plenty of help."

Jenny smiled. "Oh, they'll love that! That'll keep them busy all day."

* * *

Ben hasn't driven a car in years and is a little nervous. He also has to risk driving around with no driver's license or insurance. All he has on him is a passport for identification. There is an endless list of things they have to do to get back into the system again. This is the beginning of the bureaucracy.

"If you get stopped, just explain who you are and show them your passport," Walter tells his son. "Just don't worry about it! All they can do is give you a ticket."

"OK, I'll remember that. So, what side of the road am I supposed to drive on?" Ben jokingly asked his parents, then slowly drove away.

"Keep to the right side!" Walter frantically yelled out before realizing Ben was joking with him.

April, June, and Baby wave as their mother and father slowly drive away in the car. Seeing their father driving a car is a big thrill. They can't wait to have their turn driving.

Once they are out of sight, June looks at her watch. "So when they coming back?"

Walter shrugged. "Hard to say... Maybe several hours, but don't worry about it. They'll be back in time for supper."

"Let's go back inside, and we can play some games," Mary said, ushering them into the house.

Mary is already spoiling them by bringing out fruit salads and Pepsi drinks. They love having so much fruit available whenever they want it. No more treks up to the top of the island to pick fruit off the trees. The ice-cold Pepsi is now something they never go without.

Walter and Mary love taking care of the kids. They are always quiet and never fight with each other. Once they get their coloring books, it keeps them busy for hours. They don't care to watch television like all the other grandchildren do. They do what they are told and never complain.

After shopping for flowers, the children are in their glory, helping in the garden. It is not much different from planting the seedlings at the big orchard. Mary is surprised to see how much the girls already know about gardening. All she has to do is tell them where she wants things planted, and they do all the work.

* * *

Mary heard the forecast of thunderstorms coming in later that afternoon. Dark clouds are already rolling in, and the wind is picking up. The weather is changing as a cold front is on the way. After they finish their lunch, Mary knows that this will be a good time for the children to take a nap so they won't be scared of the storm.

Mary wants them to start getting back to a regular schedule of going to bed early and taking afternoon naps like they used to do on the island. No more hard work cutting down trees and hauling firewood. The days of the Amazon girls are coming to an end. She knows Jenny wants to keep things simple, like tending to the garden so they can gradually get used to their new environment.

Mary and Walter are in the living room watching the news when they hear the first thunder way off in the distance. They don't think too much of it at first. It's normal at this time of year to have a few thunderstorms.

June hears the thunder and quickly wakes April and Baby. They run into the living room to find their granny and granddad just sitting on the couch.

"Did that bad thunder wake you?" Mary asked. "It's just another rainstorm, so don't worry about it. Come and sit on the couch with us. It'll blow over soon," seeing they are a little nervous.

Lightning strikes nearby, and a loud blast of thunder shakes the house. April runs over to the back door, seeing how dark it is. The wind is terrible, and the chairs in the backyard are rolling all over the place. A small branch falls off the tree, crashing down on top of the patio.

"Looks like a bad one!" April tells June. "We need to get to the cave."

"Where is Mom and Dad?" June asked.

"It's OK... Your mom and dad are out doing some errands and will be back soon," Mary explained. "Just come over and sit with us. There is nothing to be scared of," trying to calm them down.

"No, Granny! We're supposed to go to the cave if a big storm comes and they are not home!" June shouted.

"That's the rules!" April added. "We're supposed to go to the cave now. Better start packing!"

April and June hold Baby's hand, going to the bedroom to get their shoes and backpacks on. Mary stands at the bedroom door, trying to convince them everything is all right, but to no avail. The two girls know what they have to do. They were always told it was very important to run for the cave if they are caught alone in a big storm.

All dressed up, and with backpacks on, June takes Baby's hand, walking back to the living room. Then they realize they don't know where the cave is.

June frantically looks around. "We got a big storm coming! Where is your cave, Granny?"

"What cave?" she asked, so confused. "Why do you want a cave? It's just a little storm. We get storms all the time here."

"We're supposed to go to the cave if a storm comes when Mom and Dad are not around!" June shouted, getting scared. "We be in big trouble if they go to the cave, and we not there. Big waves can come up and wash us away! Granny, you have to put your shoes on. We have to go!"

Mary and Walter look at each other, not knowing what to do. The storm is getting closer, and the rain starts coming down hard. The wind is now shaking the house, and the lightning is non-stop.

"Ben was telling me about how they stayed up in the cave for the big storms," Walter explained. "I guess they're not used to being by themselves."

Mary looked down at the frightened children. "It's OK... We are here with you. We can all stay in the house. There are no big waves around here. It's just a little rain."

At that moment, a big clap of thunder shakes the house, making everyone jump.

Mary cringes, knowing the storm is getting worse. "Well, we do have a shed out in the backyard. Maybe we can wait in there."

"I don't think the shed is the best place to be in this storm," Walter said but thought of an idea. "Oh, I forgot all about it! Our cave is in the den."

The girls looked at him, puzzled. "Where is the den?"

"I'll show you... It's just a short walk," ushering the girls into the den. "See, we have our cave right next to the house, so we don't have far to go," Walter explained.

April and June walk into the den, amazed. "I didn't know this was your cave! It's way bigger than ours, and you don't have to walk up the trail to get here! We don't have to go outside and get wet!"

April sits on the couch with Baby. "Wow, this is nice! We didn't have nothing to sit on in our cave. You even got a TV in yours!"

"That's right!" Mary quickly said. "We got lots of things in our cave. You can wait in here until the storm blows over."

Walter turns on the television so they can watch cartoons to get their minds off the storm. He is about to leave, only to be yelled at by the girls.

"No, Granddad... You must stay in the cave!" June shouted.

Walter laughed. "I'll be OK out here. You guys can stay in the cave."

April and June rush over, taking his hands, pulling him back into the den.

"No, we must all stay in the cave until the storm is over! That's the rules!" June said, waving her finger at him.

"We better stay in here till the storm ends," Mary said. "We can watch the cartoons in here with them," sitting on the couch with Baby.

Walter sighed. "We need to reprogram these kids and get them off the survivalist things Ben had taught them."

"He just wanted them to be able to survive out there on their own," Mary explained. "I think they're doing fine and will adjust after they have been here a while. It's only been a few days. They still got a lot to learn."

"Where is Mom and Dad?" June frantically asked. "They must have gone to our cave. They'll be worried and will be looking for us there."

"No, they know we're here, and they'll be back soon," Mary explained.

"Do Mom and Dad know you got a cave here?" April asked.

"Sure, your father used to sit in here many times during the storms," trying to calm them down.

April turns to June. "Dad never told us about all this! We going to have a long talk when he gets home!"

They all sit together watching cartoons. Baby doesn't care about the storm anymore. He has his cartoons to watch and, as usual, is laughing at the Tom and Jerry show. April and June are still concerned about their mother and father being out in the storm.

Mary forgot they had the cell phone. "Do you want to talk to them on the phone? We can see how much longer they are going to be."

"Yeah! We can tell them we're here in your cave!"

"Stay here while I get the phone," Mary said.

They don't like the idea of her leaving the den. They stand by the door, watching her while she walks into the kitchen to get the portable phone.

"How come she gets to leave the cave?" Walter quickly asked.

June frowned. "She's the boss!"

"Oh, I forgot about that," Walter replied. "I need to remember that one," just shaking his head.

Mary walks back in and dials the mobile phone number. She quickly explains that they are all waiting in the den, which is now the cave. She talks to Jenny for a few minutes, telling her all about their day. All three of her grandchildren stand next to her, waiting for their turn on the phone. They love the phones, being able to talk to anyone no matter where they are.

Mary finally hands the phone to June. "There's a storm here! We're in Granny's cave! Are you in our cave at home?"

"Oh no... We're still in the car," Jenny quickly explained. "We're not far away, and we'll be there in less than an hour. Don't worry about the storm. Granny and Granddad will take care of everything."

"So, how are they holding up?" Ben asked.

Jenny put her hand on the phone. "They thought we were in the cave."

Ben cringed. "Oops, I totally forgot about that. Are they all right?"

"They are OK," Jenny said. "They told the girls that the den is their cave!"

Ben laughed. "That was a good idea! Didn't think about that."

They all take turns talking to their mother, asking way too many questions. Baby, copying his sisters, babbling on the phone, thrilled to hear his mother's voice. They are all so excited to talk to their mother on the phone while she is away. They also add the mobile phone to the long list of things they want to bring back home with them.

* * *

Jenny and Ben finally return to the house. Still raining hard, they rush into the house soaking wet.

"So, have you been behaving while we were gone?" Jenny asked.

"Yeah, we behave real nice," April said. "We had a really good time, too! We went to a big flower store and a big huge camping store. Then we worked in Granny's garden and planted lots of pretty flowers. Then we got a big storm, and we got to stay in Granny's cave!"

"You had a busy day!" Jenny said, hugging them. "Sounds like you guys had a lot of fun!"

"It sounds like you had a better day than we did," Ben said. "I'd like to see that camping store. See anything we could use?"

"They got everything there!" April explained. "Even had those nice big tents. You can stand up when you are in them, and they even have little rooms inside! We got to get one of those to bring back home."

"It would be nice to have one of those instead of that small one we got!" remembering all those days being cramped up in it while it rained.

Jenny picks up Baby. "Have you been a good boy too?"

He started babbling for about a minute, waving his hands in the air.

"Sounds like you all had a good day," Jenny added.

"We had fun, and you ought to see their cave," June said. "I didn't know you can have a cave right in the same place."

"Oh yeah, I heard about the cave," Ben said. "Good thing they have it real close. It's a bad storm out there."

"You need to tell us some of those rules," Walter said. "We need to know what to tell them when a storm comes up. They were all dressed up, ready to hike up to some cave."

Mary gives her husband a stern look. "They were no problem at all. They are settling in just fine. It's nothing we can't handle. All children are frightened by the storms, anyway."

"Come and see their cave... It's really big!" April said, taking her father's hand, leading him into the den.

The twins are so thrilled to show their parents the cave, even though they have been in it many times before. Both Jenny and Ben played along as they looked over the den.

"Now, this is a nice cave!" Ben said, playing it up. "Just think how nice it would have been to have a cave this big at home."

"Yeah, ours was real small and poky, and we didn't even have a TV!" June said.

"They got nice chairs to sit on! We need to make some of those when we get back home," April added.

"OK, you two!" Jenny said, still holding Baby. "I think it's time for you to finish your naps," leading them all back to the bedroom.

"So, how did you get on?" Walter asked.

Ben rolled his eyes. "It went OK... We got back into the system again. We got our Social Security cards and even our driver's licenses reissued. I had a feeling Mrs. Burns had her hand in it. It's like they were waiting for us and had everything there and ready. It's still going to be a couple of weeks before we get them in the mail. At least it's done. It's still frustrating having to deal with all this government stuff and endless paperwork."

"Oh, don't worry about it," Mary said. "Sit down and rest while I make coffee. There is no rush for any of that stuff, anyway. You're home safe and sound, so just relax."

Jenny walks into the living room and hears some of the conversations. "Has he been complaining again?" sitting next to Ben, hugging him.

"Yes!" Mary said. "He's back to normal again, always complaining about something. Good thing he hasn't got a job yet. Then you'll hear him complaining about that, too!"

Jenny smiled. "Funny how you didn't complain that much before now."

"We didn't have all these problems like we do now," Ben said, frustrated with the paperwork.

Jenny started laughing. "You need to start looking on the bright side, or I'll make you take a nap too."

"You tell him, Jenny!" Mary said. "Ben, you got nothing to complain about now. You got a great wife and three perfect kids. So just relax and enjoy life."

Ben knows he better not say anything. He closes his eyes and starts thinking about his time back on the island. He has so many fond memories of all those days out fishing or walking the many trails, especially sitting on the beach next to a campfire watching the sunset. That was an easy life.

* * *

Chapter 58

Eastern Bound

When Jenny returns from New York, she is so excited about all the big news. The publishing company is going all out to promote her book. She met so many famous people and was the center of attention, constantly being wined and dined. The movie contract is still in the works, with several companies trying to outbid each other for the rights.

While in New York, she also met with her family lawyer to settle the inheritance. Apparently, her sister is fighting to keep it all. Now that the lawyers are getting involved, things are going to change. The family inheritance is going to be redistributed now that Jenny is back.

Now, they have money to spend and a big decision to make. Where to live is the big question. There is not enough room at Walter and Mary's house. The house is too small, and having five extra people makes it a little cramped. Ben's parents had been a big help, but it was too much for them. The twins are a handful and have to be watched all the time. Baby is always getting into everything.

Ben feels uncomfortable not having a job, but at least Jenny is doing great with her book. He can't get back into software development after being away for over six years. His skills are already obsolete, and he will probably have to start as an entry-level programmer since so much has changed. Also, sitting in an office all day long in front of a computer is the last thing he wants to do.

Ben knows it's his turn to watch the children. Just like on the island, they always shared the workload. Staying home with the children is the one thing he enjoys. Jenny is so busy now. She is always on the phone every day with her publisher, going over the details of the promotional tour. She has several talk shows lined up, plus a few book signings, and will travel around the country for a long time.

Sitting around the house with nothing to do is something Ben doesn't enjoy. Even the children are restless, always looking for extra chores. Cleaning up the garage and fixing up the old house is easy, but after a while, there's not much else left to do. Even the yard had never looked so good. The twins worked in the backyard for hours every day, making it look like a well-manicured botanical garden.

* * *

The day finally arrives when Jenny receives word of the settlement from her estate. She is so relieved to get it resolved. Jenny's sister, Kim, had become an embarrassment to the French community when the news media broadcast what she was doing. Kim finally had to save face but found it cheaper to settle than have a lengthy legal battle, paying all the lawyers trying to keep it all.

Jenny knows it will be the last time dealing with her sister. She is devastated, knowing that her only family member wants nothing to do with her. Jenny would give it all up just to have her parents back. For some reason, Kim hated her sister and blamed everything on her, even the deaths of their parents.

Ben is stunned when he discovers she will receive over $500,000 from her parent's estate. He is even more amazed to learn it's only a tiny fraction of what she should have received. Her sister had spent most of it on expensive houses and property in France that the lawyers couldn't touch. The only thing left is the cash and stocks Kim had in the banks in the U.S. that the courts could seize. He had no idea that Jenny or her parents had that much money. All Ben has is a credit card with a $5,000 limit that his father gave him. At least things are changing for the better.

* * *

Jenny has to make another trip to her home in Connecticut to sign the settlement papers. Also, it's time for a reunion with her aunt, uncles, and cousins. She has been reluctant to go back home because it will mean having to face the death of her parents. She has been putting it off, but now is ready to handle it.

Both Jenny and Ben know the time is right. The children are getting acclimated to their new lifestyle and being around other people. Now, it's time to move on with their lives. They can't stay with Mary and Walter forever. A difficult decision, but they know it's the right thing to do.

Mary and Walter are very close to their new grandchildren and are so sad that they are leaving. Every night, there is a big barbecue out in the backyard, Texas-style. April and June are always learning new things to cook from their grandmother and how to take care of the garden. Baby never had it so good. He is constantly being spoiled rotten with never-ending presents from his grandparents.

* * *

The next morning, Jenny, Ben, and the children are on their way to Connecticut. No more coach flights, sitting in cramped little seats. Now, it's first-class all the way. There is no more waiting in lines using the VIP check-in and being waited on and pampered to the likes they have never seen before. Ben is just not used to this lifestyle. He has never flown in first class in his entire life. Even though he has the money, it's not the lifestyle he wants.

The twins are so excited to fly on another airplane. Jenny makes sure to bring plenty of coloring books, crayons, and other activities to keep them amused. At least this time, they don't have to worry about the girls wandering around. Being in first-class, they don't want to go anywhere else. They are very content staying put, with the extremely comfortable seats and the first-class service.

"So, are you ready to see my world?" Jenny asked Ben.

"After all those years of you talking about it, Connecticut sounds like a nice place to live."

"It'll be strange seeing my old home again," she said, reaching over to take his hand. "It's going to bring back a lot of old memories. Although not having Mom and Dad there, it just won't be the same," then the tears run down her cheek.

"I know... At least you have family there. I know they'll be glad to see you, just like mine were with all of us."

"I wish they could have met you and the kids," she whispered, putting her head on his shoulder.

"I have a feeling they would be very proud of you and probably spoil the kids as much as mine did."

She chuckled. "I know," the memories of her parents flashing through her mind.

He knows that once Jenny gets back home, the reality of losing her parents will hit her hard. When she sees her parent's grave, it will give her the closure she needs. She can't do this alone. They are a family, and they all have to be there and face it together.

The trip to Connecticut is only for a few days. They booked a room at the bed-and-breakfast close to her aunt and uncle's home. Most of her family is driving in just for the weekend, and it's not anything like the huge reunion they had in Texas. There is no big swimming pool and no outside barbecues. Just a simple get together but an extremely emotional weekend for Jenny. The most difficult part is visiting her parent's graves. After that, their options are open to how long they will stay, depending on how things go.

* * *

After the long flight, they finally arrive in the town of Old Saybrook. A quaint seaside town at the mouth of the Connecticut River. Ben can see she is elated being back home again. Jenny is reminiscing about old times, pointing out various places.

They walk the grounds to stretch their legs after checking into their room at the bed-and-breakfast. The grounds are beautiful, filled with flower beds canopied by large hundred-year-old trees. The plush garden has gazebos and small ponds filled with goldfish. Ben now knows why Jenny always comes back to this place.

"Is this where your mommy and daddy live?" June asked, knowing that they were here to visit their mother's parents.

"No, we're just staying here for a couple of days," Jenny explained. "Later on, I'll show you the house where I grew up."

"When do we get to see your mommy and daddy?" June asked.

Jenny pauses, trying to think of a simple way to explain things. "Well, my mother and father used to live there. But now they're in heaven."

"Can we bring them a present like we did Granny and Granddad?" April asked with a big smile. "I think they'll like it when we give them presents and things," nodding her head up and down.

"I don't think they're going to be there," Ben explained, seeing they still don't understand. "They're in heaven up in the clouds."

"Are they on an airplane?" the girls asked, looking up at the sky.

"No, I meant they are up in the clouds. They are with the angels."

Again, the girls look up. "Come on down! We're here to see you!" waving their hands up at the clouds.

"We'll eat first... Then we'll go out there so you can see for yourselves," Ben said, giving up trying to explain things.

April and June continuously ask questions about their mother's parents. They want so much to meet them. No matter how many times Jenny explains it to them, they still don't understand that their grandparents have died.

At least Baby is at that age where all he cares about is his next meal and a clean diaper. Mostly, he wants to be able to run about and play.

* * *

After lunch and a little rest, Jenny is ready to see her old home and her parent's resting place. The house was sold long ago, but she was able to make arrangements with the new owners to visit. Seeing her parent's graves will be hard on her, but it will give her closure. What makes it worse is knowing that her parents thought she was lost at sea, never knowing what happened to her.

Driving over to her old home, Jenny sees a small flower shop. "I need to stop here to pick up a few things. Can you stay in the car with the kids while I do this?"

"No, let's take them in... They can pick some flowers out for your mom and dad. It'll be their gift to them. I think it'll be a nice gesture."

"I guess it might help them understand," she reluctantly said.

She wants to do this alone but knows he is right. They are a family, and they need to do this together. As Jenny talks to the shopkeeper, Ben walks the children around to let them pick out their own flowers. They are so thrilled to see all the various types of flowers with so many pretty colors.

Jenny waits at the counter with two large flower bouquets as April, June, and Baby run up with the flowers they picked. They gathered up a nice variety of daisies, roses, lilies, sunflowers, and daffodils. The shopkeeper carefully wraps each bundle in white tissue paper, tying them with a red bow.

* * *

Driving to the old house, Jenny gets depressed. Seeing the house without her parents being here is something she just doesn't want to do. Now that it's owned by someone else, it's not helping. On her last trip to New York, she contacted the current owners and explained her situation. The couple that bought the house knows all about Jenny and is looking forward to meeting her.

Ben really loves this place. Everything is green with huge trees. Every mile or two, there is a little colonial house or farmhouse. So picturesque, not anything close to the flat dry Texas he knew so well. With the gentle rolling hills, he can see himself walking these fields for hours on end.

Ben can tell they are getting close, seeing Jenny is getting upset, constantly wiping away the tears. They drive down a long country road filled with trees and green pastures. Seeing a white two-story colonial house out in the middle of a field, he recognizes it right away from the description she told him years ago.

Jenny pulls up into the driveway, stopping in front of the house. "I never thought I would ever see this again. I wish my mom and dad were here so they could meet my family," visualizing them both standing at the front door to greet them.

"Remember, my mom always knew I was OK. I think your mom and dad might have known, too."

"I hope they did," she whispered.

She lets out a long sigh, just staring at her old home. "Mom, Dad... I'm back home now. I miss you so much," crying uncontrollably.

"It'll be OK," he said, giving her a big hug, wondering if they were doing this too soon.

Just as they step out of the van, an elderly couple walks out of the house to meet them.

The woman walks up. "Oh, it's so nice to finally meet you... I'm Caroline, and this is my husband, Mike."

"Hi, it's nice to meet you... I'm Ben, and this is Baby, June, and April," he said, seeing Jenny overcome with emotions.

"I'm so glad to meet you all," Caroline said. "I hope you had a pleasant trip."

"Yes, it was really nice," he replied, putting his arm around Jenny.

Finally, Jenny regains her composure. "I'm so sorry... It's just hard for me to see my home again."

"We understand," Caroline said. "You've been through such a horrible ordeal, then the loss of your family. Everything is going to be OK. It's just going to take time."

As they talk with Caroline and Mike, Ben is so surprised that they know all the details about their lives. They were shocked to find out the news media had already been here interviewing the new owners and most of the people in town. He hopes they don't see any news crews on this visit. That is the last thing they need right now.

Jenny, Ben, and the children are invited in for coffee. The children are still confused, thinking that these people are their new granny and granddad. Jenny tries to explain it to them, but it's easier to tell them their granny and granddad are up on top of the hill under the tree.

Ben sits with Mike while Caroline is showing the house to Jenny and the children. The house is enormous and full of antiques. Jenny's old home is entirely different compared to the small houses where he grew up. This house is definitely out of his price range and probably his parents' too.

"You know," Mike said. "We were so shocked when we heard the news about Jenny. We heard about the story when we were buying the place. It's funny that her sister just sold everything. It's so sad to see a family suffer so much like that."

Ben nods. "Yeah, we still haven't figured that one out."

"Although the whole town was abuzz when she was found alive on that island. We even had TV crews here asking so many questions, wanting to see the graves."

"I heard Jenny's grave is still up there, too," Ben said.

"Oh yes! It's up there with her parents. They buried her mom and dad on both sides of her grave. I heard they took it hard when she was lost at sea. I wondered what you're going to do with the headstone now that she is alive. It's kind of spooky if you think about it. I don't think I would like the idea of seeing my own headstone. I hear your folks never had a grave or even a marker for you."

"My mom always knew I was alive and well and wouldn't let them."

Mike laughed. "I bet she's been telling all those people, 'I told you so!'"

Ben smiles. "Oh, she has! Mom won't let any of them forget it either. Although now they're wondering how she knew. There have been a lot of discussions going on about that."

Mike laughed. "It's one of those bonding things. My mom was like that when I was a kid. I'd be out with my friends, having fun and getting into a lot of mischief, but when I got home, she would always know. She would be standing at the front door with a big wooden spoon, waiting for me. Those were the days when we didn't even have a phone! How she knew, I never found out. It kept me in line until I went into the army!"

Jenny and Caroline come down the stairs. "Ben, I guess I'm ready to see them now," looking very uncomfortable.

"OK, guys… It's time to meet your other granny and granddad. Better be on your best behavior. This means a lot to Mom," Ben quietly said, handing their flowers to them.

"We'll be here if you need anything," Caroline said.

"Thank you for making us so welcome here," Jenny quietly replied. "It meant so much to me to be able to see the house one last time."

"You're welcome here anytime. You come visit whenever you want."

Jenny thanks them again and hugs them before walking out the back door. Ben puts his arm around Jenny. They slowly walk up the hill on the small path that leads up to a huge tree at the far end of the property.

"This is where I used to go when I was a little girl," Jenny explained. "I spent many days running up and down this path."

"Did you play with your sister here?" June asked.

Jenny is a little shaken by the question. "Sometimes," not wanting to think about her sister.

"Why don't you two run up there?" Ben asked. "See who gets there first!" changing the subject, knowing Jenny doesn't want to be reminded about her sister.

April and June race up the hill, closely followed by Baby, who struggles to keep up with his older sisters. Jenny is looking over the property, realizing how beautiful her former home is. Nothing but trees and pasture surrounds the property. The area hasn't been developed at all in the last thirty years.

Jenny and Ben reach the old tree at the end of the path. The children are patiently waiting, still confused about where their granny and granddad are. Under the huge tree, three graves face east, with a small bench at the foot of the center grave.

"Come over here with us," Ben quickly calls them over, seeing they are leaning against one of the grave markers.

"Where is everyone?" April asked. "They're not here! Are they in the house down there?" pointing down the hill.

"Let's be quiet for now," Ben said, standing in front of the three graves.

Jenny is so shocked to see her own headstone. Marked with her full name, the date she was born, and the date she was supposed to have died. On the left side of her grave is her father, and on the right, her mother. There is a small granite bench at the foot of Jenny's grave. She smiles, looking at the old bench, remembering the days when she used to sit up here when she was very young.

Jenny slowly walks up, placing one of the flower bouquets on her father's grave and then the other on her mother's. She sits on the small bench, burying her face in her hands. Tears are flowing from her eyes as the emotions overtook her.

"Daddy, why is Mom crying?" April asked.

"This is where her mommy and daddy are resting. This is where your granny and granddad are buried," he quietly explained to the girls.

"Is this heaven?" April asked.

"Yes, this is heaven," he said, surprised by her comment. "This is where they are. Why don't you give them their flowers? This one is your granny, and that one is your granddad," pointing out each grave to them.

They place some flowers on their granny's grave and the rest on their granddad's.

"What is this one in the middle?" April asked. "There are no flowers on that one!" pointing to her mother's grave.

"Why don't you come and stand over here with me," Ben said, seeing Jenny is too upset to answer and not wanting to tell them what it really is.

Baby, copying his sisters, takes flowers from his bouquet one at a time, placing them at the headstones with the other flowers. With one red rose left over, he put his last flower on the middle grave marker with Jenny's name on it.

Jenny cries uncontrollably after seeing that. Baby runs up to his mother and into her arms, where she holds him tight.

The girls stare at the grave in the center with one red rose. They both walk over and take one flower off the other graves, putting it on the center grave next to the red rose Baby placed there.

"That was really a nice thing to do," Ben said. "I think she'll like that."

April and June are getting upset seeing their mother crying. They don't understand why she is so sad.

Ben kneels next to Jenny. "I'll take them for a walk so you can be alone for a while."

"Thank you," Jenny whispered, struggling to get the words out. "There's a small path up near the trees that they might like," pointing to the far side of the big tree.

Ben picks up Baby. "Let's go for a little walk so Mom can be on her own for a few minutes."

Both June and April hug their mother, then run up behind their father on the small path leading into the trees. As they walk, Ben keeps looking back at Jenny. She is sitting all alone on the bench with her face buried in her hands, crying uncontrollably. He knows she doesn't want the children around her when she is this upset. The girls are upset too. They are just too young to understand any of this.

"How come Momma is crying?" June asked, looking back at her mother.

"Well, your mom has a mommy and daddy too, just like I do. But they died and went to heaven a long time ago while we were home on the island. She is sad because she didn't get to say goodbye to them, and they didn't get to meet you. You remember how excited Granny and Granddad were when they finally got to meet you?"

"Yeah, they were real happy to see us!" April said. "They always give us lots of toys and clothes and things."

"Well, her mom and dad would have liked to have met you as well, but they are in heaven now. Remember when we were on that plane way up in the sky with all the clouds? That's where they are now," pointing up to the sky.

"Can they come down and see us?" June asked.

"Well, I don't know... Do you remember Birdie?" he asked, trying to find a way to explain it.

"Yeah," they both said, knowing it was a sore subject.

"You remember how sad I was when I found out he died. I didn't get to see him again, and he was gone forever?"

"But we ate Birdie!" April blurted out.

He let out a long sigh. "Yes, I know! But once he was gone, we buried the rest of him in the sand and put up a little marker for him. You remember that? Well, when Mom's mommy and daddy died, they buried them up here and put up those grave markers for them."

"So, they put them in the ground like we did to Birdie?" June asked.

"Yes, this is where they are. That's why Mom is so sad. Because this is the first time she has been here to see them."

April stops and looks back at her mother, who is still crying. "They're not coming down to see us, are they?" realizing what this really meant.

"No, they're not," telling the girls, slowly shaking his head.

They both start crying. "I don't like it here... It's too sad," April said, putting her arms around her father.

"I know... Mom needs a little time to say goodbye, and then we'll leave."

Ben knows it's a far-reach trying to explain death and graves to them. They are too young, and will not remember any of this after a few weeks. As far as the girls know, they are on another big adventure to see new things. It's Jenny's time to deal with the death of her parents and not a place for the children. When they are older and can understand, they'll bring them out here again.

Ben follows the dirt path that leads up to the small forest. The path is well-worn as it meanders through the huge trees. It reminds him of the good times back on the island, walking the many trails. The girls pick flowers, pointing out all the different trees and shrubs. He is surprised at how quickly the girls get back into their old survival ways, pointing out the trees that are good for firewood.

It is not a short walk as he thought it would be. They must have been at least forty-five minutes as the trail loops around before coming out on the south side of the trees. The girls are so excited to see the Atlantic Ocean for the first time on the hill's highest point. The beach is a long way off, but it makes them feel at home. Naturally, they think they are back on an island again.

* * *

They make their way back down the trail to the old tree and the graves. Jenny is still sitting on the bench. The girls run down the hill with Baby hobbling far behind them. Ben can see they love being outside. He knows he can't live in the city, but in a place like this with plenty of land and trees. The children can play outside without worrying about cars or having neighbors right next to the house, like where his parents live.

Jenny stands up with her arms out, waiting to greet her children as they race toward her. They can't wait to tell her about their trip through the trees, seeing the ocean, and all the flowers they picked for her.

"Mom, where did the little girl go?" June asked, looking around for her.

Jenny looks at her, so confused. "What little girl?" thinking that they had met someone on their walk through the forest.

"The one that was here with you!" April said. "Did she leave?"

"I'm sorry... I didn't see anyone. Was there someone else here?"

"Yeah!" June said. "She was standing right next to you! We saw her when we came running down the hill!"

"Oh, maybe I just didn't see her," she said, so confused. "I guess I was deep in my thoughts and never noticed. She must have run off," looking back down towards the house to see if anyone was behind her.

Ben finally arrives, giving Jenny a big hug and kiss. "Feeling better?"

"Yes, a little... You know, I can just imagine Mom and Dad sitting on this bench, looking at my grave. It's funny how they put my grave up here behind the bench. Dad must have put this bench up here when I was little. Mom and I would always come up here and put flowers around it. I used to come up here and have a little picnic, read a book, or just look over the scenery. I even had an imaginary friend and talked with her all the time. When I was young, I spent a lot of hours up here. This was my sanctuary."

"It's really nice up here," Ben said, looking around at the view. "They couldn't have picked a better resting place."

She puts her arms around him. "I just wish Mom and Dad would have known I was OK and been able to meet you and spoil the children. They never had any grandchildren. I think they would have been very proud seeing how the girls loved to cook. It's so sad they never got to meet them," looking down at her parent's graves.

"Maybe you should introduce everyone to your mom and dad," Ben suggested.

"Sounds like a good idea," she said, surprised by his comment. "OK, let's all get together. I want you all to meet your other granny and granddad, my mom and dad."

Jenny walks everyone over to the bench, then stands behind the children. "Mom and Dad, I would like you to meet my family. These are my two girls, April and June."

"Hi, Granny. Hi Granddad!" the girls said, waving at the graves.

"And this is my son, Baby. Oh, his name is August, but we've been calling him Baby because that's the name the girls gave him."

Baby copies his sister and waves, chattering about something.

Jenny takes Ben's hand, pulling him over. "This is Ben, my husband and the love of my life. I wouldn't be here if it weren't for him. He made those years on the island the best years of my life!" kissing his cheek.

"Say hi, Daddy!" June said, looking up at her father.

"Hi, nice to meet you," Ben said, feeling a little awkward.

They stand in front of the graves, having a conversation with Jenny's parents as if they are there with them. She feels a little better, being able to talk to them with her family. Jenny and the girls sit on the bench, telling them all about their life on the island. April and June describe in detail how they caught fish and lobsters and how it was all prepared.

* * *

"I think I'm ready to go back now," Jenny said. "It's getting a little late."

"OK, girls, it's time to go," Ben said. "Are you going to take your flowers with you?" seeing they are still holding the flowers they picked from their walk.

"I think I'll leave mine here for Granny and Granddad," April said, placing the flowers on the graves.

"I'll leave mine, too!" June said, doing the same, carefully placing the flowers with the rest.

"So, what are you going to do with it?" Ben asked, seeing Jenny staring at her headstone.

"I don't know... It's a little uneasy seeing your own grave. I know they spent a lot of time up here, probably talking to me just as we were talking to them. That was the last thing they did for me. It probably meant a lot to them, putting my grave up here under the old tree. Maybe it'll be best just to leave things as they are and let them be on both sides of my grave."

"It sounds like a good idea."

He leans down, whispering to Baby. "Why don't you put your flowers right over there," pointing to Jenny's headstone.

Baby quickly runs over, putting the flowers he picked next to the grave. Jenny is pleased that he keeps putting all his flowers on her grave.

"We have to go now," Ben whispered. "Say goodbye to your granny and granddad."

They all stand silently at the foot of the graves. Then, one by one, they said goodbye.

"Let's go back to the house," Jenny said. "I want to thank them for letting us come up here," wiping away the tears, then taking Ben's hand, slowly walking back down to the house.

Jenny keeps stopping, looking back at the old tree, her mother, and her father's resting place. She wants so much to go back up there, not wanting to leave.

"We can stay longer if you want?" Ben asked, seeing her hesitating.

"No, it's OK... It'll always be here for me to visit. It's enough for now."

"That's right... We can always come back. It's a beautiful place, though. I can't believe you grew up here with all this. I can see why you spent so much time up by the tree, and I would have done the same. It's a magnificent view from up here. You can see everything for miles around. We even saw the ocean from the top of the hill!"

Jenny puts her arm around his waist. "I had a good life growing up here and so many fond memories. It's the only house I ever lived in, so I didn't know anything else. Mom and Dad wanted us to keep it in the family and never sell it. I can't believe my sister sold it all and moved to France!" getting angry just thinking about it.

"Well, at least she didn't sell the land with the graves on it."

"I don't think she could," she replied. "I think it was too much of a legal problem trying to sell it. At least I have my name on the deed for the entire area around the tree. So it's still in the family, and it's going to stay that way."

Caroline and Mike are sitting on the back porch when Jenny and Ben return to the house.

"I want to thank you for letting us see the house again and visit the graves," Jenny said.

"You're welcome here anytime... It was nice to meet you and your family," Caroline said, knowing this is an emotional time for them.

Jenny hugs and kisses them both. She feels much better knowing that her old home is in good hands. They are a nice couple, and she is so glad that they love the house as much as her parents did.

* * *

Having dinner out on the back patio of the bed-and-breakfast is the perfect place to relax and enjoy the flower gardens. They love eating outside, especially at the end of the day. It reminds them of all the times that they had dinner out by the beach watching the sunset.

After years of living out in the open, they never missed a sunset or even a sunrise. In all the time they spent at the house in Austin, they realized they had not seen a sunrise or sunset. Their time out in the backyard was nice, but it was too confining. Living on a small lot surrounded by a six-foot privacy fence is not their lifestyle.

"So, have you given much thought to where we should live?" Ben finally asked.

Jenny stares at the lush trees and fauna. "You know, I have been thinking about it. It would be nice in Hawaii, but maybe we've seen enough beach and humidity for a while. I thought about coming back home again, but now I'm ready for something new. I have lived here all my life, but it's time for a change. That was the reason I went for the Kwajalein job. What about that place you lived at?"

"You mean Colorado?" he asked.

"I have never been there before," she explained. "You talked about it so much over the years. I'm interested in seeing it all. I would love to have a place up in the mountains where you can go for long walks. It would be nice to experience the seasons again. For the past six years, we've only had summer! I would love to take them skiing and do all those things you used to tell us. Is Denver a nice place to live?"

"I liked it when I was there, but it's a big city, just like all the others. I don't think I can live in a city anymore, especially being around all that traffic and pollution."

"What about the other places there?" she asked. "Maybe we can check out some of those small towns up in the mountains. I remember seeing those brochures of Vail and Breckenridge. I always thought it would be a great place to live," thinking about all the places she always wanted to see.

Ben is elated to hear that she is interested in Colorado. "I know this great place where I always wanted to live. It's not far from Colorado Springs, right next to the national park. I had looked at a couple of places when I was there, and you can get ten to twenty acres of land with a house for just $120k to $200k. It might be a little more now, but it's so nice, surrounded by mountains and forests. It'll be great for these guys. They'll have plenty of room to play and plenty to do. I guess they'll go from being Amazon girls to wild mountain girls!"

Jenny smiles at Ben. "You've talked about it so much over the years I don't think you can live anywhere else. I need to have plenty of open space around me. It sounds like a great place to bring up a family. It's nice here, but I can see the difference six years have made. There are a lot more houses than there used to be. I hate to think what this will look like ten or twenty years from now. I remember the look on your face when we drove from the airport to your parent's house when you saw how much it had changed."

"That's why I'd like to be in a rural place where you know they won't be building shopping malls nearby. I would like to have plenty of land so I can walk around as well. I couldn't stand having neighbors fifteen feet from the house, like my mom and dad. There is just no privacy there and way too many people."

"Good!" Jenny said, nodding her head. "Then, we'll make that our next stop after we visit with my aunt and uncle tomorrow night."

* * *

Chapter 59

Jenny's Family Reunion

E arly the next day, Jenny decides to take everyone out to the beach. She packs a lunch for a little picnic like she used to do many years ago with her family. They have not been on a beach since they were on Kwajalein Island, so this will be a big treat.

Having to fight for a place to park the car and carry everything down to the beach is extremely frustrating. The beach is packed with hundreds of tourists. The days of having an entire beach to themselves is a thing of the past.

They find a nice quiet spot right next to the sand dunes. When everything is set up, April, June, and Baby strip off their clothes, running naked down to the water. When they jump into the water, they scream out loud. The ice-cold Atlantic water is something they were not expecting. All three quickly rush back, shivering and wrapping themselves up in towels to get warm.

When Jenny was young, she would come to this beach to see happy couples with their children having a picnic and making sandcastles. She used to visualize what it would be like when she was married and had a family. Now, her childhood dream has finally come true. She puts her arm around her husband and watches the children playing in the sand.

Sitting on the beach without a care in the world is the lifestyle they love the most. No more worrying about where the next meal is coming from or if a storm is just over the horizon. With a bottle of wine, fresh fruit, and various cheeses, they can now just lie back and enjoy themselves.

* * *

After a great day at the beach, it's time for Jenny's family reunion at Aunt Rosy's house. After driving to a small town an hour away, they pull into the driveway of a small colonial home with a well-manicured front yard. The front door of the house slams open as

Aunt Rosy runs out to greet them, followed by the rest of the family. Aunt Rosy picks Jenny off the ground, swinging her around. Everyone is crying as they hug and kiss her.

Ben holds Baby, standing with June and April, watching the big reunion. April and June are now used to these happy gatherings. That is a good thing since Jenny's family is far more emotional than Ben's family. Eventually, everyone notices Ben standing quietly with the children. Jenny walks over to introduce them to her aunts, uncles, and cousins.

Jenny puts her arm around Ben. "OK, this is my Aunt Rosy and Uncle Ted. This is my cousin Marsha, her husband Carl, and the boys Camden and Kurt. Then hiding behind them all is Aunt Gill, my other cousins Matt, Debbie, and last but not least, Uncle Bruce."

"Hi, nice to meet you all," Ben said.

"This is Baby, April, and June, who are still hiding up," Jenny proudly said.

"Mom, are they more family?" June asked.

"Yes!" Jenny said. "You have a few more cousins, but they're in California and couldn't make it here today."

"Wow! We got lots of family, don't we, Daddy?" April asked.

"We sure do!" Ben said. "There's even more over in England from my mom's side."

"Are those the ones who talk funny like Granny?"

"Yep," Ben said. "They all talk with that English accent, and all they do is drink cups of tea all day long."

"We going to see them next?" April asked.

Ben glances over at Jenny. "Maybe later on... That's a long trip," knowing Jenny is not ready for a flight to England, especially going over the Atlantic Ocean.

* * *

Everyone sits in the living room, and as usual, it's more of the same old questions. Ben is getting tired of telling the same old stories. Luckily, Jenny does all the talking, telling everyone about their time on the island and how beautiful a life it was. She always tells it better anyway and doesn't leave out any details. When they hear about her journal being published, they all want to read it.

Everyone is having a great time getting acquainted with Jenny's family. As usual, the twins are wandering about, taking inventory of everything they see. Just like with Ben's parents, Aunt Rosy loves knickknacks, and there is not a bare shelf in sight.

After a big dinner, they all sit in the living room looking through the family photo albums. Jenny sits next to her Aunt Rosy, going through them all. Ben chuckles, seeing photos of Jenny when she was young. He can't help from laughing, seeing how gangly she looked when she was a teenager, with all the different hairstyles. At least now, it's payback time for when his mother did the same, showing Jenny all of his embarrassing photos.

April and June are on both sides of their father, looking through all the old photos. Ben is so shocked to see a picture of Jenny when she was about four years old. She looked just like the twins. The resemblance is remarkable.

"Look, Daddy! We're in the pictures! Is this me or April?" June asked.

"That's your mom!" Ben replied. "She does look like you."

Ben can't believe how much she looks like the twins. "Jenny, you need to see this," passing the album down to her.

Jenny gasped. "I haven't seen these in ages. My God! I do look like the girls! Aunt Rosy, are these my mom's photo albums, or are they yours?" looking at the front cover.

"Oh, they're yours now," Aunt Rosy said. "I got all the photo albums after your mom and dad died. For some reason, your sister didn't want them. I don't know why she doesn't want anything to do with us anymore."

"She was always a little distant at times. Mom and Kim never really got along. I don't know what happened," glancing at the photos of her and her sister together.

Ben takes another album off the stack, flipping through all the pages. With all the black and white photos, he knows this one must be old. Reading the caption under the picture, he sees Jenny's parents for the first time. They were very young, probably in their twenties. He quickly notices that Jenny looks just like her mother.

In one photo, Jenny's mother was very pregnant. That must have been right before Jenny was born, seeing her sister also in the photo. After a few more pages, there is nothing but page after page of baby pictures.

"Here's a picture of Mom when she was a baby," Ben said, pointing to one photo.

"Look how tiny she is," April said. "She don't have any hair!" then giggles.

"Hey, there are two babies!" June said, pointing to one photo with two babies being held by their mother.

"That must be Mom's sister Kim. I thought she was a little older?" Ben asked, thinking it's odd seeing two babies looking about the same age.

A hush goes through the room. Ben looks up, seeing Aunt Rosy has a shocked look on her face. Everyone else in the room is also looking a little strange. Something is going on, and it's very awkward for some reason.

"Mom, is this you and your sister?" April asked, pointing to the photo.

Jenny leans over to look. "Oh, no... That can't be her. She is five years older than me. Let me see," she said, reaching for the photo album.

Ben hands the album over to Jenny, but then Aunt Rosy quickly takes it from her, closing it up. Aunt Rosy has a guilty look on her face, placing it on her lap. The room is silent. Ben can see something is definitely wrong here.

"What's wrong with everyone?" Jenny asked. "Why are you taking the album away?" seeing the odd looks she is getting.

"So, what do we do?" Aunt Rosy asked, looking over at her husband.

He nods at her. "I think you better tell her. Her family is gone now. I think she has a right to know."

"Tell me what? What's going on?" Jenny asked.

"Your mom and dad were going to tell you," Aunt Rosy explained after a long, awkward pause. "You got to understand it was a long time ago. They wanted to tell you after you got out of high school. I guess after years went by, they kept putting it off and never got around to it. That was a sad time for all of us. They didn't want to bring up the past again and all those bad memories."

Again, there is another long pause. "Rosy, she needs to know!" Uncle Ted blurted out.

Aunt Rosy puts the old photo album on Jenny's lap. "Your mom and dad removed some of the photos from your albums. They hid them for years, but I didn't. I kept all of them. You've never seen any of these. She was never forgotten and has always been in our hearts," wiping tears from her face.

Silence fills the room. Aunt Rosy slowly opens the photo album. Jenny stares at the old photos, not understanding any of this. It's the first time she has seen these photos.

"Jenny, your mother, had twins too," Aunt Rosy explained. "You had a sister. A twin sister, and her name was Amy," pointing to one photo.

"What! I had a twin sister!" Jenny cried out, so shocked, hearing this for the first time. "Why wasn't I told about this? Where is she? What happened to her?" looking down at the old photos, seeing her mother holding two babies.

Aunt Rosy takes Jenny's hand. "I'm sorry... It was an accident. Amy died when she was a baby."

"How did it happen?"

"Your sister Kim was only five years old, and she didn't understand. She was so jealous of all the attention you and Amy were getting. She was only a baby, too, and she was probably trying to help out—"

"What happened?" Jenny asked.

"She accidentally dropped her... She didn't mean it," Aunt Rosy whispered, remembering that horrible day.

"Right, accidentally dropped poor Amy down the stairs," Uncle Ted sarcastically said.

Aunt Rosy quickly turns to her husband. "Be quiet! We don't know that! She was only five years old!"

Jenny is so stunned, hearing all this for the first time. Slowly turning the pages, she sees photos she has never seen before of her and the other baby with her mom, dad, and sister.

"She died," Jenny quietly mumbled. "I had a twin sister, and she died," looking down at the photos of the two of them together so long ago.

"Amy was only a few months old at the time," Aunt Rosy explained. "There was an investigation, but they ruled it as an accident. Kim was only five, and she didn't understand what she was doing."

"I always thought Kim had an evil side to her," Uncle Ted said, getting mad thinking about her. "You noticed that when her mom and dad died, she just sold everything and left the country. The last we saw of her was at the funeral. She didn't say a word to anyone. When it was over, she just got up and left, not saying goodbye to anyone. We've never seen or heard from her since."

Jenny cries uncontrollably. Aunt Rosy motions to everyone to leave the room so they can be alone. Ben scoots over next to Jenny, putting his arm around her. He knows this is not the right time to be giving her more bad news like this, especially after losing her parents. At least now he knows why her sister ran off, not wanting anything to do with Jenny and her family.

Once Jenny regains her composure, she continues looking through the pages, seeing more photos of her and her twin sister. She notices how much they resembled April and June when they were babies. She then notices several strange pictures of the old tree where her parent's graves are now.

"What are these up by the tree?" she asked, seeing hundreds of flowers around the small bench.

"That's where they buried Amy," Aunt Rosy explained. "That small bench is her gravestone."

"Oh, my God!" Jenny cried out. "That's her grave! I never knew it! All those times I was up there."

"I'm so sorry that they never told you. Your mom used to sit up there for hours reading stories to you and Amy. She would always talk to Amy as if she were there. Maybe when you heard your mom talking to her, so you kept on telling everyone that she was your imaginary friend. After that, you always went up there to play on your own."

Jenny fights back the tears. "I remember that now... Mom would always bring me my lunch up there. We'd sit and talk together for hours. I remember she would always act like someone else was there with us and tell me it was my special friend. That was the little game we played together. Now I know why Kim would never go up there! She was always so scared to go near it! I could never understand why, but now I do!"

"Remember, she was very young and didn't know what she was doing. Your mother never forgave her. Kim knew you were the favorite and always held it against you but never knew why. She doesn't know about Amy either. Your mom and dad never told either one of you. They thought they might tell you when you two were older, but after so many years had passed, they thought it was best just to leave it alone."

"I always felt there was something odd between us. Kim was never close and always pushed me away."

"I know... Kim probably felt unwanted when she was little," Aunt Rosy explained. "Your mother never got over it. Even after all those years, the damage was done. It was so sad."

April and June slowly walk over to look at the photo album. Jenny turns it around to show them her little sister.

"Mom, you had a sister, too?" April asked, seeing the photo.

Jenny nods. "Yes, a long time ago."

"Where is she?" June asked. "Can we play with her?"

"No, she would be my age now. She is in heaven with my mom and dad."

"Is she the one up by the tree between Granny and Granddad?" June asked, quickly figuring it out.

Her comment surprised Aunt Rosy. "Yes, she is up there by the big tree near the bench."

"We gave her flowers too!" April said.

"How come you didn't tell us?" June asked.

"I didn't know," she quietly answered, running her hand over her sister's photo.

They think the center gravestone is Amy's, not knowing it's their mother's grave. No one wants to tell them the truth. Jenny doesn't want them to know either. When they are older, she will tell them about the gravestone. Until then, it will be Amy's.

"I can't believe I had a twin sister and never knew about it," Jenny said, still in shock with all this news. "It's funny how I remember sitting on that bench with Mom, having conversations with my imaginary friend. All along, it was my twin sister Amy I was talking to!"

"Can I have some of Amy's photos?" Jenny asked her aunt. "I like to show the children a little later. Maybe explain things a little better when they are older."

"You can have them all. I also have some of the larger ones in a box somewhere around here. Your mother gave them to me to keep because when you got older and saw them, you kept asking who the other baby was. It's a shame she never told you years ago. I think it was also to protect your sister from ever knowing what she did."

"That would be devastating for her to hear after all these years," Jenny said.

"She probably always sensed something from her mother," Ben suggested. "Maybe that's why she left. She didn't want anything to do with you, your family, or even any of us."

Jenny nods. "Now I know why she was always distant. Not wanting anything to do with me."

* * *

Late into the night, Jenny is exhausted. She needs time to be alone after hearing about her twin sister. She didn't expect any of this. What was supposed to be a joyous occasion with her family is now an absolute nightmare, opening an old wound. She has discovered something horrible about her past, but it's answered so many questions.

Uncle Ted returns with two boxes filled with old photos and other albums. "This is everything... Many of the ones with Amy are in the box."

"Thank you," Jenny said. "I'll go through them all and put them in a new album when we get home."

Uncle Ted gives her a big hug. "That's good... I'm glad she is back in the family again. So, have you decided where you're going to settle down?"

"We might go up to Colorado, where Ben used to live. I don't think we can be happy unless we have plenty of open space around us and far away from the big cities."

"Oh, that sounds great!" Aunt Rosy said. "I always wanted to go there. You wouldn't mind having a few guests, would you?"

Jenny hugs her aunt. "I'll make sure to get a house with extra bedrooms so we can have all of you over to visit."

"I'll let you know where we finally end up," Jenny said after many hugs and kisses. "We can all get together with Ben's family from Texas and have a great big family get together."

"You'll have to come down to Texas and meet up with my family," Ben suggested.

"We have never been to Texas," Uncle Ted replied. "I'll have to get myself one of those cowboy hats and a western shirt. I hear everyone wears those down there."

"I hope you know how to ride a horse," Ben jokingly added. "That's the only way they get about nowadays. It's a pain to ride out to the grocery store on horseback," seeing he doesn't know much about Texas and the people there.

"That's right! Everyone rides horses there. I might have to get some riding lessons before we go."

Jenny realizes Ben is pulling a fast one on her uncle. "Oh, he's just kidding! However, they do have big barbecues. You'll love those. One of his uncles has an enormous pool and has the best parties. His mother is English, so you better study up on drinking tea with a small cup and saucer. It took me a while to get used to that."

Aunt Rosy laughed. "I can just see Ted trying to drink a cup of tea while wearing one of those big ten-gallon hats. Don't worry… We've seen that Dallas show on TV. We know how they live down there. I can't wait to see their ranch and wouldn't mind riding one of their horses, too."

"So, how many cattle do they have?" Ted asked. "I'd like to try one of those roundups, where they herd all the cattle into the pens."

Ben stands with his mouth wide open. "Ah, they're retired now. They don't do that anymore," realizing his joke went a little too far.

"I'll explain it to you later," Jenny said, realizing they had been watching the Dallas television show, thinking everyone in Texas lives like that.

* * *

After many hugs and kisses, it's finally time to leave. Ben insists on driving since Jenny is still having problems keeping her composure. He wants to get her away before there is any more devastating news. He wishes they would have waited a month or two before telling her about Amy. After seeing her parent's graves, it's going to take her a long time just to get over that. At least her family is nice, considering all the problems they are having with her sister Kim.

Ben can't wait for his family to meet Jenny's family. He'll have some explaining to do if her family shows up in Texas. They might be expecting to see a big ranch like they did on the Dallas television show. That really surprises him how many people still think of Texas as the Wild West, where people still get about on horseback.

Ben then realizes he has heard the name Amy before. He remembers Jenny talking about having an imaginary friend when she was young. The strange thing about it all, Amy was the name for April and June's little imaginary friend too. Jenny might not have realized it, but she passed on the family tradition with the girls having one as well.

"So, what's next on the list?" Ben asked. "Do you want to stay a few more days? We are not on any schedule here," seeing she is feeling a little better.

"I don't know... It would be nice to spend more time with my family, but it's a little too much for me now. I'm so emotionally drained, but I think it's more important that we get a place of our own. I don't want to burden anyone by staying with your family or even mine. It's time for the children to have a place they can call home. Once we get settled in, then we can visit them, or they can stay with us. I just don't like being homeless. We need to settle down somewhere."

Ben nods. "Yeah, I know. We're kind of in limbo with no home. I guess it's on to Colorado! We'll check it out and see what everyone thinks."

"I can't wait to see the mountains! I have a feeling that if we do get a place there, I'll be seeing a lot of my family."

"Oh, I forgot to tell you about that. When I lived in Denver, my place was like a hotel. You'd be surprised how many old friends come out of the woodwork when they hear you live in Colorado, especially when it's ski season!"

"I hate to say it, but I can't wait to see the snow again! I bet the kids will love it, too."

He laughed. "I don't know... Seeing their reaction after getting in that cold water today, they may not like snow at all, or worse, the ice-cold winters in Colorado!"

She laughs as well. "That's true, but at least they'll be keeping their clothes on. I think they'll like the snow. All kids that age do. They'll be out throwing snowballs and sledding down the hills."

He looks in the mirror, seeing them all sound asleep in the back seat. "I know they'll have a good time there. Although I don't know what it is about riding in cars, but it sure does knock them out."

"It's been a long day for them," she said, checking on the children. "It's probably jet lag, and it's going to get worse with the flight going back. This is why we need to find a place to live. I can see now that traveling about like this is too much for them. The difference in the time zones puts them off their sleep. They need to get to bed at normal hours again."

"Yeah, I know… They all slept in until eight this morning. They're still on Texas time."

She laughed. "It was a shock when they found out the sun had been up for hours. It's throwing them off. Things were a lot easier getting them to bed when the sun went down. That's the bad part of traveling. It always takes several days to shake the jet lag."

"I feel the same way. Speaking of the sun going down, we missed another sunset," seeing the overcast sky.

"Well, I'm not going to miss another one," she said with a big smile. "We're all getting up real early and going down to the beach to watch the sunrise. It'll be a nice treat for the girls."

He nods. "Sure, we can go scavenging on the beach like we used to do. Maybe they can find something interesting."

She leans over, kissing his cheek. "That is a great idea! I'll bring breakfast, too."

* * *

Lying in bed, Jenny and Ben have plenty to think about, but money is no longer an issue. They can now take their time and not have to worry about getting jobs for a while. Jenny's future is already in motion, with her book being published. Ben is still in limbo, not knowing what he is going to do with his life. All he can think about is being a father to his children, which is the one job he loves the most.

Jenny let out a long sigh. "What a day... I never expected any of this. I still can't believe I had a twin sister. That is one thing I never saw coming!"

"They should have waited. It's a little too much for one weekend. I don't know how you're able to deal with it all."

"I know... It hasn't sunk in yet. It'll take a long time to get over this."

"I don't know if you remember, but the name Amy is familiar. Long ago, when the girls were young, they pretended to have a little invisible friend as well," Ben explained.

"That's right! I haven't thought about that in years. That's before the Amazon warrior days when they used to play like little girls."

He laughed. "Yeah, you must have passed on the game your mother used to play with you. I always thought it was odd how they would come up with some of the things they used to do. Always serving an extra plate of food, or pretending someone else was with them in their games."

"Yeah, that was strange," she said, thinking about it. "I must have told them the same stories my mom told me. I guess I played the same game with them when they were little and just don't remember it. Back in those days, I had them all to myself while you were up on the island. I had a hard time keeping them amused, always having to make up all those games. Somehow, that one must have stuck. At least now, I'm glad we had twins. They always had each other."

"It's funny... I always thought it was me who was responsible for the twins. We had twins in our family, but it usually skips a generation. It was always the big joke back home that I was the one that would end up with twins."

She laughed. "Well, it ain't a joke anymore. You now got them! It does make you think, though, after seeing how close April and June are. You know how they almost read each other's minds. I wonder what it would have been like if Amy were still alive."

"You'd probably be close like the girls are. From the sound of it, your mother kept her alive. She always read to her and had you up at her grave like that."

"All those times I used to sit up there on that bench playing and talking to my imaginary friend," she said, shaking her head in disbelief. "Mom never told me, but I guess that was her way of keeping her alive. We used to spend so much time up there together, always pretending someone else was there. It was like a game to me. Now that I think about it, I can recall her calling her Amy. Mom would tell me it was my special friend and that only I could see and hear her. I used to try to get Kim to go up there to play with me, but she never did."

"Maybe because she was older than you."

"I thought that too, for a long time. That was only our special place. Kim was never part of it. Now, I feel sorry for Kim. I now know why Mom treated me so differently."

"Kim doesn't know anything about it either?" he asked.

"No, I guess not," she said, shaking her head. "And I don't want her to find out about it. It might take me time, but I want to get her back. She's still my sister. She can't be blamed for something she did when she was only five years old."

"From the sounds of things, some of your family hasn't gotten over it. I don't know how they were able to keep this quiet for so long."

"I know... I can't believe they kept this from Kim and me."

As Jenny talks about her past, old memories come to the surface. "Now I think about it. I can remember how Mom always cried at my birthday parties. Even Dad would get emotional and always try to hide it from me. They were never like that when it was Kim's birthday, but always on mine. After my birthday party was over and everyone was gone, Mom always pulled out one last present and a cupcake with a candle on it. We walked up the hill and sat on the bench together. She would light the candle, and we'd sing 'Happy Birthday' to my special friend. I would help open the present and show her what she got. Mom and I would sit there for a long time talking to Amy. We'd always leave her the present and a cupcake on the bench. Thinking back, I always wondered why she used to do that. Now, I know… She always included Amy at every one of my birthday parties. I remember once Kim was on the back porch when we came down. I never forgot the mean look my mom gave her. Poor Kim looked scared and just ran off. I could never understand why Mom was like that. Now, I know!" she said, and started crying again.

He pulls her towards him, holding her tight. "Let's not talk about it anymore."

Ben knows Jenny can't stay here in her hometown. The reunion with her family was not what they were expecting. Seeing her parent's grave for the first time is one thing, but then to find out she had a twin sister who died long ago is just too much. To make matters worse, she may have been killed at the hands of her older sister.

* * *

Jenny wants to visit her parents one last time before they leave for the airport. Aunt Rosy and Uncle Ted are there as well. The small marble bench is Amy's grave marker. The top had been turned over, hiding the epitaph for Amy. When Jenny and Kim started learning how to read, it was done to prevent both of them from learning the truth.

Uncle Ted brings some tools to set it right. After removing the top, they turn it over, revealing Amy's epitaph. Jenny quietly read her sister's inscription for the first time. She wishes her parents had told her. If only she had known, it would have answered so many questions when she was young.

Jenny looks down at the white marble bench. "Aunt Rosy, I think I would like to change the headstone they made for me and change it for Amy. Then Mom and Dad can be next to her. It's not right for me to have a headstone. It's starting to make me uncomfortable."

"Your mom and dad would like that. I'll make the arrangements to have it changed."

"I wonder what my life would have been like with her?" Jenny asked, staring at the small bench, reading the words.

Aunt Rosy puts her arm around Jenny. "Probably no different from April and June. Through them, you will see how it might have been."

"I wish I had gotten to know her," she whispered, then started crying.

"Why don't you put your flowers in the vase?" Ben said, seeing the girls are getting upset with their mother crying.

April, June, and Baby put the flowers in the vases and then set them one by one in front of each headstone. The children also selected little gifts for Amy. Three little beanie babies, a dolphin, a whale, and a teddy bear. They put each one on the bench for Amy.

They walk down the hill back to the house, leaving Jenny alone to say goodbye to her mother, father, and sister. April and June don't like staying up on the hill by the tree. It's a sad place that makes everyone cry.

While they wait in the house for Jenny to return, the twins are excited to get another chance to look through the old house filled with antiques and knickknacks. They think the house is a store since there are so many shelves filled with antiques. At least they know not to touch anything, always keeping their hands behind their backs. As usual, they go back to their old ways of taking inventory of everything they see.

★ ★ ★

After about twenty minutes, Jenny walks down the hill. April and June both rush out to meet her while Ben stays with Baby on the porch. She tries to smile, seeing the girls running up to meet her. She is still upset, trying to hold back the tears. The girls hold their mother's hands as they walk back to the house.

"Did Amy like her presents?" April asked her mother.

"I think she did! They are really nice presents."

"Is she going to come back home with us?" June asked.

"Yeah! She can play on the beach with us. We can show her the cave and things," April suggested.

"No, she's going to stay here with your granny and granddad," seeing how the girls don't understand any of this.

"How come she doesn't come down here and play?" June asked. "Is she scared of us?" looking up at the hill.

"Oh, maybe a little... Don't worry. She'll be all right," not understanding why the girls are asking all these questions.

When Jenny reaches the house, Ben knows she is upset again. "Why don't you go into the house for a while? I think they have the coffee ready."

"OK... I need to sit down for a few minutes," Jenny said, picking up Baby and then taking him into the house.

Ben is about to follow her but then notices the girls are standing at the end of the porch, looking up at the old tree.

"You two want to stay out here and play a little longer?" he asked.

"Daddy, how come she just stands up there all by herself?" April asked, looking so sad. "Doesn't she want to come down here and play with us?"

"Who are you talking about?" he asked, not understanding her.

"That girl!" April said, pointing up at the old tree at a little girl standing all alone.

He looks up, seeing nothing but the old tree and the gravestones. "Oh, like Mom said, maybe she's a little scared. She'll be all right. She's with her granny and granddad," playing along, thinking they are talking about Amy's gravesite, seeing no one else is around.

April and June wave frantically, yelling for her to come and play.

"Let's go in the house for a while," seeing how the girls don't understand any of this.

June is feeling so sad, turning to her father. "If she can't come down here, can we go up there and play with her?"

"No, you better not," Ben said, not wanting the girls to run up to the gravesite on their own. "Mom might not want you up there. Remember, it's a really sad place for your mother. Let's go inside and get some cake and cookies."

"Bye, Amy!" the girls yelled out, waving at the little girl standing all alone by the bench.

June smiles. "She waved back!" waving her hands up in the air.

Again, he looks up, seeing nothing. "Oh, that's nice," waving as well, thinking they were playing one of their games.

"See!" April shouted. "I think she likes us!" frantically waving back.

"She likes the presents we gave her!" June said.

When they get into the house, Ben quickly closes the door. "That's nice, but let's not talk about this around Mom. She is really sad, and it might make her cry," he said, knowing Jenny is really on edge emotionally about her sister Amy.

"OK... We won't," the girls said, not understanding why.

* * *

As they get ready to leave, Jenny hugs Caroline and Mike. "It's been so nice meeting you. Thank you for letting us come by again."

"Remember, you and your family are welcome here anytime!" Mike said.

"You have a safe trip to Colorado!" Caroline said, hugging Jenny again.

Jenny hugs her aunt and uncle. "Thank you for everything. We'll let you know when we get settled. We'll have a big house party, and you're all invited. Don't worry about the cost. I'll get the tickets, my treat!"

"Thank you!" Aunt Rosy said, hugging her again. "We'll be there! You can count on it!"

Ben hugs both his new in-laws. "Thanks for everything. I'm so glad to see she has a nice family who cares."

"She's going to be all right," Aunt Rosy whispered. "Don't worry... These things take time," giving Ben a big hug.

Ben gets the children buckled into their car seats while Jenny says her last goodbye. He drives back since Jenny is still a little shaken, leaving her family and home. He knows it's going to be hard for her to leave and get over this.

"Goodbye, home... Goodbye, Mom. Goodbye, Dad," Jenny whispered as they slowly drove away, not taking her eyes off the old house.

"We can always come back," Ben said, seeing she was getting upset again.

"I know... We will someday," still looking back at her old home.

A little ways down the road, she can see the old tree on top of the hill behind the house. The sun breaks through the clouds, illuminating the gravesite. She keeps wiping away the tears as the three gravestones come into view. The place she once found solitude so many years ago is now a place of so much sadness.

To her surprise, she sees a small figure standing next to the bench, all alone. She wipes away the tears, trying to get a better view. All at once, she realizes it's a little girl waving at the car. Jenny puts her hand up to the window, slowly waving back. She wonders if that's the little girl the twins were talking about seeing up there.

Somehow deep down, she knew. "Amy, it was you all along... You were with us on the island, and it was you hiding in the trees. You were there with us, watching over the girls. It was you in the raft that helped me and in the cave protecting the girls," she whispers, recalling the days long ago, living on the island.

"Goodbye, Amy," she whispered. "May you rest in peace," the tears running down her cheek.

Right before her eyes, the little girl slowly vanished. Chills run down her spine. She keeps blinking her eyes, but then she realizes what she had just witnessed. Her sister, Amy, can now finally rest in peace.

"Are you OK?" Ben asked, hearing her mumbling about something.

With the gravestones finally out of view, she turns to Ben. "Thank you for everything... I couldn't have done it without you. I'm so glad I came now, but I think it's time to move forward with our lives. It's time for me to let go of the past. I know that now. The children are our future, and they need a place to call home," reaching over, holding his hand.

"You're right... Well, we're going to Colorado Springs. So, maybe we should look around for a place to live while we are there. I have a feeling you and the kids will love it!"

* * *

Chapter 60

Colorado Bound

J enny and Ben arrive in Colorado on a perfect day with clear blue skies. Pikes Peak is still white with snow, towering over everything in sight. Ben is so glad to see the Rocky Mountain range again.

"Check it out!" Ben yells out. "What a view," walking over to the windows facing the mountains.

"Wow!" the girls shouted, in awe seeing the majestic view.

"Look how clear it is out here," he said. "You can see all the details in the mountains, even the trees. They're also about twelve miles away!"

"Yeah, they got lots of them here!" June said, looking up and down the mountain range, seeing it stretching from one horizon to the other.

"It's going to be fun walking around up there! What's that big one, and how come it's all white?" April asked.

"It's called Pike's Peak, and it's over fourteen thousand feet high. That white stuff is snow, and you guys will love playing in it!"

"Wow! Can we go up on that one?" April shouted, jumping up and down in excitement.

"Oh, no!" Jenny said. "That's a little too much, even for you."

"Well, we can drive up or take the train," Ben suggested. "One day in the future, we'll hike up on the trail. We need to get in shape for that one. That's about a five-hour hike, and it's uphill all the way, going from 6,000 to 14,000-foot climb!"

"I don't think we're going to be doing that for a while!" Jenny said, shaking her head. "We need to be looking for a place to live first. From the looks of those mountains, I think I'll let you do the driving here. I'm not going to be driving on a dirt road on the edge of a cliff," thinking about all those horror stories she heard.

"Oh, it'll be lots of fun. Nothing like driving on a dirt road with no railing and a five-hundred-foot drop-off!"

"Precisely what I was referring to, and no way I'm doing that!" she replied.

* * *

When they pick up their luggage, they make their way to the car rental office. Ben makes sure to get a 4x4 Jeep so he can take everyone off-roading in the backcountry. All the first-class service is spoiling him. The rental car is already parked out front, with three baby seats in the back.

As Ben loads up the Jeep, he feels the high altitude for the first time in years. "Can you feel how hard it is to breathe up here?" wondering if Jenny is feeling it too.

"Yeah, is it always like this?"

Ben laughed. "Yep! This is nothing. We're only at six thousand feet here, but wait till you get up in the mountains. It's far worse up there. You'll get used to it after a couple of weeks. Just make sure you drink lots of water and take it slow. Don't get up too fast and don't overexert yourself."

"Oh, I see what you mean!" she said, getting into the Jeep, already feeling a little woozy. "I'm a little lightheaded already just getting in the car. If it's going to be like this, I think I'll lie around the pool for a couple of days before we do anything else."

"Yeah, I feel it too. We'll take it easy for the first couple of days. We can all use a good rest," seeing the children starting to yawn after the long flight.

"So, what is this Broadmoor Hotel?" Jenny asked. "Every time someone on the plane asked where we were staying, they were always impressed when I told them the Broadmoor. Is it really nice?"

"The best in the city, or even in the whole damn state! You're going to be pampered like never before. It'll be like going from one extreme to the other. We lived out on the beach with nothing, and now, utter opulence!"

She takes his hand. "I noticed you kept all the plans a big secret. But do we need two rooms? We can all fit in one."

"It's our second honeymoon!" he explained. "We have our own room for the first time! The kids have an adjoining room, but there is a door between the two. Just think, we can close the door and finally be on our own!"

She looks back at the children, who are already asleep. "I don't know... I can imagine what mischief they'll get up to in a room all to themselves."

"That's the best part about this place! They have everything there, even babysitting! They have horseback riding, paddle boats, swimming pools, and plenty of hiking trails. It'll be great! They'll have lots of fun."

She leans over, kissing his cheek. "Oh, I see... So, you're really taking the kids there to play!" knowing how he can't wait to show the children the mountain life.

"We'll have some time for ourselves, so don't worry! I have it all arranged!"

* * *

Arriving at the Broadmoor Hotel, Jenny is stunned by the opulence, having never seen anything like it before. The large hotel is at the foothills of the Rocky Mountains with the backdrop of Pikes Peak painted white with snow. The hotel has been famous for more than a hundred years as the playground for the wealthy.

Ben is so excited about getting to stay at the famous Broadmoor. He makes sure to get a nice room for Jenny. He wants to show her and the children a good time and knows this is the only place that will really impress them.

After checking in, it's obvious that no one knows who they are. Since many celebrities and even politicians stay at the hotel on a regular basis, no one will notice them. That is a big relief after Jenny's hometown, where people always recognized them. They were lucky to leave right before the news media found out they were there, showing up in droves with all their vans and satellite trucks.

Walking into the room, it's way better than Ben ever expected. Seeing the size of just one of the rooms, he realizes it's more than enough for all five of them. With the two adjoining rooms, it's almost as big as a house. There are no more cramped small rooms like at the hospital, and this is bigger than the bed-and-breakfast they stayed at in Connecticut.

"Wow," Jenny mumbled, lost for words, looking at all the luxurious furniture and the large paintings covering the walls.

"So, how is this for a honeymoon suite?" Ben asked.

She doesn't reply, running up and kissing him passionately. April and June start laughing, seeing their parents kissing.

"This is so nice! Now, my dream has finally come true. I always wanted our honeymoon at a place like this!"

"What! This is nothing compared to our wedding night up on the lookout," he jokingly said. "We had a campfire with music and lots of dancing! You can't tell me that wasn't nice."

She kisses him again. "Well, that was nice, but this is what I really had in mind. You forget we were not alone then either," glancing over at the children wandering around the room.

"That's why I got two rooms," walking her over to the open door leading to the other room.

She gasped. "Oh, they'll love this! Come on, kids. This is where you're sleeping tonight!" seeing the two beds and a baby crib already set up.

"We can shut the door and even lock it on this side!" he explained.

"You thought of everything!" winking at him.

"Yep... It's our honeymoon! No kids tonight!"

"We get our own beds!" April and June shouted out, running into their room, so excited to see two separate beds.

"Sure! Even Baby gets his own!" Jenny said.

"This will be like camping out on your own," Ben explained. "All three of you get to sleep in here. It'll be a big adventure," trying to make it sound like fun getting to sleep in their own room.

"It's like our own cave!" April said.

June stands with her mouth wide open. "Wow! We even got a potty in here too!" seeing the bathroom.

Jenny is getting worried. "Remember, no playing around in there. Don't touch the water taps and don't keep flushing the toilets all the time. Only after you go potty."

"You two make sure Baby doesn't go in the bathroom by himself," Ben added. "You'll have to watch him when he's in here with you. Don't let him mess around or break anything either."

"Yes, Daddy!" they both said, knowing it was still their job to watch their little brother.

Jenny is wondering if the girls, especially Baby, will sleep on their own. All three are running around so excited. They can't believe they are getting their own room, but mostly, their very own beds.

Ben, seeing they are getting out of control, hands out the coloring books and crayons. That is the one thing that always calms them down and keeps them amused for hours.

"What do we do for supper?" Jenny asked. "It's getting late... Is there a restaurant here where we can bring the children?"

"I'm already ahead of you," Ben said with a big smile. "I knew we would get in a little late, and I didn't know what types of restaurants they have here. Some are rather fancy, and we'll have to dress up to get in. Those are the ones we'll go on our own. I don't think they'll let the kids in those, anyway. So, I made arrangements for room service tonight, if you don't mind."

"That's good! I'm not ready to go out yet after that long trip. I need a long soak in the bathtub and to change my clothes. So, what's on the menu? When do we order?"

"It should be here shortly! Like I said, it's all planned. I ordered our meals when we checked in."

She is getting a little flustered with all the secrecy. "OK, Ben... I'll leave it all to you," kissing him, then started unpacking.

She knows this trip will be one surprise after another. Everything is a big secret, and she is wondering what else Ben has arranged for them. She has not seen him this happy since they left the island. Ben is back in his element here, and the mountain man has returned.

* * *

"Ah, I think it's suppertime!" Ben said after hearing a knock on the door.

Two men walk in pushing carts filled with covered silver trays. Ben thanks the waiters, then gives them a generous tip. The aroma from the food fills the room. Right away, the girls come running in, followed closely by Baby.

"Guess what's for supper?" Ben asked the girls.

Just from the looks on their faces, they already know. "Lobster and shrimps!" taking in deep whiffs.

Jenny gasped. "You didn't!" lifting one of the silver covers.

"Yep! It's lobster and shrimp night. We're going to have a fun day just like at home!"

"We even got Pepsi, and it's real cold, too!" April said, pulling out a bottle from the ice bucket.

Ben opens the main cover, revealing the shrimp platter. "Check this out! We got sautéed shrimp, battered shrimp, coconut shrimp, southern fried shrimp, and a few more I don't recognize. I told them they'd better do a good job because they'll be serving dinner to the best seafood chefs in the world!"

"It's a good thing we're eating in the room," Jenny said. "I can imagine what the chefs here would think being told off by two little girls on how they should cook seafood!"

"Exactly, that's what I thought! We'll check it out tomorrow and see where the best place to eat is. Meanwhile, it's a fun day! Let's eat!" turning on the radio for some dinner music.

* * *

After a couple of days of rest, Ben drives everyone up to the mountains. The winding mountain road keeps them all on edge except for Ben. He loves every minute of it. The small town of Woodland Park is their first stop. They pull up outside a real estate office to check out what is available in the area.

As they get out of the car, Jenny and the twins are awestruck by the scenery. The crisp, clean mountain air is something they were not expecting. At an 8,500-foot elevation, it's already too cold, and it will take time to get used to it.

"It's unbelievable how clear it is up here," Jenny said. "The view is just spectacular!"

"Oh yeah! Springtime is the best, and there will be wildflowers all over the place. I spent a lot of time up here in these hills. There are plenty of trails we can hike on around here, just as we did at home. You know, I always wanted to live here. It's nice and quiet, and there's plenty of space," looking up at the mountains surrounding them.

"Now, I can see us living up here!" looking at all the rustic log cabins not far from the road.

"Look how high those hills are! This is just like home, but there are so many here, and they are all around us," April said, pointing to them all.

"These are a lot bigger than what we had at home," Ben explained. "There are some good trails up here too. There are so many around here, and it'll take us years to explore them all."

"Can we walk around and explore like we did at home?" April asked.

"There is a good trail not far from here, and it goes around an enormous lake. I think it's about ten miles. It'd be a good one to start on."

"I don't think so," Jenny blurted out. "Especially on our first day here. We can do some short hikes a little later. I'd like to see some houses first," so excited about the idea of living in the mountains.

They visit several real estate agencies and collect listings of houses for sale. Then it's off to one of the local restaurants for a bite to eat.

Ben is surprised to see how the small town hasn't changed. He doesn't want to see this charming little town ruined like a lot of others by the typical strip malls and office buildings.

After a great home-cooked country meal, they drive to the mountains to look for prospective houses and to do a little sightseeing. Ben is in his element again, with plenty of open space, trees, and clean air. Being in the mountains brings back memories of the lifestyle he loved so long ago.

* * *

After several days of driving around looking at houses, they find one that stands out from the rest. The house is twenty-years-old on 640 acres, right next to the national forest. Trees cover almost eighty percent of the property. The back of the property skirted one of the small mountains. This one is perfect, with a little creek flowing through the property and a small pond. After seeing a few trout swimming in the stream makes the twins so excited.

The two-story house has plenty of potential with a huge kitchen, dining room, and four bedrooms. The house has to be big enough for their families, and many are already planning a trip to Colorado. It even has a separate barn that can be used for storage or for parking the car. The part they like the most, there are only a couple of houses around, with the closest almost three hundred yards away. Both Ben and Jenny know this is the one.

* * *

That night, Jenny and Ben lie awake, talking about the house. They discuss all the pros and cons and the location. The house has been empty for more than a year and will need plenty of work. Since Ben doesn't have a job, he can spend all day working on the house. He loves a good challenge and looks forward to fixing it up.

Jenny is ready to settle down with her family and start living a normal life. Having to paint and re-carpet the entire house is a little more work than she wanted to do. The kitchen will be the worst as far as repairs. Many of the appliances need to be replaced. Compared to the other houses, this one still has the best location with all the land and privacy they need.

Jenny wishes they could move into a new house and not have to do any work. Unfortunately, all the new houses that they looked at were in new communities. None of them had any landscaping done at all, and there were no trees. All the houses were so close to each other with very small yards, not much different from Ben's parents' house.

* * *

The next morning, Ben wakes up, seeing Jenny sitting by the window looking out at the scenery. "Good morning. How long have you been up?"

"I have been up for hours," she replied. "I didn't sleep at all, constantly thinking about the house all night long. It's perfect for us! Let's buy it!"

"Yeah, I think you're right," he said, so relieved she wanted it. "After we eat breakfast, we'll call them up and let them know. From what the realtor said earlier, we can probably move in right away," giving her a big hug.

"There is so much to do! We need to shop for an entire household of furniture, plates, towels, and just about everything. Just think, all we have is packed in our suitcases."

He laughed. "We had less when we arrived on the island, and we did fine."

"Well, I can get you a small tent and a sleeping bag if you want," she jokingly said.

"Actually, I think that might be a good idea. Remember years ago I told you about all those camping trips. I can't wait to take everyone out camping and sleep out under the stars again."

"Ben, you'll have plenty of time for that later. We need a home for our children and to start living a normal life again. Don't forget the girls maybe starting school soon."

"Oh, no... I forgot about that. Now, that should be interesting. I can't wait to see what the teachers think of those two, especially after eating at the school cafeteria! If they thought the airplane food was bad, the food they serve at these schools is probably downright horrible!"

She cringes. "That's going to be the least of our problems. You need to start deprogramming them. They need to learn how to act around other children of their own age. No more Amazon warrior girls. They need to start acting like little girls from now on."

"The Amazon thing is gone," he jokingly said, "but I have a feeling the mountain woman is about to start."

She gives him a mean look. "Oh no, you don't! Don't even think about it!"

✦ ✦ ✦

Chapter 61

New Home

As the proud new owners of their first home, Jenny and Ben are ecstatic and can't wait to fix it up. The house is in such a mess that it'll take a few weeks just to clean it. Ben is so proud to see his children helping out. Since they left the island, the girls never had enough things to do to occupy their minds. Now, there are so many chores to do. By the end of the day, they are exhausted, falling asleep as soon as they finish supper.

The girls love every minute of it. Getting to help fix up their new home is a dream come true, especially one with their very own bathroom with hot and cold running water.

For Jenny, this is the home she has always dreamed of since she was a little girl. A house in the country surrounded by mountains. What makes it so special is the view of Pikes Peak dominating the front view of the house. With nothing but open land around, it's so quiet. The only noise is the wind rushing through the pine trees. That is the one thing that reminds them the most of their home on the island. The only thing missing is the sound of the crashing waves.

The children are adjusting to their new home. With 640 acres to play in and explore, it's one big adventure. Every day, they go out exploring the many trails. On the edge of a national park filled with pine trees and small mountains, it's enough to keep them busy for years to come.

Ben surprises the children when he buys a new tent for them. The girls quickly set it up close to the house. Big enough to sleep four, they fill it with cots, sleeping bags, and little chairs. They quickly set up their old campsite again, adding a campfire surrounded by small wooden benches. The only thing different from what they had on the island is that everything they have now is brand new and the latest high-tech camping gear.

* * *

Ben knows the only thing missing now is a family pet. One of the things he always wanted was a yellow Labrador. Not only will a dog be good for the children, but also will provide protection. Living up in the mountains is nice, but bears and mountain lions are also in the area. A dog is one of the best ways to keep wild animals away.

After talking it over with Jenny, he set out to the city, having heard about a new litter of Labradors. He keeps it a secret from the children, wanting it to be a big surprise. He is still concerned about how they will react to having a pet. So far, there have been no problems. They are getting used to seeing other dogs and cats and know these are pets and are not for eating. The hunting and gathering days are over since they have discovered the local supermarket is the best place to get all their food.

Ben finally arrives back home with the new family member. He hid up in the bedroom while Jenny set things up. He is hoping it will not be like the last time he brought a pet home. She calls the children in from the backyard and keeps them in the living room for the big surprise.

"Well, we got something special for you," Jenny said. "We now have a new addition to our family."

Both the girls look at each other, confused. Baby starts clapping his hands, jumping up and down, hearing the word 'Surprise.' He knows it means something good.

"What do you mean?" April asked. "A new baby?"

"We already have Baby!" June quickly replied, pointing to her little brother.

Just then, Ben walks in with the new dog. The little puppy is so excited and ready to play. Startled by the animal, the twins immediately jump up, pushing Baby behind them to protect him.

"That's a dog!" June shouted out loud.

Ben sits on the floor, holding the little puppy. As soon as the puppy sees the children, she wags her tail, wanting to play. Baby isn't scared at all and pushes his sisters out of the way to get closer.

Ben is glad to see their reaction. "Yep! It's a dog… She is part of our family now. We need to come up with a name for her."

Jenny nudges the children closer to meet the puppy. "It's OK… She will not hurt you and is very friendly," seeing the girls are a little cautious.

Baby rushes forward, hugging the little dog. Cautiously, the twins get closer, gently petting the puppy.

"She's so soft!" June said, running her hands over the puppy.

"So, what's a good name for her?" Ben asked.

"How about Dog?" June suggested.

"No, we need a nice name," he said, shaking his head. "Can't you think of a nice name for her?"

"Yellow Dog! That's it! We'll call her Yellow Dog! That's her name," April boasted.

Jenny laughed. "Well, she is yellow and a dog. It makes sense!"

"No, how about something like Mable, Lassie, or Lucky?" Ben asked.

They go back and forth with various names, but the twins have already decided what they want. Yellow Dog is the name.

"You had your chance to name her," Jenny said, "but you wanted the kids to do it. So now you have to live with it!"

"OK, Yellow Dog, it is," he said, knowing he couldn't fight it.

They all cheer and start petting the poor little puppy. She is licking everyone's faces, so happy with all the attention.

Ben sits down with the children. "You need to be careful and watch over her. She's just a baby dog," seeing the little puppy is getting scared by all the noise and commotion.

They listen carefully to their father's instructions. He wants to make sure they understand the puppy is not a toy but is part of the family. The little puppy needs to be taken care of, but mostly potty trained. With new carpets all over the house, it's one of Jenny's primary concerns.

Yellow Dog quickly blends in with the children. She is their constant companion, and they are never apart. Whenever they are out playing, the puppy is always there. Walking on the many trails is still too much for her, and she always ends up in someone's backpack, enjoying the ride.

* * *

With the house now fully furnished, it's not long before all the relatives show up. With Ben's family in Texas and Jenny's family flying in, their home is turning into a hotel. That is one of the reasons they wanted this house, since there is plenty of room for guests. Their new home is a perfect place for barbecues in the afternoon out in the backyard, surrounded by the majestic mountains.

April and June are already forgetting about their life on the island. Their new home is more fun, especially with all the modern conveniences. Also, getting to see their relatives all the time helps them get used to being around other people.

Every day is still an adventure with plenty of things to do to keep them occupied. There is no sitting around the house watching television with this family. Everyone has chores to do, but after that, they are always outside enjoying life and exploring the land.

* * *

Chapter 62

Starting School

Summer has ended, and the weather is changing fast. April and June are now at the age where it's time for them to start school. Jenny wants the girls to start being around children their own age. Living in the mountains is almost like being on the island, being somewhat isolated. The only contact with other people is at the local grocery store or visiting family. She wants them to make friends at school and learn how to play like little girls and not like Amazon warriors or the mountain wilderness girls.

Ben knows this is a big step and is not looking forward to it. He is used to having the family together. The girls are always helping out, fixing up the house, and doing chores. Playtime is hiking on the many trails, fishing in the small creek on the property, or at the lakes surrounding the area.

The school is ten miles away in a little town called Divide. The town is not much more than a small rural community at the crossroads between Cripple Creek and the big ski resorts. It has the basic necessities needed to live in the country. It has an old-style general store, a few restaurants, a post office, and a gas station. If they needed anything extra, Woodland Park is only seven miles away.

There is a problem when April and June register at the local school. The principal and the teachers are concerned when they discover the two little girls are the famous Amazon twins. That one famous scene of the girls attacking the photographer when they arrived at Kwajalein Island makes them all overcautious.

Since arriving in Colorado, they have been able to keep a low profile. Rumors are spreading fast that they live in the area, but no one knows where. Now the cat is out of the bag, and the news spreads fast in the small mountain community.

Some parents are concerned about the famous Amazon girls attending school. The school district is also worried and made the twins take part in several counseling sessions before admitting them. This is being done mostly to appease the other parents and the insurance companies.

April and June attend several closely supervised mock classes with just a few children. The counselors closely watch the girls, seeing how they interact with the other children.

After several days, it's determined that the girls are very mature for their age, and they get along well with the other children. The counselors also notice that the girls love to play and are willing to learn new things. Being with other children their age is not a problem at all.

April and June treat the other children as they did their little brother. They tell them all what to do and how to do it. They quickly take control of the class, organizing all the games, but mostly teach them a few basic hand signs and birdcalls. What surprises the twins the most is finding out that none of the other children know any of the signs at all.

* * *

The next morning is the first day of school for April and June. Jenny has been crying all morning. Ben makes sure the girls have their two-way radios in their backpacks, just in case. Since the first day will only be four hours, they decide to stay in town and keep close by, going shopping and having lunch at the local restaurant. They notice they are not the only ones keeping close to the school. They recognize several parents from the class who are also at the restaurant.

April and June are so excited about their new school and talk about it for hours when they get back home. They can't wait to go back and think it was a great adventure. They are both still like sponges, always ready to learn new things. Having other children to play with makes it even better.

Just like on the island, the girls are up early, getting themselves ready. They even make their own lunches and pack their backpacks for their day out at school. What makes it even better is that they are already making new friends. They are also losing the overprotective mode that they grew up with and are acting more like little girls their own age. Learning how to survive in the wilderness is now a thing of the past.

Ben misses the girls while working on the property or doing chores around the house. He can't wait until they come back home so they can go out hiking or fishing.

He still teaches them how to live off the land, but mostly, it's just for fun. Ben tones it down a little but makes sure that they won't have any problems living off the land for several days if they do get lost. The only difference here is learning to deal with the cold weather, and winter comes early in the mountains. Their first real winter with snow will be a big change for everyone, especially after living on a tropical island where the temperature was always in the 80s.

* * *

With April and June going to school, Baby has problems being on his own for the first time. Ben decides it's time to let Baby have more responsibilities. Just as he taught the girls how to take care of their little brother, Ben is doing the same, teaching his son how to take care of Yellow Dog.

Baby is so thrilled to have someone to watch over. Best of all, he is not the littlest in the family anymore. Yellow Dog is now the baby, and someone has to look after her.

Ben knows he made the right choice with the little puppy. She is so good with the children, always running around with them and being part of their games. Baby and Yellow Dog are constant companions when the girls are at school. The two are never apart, and they are the best of friends.

Baby is not one for chores and is growing up normal. He is always out having fun playing with his best friend, Yellow Dog. He doesn't have his sister's work habits, and Jenny wants to keep it that way. Luckily, he missed out on the Amazon warrior phase. No more worrying about if there is enough firewood, food, or an approaching storm.

When it's time for the girls to come home from school, Baby and Yellow Dog sit out on the front porch together. Just like in the old days, where he sat on the small bench, waiting for his father and sisters to return after a day out over the island.

Once Ben returns with the girls from school, it's like a madhouse. The dog is barking, and Baby screams at the top of his lungs. They both run up and greet the girls as if they had been gone for ages instead of just a few hours. Baby is always so thrilled when his sisters come home from school so they can all go out and play.

* * *

Jenny finally published her book. She is now traveling, gone for weeks at a time to promote her book. The book is well-received and is on top of the bestseller list. She is famous now, appearing on all the talk shows and attending book signing events.

Ben stays home, and he doesn't mind it at all. Every time she is on television, it's a big event at the house. Ben always records it, watching it over and over with the children.

Since Jenny is the only one doing the talk shows, she is the big celebrity in the family. Ben and the children keep a low profile. He refuses to go on camera and will not do any interviews. No one recognizes him, and that is the way he likes it. They can go anywhere without being bothered. He thinks it's essential for the children not to be in the limelight. They are not the center of attention at their school, blending in well with the other students.

* * *

Ben finally gets in touch with his old friend Kyle. He had the hardest time trying to contact him. Kyle lives in his mountain cabin for the summer and has no phone or even electricity. Living in the wilderness, Kyle goes out fishing and hunting every day. During the cold winters, he returns to the city and works in one of the local sports stores for a little pocket money.

With no phone, television, or radio, it's a big shock for Kyle to hear that his best friend is back among the living again. They start right back where they left off with their weekend fishing and camping trips.

The twins love being back in the wilderness again, camping out under the stars. This type of camping is a little more comfortable than what they did back on the island. There is no more roughing it from now on, especially with all their new camping gear.

As an avid fisherman, Kyle can't wait to see these two little girls spearfishing. They don't disappoint him at all. The girls not only make their own spears but can still catch a fish with just one toss. Then, they clean and cook it themselves over the campfire, which they also made.

Ben is getting back into all the latest camping gear and gadgets. His favorite place is the REI camping store in Colorado Springs. He always makes sure he has the best of the best camping and survival gear. He takes nothing for granted after what they had endured while on the island.

Although camping is still a very active part of their lives, they are all getting soft, especially Jenny. Pooping in the woods is now a thing of the past. She insists on bringing along a portable potty. It makes things a little more comfortable, but they all know they can still survive in the wilderness with no problems.

* * *

Chapter 63

Normal Life

As the years go by, the Hughes family is now just another member of the community. Jenny's book finally fades away. The interviews and talk shows are now a thing of the past. They are just another family living out in the mountains, blending in well with the community.

The children have adjusted to their new lifestyle. August is finally old enough to realize the name Baby is not a good thing. Once he starts playing with the neighbor's kids, they all tease him about it. Nothing gets him madder than one of his sisters calling him Baby in front of his friends. That name will haunt him for a long time.

With all the money coming in from Jenny's royalties, they are now very wealthy. They settle back into their old ways again, where money and possessions are not important to them. They have everything that they would ever need. Most of their money goes into the bank for the children and their education. The rest is for their extended family. All the nephews and nieces have college funds waiting for them when they get out of high school.

Jenny and Ben love the mountain life. Every morning they are out walking on the many trails. In the afternoon, there is always a big barbecue out in the backyard. They love the outdoor life, spending most of their time outside. They live a very simple lifestyle, just as they did back in the days on the island.

During the cold winters, Ben spends most of his time on various woodworking projects. With the barn filled with the latest woodworking tools, there is nothing he can't make. All the store-bought furniture in the house has been replaced with his handmade furniture. Once the house is full, he keeps on making more furniture at the request of friends and family.

While Ben is making furniture, Jenny sits on the back porch working on her next novel. She is really in demand, and her publisher is eager for her next bestseller. Jenny still travels to book signings and guest appearances, but they are becoming few and far between. Now, she wants to stay home with her family and move on to newer projects.

* * *

Jenny and Ben fondly remember their time on the island, wanting so much to go back to visit. After reading Jenny's book, everyone wants to see the famous island as well, but it is not meant to be. Unfortunately, the military expanded the restricted area back to its original size not long after they left. That keeps everyone from the area and off their island.

Ben thinks it's such a shame that the military is blocking people from visiting the island. He always knew that it would make the perfect location for a small island resort. Their island was such a paradise. Now, it's just another island in the middle of the Pacific controlled by the military, barring anyone from seeing its beauty.

He now has all the photos taken by their rescuers on that last day on the island. Having bought all the negatives, he had them all professionally printed and framed, putting them all over the house.

He even bought a large satellite photo of their island and had it mounted on the wall. The satellite photo is so detailed that he can see individual palm trees on the beach. He can clearly see some of the paths that lead up to the cave. The lookout and all the fruit trees are clear as a bell.

Every day, he spends hours just staring at the satellite photo, remembering what life used to be like on their island they once called home. What is so remarkable is discovering that the satellite image was taken while they were there.

Ben uses a magnifying glass to look for clues to figure out where they were. He would love to see the two of them walking on the beach or playing in the water. By the shadows of the trees, he knows it was taken during the midday sun. At that time, they used to take naps under the old milo tree right in front of their campsite. Maybe that is where they were when the image was taken.

Ben never gets tired of reading Jenny's book or even the original journal. The originals have more details, but at times, it's difficult to read since she used to write so small, trying to fit as much as possible on a page. Since Jenny always wrote the day's events right after supper, the aroma of fish or even citrus is still noticeable when someone handles the papers. That always makes it more interesting being able to smell seafood after reading about her describing the freshly cooked meal they just had.

He can read any page of the journal and visualize it in his mind as if he were still there. That makes him very homesick, wanting to go back to visit. The island was such a beautiful place. They had such a peaceful and fulfilling life there, and now, he really misses it.

* * *

As time goes by, Jenny and Ben's fondness for the island grows more and more. That was the biggest adventure of their lives. The hardships of living off the island are now forgotten. They remember only the good days, which were many, but mostly, it was an absolute paradise in which they lived their lives.

April, June, and even August don't understand their parent's fixation with the island. Now, it's all a distant memory for them. The only home they know of is the one in the mountains in Colorado, where they have friends and a real home. The idea of living in a tent out on the beach is not appealing at all. They love camping, but after a couple of days, they like knowing they have a nice warm bed waiting for them at home.

* * *

Chapter 64

Hollywood Bound

After years of negotiations, it's finally official. Jenny's book is going to be made into a movie. Since the project was on and off for several years, no one ever thought it was ever going to get off the ground. Now, it's a big-budget film backed by a major studio. Once they get the final go-ahead, there is nothing to stop it.

When the news media hears about the movie, the Hughes family is back in the spotlight again. Ben still refuses to do any interviews, leaving it all up to Jenny. The children have done a few interviews, but it's clear they are having a hard time remembering things. Poor August is so out of place, not knowing anything about the experience. Although he is glad to be on television so he can boast about it with his friends.

Ben stays in Colorado with the children, while Jenny travels to California for the never-ending meetings with the writers and producers. At first, she is flying out once a week for a few days at a time. As time goes by, she is there all week, only coming home for the weekends.

Jenny is the technical advisor and makes sure she is in the studio when they are shooting most of the scenes. She wants the director to keep with the essence of the story she wrote and not do a typical Hollywood boondoggle.

One of the constant arguments she has with the director and the producers is that there is no need to change the story since the book was a huge bestseller. If they make the movie based strictly on the book, it might also be well received by the public. The director, however, has made several blockbuster movies and is always trying to change things, blowing everything out of proportion. Jenny is there to make sure it doesn't happen with this movie.

* * *

Ben flies the family out for another weekend in Hollywood to see it all firsthand. He is curious to see how they are doing the beach scenes in a studio. Luckily, they are shooting scenes of their final year on the island, where August is now part of the movie. The last thing Ben wants is to visit the studio, and the girls are the only ones in the scene.

August is now at the age where he wants equal time like his sisters. That's all he has been talking about for days is seeing his role in the movie. Unfortunately, he has this idea that someone his own age will play his part. He is going to be mad when he finds out that it's an eighteen-month-old baby.

* * *

They arrive with Jenny at the studio early in the morning, and security promptly escorts them directly to the soundstage. The security is tight. Jenny makes sure that the press does not know her family is at the studio.

When they walk onto the huge soundstage, everyone is so shocked to see the set for the first time. They re-created their old campsite, with all the sand, campfire, and tent surrounded by tall palm trees. The crew is still setting up lights, giving them time to have a good look around. They all stand in the middle of the campsite, so astonished at how realistic everything is.

"Jesus!" Ben blurted out. "This looks so real. It's almost like we're there!"

"This is the best as I can remember," Jenny explained. "Can you think of anything I left out?"

"The sounds of the ocean, and maybe the heat and humidity!" he jokingly said, looking around the set.

"Oh, they didn't leave that out. Wait until they turn on all the lights. It gets so hot in here, and will be far worse than what we had back on the island. It does feel like home in some ways, doesn't it?" she asked, glancing at the wooden hut.

Ben walks over, looking in the hut. "Did we really live like this! How did we put up with all this sand?" kicking it about with his feet.

"I know! The more I think about it, I just shudder at the idea of having all this sand everywhere. And the hut is the worst. The floor is covered with it as well. Just think, you helped deliver our three babies in this small shack!"

April looks down at the fake fireplace and starts crying.

"What's wrong?" Jenny asked.

"Mom, was it really like this? I'd always thought it was more like Gilligan's Island, but not like this. It's so sad."

"I'm afraid this is the way it was," Jenny explained, trying to comfort her. "We lived a primitive life back then. It was even worse at first. All we had was the tent. It didn't matter to us. We had some of the best times of our lives out there. I still loved to go back to watch the sunset. Then there was the fun day out on the beach with a big bonfire cooking up lobsters!" remembering those good old days.

"Don't forget all the fresh fish we had!" Ben added.

"I liked fun day the most and all the stories Dad used to tell. They always started with 'One time!'" June said, then started laughing, remembering his old stories.

"You didn't complain back then. You always liked those old stories," he said, prompting more giggles from the girls.

The girls remember those stories their father used to tell. That was their only entertainment when they were young. Now, they are always watching television, or at school, or out playing with their friends.

Jenny comes over, hugging Ben, and both start crying. They miss their old home and the carefree lifestyle of living in paradise. They have so many fond memories of their times on the island.

August doesn't say a word. He can't relate to any of this. He is more interested in kicking the sand. Seeing the fake campfire, he can't leave it alone. Like in the old days, he is always drawn to a fire, ready to toss something in to watch it burn.

June looks around. "Is this right? It's kind of small."

"Yeah, it's all too small," April said. "I thought it was all bigger than this. Even the tent is so tiny. Did we really sleep in this?" examining the small tent.

"Oh, yes!" Jenny said, wiping the tears from her eyes. "Not only did we sleep in it, but we also lived in it too. Just think, there were times when all of us were stuck in it for days when it rained. You know, that's the same tent we used to have. They still sell the same model after all those years."

"I like the ones we got now," April said. "At least it's bigger, and we can stand up in it. Ours got windows, too."

"OK, I'm sorry I didn't bring my other one," Ben said, just shaking his head. "Your mother never lets me forget that," remembering how close he came to packing his bigger tent all those years ago.

* * *

The crew is scurrying about working on the set. The director walks in and introduces himself. Ben is so surprised to see how young he is. He expected someone in his sixties, not this guy, who looks about thirty years old.

They are getting ready to shoot the scene around the campfire. With all the people running about and yelling out to each other, it's absolute chaos. The director asks Jenny and Ben to sit behind the camera while they set things up. Jenny is quietly explaining everything to the children. They are all so excited, getting to see it all firsthand. Ben is so shocked to see how many people it takes to do this one simple scene.

There is so much that needs to be done. The director is frantically trying to get everything set up for the shot. It's a big mess with all the lights, sound, and camera angles. At times, more people are standing around, and just a few are actually doing something. All this is just for one simple scene, and this is probably only going to be a few seconds in the movie.

* * *

Word gets out that Ben, and the children are at the studio. It is the first time any of the production crew and even the cast have had the opportunity to meet the elusive Ben Hughes and the children. Everyone is running out to meet them, all wanting autographs.

Ben finally meets the young man who is playing his part. Rich Bentley is one of those Hollywood hunks that all the women drool over. Ben can't help from laughing, seeing him in person for the first time. This guy doesn't look anything like him at all. Rich Bentley looks more like one of those male models in all those underwear advertisements.

"Wow, he's really a cutie!" the twins whispered to their mother, then started giggling.

"OK, girls! None of that. Remember to behave yourselves," Jenny promptly said, seeing how they were getting in their giggling mood.

"Oh, Ben... This is the famous Rich Bentley. It's almost like looking into a mirror, isn't it?" Jenny said, joking with him.

Ben holds out his hand. "Nice to see they are keeping this as accurate as possible," trying so hard not to laugh.

"Hey, dude!" Rich said, shaking his hand. "Nice to meet you! Yeah, looks like a real beach out here," not catching on to Ben's little joke.

Rich rambles on, talking the Hollywood jive. For Ben, it's almost like this guy is speaking a foreign language. Ben politely nods his head, pretending to understand. Right away, he knows this guy wouldn't last a day out in the wilderness. Ben is a little concerned about how this is going to work out. This Hollywood hunk is not that bright, but he'll probably bring in droves of young girls to see the movie.

After only a few minutes talking with this actor, Ben is getting a bad feeling. He doesn't want to be portrayed looking like some sort of doofus on the big screen. This guy has the looks, and that's probably the only reason that he got the part. Never having seen any of Rich Bentley's movies, Ben hopes Jenny and the producers made the right decision selecting this guy.

Ben gets a break when a beautiful woman walks in, interrupting them. Everyone comes to a complete stop, and there's dead silence in the studio. Being so tall and absolutely stunning, she is the type of woman who gets everyone's attention.

Aliceson Madeline is playing the role of Jenny. Seeing this woman close-up, Ben knows why Jenny is so excited about her being in the movie. Aliceson is going to be a big hit with all the men, and especially with the teenagers.

Aliceson was not even in the top ten to play the part of Jenny. Of all the actresses that wanted the role, none was willing to bare it all. Aliceson is a model, so nudity is nothing new to her. They offered her the part, to Jenny's delight. She has only done minor parts in numerous movies, so this will be her big break in Hollywood as a leading actor.

Jenny takes her hand, then walks her over to Ben. "Aliceson, I would like you to meet my husband."

"Oh, hi! It's nice to meet you," Ben uttered, so amazed at seeing this woman close-up.

"It's a pleasure to meet you, too," she replied. "I have heard so much about you. My God, you're still a hunk!" feeling his biceps.

"Yeah, I still work out a little," he mentioned, a little embarrassed with her feeling his arms.

Jenny laughs out loud. "You should have seen what he was like back then. His arms were twice the size he is now," hugging Ben.

"Check these out!" Rich boasted, flexing his arms, trying to get attention.

Ben rolls his eyes, seeing this guy showing off. "This is not an underwear advertisement," he jokingly said, seeing how this guy was posing.

Jenny takes Ben's hand, pulling him away. "Just leave him alone... He's very temperamental. If he gets upset, he'll run back to his trailer to sulk."

"You got to be kidding? What a wimp. Look at how he is standing there. It's embarrassing."

"You haven't seen anything yet. Some of these people just drive me nuts," she whispered, shaking her head. "It's best to be polite, but mostly, don't make any comments. I just let the director handle them. They are so used to being pampered and put up on a pedestal."

"So, what are they going to do when they're on location?" Ben sarcastically asked. "If they're out doing what we did, they wouldn't last a day, especially pretty boy over there," glancing over at Rich.

She laughed. "Oh, it'll be nothing but constant complaints. Just think, they are getting paid millions to do this."

"It's a shame they couldn't shoot all of this on the island. I would pay a million dollars just to go back for one day."

She puts her arm around his waist. "I know... This is as close as we're going to get to going home, so you better enjoy it!" kissing his cheek.

A loud bell sounds, putting an end to the social gathering and time to shoot the scene. Ben and the children have to stay behind the cameras to watch the short scene around the campfire.

Two little girls, playing April and June, walk in wearing what looks like rags. Standing behind the cameras are several babies playing August, all waiting for their turn, being held by their mothers. The sad part of it all, whenever one of the babies starts crying, the next one in line quickly replaces him. They all look alike, so it'll be difficult for anyone to know that August is being played by at least a dozen babies.

Ben is immediately struck by the clothing the little girls are wearing. Jenny kept it accurate, using their original dresses as a guide for their wardrobe. When Aliceson removes her robe, she is wearing a short little white sheet tied about her waist. That brings back fond memories for Ben, seeing how revealing it is.

The constant rehearsals are taking forever. Once they start filming, it's not any better. The little girls playing April and June are always messing up their lines. They keep re-shooting the same scene over and over. To make matters worse, when they get it right, the baby cries or crawls away, forcing them to start all over again.

After thirty-two takes, it's finally over. They got the shot they wanted. Ben is utterly bored, seeing the thirty-second conversation of their lives played out over and over for hours. The children are sound asleep, so bored sitting around with nothing to do. The movie industry is not glamorous at all but is mostly repetitious and extremely boring.

* * *

They return to the hotel for a break. Jenny has another talk show interview to do later that afternoon to help promote the movie. Since the children are here, they are going to join her for this one. Ben has never done any interviews and will not start now. With his dislike for reporters and interviews, she doesn't ask him anymore and knows not to push it.

After a brief rest and a quick meal, it's back to the studio for the talk show. The children are so excited to be doing a late-night talk show with an audience. All their friends at home are going to be watching. Even their school is making a big deal out of it. When they return home, the school will show the interview on a big projection television for all the students.

Walking into the studio, they are quickly escorted in to meet with the producers and the host. People are frantically talking on the radios to the control room when the Hughes family arrives. Their eyes light up when they see Ben. He has never done any interviews or even talked to any of the news media. With the entire family here, the producers think they have an exclusive.

Unfortunately, the producers and the host are in for a big disappointment. Ben will not be on camera, and he will also not be doing any interviews with anyone. He can still be very intimidating and doesn't take any crap from these Hollywood types. The interviews are for Jenny and the children, and that's the end of the discussion.

Ben sits in the green room while his family is getting ready for the big interview. Monitors on the wall display everything that's going on in the studio. He can even watch them getting fixed up in the makeup room. He feels so proud of the children who are brave enough to take part in these interviews. Jenny, however, is always nervous when she is about to do an interview.

Once the show is about to start, everyone is in the green room waiting for their turn. Jenny goes over her notes while Ben makes sure the children don't touch their faces, messing up their makeup. August is not too pleased to have makeup on. He doesn't want to look like a sissy in front of all his friends.

One of the crew comes in to escort Jenny and the children out to the stage. Ben is alone with the other guests. A young actress is here promoting her latest movie. He has no clue who she is. The entire time, she talks on her cell phone to her agent and constantly complains. Four strangely dressed guys in some band are here to play their latest hit at the end of the show. He doesn't know who they are, either. They don't say a word, staring at the young actress, drooling over her.

* * *

The big moment is finally here. Ben is so proud to see his family walking across the stage up on the monitor. They sit together on the couch. Each one gets to say a few words and say 'Hi' to all their friends at home and to their granny and granddad. They talk about their trip to the studio where the big movie is being made. August is getting a big thrill out of this. He is now old enough to handle a few questions on his own.

The interview is only ten minutes, and then it's over. They all rush back to the green room to tell their father all about it. They replay the entire interview, telling him what they were asked and what they said. Ben plays it up, making them out to be big celebrities, getting them to sign their autographs in his checkbook.

While the young actress is on stage plugging her new movie, the musicians are out getting ready to play their latest big hit. April and June want so much to see them, so Ben decides to stay for the end of the show.

They wait in the green room, watching the young actress promote her new upcoming movie on the monitors. Being only nineteen, she sounds more like a twelve-year-old, looks very immature, and it's embarrassing to watch. The worst part is knowing that she is making millions in these movies, with two more already in the works.

When it's time for the band to play, one of the crew walks in to escort Ben and his family to the far side of the stage. After waiting for the never-ending breaks and more endless chitchat from the host, the band is finally up next.

Jenny and Ben still have no clue who these musicians are. They know this is a big event, seeing all the stage crew standing around excited to see the band as well. The audience is going crazy. All the girls in the audience are jumping up and down, screaming out loud.

April and June are excited to be right up next to the stage to see the band live. With their cameras out, they are taking endless photos of these four strange-looking guys. They are growing up fast, getting into all the latest crazes, and picking up a lot from the other girls at their school.

Once the band starts playing, it is absolute chaos. The audience is screaming out loud, jumping up and down. April, June, and even August are out on the stage dancing. Never having seen a live band before, it's a big treat for them.

With all the commotion going on, no one notices the children are dancing in front of the band. Jenny sees that the twins are getting plenty of attention on the monitor. The cameras focus on April and June dancing as the band plays. From the expressions on a couple of the band members' faces, it's easy to see they are not too pleased to be up-staged by these little kids.

Ben sees himself on one of the monitors. Now, he knows why everyone was so glad to hear that they wanted to be on the stage to see the band. The studio had one camera ready to get a shot of the elusive Ben Hughes. They make sure the camera is at a distance from him, knowing how intimidating he is.

All Ben can do is smile, wishing it will be over soon. At least he knows the girls, and August is a more tempting target, getting more airtime.

After the show is over, Ben is already tired of the total mayhem and the chaos of Hollywood. He is ready to return to their quiet, blissful home in the mountains with all the clean air and open space. The first thing he wants to do is go out fishing when he gets back home.

Jenny is used to the chaos with all her travels around the country. She knows Ben and the children can't handle life in the big city at all. After just a few days, it's always too much for them. The trip to California makes them appreciate their home up in the mountains and their love of the simple life, and they can't wait to get back home.

* * *

Chapter 65

The Big Premiere

After eighteen months, the movie is now finished. Now, all they have to do is wait for the big premiere. The studio is going all out with a massive advertising campaign. Not a day goes by without seeing it on television, in newspapers, and in all the magazines.

April, June, and August are now celebrities at school, always being in the news. At first, none of the other kids understood why these three were so famous. After seeing the promos for the movie on television, now everyone knows.

The premiere will be their last promotion of the book and the film. With all the advertising for the movie, the book is back on the top ten bestseller list again. Jenny is getting tired of being asked the same old questions. She is ready to move on and promote her new novel.

The movie premiere means another family trip out to Hollywood. Ben is getting tired of all the attention. With the children getting older, he wants them to lead normal lives. Even Jenny knows it's getting out of control, and she will not go through this again. Making movies is way too much work, and she doesn't like being away from her family. She is content with writing novels from here on out, and there will not be any more movie deals.

* * *

The day finally arrives for the big event. The studio is going all out, making a big production of it. A huge stretch limo arrives at the house to take them directly to the airport, and then a private jet to California. It's a level of extravagance Jenny and Ben have never seen before.

The big premiere of the movie 'Lost Paradise' is at the old Chinese Mann Theater. A long line of stretch limos is waiting to unload their passengers on queue for the media. It's going to be a long wait with all the cast and other celebrities ahead of them.

Once they arrive at the theater, it's a media circus. Their limousine finally pulls up at the famous Chinese Mann Theater. The news media goes into a frenzy, surrounding the limo with cameras flashing. The big moment has arrived. Everyone has been practicing at home to get this right, all under the supervision of a studio representative.

"Well, this is it!" Jenny shouted, trying to be heard over all the noise. "Ben, you can do it… All we have to do now is get out of the limo, and it's just a short walk. Then it's all over, and we're done with it."

Ben lets out a long sigh. "I didn't think there would be this many," seeing the huge crowd, not wanting to get out of the limo.

"Look at all the cameras!" April shouted, knowing her father's dislike of the news media.

Jenny gives Ben a stern look. "Remember, you only have to talk with one person out there. You don't have to say much. You promised!"

"I know," Ben reluctantly said, knowing Blenda Jones would be out there waiting for an interview.

"It'll be fun, Dad!" August added. "Just smile and wave to all the people!"

"You'll do just fine… Remember how we're supposed to do this. Ben, lead the way!" Jenny said, motioning him to get out first.

One by one, they exit the limousine. Even getting out has to be done in a certain way. Ben has to be first, then help Jenny out, holding her hand. Finally, April, June, and August step out of the limousine, smiling and waving at the cameras.

Ben, dressed in a black tuxedo, has to put on a smile for the cameras. Jenny is in her glory, posing for the cameras. She is wearing a long, elegant black dress made especially for her by one of the top designers. Even the twins have matching outfits, while August has his little black tuxedo matching his father's.

With the enormous crowd yelling and screaming, it's total chaos. Ben picks up August, seeing he is getting scared by the noise and the people shouting. They keep together, slowly walking down the red carpet, waving at all the fans. Media organizers escort them along the red carpet, always surrounded by security.

Jenny is used to being in front of the media, but this is more than she expected. "Everyone, keep together!"

Ben dreads this and has avoided it for years, but now he is stuck with no way out. He makes sure to stand behind everyone else, waving at all the fans while ignoring the reporters. Whenever one yells out a question, he pretends not to hear, which is easy to do with all the noise.

The Hughes family is quickly being ushered over to Blenda Jones. She is already informing her fans of the arrival of Ben and Jenny Hughes. She interviewed Jenny several times before, but this will be the first time anyone has had the entire family together. It's going to be an exclusive. Even Ben knows it's probably a deal they have made. Nothing goes on in Hollywood by accident.

Ben knows he is now trapped, seeing how the media and security surround them. He is a hard catch, and the reporters will not let him slip away. While Jenny talks to Blenda on the live broadcast, Ben just takes it in stride, hiding behind Jenny while holding on to August. At least he knows that once the girls start talking, he is safe for a while. These interviews don't intimidate the girls, and they love to talk.

Ben is not even paying attention, looking around at all the other big celebrities. Then he notices a microphone being pushed up to his face. He turns to see Jenny and Blenda just staring at him.

Jenny can see Ben is not paying attention, tuning out everyone. Ben has no idea that Blenda has been asking him questions and is waiting for him to reply.

Again, Blenda has to repeat her long, drawn-out question, getting a little frustrated since this is a live broadcast. Ben had heard these questions so many times before when Jenny had been on various talk shows. After the long question, she shoves the microphone up to his face again, waiting in anticipation for his first interview ever.

"We're all glad to be here," Ben replied after a long pause. "We can't wait to see it on the big screen."

She keeps the microphone up, waiting for more, but Ben thinks that's more than enough. The worst nightmare for any live broadcast is a person who doesn't want to talk. Blenda is asking more questions, but Ben has had enough. Luckily, August yells 'Hi' to all his friends back home, waving frantically to the cameras. That takes the attention off Ben.

Seeing some of the other celebrities, Ben turns his back to Blenda, pointing them out to August. Jenny can see it's not going well and quickly starts talking about the twins. That's all it takes to get the attention off of Ben with all these reporters.

Walking down the red carpet, Ben is lucky enough to avoid any more interviews. He makes sure to keep a few steps behind Jenny and the girls. He can't see the point in answering the same questions over and over. After answering his one question, he thinks that's more than enough. He is having more fun waving at the screaming crowds. August is doing the same, having a good time waving at everyone.

* * *

Since it's getting late, they are quickly ushered into the theater. They sit in the back with the rest of the cast, producers, and the director. Jenny is so nervous and hopes everyone will enjoy it. So much has been left out of the film. The final cut is two hours and fifteen minutes, and is far more than she expected.

With much fanfare, the theater lights slowly dimmed. The first thing on the screen is the dedication to the people who lost their lives on that fateful day. Seeing all the photos and their names, Ben recalls all the fond memories of the friends they made while in Hawaii. That is the one thing he insisted they put in the movie. They were so lucky to have survived it all and to live a great life. For the rest of the people on the flight, it was the last day of their lives. He wants them all to be remembered and had the film dedicated to them.

The movie of their lives is played out on the big screen. Luckily, it was an astounding success, just like the book. Jenny and Ben can't be more pleased with the outcome, but they know it's time to move on. Their story is now part of history.

They promptly return home with no fanfare. Back to a normal life and lost in the obscurity of the Colorado Mountains. Jenny wants more than ever to move on to new projects and promote her latest novels. Ben loves the simple life and wants to stay home so he can take care of his family.

* * *

Chapter 66

Growing Up

E ventually, April, June, and August are old enough to understand the story of their lives on the island. What memories they had were always of the good times playing on the beach or going out fishing. After reading their mother's book and seeing the movie, they are so amazed at what they went through and realize how lucky they are to be alive.

Jenny, being an avid writer, published many novels, including numerous children's books. She has become an international bestselling author. Her inspiration came from her children's love of life and the many adventures of living in the mountains. She travels throughout the world, either on interviews or book signing tours.

Ben and his best friend Kyle go into business together, taking people out on exclusive camping and fishing tours. It's the first real job he has had since leaving Denver many years ago. To him, it's not a job but an excuse to take people out for a good time and do a lot of fishing and camping.

April and June blend in well at school but are always in trouble. Their ability to secretly communicate with each other is causing issues for the teachers. Every time they take a test, both end up with the same answers. The teachers initially thought they were copying from each other. Even when the teacher separates them to opposite ends of the classroom, that doesn't stop them. Their subtle hand signals and gestures are enough to share information across the classroom.

Being identical twins, April and June find it so easy to change places. The only difference between the two is that June is a little slow in math. They secretly swapped classrooms, and April always did the math tests for her sister.

They learn never to wear the same outfit to school. When they swap clothes, even their friends can't tell them apart. No one ever caught on, and it's like a big game to them. Unless it's something about cooking or venturing out into the mountains, they are not interested in anything else. As long as there are no math questions, no one is to the wiser.

* * *

As the years go by, one of Ben's worst fears comes true. The twins are getting interested in boys. They have grown up into beautiful young ladies. Many of the boys at their school long to date the Hughes twins, but they are so intimidated by them. Everyone in the school knows their reputation for being Amazon warriors, but they have also excelled in self-defense with black belts in karate.

To make matters worse, any boy who has the nerve to ask April or June out on a date has to face their father. Everyone knows Ben's reputation, and the rules are clear. If a boy wants to take one of the girls out on a date, he must first meet their infamous father. The girls don't mind since they know anyone who will go through all that must really be interested.

Ben makes all the prospective boyfriends go through this little ritual. At times, he plays it up, being extremely intimidating. The poor boys are terrified, shaking in their shoes. He makes sure to let them know they will have to face him if they get out of hand with his girls. He never worries about it since he knows the twins can defend themselves exceptionally well with their karate and all the other things he taught them over the years.

Anyone who goes on a date with April or June is respected at school. Not that he dated one of the beautiful blonde twins, but he mostly survived to tell about it, especially after having to endure the excruciating meeting with their father. Several never got past Ben and ran off home, terrified of the overprotective father.

August has a bigger problem when it comes to girls. He doesn't have his father to deal with, but has his two sisters always looking after him. They are even more discriminating than their father. Any girl their little brother wanted to go out with had to meet their approval and standards.

April and June can always tell when some girl is interested in their little brother. These little girls constantly follow them around, being overly friendly, hoping to get approval from his older sisters.

August has many friends and is always over at the house after school and on the weekends. Apparently, none of them eats at home and show up hungry all the time. April and June love having a hungry crowd to cook for, constantly testing some new dishes. One of the rules for eating at the house is there will be a big discussion about what was good or bad about the meal. After cooking for so many years, the twins always won them over.

All of August's friends have big crushes on his older sisters. He knows how to get back at his sisters by having all his friends over for the night. April and June dread it the most, having a house full of horny little teenagers lusting after them. No matter where the twins go, August's friends are constantly following them around and staring at them.

* * *

Eventually, one by one, the children leave for college. Soon after, they get married and have children of their own. April and June are never far apart from each other. They take after their mother's side of the family, owning a restaurant in Denver.

August surprises everyone by going to medical school. Jenny is ecstatic about having a doctor in the family. August is not the outdoor type and cannot cook anything even if his life depends on it. He ends up being so different from everyone else in the family. He doesn't have the survival instinct and grows up normal.

Jenny and Ben continue to live a simple life in their ranch house up in the mountains. The house is the central focus and meeting place for the family. On every holiday, the entire family is at the house for a big feast. Distant relatives are always spending the week at the house, enjoying the mountain life. Whether it's winter or summer, the house is always busy and filled with people.

Ben always has Yellow Dog to keep him company over the years after the children left the house. Every day, they go for their five o'clock walk out on the trails through the mountains. At times, Ben lets Yellow Dog lead the way. He follows along for a change of pace, always interested to see what path the old dog takes through the dense forest. When the path splits into two separate trails, Yellow Dog pauses for a few seconds to look each one over. For whatever reason, she selects one over the other. It's a big mystery to Ben why she decides which path to take, but it always makes for a challenging hike for the two of them.

Yellow Dog is a faithful companion but is stuck in her old habits. Although it has been years since the children left home, the old dog still sits out at the end of the driveway, waiting for the school bus. She has been doing this since she was a puppy. The bus driver honks the horn every time he drives by the house. The children on the bus always wave and yell out to her. When the school bus drives by without stopping, sadly, Yellow Dog walks back to the house, lies on the front porch. After so many years, she just doesn't understand why her best friends, April, June, and August, don't get off the bus as they did so many times before.

Everyone who grew up in the area knows about Yellow Dog. Many of the children who rode the school bus have seen the old dog sitting out by the road every day coming back from school. Now, years later, driving their own cars, they always honk their horns and wave when they see Yellow Dog waiting for the school bus. She always barks, wagging her tail every time.

Yellow Dog becomes even more famous when someone takes her photo while she waits by the road. With Ben's permission, they publish it for a poster using the caption 'Faithfulness' on it. Copies of the poster are placed at the main entrances of the elementary, middle, and high schools. One copy is put at the City Hall. Yellow Dog ends up being the official mascot of the small mountain community.

* * *

After eighteen good years, Yellow Dog finally passes away. She is the first loss in the family, and Ben is hurting the most. She was his closest companion after the children left home. They were always together, either hiking the trails or camping and fishing. She was very much a part of the family. Now that the children are older and have lives of their own, and with Jenny always traveling, Ben is all alone for the first time.

They bury Yellow Dog under the huge shade tree, where she always took her naps. They have a funeral, and everyone in the family attends, including several close friends. For eighteen years, Yellow Dog brought love to this family, and she is dearly missed.

Ben is so lost without his faithful dog. Jenny cancels most of her interviews to stay at the house for a while. She can see Ben is not himself. He spends hours just sitting on the back porch staring at the small headstone of his old friend. He doesn't go on any more walks and has been lying around the house for weeks.

Kyle knows that no one living up in the mountains should be without man's best friend. He tries to persuade Ben to get another dog, but Ben is not interested. There can never be a replacement for Yellow Dog. He thinks it just wouldn't be right to bring in another pet.

* * *

After several months, Kyle surprises Ben one day. He brings over a little brown Labrador puppy. He knows that once Ben sees the little puppy, he won't be able to say no. She is the friendliest little dog, always looking for attention. Kyle is right all along. Ben can't say no and promptly gives her the name Brownie.

Ben starts training Brownie to walk with him on his daily hikes on the trails. The first thing he does before his walk is to go over to Yellow Dog's grave. That always brings a tear to his eyes. Standing next to the small grave, he looks down at the headstone bearing her name, remembering all the fond days they had together. He always talks to his faithful old dog as if she is still alive. He tells Brownie all about his old companion and all the good times they had together.

Ben always carries Brownie's leash with him. Luckily, he has never had to use it. Just like Yellow Dog, Brownie walks right next to him and never wanders off. One of his biggest fears is that she would see a deer or a rabbit and chase after it, getting lost in the dense forest.

After a while, the little dog knows it's time for their walk, seeing Ben carrying her leash. One day, Ben leaves the leash behind, knowing Brownie doesn't need it. He is so amazed to see the little dog running back to the porch, picking up the leash and carrying it in her mouth. She doesn't want to leave without her leash, dragging it along as they go on their walk.

From that day on, the little dog always picks up her leash when it's time for a walk, dragging it around in her mouth. No matter how many times he tries to take it away and carry it for her, she always barks until he gives it back. That is a big mystery. For some reason, she doesn't think it's a proper walk unless she gets to carry her own leash.

* * *

Chapter 67

Farewell

As the years pass, the Hughes family grows with more and more children. With all the grandchildren and eventually great-grandchildren, the old house is always crowded, to Jenny and Ben's delight. It's like starting all over again with all the little children running about and babies crawling around. All the children love staying at the house with acres of land to run about and play.

During the summer, Ben sets up the tents so all the children can camp outside in the backyard. At night, he lights a big campfire and tells tall stories. Most of the stories are always about the good old days on the island. The stories are getting better and better over time. Wrestling with sharks or a giant octopus still has the grandkids on edge.

Jenny also spoils them, always showering them with gifts. She lets them have a sneak peek of one of her new children's books. At times, she gets them to help with the story or even includes them as one of the characters. The grandchildren always get the first ones off the press. Each book is personally signed and dated. When the Hughes children show up at school with one of Jenny's books months before anyone else can buy one, it's always a big hit with show-and-tell.

There is always a big party at the Hughes' house every weekend or when school is out. Many people often mistake the house for a daycare center, with so many children running around. With all the swing sets and wooden forts Ben has built, it's the envy of all the local children.

* * *

Time takes its toll, and Jenny's health is failing. Traveling across the country to promote her latest novel is getting too much for her. After recovering from a mild heart attack, she stays at the house, very adamant about finishing her new book.

With Thanksgiving just days away, she is so frustrated not being able to help with the cooking. April and June are there to ensure their mother rests and to handle the big family feast.

As usual, Thanksgiving is another big family affair. The house is full of children constantly running around. Ben is in his glory, taking them all on daily hikes up on the snow-filled trails. He always makes sure that the children have fun.

The house is like a big summer camp with various activities going on every day. Ben teaches them how to make things out of wood or survive out in the wilderness. The secret hand signs and birdcalls are always a favorite. The tall Texan tales are getting bigger than ever. Wrestling with a bear he met on one of his many hikes and seeing Sasquatch is always a good one.

* * *

After the long Thanksgiving weekend, Jenny and Ben have the house to themselves again. As usual, August is the last to leave, checking on his mother to make sure she is OK. Jenny is on the back porch in her favorite rocking chair with her thick blanket to keep her warm. Thanksgiving is over, and now she is looking forward to the Christmas holidays.

Once everyone has gone home, Ben gets ready for his daily walk. "I'm going to take Brownie out. Are you sure you're going to be OK on your own for a while?" he asked Jenny.

Jenny smiles. "Oh, I'll be fine... With all the commotion going on in the last couple of days, I could use the peace and quiet. I need to get this finished by Christmas. They keep asking me if I'm going to make the deadline," glancing down at her latest handwritten novel.

"Let them wait," Ben said, getting annoyed with her publishers. "Take your time and finish it when you're ready!"

She let out a long sigh. "It'll just take me a week or two. Then I can relax for a little while. We need to get ready for Christmas. Time really flies. All the kids will be on their Christmas break, wanting to stay here."

"We just got them all out of the house, and you're already planning the next visit. Yeah, they are already talking about spending the week here for Christmas. I need to fix up the place and get everything ready for that. I'm going to make sure the girls help out with the cooking as well. It's getting too much to feed them all nowadays."

She laughed. "You're telling me... It takes three big turkeys to feed them all! It was a good Thanksgiving. Those girls of ours sure know how to cook for a crowd. Everything worked out fine, didn't it?"

"Oh yeah, everything was cooked to perfection. I think it's more of a challenge with our family than what they get at the restaurant."

"With all the kids running around and trying to cook, I'd say it was!"

"They're all getting to be like little food critics. It seems like we can never have a meal without everyone over-analyzing how it was prepared and the presentation. They'll all probably take after you and the girls and become chefs from the sounds of things."

She laughs again. "Some are already helping out at the restaurant now. In a few years, we might have a few more restaurants in the works. The girls are going to make sure it's a family business like we used to have," remembering the old days of helping her parents with their restaurant.

With Brownie ready to go, Ben leans over, kissing Jenny on her cheek. "Love you... We'll be back shortly."

"I love you too!" sitting back, watching her husband walk away.

Ben turns and gives one last wave to Jenny before stopping by Yellow Dog's grave, as he has done so many times before. He stands with Brownie for a few minutes, paying respects to his old friend. He still talks to Yellow Dog, telling her all about the big Thanksgiving dinner they just had.

Ben starts to shiver, feeling the temperature drop as a breeze comes down off the mountains. A sliver of sunlight breaks through the base of the dark gray clouds. Ben closes his eyes, tilting his head back, feeling the warmth on his face, basking in the sunlight. He slowly turns to see the spectacular view. The narrow sunbeam drops out of the clouds and illuminates the house, while the surrounding area is dark and gray.

As the sunbeam fades away, a horrible pain jolts him, ripping through his body. He does not know what it is, putting his hand up to his chest. The air is so cold, as if the temperature suddenly dropped 20 degrees. A moment goes by, and all the pain is gone. He feels a tingling sensation, like being in an electric field. His body feels warm all over. Then, he feels a sense of absolute serenity.

Brownie whimpers, starting to act strange. Ben almost stumbles, trying to comprehend the experience. In an instant, he fully understands. Slowly, he turns to look back at the house, seeing Jenny's head lower as if she had fallen asleep. Her arm slowly drops to her side, and the writing pen rolls across the wooden patio.

Right away, he knows. "Oh God, no! Jenny! Jenny!" running over to her as fast as he could.

As soon as he reaches her, he knows it's too late. Her lifeless body slumps in the chair as if she has fallen asleep. He put his arms around her, holding her as he wept uncontrollably. He frantically calls August on the phone. Luckily, he had just left, and within minutes, he was back at the house.

As a doctor, August is used to these situations, but he is unprepared for this one. Seeing his mother looking as if she is asleep is too much for him to bear. He gently puts his hand on her neck, checking for a pulse. He turns to his father, then simply shakes his head and starts to cry. Neither one of them said a word. There is no need for words. They both know she is gone.

"Oh, Jenny," Ben cried out, taking her hand, holding it tight. "I love you so much... I'm sorry I wasn't with you to say goodbye," as the tears flow from his eyes.

August takes her writing pad from her lap, glancing down at what she had written. His eyes open wide as he reads his mother's last words.

"Dad, she wrote this before she passed away," he said, holding it up to his father.

Ben takes the tablet, seeing she had been writing a message right till the end. He can't believe his eyes as he reads the note.

'To my love. My time has come. I watch you and Brownie go for your afternoon walk. I know I couldn't have asked for a better life than the one I shared with you. Tell the children I love them all and for them not to be sad. I have been blessed with such a wonderful life. I love you so much. We will always be together. We will never be apart. Walk the beach. Watch the sunsets, our island home.'

The last words she wrote are almost illegible, but he knows what she was trying to tell him. He stares at her last words, taking her hand again, struggling with his emotions.

"Jenny, I love you too. I always have from the first time we met. We will always be together. We'll walk the beach again," not wanting to let her go.

* * *

Word of Jenny's death hit the news media throughout the world. Jenny wrote over thirty novels, with twelve being bestsellers in seventy countries. She wrote over fifty children's books as well. She is going to be missed, especially by all the people who love reading her many novels.

Jenny's funeral service is at the house. Only close friends and family attend. Many of her fans want to be there, but Ben doesn't want this to be a public affair. He bans all news media from the service, refusing to do any interviews.

The news media arrive from all parts of the world to the small mountain town, but the police keep them miles away from the house. Even local helicopter services refuse to take camera crews near the Hughes' home in respect for Jenny. The police close the road that leads to the house to anyone who doesn't live in the area.

* * *

Ben lost interest in everything, spending most of his time in his reading room gazing at the old photos of Jenny over the years. His favorites are from that first roll of film he took while on the beach in Hawaii the day before they left for Kwajalein. Little did Ben know back then that it would be the first day of their wonderful life together. Now, he is alone after all those years and is lost without her.

Jenny's urn is placed on the mantel above the fireplace in the bedroom. Behind the urn is one of his favorite photographs he took of her several years ago. Lying in bed, he just stares up at the image of his loving wife, unable to sleep.

Ben's reading room is also referred to as the island room, where all their mementos and photos are on display. He spends all his time reading Jenny's book, reliving their lives back on the island, or he just sits and watches the movie. He fondly remembers those years and all the adventures they had together.

His one regret in life is not being able to go back to visit their island. He wanted so much to return with Jenny just for one more walk on the beach and to watch the sunset. Now, it's too late, and the trip would be too much for him anyway since he is getting old and frail. With Jenny gone, there is no point anymore.

Friends and family are always there to help cheer him up, but it doesn't help. Even with all his children, grandchildren, and great-grandchildren, Ben has lost the will to live. Slowly but surely, his health is starting to decline.

He just sits in his reading room, surrounded by all the photos of Jenny, talking to her as if she is still alive. Everyone in the family is getting concerned about his health. The tall, strong wilderness father they love so much is now very weak and frail.

August, a prominent doctor in Colorado Springs, tends to his father's ailments. He knows it's only a matter of time. His father's mental health is getting worse. On his daily visits, his father is always asking where Jenny is, not remembering she had passed away. Every day, Ben sets her place at the dinner table and cooks for two people. He always walks around talking to her as if she is still with him.

* * *

Ben is at his lowest during Christmas. Only a month since Jenny had passed away, he missed her so much. Christmas is not the same without her. Even with all the family staying with him, it doesn't help. Everyone knows it's going to be a sad Christmas without their grandmother.

To make matters worse, their grandfather is not the same. No more campfires and no more walks out on the trails or tall stories. Ben sits in his chair, keeping to himself.

Seeing the one last unopened present left under the Christmas tree makes everyone feel uneasy. That was the last gift that Ben made for Jenny. He has been working on it since the summer. They are all so sad seeing it under the tree, still wrapped up in banana leaves.

When they sit down to eat, Jenny's chair at the end of the table is empty. No one dares to sit in her chair, where a place setting has been set for her. Ben doesn't say a word, just stares at the empty chair, and it makes everyone so uncomfortable.

August stands up to give the toast. After the room is quiet, he thanks everyone for being here. He talks about his mother. How beautiful she was and how much they all miss her. As they all raise their wine glasses to toast their mother, grandmother, and great-grandmother, Ben starts crying uncontrollably.

August helps his father up from the table. For Ben, it's just too sad. He misses Jenny so much and doesn't want to ruin everyone's Christmas, but he can't hold back his emotions anymore. He retires to his bedroom and lies in bed, not wanting to be reminded of the holidays, which makes him miss Jenny even more. Life is not the same without her.

* * *

After a very long winter, the snow finally melts, and the flowers are blooming. The entire family is at the house to be with Ben for Easter. Ben is still under orders from August to keep in bed. He is a little uneasy on his feet. After several bad falls, someone always has to be with him.

Easter was always Jenny's favorite time of the year. Just like on Christmas, they all know Ben will be depressed that she is not there. Everyone is there to help cheer him up.

Ben loves having everyone at the house. The one thing he hates the most is being all alone. With all his great-grandchildren running about screaming, he is in his glory. They all congregate in his bedroom, sitting up on the end of his bed. He tells them endless tall Texan stories, to their delight. He still can create stories off the top of his head, always including their names, making them all part of the story.

Ben loves to read aloud Jenny's book to his great-grandchildren, telling them about their island adventures. Many are too young to fully understand the story and how important it is to the family. Most think it's just another tall tale, not knowing that the two girls and the boy in the story are really their grandmothers and grandfather.

He knows it all by heart, having read it so many times over the years. He always keeps the book on his nightstand. Not a day goes by that he doesn't pick up the book to relive a very wonderful part of his life. Although his memory is fading, he still can remember those days on the island as if it were yesterday.

"Suppertime!" someone yelled out as Ben read to all his grandchildren and great-grandchildren.

"OK, that's enough for now," Ben said, closing the book. "You better run along and get something to eat before it's all gone!"

"Thanks for the story!" they all shouted out, running out of the bedroom.

"Better slow down... Come back after supper, and I'll read you another one," he mentioned, then started chuckling, seeing how everyone acts like they have not eaten in days.

After everyone runs out of the room, the only one left is Mary. She is the youngest of them all, just five years old, and is as cute as a button. With her long blonde hair, she resembles April and June when they were her age. He always gets in trouble, mistakenly getting her name wrong, calling her April or June. With so many great-grandchildren, he still has trouble keeping up with all their names.

Mary loves spending time with her great-grandfather. She intensely listens to all his stories or the many books he reads to her. She laughs when he talks to his invisible friend named Jenny. Mary plays along, thinking it's just another game, and they both sit together for hours talking to their invisible friend.

Sitting next to her great-grandfather, she stares at the picture on the cover of Jenny's book. A silhouette of a couple walking down a palm-covered beach with three children in hand, with the sun setting in the background.

"Is that the people in the story?" Mary asked, pointing to the book cover.

Ben looks down at the cover. "Yes, this is me and your great-grandmother. This is your grandmother June and her sister April. The little one is August, but we used to call him Baby at the time."

"That's cause he's a baby doctor, right?" she shouted, then started laughing.

He laughs as well. "Yep, that's right! Better not say that to his face. He gets mad when people call him Baby!"

Mary giggles, hearing how August used to be called Baby. August went through hell when he was growing up. All the kids teased him about his nickname. Now, at six-foot-tall, not too many people can get away with calling him Baby, except his two older sisters.

"You better get some food," he said. "With all the people here today, you might miss out. They got some good food out there."

"I'm not hungry," she simply replied. "I want you to read me another story!"

"Another one? Which one would you like to hear?"

"I want that island one again!" she said, pointing to the same book he was just reading to her.

"You must like this one... It's my favorite, too!"

"Is this your friend?" Mary asked, pointing to the silhouette of Jenny on the book cover.

"Yes, it is... That's also your great-grandmother. She is the one who wrote this book about our life on the island. She also wrote all those over there," pointing to the bookcase filled with books.

"Wow... She did all those too!"

He tells her all about her great-grandmother and that she is in heaven. He tries to explain it so that she can understand. Thinking about Jenny, he realizes it has only been a few months since she passed away, but it feels more like years.

"That's Granny in there, right?" she asked, pointing to the urn on the mantel above the fireplace.

He looks up at the urn containing Jenny's ashes in front of a big portrait of her. "Yes, that's where we keep her ashes, so she can always be with me. That's her picture up there too," starting to feel tired.

* * *

Everyone gathers in the big dining room for supper. Getting all the children together at the long table is an ordeal. They are all hungry, as usual. This is a family that loves to eat.

August comes walking in. "Just like old times!" seeing all the children at the table eating.

"Hi, Baby!" June said, hugging her brother. "Glad to see you can make it on time for supper," teasing him by calling him his old nickname.

"Hey, June... I see I'm on time for the big feast!"

The entire house lit up as the sun broke through the clouds. "Just my luck," August added. "I have been running around all day long, and now the sun comes out. It looks like spring is almost here," glancing out the windows.

"Oh, finally! I could use some nice warm weather after this long cold spell we've had. I just can't stand this cold anymore," June replied, starting to shiver.

"It's still cold out there, but at least there's a break in the clouds," he added.

"Hi, August!" April said, walking in from the kitchen carrying more food. "Just in time... Better check on Dad and see how he's doing before you get something to eat."

"So, has he been staying in bed?" August asked.

"Yeah, he has been in his room with all the kids, telling them stories. He even made them watch the movie again!"

"He never gets tired of all those old stories," August said, shaking his head. "At least the grandkids will know about the family history and our big adventure."

"You need to remind him to leave out the part about the land sharks and the bogeyman," April said. "The little ones have been wanting to make sticks and go out hunting!"

"He's also been teaching them hand signals," June said. "The little buggers have been doing it all day long, driving us all crazy."

"Dad has been teaching them some new ones, too," April added. "There are a few I haven't seen before."

"He is trying to make them all into little Amazon warriors," August said, shaking his head again. "I'll have another little talk with him. Better check to see if they made any more sharp spears. They probably got them hidden out in the backyard."

June realizes one of the little ones is missing. "Mary! Come in here and sit down at the table. Let your great-granddad get some rest!"

"I'll have my supper with Dad and keep him company," August said. "It'll be a lot quieter in there too. I'll let you guys have all the fun keeping the kids from having a food fight."

June lets out a long sigh. "Thanks a lot!"

The house gets dark as the clouds return. "Well, that was nice while it lasted," August remarked. "Feels like winter is back," noticing how cold it is.

"Yeah, feel that cold air," June replied, moving closer to the fireplace. "You need to see what's up with the heater."

"I don't think it's the heater. It feels like one of the kids left the door open," he added, noticing a blast of cold air running through the house.

Just then, slowly but surely, Mary comes strolling into the living room. She walks up to her grandmother, holding up a small ceramic souvenir to show her. The most prized possession. The little ceramic island that April and June got for their mother while they were on Kwajalein Island.

"Oh, that's pretty," June said, a little startled seeing Mary carrying away one of her father's favorite island mementos. "You better let me have it so you don't break it."

Mary quickly pulls it back. "No, it's mine... Great-granddad, and that lady said I can have it!"

June kneels in front of her granddaughter. "Oh, he did! Well, you must be really special because he doesn't let anyone mess around with his island things."

"That's a real taboo around here!" August added. "Maybe you should put it back. You don't want to break it."

"No! They told me I can have it!" Mary shouted out, holding the small ornament.

Heather rushes over, seeing her daughter with the ornament. "Mary, why don't you take it back to your great-grandfather so he can hold it while you eat?"

"I can't... He told me he's going away," she explained, shaking her head. "He won't be able to tell me any more stories. So, he let me have it to remember him! It's mine now," making sure no one is going to take it from her.

"So, where is he going this time?" June asked, a little perplexed by her granddaughter. "Better not be going on another fishing trip!" thinking her father might be planning another trip with his friend Kyle.

"No, we were talking to that nice lady in the book again. He told me he's got to go away with her. Something about home sweet home. What does that mean?" Mary asked.

June shrugged her shoulders. "Home sweet home? I guess that's here. It's the only home we have, so this must be our home sweet home that Dad was telling Mary."

"Why is he saying he is going away?" August asked June, a little confused by all this. "Who's this nice lady she is talking about?"

"Oh, it's probably one of his stories or big adventures," June explained.

"So, where is he going?" August asked little Mary.

"I don't know... He just went to sleep," Mary explained. "Something about it's his time. That nice lady told me she was here to be with him and to take him home. I think she said they're going to the beach," pointing down the hallway towards the bedroom.

June quickly looks up at August, then frantically runs to the bedroom. Everyone knows something is wrong. Hearing June crying out loud, everyone rushes down the hall into Ben's bedroom.

June is at his bedside, holding his hand. "No! No! Don't go... Please don't go!" crying hysterically.

August is on the other side of the bed, frantically going through his medical bag. April runs in, seeing her father lying motionless on the bed, still holding her mother's book to his chest. August has his stethoscope out, trying to hear the sounds of a heartbeat. They all know the inevitable has happened. Their father is gone.

All the children are quickly ushered out of the bedroom. August continues to check for vital signs but knows there is nothing he can do. He looks up at his family, then slowly shakes his head, letting them know his father is gone.

Ben passes away quietly, in the same way Jenny had. August was told by his father long ago not to revive him but to let him rest in peace. The one thing Ben wanted was to be in his home, surrounded by his family, when it was his time to leave this world.

* * *

Later that night, everyone gathers around little Mary. They all want to know what she had been talking about with her great-grandfather before he died.

"Can you tell us what happened?" Heather asked her daughter. "What did he tell you?"

"He told stories and read me that book again," Mary explained, still not understanding what had happened.

"What else did he tell you?" April asked.

"Nothing, we just talked," Mary replied, wondering why they were asking all these questions.

"Did he talk to his special friend?" June asked her granddaughter.

"Great-granddad always talks to his special friend!" Mary said with a big smile. "She is my friend too! We both talked to her."

"Do you remember her name?" Heather asked, wondering if she had been making it all up.

Mary thinks for a few seconds trying to remember. "It's Jenny! Yeah, that's her name! That's the lady in the big picture in the room. We always talked to her. She's really nice, and I like her. She is the one who told me I could have the little island," then holds up the small ceramic ornament of Kwajalein Island for everyone to see, so proud that she gets to keep it.

"Oh, that's a pretty one," June said. "April and I picked that one out for our mother when we were your age."

"I know she told me!" Mary said, nodding her head up and down. "It's her favorite one. That's why she wanted me to have it!"

Everyone in the room looks at each other, so shocked. All are wondering if the little girl truly understands what she is saying.

"You remember when he told you he had to go?" June asked her. "Can you tell us what he said?"

Mary stands quietly for a moment, trying to remember. "He just said it's his time now, and he's got to go. I asked him where he was going, and he told me he was going home."

"What did he mean by that?" June asked.

"I don't know!" Mary said, shrugging her shoulders. "I told him he's already home. He gave me a big hug and said he loved me. Then he went to sleep. That nice lady said they're going back home again. It's a big secret! A surprise!" then starts giggling.

There's not a dry eye in the room. Everyone tries to keep their composure, and it's so quiet while everyone listens to the little girl.

"You talked with a lady? She told you things?" August asked, still wondering who this person is.

"Sure! We talk all the time!" she explained, nodding her head. "She's the one in the big picture on the wall."

"How can that be!" August blurted out. "That's Mom!" looking over at June.

"I don't know," June whispered. "Mom has been gone for months. Heather and Mary have not seen her in over a year. They moved back right after Mom died."

"I don't think she remembers her," Heather added. "Mary was only three years old the last time they met, and that was when Granny came to stay with us for the weekend."

"I think Dad has been telling her too many stories, and she's getting them all mixed up," August said.

"Dad has been walking about talking to Mom like she's still here," April explained. "Maybe she's just playing along, thinking it's a game."

"I think you are right... So, Mary, what's this big secret?" June asked, getting a little curious.

She laughed. "I'm not saying! It's a really big surprise! That lady said everyone will be so happy! You'll really like the surprise!" jumping up and down so excited.

Mary is so confused with all the questions. "So where is he going, and when is he coming back?" but no one has the heart to tell her the truth.

June kneels down and gives Mary a big hug. "He is not going anywhere... He'll always be here with us," then starts crying.

* * *

The next day, August stays at the house while everyone else has gone back home. What is supposed to be a joyous family Easter weekend ends so tragically. The old house is now empty and so quiet. He feels lost without his mother and father sitting in the living room, remembering all the fond times growing up with his family.

He looks around at all the family photos covering the walls. His father was always taking someone's picture. Every wall in the house is filled with pictures of the family and the different places they have been. Even the bookcase contains photo albums going back to the very first day when his parents bought the house.

All the furniture in the house is handmade by his father. Those few years living out on the island made his mother and father so self-sufficient that most things they owned they made themselves. They never relied on others and were always there to give a helping hand to someone in need. They lived such a simple and beautiful life.

Ben had arranged for August to move into the house with his family when he was gone. August wants to start his own clinic, and the house is centrally located in the community, which will enable him to work from home. The only condition Ben had was that Brownie came with the house. August knows she will be a good companion for him and his children, too.

August is about to leave to meet with the lawyers when Brownie comes up to him, carrying her leash in her mouth. They all have been taking turns walking her while Ben was ill. With everything going on in the last few days, he forgets all about Brownie. She has been wandering about the empty house, looking for someone to take her out for her daily walk.

He kneels, petting the old dog. "I'm sorry, but I can't take you for a walk today, but maybe later when I come back."

Brownie just whines and whimpers, not understanding why no one wants to take her for a walk. She sits on the porch, watching August get in his car and drive away. With her leash still in her mouth, she bolts around to the back porch looking for Ben.

She runs all over the property, searching around inside the sheds and the small barn, finding no one. She runs back to the house, through the trapdoor, searching inside the house again. Going from one room to the next, she desperately looks for Ben, whimpering the entire time.

Finally, she walks into Ben's bedroom. Finding no one there, she jumps up on the bed. Slowly dropping the leash on the pillow, she starts howling. Somehow, she knows her best friend is gone. Still whimpering, she lies on the bed with her head on the pillow. Brownie is now all alone for the first time in her life.

* * *

After Ben's funeral, everyone arrives at the ranch house for the wake. All the family and friends are there to pay their respects. In the living room, above the big fireplace, is the portrait of Jenny and Ben. Right underneath the portrait, on the mantle, are two urns containing their ashes.

The backyard has huge canopies filled with tables and chairs, catered by the best chefs in the state. There is also a live band for entertainment. Hundreds of friends and families attend, celebrating the lives of Jenny and Ben Hughes.

At the end of the day, after everyone is gone, only the immediate family is at the house. They all gather in the living room. August is in charge of the estate and the reading of the will. He walks up to the fireplace to give the last toast to their mother and father. He holds up his wineglass, tapping on it with a spoon to get everyone's attention. Everyone quietens down, slowly gathering around him.

August, in a somber mood, takes in a deep breath, trying to keep his composure. "I want to thank you all for being here to say goodbye to a great man who just happens to be the best father one could ever have. He had a good life and many friends, but mostly a loving family. I know that when Mom died not too long ago, he couldn't go on living without her. Dad knew his time was near, but he didn't mind. He wanted to be with Mom again and told me not too long ago that he was so proud of his family and wanted us all to live long and fruitful lives. He also said that he and Mom had a glorious life together and wouldn't change one thing."

August holds up his glass, looking up at the portraits of his mother and father. "To the best mother and father in the world, rest in peace!" taking a sip of the wine.

Everyone follows suit, raising their glasses, toasting Jenny and Ben. April and June walk up to their brother and start hugging each other. Their mother and father, who meant so much to them, are now gone. Even with everyone in their family surrounding them, they feel so alone. Jenny and Ben's family grew so much over the years with three new generations. They had three children, then nine grandchildren, and in the end, ten great-grandchildren.

August takes out an envelope from the inside pocket of his jacket. He opens it up, curious about what his father has in store for them. The envelope has been sealed only to be read aloud with all the family present. There is no animosity about the distribution of the house and the family's wealth. Jenny and Ben were always generous, helping everyone financially. Money was never an issue, nor were any possessions.

August opens up the envelope, looking at the contents. Everyone stands patiently, waiting for him to read it aloud. Seeing the shocked look on his face, whatever it is, really startles him, leaving him lost for words.

April turns to August. "What is it?" seeing he is getting upset.

"You're not going to believe this!" August blurted out, quickly composing himself. "Mom and Dad are going back home to the island. Dad had arranged for their ashes to be taken there, and we are all invited to the ceremony!"

The news shocks everyone, and they can't believe it's true.

"That can't be right!" April said. "They're not going to let us all go there. It's still a restricted area!"

"All the arrangements have been made, and it's official!" he explained, holding up the documents. "Apparently, Dad finally found someone up in Washington, DC, who was a big fan of Mom and cleared everything for us. We are all finally going back home after all this time!"

"I can't believe he never mentioned this to anyone!" April said, quickly reading through it, shaking her head in disbelief.

"He always wanted to go back with Mom," August said. "I think he knew it wouldn't be the same without her. Nevertheless, I guess now they will get to return together. They got their last wish. This is one hell of a surprise."

"A surprise! A big secret, that's what Mary told us," April said.

"How did she know?" August asked, looking over at June. "None of us knew any of this."

"I do not have a clue," June mentioned. "We need to have another long talk with her again. I just wish we were there with him."

"I know," April said. "There was so much going on that day. At least little Mary was with him at the end. He must have told her about it."

"From what she has been telling us, it's just too hard to believe," June said. "What's real, and what's the tall stories? She said Mom was there and even talked with her. I don't think she really knows," wiping the tears from her eyes.

"It doesn't matter now," August added. "They got their last wish to go back home. That's all that matters now."

* * *

Everyone is astounded by the news. August, April, and June knew it was their father's one last wish to visit the island. At least they know their parents will have a beautiful resting place. The island is where their lives started together, and now it will be where they will spend eternity with each other.

August makes all the travel arrangements for fifty people to attend the final farewell. Ben's surviving sister and her family will attend, plus some of Ben and Jenny's closest friends. August was too young to remember life on the island and can't wait to see it for himself.

The news media quickly jumps on the story. Since the Hughes' adventure was years ago, it was long forgotten. Now, with all the media attention, everyone is interested again. Their story of survival is now being retold all over the world. The movie is being aired again on television, as well as the documentary about their adventure. The news media is even replaying old footage of when they arrived at Kwajalein Island many years ago.

Jenny was well-known throughout the world as a best-selling novelist. Many always assumed her first book was fiction. Now, they are learning the true story of this small family. Jenny's book about their ordeal and adventures has become a classic novel throughout the world. Again, it's back in print and on the top ten bestseller list after all those years.

* * *

Chapter 68

Going Home

The Kwajalein Island base commander, Colonel Ken Wells, arranged a short reception for the weary travelers. He reviewed all the archives in the Hughes' case. Even though it happened well before his time, the story is well-known to everyone stationed on the island.

Kwajalein has changed over the years, but it's still the major transit hub for the Pacific Defense Shield for North America. The monument at the base entrance contains all the names of those lost, including Ben Hughes and Jenny Mason. The only crew they lost in transit in all those years.

Arrangements are being made for the Hughes family and friends to stay the night in one of the barracks. At first light, the Langa-Moa hydro transport will take them out to Mocker Island for the ceremony. The trip to the island will only take a few hours, unlike the several days it took all those years ago in a catamaran sailboat.

The family can visit Mocker Island for only one day. At sundown, they will have to leave and immediately return to Kwajalein. The news media cannot attend since it's a private event. One military photographer will attend the ceremony to record the event. Once the security group clears them, they will release the photos and video to the Hughes family.

After fifty years, all that is known about Mocker Island is that it's near a secret military outpost. The only time civilians were allowed near the islands was when Ben and Jenny were discovered. After all the initial media attention, the military closed off the entire area, barring anyone from visiting the small, pristine island ever again.

* * *

The flight to Kwajalein Island is long and strenuous. The private jet arrives on the small remote island with all the friends and family of Ben and Jenny Hughes. What is somewhat ironic, their return is almost fifty years since that fateful day.

The private jet comes to a stop just in front of the honor guard. The military is going all out as if it's one of their finest being laid to rest. Being a quiet little remote island in the middle of the Pacific, it's a major event for everyone working on the island.

When the pilot cuts the massive engines, like clockwork, the ramp is pushed to the front doorway. The Colonel and his top staff, in full dress uniform, immediately race up the steps to greet their guests.

August is so relieved to be on the runway at Kwajalein. He dreads this last leg of the trip from Hawaii. It was the same flight his parents had been on that had never arrived. He tries to imagine the ordeal that they must have gone through. Knowing their plane was going down hundreds of miles from land is terrifying, and he shudders just thinking about it.

A gust of hot, humid air fills the plane as the main door opens. As Colonel Wells and his staff walk in, they are astounded to see all the passengers on board. They find it hard to believe that most of these people are the descendants of two lost souls who were lucky enough to be washed ashore on a small island almost fifty years ago.

The Colonel notices a large container on the front row of seats surrounded by flowers. He just stares at it, so astonished, knowing that it contains the ashes of Ben and Jenny Hughes. As a young boy, he read all the books, watched the movie, and documentaries about these two famous people. He still remembers watching the live broadcast on television when they arrived all those years ago. Now, sadly, he is responsible for bringing them back home to their final resting place.

"Welcome back, Mr. and Mrs. Hughes," the Colonel whispered, looking down at the container. "It's an honor to escort you home."

August gets up and walks over to the Colonel. "Hello, I'm August Hughes," extending out his hand.

"It's my pleasure," Colonel Wells replied, recognizing August from his photos, shaking his hand. "I'd like to welcome you and your family to Kwajalein. I also want to give you our deepest regrets for the loss of your mother and father. They were a big influence on my life and part of the history here on the island."

"Thank you... I also want to thank you for making their last request possible."

The Colonel introduces August to the rest of his staff. August calls April and June over to introduce them. The Colonel feels awkward, seeing all three standing right in front of him. They are celebrities and a legend on Kwajalein. Now, he is face-to-face with all three and finally getting to meet them personally.

Everyone disembarks from the aircraft and waits in the procession line. April, June, and August remain on the aircraft. They stand next to the container, waiting for the procession to begin. Two honor guards enter the aircraft to carry Jenny and Ben's ashes. A dozen honor guards march up in unison, stopping at the base of the gangway, standing six abreast and facing each other.

With the beat of the snare drum, two honor guards appear at the doorway carrying the flag-draped container. They slowly step down the ramp, followed by April, June, and August. When they reach the bottom of the ramp, the drummer stops. The honor guards snap to attention in unison, saluting as the flag-draped container is carried past them.

Two military cars and a bus stop just short of the aircraft. The Colonel and his staff stand in the procession line to greet and console the friends and family before they board the transportation to the barracks.

The Hughes family and close friends settle into their rooms after traveling all day long. All the children are sound asleep after the long flight. A large buffet is in front of the barracks. Those who can stay awake gather in front, talking to all the people who work on the island. Everyone wants to hear all the stories again. Hearing it firsthand from the actual family who were part of this history keeps them all captivated.

* * *

Early in the morning, everyone gathers at the front of the barracks, waiting for the bus ride to the Langa-Moa transport ship. Many of the younger children don't understand what is happening. Most think this is another big family vacation, and they are ready to play and have a good time.

The crew of the Langa-Moa transport ship is preparing to cast off. The ship looks more like a huge catamaran. It's the latest high-tech military transport that skims the top of the waves, reaching speeds up to forty knots.

There is a sense of urgency in the air. The military is rushing to get everyone on board to keep things on schedule. The security is extremely tight. Everyone has to be cleared by the security detail before boarding the Langa-Moa. After several failed attempts, there will not be any more unauthorized people sneaking onto the island.

When the sun peaks above the horizon, the large ship slowly moves away from the pier. April and June recognize some of the landmarks from when they were first here. They can still recall the memories of that day when they arrived with their mother and father.

The Langa-Moa is fast as they said it would be. When it picks up speed, it lifts almost out of the water, skimming on top of the waves. It takes only a few hours to reach Mocker Island. It is nothing compared to the days it initially took to go from their old home to Kwajalein Island.

They couldn't have picked a more beautiful day. The ocean is calm, with a deep turquoise blue color. An extremely clear morning with small white clouds dotted along the horizon, and a perfect picture of the South Pacific Ocean.

* * *

"Good morning, everyone," the captain announced over the intercom. "Just to let you know, we are coming up on Mocker Island in a few minutes. If you move to the front of the vessel, you should be able to see the top of the island just over the horizon."

Everyone runs forward to get their first glimpse of the famous island. It is so quiet as they all look out the forward windows. No one can see anything but the blue ocean.

"I think that's it over there!" someone yelled out.

"You can see the island now," the captain announced. "It's the dark spot directly ahead, on the horizon just between those two clouds."

The island is small at first, then slowly becomes more prominent in the vast ocean. April, June, and August hug each other after seeing the island. An incredibly emotional time for them, never thinking they would ever see their old home again.

"I can't believe this!" April shouted. "We finally made it back home!"

"I wish Mom and Dad could see this… They wanted so much to come back. Especially having the whole family out here," June said, wiping the tears from her eyes.

"They are here," August whispered, glancing over at the container holding their ashes. "They are coming back home to live together in paradise."

The island fills the sky as the ship slowly approaches. Everyone is so excited, already recognizing some features and landmarks. April and June can't wait to get on the sandy beaches and explore their old home again.

"We'll circle the island first before landing on the south side," the captain announced. "It'll give you all a few minutes to get ready to disembark."

Since they arrived during high tide, the ship had no problems coming within a hundred feet of the shoreline. All the passengers move to the port side for a better view of the allusive island as the ship circles around it. Everyone is astounded at how small the island is, seeing it up close.

As the ship slowly ventures around the island, there is nothing but one long, pristine beach lined with tall palm trees. They all know it's such a waste that this little island is off-limits to everyone. The island would be a glamorous hideaway resort that attracts thousands of people if it were only located somewhere else in the world.

The big moment arrives when the Langa-Moa returns to the southern shore. The captain searches for a place to beach the ship. When he sees the perfect spot, the captain barks out orders, and the crew runs about the deck to prepare for the landing.

The ship slowly approaches the beach, coming to a stop as its keel digs into the soft sand. The crew works fast, lowering the forward gangplank and pulling it out just short of the beach. Two crewmen drag the anchors out on the sand to help lock down the ship to prevent it from drifting away. The rest of the crew are dragging out big tubs of food, drinks, and tents to set up the base camp.

"Welcome to Mocker Island!" the captain announced. "We'll be docked here for approximately forty-five minutes before the tide changes. Then, we'll anchor the ship about a hundred meters out for the duration. A small boat will transport you to and from the island for most of the day. Tents and canopies will be set up on the beach for shade and refreshments. You may now leave the ship."

A big cheer comes from the crowd as all the passengers rush to the front of the ship. All the children are up front with their swimming suits on, with pails and shovels in hand. They can't wait to hit the beach and have fun. When the crew stabilizes the gangplank, it's a mad rush. All the children run as fast as they can, stomping their feet on the metal plank, making it bounce up and down.

April, June, and August are the last ones off the ship. They had been waiting for this moment for as long as they could remember. They stand quietly at the end of the gangplank, looking over the island. Right away, April and June recognize this as the same place where their rescuers had their camp. Also, it's the same place where they got on the little dinghy when they left the island. About a hundred yards down the beach, around the bend, is their old home.

Everyone quietly gathers around the front of the ship, waiting for April, June, and August to take their first steps back on the island. Slowly, they make their way down the steps, with August carrying the urns in the padded container. As they step on the sand for the first time, their friends and family applaud, welcoming them back home.

The crew quickly sets up the canopies on the beach. The tables are filled with small snacks and various ice-cold drinks. A beautiful setting for a day's outing, and the crew makes sure the passengers have everything that they need. Even though it's still early in the morning, the heat and humidity is already a problem. The canopies will be the only protection from the sun's fierce heat on the open beach.

The ceremony is to take place at the lookout far up on the island. The lookout is the most beautiful spot on the island. After over fifty years, no one is sure it still exists. The biggest challenge is the long hike. Getting everyone up on the island is going to be a problem in the timeframe given. The ceremony has to be completed by sundown. After that, everyone has to be off the island.

* * *

After a brief break, everyone is ready to explore the island. Even though it's still early, the heat and humidity is already overbearing. Many are wondering how anyone could enjoy this climate. After years of living up in the cold, dry mountain air in Colorado, this is far worse than anyone expected.

Ben's sister, Kelly, and his best friend, Kyle, decide it will be best to sit in the shade under the canopy, enjoying the view until it's time for the service. They also are very frail, and the long trip is already taking its toll on them. They watch over the container while everyone else is out exploring.

Kelly knows it will be her only chance to experience the paradise she had heard so many times from her brother's stories. Just sitting on the same beach is more than enough for her. She looks down the beach, imagining in her mind her brother and his wife living here without a care in the world. Seeing all the children running around playing in the crystal-clear water, she can now see how this is indeed a paradise and why her brother never wanted to leave.

"Welcome home, little brother," she quietly whispered, looking down at the padded container with the urns of her brother and sister-in-law. "I know you'll find peace here," as the tears ran down her cheek.

* * *

April and June are having a hard time recognizing the old landmarks. For some reason, the island looks so small from what they remember. To their surprise, the one thing that has not changed is the peak that towers over the island. After all those years, one look at the peak, and they know exactly where they are, but everything else looks so different.

Right away, they can see there are a lot more trees. Even though it's high tide, the beach used to be twice the size it is now. The beach looks as if it's eroded away. Or the palm trees have encroached farther out on the beach. They soon realize that finding their old campsite is going to be more difficult than they initially thought.

The beauty of the island astounds August. The water is so clear, and the sand on the beach is just perfect. His only regret is that he can't remember any of this. The movie made about their lives doesn't do it justice. The island is far better than he could have ever imagined. He wishes he had been a little older at the time. At least his sisters have some vague memories of their time here.

August tries to imagine what it might have been like being stranded here and trying to bring up a family. If it were not for that one day when the tourist just happened to be anchored off the beach, they might have spent their entire lives out on this desolate island.

April and June walk the group down the beach. Everyone knows all the details and landmarks so well described in Jenny's book. Before they left home, they all got together and meticulously went through the book, drawing out the various landmarks that were referenced. Now, it is evident that so much has changed.

Walking around the bend on the beach, April and June suddenly stop, grabbing each other's arms. Despite all the changes on the island, they both recognize the little strip of beach they once called home. They get a second wind, walking as fast as they can.

Finally, they discover the dry riverbed that marks the entrance to the big freshwater pond. April and June run into the dense trees following the riverbed. Seeing the big pond brings back so many fond memories. The cliff is still covered with ferns and flowers. A small waterfall still trickles down the cliff face. Unfortunately, the pond is not as big as it used to be, only a foot deep, filled with silt over the years. The scene is far more beautiful than anyone could have ever imagined.

August is so glad to have a photographer here to record all of this. He gets everyone lined up to take their photo on the ledge just above the pond among all the ferns and flowers. Now, everyone will finally be able to see the beauty of this island.

* * *

After a quick break, everyone is eager to find the old campsite. Discovering the large pond, everyone now ventures farther down the beach. April and June are always looking up at the peak, seeing that they are getting closer. Their old campsite was near this area, but it just looks all the same. It's just a dense forest with tall palm trees and ferns covering the ground.

April comes to a complete stop, grabbing her sister's hand. Looking toward the trees, June fails to notice the huge boulder sitting twenty feet out in the water.

"What is it?" June asked, seeing her sister staring out at the ocean.

April points over to the small boulder. "I think that's it! That's got to be the top of the boulder that was in front of the camp. That's where we used to keep the fish in the little tidal pool at the base of it!"

"No, that can't be it! It's too small and way out in the water. The one I remember was right on the shoreline, and it was huge."

"I'm positive that's got to be it!" April said. "Just think... With the beach half-gone, that would place it out in the water. Look, there are no other boulders anywhere on the beach. That was also the tallest one around, and it's now the only one here, even though it's in the water. It's also about the right distance from the big pond. If that marked the edge of the water, it would make the beach about the right size, the way it used to be. This has to be it! The camp has to be here!" then she turns, walking towards the trees.

"It's hard to tell," June said, quickly following her sister. "I don't remember the beach being this steep!"

"I know... I remember it being somewhat flat. The trees are a lot closer to the water than they used to be. If that is the big boulder in front of the camp, then we must have lost more than thirty feet of sand."

"If that's the case," June said, "I wonder if the tree line had moved closer to the water. No telling how far back the old camp is from the beach. These trees look pretty close to the boulder out there. These could be new ones grown long after we left. The old tree line may be over ten feet back."

"If this is the place, then the old Milo tree is gone too."

"You're right! I don't even see it. That was right out on the beach, too. I remember the days when Mom made us take a nap under it. It's a shame it's gone. That would have shown us exactly where the camp used to be."

"It was probably washed away years ago."

They slowly make their way into the dense trees and brush. Everyone follows along except for the children. August remembers stories of big black scorpions, deciding the youngest ones should keep on the beach just in case. The children don't care since all they want to do is play in the water or make more sandcastles.

August quickly discovers that the old stories of the humidity within the trees is nothing compared to actually experiencing it. He feels as if he has just walked into a steam room, with the sweat dripping off his face.

Everyone wanders through the trees, looking for signs of the old campsite. What was once a small clearing is now a dense jungle. With so many fallen trees on the ground, it's difficult to walk. Eventually, they reach the gradual foothills that lead up to the peak, finding nothing.

Again, everyone spreads out, moving back towards the beach. Many are starting to think it's all probably buried deep under the sand or maybe just washed away over time. The thick brush and all the fallen branches are now covering the ground, making it worse.

Everyone is so disappointed not able to find the old wooden hut, expecting to see parts of it still standing even after all these years. One of their biggest fears is that some tourists might have gotten on the island shortly after they left, using it for firewood.

April knows they are in the right place but wonders if anything survived after fifty years. She walks out to the edge of the beach so she can see the boulder out in the water. From there, she goes back into the trees, looking for signs of their old home.

April's grandson, Paul, is there to help, running around and kicking the dead leaves and branches. Suddenly, he trips, falling flat on his face. April rushes over to help him up. Paul brushes himself off and starts kicking the fallen leaves again as if nothing had happened.

April notices what her grandson has just stumbled over. A large, round, black rock buried halfway in the sand. She brushes away the leaves to find another rock right next to it. Paul comes back to help, seeing his grandmother has found something interesting. She quickly clears the area to find a small circle of lava rocks buried deep in the sand.

"I think I found it! This looks like the old campfire!" April shouts, waving everyone over.

"You think it's ours?" June asked, helping to clear the sand away.

April nods. "This has to be it! It's about the right distance from the beach. The big boulder is right out front!" she shouts, looking around, trying to find more.

"OK, everyone! I think we found it! Let's clear this area and see what else we can find," June said, pushing away the dead leaves with her foot.

April stood up, looking around. "My God! Look at this place. It used to be a big open area with nothing but sand on the ground. None of these trees were here. It's a good thing that the boulder is still out there. We would have never found it."

"You're right," June said, looking around at what used to be their campsite. "It's been a long time. These all have grown since we've been gone. I have a feeling that a lot of the old trees are gone, too. They either died off or were blown down with the storms," seeing all the dead trees covering the ground.

April quickly turns to face west, to where the hut should have been, but sees nothing. No signs at all that the old wooden hut even existed. The entire area is filled with new ferns and palm trees.

Everyone gathers around to help clear the area, pulling up the small ferns and dragging away the dead palm leaves. Then, someone uncovers a bamboo branch with a rope tied around the end. Removing the rest of the sand, they discover the remains of one wall of the hut. Their old home finally sees the light of day once again.

"We found it!" June excitedly yelled out. "This is one of the walls of the hut!"

"This is it!" April shouted, so relieved. "I can't believe after all this time, most of it is still intact," examining the wall of their old home.

"Let's clear this entire area. The rest of it's probably here too."

Within a few minutes, they uncover the remnants of the old hut buried underneath the sand. To their disappointment, the storms and typhoons over the years had destroyed the small hut. The walls and the roof remained somewhat intact since it was made from wood, bamboo, and vinyl from the old raft.

"Oh, look what I found!" April said, struggling to pull up one of the walls. "It's our old table and one of the chairs Dad made!"

Everyone rushes over to help drag away the heavy wall. With the old bamboo wall pulled away, the broken remnants of the old furniture are right underneath it. Buried in the sand and saturated with water, the wood is so brittle that it falls apart as soon as they pick up the pieces.

"I remember this so well," June said, then started crying, seeing it all falling apart. "I wish we could put it back together again and take it back with us."

"Well, we can still take some of it back," August suggested. "It's all broken, and some of it has wood rot, but just knowing Dad made it, I'd love to put this with all our island mementos."

"I know... This is part of our family history. I need a bag to put it in, and I'm bringing it all back home. I don't care if it's all broken pieces of wood. It means a lot to me."

"So, I wonder what happened to Mom's bed?" April asked. "You think it would be here with the rest of this."

"No telling," August said. "It could have been picked up with the wind and blown away. It can be anywhere under all this sand," looking around.

Seeing the wooden walls on the ground, it doesn't take August long to figure out that the two tall trees in front of him were once attached to the hut. The other two trees had fallen years ago, still lying on the ground. Standing in the center, he can now see how small it was, only seven feet square.

Now they have the exact location of the hut, so everything is being cleared out. Everyone helps pull the remnants of the bamboo walls and the plywood floor away. A partially buried pile of firewood is all that remains. It is the last of the reserves they stored under the old wooden hut.

August turns to his sisters. "I can't believe it! Just think, we were all born right here in this very spot. I never thought I would actually get to see the place we were born. God, just look at all this! I can't imagine Mom giving birth way out here in the middle of nowhere. I don't know how they did it," shaking his head in disbelief.

"It explains a lot about Mom and Dad," June said, looking over the remnants. "They were really the strong outdoor types who never relied on anyone else. They knew how to take care of themselves no matter where they were."

"Yep, that's the truth," August said, nodding his head. "They did love it out here. Now, after being here, I can see why," looking out to the beach.

April looks down at the remnants of one of the walls. "It's hard to believe how small everything is. I always remembered this as a lot bigger."

"You know, I can still see it now!" June explained, looking at the trees that marked their old home. "It had a little door at the front here. There was a small window opposite the door and one on the beachside. The bed was there, and the table over at this corner," pointing it all out to everyone.

"It's hard to believe Mom and Dad built all this with a wire saw and some old rope," August said. "Can you imagine all of us crammed in here on those rainy days? How did they do it?"

"This is nothing," April said. "Wait till you see the cave! We were in there for days at a time!"

"I hate to see how small that is!" June added. "If it's anything like what we see down here, it's probably nothing more than a hole in the side of the cliff."

"This hut was a luxury for us, anyway. If you remember, they only had the small tent to live in before Dad built this."

"I guess with Mom pregnant with you two," August said. "That was a big incentive for Dad to build a more permanent shelter. I just can't see them living out here with nothing but that small tent or even the hut!"

"Yeah, from what Mom used to say, it was a scary time for them," June said. "With Mom being pregnant, it was the only time Dad wished they were rescued and off the island."

August chuckled. "Knowing how squeamish Dad used to be, I don't know how he helped deliver us in this tiny wooden shack."

June laughed. "Yeah, luckily, it was dark... Mom always said he never wanted to go through that ever again. But at least it all worked out. We're proof of that."

The center of the campsite is the campfire. They place markers on the ground where the tent, hammock, and hut used to be. With everything marked out, it's now clear to everyone how small the camp was.

They were hoping to find some mementos to bring back, but now they can see there is nothing left. They fill one sack with remnants of the old table and chair and some of the firewood. It's not much, but it does have a lot of sentimental value.

* * *

Slowly, one by one, everyone walks back to the beach to cool off. April, June, and August are the last to leave. They hug and hold each other. It's a very emotional moment standing next to the campfire, looking over their old home. Now, since everyone is out on the beach, it's the first time hearing the wind blowing through the trees and the crashing waves in the distance. A sound so profoundly embedded in their memories.

Reluctantly, they turn and walk out together. Then, for some reason, April stops, turning for one last look at what was once her birthplace and a very happy home. She then realizes that she is standing in the same place when she was a little girl on that last day on the island. For a moment, April can see the campsite in her mind as it had looked so long ago. She feels so sad that it's all gone, washed away with time.

"Oh my God!" she shouted, remembering the little Christmas tree. "How you have grown!" seeing the huge Travelers Palm tree.

She walks over, putting her arms around the tree that now towers over her. The tree that was once small and decorated with flowers and ribbons is now fully grown.

She looks back over at the campsite, and the tears running down her face. "Goodbye, old home," with one last wave, she turns to join the others back out on the beach.

Knowing that this is the actual campsite means the trail is not far away, and the next stop is the small pond. The crewman calls the ship, informing them of the news. The captain gives the order to pack up the base camp, moving everything back to the Langa-Moa. Once the small pond is located, he is going to move the base camp there. Later in the day, when everyone returns from the ceremony, it will save a few hours not having to walk back to where the base camp is currently located.

* * *

They find the dry creek bed a hundred yards down the beach leading to the small pond. A crewman signals the ship to set up the new base camp. Again, the tents and tables are being set up, and lunch is going to be served before the long walk up the trail.

August stands quietly, looking over the small pond. Of all the places on the island, this is the one that meant so much to him. He always tried to picture this place in his mind from his mother's descriptions. After seeing it firsthand, he now knows why his mother loved this one spot more than anywhere in the world. She always told him stories of how she used to bring him here every morning to bathe him while his sisters played in the water. She always called it her little Eden.

While the rest of the family is eating lunch, April and June explore the area around the small pond, so amazed at how everything is so overgrown. The pond is almost gone, with just a small puddle in its place. With all the years of rainwater rushing down from the hills above, it's almost completely filled with silt and sand. The pond is the one place they fondly remember and are so saddened to see it has changed so much over time.

The trail is still there, but it's heavily overgrown with trees and shrubs, like everything else. April doesn't want to wait, so eager to hike up the trail. Being a doctor, August has to persuade her that she is not as agile and young as she used to be. Also, it's not the best time of the day to make such a strenuous hike.

* * *

Everyone takes a break, sitting in the shade under the canopies. The children are running around, having the time of their lives. Many are out in the water, enjoying themselves. Some of the crew are out fishing, catching some fish to fry up.

August knows his mother and his father didn't want everyone to be sad. The island is an absolute paradise, and there is nowhere better in the whole world to celebrate the lives of their parents.

Kyle sits under the canopy, drinking beer and telling everyone his old fishing stories. Kyle is now the sole owner of the Rocky Mountain Fishing Adventures. Ben gave his half of the business to his best friend and business partner. Neither of them did it for the money. Kyle no longer goes out fishing or camping now that his best friend is gone. He has also lost interest, letting the younger generation take over the business.

He had heard all the stories about this island paradise. Seeing it firsthand, he now knows why his best friend never really wanted to leave. Sitting on the beach, he knows this will be a great place to spend the last few years of his life.

"You know... I just might stay out here for a while," Kyle mistakenly mentioned to the captain. "No one will know if anyone is out on this island, anyway."

The captain looks over at the old man. "Sorry, don't even think about it... Ain't no one going to be left behind. We're going to count every one of you several times to make sure we have everyone on board before we head out. This will probably be the last ship docking here in our lifetime. I got my orders."

"That's a damn shame!" Kyle replied, seeing everyone was having such a great time. "There ain't no good reason to ban people from coming out here. I don't know what they're doing around here, but I can tell you now, it ain't that important."

The captain nods his head in agreement. "I know... It's a shame it has to be this way. Hell, I don't even know what's going on out here, either. All I do is shuttle people and supplies around from one place to another. Worst of it all, it's always at night. Would you believe that after six years, this is the first time I have been out in this area in the daytime!"

Kyle laughed. "I bet they had a run for their money when all the tour boats started coming out here after they found Ben and Jenny!"

"Oh, you know they did! Between you and me, I heard they had to shut down operations until they got Congress to reinstate the original boundaries. It was one thing getting the occasional aircraft or ship getting a little too close, but the tourists just went where the hell they wanted. Most of them didn't have a clue that this was a secure area. That was a hell of a mess back in those days."

"I guess it's like Area 51 out in Nevada. Once people found out it's there, the show is over."

"Well, there is no sneaking up on some mountain ridge to get a look around here," the captain explained. "Out here, they can see you well before you are even near the island. With all the satellites and underwater sensors, nothing goes on without them knowing about it.

Hell, they're probably watching us right now from some satellite camera up there," looking up at the sky.

"Those bastards!" Kyle shouted, giving the finger to some obscure high-power camera in orbit, watching over them.

* * *

As the hours go by, many take naps in the shade, resting up for the big hike. The more adventurous explore the island. The children, with so much energy, are still playing out in the water while others make sandcastles or try to catch some fish.

Kelly is the caretaker of the two urns, which are still in the padded case. She always makes sure the container is with her, never letting it out of her sight. The crewman sets up a chair for her so that she can sit in the shade next to the small pond. Kelly wants to spend time alone to admire the beauty of the place.

She rereads Jenny's book while on her travels. She goes back through the pages where Jenny talked about this very spot. The passage in the book describes the small pond so well. She feels as if she has been here before. Such a beautiful place, even though the pond is almost gone.

She can imagine in her mind her old friend Jenny here at the pond bathing her little babies. She is so sad that they are all gone. Now, she is the last one alive in her family. Her brother Sam, as well as her husband, passed away years ago. In a matter of a few months, not only had she lost her sister-in-law, but now her younger brother.

Kelly is so glad that she was able to make the trip. She will hike up the trail for the ceremony and wouldn't miss it for anything in the world. She is doing this for her little brother and her longtime best friend, Jenny.

April and June join their grandchildren out on the beach, showing them how to make the best sandcastles. It brings back so many fond memories of those few years when they were here, seeing all the children having fun. They feel so sad looking up and down the beach, knowing that this is the place where they used to live. At times, they can even visualize their parents playing on the beach with them. They feel so sad, knowing that their parents could not return to the island home they loved so much.

* * *

Chapter 69

The Last Trail

L ate in the afternoon, everyone is ready for the walk up the trail. With the ceremony scheduled to begin right before sunset, June is confident that three hours is enough time to reach the lookout. Once it's over, everyone needs to hurry back and be on the ship before it gets too dark.

August has the task of carrying the urns. The padded case has two big straps, using it as a backpack. He has been practicing this for weeks at home, carrying a heavy backpack while hiking every day through the mountains. Now, with just the urns, it's much lighter, but he knows it will be a problem with the heat and humidity.

April is the first to walk up the trail. Just like in the old days, she makes a walking stick from an old tree branch, trimming it off with her knife. June quickly follows suit, making a walking stick as well. Their father taught them to always be prepared and take nothing for granted.

One by one, they slowly make their way up the narrow trail. August makes sure everyone has plenty to drink. Even though many prepared themselves by hiking for weeks on the mountain trails, it was not enough to prepare them for this.

Kelly and Kyle don't see this as a grueling task but as a right in life. When they return home, they can tell everyone they walked the famous trail to the cave, but mostly, they lived to tell the tale.

The walk up the trail is more of an educational tour for the Hughes family and friends. At various rest stops, April and June are pointing out all the interesting sites. They continue their father's tradition of teaching the children how to live off the land, explaining which trees are best for firewood and which plants can be used for making hats and baskets. The children listen to every word. All are pretending they are Amazon warriors trekking through the dense, dark jungles.

After almost fifty years, April and June are so surprised at how much they can remember. The old trail is overgrown, but in essence, everything is still the same. What makes it so sad is knowing that the only thing that has really changed is that their loving parents are not here to share this experience with them.

* * *

In a little more than two hours, the first group reaches the lookout. April is the first to see the small flat area overlooking the island, now covered with tall grass and shrubs. No more well-manicured short grass, she once remembered. Right away, she knows that it's going to be a lot of work to clean everything up before they can start the ceremony.

As April gets closer, she can't believe her eyes. The orchard is now massive, filled with an abundance of oranges, lemons, and grapefruits. She runs over, standing in front of the trees in awe. The trees she planted from seedlings are now towering, far above her, full of fruit.

"Well, my babies have grown up here too," she whispered with a little smile. "Did you guys miss me?"

"I wonder what the big orchard looks like on the other side?" June asked, looking up in amazement.

"It must be huge if it's anything like this!" April replied.

"Come on!" quickly pulling off several oranges. "There's plenty to go around!" passing them out to those walking up behind her.

June points to a group of fully laden trees that lead up to the cave. "Look at those over there! They're the ones we planted up by the trail! Look how big they are!"

"Wow... Just think. We planted all these from just little seedlings, and look at them now."

"I don't know... From the looks of things, I think there are a few more here than what we planted. Many of these might have grown on their own."

"I think you're right," April said, spitting out a few seeds into her hand. "I'm going to take these home with me and put them in my greenhouse! This is our only chance we have, so I'm taking back as much as I can from this island."

June nods. "Good idea!" putting the seeds into her pocket as well.

* * *

August finally arrives, walking straight past everyone, ignoring the orchard. The fruit trees don't catch his attention at all. Slowly, he makes his way through the tall grass until he reaches the edge of the cliff. Seeing the view from the lookout for the very first time, he is absolutely stunned. He stands in awe, looking over the island far below.

April and June notice their brother standing all alone at the edge of the lookout. They walk over to be with him. All three look down at the beach far below. What was once a huge ship now looks like a little toy from this height. They stand with their arms around each other, taking in the beautiful view without saying a word.

"I can't believe I'm actually here!" August said, carefully putting the container on the ground. "It's like a dream. Mom and Dad were right about this place. It doesn't get any better than this!"

"That's right!" April said to her brother. "You really haven't seen this yet... I can remember this view as if it were yesterday. We spent a lot of time sitting up here, enjoying this. You never forget something like this."

June kneels down, putting her hand on the container. "Welcome home, Mom and Dad," she whispers, realizing this is the end of their journey in life, then cries uncontrollably.

"It's OK... This is what they wanted," April said, then cried as well.

August helps June up, trying to comfort her. He also feels overwhelmed with emotions. Leaving the ashes of their parents here is going to be difficult. No one will ever be able to visit them ever again.

* * *

Slowly, one by one, the last of the group makes their way to the lookout. No one thought the grass would be so tall. After a quick break, everyone stomps down the tall grass to flatten the area for the ceremony.

"Granny! I found something here!" one of the children called out, uncovering something hidden up in the grass close to the edge.

June rushes over, astounded to see the old wooden bench her father had made. "Oh, my God! I can't believe it's still here! Help me clear everything away," kneeling down, pulling up the tall grass growing around it.

April walks up, so shocked. "Oh, God! I forgot all about this being up here!" holding her hand over her mouth.

Everyone quickly gathers around, looking at the old, weathered wooden bench. Now, it's almost like a monument, so famous in all the stories.

August races over. "I didn't know about this! Did any of you?" so surprised, seeing the inscription.

Both April and June shake their heads. They are astonished at seeing the inscription for the first time.

"Home Sweet Home," he reads aloud, the tears running down his face. "April, June, August, Jenny, Ben Hughes 1997 - 2003."

"I remember this bench so well," June said, running her hands over the inscription in the wood. "We used to sit here eating oranges while we looked out over the ocean. But I don't remember this writing."

"You're right!" April said, looking at the bench. "I bet Dad did this on the last day before we left."

"Dad made several trips to the cave, storing everything away that day. I can't imagine what he went through on that last day, inscribing this. Dad loved it here so much and never really wanted to leave. But he did it for us," June explained, wiping away the tears.

"I remember Mom telling me how he hated having to leave," August said, looking down at the small bench. "They always thought that one day, they could come back and visit. It's a shame they never had the chance."

"It makes me so mad when I think about it," April said. "It wouldn't have hurt anything by letting them come here. Why did those people have to wait so long until it was too late?"

"We can't change the past," August said. "We're here now, so let's make the most of it," not wanting his sisters to get worked up about it again.

June turns to April. "He's right... We need to make the most of it. This is our only chance. I want to see the cave! You want to go with me?"

"We better go now," April replied, nodding her head. "We don't have much time left. The sun is getting low on the horizon."

"I'd like to go as well," August said. "I can just imagine what that looks like!"

"Better leave the container by the bench for safekeeping," April said. "I don't trust leaving it out here so close to the edge of this cliff," walking over, retrieving the case, and placing it right next to the bench.

August looks at his watch. "We still have a little over an hour, but that's all the time we have. We need to start the ceremony well before sunset."

April kneels and opens the container. She carefully pulls out the two urns, placing them on top of the bench. Tears start running down their faces seeing the urns again.

"Don't worry," she said, running her hands over the urns. "We'll be back shortly."

Kelly and Kyle walk up, carrying their folding chairs. "You kids go and do all the things you need to get done. We'll watch over Jenny and Ben."

"Thank you," June replied. "We won't be long. It's just up the hill, a short distance from here."

Kelly promptly puts her chair down next to the bench, followed by Kyle. They both sit down to rest, enjoying the fresh oranges and the spectacular view. For Kelly, this is a major achievement in her life. To be sitting here is something she thought would never happen. The walk up the trail was exhausting, but to do it at her age was an accomplishment. She sensed her brother was encouraging her on every step. To sit in this place of solitude, her brother and sister-in-law's final resting place, is a lifelong dream.

* * *

June leads the way up the trail to see the cave for the last time. All the grandchildren are ready to explore, and the cave sounds like fun, and all follow along. The others stay on the lookout to rest up from the grueling hike and to get ready for the service.

June quickly reaches the ridge of the trail, the crossroads to the rest of the island. The path is still here and well-worn. With the canopy of trees overhead, not much brush or grass grows here. Nothing has changed.

To the right, the small trail goes around the peak, then up to the top of the island. That is the one and only place they were never allowed to go.

The trail that leads straight ahead goes down to the other side of the island. The path they walked so many times with their father, getting firewood and fruit from the big orchard. All that hard work dragging tree branches up here to be cut for firewood. A never-ending task, but the twins enjoyed every minute of it.

To the left, the trail leads to the cave, their second home on the island. Now, it holds all the possessions they left behind. Their only hope is that everything is still intact and no one else got to it after they left the island.

June waits for her brother and sister to catch up with her. Time is getting short, and this is something everyone wants to see for themselves. After a short wait for the rest to arrive, June clears a path through the thick, overgrown brush. She sees a large group of boulders right in front of the cave entrance. They all stand motionless, so shocked to see how small it is.

"This can't be it!" August blurted out. "Are you sure this is the one?"

April wipes the tears away from her face. "This is it, our old cave and home," slowly approaching the cave entrance, peering into the darkness.

August is overcautious. "Wait a minute! Don't go barging in. There might be wild animals still living in there!"

June hesitates, then looks back at the crewman, who has a flashlight ready. "George, can you look in there and see if it's OK? It's too dark to see anything."

"Sure, I'll check it out first. There could be rats, or worse, scorpions. You might want to stand back just in case something runs out," shining the flashlight into the cave.

Even with his flashlight, he can't see much. After being out in the bright sunlight, he needs a few minutes for his eyes to adjust to the darkness. Slowly entering the dark, musty cave, he notices a lot of things strewn all over the cave floor. He is ready to run if he sees anything move. His worst fear is something dropping on his back from the low ceiling. He picks up a small rock, tossing it into the back of the cave to scare anything out. Nothing moves at all. There is nothing but dead silence and no critters scurrying around.

April and June slowly follow the crewman, trying to make sense of all the dark shapes in the cave. They cautiously stand just within the entrance, waiting for their eyes to adjust to the darkness. Getting brave enough, they slowly move deeper into the cave.

"I don't remember it being this small," June said. "It's really cold in here too!"

"I know!" April replied. "Can you believe we lived in here for days during those storms?"

"Look!" June shouted out. "It's all still here!" as the crewman points the flashlight at the back wall.

April gasped. "My God! Look at all the firewood that was left over! Even the camping gear is still here!"

They slowly make their way to the far end of the cave. On top of the large pile of firewood, is the remains of all their camping gear and the various things they collected while they lived here.

"Look! The old cast-iron pot is still here on the floor. That was the last thing Dad stored away before we left that morning," June said, picking up the old pot.

"I can still remember him carrying that away. Hard to believe it's been sitting here for all those years."

June carries everything out of the cave. The old fishing rod is now an antique and probably worth a lot of money. Even the diving mask and fins had seen better days. The plastic had hardened and is covered with mold. The radio and the solar charger are a sight for sore eyes. Those were their best memories of fun day out on the beach dancing to the music. Luckily, everything is still where their father had stored it so long ago.

"Remember this?" June asked, carrying out their old sleeping bag.

"Now, that is something I do remember!" April said.

"I can't believe we all used to crawl into this at night to keep warm," June said, opening it up on the ground.

April cringes. "Look at all the mold. I don't think I'd want to sleep in that now!"

"Yeah, the bugs have been in it too. Let's see what else is in there!" running back into the cave.

"Look! It's Mom's old writing table! We need to take this back with us."

June looks it over. "She regretted not taking it with us when we left. Dad did a good job of making it. It's really held up over time!"

"It's one of the things I can still remember," April said, brushing the dust off. "At the end of the day, Mom always sat down to write in her journal on this old table."

"You know... We need to take all of this back with us. This is our only chance. If we don't take it now, we never will. There's no way I'm leaving any of this," dragging everything outside.

"I got it!" April shouted from the back of the cave. "It's here!" running out with a walking stick.

June starts weeping. "My God! It's Dad's walking stick. I'm so glad we found it!"

"This is coming home with us. I can't believe Dad left this here."

"I thought Dad wanted to leave all this in case someone else is stranded here," August said, seeing how they were hauling everything out.

"No, we're going to take it all back home with us," June said, shaking her head. "It's been fifty years, and no one has touched this in all that time! These are our keepsakes."

"I think that's what Dad intended," August said, not wanting to argue the point. "Leave it here for someone else who may get stranded."

"She is right," George explained, carrying out the old cast-iron pot. "From the looks of things, no one has been in this cave since you left. The way they track things around here nowadays, ain't no one going to be on this island for years to come. It's unlikely anyone is going to be stranded here. They are not going to make that mistake again."

"We're not going to get another chance," April added. "We need to take some of this home."

"I guess this is not going to be much help to anyone," August said, picking up one of the Styrofoam cups and then seeing it disintegrate in his hand.

"This has more sentimental value for all of us," June explained, rummaging through their old things, "but it's not going to be much value to anyone after all this time. Most of it is already falling apart."

"Some of these camping things can still be used," August said, still not convinced.

The captain, walking up behind them, overhears the discussion. "You can take it all back with you. From the looks of things here, it's not going to be much use to anyone. We have an extra tent and some old sleeping bags we can exchange for all of this. If one day, someone does get stuck out here, at least they'll have some new gear to use," looking at all the antique cookware and camping gear.

"Thanks, that will make Dad happy," August said, shaking the captain's hand. "Most of these things helped them survive here. That's why he always insisted on leaving almost everything behind just in case some poor soul is stuck out here like they did."

The captain nods. "I'll make arrangements to have a few things brought up here. Are you all finished? We need to move back down to the lookout. The Padre is here and ready to start the ceremony."

"Better take what you want then," August said, glancing over at his sisters. "We'll help you carry it all back."

At that, April and June are back in the cave, seeing what else they can find. Everyone picks up what they can, carrying it all down to the lookout where the others are waiting.

August enters the cave, seeing his sisters rummaging through everything. The cave is one thing he is glad he can't remember. In addition to his fear of flying, he also fears being cooped up in confined places. Somehow, he knows this is where he got it. The damp, old, musty cave is almost emptied of its contents except for the firewood. His sisters leave him holding the flashlight while they are outside, going through all their old possessions.

August feels so sad, standing all alone in the cave looking at the four-foot stack of firewood. It was days' worth of hard work stored away for those rainy days. He can almost visualize his father out here, chopping down trees with nothing but a small handsaw. When this was cut up and placed here, his father did not know that their rescue was probably just days away. Unfortunately, all that hard work was for nothing, sitting here untouched for almost fifty years.

Just as he turns to leave, the flashlight's beam lit up a small white object tucked between the firewood and the back wall of the cave. He bends down for a closer look, seeing it's nothing more than an old rag. He pulls it out and can't help but laugh, seeing what it is. The old rag doll his mother had made was accidentally left behind. Nothing more than a piece of cloth wrapped around some Styrofoam. The head has two little buttons for eyes and a stitched-on smiley face.

"Does anyone want to claim this one?" he asked, walking out, holding up the little rag doll.

April and June are stunned when they see their old doll Booboo. They immediately jump up, running over to see the first little doll their mother had made them.

April takes the fragile doll, cradling it in her hand. "I thought we lost her. She was in the cave after all!" and starts crying.

"I can't believe she was left alone for all those years," June said. "Where did you find her?"

"It was wedged up between the wall and the stack of firewood. One of you two must have stuck it in there and forgotten about it."

June laughed. "Don't blame us! You used to play with her too. It could have been you who hid her in there. You never did want to share her," prompting a few giggles from some of the children.

Both April and June take turns cradling the little rag doll. When they were very young, they always talked about going back to get her. They never forgave each other for leaving her all alone here on the island. After all those years, they have finally found their little doll.

* * *

After storing everything away in bags, the children help carry it all down to the lookout. All that remains is an old seat cushion from the fatal flight, remnants of old Styrofoam cups, and plastic soda bottles. They find an abundance of rope of all sizes coiled up but only take a few.

Seeing what was once so valuable is now so worthless is a little strange. Most of these things had been washed up on the beach over time, which made life easy for them while on the island. Everything is so brittle that it falls apart in their hands or is already in pieces. They place anything with any sentimental value in the last sack. Carefully, they gather up the rest, putting it all back.

April, June, and August are the last ones at the cave. They stand at the entrance for the last time. April and June have so many fond memories here. During the big storms, this was their home, and where they helped their father with the daily chores. He taught them everything about surviving in the wilderness so that they could take care of themselves in case something happened to him. The cave is where they held the family rite of passage and were presented with their own walking sticks from their father.

As they had done so many times before, both April and June know what each other is thinking. While August gathers up the last of their things, April picks up her father's old walking stick. They both approach their little brother, standing quietly in front of him.

"What is it?" August asked, knowing something was up, seeing the way they were looking at him.

"It's something Dad was never able to do for you," April explained, holding out the walking stick. "It's a family tradition for those who walk the trail to the cave for the first time. Dad made us our very own walking sticks and presented them to us here at the cave. We think it's appropriate for you to have his walking stick. I know he would have wanted you to have it. You earned it by walking the trail," handing it to her brother.

August didn't expect this. "I never did get the chance," finding it difficult to speak, slowly taking the walking stick.

"You earned it," June said with a big smile. "You made it to the cave on your own. Dad would have wanted you to have it," remembering the day when her father presented her with her very own walking stick.

"Thank you," August mumbled, getting very emotional. "This means a lot to me, and for Dad too," wiping the tears from his eyes.

April and June hug their brother. They have finally completed the family tradition. August tries to control his emotions, but it's just too much for him. They have so many fond memories of growing up here. They hug each other one last time, slowly walking down the trail to the lookout, where everyone has already gathered.

* * *

Chapter 70

The Ceremony

The padre stands next to the two urns, silently reading passages from his Bible. Everyone gathers at the edge of the lookout. All are admiring the beautiful view and the setting sun. They couldn't have picked a more perfect day with the small clouds beginning to turn a burnt orange color.

Mary, seeing her grandmother, runs up to greet her. June hugs her granddaughter, leaning over to show her the little doll Booboo.

Mary cringes, seeing the little raggedy doll. "Oh! What's that?"

"This is our little friend Booboo," June explained. "This was our first little doll. We used to play with her when we were your age. Isn't she pretty?"

"It's all dirty!" Mary blurted out, stepping away from it.

"Well, she does need a little cleaning up. She has been out here alone with no one to play with," brushing off the dirt and mold.

"Hi, Booboo!" Mary said, taking the little doll, then started hugging it. "I'll play with you... I'll clean you up when we get home and put you in the washing machine. Then you be all nice and clean!"

"Well, let me try to clean her up first," June quickly said, taking back the doll. "She is very fragile, and we have to be very careful with her," trying not to think what would happen to the little doll if it was put in the washing machine.

They join the rest of their friends and family. They all hug each other, telling everyone what they found in the cave. Two crewmen from the ship walk up carrying the small white granite marker with the plaque bearing the epitaph of Jenny and Ben Hughes. They carefully place it next to the wooden bench.

After a few minutes, the Padre looks around, seeing everyone is present. "Are we ready to begin?" glancing over at August.

August simply nods, motioning everyone to gather around. Everyone circles the Padre, who stands next to the two small urns placed on the wooden bench. The timing couldn't have been better, with the sun just over the horizon. The clouds slowly turn red against the deep blue sky. A cool, gentle breeze is blowing from the east.

The Padre never met Jenny or Ben but knew all about their lives and many adventures living on this island. He spent the last ten years on Kwajalein Island to boost morale and give spiritual guidance to a small group of people far from home and family. He always used the stories of Jenny and Ben as inspiration in his church services, in taking life, however bad it could be, and then turning it around, making it into something glorious.

The padre starts the service by reading several passages from his Bible. Then he talks about Jenny and Ben, honoring their lives, their passion for life, no matter what was dealt to them. He talks about their three children, April, June, and August, which made Jenny and Ben's love of life even greater. Now with children of their own, and even grandchildren, it is the best reward that any parent could have hoped to achieve.

As the sun slowly sets, the Padre calls August, June, and April to step closer. They slowly walk up to the small wooden bench where the two urns sit with prominence. The Padre reaches down, picking up the urn containing the ashes of Jenny Hughes. He turns and carefully hands it to June and April, holding it together. Reaching down again, he picks up the urn of Ben Hughes and hands it to August. They can't help reading the inscription their father had made on the bench one last time, 'Home Sweet Home.'

"Please step forward while I read the passage," the Padre said, holding out his arms.

They slowly walk over to the edge of the cliff. The Padre stands between them. A gentle breeze blows up as a sign that the day is ending. The music starts to play after a few moments of silence. Everyone is singing the words of the song Amazing Grace.

April, June, and August are having a difficult time trying to get the words out in a broken voice, so overwhelmed with emotions. At the end of the song, the sound of a solo bagpipe continues playing. August then carefully removes the top of the urn. While April holds her mother's urn with both hands, June opens the lid.

The padre, projecting his voice, reads out aloud. "Forasmuch as it hath pleased Almighty God to take unto himself the soul of our dear brother Ben, and sister Jenny here departed, we, therefore, commit their bodies to the ground, earth to earth, ashes to ashes, dust to dust. The Lord blesses them and keep them. The Lord makes his face to shine upon him and be gracious unto him. The Lord lift up his countenance upon him and give him peace… Amen."

Slowly, as the Padre speaks, August, April, and June tilt over the urns. The ashes of their parents scattered over the edge of the cliff, drifting down on the island far below. Everyone stands for several minutes with their heads down as the Padre gives the last prayer. April cries hysterically. Her brother and sister try to console her, but they can't control their emotions any longer. They hold each other, standing next to the edge of the cliff. It is the end of a very fruitful life of their loving parents. A generation has finally passed on.

One by one, friends and family walk up, placing a flower down by the plaque, hugging and consoling August, June, and April. They thank the padre for a beautiful service, then slowly turn to make their way back down the trail. The ship is already on the beach, waiting to take them away.

* * *

With the sun setting, there is no time to waste. Everyone has to be off the island before it gets too dark. The captain stations his crew at various points on the trail. They all have flashlights to help guide everyone down if it gets too dark. The walk is long, but going downhill will not take much time as it did walking up. The temperature drops dramatically as the cool breeze comes off the ocean, helping the weary group.

Everyone walks down the trail back to the beach. The captain and several of his crew wait at the lookout. April, June, and August have a private moment to themselves. They sit on the grass next to the grave marker, covered with flowers. It's a very somber moment for them, with all the memories of their time with their parents playing through their minds. They don't want to leave this beautiful island. A place they once called home. Knowing that no one will ever be allowed back to visit the grave makes them all so sad.

The island is so quiet, with the only sound coming from the slight breeze working its way through the trees. The sky is glowing orange with the sun well below the horizon. They couldn't have asked for a more beautiful day to say goodbye to their loving parents.

April, June, and August are so emotionally drained. They reminisce about all those times that they had as a family, from the first days on this small island paradise to the many adventures in the Colorado

Mountains. They had such a great life with their mother and father and would not change one thing.

The captain slowly walks over. "I'm sorry... It's time we headed back to the ship."

August nods. "Thank you... We're ready."

They slowly get up, standing next to the old bench. Each one runs their hand over the inscription 'Home sweet home' their father had put on the bench, placing one last flower on the grave marker. April places one flower in each urn, sealing them up. She then puts each urn together under the old wooden bench. A perfect fit, almost as if it were made for this purpose. It was their mother and father's favorite place in the world. Now, they will have eternity to watch the sunset together.

"Mom and Dad wouldn't have wanted it any other way," August said, looking down at the grave marker. "Now, they can always be together, looking over the island and watching all the beautiful sunsets."

"Goodbye, Mom... Goodbye, Dad," April said in a broken voice, taking her sister's hand.

"Goodbye, Mom," June said her last farewell, reaching over to take her brother's hand. "Goodbye, Dad... I love you," she whispered, then started crying.

August stands between his sisters, looking down at the two urns. "Goodbye, Mom, Dad... Thank you for the life you gave us. You will always be in our hearts. We will never forget you. We love you always."

They hold each other for a moment, then slowly turn to walk back towards the trail. The captain and his first officer are quietly waiting. Even for them, it's an emotional time and difficult to watch and not be affected.

A crewman runs up the trail carrying a large duffel bag. He immediately stops after seeing the family and all the flowers next to the small bench. He feels so uneasy since it reminds him of his own mother's funeral not too long ago, still feeling the pain of her loss.

"Sir, I got everything you requested," the crewman whispered to his captain. "I have a tent, several sleeping bags, cookware, and a few utensils. I also put in the flare gun, a short-wave radio, and a medical kit."

As they approach the captain, August overhears them talking. "Thank you for doing this. It meant a lot to Mom and Dad to know there are always supplies here for someone."

"I thought that if anyone did get stuck out here," the captain explained, "they'll need a survival guide. So, I brought my copy of Mrs. Hughes' book about her times here," pulling the book from underneath his jacket, handing it to the crewman.

"Even better... Thank you!" August said with a big smile.

"Run up and place everything up in the cave," the captain orders the crewman. "Hurry, we don't have much time."

"Yes, sir!" then quickly turns, running up the trail carrying the survival gear.

* * *

On the walk down the trail, no one said a word. The captain and the first officer quietly follow behind. As April and June walk, their minds are filled with memories of their times on this old trail with their mother and father. They never thought that being back on the island would revive so many vivid memories of their time here. For such a short and early part of their lives, those few years were the most memorable.

August walks so proudly down the trail with his most prized possession, the walking stick his father had made. He finally walked the trail to the cave, his rite of passage. It means so much to him and is something he will never forget.

No one wants to leave. April and June wish they could stay here and experience life again, as they once knew it so long ago. To live life as it was meant to be. They want to show their children and grandchildren how beautiful this place is. They want to be able to pass on the knowledge that their mother and father gave to them. Deep down, they all know it's so wrong for this island, their old home, to be barred from any future visits from anyone. This one day is the last time anyone will step foot on the island, and it hurts so bad knowing it.

* * *

Once they reach the beach, only the grandchildren are still out playing and having fun. Within minutes, the last crewman is back on the beach after placing the survival gear in the cave. He is the last one off the trail, making sure no one is left behind.

Now, well after dusk, they barely have enough light to see. The ship is lit up and docked right up on the beach, with its center catwalk extending out on the sand. Two crewmen are standing on the bow of the ship, keeping a close watch on everyone. The security group is keeping a constant vigil on all the passengers, including the crew as well. They keep counting over and over when anyone gets on or off the ship.

The youngest children are the worst, always having to keep track of them. They are constantly running on and off the ship. Some of the more adventurous ones are jumping off the ship into the water and running back to do it again. They are keeping the crew extremely busy. They don't care about the rules, and nothing will keep them from having a good time.

As April, June, and August walk up to the ship, several friends and family rush up to greet them. An emotional time for everyone, and no one wants to leave, especially the children. They are still enjoying themselves, running in and out of the water and making sandcastles on the beach.

What surprises them the most is seeing the huge stack of wood on the beach. Kyle wants to have one last bonfire in memory of his best friend. With all the children having fun playing on the beach, it would not be right not to have a huge bonfire for the last fun day on the island.

The ship's bell rings, indicating it's time to leave. Several crewmen run out to the beach to inform everyone to board the ship. None of the children wanted to go, and their parents gathered them up and escorted up the gangplank back onto the ship for the last time.

A few of the rambunctious ones quickly run to the top deck, jumping back into the water again, thinking that this is a big game. The captain orders the crew to take all the children to the cabin below, ensuring they don't jump off the ship again.

June's grandchildren, Sam and Mary, are the only two still running around on the beach. They run into the trees towards the small pond to hide. June and her daughter, Heather, chase after them, followed by one of the crewmen.

This is the one thing that the captain doesn't want. Having passengers hiding in the trees will delay their departure. With it getting dark, it will be a problem if they got lost. He quickly gives the order that no one else is to leave the ship.

After years of transporting equipment and military personnel to top-secret installations, these children are far more trouble than anything the captain has dealt with before. The children don't obey his orders, always laughing at him and making fun of his crew. He knows they are having fun and doesn't want to leave, but he has his orders.

June and her daughter are so frustrated chasing after the two children. They don't have much time left before it gets too dark to see anything. Getting lost in the trees is bad enough during the day, but at night, it's going to be a serious problem.

Finally, Heather finds Sam hiding behind a tree. The crewman quickly escorts him back to the ship. Many on the ship let out a loud cheer, seeing the lighter side of this. August is not amused, and he knows these two little ones are going to get punished when they get back home.

Little Mary is more elusive. She keeps quiet in her game of hide and seek. They are calling her name repeatedly. Now, they are all starting to worry. It's getting dark fast, making it even more difficult to see. The last thing they want is a five-year-old lost on the island.

* * *

As time goes by, and with no sight of anyone emerging from the trees, the captain orders several more crewmen with flashlights to help with the search. They are already late and are supposed to be off the island. Communications about their status are already coming in. He is going to have a lot to answer for if they are not off the island soon. The people in charge will not be kind if their departure is delayed. His career will be over if he has to call in for additional help to find a little five-year-old girl who got lost.

June and Heather frantically look for little Mary. Their anger turns to fear as they chase through the dense trees, looking for her. Occasionally, they hear her laughing in the distance. They panic, knowing there are only a few minutes of light left before it gets too dark.

With five crewmen with flashlights, they all spread out, searching for the little girl. What they don't know is that she can see their flashlights. She knows where they are and can keep hidden from everyone else.

"Listen," June whispered. "I think I can hear her," coming to a complete stop after chasing through the trees.

Everyone quickly stops, standing quietly, listening for the little girl. Right away, everyone hears a little voice just beyond the trees. They turn off the flashlights so that Mary will not know they are on to her. Slowly, they follow the sound of her voice.

As they walk out from behind a group of trees, they finally see her in the distance. What strikes them as odd is seeing her standing alone, looking up into the trees as if she is having a conversation with someone. At least she is not trying to hide or run away, just standing there talking and laughing at something. Then they can hear another voice. Someone else is there, hiding among the trees, talking to her.

"Mary!" her mother yelled out once she got close. "Don't you run off! They're all waiting for us on the boat!"

Mary turns, seeing everyone coming towards her. She just smiles, waving at them, and doesn't run away.

"Don't you run away!" Heather yelled out, running towards her daughter.

Mary turns and looks up towards the trees. "OK! I have to go! Bye now!" she said, running towards her mother and grandmother.

Heather quickly grabs Mary, scolding her for hiding out and scaring everyone. The crewman turns on his flashlight, running over to where she was standing. He is so shocked not finding anyone there. He thought she was talking to someone else. Two others join in to search the area for the other person. The crewman radios back that they have found her, escorting June, Heather, and Mary back to the ship.

The last crewman stays behind, searching through the trees, looking for the other boy or girl. He is on the radio informing the security officer that he still can't find the other one, requesting more help. He is surprised to hear that everyone has reported in, and now he has orders to return to the ship. With one last look around, he heads back. He figures whoever it was must have run back along the beach and is back on the ship.

June, frustrated, escorts Heather and Mary back to the beach. As they approach the ship, Kyle stands at the end of the gangplank. He holds a large wooden stick with rags wrapped around the end.

"June, would you like to do the honors?" Kyle asked, lighting the handmade torch.

She turns to look back at the huge stack of wood on the beach. "Thank you... It would mean a lot to me. It's a nice gesture for Mom and Dad," quickly realizing what he is asking her to do.

She slowly turns with the torch in hand, walking back out on the beach to light the last bonfire. With everyone now on board, they all watch as June stands quietly out on the beach all alone. Now, with the darkness setting in, the small torch illuminates everything.

June stands motionless, staring at the huge stack of wood. Just like the ones they used to have on fun day. She slowly lowers the torch, placing it within the base. The dry wood quickly catches on fire. She steps back, watching as the flames slowly grow taller and taller. The fire quickly illuminates the trees in front of the small pond.

The flames of the bonfire bring back so many fond memories. June can still visualize running down the beach after being out with her father, carrying loads of fruit and firewood. She remembers their times together, singing songs and having a great time on their many fun days out on the beach.

June feels a deep sense of loss. "This is for you, Mom and Dad… Thank you for everything. I hope you both find happiness here again. May you walk the beaches together for eternity and see every sunset together. This is indeed a paradise, and now, heaven. May you rest in peace," she whispered, slowly turning, walking back to the ship.

With everyone accounted for, the crew prepares the ship to leave the island. Standing at the foot of the gangplank, June pauses for a moment, looking at the pristine beach. She feels so sad knowing that her mother and father never had another chance to see their island again. Now, she knows why they found it so hard to leave, with all its beauty and solitude.

"Goodbye, Mom… Goodbye, Dad," she quietly whispered, looking back towards the lookout where her mother and father's ashes were scattered. "I know you'll find peace here," bowing her head, walking up the gangplank.

Everyone stands quietly on the forward deck as June returns to the ship. All that can be seen is the massive bonfire out on the beach. The fire is so big it lights up the entire area. No one said a word. Everyone stares at the flames, remembering the lives of Jenny and Ben.

April, June, and August stand together, holding each other to watch the roaring bonfire. The last of the famous fun days they loved so much. Their way to celebrate life on the island. They fondly remember those nights of dancing and singing songs with their mother and father.

"Goodbye, Great-granddad!" Mary said, then started waving. "Goodbye, nice lady!"

"That was nice of you to say goodbye," June said, picking up her granddaughter, hugging her tight. "I hope your great-granddad and granny like it here."

"Yeah, he said he's glad to be back!" Mary quickly replied. "That nice lady said she likes it too!"

"What did you say?" June asked, looking at her granddaughter, a little startled.

"They like it here!" she shouted, excitedly pointing over to the trees. "Great-granddad and that lady in the picture was hiding with me. We were playing hide and seek, and nobody could find us! We had lots of fun!"

"You did what?" June asked again, not understanding. "You were hiding with someone?"

"Yeah! It was great-granddad! We had a good time! But, he said it's time for me to go cause I might get in trouble with Mama."

"You saw your great granny and granddad?" thinking she is making up more of her little stories again.

Mary nods her head up and down. "Yeah! They were playing hide and seek with me."

"Oh, that's nice," June said, going along with the story.

"Granny, is that heaven?" Mary asked, pointing to the island.

"Well, heaven is where you go after you die," June explained, still a little confused. "It's where they have angels. What made you say that?" putting Mary down as they are being ushered on the deck by the crew to clear the way to store the gangplank.

"That's what great-granddad told me," Mary said, holding her grandmother's hand. "He wanted to thank you for bringing them back to heaven. He said not to cry and be sad. This is supposed to be a happy day."

June is so shocked, not believing what she is hearing from her granddaughter. Maybe she is just too young to understand what she is saying. Mary was her father's favorite since she was the youngest. He always told her so many stories. She wonders if her little granddaughter really understands why they are all here.

* * *

The ship slowly backs away from the small island. Once clearing the beach, it slowly turns around, then heads out. June takes Mary's hand and walks her to the rear deck to look at the island for the last time. The island is now nothing more than a silhouette against the dark sky. The flames from the bonfire get higher and higher.

April and August join little Mary and June, holding each other. They will never forget this day.

Heather comes over, standing next to her mother. She picks up Mary so she can see the island over the railings.

"Oh, this is nice... So, where did you get this?" Heather asked, noticing a necklace around her little girl's neck.

"That nice lady gave it to me," Mary explained, holding it up to show everyone. "She said I can have it!"

Both April and June look over in absolute shock seeing the necklace. Around Mary's neck, is a huge black pearl at the end of a gold chain.

"Oh, my God!" June shouted out. "Where did she get that?"

"I don't know!" Heather said, startled by her mother's outburst. "Mary, where did you get this?"

"It's mine! She said I can have it!"

April gasped out loud. "That's Mom's pearl necklace! She's found it!" leaning over for a closer look.

"Mary, it's very important," June explained, trying to remain calm. "No more stories… You need to tell us where you got this."

"I told you!" the little girl said, pointing over at the island. "That nice lady gave it to me. It's mine!" holding the large pearl tight, not wanting anyone to take it away.

"Who gave it to you?" June asked again. "What did she look like?"

"That lady! You know, the one in the picture in Great-granddad's room? I really like her. She gave me the little island, too! Remember?"

"What! That's Mom!" April blurted out, not believing what she was hearing. "Mom gave this to you?"

"What are you guys on about?" August asked. "What did she find?"

"It's Mom's pearl necklace," June explained. "Somehow, she found it!"

August gasped out loud. "You got to be kidding! Mom always regretted losing that. So, where did she find it?"

"I'm not sure," Heather said. "That's what we're trying to figure out. She said some lady gave it to her."

"Some lady?" August asked. "Someone here gave it to her?" getting confused.

April is utterly shocked. "No, she said Mom gave it to her! I don't understand. How can this be?" looking back at the island.

"What? That can't be right," August said, scratching his head. "How could Mom give it to her when she lost it years ago before we left?"

"No, she saying that Granny gave it to her while she was out playing hide and seek," Heather added.

"Mom died months ago," August mumbled. "Mary doesn't understand what she is saying. She probably found it on the beach or maybe up at the cave."

June examines the large black pearl. "I don't understand it either, but somehow she found it. It's the one Mom had all those years ago. There is more I need to tell you. Something else happened when she was out hiding in the trees. She was saying that Mom and Dad were out there playing with her when we found her."

August is dumbfounded. "No, she doesn't understand... She's just playing one of her games."

"That's what I thought, but after hearing some of the things she told me," June explained. "Let's not go into it now... It's been a long day. I'll tell you later. We'll need time for all this to sink in," feeling so emotionally drained with the day's events.

They all look at each other, wondering if any of this is true. Little Mary was the last one to talk with their father. On the day he passed away, the little girl talked about the nice lady being there with him and how he was going away with her to the beach. What shocks them all is that the nice lady she was referring to is actually her great-grandmother, Jenny.

Mary didn't really get to know her great-grandmother since she always traveled. She doesn't fully understand what is happening or why they are all here. She has not even been told that her great-grandmother or even her great-grandfather had died. They all have so many unanswered questions, but this is not the time or the place to go into it. This will be something they need to discuss when they return home.

* * *

As the ship slowly leaves the island, the family and friends gather on the rear deck. No one said a word. Everyone waves farewell, watching the small island disappear into the darkness. The last of the fun days and the last time anyone is to step foot on this little paradise they once called home.

What astounds everyone is how the huge bonfire can clearly be seen even though it's miles away. Any ship or airplane in the area could easily see it. For all those years, Jenny and Ben had bonfires out on the beach, so someone should have seen it. Any high-altitude aircraft should have been able to see that someone was on this tiny island, especially at night.

The ship gains speed, and the huge bonfire slowly diminishes until it passes below the horizon. Their one day on the island has come and gone. They got their one wish to visit their old home and to lay to rest their parents in heaven. A generation has passed, but will not be forgotten. Jenny and Ben Hughes will always stay in the memories of all their family and friends and those whose lives they have touched.

* * *

Chapter 71

Epilogue

The story of Mocker Island is well known to all the military personnel in the area. Unfortunately, several months after the funeral, curiosity gets the best of one of the crew on a patrol flight returning to Marshal Island. The unauthorized low flyby gives the crew a close look at the famous forbidden island. With the aircraft fitted with high-resolution cameras used to identify any ships in the area, one crewman wants a souvenir, taking several unauthorized photographs.

Later, when the photographs are printed out, it's quickly discovered that there is a major security breach on Mocker Island. Close scrutiny of the images clearly shows two sets of footprints on the beach. With the most advanced surveillance system in the world, no one thought it would be possible for anyone to get within a hundred miles before being detected. Many who had tried were discovered and turned away, not even getting close enough to see the island.

Although the security is supposed to be foolproof, the truth of the matter is that someone got through and is now on the island. The chances of anyone being stranded are nearly impossible, but someone was able to get through all the security again.

The military officials concluded that somehow two people had intentionally made their way to the island to live out their lives there. Now, they have the task of removing these two from Mocker Island. The security group wants to find out how anyone could get past the most secure military system in the world.

* * *

After several days, the head of the security group has concluded that the only way anyone could get on the island was during the Hughes' funeral using the Langa-Moa. Somehow, two people sneaked onto the ship and then onto the island without being detected. The captain and the crew of the Langa-Moa have been summoned for an inquiry.

Initially, the investigation found nothing. None of the crew saw anything suspicious, and no one had been reported missing. The security cameras on the ship recorded the entire trip from the moment it left Kwajalein until it returned later that night. Even after comparing the photographs of the crew and passengers with the video, everyone has been verified. There is no evidence that the Langa-Moa had slipped up, leaving two people on the island, and it leaves them all bewildered.

The only conclusion is that there must have been a stowaway. Two people might have hidden on the ship long before the voyage to Mocker Island. When the ship was anchored off the island, it would have been easy to jump off the stern of the ship undetected while the rest of the passengers were disembarking from the bow.

This is a real embarrassment to the security detail assigned to Jenny and Ben's funeral. They are very adamant about correcting the situation and putting their reputation back on track. A small ship is immediately dispatched to Mocker Island to investigate and remove these two people. It will be the first ship to arrive on the island since the funeral and the last.

* * *

The security ship arrives at Mocker Island. A scouting party is immediately sent out to find the trespassers. Whoever these people are, most likely, they don't want to be found. The scouting party goes in as quietly as possible. Using the latest portable infrared detectors, they can easily spot anyone trying to hide behind the trees and thick foliage.

Searching the island for hours, they find nothing. No footprints are on the beach. They even go inside the cave, and everything is still tightly sealed as the crew of the Langa-Moa left it. It's apparent to everyone that there is no one here and no evidence of a camp or even a campfire to indicate that someone had been living on the island.

By the end of the day, the scouting party had secured the island. There is no one else on the island, and there are no signs that anyone has ever been here. Even with several low flyovers with heat-sensing monitors, they have detected nothing except the scouting party out on the beach.

The entire event is now a big mystery. They conclude that the footprints just might have been an illusion, or maybe from an animal or a bird long gone. The case is closed, and the scouting party is ordered to return to base the next day at sunrise.

* * *

Early in the morning, they break down the camp. To their dismay, they discover two sets of fresh footprints on the beach. These are not from any birds or animals. They are human footprints, and it looks as if two people are on a morning stroll, barefoot, on the beach. The footprints even go right next to the camp.

Initially, it's thought someone in the group is pulling a joke. After examining the footprints, they can see these are from two different people. One footprint is smaller, as if it's from either a young person or a woman. When they measure the smaller one, comparing it to all the crew, it's clear it can't be any of them.

The scouting party runs down the beach following the footprints. Eventually, the two sets of footprints turn from the water's edge, leading to the tree line along a small dry creek bed. They run into the trees, following the footprints using their sensors to detect any heat patterns of these elusive trespassers.

Everything comes to a sudden stop when the footprints end at the small pond. The trespassers are close by because the footprints are fresh. They all stand around the small pond in disbelief. Two sets of footprints lead right into the pond, but there are no signs of any leaving.

The entire area is scanned again with infrared detectors, but nothing is found. Only a few feet away is the beginning of the trail that leads up over the island. They have no choice. The island is thoroughly searched again for these two elusive people. After another day of searching, there is no evidence that anyone else is on the island. Now, this is a big mystery to everyone involved.

Orbiting satellite cameras are continuously focusing on the small island. The military's most sophisticated sensors are permanently set up on the beach. The sensors can detect any heat, motion, or sound and monitor everything twenty-four hours a day. All the information is sent to a satellite and then directly to the security center. The sensors are so accurate that every time a bird lands on the beach, it's detected. Anyone coming near the beach can now be seen during the day or night.

The results of the extensive search reported nothing substantial. The infrared sensors keep coming up with nothing, but the satellite images still show footprints on the beach. After recalibrating all the sensors, they discover that none are malfunctioning. They add more infrared sensors to the other side of the island, but it doesn't help.

* * *

After monitoring the island for several weeks, the search is permanently called off. Footprints can clearly be seen, but the people who made them are never found. With no proof of anyone being stranded or even living on the island, the case is closed.

The island is sealed off, barring anyone from stepping foot on its pristine beaches. There are no more unauthorized flybys. The area around the island is now off-limits, even to all military ships and aircraft.

The small island will never be seen again. However, deep down, everyone involved has a good idea of who left the footprints on the beach. They are from the spirits of Jenny and Ben Hughes on one of their many walks on the island paradise they call heaven.

* * *

The End.

www.ingramcontent.com/pod-product-compliance
Lightning Source LLC
Chambersburg PA
CBHW052338020726
47503CB00001B/9